GIANTS IN THE SHADOWS

Book III of The Manipulators Trilogy

THE CONTINUING CAST

Valentino Erice: The daring young immigrant who parlayed his raw courage into a formidable financial empire, only to become the target for destruction by an international cartel of power brokers.

Tina Erice: Val's only daughter, a beautiful woman and heiress to a fortune. When the one man she desires rejects her she chooses power as a substitute for her fiery passions.

Benne Erice: Born under a shadow of veiled intrigue, his manipulative genius is haunted by constant reminders of his inevitable destiny.

Whip Shiverton: He believed the world should be served to him on a silver platter, and he steamrolls the Shiverton political machine to victory despite all the odds against him.

Ted Shiverton: The favorite son of a wealthy Irish-American family, he was literally born to power. The White House is his until tragedy strikes.

David Martin: The enigmatic government agent who relentlessly pursues his suicide mission despite the roadblocks and deceptions of the Erice family.

Jolie Barnes: A white trash, backwoods gal who uses her body to reach stardom on Broadway, and finds the same methods work in the White House.

Renzo Bonaparte: The tough Brooklyn kid who'd fight, fornicate or marry his way to the top. And for him it worked, until one woman stopped him cold.

Maureen O'Mara: The beautiful Irish actress who'd do anything for a fix and an escape from reality . . . and who one day awakens to find she's destroyed the only man who could help her.

Mourous Benkhanhian: The gnome-like IAGO chieftain who casts a giant shadow of indescribable power. The one man who can shake the politics of the world, perhaps control the White House itself.

Neiland Milton: The former vice-president who sells his soul to IAGO for a chance at the presidency of America, and finds that even his ambition, ruthlessness and greed are no match for his new masters.

E. L. Lamb: The crusty old Texas tycoon who uses his billion-dollar petroleum empire as a weapon aimed at the Shiverton oligarchy.

Prince Ali Mohammed: Dynamic head of an oil-wealthy Arab Emirate, and champion of a new breed of businessman whose destiny is to rule from the podium of IAGO. His one mistake is to fall in love with the wrong woman.

Princess Jamila: The sensuous Arab princess, sister to Prince Ali Mohammed, whose incestuous love turns her to alabaster and ice until Abdul's primitive passions set her afire . . . and against Ali.

Abdul Harrim: The handsome terrorist, seething with satyr-like sexuality. His ambitions for the Fedayeen movement are handily implemented by his expert debaucheries and sadistic murders.

Bahar-Bahar: A crafty, subversive assassin and head of a splinter group of the Fedayeen with nihilistic aims for the overthrow of all world oppressors.

The Man: Who is The Man who stalks by day and night until his last contract becomes his undoing?

Dear Reader:

Giants in the Shadows brings to a conclusion the Manipulators Trilogy, in which *The Manipulators* and *Born To Power*, respectively, were volumes one and two.

You have already met the characters described in the opening pages. You were introduced to Valentino Erice and his family; you shared in his beginnings, his highly enlightening and frightening street education, his love and marriage, and the birth and tragic deaths of two sons and a daughter; and his connection with the order of the double headed griffin and the Sicilian Mafia. All this served to shape the world of Val Erice and the empire he created.

You met an international cartel of power brokers, IAGO, terrifying men with unlimited power who shape the world in which we live. They are the unknown, unseen Giants in the Shadows who control the political and financial decisions affecting the entire world. Do they exist, you ask? Ask yourself this question when you observe the manner in which dark horse political candidates spring seemingly from nowhere to win high office; ask yourself this question when you watch phenomenally spiralling inflation, the incredible rate at which the price of gold is soaring, the unbelievable oil crisis, the Middle Eastern disputes and why they are not resolved intelligently. These power brokers exist; perhaps not under the name of IAGO, but they are to be found throughout the capitals of the world, and wherever money causes the heart to palpitate faster than love . . .

These giants in the shadows are electronically connected to the pulse of world politics. . . . They decide who shall be rich, who shall be poor, who shall be famous, who shall live . . . and who shall die.

In *Giants in the Shadows,* be prepared for the exciting conclusion to the Manipulators Trilogy. The fiery passions of this novel begin in the midst of a Middle Eastern crisis and take you back to Washington and Las Vegas in a spellbinding tale of mystery, adventure, romance and death.

—*Gloria Vitanza Basile*

BOOK III, *THE MANIPULATORS* TRILOGY

GIANTS IN THE SHADOWS

GLORIA VITANZA BASILE

PINNACLE BOOKS   LOS ANGELES

This is a work of fiction. All the characters and events portrayed in this book are fictional, and any resemblance to real people or incidents is purely coincidental.

GIANTS IN THE SHADOWS: MANIPULATORS III

An original Pinnacle Books edition, published for the first time anywhere.

First printing, December 1979

ISBN: 0-523-40708-4

Cover illustration by Norm Eastman

Printed in the United States of America

PINNACLE BOOKS, INC.
2029 Century Park East
Los Angeles, California 90067

To the memory of my father and mother,
Mr. and Mrs. A. Vitanza

BOOK ONE

What hand is that which writes the end
Before a life begins,
Whose right is it to pick and choose
Declaring good from sins . . .

CHAPTER ONE

A marvelous stillness pervaded the world as a new moon hanging low in Italy's western sky began its ascent to the heavens, illuminating a thousand spectacular stars in its path. A gasp of appreciation escaped the lips of a few of the guests standing at the edge of the lionshead-balustraded terrace of the Moorish-inspired villa belonging to Sheikh Ali Mohammed Izmur, situated high on one of Rome's seven hills.

Whip Shiverton, weary after an exhaustive European tour, stood gazing at the magnificent panorama, missing Tina desperately. A certain eagerness crept into his sapphire eyes at the thought of returning home to her shortly.

Sounds of excitement and lilting laughter echoed from inside the villa, intruding upon the mood and sentiments of the group watching the magic of nature, drawing them back to the festivities. Valerie Shiverton, Ted's widow, linked her arm through Whip's as they ambled leisurely back inside.

"I've never been so excited, Whip. Isn't this the grandest, most opulent villa you've ever seen? Nothing like this in America," she added, clasping a free, fluttery hand over her breasts, speaking in that affected Southern voice of honey and molasses that at times galled Whip. She continued, "I suppose I should be flattered at the attention lavished on me in your company, Whip. In all honesty my body needs a man's touch to make it come alive." Her eyes challenged him.

Speaking with limpid arrogance and measured gratification, he muttered as he patted her hand, "My dear Valerie, you never disappoint me, do you?"

She gave him a brief, sharp look, unsure how to take his words. Whip led her to a sofa where she sat demurely, careful to drape the folds of her turquoise Qiana jersey gown to one side. Aware that every eye in the room was upon them, she smiled at him calmly. The White House years had done this for her—instilled her with the confi-

3

dence she needed. No one need know how scared and nervous she really was among all these staring strangers.

Whip leaned over and handed her a hollow-stemmed glass filled with Dom Perignon, brought by a servant in gold livery. Valerie accepted it, her eyes welling tearfully as if on cue. "I'd toss all this away if we could bring Ted back. You do believe me, don't you?" She needed solace and sympathy and above all, love, even if it was false.

She's a genius at tricking herself, thought Whip, watching her sip the champagne, her eyes sweeping the room, sizing up the males in attendance. Whip smiled inwardly. *Good old Valerie, running true to form.*

Valerie caught Ali Mohammed's meaningful glance. Standing in a circle of other guests, he blatantly ignored them and focused on her in a way that pleasurably turned on all her senses. In a quick transition she confided to Whip, "I declare, he makes me feel positively indecent. He looks at me as if I'm not wearing a stitch of clothing, Whip." She reached for a cigarette from a stunningly crafted crystal bowl resting on a low glass and gold table.

Whip scanned the room in the direction of Valerie's interest and locked eyes with their host, the prince. They nodded briefly. Turning back to Valerie, his cigarette lighter ready to light her cigarette, Whip's brows arched slightly.

"Careful, girl, you're smoking something potent in that."

Valerie shrugged indifferently. "It isn't the first time I've smoked Colombian gold. Oh, don't look so shocked," she pouted delicately.

Whip's mind was elsewhere. He and Ali had been playing games for the past hour, each sizing up the other from a distance. Accompanied by both the Italian and Arab ambassadors, the proper protocol had been observed earlier. He and Ali had shaken hands, exchanged pleasantries, each the epitome of polite cordiality. Ali, more restrained of the two, made frivolous and superficial chatter. Before moving on to his other guests he suggested that he and Whip should talk later over coffee.

"You do remember we were once schoolmates, don't you?"

Whip grinned. "However do you think I could have forgotten the inimitable Ali Mohammed Izmur?"

Almost on cue Whip was whisked away to meet an

4

ambassador, a chancellor, oil tycoons, Swiss financiers, actors, actresses, directors and producers from Cinecittà— all conversing in their native tongues.

The atmosphere reeked of an opulence beyond credibility. The Moorish villa overflowed with elegantly dressed men and women, some draped decorously on low pastel damask sofas under domed archways, some standing on marble floors strewn with priceless Persian carpets. Statues carved by genius sculptors graced several private alcoves where collections of gold ingots and precious gems were displayed in locked cases embedded in the walls, protected by an intricate set of burglar alarms linked to the unique spotlights illuminating them. A banquet of gourmet food displayed on stunning Royal Doulton china encrusted with gold had been prepared by master chefs. Blocks of ice carved in the form of Egyptian and Roman gods graced the table, set on platters of gleaming silver. Urns placed strategically throughout the villa exuded the fragrance of musk. A profusion of enormous, blood-red Belle of Portugal roses were arranged in porcelain vases.

Valerie, encircled by a covey of admirers, both men and women, found herself being flattered guilelessly. Instantly compassionate, they expressed their concern over her recent widowhood; then, as quickly, they resumed their fluttering social overtures, flitting from one circle to the next holding Valerie's hand, as their senseless conversation continued among the endless sea of faces alien to her.

Soft, scintillating mood music played by a sizeable orchestra hidden behind fluttering, transparent scrims provided a romantic background. The low-keyed conversation increased in volume periodically as laughter waxed and waned. A few of the more amorous couples were dancing the latest American craze, the twist.

Whip was as impressed by the Oriental splendor as Valerie. On their arrival they had been greeted by servants bearing flaming torches, who escorted them from their limousine. Inside the villa, ornate golden lanterns with cutout designs created mesmeric light patterns on the floors and walls. At the center of one grand salon was a fountain; its lighting and flow of water were controlled electronically. Sofas and low chairs were placed nearby for guests who lingered to view the exciting colors that changed as if by magic.

Whip, no exception to the other gaping, wide-eyed

guests, found the lighting display intriguing. As he paused to watch the magic fountains, waiters served him Beluga caviar and champagne. About to sip the Dom Perignon, he was arrested by the sound of a woman's husky voice.

"Dahlink, do pay attention to what I am sayink," said the stunning woman whose name, he later learned, was Eva. She was an overblown Swedish actress who resembled Anita Ekberg.

Both Whip and Valerie glanced at her. "Are you speaking to me?" Valerie asked, squirming under the impact of the woman's commanding eyes.

"But of course, dahlink," Eva laughed throatily. "Prince Ali is trying desperately to flirt with you. Do be a luv and stop avoiding him."

Flushing under Whip's cool, censorious eyes, Valerie, unable to help herself, turned and caught the expression in Ali's eyes. She did her best to exude an alabaster and ice appearance. Valerie did not know that after their encounter at the presidential galas in Washington, where they first met, Ali had assiduously compiled a dossier on her that gave him insight into her burning sensuality, discreetly obscured by the virginal manners she'd learned to assume before the unsuspecting public.

"Eva is right," said Ali, moving in and holding Valerie's elbow. He steered her away from the others. "Eva can read my mind like a psychic." They left the others looking after them knowingly, Whip doing a slow burn.

Ali walked her out onto the moonswept terrace where a warm breeze rustling through the citrus groves perfumed the air with orange blossoms, helping to promote a mood of indolence. Valerie trembled inwardly, excited by Ali's clean, masculine scent. His deeply penetrating eyes, the bold audacity of his inexorable manner—everything about him shook her resolve. Old uncapped emotions stirred close to the surface. She thought, *He has to be the most exciting man in the world.*

Unsettling tremors coursed through her as they clinked glasses. A wave of warmth permeated her body. She gave a start, afraid to look into his eyes for fear he'd see the truth.

"I've waited a long time, Valerie. I'm not a patient man," he said as if he saw through her.

She felt the color flush her cheeks. "I do declare you fluster me. I-I d-don't know what to make of you."

"Flustering is for children. We, my dear, are both adults." Leaning towards her, he nuzzled her neck, then,

6

his eyes fixed on hers, he kissed her, properly this time. Valerie fell limp against him.

Ali knew his women. He whispered in her ear, making exciting animal noises to step up her passion. He sensed she was without will or volition. Giving in to his seduction, kissing him back with abandon, she sank against him.

She wasn't certain how or when it happened. Deliriously, emotionally aroused, they had escaped the other guests. Now they stood intimately embraced in Ali's private quarters upstairs in the villa. Floating on a champagne high, plus the pot or whatever else she'd taken, Valerie felt all aquiver and slightly disoriented. A blur of impressions formed in her mind.

Lying naked on the bed with Ali, she stared up at the thousand glittering reflections of their bodies in the mirrored ceiling over the elegant oversized bed. His powerful, darkly tanned body, lean and muscular, enveloping her protectively, was gentle, yet fiercely sensual. His murmurings, soothing and stimulating words of erotica, thrilled her beyond description. He stroked her masterfully with feathery light fingers, bringing her back to new excitement, time and again. She had climaxed several times before he penetrated her with acute ferocity, leaving her gasping, wanting more. Savage, sensual tremors shot through her, shaking her compulsively. Her eyes, startled and wide open, watched him in his ritual of love; his eyes were like glittering black diamonds. Grabbing her face between his two strong hands, he stared into her eyes, his body building to a crescendo of feverish thrusts. A low wailing sound escaped his lips. Beginning deep inside him, spiraling up and through his throat came an animal sound that sent them both into paroxysms of passion.

"Stay with me, aboard my yacht. I need to know you better," he whispered to her when his voice returned.

"Oh, I will. I will," she murmured ecstatically, giving Whip no more thought.

Ali reached for a bottle of iced Dom Perignon standing in the silver bucket near the bed. He poured two glasses, and handed her a solid gold lidded bowl. Valerie accepted it wonderingly. She lifted the lid, exposing a mound of white powder with a tiny spoon stuck in it.

"Help yourself," he said quietly. "Then wait for the real thrills." He handed her the champagne. "In case you become dehydrated."

Valerie snorted. Icy shocks coursed through her nostrils, exploding in her brain. Her eyes brightened as the dope hit her. A wet hot rush melted between her legs. She stood outside herself, hearing her voice say, "You have a villa filled with guests."

"I have only one guest, you. There's no reason to think of anyone else." They clinked glasses. "To us, *ma petite amour*."

Ali's mysterious eyes jarred her composure. Her throat felt parched, even as she sipped the champagne. Even if she wanted to, she could never escape him. She cared for nothing beyond this moment. She wanted to believe that the past had never happened, and her future was about to begin. Yet something nagged at her insistently. Her hand flew to her temple as if it could stop the giddiness she experienced. "I-I m-must get back to W-Whip. He must be frantic."

"He's old enough to care for himself. Stay. I want you here with me."

She tried to wriggle out of his arms. Ali held her pinned to the bed, concentrating first on one breast, then the other, until he had devoured them both. Valerie, a master at orgasm, continued to exhaust herself as he touched her off, again and again. In a moment of clarity, Valerie admitted something she'd found impossible in the past. Here was a man who could control her. The thought gave her a jolt of fright. She tried to sit up, watching him, until a series of small inner explosions dissolved her inner panic, allowing her to succumb to his mastery. Ali Mohammed was a new and exquisitely terrifying experience to her. In these moments she became hopelessly addicted to him.

Ali slid himself up to frame her hot dry lips with his. He penetrated her body as shudders rippled through her.

Unaware of the torrid sexual interlude enacted in Ali's private chambers with Valerie, Whip floated through the next two hours hardly noting her absence. Converged upon by countless guests tossing names at him as if he should know them intimately, Whip cocked his ears at certain ones. Eric Von Rhome and his wife Felicia, of the Munitions Von Rhome, exchanged pleasantries with him. Felicia, a pulsating stick of dynamite with the obviousness of a street hooker, cooed, "You must be our guest in Cannes before you return."

Whip thanked her but apologized that there was no time on this trip. "Perhaps another day?"

Abdul Harrofian, eldest of Lord Harrofian's offspring, made small talk with Whip. "My three younger brothers

8

would have been here but they had other pressing matters. All playboys, they haven't the business acumen between them to raise the price of a postal stamp. Their only goal in life is to seduce every woman between Paris and Istanbul and live to boast of it."

"What a noble ambition," said Whip.

Aimee Skouras Harrofian, daughter of a Greek shipping tycoon and Abdul's wife, linked her arm through Whip's. "Is it true, dear boy, that you intend to run for the American presidency? My dear, aren't you the least bit concerned since your brother was cold-bloodedly murdered?" Her words hung like an icy pall over the group. Icicles of frozen silence descended.

Spoiled, stunning, daring, impervious to anyone's opinion but her own, Aimee seemed intent on starting minor revolutions with her bold audacity. Whip tactfully removed her hand from his arm.

"My dear Mrs. Harrofian—it is Harrofian, isn't it?"

"Call me Aimee, if you desire."

"Very well, Aimee, if you desire. Your first question is premature, your second in bad taste. Do you have a third?" he asked pleasantly.

Aimee's face turned crimson, her eyes darting to her husband for support. Abdul seemed content to let her stew in her own juices. The plucky lady snorted and turned back to Whip like a champion. Her brows rose. Tilting her head slightly she clapped her hands. "Bravo, I accept your reply in the same manner in which I asked the questions. You're an excellent wrist slapper. I deserve your rancor. My dear, you have certain admirable traits so lacking among these—uh—people. May I call you Whip?" She gushed, "No one here would dare put me in my place—or as you Americans quaintly put it, put me down." She gave him a cool, judgmental look. "I'll expect you and Valerie for lunch tomorrow aboard our yacht—"

Whip smiled tightly. "Sorry, Valerie has other plans." He glanced about, missing his sister-in-law now for the first time. The woman was clutching at him, trying to evoke a promise from him.

"Come along then, Whip. I want to talk with you. I want to know how you really feel about your brother's death."

Whip replied, "At least I'll never have to say goodbye to him. Excuse me," he muttered to the others, aghast at Aimee's bad timing. "Excuse me for being underwhelmed."

Kevin O'Brien and Tom Murphy, two Secret Service

agents who had arrived with Whip, moved in swiftly at his eye signal.

"Where the hell is Aphrodite?" It was a code name for Valerie. "I haven't seen her for over an hour," snapped Whip.

O'Brien tensed. The agents exchanged concerned glances.

"I'll mosey about. You stay with Sir Lancelot," he told Murphy, using their code name for Whip.

Murphy was dressed in formal clothing, as was O'Brien. His six-foot stature, ruddy complexion and tight-lipped expression quickly identified him as an American; his manner marked him as an agent. Other guests paused briefly to observe him, then turned back to their own activities.

Murphy sauntered into the next salon where pornographic films were being shown to a scattering of sexually impassioned guests. The pungent aroma of pot, hashish and alcohol hung in the air, their inhaled effects already clouding Murphy's senses. Peering into the darkness, half expecting Valerie to be here, he left, unable to locate her.

Walking along one of the marble corridors Whip passed Murphy, silently questioning him with his eyes. Murphy shook his head. "Where's our host?" asked Whip, recalling Ali's amorous advances to Valerie.

"Haven't seen him either," muttered Murphy, biting his underlip. His professionally trained eyes swept the area, noting all the exits.

"Give it ten minutes, then do what you have to to find her. I'll be in the study using the phone."

Murphy glanced at his watch, noting the time. He stepped into the room before Whip, snapped on the overhead lights and searched the study thoroughly. He nodded to Whip, and paused briefly before closing the door behind him.

"I'll be outside the door. I'll send O'Brien to locate Aphrodite. He may know of places I couldn't find." He nodded to two of Prince Izmur's darkskinned, bearded sentries as they passed in the corridor.

Whip was across the room in giant strides and, seated behind the impressive gilded desk, he stared at the phone for a few moments. Voices speaking in a garble of languages reached him, Italian, French, Arabic. He had more important things to do than eavesdrop. He picked up the phone and gave the overseas operator a number to call in Las Vegas. He gave her his charge number and waited for Tina to answer the phone. It was ten A.M. in Nevada.

He didn't count the number of rings, but after several of them he hung up, dejected. He tapped his fingers on the desk.

Where in hell is she? Why in hell isn't she where she's supposed to be? Provoked and irritated, he drummed a steady staccato on the desk.

Tina, Tina, why the hell aren't you here with me, where you belong? . . . Because you, Whip, are a jerk! If you had any sense you'd have claimed her before this. When you return home, you either marry her—or forget her. Lay down the law to her!

With this decision made. he helped himself to a thin cigar retrieved from a handsome humidor on the ornate desk, sniffing it before biting off an end to light up. He was anxious to return home now. The European trip was becoming a bore. Ambassadors, dignitaries, even minor royalty had come forward promoting their daughters, nieces, friends—anyone wearing a skirt—proposing some sort of arrangement since he was a bachelor and so far from home.

Dammit, Ali! Get off the stick. Let's get our talk over with.

He drew on the cigar expansively, about to leave. The sound of a soft knock on the door at the far end of the room arrested him. A stunning young woman dressed in a revealing gown of diaphanous white chiffon floated into the room like a breath of spring. Her low-cut gown set off twin beauty marks, fetching moles mirroring each other on either side of her cleavage. Her sparkling mysterious eyes held his.

Whip, a charming man, attempted to convey an eloquent greeting. "Uh—hello," was all he managed.

"*As-salaam Aleikum.* I am Princess Jamila Rhadima Izmur, sister to Prince Ali Mohammed Izmur, soon to reign in our nation as lord and master of all," she said in a detectably imperious voice. "Forgive my impertinence. Although we have not been formally introduced, Mr. Shiverton, *effendi,* many are the splendid things I have heard about the man with whom my brother attended Harvard." She spoke with a slight accent.

"The house of Prince Izmur is your house," she said, walking to a handsome sideboard of carved rosewood. "May I offer you the wine of our people?"

Whip nodded. Speechless and stunned by her beauty, he watched her swing from the hips like a thoroughbred. Her well-rounded curves were instantly detectable as she

11

moved against the shimmering sheer fabric of her gown. Whip was unable to subdue his excitement, caused by the merest movement she made. Her jet black hair, pulled up off her neck, had been twisted into a coil with white bugle beads and pearl strands and hung over one shoulder like an ornate pony tail. Moving like a graceful gazelle, she poured the darkish purple wine from a delicate lead crystal decanter into two solid gold cups.

When Whip could breathe he noticed that her amber skin, tinted with gold, glowed in the subdued lighting. His eyes, however, were trained on the twin moles over each breast. They appeared to have been painted on with the express purpose of exacting an exciting response. She carried herself with a proud hauteur.

But, oddly, Whip got the distinct impression that she was very young, playacting at being a grownup. Because of the expert application of sophisticated makeup it was not an easy task to determine her age.

"I assure you, the pleasure is all mine," he said when speech returned to him. "Why didn't I meet you earlier, Princess?"

"Please, Mr. Shiverton, you may call me Jamila. My brother, lord and master of our house. asked that I entertain you until he arrives to converse with you. I'm happy I was not forced to pull you away from that swarm of female predators in the salon."

Whip raised the gold cup in a silent toast, sipping the wine delicately. He grimaced, hesitant to offend her, at the thick, unpalatable, syrupy taste. "Don't you approve of Westerners? I detect a slight hostility—"

"Most Westerners are shallow." A tight smile formed around her full and pouting lips. "Their words are as thin as a mirage and cannot be trusted. Your women, especially, are different from ours. They take too many liberties. They are totally without scruples. Shall we drink again to your pleasant visit with my brother?" She poured more wine for them, failing to see Whip's grimace of distaste. She raised her glass to his.

"I prefer drinking to your beauty, Princess," he said somewhat mockingly. The elixir was spicy and now seemed warm on his tongue and more palatable than the first sip. "Why do I detect a peculiar sullenness in your Arabic beauty?" he asked teasingly.

Jamila shrugged petulantly. "I see I'm not clever at hiding my thoughts." She placed her cup down and turned to him imploringly. "My brother, the prince, has become

12

smitten with the charms of your brother's widow. Imagine? He is thinking of marrying her."

Whip's thoughts braked instantly, her words having a stunning effect on him. "I beg your pardon. What was that you said?"

Jamila repeated her words, indicating at the same time her own displeasure over such an alliance. Whip became instantly reserved.

"I find it strange, Princess, and a bit awkward, that you should take the liberty of speaking presumptuously of your brother's intentions. You may be reading the wrong things into a gesture of friendship and mutual admiration between two human beings."

"I assure you that my brother, the prince, lord and master of our house, shall speak his intentions at the proper time. I was merely curious to observe your reactions. I can see you are as offended as I at the thought of such an alliance—"

"I never said—" Whip was cut off instantly.

"It's true. You said nothing. As Allah is my witness, your displeasure is written in your eyes. Such a union would be as distasteful to me as to you." She moved in closer. "For your influence in dissuading your brother's widow from such an alliance I would do anything."

There was no mistaking her words. Whip studied her inscrutably.

She turned from him, blushing under his penetrating gaze. "They are both upstairs, where they've been for nearly two hours. They are in my brother's bedroom," she insisted, as if she had to paint a lurid picture for Whip before he could understand her words.

As angry as Whip was at Valerie for stupidly flaunting her sexual prowess before such people, he was equally as annoyed at Jamila for what he considered to be malicious spying and telling.

"You are incredibly indelicate, Princess," he told her tartly.

Noting the intensity of anger sparking his icy eyes, she lowered her own in practiced demurral. "You are angry with me," she said. "You are probably thinking me a terrible person for spying on my brother. Well, perhaps I am. Is it wrong that I feel this woman would be a bad influence in Ali's life? But when do men think with their brains when it comes to asserting their manhood? Yes, Mr. Shiverton, I will do almost anything to prevent a union between them."

13

"Anything?" Whip wanted to teach this bit of baggage a few manners. His eyes bored into hers until a crimson flush spread across Jamila's face and neck. Demurely she dropped her eyelids so he couldn't read the excitement she felt in his presence along with the hatred she felt for all Americans. To Jamila, they were all supercilious, filled with the wrong values.

It came as a stunning blow to Whip that Valerie might consider such an alliance, if what this woman told him was true. Come to think of it, he hadn't had much trouble convincing Valerie to make this trip with him. Why, the very thought that Ali and Valerie had something going between them . . .

A peculiar languor overtook Whip, a slow warmth flowing through him that seemed to melt his inhibitions and reduce his resistance to nothing. He became aware that Jamila's dark, shadowy eyes were watching him, waiting, searching for his reaction.

"My brother, who will soon be the reigning monarch, must have a male heir. He presumes that the woman Valerie is somewhat of a brood mare. He feels certain she can provide him with an heir—and more if necessary. I have exhausted all weapons of arbitration with him. I suggested he take her as his concubine. My brother refused. The woman who was the First Lady of your land is not to be so dishonored he argued. And then what do you think the foolish man tells me? He is willing, if need be, to divorce all his other wives. Oh, Mr. Shiverton, Allah would indeed be grievously offended. Is that not so?"

Whip stiffened and forced a smile. "That might prove costly."

Jamila stared blankly. Laughter fell from her lips and for a moment she relaxed. "I see you are thinking as a Westerner. In our country a man has but to declare before four witnesses of Allah that he wishes a decree of divorce, and it is done. Praise be unto Allah, it is by far a saner rite than the one by which Westerners abide."

Whip watched her pour more wine for them. "This wine dazes me. I find it heady," he said, dabbing at the beads of perspiration dotting his brow.

"It is the fig wine prohibited by Moslem law."

"Yet you drink it?" He was fascinated by the twin moles.

"Are not the forbidden fruits the most delicious? Because it is forbidden to us does not mean we should de-

14

prive our guests, Mr. Shiverton." She approached him, a suggestion in her eyes.

"Then I feel most privileged to drink it with you." He accepted the wine she held out to him.

Jamila stood very close to him, the sweet scent of her perfume added to the slight intoxication Whip felt from the wine. He detected a slight uncoordination of movement, a slurring of his words and a marked giddiness. He took another sip, and put the gold cup down. He reached for her, pulled her to him and kissed her. His ardor surprised him but didn't deter him.

For an instant he felt her stiffen, pull back, then suddenly succumb to his embrace. His sensuous mouth covered hers and instantly Jamila kissed him back ardently. She felt powerless against the flame of his passion. At this precise moment, the door opened.

"Mr. Shiverton," called Ali Mohammed. "I have a surprise for you." He stopped short at the sight of Jamila in Whip's arms.

Whip disengaged himself from the girl with noticeable reluctance, glancing casually at the intruders, his eyes hazy and unreliable. Blinking hard he peered beyond Ali, staring dumbly at the stunningly dressed woman standing to one side of their host. Jamila, uneasy under Ali's cold and reprimanding eyes, retreated from Whip self-consciously. Whip blinked again, rubbing his eyes with his knuckles. He swore it was Tina standing next to Ali. Was it?

"I believe you know Mrs. Bonaparte." Ali turned to Tina.

"Madam, this somewhat wilted and shameful flower is my young sister, Princess Jamila." He spoke to his sister in a rapid patter of Arabic. The girl bowed her head low and, salaaming to Whip, then to Tina, left the room hurriedly.

"If you will excuse me, Whip, I have matters of a personal nature to discuss with my sister." He closed the door behind them.

They stared at one another in the silence. Whip smiled sheepishly and pointed to the phone. "I-I was just trying to call you."

Tina stood resolute.

"Does it look bad?" he asked with a little boy quality in his voice.

She nodded. "Perhaps more to your host than to me."

He sighed, relieved. "I don't give a fig about him. I care what you think." He moved towards her, taking her hand and leading her into the room. "Where the devil have you been? Have you any idea—" He stopped. "I guess you were on your way here."

Tina watched him squirm.

"I tell you it was nothing. There's nothing between us. You do believe me?" She nodded. "Then why do I feel like shit?" He tossed his hands into the air in a gesture of helplessness.

Tina felt worse than he did. Excited and ebullient at the prospect of seeing Whip, she believed it wasn't fair to drop in on him out of the blue while he was barnstorming Europe, without any warning. She had told Amy so, when she insisted on her making the trip. She had no right to be angry or jealous. She had no real ties on Whip. Legally she was still married to Renzo.

"Why apologize? I understand. Really, I do."

"You don't," he muttered accusatorily, mopping his brow. Every pore in his body was seeping sweat, he thought. "You don't understand at all. Will you let me explain properly "

"You already did," she said, turning to leave. "I've no right to be here. I let Amy talk me into the trip because I ached for you. I came as an emissary of my father to let you know that should you decide to run for the senate, he'll be behind you to the end." She felt awkward. "This trip is a prelude to announcing your decision to enter a political campaign, isn't it, Whip? All America is speculating on your intentions."

Whip lit a cigarette with shaking fingers. *Damned fig wine—or whatever in hell it was!* He offered Tina a smoke. She declined. Unable to bend to his silent appeal for understanding, Tina maintained a forced and distant manner.

"Forgive me?" he pleaded huskily.

"There's nothing to forgive."

"Then why are you so far away from me?" He extended his arms to her. She turned from him, her eyes searching the room erratically to keep from looking at him. She knew she'd fall into his arms in a second, otherwise.

He walked closer to her, his eyes fully approving the elegant champagne-colored Schiaparelli chiffon gown worn in a Grecian style with one shoulder uncovered. Her coppery flawless skin glowed against the pale fabric. Whip placed his hands on her shoulders and pulled her to him, inhaling her fragrance. He held her tightly against him,

16

not kissing her, just holding her until their heartbeats beat as one.

She broke down and whispered, "Let's go, Whip. I've booked accommodations at the Villa Garibaldi. No reporters, no prying eyes, just the two of us."

He felt relieved. He pulled away from her. "Not now. I can't leave until after Ali and I have talked."

"How long will it take?" She tried disguising her disappointment.

"I don't know. Please trust me, Tina. The full intention behind this trip to Europe was to flush out Ali Mohammed. It's imperative that we talk."

Tina's eyes searched his. She experienced a modicum of dismay and discomfort. "I shouldn't have come," she said flatly.

As excited as Whip was that Tina was here, he was equally as disturbed should anyone suspect the relationship between them. Especially Ali Mohammed. Amy, the meddling fool, meant well but she had no comprehension of the awesome complications underfoot nor could she understand what might happen if certain interested parties got the slightest hint of the love he and Tina shared. He had to be cruel, there was no other way.

"Yes," he said tightly. "You shouldn't have come here."

Hurt, confused and suffused with mortification at his cold withdrawal, she searched his frigid eyes for an answer. Moments before they had been aflame with desire and passion; now, two icebergs eyed her from an incalculable distance. She turned abruptly with marble-like majesty and, masking the rejection and shame sweeping through her, left him alone in the room.

He stared after her, his heart shrinking into a sterile unfeeling mass that gagged him. How could he have spoken to her as he did? His scorpion-like tongue had lashed out at her, stinging her with his deadly venom. He moved out onto the terrace, his hands thrust into his pockets, his body rigid as he seethed with self-anger. He couldn't lose all he'd worked for, he rationalized. Tina would have to understand. Later, he'd explain it all to her. *God, make her understand the pressures I endure!* He couldn't permit his previous intentions to be watered down by his love for Tina. He had to carry on. He had to. The more he argued with himself the more he upbraided his stupidity. Yet as common sense replaced his emotional reaction the more intensified was his belief that he'd done the right thing in discouraging Tina's presence here. He couldn't afford to parade his love for her before the world like a smitten schoolboy, not yet.

Jamila watched Tina leave the villa from the upper balcony, a triumphant glitter in her eyes. She turned around and allowed her eyes to rest on the door leading to Ali's suite of rooms. Other than a few guards patrolling the corridor, the area was deserted. Slowly she moved towards the door, nodding to the sentries in passing. Now she would deal with the woman with whom her foolish brother was apparently enamored—the widow of the late American president.

The villa was ablaze with a myriad of lights when Tina rushed out the front entry door, her floor-length chinchilla dragging behind her. She glanced up and down the shadowy drive lined with sleek, low-slung Ferraris, glittering Mercedes, highly glossed Rolls and a few mirror-polished American limousines, looking in all directions for her driver. Catching sight of the liveried doorman approaching her, tipping his hat, she gave him the make of her auto, still trying to subdue her inner rage and humiliation.

"Madame! Madame, please wait a moment!"

Tina turned slightly to see Ali Mohammed rushing out the door after her. "Please, you mustn't leave. I assure you nothing happened to warrant your being so upset." He sighed dolefully. "Alas, it seems I am committed to suffering the continual intervention of a young and foolish baby sister who believes her sole mission in life is to rescue me from whatever it is she feels to be detrimental to me. She especially frowns on any thoughts of American alliances. I assure you, madame, that Mr. Shiverton could have been in the company of the princess for but a few moments. My dear, when that shameless girl decides to turn on her charm there are few who can withstand her. It would grieve me if you permitted so insignificant an incident to drive you away."

"What must I do to assure you, Sheikh Izmur, that I am not leaving for any other reasons than personal business? There is nothing between Mr. Shiverton and me. I'm here as a guest of his sister."

Ali bowed politely and said discreetly, "How long will you stay in Rome?" He opened a platinum and sapphire jeweled cigarette case and offered her one. Tina shook her head. Ali lit one for himself. "Please call me Ali. All my friends do."

18

"I'll stay a day or two and do some shopping, I suppose."

"Where are you booked?" Ali clicked shut the matching platinum lighter.

"The Villa Garibaldi."

He took another probing look at her. "Indeed? How is it that a young woman, a foreigner at that, should find such a place? It's quite remote."

"Yes, isn't it? But it's so enchanting. My father owns the place. The least I can do is patronize his establishment, don't you agree?" She looked past him in search of her driver.

If Tina hadn't been so upset over Whip she might have noticed the sudden change in Ali as realization of her true identity struck him. "I can't tell you how many times I've tried booking into the Villa Garibaldi and haven't made it. I had to buy this place instead," he said teasingly.

Tina smiled. He was charming, his accent fetching.

"Is there no way I can induce you to remain longer? I promise the guests can be amusing at times."

Tina laughed aloud, more at his amusing facial grimaces. Ali, hoping to detain her, quickly said, "Actually they are very boring. They represent the so-called jet set, the last dregs of café society. But when they put their minds to it, they can be amusing."

"I'm afraid I have other plans," said Tina as her limousine pulled up before the entrance.

Ali leaned over and kissed her hand, holding on to it tightly. "I haven't seen or met a woman as exciting as you in a long while, Madame Erice. That is your name, isn't it?"

Her eyes locked compulsively with his. She drew her hand back, an uneasy feeling sweeping through her. "How did you know—"

"Everyone in Rome knows the Villa Garibaldi is owned by the American financier, a remarkable man, Valentino Erice. He is your father?"

Tina was uncertain why she resented the manner in which Ali spoke of her father, however laudable and complimentary it was. He seemed to disdain the name while holding it in oblique respect.

"May I call for you tomorrow for lunch? There is an intimate restaurant at the beach near Ostia Antica that will thoroughly enchant you. Trust me. Besides," he added,

19

"anything I can do to make the daughter of Valentino Erice enjoy Rome, the closer I shall arrive at that time when the Villa might be open to me."

"Sheikh Izmur, you are incorrigible. From what I've learned about you in the short time I'm here, you could buy and sell the Villa Garibaldi ten thousand times over."

He feigned being terribly downcast. "I hope you won't hold my wealth against me. It can be a terrible stumbling block at times." He grinned amiably.

"Yes, I find it so." She gave him a measure of his own kind and entered the limousine. Ali closed the door behind her.

"Lunch tomorrow. I won't take no for an answer."

As the car rolled leisurely along the curved drive to the gate, Ali stood for several moments watching it until it was lost in the darkness, out of sight. He tossed his cigarette to the ground, grinding it out with the toe of his patent pump.

A puzzled frown crept into his face as he attempted to piece together the relationship between Whip Shiverton and this terribly attractive daughter of Val Erice. Benk- hanhian had advanced the theory that Whip Shiverton was not held in good repute by Val Erice, who wouldn't sup- port Whip in his political endeavors. Coincidence that Tina Erice should appear in Rome at the same time Whip did? Possible, but hardly probable in this case. He'd seen the look of intimacy passing between them, and could recognize the presence of love on the spot.

A pang of jealousy shot through Ali. Taking hold of himself he frowned and reprimanded himself, assuring himself that the world was filled with women like her. Yet something about her was unique . . . something be- neath that surface . . .

He glanced at his watch. It was nearly 11:00 P.M. Where had the night gone? He glanced about the grounds. Private sentries were still on watch. They'd be changing shifts at midnight. As he entered the villa, his thoughts centered on Valerie. What an enormous capacity for sex! He disliked her excessive use of drugs. But then most women today were no different.

Inside the villa, sweeping past the doorman who sa- laamed to him, he nodded to a few guests in passing. He checked with the caterer to make certain there were enough refreshments provided. A few guests were danc- ing, but most were gathered in the next salon viewing the pornographic films, freely imbibing their own intoxicants.

20

He ordered the servants to open more windows and doors.

When it dawned on Ali that he was deliberately delaying but could no longer prevent the inevitable, he headed for the study to confront the American maverick, Whip Shiverton.

CHAPTER TWO

Whip, admiring a formidable gun collection in the built-in cases along one wall, turned and walked towards Ali when he entered the study. Ali was all apology.

"I say, my timing was off. I hope it wasn't awkward."

"Is Mrs. Bonaparte still here?" Nonchalant, he hoped he showed little emotion.

"The—uh—charming lady left for the Villa Garibaldi. I regret that my sister behaved abominably. I assure you she shall be severely dealt with."

"You needn't deal with her at all. I take full blame." He smiled, and glanced at the carafe of fig wine.

"The fig wine was a bit much for me. Too overpowering. Let me tell you it packs a terrific wallop."

"Fig wine?" Ali frowned, his eyes falling to the lead crystal decanter. "Fig wine?" he repeated, holding the glass stopper to his nostrils. He inhaled delicately. Replacing the stopper, he picked up the remains of Jamila's glass and touched the contents with the tip of his finger. He touched his tongue to the liquid. He shook his head, forcing a tolerant smile to his lips as he would at the discovery of a child's mischief.

"The princess, that little minx, had every intention of seducing you, Whitman." He shook his head, exasperated.

Whip's brows rose at the thought. "You'll have your problems keeping a long list of suitors away from her beauty."

Ali became overly dramatic. "You see what happens when we try to westernize my people? They get out of hand. Jamila laced the wine with a powerful aphrodisiac brewed from the extract of pomegranate and dates, mingled with a narcotic we call *qat*. Combined, the ingredients affect the central nervous system, stimulating it in various ways. Do your arms and legs feel watery—weak? You must be sweating excessively?"

He nodded, embarrassed at having been taken in by

22

Jamila. What was it Ali called his sister? A child? Perhaps Ali ought to take another look at her. She was no child.

Ali spoke Arabic into a phone and hung up. "I've ordered you some black coffee. I'm certain it will help your head."

"Why the formality? You called me Whip in school," said Whip.

"I believe I've always called you Whitman. I detest nicknames."

Whip shrugged. "Suit yourself. I may call you Ali?"

The coffee came in moments. Whip had two cups of the bitter black syrupy fluid and protested when Ali began to pour a third.

"That's enough. Thank you. That's a bit much to take."

Ali laughed. "Come, suppose we take a walk in the garden. The fresh air will do you good. Are you up to it?"

"Anything but no more coffee," Whip replied, daubing at his moist face and neck with a handkerchief.

They walked together in silence, out onto the terrace, down another flight of stairs and onto the garden path, through a lovely garden of blooms and shrubbery barely visible under dim spotlights.

The small talk has ended, thought Whip. *Good. Now to get to the nitty gritty.*

Whip lit up a filter tip and offered one to his host. Ali smoked his own, a Turkish brand. Taking time to light up, he clicked his lighter shut and fell into step alongside Whip.

"A deplorable accident, that in West Berlin. Did they catch the terrorist who tried to do you in?"

"Terrorist? You know more than the police. I'm not certain. I left within the hour following the incident. . . . How do you figure it was a terrorist plot?"

"I was watching the telly when it happened. I recognized the fool. He and his kind always attempt to advance their personal philosophies. They can be hired to promote any radical cause for a goodly sum of money."

"Communist inspired?"

Ali shrugged. "The jackal is always identified as a jackal unless he wears a disguise. Then it becomes difficult to identify him. Not impossible—just difficult." Then, on a lighter note, he asked, "Why don't I see you in the pleasure pots of the world?"

"No time for pleasure pots in recent days. Tell me, Ali, why do you make yourself so scarce in Washington?"

"I leave Washington and its ridiculous intrigues to my embassy and its peculiar breed of men trained especially for the stuffy, time-wasting protocols of supercilious men."

"I've always wanted to talk with you, thank you for your generosity and that of your father, for the substantial campaign contribution made on behalf of Ted. I'm sure if he had lived he'd have thanked you personally."

"But he did. Ted and I had lunch the week following his inauguration." Ali inhaled deeply, exhaling slowly.

Whip gave him a sharp, quick look and his face became heavy and tight. *Why hadn't Ted mentioned this?* he wondered, keeping his reaction minimal.

"You see, Whitman, our nation wanted to cement better relations with the Shiverton administration than those endured with previous chiefs of state. Since 1948 our nation, unfortunately, has been forced to undergo several transitional and precarious periods when aliens stealing and occupying our lands by force succeeded in pushing back our borders, playing havoc with the lives and properties of our people. They laid claim to our natural resources indiscriminately. We were forced into chaos as larger nations chose to play God—Allah if you will—using us as pawns. The disorder and turmoil in the Middle East doesn't escape you, does it?"

"Hardly," replied Whip, an intent expression in his eyes.

"Would it not therefore be sensible for the two future leaders of our countries—mine and yours—to sit down, discuss our grievances and offer probable solutions in mutual agreement?"

"Future leaders, Ali?" Whip gave him a bland look.

"My father, the Prince, is dead. I am soon to be crowned in his stead. Upon the death of my uncle, the King, I stand next in line. And you, my old Harvard friend, will one day become an American president. Correct?"

"You're a bit premature. I have yet to declare my intentions. Why should you be so presumptuous?" He laughed lightly.

It was Ali's turn to laugh. They were like prizefighters sparring about in the ring, each wary of the other and unsure where the real strength lay, in a powerful right jab or a left to the jaw.

"You are too intelligent to underrate my sagacity in such matters." Ali paused and laughed again, showing even white teeth dazzling bright against the coppery glow of his suntan. He extinguished his cigarette and inserted another into the slender platinum holder and before lighting it, turned to Whip. "You have come to Europe giving off the scent of both the fox and the lion to all who stand in the wings to watch this marvelous performance. You are the fox who knows all the traps and snares and your roar is that of the lion when he frightens away the wolves and jackals. Do you insult my intelligence by denying your own drama?"

Whip continued to smoke in silence. Music from the dance orchestra floated from the villa down along the sloping garden and reached Whip's ears. For an instant he thought of Tina and the enormous hurt that had welled up in her eyes before she left, and he felt a pang over his heart as the blood rushed achingly through his veins. He turned to stare out at the night scene of lights in the valley cradling the Eternal City of Rome. The dome of Saint Peter's Basilica was lit up at the center of a halo of lights scattered throughout both old Rome and the new. The heady scent of orange and lemon blossoms intoxicated his senses. If only life could be as simple as this moment, he thought, before his own mind grinded gears for his reply to Ali Mohammed. Still he was unable to speak. Ali made an additional comment.

"You know, Whitman, you are more the prince than Ted was. You know how to employ the nature of men."

"How do you figure that?" retorted Whip quietly.

"A wise prince—leader if you will—who continues to support a cause, long after the forces that induced him to do so no longer exist, is a fool. Because all men are naturally evil and will not observe their faith towards you, you must not hold fast to your principles and observe your faith to them."

Whip asked, "You presuppose all men to be evil?"

Ali laughed from deep within his belly. "You amaze me, Whitman. I cannot believe I am in the presence of the man who made the earth tremble during his days as attorney general." Ali shook his thick head of curly hair and rubbed his cheeks and chin contemplatively. "How many treaties of peace have been made null and void, how many business alliances have been broken by the faithlessness of leaders? History has marked them well.

25

Only he who knows best how to play the fox has been most successful. And," he emphasized with animated hands, "at times it is necessary for a leader to be a hypocrite and a dissembler. From the time man became a thinker the successful men, leaders of nations, think only of deception and find excellent reasons for these same deceptions. No one has developed greater skill in pledging his words. No one affirms his pledges with greater oaths and observed them less than certain recent leaders who have come into worldwide prominence. You are well aware of whom I speak. You may ask why are they successful in their deceptions? Because they know well the weakness of men."

Whip turned to face his adversary, their eyes locking compulsively in the ambiguous shadows of the muted lamplights.

"Your brother Ted apparently didn't know the inner nature of the men of whom I am speaking. My nation gave Ted millions of dollars for his campaign because we believed in his astuteness and fairness. But Ted gave them arms and ammunition and antiaircraft missiles to be used against us. Why?"

Whip tensed. He felt his blood run to ice paralyzing his senses. "I cannot answer for my brother. Without a clearer exegesis of the facts it would be folly for me to explain."

Ali, biting on the cigarette holder, continued as if Whip hadn't spoken a word.

"A leader must appear to be merciful, faithful, humane, devoutly religious, upright, and astute in his dealings with others; he should even be so in reality. But his mind should be so trained that when the occasion requires it he must change to the opposite position." Ali extended his hand, pointing it to the villa, and they began the slow walk up the incline.

"It's perfectly understandable that a leader can't always perform those things which place him in an excellent light. He's often obliged to act contrary to humanity, charity and religion. It is, however, vital for him to have a versatile mind capable of changing readily—not to swerve from good, mind you—but to resort to evil if necessity demands it."

Whip wanted to ask him why he was so intent on offering a treatise on ethics, morals, protocol and decorum. Instead he listened intently as they moved along the gravel

26

path. An occasional chirping bird intruded upon their minds.

"Contrary to the image you projected as attorney general, as president you'd have to be most cautious not to allow anything to escape your lips that isn't indicative of charity, integrity, humanity, uprighteousness and piety."

Whip shook his head, forcing light laughter. "Again with the president business. I tell you, Ali, you are premature."

Throughout their conversation Whip became acutely aware of the armed sentries stationed strategically along the path. Dressed in desert robes, their black eyes iridescent, they held their guns at the ready prepared for any emergency. They bowed their heads reverently as their master passed them.

"Leaders of men are judged by the results of their labor—"

"The end justifies the means. Is that it? What exactly do you want to say, Ali?"

"I am doing a bad job. The diplomatic, circuitous route isn't my cup of tea. Bear with me, please."

They climbed the steps to the formal terrace, scaling a few more before reaching the patio at the rear of the villa, and entering the study. Whip gazed around, impressed by the library of first editions. "You don't really pack these when traveling to your homeland?"

"I have duplicates in all my homes. Even I need time alone to meditate or read. I haven't learned the knack you Americans have acquired for burning yourselves out around the clock."

Whip sat opposite the gilded throne-like chair Ali was seated in. He smiled. "Believe me, it's a rumor the Communists spread to undermine the morale of the nation. We aren't nearly as decadent and self-indulgent as you noble Easterners. We may be advanced in modern technology. But it's clear we haven't begun to implement the ingenious devices you Arabs have perpetuated for centuries to arouse your passions. Your country is, after all, the cradle of erotica. Our progress was spoiled for too long by Victorianism."

Ali laughed heartily. He poured wine from a delicately crafted gold carafe, filling two crystal goblets and handing one to Whip. "I assure you this is the forbidden fig wine of our people, *without* the added properties of a gazelle's sweetbreads or of *qat*. It contains none of the pomegran-

27

ate ferment Jamila prepared for you earlier." He shook his head thoughtfully. "Can't imagine why she intended to seduce you."

"Should I feel offended or complimented by your remark?"

They clinked glasses as Ali gestured vaguely to dismiss both the thought and his remark. They drank in silence. Whip savored the rich liquid as it splashed on his palate.

"My colleagues and I have witnessed a total change in your personality, Whitman," Ali began, lighting up a cigarette. "We know you in the past to have been a courageous, grave and determined man. You've maintained yourself in such esteem, it would be difficult to conspire against you or attack you."

"Oh, for God's sake," said Whip. "That fellow in West Berlin didn't think so."

"That was something else. That man was a radical, a malcontent, a poor, misguided fool provoked by conspirators itching to promote a confrontation between our nations. Two things a president must fear: attempts against him by his own people or attacks from without by powerful foreigners."

No one had been more loved and adored by the masses than Ted Shiverton, thought Whip, watching Ali remove a gun from a wall case.

The difficulties surrounding the conspirators of the world are infinite. Few ever come to a good end, because he who conspires seldom does it alone." Ali examined the gun.

Whip tensed. The feeling that he was standing at the edge of the world, slowly losing his balance, wouldn't leave him. *Come on, Ali. Talk. Tell me what I've come to hear.*

"A conspirator fears jealousy, apprehension of punishment, even unsuspected death. The leader, on the other hand, has on his side the law, the support of his friends, a government that protects him and the majesty of his office."

Where the hell was all this when Ted was killed?"

"Earlier you mentioned—uh—colleagues. Who are they?"

"Colleagues? Did I say that?" He was handling an 1873 Colt Peacemaker. "This is the famous revolver that made all men equal in your American pioneer days. Did you know that?" Ali balanced it, pulled back the ham-

28

mer, and squeezed . . . a loud click. "It's in excellent working order," he boasted. He removed another after replacing the first. "Texas Patterson .40 calibre, 1836. You load the muzzle with powder and ball," he said with pride.

Whip patiently waited for Ali to make his point. He wasn't disappointed.

"It's a strange thing. People see only what you seem to be. Few really know you as I do." Ali rubbed his jaw, smiling in reflection. "I came into contact with your irresistible force on the gridiron at Harvard once."

"Sorry as hell about it. It couldn't be helped."

A deep silence fell between them as Ali returned to his seat to sip more wine. He stared at the spiral of smoke escaping from his cigarette. Silence was pierced by the sounds of barking dogs. Ali gave a start and moved anxiously towards the terrace. Two Dobermans on leashes leaped towards him, breaking their choke chains. Ali petted them fondly, calling to an approaching guard. "What happened?" he asked in Arabic.

Whip saw him move towards four sentries in desert garb. They huddled, speaking in excited but hushed tones. Ali handed the dogs back to their trainer, nodded to them and waved them back off the terrace. He rejoined Whip in the study.

"Sorry. Seems we had a bit of a security problem. Would-be prowlers. Unfortunate . . . One won't have the use of a leg. The Dobermans strenuously object to uninvited guests."

"Anyone I know?"

Ali shrugged. "Do you know a man named Bahar Bahar?" His keen eyes, lidded at half mast, enabled him to peer at Whip without his being aware of the scrutiny. Whip played the name over on his tongue several times, shaking his head dubiously.

"Bahar Bahar? No. Afraid not." Inwardly his guts churned. West Berlin authorities had confirmed that his assailant was a Palestinian terrorist from a splinter group. Name of Bahar Bahar.

"He'll not be trespassing on our land again. He would be dealt with by the Guardia, under Italian jurisdiction. In my country he'll be charged with a crime against the state."

"The state? How do you figure it?"

"The crime was against me. I am the state in my nation."

29

A flicker of annoyance crossed Whip's face. Ali, quick to see it, scoffed. "You Americans, so easy to forgive, so temperate in your punishment of criminal offenders. The number of criminal offenders declaring residences in your state and federal facilities is mind-boggling. You realize you only prolong the inevitable. A hating man is never done with loathing."

"Dammit, Ali," Whip was losing his patience. "You studied the same law I did. The system of jurisprudence prevailing in the American system isn't perfect. It is something one man can't abolish, however. In a democracy the majority decides an issue. Americans feel it to be more humane to rehabilitate the criminal——"

"And give lightning the opportunity to strike twice in the same place." Ali's smile evaporated.

For an instant Whip saw beneath the mask of pleasantry a hard, impersonal sovereign unused to being countermanded, a man whose word was absolute. He thought, *What I'd give to get inside his mind*. Whip loosened his black tie. "Do you mind?"

"Think on my words. You Americans ought to do something about your liberal ways—stupidity pawned off as democracy." Ali realized by Whip's expression that he'd gone over the line.

"Whitman," he said, pausing for dramatic effect. "May I suggest, if you really want the Presidency, it can be insured for you."

Whip, sat forward in his chair, his cynical expression turning bland. "My dear Ali, if I want the presidency, I don't need you to insure it. My campaign tactics got Ted elected, didn't they?"

"Determination plus the assistance of several million dollars, my dear Whitman, is what won the election, plus a last minute change of plans by my colleagues."

Something exploded in Whip's head. He had to wait until all the pieces fell into order in his mind before he could make sense of what followed. Whip became unaware of the passage of time. He listened, spellbound, in utter disbelief as Ali unfolded a most astounding melodrama. Whip heard a revelation of facts that boggled his mind.

Whip remained in Rome for the next two days, listening, talking very little, never giving a concrete answer when a question was asked of him. For relaxation he played a few vigorous games of tennis and swam to limber his muscles when he felt the fatigue of restlessness

30

engulf him. He listened raptly when Valerie begged him to understand her sudden, unexpected romance with Ali Mohammed. He suppressed his indignation and personal feelings.

Whip spoke sternly to her, carefully pointing out that her former image as First Lady would be shattered if she chose to have an indiscreet romance with the Arab chieftain. He suggested what she might encounter back in America if the relationship didn't work.

Valerie could not be convinced that she hadn't the right to do as she chose. "He's settling several million dollars on me and tells me he wants to adopt the children." At the furious expression on Whip's face, Valerie hastened to add, "Of course I won't allow it. They are Shivertons and Shivertons they'll remain. Please, Whip, help me to handle it properly. I don't want Ted's image to be sullied."

"What in hell do you need more millions for? You're already an heiress and Ted left you well provided."

"But not enough to live this life!" Valerie pouted. "It's the only way to live, Whip. Rome, Paris, London, the Riviera, the whole world! What else is there?"

"There's America," he said quietly, studying her as if seeing her and a new brand of women for the first time.

"Oh, that," she muttered. "It's old hat. I want new and exotic thrills. I want to be where I can live a private life and do what I want . . ."

It always amazed Whip when he heard Americans take America for granted. There was no place like it on earth, despite its many shortcomings. True, it was still a young nation boasting the growing pains of its few hundred years. But where would it be in another century or two?

Thoughts of America made him sick for hot apple pie, hot dogs, and cheeseburgers, even though they were considered gauche by the elite. Then, of course, there was Tina whom he missed more than life itself.

He and his entourage headed back home before the week ended. Valerie remained behind for another two weeks, promising she'd be most discreet. It was agreed she'd wait a respectable length of time before shedding her widow's weeds. Oddly enough she agreed to this stay of ceremony but only after Ali Mohammed insisted on it.

CHAPTER THREE

Two days before Whip left Rome, Tina made her exodus aboard a TWA transoceanic jet, paying little heed to her fellow passengers. She wallowed in the gloomy thoughts assailing her senses, admitting her folly in making the trip to rendezvous with Whip. Thoughts that her sentimentality might have jeopardized their relationship irked her, fragmenting her composure.

Apparently neither she nor Whip were prepared to make commitments to each other. Not a telephone call had come from him in the two days she remained in Rome. *Not one!* Wondering at the fragility of their love, she thought that perhaps she wasn't capable of loving one man totally, not in the strictest sense of love. Had she seen too much in her young life? Had she viewed deception at too close a range?

Following their sexual sojourn in Manhattan when the revival of their feelings spiraled into love, how certain she'd been that this was the real thing—the love of her life. She was no neophyte. Loving a man in a mature sense meant loving everything about him. It came as a crushing blow to her when she realized the impossibility of such a task. How was it possible to love everything about a man? Certainly there was as much to dislike in a person's behavior as there was to love. Such insights caused whirlwind conflicts in her. Since the good in Whip far outweighed the bad, she concluded the negatives would merely fall by the wayside and be ignored. Therefore she chose to love him.

But did she? Had it really been so simple a problem to resolve? Or was she merely delaying a day of reckoning within herself?

The stunning impact of his cold dismissal, his brutal lack of consideration had offended, revolted and angered her. How different it had been when she spent a week of ecstasy with him after Ted's death. Between them had been love, cohesion, and the inclination to overlook any

32

shortcomings. Now, after a bitter rejection, Tina experienced suspicion and alienation followed by frightening inner conflicts. The birth of a new hostility spread through her coupled by a desire to push from her mind anything connected with the name Shiverton. She felt as she had with Renzo when the veil of deception fell from his face and she saw him for what he really was.

Tina lapsed into a meditative silence, where she hoped she could erase all thought from her mind. Unfortunately a procession of images waiting in the wings of her mind moved swiftly into action, dancing across the stage of her skull. First, Jamila, wrapped in Whip's feverish embrace. His startled embarrassment when he recognized Tina. The hostile attitude when Ali Mohammed stumbled onto their intimacy. His hasty apology, too stagey to suit her. And to top it off, Ali's reaction at her identity as the daughter of Val Erice. Strange, her father had never mentioned knowing the prince.

The more Tina dwelled on the peculiar circumstances surrounding Whip's unusual behavior, the more she convinced herself he was up to something. The hurried trip to Europe, Valerie as his companion. Valerie, of all people!

Enigmatic words spilling uncomfortably from his lips. What was it he'd said so cryptically? *I can't leave. I made the trip to Europe to insure a meeting with Ali Mohammed.*

The only benediction she could give Whip were his very words. They helped keep her sanity. As she continued swimming through the hazy mist of adverse thoughts an inner stabilizing voice whispered over and over, *This, too, shall pass.*

Sheikh Ali Mohammed Izmur . . . *Sheikh Ali Mohammed . . .*

The more she tried to dismiss him from her mind, the more he intruded on her thoughts. Much about Ali disturbed Tina. On the plus side, he was handsome, certainly no fool, well educated, polished in international diplomacy and exceedingly charming. The day after they met, he called for her at the Villa Garibaldi and took her to lunch, as he said he would. On the minus side . . .

Lunch was at a charming bistro overlooking a sandy beach at Ostia Antica, at the edge of a city built up of the excavations of antiquity. His manners were impeccable. Solicitous of her, he was concerned that she'd leave Rome harboring feelings of anger against his sister

33

Jamila and Whip. For too long Tina felt as if he were inquiring too deeply into her relationship with Whip, as if driven with purpose. She had denied the relationship repeatedly.

"Your assumption that I'm having an affair with Whip is purely whimsical," she insisted adamantly at one point.

"If I seem to be pressing, it's because I have ulterior motives. I find you most provocative, Tina. I'm flirting with you and bungling it. I suppose American women have always intimidated me."

Tina, aghast, sputtered, "But—but you've just asked Valerie to marry you! Are such sacred rites taken so lightly in your faith?" Tina had been chafing at the bit ever since Valerie called her at the Garibaldi to impart the stunning news.

"Who can explain what happens when two people meet and the explosions begin? Surely you've experienced such feelings?"

He waited for her reply. Tina, tilting her head and flashing him an indulgent smile, said, "I'm not the type to hear bells ring, cupids sing, or whatever it is women claim they hear."

A gust of gentle wind crept across the sand, ruffling her hair in the breeze. The sound of the white-capped surf rolling in from sparkling Mediterranean waters was lulling and peaceful. Ali, gazing at her, reached across the table to take her hands in his. "Don't you hear anything now, Tina?"

She blushed. She tried to withdraw her hands, but he held them fast. He was intent on dissolving the invisible barrier between them.

"You're more beautiful than I remembered. Last night you were stunning. Today, an added dimension has crept into your beauty—soul. So few Western women have it. Oh, they have chic, *savoir-faire*, a knack with decor, but few have soul. It's a rare and elusive quality, Tina Erice."

"Uh—Tina Erice Bonaparte. I'm a married woman."

"A fact that can be easily remedied," he suggested. Curious about her, he asked her numerous questions about herself. She complied with noticeable restraint, citing a few highlights of her young life. When she could she maneuvered the subject back to him.

Ali spoke of himself freely as if his life were an open book to anyone interested enough to inquire of him. Like Tina he did not go into depth about his personal

34

life or about his country. They fenced skillfully for a time, never drawing blood.

"What a tremendous responsibility thrust upon your shoulders in your country. You're very young to become the leader of so important a nation."

He shrugged indifferently. "I'm a year younger than Whitman. If he's able to run a nation, should I be less capable? Remember, I was born to power."

Tina felt the impact of his words. They clung cohesively in her mind. *I'm a year younger than Whitman.* . . . Tina gazed at the sandy beach where a gang of street urchins were playing a game with rules only they were privy to. Earlier when Ali drove her through the Coney Island atmosphere he told her that Ostica, once Rome's military and commercial port, was actually an entire city excavated from ruins.

Everything was so old and ancient here she found it difficult to bridge the present with the past. Now, the present was becoming too complex. His last statement whirled in her head. She felt dizzy.

She sipped her wine, and thrust her hands in the pockets of her jeans jacket, tailored to perfection for her by Cardin.

If he's able to run a nation I am capable of doing so, since I was born to power. Those were his words. Was it possible Whip *did* seek the presidency? Why should she be so surprised? Rumors circulated wildly back in the States. The betting men in Las Vegas were already taking odds against it.

Ali watched her too intently. She began to squirm uncomfortably. Many things threatened Tina. The most prominent was Ali's reaction to her being the daughter of Val Erice. It wasn't a known fact that Val owned the Villa Garibaldi. Yet, synonymous with the exclusive hotel in Ali's mind was the name Valentino Erice. He'd been too quick with the knowledge, the name easily within his grasp. Knowing how careful Val had been to keep his business hidden from the public, this fact made her feel squeamish.

Tina suddenly felt an urgency to flee Ali Mohammed's company, to leave Italy and get back to Long Island where she felt safe. She'd made plans to visit Sicily, land of her father's birth, but the instinctive feeling of impending danger shook her.

"Please take me back to the Villa Garibaldi," she told him.

The frozen look on her face, the noticeable agitation of rising hysteria, precluded any attempt on his part to dissuade her. He tossed a handful of lire on the table, more than enough to pay the bill, and helped Tina out of her chair. Standing there a moment, in a spotlight of sun, Ali was unable to hold back the comment,

"My dear Tina, you are extraordinary. You have the gift of life. Everything around you comes to life. You smile and the sun rises in its heaven. We will be together, you and I. Mark my words. When we do, it will be because you will it."

They drove back to Rome in his steel blue Ferrari convertible in silence. Only the high-powered roar of the powerful engine was heard, for each was absorbed in private thoughts. Tina, trying to fathom his last cryptic remark, thought his strange, prophetic words farfetched and improbable.

She would never know how much she meant to this prince among men. On this day he might have been persuaded to forget that Valerie Shiverton ever existed. If she had only shown the slightest inkling of interest . . . His fancy had been totally captivated by this trim-figured woman who had by her comportment excited him more than any woman in his life. Was it because she appeared so remote? So totally self-sufficient? What was it?

At the Villa, Tina wished him well. She made some flimsy statement about inviting him to Las Vegas.

"Perhaps one day you'll be my guest, your highness."

"In the numerous times I visited your American Monte Carlo, I never saw the likes of you, Tina. If I had, I assure you I might never have returned to my homeland." He spoke with serious overtones, in a manner Tina took in jest.

Before leaving her Ali drew her to him and kissed her lightly on the lips. Tina blushed again and forced herself to deny the excitement she felt. She looked deeply into his eyes and what she read in them both confused her and caused her to flush again. She quickly walked away from him and entered the Villa Garibaldi angry at herself for acting in such a schoolgirl manner. *He's just a flirt. All men like him do is try to make every woman they can. They are incapable of any feelings other than lust and the urge to conquer,* she told herself.

Her eyes snapped open suddenly at the jarring drone of engines. Sudden air turbulence rocking the plane caused

36

her stomach to sink sickeningly. A glance at the other passengers who hadn't minded the abrupt changes taking place pacified her somewhat. She finished her coffee, barely touching the sandwiches, and placed the tray on the empty seat next to her. She pulled her leather coat around her shoulders, chilled by the temperature drop, and closed her eyes hoping that sleep would engulf her. She had much to discuss with her father when she arrived in Long Island.

He was puttering about in the garden supervising a crew of workmen busy building a formidable greenhouse adjoining the main house. Val felt lost in the winter months when he was unable to occupy his spare time among the living things he loved to grow. For him it was therapy; time to relax and concentrate only on things he could do with his hands. Now, soon, before the onset of winter he'd be ready so his time wouldn't be frittered away on useless things. Absorbed watching the men perform their craft he suddenly noticed them pausing in their labor to gaze beyond him. A few workers whistled appreciatively.

Val turned in the direction of their interest, squinting against the sunlight. His eyes lit up joyously at the sight of the lithe figure in blue jeans and a sheer lacy cotton blouse sauntering towards him. No one could have been more astonished than Val as he opened his arms towards her.

"Tina! What are you doing here? You're supposed to be in Rome." He took her hands, kissed her and hugged her dearly.

"Come, come see the new hothouse."

"Not now, Father. Can we talk?"

Val glanced sharply at her. "You don't call me Pop any more?" He smiled. "I understand. It's serious talk you want."

"You know me like a book."

"Come, we go to the gazebo, eh?" They walked side by side over the gravel walk crunching the stones underfoot. In the shaded alcove Tina sat down, fanning herself.

"It's never been this warm in June, phew."

Val shrugged noncommittally. He wiped his hands on a towel, then daubed at the sweat on his brow. He poured two glasses of iced lemonade from a thermos container and handed one to his daughter. He took the other and sat down in one of the patio chairs.

37

"Who's Sheikh Ali Mohammed Izmur?" she asked lightly.

"I'm supposed to know him?" Val shook his head dubiously.

"He knows you."

Val sighed. "Many people know of me."

"He knows that you own the Villa Garibaldi."

Immediately Tina's words elevated the conversation to a different plane. Val sipped his iced drink and inhaled the fresh scent of lilacs growing in a vine over the gazebo. Val's eyes trailed back to her as Tina began to talk. She told her father of their meeting, mentioning the names of those guests she'd met at the party held in Whip's and Valerie's honor and describing in detail the opulence of Ali's villa. She found herself gushing over Ali's charm.

"At lunch before I returned home, he told me he'll be the reigning monarch in his nation shortly."

Val, listening solemnly, minimized his interest at the names Harrofian and Von Rhome. He wanted to ask, wasn't the Benkhanhian heir present at the festivities?

"That's not all, guess what?"

Val's interest was piqued. "Don't keep your father in suspense."

"The Prince has asked Valerie to marry him. Can you beat that?"

"What better insurance?" muttered Val knowingly, words he hadn't meant Tina to hear.

"Insurance for what?"

Val feigned indifference. "Did I say insurance? Insurance?" He touched his hand to his forehead in a gesture of forgetfulness. "Lately I grow confused." A weak excuse, but an effective one.

"That'll be the day—you get confused? Hah! Anyway," she continued, "he's willing to wait for the proper passage of time. I marvel at the dispatch with which this romance budded. He told me romances often spark without warning, that you must take advantage of the flaming passions, for they pass all to swiftly." She had the good grace to blush at the echoing of Ali's words. "American men should take lessons in romance from such a man. He oozed with vitality." Then on a more serious note she added, "Know what, Pop? I didn't believe him." Her eyes fell to the doodling Val was performing on a notepad.

Val's eyes lifted from the doodling and met his daughter's in a manner conveying sharp interest. "Why didn't you believe him?"

"Don't ask me why. The way he spoke, deliberately with precise words. It's not my affair what he and Valerie decide to do with their lives, yet he took time to explain as if it were imperative that I understand."

"Harumph," muttered Val, clearing his throat. He was writing over and over again the name Ali Mohammed Izmur. Sheikh Ali Mohammed Izmur.

"First tell me what Amy's brother had to say about these interesting developments. Then, Tina, if you will, tell me why you returned home so suddenly?" His eyes searched hers critically.

"I don't know what Whip thinks. I didn't ask." She sipped her lemonade and poured them both another drink. She handed Val a refill and took hers back to her seat, deliberately avoiding Val's penetrating, thoughtful gaze.

"Before I reply to your second question, I want you to talk with me." Now she looked at him challengingly, but Val averted his eyes.

"Yes. About what?" Val sipped his drink sparingly.

"What's going on, Pop? Something is troubling you, isn't it? Ever since Ted's death—" She paused thoughtfully. "No, it was before that. I'm not certain how much before. Don't deny it, Pop. Not to me. I may be your daughter, but I know more than I let you think I know. The concentration of our business in Las Vegas. The slow liquidation of our assets in the East. The total separation of our name from Joey's business and the formation of so many corporations—Why?"

Val placed his glass on the nearby table and looked hard at his daughter, thinking as he did, *If only she'd been born a man*. Then, as if she had read his mind, Tina said with noticeable irritation, "Father, I'm not sixteen—or eighteen. Nor am I a man. If I'd been your son, I wouldn't have had to ask you these questions. You'd have already told me. Why should it matter if I'm male or female? I'm still the seed of your seed—the blood of your blood. I want to know all there is about you—from your lips to my ears—now, while we're both alive and can appreciate each other."

It was a poignant moment in which Val's heart swelled with pride until he felt it would burst. He rose to his feet and taking Tina by the hand led her back over the path towards the house.

Catching sight of the swing hanging from the tall oak

39

tree, Tina exclaimed gleefully and sprinted towards it. She sat in it and propelled herself into the air for several moments until she soared above the ground feeling as free as a bird. In a quick transition as she caught sight of Val glancing up at her like any adoring father, she brought herself back to the present and slowed the swing to a halt.

Running to his side, out of breath she asked, "How come the swing is up again? That took me back a few years," she smiled.

"Joey brought the children here last weekend. Like all children, they love to swing through the trees. We didn't dismantle it."

Tina nodded and followed him inside. In moments they were in Val's study. Standing before his desk, he pulled her into his arms gently holding her as he had when she was a growing child. After a moment, he disengaged his arms from her and sighing heavily walked to the window overlooking the tennis courts.

A series of mental images returned to him. The courts were suddenly filled with laughing voices and competitive young men and women swinging their racquets. There was his son Jimmy, and Tina and Bob Harmon and young Benne with his horde of young schoolgirl flirts who chased him. Then as the scene dissolved and silence returned Val was unable to pull himself away. He continued to peer with nostalgia, at the sun-drenched lawns and dazzling white tennis courts.

"You should have really been a son."

"But I'm not. Face that reality. Get over that hurdle for my sake if not yours, Pop. I need answers to many questions. Don't shut me up by telling me I should have been a man. Won't you tell me what I want to know?" she pleaded.

Val turned from the tranquillity of the scenery. "I wonder if you can handle everything in your mind."

"Won't you trust me?" she agonized. "Is it always to be this way between us, Pop? Because I'm a woman you fail to see what's really inside my mind."

"It's not a matter of trust." Val sauntered back to the desk and sat down facing her. "Women as a rule don't have the capacity to dwell within themselves. They need a counterpart, another human being to make them feel whole. If the knowledge I impart to you presses upon you too heavily you might be inclined to confide in the

40

wrong person. The last thing in my mind is to make you vulnerable."

"Why not? What's there to fear in my sudden vulnerability? What can happen to me? Tell me, I need to know." Tina sat in the chair facing him, one leg crossed over the other.

Val remained silent and contemplative for the next few seconds.

"How long can you be spared from your responsibilities at the Pyramids?" he asked softly. "Can Las Vegas do without you for a time?"

"Your son Benne is doing superbly. Haven't you heard?"

Val stood up and moved behind his highbacked leather chair, and leaning over it pursed his lips as he stared interminably at his daughter as if he were trying to peer inside her mind to determine the character that was contained in it.

"It isn't anything I can tell you in a moment, a day, week, month, even a year. It will take time. I can only lead you over the path slowly to see how you handle it in your mind. There is something solid in the way you handle yourself. I've noticed this about you over the years, then there've been times when you literally seem to fall apart and become emotional. Emotional women are intensely frightening because you can never outguess them or predict their behavior at any given moment."

Val removed the curious figure of the double-headed griffin from the curio cabinet and returned with it to his desk. Seated, he began to speak quietly. "Diana the huntress was a special woman whose skills increased by learning the habits of her prey. To make herself invulnerable to her enemies, she skillfully changed her own habits, never doing a thing the same way twice. She became wise learning of the powers on earth that guide men, animals and all living organisms."

Listening to Val increased her puzzlement and impatience. She wanted to interrupt, to ask him to explain his cryptic statements. For fear she'd lose what she'd gained these past moments, she kept silent.

Val cautioned her not to discuss with anyone else the things he revealed to her this day. Sensing she was on the threshold of something spectacular, she sat forward on her chair like a cat ready to spring at its enemy. "Does Benne know about all this—whatever it is?" she gestured animatedly.

41

"Not entirely."

"Does Joey?"

"No."

"Why not Joey?"

"He's never asked. He chose to live his life as he desires. I respect his wishes. He doesn't have to live in the manner of his father."

"I don't like that, Pop." She evinced stern disapproval.

"What you like or dislike is of little importance. You do not have to live your brother's life—nor does he have to live yours or anyone else's life. He needs no one to explain or defend his way of life. One must be responsible for his own actions in this world. Until you do this and become void of animosity towards anyone including yourself, you'll never become a huntress like Diana." He popped a pill into his mouth and washed it down with water.

"The more you learn, the more you'll be responsible for," Val's voice continued.

Tina's eyes were fastened to the double-headed griffin, hypnotized as it were by the curious shape and form, wondering what this monstrosity actually had to do with the questions she had asked her father.

Patience, Tina. Be patient. Pop has a reason for laying so elaborate a foundation before he begins to construct a building on it. Listen to him . . .

His voice droned on. "The first thing we must dwell on is the removal of all fear from your mind—totally."

CHAPTER FOUR

For a long while after Ted's death Whip had reflected the tone of Washington: subdued, strained, deeply aggrieved and silent. He moved in shadowy ambiguous ways filled with unspeakable sadness. The very heart and soul had been expunged from this figure of quiet desperation, thought the outside world, viewing this haunted soul who wandered aimlessly in circles where seemingly he belonged, yet he was unable to fit in any more.

Threats followed him all hours of the day and night.

"Stay out of politics or you'll get what was meant for you and he got instead. Don't investigate the Custer affair unless you want to be the mark of an assassin. We weren't fooling in Ted's case. We warned him—he ignored us. Be a wiser man and live!"

Whip, impervious to such threats, got so he could spot the crank letters by the envelopes in which they came. He burned them in an incinerator in the rear yard of the Georgetown townhouse.

Upon his return from Europe Whip continued to maintain a low profile; he completed his term of office as attorney general, but retired temporarily from public life, attending only those functions where protocol demanded his presence. His old friends and companions discerned noticeable changes in him. He'd become a totally different man; a far cry from the despot of the past and no longer the clown with whom many had partied on occasion.

Astute politicians speculated that Whip's European exposure was premeditated with every intent to toss his hat into the ring. Was it possible they'd been wrong? What took place when Whip met with certain international moguls overseas? Had the assassination attempt in West Berlin frightened him off? Those in the know, those politicians maintaining links to IAGO, kept their mouths closed, their eyes and ears open for new developments to report.

Washington would never hold the magic it did during

Ted's administration with the New Horizon men. No one was more aware of it than Whip, who went on about his business for a time avoiding the fanfare of publicity where he could. In the past he'd entertained neither the compulsion or the compunction to occupy the Oval Office. He hadn't seriously considered the idea until his encounter with Ali Mohammed Izmur. Only then, although technically no such blueprints existed in his mind, had the germ of the idea filtered into his thinking.

One day a curious series of events began to manifest itself in Whip's life. He heard it clearly. The familiar chanting commenced: *Shiverton for President! Whip Shiverton for President!* Wherever he went, whomever he talked with it was the same. Willing supporters pressed. The people demanded in ceaseless chanting:

"*Shiverton for President! Shiverton for President!*"

Crowds flanked him in all the major cities. Whip, smiling tolerantly, would wave to the flanking mobs and turn his back on their stout demands.

He sat on the Fordingham Committee's Investigatory Board, appalled at their gross negligence in questioning witnesses. Their ineptness concerning every facet of the case under scrutiny was shocking to him. Basing their findings on inconsistencies—not supportive evidence—and only on that which supported the lone assassin's theory of Ted's death, galled him. Wisely he kept his silence. His name appeared on several documents indicating that he concurred with the Committee's findings when in fact he was bitterly opposed to their bungling. Whip had never played a more dangerous game and he knew it; wearing two faces, perilously so, enabled him to scrutinize countless highly classified documents to which he otherwise might have been refused access, in hopes they might shed light on Ted's assassins. He would overlook nothing.

The Georgetown brownstone contained some of the most sophisticated electronic equipment the Justice Department could devise, affording him a modicum of protection to house his and Ted's numerous personal files. Perusing Ted's files he found in them invaluable information he'd forgotten about and at one time considered too trivial for consideration. Daily he dictated his findings, thoughts and conclusions and what he recalled of Ted's involvements beginning with Ted's announcement to run for president and what took place following his inauguration, up to and including the assassination.

He believed with conviction that the answers to the

giant riddle of Ted's death lay buried in the files surrounding him in his study, so that's where he began. Picking up from where Ted left off before he left for Custer, Whip's rapier interest concentrated on the income tax returns of those three Texas billionaire oilmen whom Ted had spotlighted for income tax evasion: E. L. Lamb, Merkle and Larchmont.

Since the Joey Erice kidnapping attempt Tex Merkle had aroused Whip's curiosity, so he was the first to be scrutinized by the former attorney general. But after reviewing his late father's file, the name E. L. Lamb became too dominant a person to ignore. Eastland Larchmont, although involved with the triumverate known as the TFL Corporation, didn't figure as prominently in Shiverton business as the others. One fact, however, stood out like a beacon in a stormy sea. The three oil moguls were inseparable. That is what intrigued Whip to hell and back and stirred up smoldering fires in his mind.

Whip paced the floor all night, smoking, drinking black coffee by the gallon until he was wired together on nerves alone, popping bennies by the handful, concentrating on each vital fact until he knew it intimately.

He got out all the dossiers on these men, adding to them the information fed by his sources, and studied them over again.

Through all this, Whip was unable to dismiss from his mind the lengthy and enlightening conversation he had with Prince Ali Mohammed, who had been officially declared the sovereign in his country. Whip had given Ali no answer when he tossed the presidency at his feet except to contend that he had no ambition for high office.

What he'd learned from Ali was of mind-boggling importance. Whip recognized the inherent dangers both politically and on an international level. The situation had to be carefully dissected, evaluated and controlled or a series of projected diplomatic coups would boomerang into disaster on so grand a scale that minor nations could be blown off the map, taking with them millions of lives and causing a violent wake of destruction.

CHAPTER FIVE

The sky was clear; a pink, pearly glow suffused upward from the eastern border of the ocean. The Ligurian Sea was dotted with sleek, imperious yachts and cruisers belonging to millionaire playboys and oil tycoons. Other colorful ships, some as ancient in appearance as those built by the Phoenicians centuries before, bobbed up and down in the early tide of what appeared to be a placid sea of mirrored reflections.

"What an ungodly hour to be attending a meeting!" Neiland Milton complained to his companion Carlos Rajos as they sat in the rear of a chauffeur-driven Rolls Royce scaling the narrow spiralling mountain road winding through the Maritime Alps to the medieval castle of Mourous Benkhanhian. Up ahead the magnificent estate sprang to life as if it had been carved from the mountain itself.

Carlos merely nodded and looked out at the vast scenic display of the French Riviera, silent at this early hour. Up ahead the palace stood like a silent sentinel, a feudal fortress that once had housed kings and queens and the crusaders marching on pilgrimage to the Holy Land. It still impressed him as it had on his initial visit and he understood Neiland's enthrallment. He'd taken time to study the castle's background, explaining that the estate had been converted to suit the tastes of its master, Mourous Benkhanhian.

"It's his monument, Neiland," Carlos added. "After his death it will continue to exude the character and nature of its master—or Benkhanhian threatens to haunt the place."

Neiland Milton, of course, observed everything with wide-eyed solemnity.

The palace itself, one of many owned by IAGO, was used for clandestine meetings of this power-saturated consortium for the purposes of determining which nation would fall, which would survive and how the spoils would

46

be divided. On this day the gathering of power brokers were preparing to determine the identity of the next American president.

Some time ago this covey of financial wizards had decided that Samuel T. Linden wouldn't seek reelection. From out of the magic hat labeled United States of America they had plucked the name of the most likely political rabbit, Neiland Milton. Today they would ascertain the prolificacy of this rabbit and whether or not the magic hat would remain intact or crumble to dust.

When word reached Milton at his home in Florida that he was once again to be groomed for the presidency —if he met IAGO's qualifications—his thoughts rolled back to the pre-Shiverton days when he'd been informed that his running mate would have to be someone other than the exceedingly popular Howard Halsey. Because IAGO felt that Halsey would defeat Milton at the polls, they conjured up the dark horse candidate, Ted Shiverton.

Milton laughed aloud at the recollection. Carlos Rajos glanced at him for a moment, then returned to his own thoughts.

Milton's laughter was over an inside joke. *What a farce the elections had been, and still were for that matter,* he thought. For a long time after his defeat he'd given much thought to his political career and his rapid decline to near oblivion after the Shiverton machine steamrolled to power. It had all happened too swiftly, and so unexpectedly that no one, no political sage, could have predicted the outcome.

Now, here he was again, six years later, to be considered as proper timber for the White House. So IAGO hadn't forsaken him! They hadn't buried him alive in the ashes of political defeat and the financial losses incurred in the Namtu–Bodicam and Lojuria fiascos in the Far East. To be so honored was a sign of acceptance by the IAGO hierarchy. No more than a volcano once activated could stop erupting, so did Neiland refuse to become subdued.

Shiverton's presidential victory had created enormous losses and personal defeat in business for him. Now, as flurries of excitement stimulated him he puffed up with arrogance. He'd show them how to pick up the pieces, march into the White House and mend the giant rips in IAGO's pockets made by previous administrations during his absence from the capital.

Milton gazed out the window of the Rolls at the magnificent panorama of French countryside. Rolling vineyards, immaculately kept, stood lush with the promise of a fruitful harvest. Here and there a redfaced peasant glanced up from his work and waved to them. A mother nursed her infant by the roadside.

Reaching the crest of the mountain the limousine paused momentarily at an electronic gate until it rolled open, then wheeled through the opening and traveled the hundred yards to the palace courtyard.

Earlier when Carlo's Venezuelan jet crossed the Atlantic he confided to Milton, "The men in Europe are nothing like those rugged men of pioneer stock you met in Washington or at Golden Bar Ranch in Texas. These men are ruthless and deadly."

Very well, they had arrived at last. Out of the Rolls, ushered into the castle by a sinister, scar-faced heavy, whom Carlos hastened to explain doubled as a guard. "He once held the honor of being the sharpest shooter in France, winning countless medals for his skill. From time to time he is used for assassinations. There is no one like him, *amigo*."

Milton listened, drinking in the imposing architecture along with the outline of the well-muscled, militarily disciplined guard, braced stiffly, speaking into a wall phone. Replacing the receiver the sharpshooting guard raised two fingers into the air as if he were pontificating before a religious congregation. He half spoke, half whispered imperatively, *"Allez, allez, monsieurs, s'il vous plaît. Allez!" Allez!"*

He ushered the guests along a marble-floored foyer that branched off into six exits, through what had to be the tallest doors in the world, carved with scenes of the Crusades, and with solid gold handles. Milton nudged Carlos, desiring to point them out to him, only to elicit a disdaining frown from the guard whose attitude irked Milton. Carlos signalled a silent recital of displeasure with his eyes and stood aside allowing Neiland to enter before him.

It occurred to Milton that the thundering of his heart must sound like rousing drums in the elegant high-domed chamber and would instantly bring guards bearing bright flaming torches as he inched closer to what seemed a scene from out of the pages of antiquity. He felt he'd been ushered into the grand salon of the Inquisition.

Twenty-four men sat around an enormous oval table of gleaming Cordovan mahogany in thick burgundy leather chairs drinking from Austrian cut-crystal goblets, using solid gold ashtrays with crystal liners. Each man, resembling an indolent pasha, smoked cigars or cigarettes using solid gold holders. For an instant it struck him that they were playing roles for a stupendous De Mille production. Feeling the earth-jarring vibrations of power emanating from them dispelled further thoughts that this could be a fantasy. But, steeped in foreign protocol, both he and Carlos Rajos appeared to be impervious to their surroundings.

Inwardly, Milton's heart was pounding as it never had before. He felt stunned and unusually breathless. Shit, he was impressed! Really impressed! Later he'd confide to Carlos that he had never been so intimidated by so much power under one roof.

Carlos, no virgin with IAGO, had been seduced by this ignominious cartel through his own indebtedness to the French and British banks who financed his growth in Venezuela. No slouch in the field of financial wizardry, Rajos demonstrated a talent in dealing with Americans, thereby facilitating international business relations with them. Thus he'd created for himself a special treasure room in the Sphinx-like bosom of IAGO. The reason Carlos never revealed to Milton the full extent of IAGO's power was because IAGO revealed to Rajos only what they wanted him to know.

This relationship pleased Rajos. He had no burning itch to learn more than he knew. Comfortable with the role playing, he had functioned profitably and insured the longevity of his banking business. He lived royally, basking in the limelight of VIP's in each of the nations he dealt with. This spotlit, however, his rise in the hierarchy of IAGO. Rajos had no objections. His position as spokesman for both IAGO and their adopted godsons of power suited him and relieved him of responsibilities which might otherwise weigh him down. For twenty years the marriage had been successful; he wanted no change.

The man who would be the next American president studied the splendid appointments as he sat stiffly in his chair. Chinese, Persian, Turkish art treasures graced the enormous chamber; exquisite lamps, carved ebony tables, hanging tapestries and oils, all of it encountered his eyes in bewildering profusion. A man from humble beginnings, Milton gasped at the mammoth cut-crystal chandelier glittering with low-keyed lighting; paintings the envy of the Louvre; wall hangings woven by the hands

49

of angels; thick, lush Peruvian carpets of imperial quality gracing the sleekly polished hardwood floors. He'd never seen anything quite like this.

Milton, coming out of his reverie, concentrated on the faces of the men; he recognized none in the subdued lighting. He thought that if these men were integrated with another twenty-four, he'd have difficulty recognizing them individually, for they all looked alike. Nothing separated one from another. In place of hearts he felt certain these men had built-in Victor calculators and spouted from thtir lips yards of tickertape each morning.

These were the men of IAGO! Beyond the stage of multimillionaires, they were the giants of industry, the omnipotent, omniscient plenipotentiaries who ruled governments and together were more redoubtable than any five nations bound together. These men had led nations into World Wars I and II and into every other international uprising in between and after. Never prominent, avoiding publicity as if it were the plague and striving for anonymity, these kingmakers, president makers, creators and destroyers of empires guided the destiny of mankind.

Carlos was right; the TFL combine were pussycats in comparison to their parent organization. Unable to dismiss the feeling that he was on a gigantic motion picture set, he glanced at the actors, all in place, the lighting geared to keep their faces in partial shadow, whether for effect or concealment. It was all too grand, too ostentatious, too perfect. The fire on the hearth, brightly lit and crackling, appeared to be a picture, as if the logs weren't logs at all but an electronic apparition with colored lights simulating a bright fire.

A sudden shiver exploded at the base of Milton's spine and he felt the rippling of electric shock throughout his body. Something told him to flee this crazy scene. Earlier Rajos had confided, "The men you'll meet will elevate you to the presidency. Make no mistake about it, you'll see them once—never again unless they decide to promote you into the hierarchy of IAGO—or to destroy you. Communications with them are through me. It's a one way street, *amigo*. You pay a terrific price for the realization of your dreams. Your option was picked up— the rest is up to you."

Very well, thought Milton, *I've traded my soul in a Faustian way with the very devil himself.* As he sat in their midst giving credence to their ideas, he expected their tongues would spit fire and damnation before his eyes.

"You understand what's expected of you?" asked Mourous Benkhanhian, addressing himself to Milton. In his late seventies, his black fiery eyes were still hypnotic; his jowelled face and thick neck gave him the appearance of a bullfrog. His pudgy fingers thumped the table. "Well, then, ask your questions, unless Señor Rajos has managed to brief you satisfactorily."

Milton cleared his throat after he sipped the demitasse served him; he had judiciously refrained from alcohol. "No complications in the future? Sam Linden won't seek reelection?"

"Linden will finish his term of office and retire," replied Benkhanhian with seeming annoyance. "The path to the presidency will be smoothly paved. Summarily it's to your advantage to follow all directives to the letter. Shiverton, elected to office in that stunning, unexpected victory, was uncooperative; he suffered insurmountable setbacks. The men of the New Horizons were besieged with problems they were unable to overcome." His thick British accent was as difficult to understand as Sir Winston's became in his declining years.

"Point in fact," Benkhanhian continued, "Shiverton's successor, approached by our people, cooperated with us. For a time we did his thinking for him. Point in fact, he was a fool. Unable to control his pride, and his humiliation at having evolved into an unpopular president, he did manage to suppress the true findings in the Shiverton assassination. The havoc and chaos that happened in your land is something historians, philosophers and sociologists will attempt to explain to future generations and like much in history the truth is buried with skeletons of the past." He snorted contemptuously. "It's a simple explanation. He was expendable because he interfered with and deterred our progress.

"Point in fact—your administration shall be sedate. You'll be bothered with the nagging Far East problem for a time and involve yourself in affairs of state at an international level; something geared to be equally demanding and to take the pressures off you on the domestic front. Point in fact: our newspapers worldwide will back your moves and suppress a public outcry should any arise. Point in fact: upon completion of your first term, with an alluring bait to insure your reelection, the public shall receive an announcement of a full settlement in

51

the Far Eastern bottleneck, followed by a progressive disarmament program. The public will sigh in relief and hail you as a hero. It will take a full term of office for IAGO to settle her differences with Far Eastern factions," he added, anticipating Milton's questions.

"Follow our directives, Mr. President," said Benkhanhian in his tired Oxford accent, putting the psychological spur to Milton's rib, "and power you never dreamed of will be yours. The name of Neiland Milton will become synonymous with the greatest of American presidents elected to office."

Observing Milton's reaction Benkhanhian assured himself he'd bagged Milton. The IAGO chieftain was wrong. He had misconstrued the tight smile on Milton's lips as a gesture of sequacity, a nonresistant surrender to the lure of the bait dangled before him.

Benkhanhian would never know how wrong he was. Milton had checked an impulse to laugh all right, but it was an ironic smirk brought on by the blatant use of the words *elected to office. Elected, indeed!* thought Milton, suppressing his indignation. The irony of American founding fathers struggling so hard to devise an equitable electoral system to place a man into high office with a minimal amount of corruption struck him as comical. All that nonsense, primaries, conventions, campaign stumping—none of it really mattered a damn! His own struggle up the slippery slopes to the vice presidency hadn't counted. All that mattered was bringing yourself to the attention of these political impresarios who wielded batons of power, laying your heart and soul bare at their feet. If you possessed the stuffings they needed—and they knew just how to pull the stuffings from a man, examine them and show him up for what he was worth—you'd be bought and paid for to eternity or until such a time as you became expendable.

For a time Milton felt as if he'd been tossed back and forth between these president makers like a dilapidated bean bag. It didn't matter. He wouldn't be in their presence if they hadn't already come to some decision over his future.

He felt a hand on his arm. It was Carlos in a signal it was time to leave. Without so much as a farewell, they were dismissed. Just like that! Nothing incensed him more than to be dismissed like a common lackey.

Before he had an opportunity to either thank them or tell them to go to hell, they'd been ushered out of the grand hall, back into the foyer, out the door into the waiting limousine. It left Milton with a feeling of incompletion, of anger and resentment at being treated like a commodity. Venting his frustration to Carlos, he was unprepared for the answer.

"Well, Neil, aren't you just that? A commodity—a machine given attention, care and money to efficiently perform the proper duties programmed by them through me? Which, by God, you had better be prepared to perform well."

"You forget one important factor, *amigo*. I am human just as they are human but refuse to admit the inconvenience." He watched his friend Rajos lighting up a Havana cigar with a platinum lighter. "You still get those Cuban ropes?" he asked.

"You forget, *amigo*, Cratos and I are still good friends."

Milton glanced sharply at the Venezuelan as they came off the winding hill towards the sea. "I forget nothing. Perhaps one day you'll introduce us?"

"With pleasure, *Mister President*," he said too silkily.

"Cut it out, Carlos," Milton snapped sourly and remained uncommunicative for the remainder of the trip back to Washington.

Milton had never been an overly patriotic man, nor did he fall into that class of people who shed tears when the Stars and Stripes passed by in a parade. He had fought in a war for his country. He passionately believed in America and what she stood for, one nation, indivisible, with justice and liberty for all. To his way of thinking, there was no better place in the world. He'd always believed this even as a child in a small country town where his parents struggled to eke out an existence in a modest Mama and Papa grocery store. He had worked his way through school, fought in World War II, traveled the world over and back coming to the conclusion that the rich—not the meek or the poor—would inherit the earth. He'd seen the power of money open doors for some and the lack of money shut doors for the have-nots. Qualifications didn't matter. It wasn't always the best man who came out on top. Politics were as fixed as a crooked horse race. Nobility didn't exist in politics. Only riches counted. Milton's determination to acquire riches was perfectly suited for politics. How else could he get rich faster? Sitting on his can in some funky role as junior law partner taking leftovers, the small fee cases no one else wanted? Not for him. He aimed high.

He felt no embarrassment at being the pawn in a universal game. But he was irked at being treated with less consideration than a serf. Who if not an American president could extract respect from these cold, iron men of IAGO with their plastic faces and mechanical hearts? Torn between the ego-shattering prospect of being their puppet and the desire to assert himself, he came to terms with himself. He wished he'd never seen them. His job would have been easier if he hadn't laid eyes on these deadpanned gnomes from Zurich who pushed the buttons of the world.

Two months after his candidacy for the President was announced, Milton and Rajos were fishing off the Florida Keys in a lazy day of rest before firing up rockets for the proposed campaign. Milton, unusually quiet and reflective, sat drinking for most of the day. Carlos, sensing his mood, remained equally as quiet. The swollen tangerine sun began nodding towards the horizon before Milton finally spoke up. His voice was thick.

"They killed Shiverton, didn't they?"

"Who?"

"Christ, you know who. Do I have to spell it out?"

"I don't know. It's not my field."

"You've had thoughts on the matter, haven't you?"

"I'd be lying if I said no, *amigo*."

"And?"

"And what?"

Milton smirked, as he laid his reel into the proper slot along the aft rail of the fishing trawler. He began to unstrap himself from the swivel chair on deck. "They knocked off Sam Linden too, didn't they. No, no, no, it's all right, don't bother denying it. I'm a big boy. I know the score. I can understand why Shiverton was wasted, but why Linden?"

Rajos, on his feet, moved towards the cabin, returning with a thermos of coffee and two cups. He poured the hot liquid, his eyes peering about the craft for the skipper and his aide. They weren't within earshot. Placing the thermos at his feet, he sat down again, and raised the volume on the radio. For a time they listened to the waves slapping against the rocking boat.

"I told you they were piranha."

"Yet you've survived all these years."

"I don't make waves."

"Is that the answer?"

"—Neither do I have a God complex."

"And I do? Is that what you're saying? I have a God complex?"

"You want to be president. That makes you vulnerable. It's that simple. You want something they can provide for a price. You bought the deal."

"Yeah, I bought the deal all right. That makes me vulnerable."

The illusion had burst, fragmenting into a thousand doubts.

Grateful for the Venezuelan's friendship, even if he was a high-salaried IAGO flunky, he preferred taking orders from Carlos. He had a unique way of softening the sharp-edged directives from IAGO.

At the next election, Milton became President of the United States, just as IAGO had predicted and delivered. He'd defeated the opposition by a conservative measure of votes. It was to be Neiland Milton's America for the next four years—and of course IAGO's.

With an air of judicious virtue, Milton in the following months showed his strength in foreign affairs, just as IAGO had predicted. The internal strife threatening the nation and the growing economic crisis was handled with a modicum of ease. IAGO's insistence that he place more of their men in top government positions created a wave of controversy among the opposition. The men President Milton appointed to the Supreme Court, as ambassadors to foreign nations, or members of select committees would sit behind their desks taking on their new roles with few people the wiser. He learned how easy it was to fool people, divert them. Offer them two cherries for a choice plum and while they savored the flavor of cherries, replace the plum with a prune and no one would be wiser.

Diversion was the answer. Keep them busy and guessing. Do one thing, tell them another. Keep things buried under rubber-stamped labels of *Top Secret—Highly Classified Information* or other top priority codes. Tell the nation nothing, then label it *Strictly Confidential* or *Security of the Nation at Stake* or *Executive Privilege*. A dozen other smokescreens could be invoked should illegal or covert acts be discovered. All the previous administrations had done it—why not his?

CHAPTER SIX

Six months! Six long months! Princess Jamila Izmur, stewing and fretting, paced the confines of the fabulous palace her brother had built for her. The effects of her interference in her brother's life where Valerie Shiverton was concerned were devastating to Jamila. All she'd attempted to do was show the oversexed, conniving bitch up for what she really was and for that she was doomed to living in a state of exile. So enraged was Jamila she could hardly think straight.

Of what use was this incredibly stunning palace made of marble, appointed with solid gold accessories, built on five hundred acres in the middle of a desert, miles away from civilization, if she had to live here alone? Marble walls and floors throughout; lush gardens; a sparkling, freeform swimming pool running the length of the palace; an aviary containing rare tropical birds; waterfalls and verdant shrubbery; a theater seating two hundred, fully equipped with the latest in film projection and screens; first-run films delivered twice a month from Rome; a heliport used once in six months when Ali came calling; what more could a person desire? Princess Jamila lacked nothing—nothing except Ali's love and trust and her freedom. Freedom from this prison.

Her hatred for Valerie Shiverton was compounded by her dislike of Ali's actions. How could he do this to her?

Jamila, resentful of Ali's attentions to Valerie from the start, wondered what Ali saw in her and why he pursued her. Foolish Jamila! From the moment the American stepped foot in the Rome villa and she noted her brother's interest in the woman, she should have realized there was more to the gala than the formality of entertaining the American attorney general.

Seated by the luxurious pool, smoking hash in a glass pipe, she glanced at the gaily chirping birds and cried aloud in an impassioned voice. "By the beard of Allah! I'm worse off than any of you. You are cared for, fed, watered and housed, but you have no brain to drive you mad. Nothing inside you urges you to freedom. Nothing in your mind compels you to concern yourself with the world of people who wallow in misery, because you sit in luxury among possessions you do not need." She laughed aloud, her voice causing a few docile love birds to scurry about, flapping their wings, retreating to the far end of their abode.

"Allah, be merciful. Of what use am I to anyone here in this mausoleum of gold, marble and glass? I am not dead. I am flesh and blood, alive, with human passions and emotions in need of nourishment! Yet I am doomed to sit here alone, allowing depression to drown my soul and slowly drain from me the gift of life. Out there is a world of live people. Surely I could be of use to someone—if not to Ali!"

Jamila, sent to America at the age of fourteen to be educated, detested these supercilious schoolgirls born of rich, wasteful parents who had no time for them, just as Ali had no time for her. Four years later she returned home quite Americanized, with the barest trace of an accent. Ali, proud of her, permitted her to hostess the many social functions to which he was committed as sovereign.

Oh, how she'd enjoyed being Ali's hostess in Rome, Paris and on the French Riviera to all the exciting celebrities and titled nobility. For a time she'd really found it scintillating. She'd tried discouraging Ali's numerous American mistresses as well as those titled European whores who were too eager to jump into Ali's bed on a permanent basis. Skillfully, cleverly, without overt threats she had managed to scare off a few of the more timid creatures by threatening to disclose to her brother the countless other paramours they entertained in his absence.

Jamila's interference with Ali's torrid love affair with Valerie Shiverton had been the last straw. Ali had had enough of her schoolgirl foolishness. Naturally he'd never confided in Jamila the real reasons behind his amorous approach to Valerie, so when she set about hampering his work, he was forced to take action against her. For a time she remained careful, regardless of what she suspected, surmised, disliked, even loathed about Valerie, but it was impossible for her to close her eyes to Ali's alliance with the American.

Jamila sadly inclined her head like a fallen bright bird.

Then suddenly she sat up, alert. *Well, it's over! I've had enough. I refuse to stay here and remain a prisoner!*

If she remained in bondage she'd be in worse straits. A letter received only this morning from her brother advised her to prepare herself for a visit at the end of the month. Sheikh Al Shammar Jebel and his son Dubai were arriving to talk marriage terms with Ali. Her exile, bad as it was, was palatable, but news that he intended to bind her in marriage to someone she hadn't met appalled her. Why had Ali taken pains to rear her in America if he intended to force on her the antiquated Moslem ways?

Such brooding thoughts incited her to action. At dusk, when most of the servants prepared for bed, Jamila dressed as a Bedouin and with a small backpack flung over her shoulders headed for the nearest village, taking only a gold, diamond-studded scorpion amulet, a gift from Ali on her eighteenth birthday, a pair of Levis, a shirt and sandals, and a pair of solid gold candlesticks she intended to sell for food and lodging.

The shrewd and conniving dealer in gold haggled over the price of the gold candlesticks. Even with his incisive bargaining powers, she came away with enough money to travel across the Persian Gulf to Kuwait where, with the aid of a forged passport in the name of Jaqualine Devon, an American name manufactured out of thin air, she booked air passage to Damascus, a city seething with rebels. The smell of insurrection permeated the air.

In Damascus she tinted her jet black hair to a lighter shade of brown hoping to conceal herself from any spies Ali might send in search of her. She changed into her Levis and shirt and bought a canvas tote to house her cosmetics and papers and set her eyes on Beirut in Lebanon.

The distance from Damascus to Beirut was fifty miles by rail. To Jamila it seemed five hundred. Loud-voiced crowds pushed, shoved and mangled her as they rushed to make frenetic connections. The words on everyone's lips spoke of the crushing blow dealt the Palestinian rebels by the Jordanian king in a recent coup against them. The fear in every man's heart was that Israel, backed by American forces, would obliterate the Arab nations.

Listening without comment, as pangs of guilt about her icy detachment over the state of affairs fought to surface, she concentrated on her own plight—getting away from the Middle East as swiftly as she could.

Through the dirty train windows she saw streams of travel-weary Bedouins making their way to some destination in the desolate stretch of desert ahead.

Where would she go to escape Ali and find a life meaningful enough to absorb her thoughts and energies? This exodus from the palace would be unforgivable in Ali's eyes. She'd sampled his anger and seething temper when he had her beaten before he banished her from his sight. Very well, then, the jungles of the world were out there waiting for her. Surely she could get lost in one of them? She was so absorbed in her thoughts, Jamila hardly heard him speak.

"Are you a stranger here?"

She turned, staring into the face of a pleasant-mannered young man, a year or so older than she. He was dressed in the fatigues of a Syrian soldier. Why he spoke to her in English she was to learn later. Thinking quickly, and recalling what she'd heard, she appeared hesitant.

"I hesitate admitting I'm an American," she lied admirably.

"Then you're leaving the country? It's wise to travel to Beirut, I hear the entire USA Sixth Fleet is waiting in the Mediterranean prepared to escort its children home. Running home to father, are you?" His irony, as obvious as the rebellious anger he tried to disguise, was laced with rancor.

"Yes, I suppose so. It's infernally hot, isn't it?"

"Do you have your papers?"

Jamila tensed. She clutched her bag, instantly resentful, as her royal spine arched stiffly. Just as quickly she relaxed.

"Is this an official request or one of personal interest?"

"Both." He wasn't about to tell her that he, too was on the run. He was a Palestinian rebel with the feyadeen, one of the many terrorist groups that had been pulverized by the Jordanian Army's surprise attack. He could take no chances. He held out his hand authoritatively.

"I'm with Internal Security," he said for added emphasis.

They both laughed about it later, but at that moment Jamila, who did not want to create a scene, handed him her papers. She felt they were in order. She'd just paid a handsome fee to insure them. She handed him the passport and necessary travel visas, watching him critically, hoping to read his thoughts.

Bahar Bahar examined them carefully, a slow smile

playing at the corner of his lips. For an instant his dark, probing cold eyes showed a glimmer of warmth. He glanced up into her eyes until Jamila became unnerved. She quickly averted her eyes, scanning the faces of the other passengers to see if they were being observed. Luckily, in so crowded an area, the people were absorbed in their own affairs and had no time to concern themselves with others.

Jamila wiped the sweat from her brow. Her body was drenched with perspiration. Dark rings were spreading under the arms of her khaki shirt. Across her back where the sweat had concentrated the fabric stuck to her skin. She felt grubby, tired and nauseous at the pure animal odors of uncleanliness mixed with the stale smells of food and overripe fruits the passengers were eating.

"Are you finished with my papers, uh—what is your rank? Captain?"

Bahar nodded. "Jabal Hassim does a fine job. Tell me, Miss Jaqualine Devon, what did that thief charge to forge these papers?"

Jamila gasped. Grabbing the papers from his hand she stuffed them into her tote. She wanted to put him in his place.

"He works for us, Miss American stuck-up," he said conspiratorially. "Look, we'd best help one another. We are both in a devilish predicament. At the border our papers will be inspected. Pray Jabal's artistry goes unrecognized . . ."

That's how it began between Jamila and Bahar Bahar. He helped her past the border inspection with little difficulty. In Beirut he helped her find living quarters until she decided on a destination. A few days after their arrival in Beirut, she glanced through several old newspapers she found in the rented flat and saw his photo on the front page. Allah be damned! He was the Palestinian rebel who'd attempted the assassination of the American attorney general in West Berlin! She quickly buried the paper at the bottom of the pile when she heard his familiar footsteps running up the stairs with a noticeable limping sound.

"Jaqualine!" he called to her as he rushed inside. "Do you still intend to go to America? We both know there's no one waiting for your safe journey home, don't we?"

It was a moment of truth. Jamila nodded.

"I'm not one to pry. We all have things we prefer to keep secret. If you can wait a month I can get you there with a hundred exchange students bound for UCLA in Los Angeles."

"My passport's American. There'll be no difficulty—"

"Your passport's a forgery. It will be discovered before you leave Beirut. Trust me. I'll handle everything."

It occurred to her to wonder why he was overly considerate of her. In her anxiety to escape her brother she didn't dwell on it.

That night he took her to dinner at a small café where other people their age congregated, mostly students, she was told. They ate a hearty meal and drank wine and listened to a few impassioned, politically inclined soapbox orators. Jamila was astonished at their zeal. She listened politely, admiring their political know-how, at the same time thinking them too radical and uninformed on the philosophies they espoused. Most were too militant, vociferous and illogical, unable too see any side except their own viewpoint.

"What do you think of them?" Bahar asked pointedly.

"If they didn't hate so much they might see things clearer." Jamila's words surprised even her. She grew thoughtful.

"You think it's fair what America does to us? Forcing us to swallow anything the Jews dish out? Why don't they mind their own affairs and leave us to our own? No! They come with missiles, nuclear weapons and the entire USA fleet to champion the Jews. We have the world by the testicles, where it can hurt them most— our rich oil deposits. And what happens?" Bahar was fired up. "Our own leaders sell us down the river. Look at them! Yankee imperialists. They've all succumbed to Western pressures. The sheikhs, the Bedouin chieftains, princes, even kings have become their pawns. Have you seen the way they live while the rest of us starve and labor for a mere pittance? And their palaces are an abomination!"

Jamila glanced sharply at him, a hot flush surging from her toes to the top of her head. He was telling her things she'd felt deeply inside her but couldn't articulate without bringing further wrath upon her head by her brother or her royal cousins.

Two young men dressed in army fatigues entered and approached Bahar, sitting down at their table. Bahar introduced them to her. "Jaqualine Devon, meet Abdul Harrim and Sharif Bey," he muttered and instantly addressed them in their native dialect, chatting furiously

61

with animation. Periodically the man named Abdul Harrim stared at her with cool, calculating eyes that made her feel uncomfortable. Abdul appeared to be assessing her, making mental notes of her behavior: the way she smoked, sipped her wine, her poise and the way she sat.

Bits and pieces of their conversation came to her. From what she was able to make out, they were discussing current developments in the recent hijacking of three airliners on a deserted strip of desert land known during World War II as Dawson Field. The airfield, located in northern Jordan, had been christened Revolution Field by El Fatah and his guerrilla terrorists. Negotiations had been under way for the past few weeks between the British, German, Israeli and Swiss governments and pressured by the Palestinians demanding the release of terrorists from Israeli jails.

The airliners forced to land on the field in Jordan were Swiss, American and British. Although America held no terrorists in custody, the TWA craft was included in the hijacking to exert influence on the Israelis. It seemed that the feyadeen had considered themselves in a bargaining position for the release of 450 terrorists from Israeli jails and the one woman hijacker held by the British. The whole world, it seemed, was in a turmoil over the action of the feyadeen. International spotlights were turned on them.

King Hussein, who in the past had managed to steer clear of dramatic conflict with the Palestinian rebels, moved to action and devastated the guerrillas, Bahar testified to his companions. They lamented the fact that King Hussein was influenced by the U.S. initiative calling for a ceasefire between Egypt and Israel. Accepted by the Egyptians, it now had the support of Russia.

As Jamila listened, she got the distinct impression that whatever happened, whatever crisis befell the Middle East, these three men were an active part of making that something happen.

She learned that the Syrian army, backed by Russia, were prepared in a limited way to help the feyadeen by intimidating the Jordanian army, but wisely chose to withdraw when they realized that they would have given the Israelis a cue for tossing their air power into the fray.

The manner in which these men strategically placed the strength of the larger nations was uncanny. They boasted that their violent terrorist methods were more effective than negotiations and in the end, their boastings proved true. The Israelis released the terrorist hostages and the woman hijacker jailed in Britain was also given her freedom. This news may not have mattered much to the ordinary citizen, but to Princess Jamila Rhadima Izmur, this startling and jarring truth brought about a change in her ideals. That a group of rebels, dissatisfied with the way their country was being run, could actually coerce powerful nations to give in to their demands was nothing short of miraculous.

She listened avidly to the rebels, paying attention to their objectives which sounded reasonable to her. In all this time, she barely noticed that Bahar walked with a decided limp. He was a master at covering up what he described as a bite from a mad dog that nearly tore off half a leg. She didn't make the connection for a long time, she was too busy trying to grasp new ideas. Listless, discontented, and critically in need of some answers to her inner turmoil, Jamila began feeling like a fish out of water, as if she didn't belong in this world. What was there in store for her, she wondered. Where would she end up?

One day Bahar showed up displaying a cheery ebullience.

"You leave next week for America. It's been arranged," he announced as if he'd accomplished a miniature coup.

Jamila was relieved. At least things wouldn't be as limited for her in America as they were for her here in Beirut. Every day she had read the papers meticulously, trying to find some account of her disappearance, something to indicate that her brother cared enough about her to find her. There had been nothing.

That night, Bahar made love to her. It was a total failure. It was a physical release they both needed, nothing else. It left her feeling deflated and ambivalent about many things. One thing in her favor, there'd be no sticky romantic entanglements to get in their way. She was grateful for this.

That last week, as she prepared for departure, numerous people stopped by to chat with Bahar, speaking in hushed whispers and staring at Jamila in a way that irked her. Before she could air her grievances with Bahar, it was time to leave.

The day of her departure Jamila was shocked to find Bahar boarding the plane with her. "I, too, go to America as a student," he told her simply. At her astonish-

63

ment, he added, "I thought you'd be pleased having a friend to talk with."

"But how?" she asked. "From where did the money come? A few days ago you were broke. Even I haven't enough."

Bahar laughed, patting her hands, seated next to her in the TWA jet. "We have friends, my dear Jaqualine. We have many friends."

She didn't know it then, but one day those words would haunt her. They were driven from LAX to a rented flat in Westwood Village close to the UCLA campus. Shortly after their arrival Bahar suggested she should enroll in a secretarial school to learn the necessary skills to enable her to get a worthwhile job. There were moments when Jamila would have picked up the phone in a minute to call Ali, if thoughts of being returned to that gold and marble mausoleum hadn't deterred her.

So, for Jamila, came the determination to study hard and become independent of everyone, never knowing, never fully aware that forces were steadily moving her to an inevitable fate with other notable Americans, who couldn't possibly know of the plotting, planning and meticulous strategy employed by a few ominous giants seated in the shadows of empires, moving pawns into place.

A year later, Jaqualine Devon returned one day to the apartment she shared with Bahar to find the sickly, pungent odors of hashish and pot hanging stale in the air; a half-dozen men were scattered about on the floor and chairs talking with Bahar.

They were talking heatedly, drinking, smoking, too intent in their conversation to have noticed her. Good, she had no burning itch to converse with them. Bahar's friends were a strange sort who all looked alike: dark-skinned, coal-black hair worn long, thick mustaches and downcast expressions, rarely laughing. It bothered her that Bahar had no visible means of support, yet he always came up with the money to pay the rent, buy food, and indulge in the luxury of dope and drink. She had no right to question him and intended to reimburse him for the monies advanced her. She thought of selling her diamond scorpion amulet on countless occasions, but couldn't, knowing it was her only link to her brother.

In her room, as she undressed and slipped into Levis, Bahar's voice reached her ears clearly. She didn't mean to eavesdrop.

"Word is that President Milton will not finish his new

term of office. That brings us to the business at hand. The target must not be elected to office. Those are our orders. We are watching, listening, and have infiltrated his organization. The moment he launches his plan . . . The subject we discussed earlier is learning skills, doing well. However, she needs someone more virile than I to stimulate her and keep her in line . . ."

The conversation lagged; voices grew dimmer. Jaqualine sorted through her school work, setting the best papers aside in a portfolio. She excelled in typing and shorthand. Her instructor promised to place her in an excellent position, possibly with a motion picture production firm that did films in the Middle East, due to her multilingual talent; she spoke Arabic, French, Spanish, English and Italian.

"What will her brother do when he learns of her whereabouts?"

Jaqualine cocked an ear. The words came in bits and pieces.

"He won't find her. It's been a year." More gibberish. "We'll continue negotiations at our end."

Her bedroom door was partially open. Footsteps sounded along the bare wood floor. The bathroom, no doubt, she thought. A shadowy figure coming towards her faltered, apparently surprised at her presence. He did not enter the bathroom, instead he walked forward and pushed open her door. She buried her head in her portfolio.

"Jaqualine?" a familiar voice.

She glanced up, searching his face.

"Jaqualine, don't you know me?" He smiled ravishingly. "I'm displeased that you don't remember me. I am Abdul Harrim. May I sit with you? I am bored with their chatter, their empty boasts and all that idealistic shit they regurgitate every day."

He sat on the bed and glanced askance at the crowded room, and its meager furnishings. "Not the suitable place for a princess, the sister of Prince Ali Mohammed," he said, lighting a joint.

He took a hit and handed it to her. "Help yourself. Don't look so shocked. I've known about you since we met in Beirut. It makes no sense you staying with Bahar. He can do nothing for a real woman." He leaned back, sure of himself, his eyes laughing.

She took a hit, handed it back to him, and replied icily, "Look, Abdul, I am Jaqualine Devon. Bahar is a friend about whom you needn't make disparaging remarks. He's been kind to me."

"It's his job, Princess," Abdul laughed at her discomfort. "He knew you from the start—we all did. Get used to it. You're being groomed to serve us in the best way you can."

She gave him a piercing look and drew herself up arrogantly. "So that's your game, is it? Ransom? You'll not squeeze a handsome ransom from the prince. He'll pay nothing to get me back. We loathe each other."

He laughed again. Oh, how she hated that superior laughter!

"Then you don't know? For over a year now, our brothers in the Middle East have been paid a profitable sum to insure your life."

She stared at him, her face a mask of concealed emotions. So she hadn't been clever after all. They knew her from the start. Bahar, at the center of the intrigue, was the deceptive one. Why? Why had they encouraged her to think she'd been clever? What did they need from her? By the beard of Allah—if they were thinking to bring harm down on Ali's head . . .

"Why did you run away in the first place?"

She gave him the answers she assumed he wanted to hear. "I couldn't live in the midst of opulence, while thousands starve—"

"Then you don't stand on the side of the oppressors? Men like your brother?" He had the languor of a sleek jaguar.

Abdul handed her the joint and pulled her from the chair to the bed. Jamila found it difficult to hold the smoke; her throat burned and she coughed. "This is foul. Hash doesn't do this to me. What in hell do you call this?" She stared at the rolled cigarette.

"Crystal—something new—angel dust. The high is fantastic." Abdul reached for her and kissed her ardently, fired by his lowered inhibitions. She pushed against him. *The idea that he can take liberties with me* . . . A wave of warmth rushing through her relaxed her instantly and she succumbed to his kisses.

Curious sensations . . . unexpected blurring . . . knees feel like water . . . kiss—kiss—kiss me again . . . She should loathe him for his effrontery; instead she wanted to be kissed. He stopped and forced her eyes to look into his.

"Don't expect me to apologize. I've wanted to make

love with you from the moment I met you in Beirut," he smiled brazenly.

She eyed him warily. He was just under six feet, slim-hipped, hard-muscled, with a coppery tan skin and mid-night-blue eyes. He looked like an American college student; bluejeans, cutoff sweatshirt showing off his muscled forearms, dark hair streaked with golden highlights. Something else was incongruous—his precise movements, a practiced, premeditated walk as if he'd been in the military.

Vaguely she heard sounds of Arabian music coming from the next room. The earlier talk had abated. More ruffled at her own ambivalence than she was at his forward manner, she tried to recall what she'd heard earlier. Her eyes felt swollen and distended and for some reason she saw things through tunnel vision. Something Bahar said earlier nagged at her. *She will need someone more virile than I to keep her in line* . . . She giggled and asked aloud, "Are you that someone, Abdul?"

It didn't make sense, so Abdul did the next best thing, drawing her to him with more fervor. When it dovetailed in her mind she felt anger. She resisted, shoved hard against him, pounding her fists on his shoulders. He released her, frowning angrily, the muscles in his cheeks twitching. She raised her hand and brought it crashing against his face in a loud smarting slap. Abdul grabbed her shoulders, shaking her, forcing her to quiet down.

"How dare you? Bastard!" she shouted furiously. "What gives you the right to come in here and treat me like a common slut?" She continued to resist him until Abdul slapped her hard. She gave a start and withdrew, her hands flying to her smarting cheek.

"Shut up, you fool! I didn't come here to take advantage of you." His sudden roughness had a calming effect on her.

She wasn't sure what happened or how. One minute she was flailing her fists against him, then suddenly they were around his neck clinging to him, her neck bending back under the onslaught of his mouth against hers. There was an urgency about their coupling, a desperate need as their hands uncovered each other and then suddenly without preamble he was on top of her, thrusting deeply and moving in rhythmic cadence until with a loud burst of despair they climaxed with breathless exhaustion. They hadn't taken time to undress completely.

They lay panting, side by side, buried in each other's

arms without thought of anything or anyone beyond the room. She'd never been taken like this. They became two savage animals in a new, exciting experience that ended too quickly for her. She wanted to recall every precious moment. Abdul's arm tightened around her, forcing her to look into his eyes, as he stroked her face tenderly with his free hand. She didn't want him ever to leave her.

A thousand thoughts clouded her consciousness. She was a princess and he . . . She didn't even know him! A perfect stranger had seduced her in a way that brought a crimson blush to her cheeks. She berated herself. A princess acting like an alley cat! Suddenly angry at herself she cursed internally. *Make up your mind, Jamila— Jaqualine, or whoever the hell you intend to be. You're not a princess here—not in this setting. Here, you're like the rest, no better, no worse than the others. You made your choice, so get off your royal ass and be human.*

"You're thinking this man Abdul is a commoner—like so much dirt under your royal feet," he whispered, caressing her.

About to refute his words, she was stopped by his greedy expert lips over hers. Then he whispered, "You are a woman and I am a man. Regret nothing. Be glad to be alive. Here in this room nothing exists beyond us."

He was ready for her again, his hardness between her legs testifying to his virility. Entering her he creatively brought her back to the heights in an earthy manner that caused her to tremble noticeably. His movements, slow and precise, his whispered endearments as he described what he was doing to her every step of the way, turned her on. She clutched at him, scratched his shoulders and back with her sharp fingernails, with the ferocity of a jungle cat. "Look at me," he whispered. "Look at it, see how big I make it for you? It is all for you, Jamila."

She couldn't take her eyes from the miraculous pole of flesh that seemed to have a life of its own. Swollen, engorged with blood, she couldn't believe that he could fit it into her small orifice. She clutched at him, drawing herself closer. "More," she cooed. "More, please. How have I lived so long without you?"

Abdul watched her explode and in the shadows it was difficult to see the self-satisfied smile on his face.

"Yes, little princess, and now you'll take it the way I love it!" He rammed his cock inside her hard and furiously until Jamila screamed aloud with ear-piercing moans before she came in violent spasms and shudders, threatening the breakdown of the bed.

For several weeks, Jamila craved him; Abdul was there to sate her desires. But she was a torn woman in the grip of conflicting emotions. No doubt she'd become addicted to Abdul; both loving and loathing him for having brought this dependency on her. But in the back of her mind, she questioned the intent behind his kindness. She'd been taught as a child that commoners always expected favors in return, double what they'd given as a gift. But every time her concerns filled her mind, her body would turn traitor and she'd squirm, as the memory of their last sex burned her with desire.

In time she came to know him better. He seemed devout in his desire to return to their homeland and help to create a better, healthier and saner society, free of all oppression. She believed him.

There were times when he was aroused to oratorical zeal. In those moments she'd listen, carefully forcing her love-addicted eyes to examine the underlying truth of his nature. He would pace the room erratically like those birds she'd left at home, caught in the restrictive confines of a caged environment. Then she would observe in him the desperation of the poor and deprived souls in the Middle East who had no chance to rise against their oppressors. Then her heart would go out to him, for embodied in him were the nameless faces of an army of hopeless men.

Gradually a metamorphosis was taking place. At a gathering of Bahar's friends, it was Abdul to whom the others showed the most respect. They would listen to him expound on recent activities occurring in their homeland. As their enthusiasm grew and became more prominent, so did Jaqualine's apathy grow towards all things of the past. She didn't seem to care about anything except Abdul and their lovemaking. She counted the minutes when they were apart, trying to close the gap on their separateness.

At times she became aware of and wept at her own seduction, but like a misguided whore, too overwhelmed by passion and lust, she didn't care highly enough about herself to realize who and what she had been. She cared even less about what she had become.

CHAPTER SEVEN

Four Years Later

Whip Shiverton had made bold strides in the political arena. He bid for a senatorial post once held by his brother and was elected by an overwhelming majority of votes. The people, still enchanted by the Shiverton mystique, created another hero they desperately needed. But during this time of activity and stress Whip had come no closer to solving the baffling mystery of Ted's death. There were numerous conjectures, unfounded and contrived rumors, but few real facts.

Senator Whip Shiverton had changed. Where had the hardnosed, two-fisted acerbic orator gone? The loner, the isolated human being, who'd been his own counsel for so long, had become another person. Was it possible, asked those who knew him well, that this gregarious, warm, smiling man, this new champion of the people, was the same Whip Shiverton who had been the oppressive tyrant of the past? After Ted's death, Whip suddenly associated openly with radicals, anarchists, and leftist journalists and elected officials. Men whom in the past he wouldn't have given the time of day were dragging Whip into the muck with the rest of the questionable parasites. Whip Shiverton had become an enigma. Those who knew him best felt there was a diabolical plan fermenting inside him, aimed at a concealed target. Those who were his enemies worried because they had something to worry about.

Only one thing had inspired Whip to convert his personality into one as charismatic as Ted's—an unrelenting, burning resolve to bring his brother's killers to justice. Whip alone knew the direction in which he was headed; this he kept a secret between himself and his God.

He and Tina seemed unable to come to terms with their love. Just when he decided nothing else mattered than their happiness, something like a wedge of darkness pushed them apart, keeping them at the edge of personal fulfillment. There were powerful disruptive influences within the intricacies of his subconscious mind. When they did surface, it was as if another person to whom he'd never been introduced took complete control of his actions and feelings, manifesting enormous power directed to the elimination or destruction of whatever stood in his way.

Whip often wondered about the calibre of workmanship that created both Tina and himself. Either they were born with the power to elevate their thinking beyond that of the average man, setting their sights on a future plan privy only to them or they considered themselves omnipotent enough to navigate the waters of destiny into doing their bidding—not the other way around.

Tina, often in a quandary when confronted with Whip's inconsistency of thoughts, was unable to understand him. He'd confess his undying love, then in the next moment she might as well be alone for his mind would wander far afield from her. On these occasions she'd dig herself a trench of silence and wait, unsure what she waited for —a miracle perhaps? How often had she accused him of living in the past?

Over dinner at the Manhattan townhouse she repeated her timeworn admonitions. "You've got to think of your own life. Ted is dead. You can't resurrect him, not if you find ten assassins."

Whip was vulnerable tonight, thinking sorrowfully about the unfulfilled plans Ted had wanted to put into effect as president. He'd been lamenting his anger for nearly an hour.

"—And then one day before Ted could fulfill his dream, ping—bing—boom, cut down by a worthless maniac or two—or three or four."

"You're reaching for the moon, Whip," she said with dread.

"No, Tina, the moon is reaching for me," he said ominously.

At that moment, Tina felt she no longer had strength to combat the forces of Whip's destiny. Frightened, shaken with an alien sense of inner defeat, she left him that night and returned to Las Vegas a determined woman. Either he would quit politics, settle down into another profession and decide on a future for them, or she wouldn't see him again. Changes were occurring in Tina also. The past several years had taught her plenty. Her sparse love life caused her to involve herself in the excitement of the empire created by her father. She no

71

longer sat back contemplating a future based on the efforts of someone else. She was becoming her own person, accepting the frightening nature of self-knowledge and in so doing canceling out some of its awesomeness. She had come to terms with herself and decided that playing second fiddle in any man's life wasn't for her. For too long, she'd been in competition with the darkness of Whip's secret thoughts. What went on inside his head since he returned from Rome she had never learned. Whatever it was had made him a changed man.

What Tina didn't know was that the circumstances leading up to this tremendous change in Whip and what subsequently happened had nothing to do with his love for her.

Months after Whip returned from Rome, he was at the Justice Department searching through some files when a voice honoring his title of attorney general called to Whip, "General!"

Whip glanced from the file into the piercing blue eyes of a strapping man with snowy white hair and a craggy face.

"Chief Bowman, what a surprise!" Slamming the drawer of the file shut he extended his hand.

Behind Bowman's dark glasses was a gaze of friendliness that warmed the room. "It's been a helluva long time. Since you mustered out of O.S. in Rome."

"What are you doing here? I thought you'd retired."

"Retirement isn't too far away," he said ruefully. "Come to my office. Warm up with a hot cup of coffee." It was an imperative request, and he hoped Whip caught his inflection.

About to decline, Whip found himself agreeing. "I could do with a little hot brew about now, Chief." Picking up his briefcase, Whip followed Bowman out of the noisy room with its clattering typewriters, voices raised in argument and ringing telephones and moved along the sterile corridor. They entered an elevator, descended to the basement and walked through more corridors. Whip wondered where in hell Bowman was heading.

He was ushered into the nondescript office of the BSI chief and stared blankly at the misleading nameplate on the door.

"Whirlwind Enterprises? What in hell? Exactly what does that mean? Why the subterfuge?" Whip shook his head. "I thought I knew every occupant in this concrete jungle."

"A decoy to keep out the nosey," Bowman said, locking the door behind them. "I can't tell you how many times I've tried contacting you, General, without the Washington goons learning of it. I've called your office, left a cover name hoping no one would tie my name to yours and end up doing some fancy arithmetic."

He busied himself making a fresh pot of coffee as Whip put down his briefcase on a sturdy wooden government-issue chair.

Whip, chilled by the cooler temperature in the basement, shuddered involuntarily. A violent rain storm outside had lashed at him earlier, nearly drenching him. He could still feel the dampness clear to his skin. He removed his Londoner trenchcoat, laying it over the back of a chair.

"Now, if only you had a roaring hot fire on the hearth—"

The hot coffee hit the spot, warming them both.

"When I think of how I conspired to reach you, even using outmoded cloak and dagger procedures, General, when you were right here in this building," he grinned impishly. "Suddenly here you are under my nose. Well, I wasn't about to worry about us being seen. Now that you're through as attorney general . . . Well, I'll get on with it," he muttered, watching Whip warm his hands on the coffee mug.

The chief began a story that would change the course of Whip's life. Three hours later he was wrapping it up.

"Shortly after Ted's inauguration he met with me to discuss this highly classified subject. We, the BSI, were out of funds. I couldn't see abandoning the project after twenty years, so I went to see President Shiverton. He took instant interest in the project and I was damned grateful for his cooperation. Two weeks later the President called me advising me we had the necessary funds to take us through his term of office, with the proviso that he'd review our work and if he thought it appropriate, and he succeeded in winning a second term of office, it could continue.

"Well, sir, we're back facing the same predicament—out of funds. Somehow I got the feeling Ted wouldn't have wanted me to go to President Linden with my cry for help. Your brother was the first president in twenty years who didn't treat the BSI like a contagious disease to be exterminated at any cost."

Whip interrupted him tersely. "Look, chief, a certain

73

protocol must be adhered to in such matters. I'm in no position to be advising you, not while President Linden is still bent on sparring with the ghosts of my brother's administration."

"I understand, General."

"Saint Michael! Please call me Whip. Anything but General. I'm no longer the attorney general," he snapped impatiently.

"I've no intention of promoting deception with President Linden." Bowman spoke with cool reservation. "Your brother swore me to secrecy. Only he and I knew the BSI was funded by him personally."

Whip's head angled sharply, scowling at the implication of Bowman's words. He glanced furtively about the room, then listened as Bowman told him more. His disturbance increased.

"I find it hard to believe Ted would fund such a venture—" He paused. "What do you want from me?" He had to know more.

Anticipating his curiosity and his reluctance to show his feelings candidly, Bowman handed Whip a large manilla file.

"Suppose you peruse the contents. You'll learn why Ted decided he couldn't let our department flounder and die, doomed to a burial in the catacombs as a foolish, useless expenditure." Bowman sipped his coffee and leaned towards his guest. "If Ted hadn't met the end he did, I might have rolled these files into the storehouse, had them microfilmed, burned the originals, forfeited all rights to them and gone on pension. For too long I watched the continued coverup of his assassination while those in power continue to distort the goddamned facts. Shit—I've grown embittered. My resentment against the system that impugns the work of the BSI boils my liver! Goddammit, Whip, contained in these files is enough information to burn their hides. One man alone can't hack it. I'd wind up dead from an assassin's bullet like Ted— or disposed of in some way that looked like an accident. I'm not afraid of death, hell, I've faced it countless times, but to die for nothing . . . This self-ordained group of righteous bastards, empowering themselves with the right to control life and death . . . Son-of-a-bitching egotists intend to control the fucking world! Someone's gotta stop them!"

Whip, only half listening as he thumbed through the

file, jerked his head up in astonishment as he studied Bowman.

"Then you don't know? You've never been briefed on IAGO?" He studied Whip with more intensity, as if he were trying to read his mind. "The president *didn't* confide his fears?"

Whip tried to subdue his inner excitement, masking his emotions skillfully. The thought that he was about to learn more stirred him beyond belief. He reset his actor's mask into place.

"Egotists who intend to rule the world?" he scoffed. "Really, chief—"

The rain outside lashed furiously against the building. Whip's mood, as somber as the shrouded light working its way through the abbreviated opaque windows in this unusual office, reflected in his eyes and communicated his concern to Bowman.

"Don't underestimate IAGO. At my first encounter with your brother, I got the distinct impression he already knew of them."

Whip recalled Ali's words concerning certain colleagues of his; those nameless power brokers who'd insure the presidency for him whenever he gave them the word. What a goddamned puzzle! He knew he was closer to solving it than he might have wanted. First there was more to learn, more questions to be asked. To sit opposite Bowman and jockey for position without tipping his hand was difficult, but profitable. He needed the answers.

So did Chief Bowman. "Senator, please explain your relationship to Prince Ali Mohammed Izmur," he said matter-of-factly.

"What do you mean, my relationship?"

"The only way to progress is to trust each other. I'm not prying. But the recent marriage of Ted's widow to the prince is a bit curious."

"We tried to discourage the alliance, but Valerie is not the type to be dissuaded from what she wants."

"If I suggested the prince's interest in Ted's widow is primarily to keep her from talking about Ted's death—"

"It's crossed my mind."

"Good. You're aware of the ramifications." He poured more coffee for them. "Recent information reached us indicating that the prince may replace a very special man in the hierarchy of IAGO, a man who's controlled it since its inception. It would be of interest to us to learn when it takes place and why him."

"Maybe he's the best qualified," quipped Whip. "How the hell should I know?"

"You do grasp the importance of placing an Arab chieftain at the head of IAGO? Especially with their hatred of the Jews in Palestine, whom they feel unjustly appropriated their lands."

"That too has crossed my mind."

"The man who attempted to take your life in West Berlin is a terrorist member of a splinter group of the PLO."

"The Prince mentioned the rascal's affiliation with them."

"Prince Izmur told you this?" Bowman retreated into a veil of thought. "What else did His Highness talk about?"

"Numerous things," said Whip. "He honored me at a gala—"

"Yes, yes, we know all that from our agent in Rome. You were there for three days, in which you became friendly."

"We were Harvard classmates—"

Bowman nodded knowingly. "There wasn't much love lost between you. The prince has been known to say unflattering things about you."

"At least he's in step with the majority."

"That isn't amusing Senator." Bowman's face turned to marble. "They aren't amusing people. They're dangerous. Don't view our conversation in so frivolous a light."

"Sorry, I mean no disrespect," said Whip, at once apologetic. He sat up stiffly. "Do get on with it, chief. I'm aware of many things I might have scoffed at before Ted's death. I don't mean to be frivolous."

"As long as we understand one another. Your brother and I worked covertly in this. Not one of his advisors knew of this amalgamation between us, so you have every right to disbelieve what I'm saying."

Whip shook his head, wagging a hand at him. "I came across a file among Ted's very private papers, giving me insight into your work. Dispel your fears. It was cryptic, difficult to understand. Perhaps we can review the contents and you can illuminate the more salient points."

Bowman nodded. He lit up a cigarette and puffed thoughtfully for several moments. "Did you also learn from Prince Izmur that he is exceedingly interested in a special friend of yours?"

Whip's brows shot up. "Who?"

76

Bowman blew smoke from his lips. "Tina Erice Bonaparte."

Whip sat up erect, the fine hairs on his body standing on end. "W-why would that interest me?" he asked guardedly.

"I thought we were friends. No more games between us. We'll make a pact. As it is I took a terrible chance talking to you upstairs where prying eyes might have seen us together."

"Do you know everything about me?" Whip asked tightly.

"Everything."

Their eyes held briefly. He could feel his skin crawl as he and Bowman regarded each other. He was aware that this was no fly-by-night operation thought up by some fancy-spending bureaucrat. There was more on his mind than being concerned that Bowman might know how many times he took a crap each day.

"How long to fully brief me?"

"Six months, maybe sooner."

"Six months!" Whip whistled softly. He felt as turbulent inside as the fulminating elements outside. Rolling claps of thunder startled them as bolts of lightning zigzagged across the sky, lighting up the dismal basement office. Silence filled the room.

"Does Neiland Milton know of your existence?"

"I hope not."

Whip's eyes held his, briefly. In Bowman's he read a great deal more than he cared to elaborate on at this time.

Thus began Whip's indoctrination into the power structure of IAGO. If in the past he'd considered his astuteness in domestic and foreign affairs formidable, he was shot down instantly. IAGO's nefarious activities on a worldwide basis, designed to manipulate the forces of good and evil for their personal aggrandizement, boggled his mind. A kaleidoscope of faces marched across the memory of his mind, and the names of E.L. Lamb, Larchmont and Merkle, having caused him many a sleepless night, now cropped up in the IAGO dossier. Shit! He should have known there'd be a tie-in somehow.

The day those two insufferable popinjays with the incredible names of Arthur Glass and James Mirror left the Manhattan townhouse, Ted had ambiguously alluded to their father's estate, suggesting that Whip familiarize himself with the files. Whip wondered if it had been the contents of their dead father's files that influenced Ted to personally fund the BSI investigation. Whip never forgot that Tex Merkle had figured prominently in the Joey Erice kidnapping.

The Erice kidnapping. How long ago had it occurred?

He recalled that night when Val Erice called them during the Christmas holidays to relate the incident of the kidnapping. He knew Val well enough by reputation to know he wasn't on a fishing expedition. Whip had kept Val waited outside a telephone booth in the freezing snow while he personally made a telephone call to the oil tycoon in Texas.

"It's Christmas eve—or don't you big politicians in Washington celebrate Christianity?" came the west Texas drawl of the hardnosed, stiff-backed oil man, in an angry bellowing voice.

Whip had laid it all out to him and with aplomb took it upon himself to deny that a man with as much at stake as Merkle would dare to commit so debasing an act as kidnapping.

"I suggested you'd never be party to so outrageous a crime. Confirm my belief in you, sir."

Sputtering, stammering, mumbling incoherently he'd managed a thank-you of sorts and appreciation for Whip's concern.

Whip's voice became sterner. "You understand if such rumors prove true the arm of my office would have no recourse but to investigate and prosecute—"

"I assure you, Mr. Attorney General, I've had nothing to do with such foul, absurd and unfounded allegations. Accept my word as a gentleman and an American patriot," his west Texas drawl thickened noticeably, "Tex Merkle wouldn't be a party to such foolishness."

Whip's voice never sounded silkier. "Understand, I didn't believe the wild rumor, sir. But I'd have been remiss in my duties if I hadn't checked with you first. I always believe in going directly to the source."

Thereupon the Texan had thanked Whip for his concern and wished him a merry Christmas. Later when Whip learned the bluff had paid off and Joey Erice had been released unharmed, he not only marveled at Val's strategy, he'd been grossly incensed that Merkle, regardless of his financial clout, would have tried to perpetrate a crime, manipulating the federal laws, as it were, to satisfy his own personal vendetta.

Whip couldn't know the complicated network of Merkle's mind. The oil tycoon, an astute man, had no desire to tangle with the redoubtable maverick attorney general. How, he wondered, had the kidnapping been traced to him? Whip's call convinced him that he wasn't unknown to Shiverton. This fact troubled him acutely. It served no purpose if the umbrella of anonymity he wanted to preserve no longer shielded him or his involvements. The perturbed Texan could gladly do without Shiverton's scrutiny.

Having felt the spurs put to his ribs, he moved swiftly and did what Val Erice predicted—he called off the kidnapping attempt. Using his code name, Gusher, given him by several old underworld friends, he ordered his contract man to call off the abduction and issued further orders to trace the leak back to him. This ended the unusual kidnapping attempt against the Erice family. Whip would learn shortly thereafter that the affair had been implemented as a tool to pressure Val into abandoning his holdings in Las Vegas.

Had Whip found the time then to pursue Merkle's background more thoroughly he might have stumbled on the chain of command linking the TFL combine to IAGO. Who could have known then what he was privy to in recent days?

"It makes sense," Whip told Bowman one night in the seclusion of the Georgetown brownstone. "TFL had to forego IAGO's plans to control those lands in Vegas held by Val Erice. What galling bile for Howard Hughes to swallow when he couldn't best Erice."

"He was exiled to a tropical island—" began Bowman.

"You mean—you mean to say that Hughes belonged to—"

"IAGO?" Bowman nodded. "They felt he should have closed the deal long before, despite the screams from Washington claiming monopoly that were echoing across the land."

Whip shook his head, bemused at all this. "Getting back to Tex Merkle—"

Bowman nodded. "Following his call to his contract man he placed a call to Manny Marciano in Vegas. Concerned over his possible culpability in the Erice kidnapping, he ordered Manny to fix it with his old cronies to make it look like a real mob job. Marciano, assuming the responsibility of sewing a frame, by integrating facts with

79

fiction tried to find someone with a grudge against the Erice family. Nothing washed. The ex-hood could find no one on whom to pin the guilty jacket."

After Chief Bowman left for the evening, Whip sat in a solitude of conflicting thoughts as he studied the corpulent files of the three oil men who made up TFL. Their backgrounds were so similar that they could have all been one man, he thought.

Self-made men. Loners, schemers, dreamers; all made fortunes during the early Texas oil strikes by buying up oil leases. Before this, shady oil swindles, stock manipulation, and fast-talking con jobs. Their backgrounds didn't differ from those of the clawing, scratching, two-tongued diamond-backed scoundrels who discovered those overnight bonanzas of gold and oil in the 1850s.

Some time prior to World War I the activities of these men became obscured. They came from opposite ends of the earth and found each other by a common bond. Suddenly their lives became private. They moved into highly secluded estates away from the limelight and publicity most Texans thrive upon. You could read any paper to learn what their individual companies were doing—how many gushers of oil daily erupted into tens of thousands of barrels. Their contributions to charities occupied four-column spreads in the paper—but their private lives remained private.

Whip discussed the possibility of moving the BSI files to his house. Chief Bowman balked instantly. "Should anyone get on to us, the possibility of a spook laying a blanket of surveillance on you with a probable break-in and entry would be heightened if you harbored the files. Presently we remain obscured by a tight network of bureaucratic red tape. Your comings and goings in the Justice Department would bring less attention to our project than if we met at your place."

"In other words, no," said Whip.

"I do get wordy at times."

"You'll need funds. Have you considered your survival?"

"I've passed that ball to you, Senator. Whether you run with it for a touchdown, drop it, or fumble is up to you." Bowman smiled a lazy smile.

Whip nodded. They talked for a time. Newspaper headlines tying Tubby Garnet to the Los Cuaycos government and Delfino Cratos had broken that day. "What's your theory, Chief?" he asked.

"The silencing of an alleged assassin, in this case what Garnet did to Coswalksi, means only one thing—conspiracy. Assassins are always sent to kill the best of a nation's competitors. Read it, Whip, it's all in our files."

Whip's eyes clouded over. "Why would the BSI be investigating the Los Cuaycos situation? Is there a link to Ted's assassination?" As soon as the words left his lips he realized the absurdity of his questions. "We'll do it your way, Chief. We'll start with TFL Corporation. If they are the holding company for Golden Enterprises, we've pierced the corporate veil. Lamb, Larchmont, Merkle—right?"

"They're only shadows for the real clout."

"IAGO?"

"IAGO."

"These men, Neiland Milton's strongest contributors, were about to be investigated by Ted for income tax evasion as soon as he returned from the Custer trip. But he never returned."

On an afternoon some six months later, Whip met Cliff Bowman at Killadreenan Downs, his farm in Virginia where he and Ted had maintained a stable of excellent breeding horses. Whip needed a swift canter on a horse and the chief rode with him.

The woods were filled with dead leaves, thick moss and an overgrowth of vines. Here and there splotches of snow dotted the brown countryside. Next to autumn and its palette of electrifying colors, tawny burgundies, golden oranges, and varying shades of green, Whip loved the slumbering wintertime when nature rested beneath the snow waiting to bloom into spring.

The swift pounding of horses' hooves as they thundered up one hill and down the other didn't pound as much as Bowman's heart. He called for time out.

They reined their horses and broke into a slower canter as Whip led the way to a rushing brook at the edge of the property. There they dismounted and allowed the horses to drink their fill of water and graze for a time.

For a time they both drank in the austerity of nature as she marked time in the wings of winter, preparing to shed her white mantle for the fertility of spring. Bowman sensed Whip's need to talk. It was no accident that he chose to speak freely in the woods where they weren't concerned with eavesdroppers.

"The proposed uprising of the Los Cuaycos nationalists led by the CIA spooks was Milton's baby. The Swineherd Bay fiasco, planned as a wedge to reenter the island, overthrow the Cratos regime and reestablish the Tabasis government, was Milton's brainchild. On the day of the invasion, I recall, the White House received a rash of tense, highly agitated dignitaries, including Milton himself, personally urging Ted to send U.S. troops to back up the planned invasion. Ted, having already considered the invasion a doomsday tactic, had called it off.

"How can I begin to describe the bedlam that day? Milton had brought with him formidable affidavits from the Department of Defense and from former President Pleasanton advising Ted to invade Los Cuaycos.

"In good conscience, Ted declined. He set aside Milton's suggestions on the grounds that such tactics employed by the USA would be construed as aggressive acts of war which would offend the OAS and violate all that democracy stood for among our Latin American neighbors. Moreover it would add to the stress with Russia."

Whip sat down on a felled log, hunched over, his arms on his thighs, tapping his leather riding boots with a twig. Chipmunks scurried past them.

"Ted was firm. He stood pat against all sorts of militant opposition. I was so proud of him, really. He was something to behold in a crisis. Later that day, however, under unbelievable stress, and against his better judgement, he relented and permitted the invasion to commence. He wasn't aware then he'd been handed a mess of garbage by his intelligence gathering forces. The reports, slanted to appear that the invasion would occur simultaneously with a coordinated attack by underground resistance forces were of course falsified. No one on the island was armed and waiting to perform a miraculous coup with the invading nationalists. No one. . . . The rest is history."

Whip dully recalled those nightmarish moments that would haunt Ted's presidency for eternity. He continued, summing it up: "The invasion without supportive internal power didn't stand a chance in hell of survival. Those poor, unfortunate souls who lost their lives for a worthless and shabby affair will never be forgotten.

"Milton, as vice president in the Pleasanton administration, had committed air power to Lojuria in the Far East to back up the CIA zombies responsible for the dirty politics overseas. Milton's efforts backed the terrorists. He committed millions of American dollars to the despot who later became responsible for burning alive a group of religious dissenters." Whip stopped abruptly, and stared into Bowman's eyes. "He's one of them, isn't he? Neiland Milton belongs to IAGO. You realize the kind of power I'm talking about?" Whip paced over the dry leaves. "He's back in his office now, stronger than ever."

Bowman nodded. Good, it was taking hold of Whip.

"Milton belongs to IAGO. No ifs, ands or buts." He shoved his fist into the open palm of his hand. "Just as I might have belonged had I acquiesced to Prince Izmur's courtship."

"They approached you? Offered you the presidency?"

Whip nodded. "All I had to do is sell out a plucky little nation. Shit, Chief, I was there in World War I. Why the hell didn't America annex Sicily, as we should have? She'd have been a worthwhile ally, considering her strategic location. Then, this trouble in the Middle East—"

The sharp crack of gunfire sounded unreal. Whip's body suddenly jerked up and back as a look of pained bewilderment scrawled across his features. He groaned aloud, "Ughhh." The horses nearby whinnied with flaring eyes.

Catching Whip as he pitched forward into a pit of darkness Bowman held him and ducked into a nearby bush, landing flat on his belly, Whip under him. His breathing came in labored gasps. The burden of knowing Whip, shot, could be dead panicked him. When he felt it safe to lift himself off he turned the senator over on his back.

Two hours later, under an alias, Whip lay in the intensive care ward at Arlington Hospital fighting for his life as skilled physicians worked over him. A bullet entering the left temporal area had exited Whip's cranium at the left rear, incredibly missing the vital gray matter by a slim hair.

Every means at Bowman's disposal were used to keep the event out of the newspapers. Despite Dr. Lovely's admonition that Whip should remain in the hospital for longer than the five days he was there, Whip insisted on returning to Georgetown. Two weeks later, after a series of strange, anonymous phone calls, and the receipt of sympathy cards sent by unsigned well-wishers, Bowman insisted he should move to New York, where access to his quarters would be more difficult.

Several BSI agents and close friends of Whip's, including Kevin O'Brien and Tom Murphy, took turns guarding him around the clock. Bowman personally conducted the investigation, covertly of course, but was unable to get anywhere with the few clues available to him. The identity of Whip's assailant remained a mystery.

On an unusually warm day in March, when the snow was nearly thawed, Whip was poking through the plants on the terrace, pausing now and again to observe the activity in Central Park, when the phone rang. His first reaction was to let it ring. Then, recalling that it was here in this apartment that he and Tina had been reunited the first time, he thought wildly that history might be repeating itself. He scurried inside. No such luck. It wasn't Tina.

Kevin O'Brien's voice at the other end sounded excited.

"I've got something hot for you, Sir Lancelot. Can I buzz on over? It's about our dear friend, Venus de Milo."

Whip hesitated a moment, then replied tersely, "You've got it, buddy. Come on over." His curiosity piqued him as he hung up the receiver. A quiver of the old excitement shot through him. The code name for Jolie Barnes had been Venus de Milo. *Now what in the hell had O'Brien uncovered—and why?* All covert surveillance on Jolie should've ended with Ted's death. While he lived, wiretaps and full surveillance on Jolie had been a necessity. A wealth of information resulted from such tactics. Hidden cameras rigged in her apartments following Ted's near-fatal shooting had revealed Renzo's infidelity to Whip. How Tina could remain with such a full-blown rat was an unsolved mystery to Whip and a constant source of irritation now that he'd shared intimacies with her. Lately he missed her more than life, but wouldn't call.

In the projection room, O'Brien loaded film into a projector and described this stroke of luck in uncovering the film. "I mean—six years after Ted's death! Someone goofed. This was dumped into my lap by a slimy character for the price of a fix. Dumb bastard didn't know what he had. Anyway a friend of mine bought it for twenty-five bucks. We watched it with a few other stags and I nearly crapped in my pants when I saw it. Luckily my buddy's sound wasn't working.

"Well, old friend, I asked to borrow the film. My buddy hesitated. So I gave him a fifty for it. You'll see what we've got in a minute."

The screen filled with bright light and the lifesize figure of Jolie Barnes. She was in bed, in the New York apartment. Renzo, naked, lay alongside her. Having seen them in this posture so many times, Whip was hardly affected by her. The screen grew animated, drawing his full attention. His internal dialogue shut off instantly at the sound of their voices.

He called out to O'Brien, quickly. "How old is the film?"

O'Brien's voice came at him as the agent returned and sat alongside Whip. "Who knows? A few years old maybe? Why?"

"It's important. Can you find out?" His attention was on the screen and he listened intently as O'Brien left to make his calls.

"Look, baby," Renzo's honeycombed voice pleaded. "I'll be riding high soon, in real style. Go along with me a little longer. I can give you anything your heart desires."

"That include marriage?" Jolie asked, up on one elbow.

"No, goddammit! I told you no. There's things I gotta do first. Stick with me and the moon'll be yours."

"No, you look, baby," she replied, pushing him from her. "I'm through being a clothesline for you and Tina to hang your dirty wash on. The sooner you get that through your head—" She squirmed out of his embrace, shoving herself militantly up against the headboard.

Renzo sullenly lit up a cigarette and took a few drags. "I got problems, kid. I mean real problems. Be patient a little longer. Listen, those Shiverton boy scouts ain't never held a candle to the kind of power we got clenched in our fists."

Whip tensed and sat forward in his seat. That remark out of left field caught his interest. He heard a beeper sound, a signal for him to pay attention to this portion of the film.

"Got it, Kevin."

On the screen Jolie countered Renzo's remark hotly.

"Boy scouts! You call them boy scouts?" She grew recklessly brave. "There'll never be a president as fearless and brave as Ted Shiverton. You shut up! Just shut your trap!"

"He's dead, ain't he?" Renzo snickered, his bleary eyes blinking lazily. "No one fools with the big boys and lives to talk about it. Small fish outa school is what they were. Now, one's gone. Phew, how that power structure crumbled—like cookies. Watch what happens to that loudmouthed punk, the senator. Without his brother around to wipe his snot nose, he's a nothing—a has-been."

Whip touched the bandaged area of his head significantly. *Something had happened to the loudmouthed punk, all right,* he thought, wondering how odd that Renzo should know so much.

"A lot you know!" snapped Jolie.

"A lot you know," he aped back. "I know plenty."

Whip hadn't known the extent of Jolie's affection for Ted. Listening to the next portion of the film he got a measure of it. He saw clearly that Jolie seemed intent on prying information from Renzo. She plied him with liquor, encouraging him to boast freely.

"You want me to believe you love me when you won't tell me what the rewards are if I stick by you. You wanted me to give up my Mister X, but you won't commit yourself to me. Hah!"

"You want I should walk away from millions after working so hard? Never, sweetie. You ain't gonna find me doing that. Goddammit! I don't love Tina—never have. It's business. Just damned good business. As long as I'm in the family there ain't nothing I can't do. The old man ain't got long to live, and that leaves Joey and Tina. I can handle Joey—even Tina. That ain't saying much for that boozed, pill-popping broad."

"You're forgetting Benne," she said, checking her anger.

"Benne? Hah! He's going nowhere. Him with his Harvard education. Nothing in the world can stop me once I've made up my mind. Including getting you, you blue-eyed sweet tomato." He reached for her, snuggling her close to him. "Haven't I always taken care of you?"

"I like Benne," she said, shrugging out of his embrace. "He's strange. It's hard to get through that wall of reserve, but I know where I stand with him. I'm a great lay—no more, no less." Then, wistfully, "About Mister X, don't concern yourself with him. He's out of the picture—for a long time now."

"You ain't just saying that, kid?" His bleary eyes were heavily lidded. "You ain't just saying that? The biggest competition I've ever had and you say it's ended? *Kaput?* Who the hell is he?"

"It doesn't matter, he's gone."

"And if he comes back into the picture? Where does it leave me?"

"He's dead, Renzo, drop it!"

"Serves him right. He had you too long." He grew surly.

86

"Shut up!" she exploded. "SHUT UP!" She shook with rage and reached for a sheer peignoir.

Renzo rose unsteadily to his feet, obviously snockered. "You still love him, kid?" He shook his head as if the thought was inconceivable to him. "Hey, you got any milk? Bring me a gallon, will ya? What did you give me —rotgut? Shouldn't have drunk so much. It's a bummer. Sorry if I'm out of line. I got outa line, didn't I? You went with him a long time. It's all right you got feelings for him . . ."

"Just don't put him down to me, hear? Lie down, will you? I'll get the milk." Seeing his apparent distress she led him to bed.

Jolie moved out of the shot, leaving the room. On the screen Renzo got up and wobbled to the chaise longue, scanning the contents of a table nearby, casually at first, then with intent interest.

Whip tried to make out the contents: scissors, a scrapbook, glue, a pile of newspaper clippings. His eyes fixed on Renzo.

Nodding stupidly, fluttering his eyelids, in the stupor of a heroin addict after a fix, Renzo tried to flip open the cover of the scrapbook in a limp-wristed, rubbery movement that seemed too much of a strain. He struggled to blink, then fell against the chaise, trying to clear something in his foggy mind. His eyes snapped open and he stared into the camera lens.

Watching him, Whip felt certain Renzo either suspected or detected the hidden camera. He tried once again to lurch forward and shake off the alcoholic stupor. No luck. He fell back defeated and unconscious.

Overhead the camera continued to grind out film. Whip watched the screen, never taking his eyes from the man who married Tina. Reaching for two pain pills, he washed them down with a tumbler of water.

Jolie came back on camera carrying a tray with a glass of milk. She paused, disturbed by what she saw on the table. She set the tray down, and picking up the scrapbook thumbed through it. Catching sight of Ted's familiar poses, Whip assumed that what she held was a scrapbook of Ted's career.

Jolie opened a drawer, hiding the book and clippings of Ted, replacing them with a large scrapbook of herself, inscribed with JOLIE on the cover. She covered Renzo with a silken coverlet and let him sleep off the booze.

The screen went blank, rolling to an insert with a memo from Kevin O'Brien: *Be Patient. Film Spliced Together for a Time Lapse.*

Whip nervously flicked his fingernails until the screen lit up once more.

Renzo, moving under the coverlet, sat up, holding his aching head. He rubbed the back of his neck slowly and with effort tried to stand up. He staggered brokenly for a few steps, holding on to the furniture as he negotiated his way to the bathroom. For no apparent reason he turned to the chaise longue, blinking his puffy eyes, searching the table. He opened the scrapbook excitedly and frowned. Tossing it aside, he disappeared through the bathroom door.

Another camera picked him up inside as he got under the shower, letting it run fast, making the usual sounds as the feeling of cold water made him come alive. The water turned off, Renzo came leaping out of the stall, grabbing a towel, cursing aloud and running into the bedroom once again.

In the bedroom under the probing eyes of the first camera, Renzo, dripping wet, peered up searching the ceiling. At one point he was staring directly into the lens. "Son of a bitch! Fucking little cunt!" He cursed, spotting the camera. He dragged a chair over to the spot and with a tissue in his hand proceeded to stuff the lens with it. The picture blanked out. Forced to rely only on the audio, Whip heard Renzo's angry voice.

"You fucking cunt! You'd do this to me?"

"What's wrong?" cried Jolie in alarm. "Stop it, Renzo, you're acting like a madman. You're wrecking the place!"

Whip heard noises: sounds of furniture toppling over, a prolonged scuffle, heavy breathing, slapping. The tissue partially fell out of the lens, affording Whip a better view.

"Not until I find the fucking microphone." Renzo tore up the place. He stopped abruptly and leveled a lethal glance on Jolie. "You're in on this, ain't ya, kid? Ya trying to hang something on me? Who put you up to it?" He pointed to the ceiling. "A fucking camera, kid. That's it—" He swung and clouted her on the side of her head. "*Fucking whore!* You're doing this for Benne, aintcha? The family's got to you!" He struck her time and again until Jolie, bleeding profusely and knocked senseless, fell against the furniture, upsetting tables and chairs. Reeling back, supported by the wall, she tried to catch her breath and ward off his blows.

"You're crazy. I don't know anything about this." She wouldn't cry—not Jolie. "What's Benne got to do with this?"

"No you don't, you fucking cunt! You ain't gonna get me to spill to you." He ranted and raved with the fury of a scorned lover.

Whip, tense, with clenched fists, lost the video portion. The audio afforded him a few moments of sound.

Renzo, cursing and raving, let loose a gasp of contentment. "Ahhhhh you little fucker. I found you!" Having located the microphones, he uprooted them.

O'Brien, the John Wayne-lookalike, returned to the room, a brooding expression on his face. He shuffled about on his feet. "You're not gonna like this, Senator. The film is no more than two weeks old!"

"That's impossible!" His astonishment was evident.

"Not when you hear what I have to say. The chain of command never broke down. Got it straight from the horse's mouth. Venus de Milo has been kept under surveillance because someone failed to rescind the orders after Ted's death. Agents have gone in to collect the film and reload the equipment periodically, stashing the film in the file room. The vault is overloaded."

"I don't understand, Kevin. How did your friend get this tape?" asked Whip, pondering the ramifications of this stew.

"Beats the hell outa me. Someone did a five-fingered exercise and lifted it. Someone on the inside who didn't know the fuck about nothing. God knows how many other films have been lifted."

Whip's startled glance and concerned expression got to O'Brien. He paced back and forth in marked agitation.

"Jesus Christ! We're gonna have to track it down. That's all there is to it!" he muttered angrily. "Who the hell fucked up on this?"

"After six years you think we can find out? Talk about bureaucratic red tape. Sheeeeit!" O'Brien, as angry as Whip, mopped his brow. "Can I fix you a drink? I need one myself."

Whip nodded and paid no attention to his bodyguard behind the bar as he paced to and fro before him. *Six fucking years of surveillance! Christ, the file room must be loaded with canned reels of film. Someone must have figured he'd make a killing. What a racket!*

89

"It wouldn't take a hayseed to figure out there's been no real activity on the assignment," said O'Brien. "Listen, Whip, the best among those government clerks gotta look to find dough these days. He must have figured no one would ever miss them."

"We've got to confiscate the rest of the film. We just can't leave it there to be peddled on the streets as porn. Someone has got to recognize the stars and then the price will go up."

"You don't mean what I think you mean?" O'Brien piped up aghast. "Just don't let me think that you mean me. You don't want me to risk that kind of a rap—do you?" he asked weakly.

Whip took the drink from his outstretched hand, and sipped the scotch as O'Brien gulped his down. He pondered the situation, then, shaking his head, gave O'Brien a glimmer of a smile.

"Wouldn't think of hanging you up. I got a better idea. Look, friend, drink up. Take the night off."

"Oh, no, not again," protested O'Brien. "I let you out of my sight once and you got bagged, real good. Uh, uh."

"Then go to bed. See you in the morning." Whip closed the door behind the imposing Irishman, snapping a dead bolt into place.

Whip sat through the film three more times, then placed a call to Cliff Bowman. He explained the situation—the oversight on the part of the New Horizons men. "I've got to get the contents of that vault, Chief."

"You know what you're asking of me?" he replied, a smile in his voice.

"I know. I know. Uncle Sam doesn't have to know? I mean the heist could be done in broad daylight while everyone's on duty."

"Senator, how you carry on." Bowman laughed heartily.

"Let the record show we use no names over the phone."

"Your lines were swept clean less than an hour ago. Dammit! We found four taps this time."

Whip thanked him, hung up and thought about Bowman's words.

The next day at approximately noon two burly agents entered the file and records room at the Justice Department, steering a four-wheeled hand cart along the narrow aisle to the door at the far end of the large, busy room. No one paid them any heed. One man knocked on the door. The door opened. A harried clerk peered out at them and grasped the papers thrust into his hands.

He checked the order and shrugged, pointing to a bin numbered and coded cryptically. The agents went in and indolently emptied the files, placing the contents onto the cart in large cartons. They signed one order, and left it with the clerk. They took with them an assignment of goods, signed for by the clerk. The agents left with their cache of films, nonchalantly wheeling back along the corridor, without raising one inquisitive eyebrow in the building. Down the freight elevator they went, loading their goods into a van.

Within the hour, the van brought the prized items to a preplanned destination.

At approximately the same time, Whip Shiverton and his aides, O'Brien and Murphy, entered the lobby of Jolie's apartment building. The trio rode the elevator to the tenth floor, walked down two flights and knocked on Jolie's door.

Jolie opened it. The two agents moved in swiftly, brushing past her. Her expression of surprise turned to indignation until Whip removed his dark wraparound glasses and she recognized him.

After searching the apartment, the two agents left them alone together.

"Sorry about the cloak and dagger procedure, Miss Barnes," Whip apologized after his men closed the door.

"To what do I owe the pleasure of this attention?" she asked.

"I'm happy you still remember me. It makes the awkwardness of our meeting less uncomfortable." He followed her into the all-white living room, whose decor he knew by heart, and sat down in the low seat across the coffee table from the sofa. Jolie was wearing a white jersey jumpsuit, revealing in all the right places. Whip understood why Ted had been enamored of her.

"Do you mind if I raise the volume control on the speaker?"

"Not if you can tolerate my singing."

Jolie moved to the bar. "Drink?"

"Scotch over ice is fine. Thank you."

She fixed his drink and poured a diet cola for herself and returned to him, handing him his drink before settling onto the sofa opposite him.

"First, let me thank you for all the years of pleasure you brought Ted. He thought a great deal about you."

Jolie's face screwed up into a puzzled look. "Now? After so many years?" She leveled her eyes on him, tentatively trying to fathom him. She shrugged, then, "I suppose now is as good a time as any." She glanced about the room. "You know, whoever said that time is the healer of all wounds was having a pipe dream. I should get rid of this place. It contains too many memories of Ted. He spent as much time with me as possible under the conditions."

"I know." Whip sipped his scotch, hoping the huskiness in his throat would melt, then dove headlong into a preamble.

"I'm not certain what I can say without incurring your wrath, Miss Barnes. Let me say this. We did what we did for security reasons. What I'm trying to say is when the president is intimate with someone naturally we cover him for protection." He cleared his throat and studied the faint bruises on her face until she squirmed under his scrutiny. He apologized. "Uh—all that is our fault." He indicated her face.

"What are you talking about?"

Whip explained, adding, "I can't apologize enough, really."

Jolie slowly removed the dark glasses she wore, her lips falling open into a somewhat astonished expression. "I'm not certain I understand . . ."

"What I'm trying to tell you is we failed to remove the wiretaps and listening devices on your premises, here."

Her astonishment as she fit together the pieces brought a premature mixture of relief and a secret smile of satisfaction.

"Look, Miss Barnes—"

"Call me Jolie."

"Look, Jolie, I'm not the diplomat my brother was. It's not part of my character to hide behind innuendo or intrigue. Your phone calls, here and in Vegas, have been monitored, taped. All activity on both premises has been filmed—"

Jolie got the picture. She was aghast. "How long—how long has this been going on?"

"Since the senator became president."

"You've been given a command performance of all my activities?" she asked icily.

"One trusted secret service agent and myself. That's all."

"That's all? That's enough, by God! Just what do you intend doing with my—with those films? After all these years?"

"Nothing. We'll burn them all. It was an oversight."

"Am I supposed to thank you for such favors?"

"You've every right to be angry. You see—uh—Jolie—"

"Call me Miss Barnes," she snapped coldly.

Whip nodded. "I deserve that. I don't want to come off sounding like an ass. What I'm trying to say is— I've come to know you fairly well through the, uh—"

"Dirty movies?" she said scorchingly.

"I've never considered them as, uh, dirty movies . . ."

"Really? They didn't turn you on? Lordy, what more would it take to turn you on? We did everything and anything God or man invented—even those things yet to be discovered by most lovers," she retorted snidely.

He coughed to cover his embarrassment and grew angry with himself for acting like a schoolboy. He clearly saw the charms to which Ted had been addicted when he was alive. Dammit, he had no emotional ties to her. *Get on with your business, Whip!*

"Miss Barnes, Ted's dead. You owe us nothing. I, especially, am beholden to you for the slice of happiness you gave Ted." He rose to his feet, moving about the room, pausing now and again to admire a rare piece of art, a Modigliani and a Picasso, pleasantly surprised that she appreciated art. "I have to learn the identity of Ted's assassin if it takes the rest of my life," he said quietly in an unassuming voice. "You can help me, if you will."

Jolie was stunned. She looked at him, blinking hard.

"I don't believe this. So many years after his death and you don't know who it was that killed your brother?" She stopped abruptly at the look of exasperation in Whip's eyes.

"I understand none of this—" she began tremulously.

"Apparently the government has its reasons for trying to convince the public to believe all the trash that's published. The truth is, I don't believe it. My colleagues don't believe it. What Renzo told you before he inflicted those bruises on you confirms my personal suspicions."

Jolie paled. She was already a step ahead of him. Slowly she shook her head from side to side and appeared disorganized for a few seconds. Then as it dawned on her she muttered, "Oh no. No, you don't, Mr. Shiverton. There's no way I'm gonna play Mata Hari for you. You saw what he did to me when he thought I was responsible for the hidden electronic equipment?"

"He's involved with the Erice family and for—"

93

"What involved?" Jolie interrupted. "He's married to Tina—"

Whip shook his head. "I don't mean that. My interest in Renzo is for different reasons." She gave him a bland look. "You recall that night in Washington when Ted was shot by an unknown assailant?"

"I'll never forget it."

"Recently my office received a provocative and revealing film of what happened that night—"

"You had a camera there too?" she exclaimed stunned.

"Our sources reveal that Renzo was the man who shot at Ted."

Jolie's blue eyes widened, then she scoffed. "With all due respect, Mr. Shiverton, you're crazy—off base."

Whip refrained from answering. The look in his piercing blue eyes was answer enough. Jolie broke eye contact first. She rubbed her hands together, her eyes darting here, there, any place but at him as she thought about his words.

"He hasn't the guts to shoot anyone, least of all a president . . ."

"Suppose Renzo had no idea the target was Ted or that Ted was the Mister X to whom you periodically referred." Whip ignored the tight look she gave him at the revelation of such intimate secrets. "Suppose, instead, that he was insanely jealous of your romance with this, uh, Mister X. An ego-shattering thought, that someone, anyone was beating his time. And following you he lay in waiting on the balcony. What a blow to his manhood to actually see you in another man's arms, making love, enjoying it."

Jolie, listening, grew frenzied. How could Renzo have been so stupid? She felt sick to her stomach.

"It's possible the lights were so dim he couldn't make Ted out in the dark. He took a potshot at the competition to prove he's top dog—"

"Anything's possible."

"Then it's possible he knew Ted was your lover."

"No, I don't believe that."

"He might have informed his associates, who in turn decided it was a perfect setup for an assassination attempt."

"No! He hasn't the guts, I tell you!" She stopped abruptly.

"I understand your feelings. How long have you known Renzo?"

94

"Ted understood about the men in my life. I made our time top priority. After all, what future is there for a president and a former call girl? He didn't want to know about the others."

"I'll respect his wishes. My interest is in the remarks he made about the Shivertons the night he beat you up, Miss Barnes."

"Call me Jolie," she said, the strength drained from her.

Three hours later, Jolie agreed to help Whip. If it was true and Renzo was inextricably caught up in the treachery and betrayal of Ted Shiverton, she wanted nothing to do with him.

"I don't trust him. He's fraught with blind ambition. In the past I laughed it off, minimizing my own premonitions. I-I don't think I can continue in the relationship knowing—Really, I don't think I can."

"If you keep our meetings as secret as you kept your love affair with Ted," he said in parting, "we'll come out on top."

CHAPTER EIGHT

Benne Erice boarded the American Airlines jet to Long Island with his bodyguard, Monk Garret, and settled down in the first class section. Before the jet was airborne, Benne was wrapped up in his thoughts.

In the past few years everything had worked for Benne with the exception of his relationship with Jolie Barnes. He hadn't wanted to fall in love with her, and told himself not to be so possessed with a woman's thighs; that her lips, as irresistible as they were, were no different than any other woman's. For too long this pulsating woman who made him quiver with excitement had insisted on keeping their romance on the back burners. Benne was straining. One way or another he had to decide about her playing a major role in his life.

In recent days something about her was different; her attitude and personality had undergone remarkable changes. He'd found more admirable traits in her than he was aware she possessed. He didn't give a damn what others thought, but in contemplating what problems marriage to her might pose to his family, he was forced to pull off the bandaids from the blistering sores of her past and found the sordidness hadn't healed at all. Jolie denied nothing; she laid her story before him with such honesty that she succeeded in reinforcing Benne's respect for her.

Today, he wondered how he'd break the news of his affections for Jolie to his father without incurring parental disfavor.

He knew about her longstanding affair with Renzo. Jolie told him it was over and he believed her. Recently he'd punched out a private eye for telling him they had shacked up again in her New York apartment. No woman in the world worth having should cause doubts necessitating the enlistment of a private eye. He pulled the man off the job, sullenly. There were too many exciting things in the near future for him to be so concerned about a woman.

Benne became visible in politics; his friends were courting him to run for the state senate. Having imposed a rigid moral ethic on his life long ago, his indoctrination to politics had left him with a taste of ashes in his mouth. He wasn't one to shortchange his obligations in life, yet the thought of serving his country in an unpalatable manner created doubts in his mind that wouldn't dissolve. He dozed off for a time.

Monk Garret, scanned a racing form, glanced periodically at Benne. He grimaced indifferently, aware of what ate away at his boss. Women! Bah! Benne's satellite, as quick to form judgments about dames as he was in picking one horse over another, had watched the intimacy between Benne and Jolie bloom and flounder over the years. Once after catching a torrid performance of hers Benne couldn't stop raving over her talent for several days.

"She's terrific, isn't she?" he commented to Monk.

"I've seen her kind the world over, boss," he replied. "They belong to any man for the price of a drink or a fix. In her case maybe it's a few diamonds or a mink."

The scowling black look in Benne's eyes brought the instant recollection to Monk's mind of the swift brutal kicks Benne had delivered to his bullet-shattered shin following Joey's kidnapping years before. Wisely Monk made no further comments concerning Jolie, nor did he become loquacious on the trip east.

In Las Vegas, Renzo sat in his office in a dark, gloomy and reflective mood, the oft-spoken words of Manny Marciano whirling around his head.

"Don't ever lose your cool, Renzo. You gotta be a prick to stay on top of things. Keep away from the jerks. Our day is coming, then we'll swing high, wide and handsome. You can afford to be a nice guy then."

Renzo cursed aloud, "That day had better come soon, Manny!"

On his feet he kicked back the chair furiously and poured himself a stiff slug of bourbon from a bottle on his desk. He gulped it in one swallow, grimacing distastefully. He wasn't about to think of Jolie Barnes and how he left behind him in New York a bruised, whimpering and distraught broad. One day he'd have to right the wrong he'd done Jolie and that didn't sit well with him. Besides the broad had really shafted him.

But that's OK, he told himself, feeling the bourbon warm his insides. *The victory will be mine in the end!*

A week ago his spies tipped him off that Benne Erice would be making a trip east, the exact date unknown. This was of no consequence to Renzo; what did matter was the nature of his conversation with Marciano a few days ago.

Marciano, brusque, feisty, condescending at times, but always in control, never dressed as spiffily as Renzo. Fat men seldom looked well dressed even in five-hundred-dollar suits. He could care less, he told Renzo as he poured two Jack Daniels for them. Sipping his drink grandly, Renzo had pursed speculative lips. "It's gotta be for a good reason else the old man wouldn't have pulled Benne out of Vegas now," he told the aging entrepreneur meaningfully.

"Whassa matter, kid, you worried?" Marciano asked, standing before a gilt-edged mirror examining the puncture marks on his hairless skull, tracing the pitted grooves of his recent hair transplant. "Hey, how about this, kid? Planting hair on your head like they plant flowers. Heh, heh, heh. As long as they don't come out pushing up daisies, eh? Heh, heh, heh," he cackled dryly. Glancing at Renzo's dour expression in the mirror, he replaced his brightly colored knitted golf cap on his head.

"Gotta keep it warm so the seeds grow," he piped up humorously. He tried cheering his guest. "C'mon, so why are ya worried?" Grabbing the Jack Daniels, he carted it back to his desk.

"Listen, kid," he began solicitously. "When TFL moved in on Hughes, he sweat bullets, didn't he?"

Renzo shrugged and nodded reluctantly.

"That sonofabitch hotshot is cooling his ass somewhere in the tropics—who the fuck knows where. You know who put him there? Our people. I mean we got clout on our side. Erice ain't bigger than Hughes, is he? I'm telling ya, don't worry." He poured more of the Daniels for them. "*Salute*," he muttered, swilling down his drink. He made a thick scratchy sound at the searing liquid coursing through him. "Pretty soon, you and me ain't gonna be anoni—anono—"

"Anonymous." Renzo supplied the word.

"Yeah, that. They'll take care of us. We done right by them."

"You'd better be right, Manny. I've played third fiddle too long." He gulped down the bourbon and lit up a smoke.

"Third fiddle?"

"First it's Benne, then Tina. Me, I'm last like a schmuck! While we're on the subject—how the hell do you come off taking Jolie Barnes away from the Pyramids? I gotta read about it in the trades, goddammit!"

"Whya asking me?" He reached under his golf hat to feel the puncture marks again. "Ain't my idea, kid. Her agent contacted my booking agent. She's bored, needs a change. It happens, kid. Whassa matter, you ain't shacking up with her no more?" His fingers continued to worry the depression on his skull. "Son of a gun, ain't this a kick in the ass? What will they think of next?"

Renzo glanced blackly at his host. "Knock it off, will ya?"

"I was just curious. It ain't kosher to break with the Pyramids when ya got points there. Maybe the broad don't know what I know, huh? It makes ya think. Benne beating your time?"

"You kidding? All I gotta do is snap my fingers and the blonde bombshell explodes only for me. Lately I've been cooling it like you told me. She's mad 'cause I don't fall all over her. Besides I got more on my mind than to think of some dumb hustling broad." He helped himself to more bourbon.

Behind Manny's dark glasses his eyes pierced through the smoky haze and fixed on Renzo. *Yeah, yeah, kid. That'll be the day. Just don't pass that shit off on Manny.* "For openers, she ain't no dumb hustling broad. Something else don't add up. If Benne Erice is crazy about the bombshell, as I hear told in Vegas, why is she leaving the Pyramids? It don't add up, pal. Ya hear?"

"What do I know what you hear, Manny? I don't like being screwed by you. What's Val gonna say?"

"Listen, kid, for sound business reasons, the Golden Oasis ain't gonna decline to sign a crowd-drawing star who plays to S.R.O. audiences in Vegas." He waddled across the room and sat down at his desk, his eyes scanning the file sent him by the old man in Vegas. "G'wan, go back to your place and don't worry, eh? I'll keep ya posted on what happens. Some of our boys will pick up Benne at the airport. They won't let his shadow out of their sight. Whatever Val has up his sleeve, we'll know soon enough."

"What about his real shadow, Monk Garret?"

"What about him?"

"You get a make on him like I asked? Shit, Manny, I asked you over a year ago to find out about him."

"I didn't find out anything. He's a loner, the usual

contract man, a small-time punk used in the Erice snatch job. Shit! That Benne ain't so smart! Imagine hiring a punk that was gonna do in his kid brother. Why are you worried?"

"I don't know. Honest to God I don't know. That sonofabitch gives me the willies. When I see him, I get the feeling he's walking over my grave."

"Hey, you ain't letting some jerk-town dime-a-dozen punk get to you, are ya?" He noticed Renzo's pale, drawn expression.

"For the record, he ain't no jerk-town, dime-a-dozen punk, *paesano*. I wish to Christ he was." He turned slowly and walked out the door.

Marciano stared into space, thinking, *For once you're right, Renzo, old boy. He ain't no jerk-town, whatever the hell else I said.* How could he tell Renzo that Monk Garret was without contest one of the most respected— *internationally* respected—hit men in the world?

He sat brooding, reflecting on his own insecurities. The old man in Dallas confided that Garret worked for him once. *What the fuck's wrong with Benne Erice? He's got no sense hiring an iceberg like Monk Garret. And if Benne's short on brains what the hell's wrong with Val, that he should let his kid do a stupid thing like putting an ex-hit man on the payroll?* Marciano shuddered inwardly, trying to figure it out. *Aw, shit! Why the fuck should I care?*

He leaned forward to open the manila file, scanning it avidly, each line bringing firepoints to his eyes and new excitement to his spirit. *Where the fuck did the old man get wind of this?* He placed his glasses on the bridge of his nose, and devoured every word in the report. Without taking his eyes from the papers, his hairy hand reached for the phone and dialed a Los Angeles number. While he waited for the connection, he stuffed a cigarette between his teeth and lit it with a desk lighter.

"Eddie—you know who's talking? . . . Good. Listen to me good, kid. You still servicing that broad, what the hell's her name? Dancey Darling? She paid what she owes us? . . . How much? Shi-i-t! Ten grand? Fucking asshole! You let her on the hook for ten grand?" Manny chewed his cigar savagely. "All right, all right, you tell her she's got a chance to pay us back and earn another twenty grand. Don't worry—we'll get it back. That stupid cunt junkie ain't got the brains she was born with. She's a scrambled egg. Listen, here's what's coming down.

100

I'm sending someone to see you. He'll pass the word—can't trust the fucking phone."

He waited fifteen impatient minutes before dialing the phone again. "Renzo, get your ass back here. Yeah, yeah, it's important. Can't talk. Just get here." Manny slammed the phone, ground out the cigarette and reached for a slender Cuban cigar, smuggled by friends from Cuba, savoring it with each puff he took.

One week later, late at night, a cab pulled up before one of those fleabitten traps on Hollywood Boulevard near Western Avenue. Intense traffic whizzed by him as the cabbie opened the door to let his fare out. The woman, a real knockout, had seen better days. Dressed in tight pants, a thick sweater, her hair wrapped in a long silk scarf, Bedouin-style, and wearing dark glasses, she didn't look the type to frequent so funky a neighborhood where the most scurrilous of dogs and degenerates hang out, thought the driver as she paid him the fare. She gave him a sizeable tip and for this he felt duty bound to warn her.

"Be careful in this neighborhood, lady. Anything can happen."

She nodded and walked briskly towards a lighted sign shaped like an arrow with blinking lights pointing to a darkened doorway where another sign read *The Sinaloa.* Pausing, the woman glanced in both directions and then disappeared inside.

The taproom was nearly deserted. A few stragglers seated at the bar talking with an ape of a bartender glanced intermittently at the television overhead where a wrestling match was in progress. The odor of stale beer, wrung-out bar towels and stale smoke clung to the air and added to the musty odors of a time-worn building in sad need of renovation. The smells were enough to make Dancey Darling turn up her nose disdainfully. If she weren't in such dire straits and in desperate need of a fix, she wouldn't have agreed to make this connection—*never in a million years!*

Inside, the shabby room felt more depressing than the streets. Her eyes, growing accustomed to the dark, enabled her to locate the last booth along the wall where she'd been instructed to wait. She slid behind the warped wooden table top burned with blackened scars of neglected cigarettes and quickly lit up a joint.

Dancey Darling had sunk to the bottom of the barrel —rock bottom this past year. Miraculously, she had managed to salvage her home for the next six months. After that she'd have to look around for new lodgings. But at least for six more months she'd have a crash pad, a place to forget the stinking, fucking world that helped screw her up—good.

Without funds or the prospect of employment she'd survived on what she'd been wise enough to put in annuities to combat occasions of unemployment. Soon, even these reserves would be gone. No one in Hollywood would touch her. Known as the biggest cock teaser in Tinsel Town, she was shunned by those studio moguls who'd used her, making her a part of this alien world where to survive she'd been forced to hide her head in shame and forget the staggering price she'd paid for becoming a star. A star! What a laugh!

Scripts sent to her remained unread, stacked high in the bare living room of her house. Once furnished with impeccable taste, the furniture was now slowly siphoned off to pay this debt and that until only one or two pieces remained in the sprawling hacienda in swank Bel Air.

Dancey lived between fixes with nothing else on her mind to help dull the terror and pain she lived every twenty-four hours a day. Pain, anger, hurt, humiliation, insecurities swirled around her befuddled brain waiting for a euphoria, the high following each needle jab—then followed by a hot rush and the blurred imaging. Then, as the inner glow transported her away from the false promises made by backstabbing, whoring pimps who ran the fucking industry, she would fantasize as she had in the early days of her career, when as Mau O'Mara she didn't give a shit what the world wanted.

Who cared for Dancey Darling? Not a fucking prick in town—except for her adoring fans. They meant well, but what good were they? To them she was a marble goddess to be revered, worshipped from afar. Dammit, couldn't they see she was just like them? She was flesh and blood with the same emotions, passions and desires. Yet for them she must remain on a pedestal in goddesslike perfection. Yeah, well, hell, life wasn't like that at all. "Goddammit!" she'd screamed one night in the middle of a recurring nightmare. "Won't someone hear my cry for help? I need you out there! Help me. Will someone who cares help me? I'm drowning—drowning—drowning . . ."

She had awakened lying in a pool of sweat, alone, afraid and filled with an unknown terror. For countless days after she'd sat before a mirror staring at her image, lightly tracing her spectacular bone structure, hour after hour, posing as if a camera trained on her was filming every living, breathing moment of her life.

"You've forgotten where acting begins and reality leaves off, my dear," she'd been told by countless psychiatrists who'd plied her with uppers during her depression and downers when she was scaling too many heights. "There comes a time when a normal, well-adjusted, mature human must part with childhood fantasies and become a part of reality," they'd told her.

"But how the fuck do I do this?" Dancey had asked in utter frustration. The shrinks would only nod their pious heads and mutter inconsequential bromides. "In time we'll find a way."

One day Dancey's body, unable to take the pill-popping tirade, rebelled. Pills to awaken her, pills to put her to sleep, pills to quiet her nerves, pills to tinkle and pills to evacuate what little nourishment she'd ingested! It was a never-ending merry-go-round that finally came to a skidding halt when her own body stopped and thumbed its nose at her. "You won't take care of me, kiddo," it seemed to say, "so I don't take care of you!"

Everything had gone haywire inside her. Whatever it was controlling the involuntary muscles of the body and the central nervous system had gone berserk, refusing to do what nature had intended it to do. Hospitalized in England, fed, cared for until her body began trusting her again, she was granted a reprieve and restored to life. She rested, recuperating in the glorious English countryside, taking long, refreshing walks along the seashore where she communed with nature and forgot the pressures of being a movie star.

Nearly a year later—all this having happened after she'd encountered Benne Erice in Hawaii—she felt well enough to consider more movie roles. She returned, feeling invigorated and strong enough to take on all those Hollywood barracudas. After four weeks on the picture it all returned: stress, anxiety, strain, the need to please her coworkers, the director and producer brought back all the old insecurities. She was unable to differentiate between Mau O'Mara and Dancey Darling. Whoever had fixed her body had forgotten to unscramble her brains and put her head back in order.

Well, fuck them! Fuck them all! Dancey Darling will do as she damn well pleases!

103

So what if every man she met loved and left her? She had balled the president, the president's brother, and if she'd wanted, she could have balled the whole fucking cabinet! Why should she be depressed? She lived better and more excitingly than ninety percent of the women in the world—hadn't she?

She'd seen miles of faces in her dreams, an endless parade of men's faces. One night they all became one face, the one man who might have been able to save her if he'd taken the time to know her—Benne Erice. To Dancey he became all the men who'd betrayed her and would continue to betray her for all eternity. He had abandoned her when she needed him most. In her distorted, neurotic, spiralling brain, a built-in computer programmed to project one face alone bedeviled her. Benne Erice became the one man on whom she blamed her troubles. The drugs had convoluted her logic, twisted and warped her mind. Nothing mattered or made sense to her except the fix; it gave her temporary peace until the nightmares began again. For this brief period of euphoria she lived; for this she'd do anything. The fix became her god.

Dancey's shaking, trembling hand, holding a cigarette found its way to her mouth where she shoved it between loose rubber lips. A hand appeared from behind her, holding a lighter steadily, its flame causing her to recoil momentarily. She lit the cigarette. The lighter was clicked shut and the man holding it slipped into the seat opposite her in the booth.

"Sure you weren't followed?" he asked in a hoarse whisper.

Glancing over the rims of her large dark glasses at the man dressed casually in leather trousers, shirt open at the neck, with a matching leather jacket over his shoulders, she studied his features. Sunglasses concealed half his face. He wore a glittering array of gold chains around his neck and gold rings on his fingers. She wondered if he wore them on his toes, also. One medallion stood out, a zodiac amulet; Sagittarius. Her eyes focused on a second man, a real weirdo, an oddball wearing a white fright wig and mustache. He sat next to King Midas without expression.

"If the choice were yours where would you go?" asked Midas.

"Wherever the poppies bloom in June," was her cryptic reply.

It was a code. Midas nodded. "Good, you know what to do?"

"It's been a while. He may show no interest in me."

"It's your job to make him interested."

"He's a nice guy." She faltered. "You won't hurt him—"

"Listen, cunt. I've been told to up the ante, five G's. The boss thinks you're worth it. Me, I don't trust junky cunts. What I'm saying, sweetie, is I think you'll fuck up. Your track record ain't what you'd call on an even keel."

"Fuck you, prick!" She dabbed at the crystalline beads forming on her brow. Her eyes darted to the weirdo's white wig.

"Who the fuck dreamed him up?" She indicated the weirdo.

"None of your business. Concern yourself with that snow country you dig so much."

Dancey's loathing for him and all men like him who preyed on her weakness to get what they wanted spilled over onto her face.

"Find out where he's going, with whom and when. Do that and we'll keep you in poppy powder for a long while."

Dancey, on fire, stared at the amulet, totally fascinated by it. Shaking, she puffed on her cigarette.

"What will you do with him?" she asked, her guts churning.

"The less you know, the better."

"When do I get the bread?"

"Some now, the rest when the job's finished."

"N-nothing will happen to h-him?"

"Take it or leave it!" he barked roughly, moving to leave.

"No! Wait! O.K. I'll do it." She held out her hand.

"Are you some crazy broad? I ain't dumb enough to bring it with me. Go home. You got a surprise package waiting."

"Fucking bastard!" She tried making him out in the darkness.

"Look, don't make no mistakes. The boss don't go for mistakes."

"Fuck you! Fuck you, too, Whitey!"

"How's about a drink to seal our bargain?" queried Midas.

"The only thing I'll drink with you, prick, is arsenic."
She picked up her bag and left the Sinaloa. Outside she
looked for a cruising cabbie. Finding none she entered
a phone booth two doors away. About to leave the booth,
she glanced up and quickly retreated leaving the door
ajar to keep the light off. The men she'd just dealt with
at the Sinaloa emerged in the company of a third man,
a burly, apelike predator. The trio boarded a black, late-
model Mercedes and drove off, but not before Dancey
caught sight of the Arizona plates. She etched them into
her consciousness, still wondering at the white-wigged
weirdo and what part he'd play in this upcoming impro-
visational nightmare.

Dancey wasn't the only one puzzled over the presence
of the weirdo in the white wig. Renzo, seething with indignation, was gonna let Manny Marciano taste the sting
of his wrath. He didn't like witnesses around to remind
him of his dirty business. Manny's orders to pick up the
bizarre-looking man and take him along to rendezvous
with the poppy-seed, bird-brained whore worried him
the minute he laid eyes on the queer. Renzo wanted no
living testimonials to his criminal involvements. Fucking
asshole!

If Manny had no control over this piece of business,
the least thing he could do was protect Renzo's ass. He
didn't like this at all. His vague recollection of being
beaten up outside the Golden Oasis was linked with memories of a white-haired man. Coincidence? Hah!

CHAPTER NINE

In New York, Val waited patiently for Benne's arrival. After six years he'd finally brought the secret negotiations between himself and the Sicilian Dons to a successful culmination, to the satisfaction of all parties.

It was over—a sheer victory. The land in Las Vegas, the choice plum he'd wanted for so long, was his, in exchange for certain Sicilian properties plus a million dollars in cash. What remained was for someone to transport the money to Mexico to a predestined rendezvous where the deeds would be turned over on receipt of the million dollars.

Following his last encounter with Mourous Benkhanhian Val had become a recluse. He saw few people, hardly played golf and ran what business he could from this comfortable retreat. He remained isolated on the island, with Christina and the vigilant guards who patrolled the grand estate around the clock.

Today as he walked about the grounds inhaling the crisp, cool air, he tried to rationally think over his now threatened future and the immediate past which he still had to reconcile in his mind. Never an impulsive man, he continued as usual to plan every aspect of his life strategically, rarely if ever making snap decisions. Now, as he walked along the path behind the house leading into the nearby wooded area, waiting for Benne to arrive from Las Vegas, he wondered if he'd been overly zealous in this last business coup concerning the lands in Las Vegas, those choice lands he had coveted for so long. He'd grown older since the tragic death of Ted Shiverton and had lost much of his sparkle.

But today nothing could mar his happiness. He was ebullient over Benne's homecoming. He found himself listening for his son's roaring laughter, the sound of his frank, heartwarming voice with the usual mild outpouring of obscenities that Val believed he did purposely if only to get a rise out of Val, which predictably followed.

Val's boots crunched over the rock gravel path noisily as he moved along. He pulled his scarf closer to his neck and turned his back to the wind looking at the grand old house. What was wrong with him? A peculiar sensation of isolation and impending doom came upon him. Why couldn't he shake this growing cynicism? Things had never been better for the Erice family. But Val had reason to be concerned. Communicated to him by silent invisible forces, which he had learned never to deny, was the distinct feeling that someone, something, was watching and waiting, marking time before striking.

He shuddered. Winter was upon him even though the heavy snow hadn't put in its appearance. The wind lessened and he could walk the path more comfortably, inhaling the pleasant smoky scents heralding winter. He could almost smell the tantalizing, savory aroma of fresh-roasted chestnuts, the sweet, honeyed, spicy odors of holiday cooking, even hear the familiar chanting at football games shouting, "Hot buttered popcorn and spicy hot dogs." The air invigorated him. How many more winters would he be privileged to enjoy?

Val thought of Benne, forcing bleaker thoughts from his mind. The news that Benne was being courted for the office of state senator in Nevada stirred Val's pride. Simultaneously, the atavistic Sicilian in him shifted about in uncomfortable disquiet. He knew too much to accept the idea of his son's political involvement in so facile a manner. What concerned him was Benne's complacency. That he hadn't seen fit to discuss his plans fully with Val gave him hope that it was only a rumor, nothing more, nothing serious.

No question existed in Val's mind that his fears lay in the future. It was the past, and what had happened to Ted Shiverton, however, that colored the future in vivid and frightening speculation. This new business, the land coup in Vegas, would be Val's final one. Ah, yes, he had much to confide in Benne and he steeled himself for the ordeal.

Seated on the split rail fencing at the edge of his property, he noticed the heavy spillage of acorns from the stately oaks. A few squirrels, a mother and her babies, darted here and about, as Val picked up a twig and drew aimless patterns in the dirt, while pondering the thoughts running rampant in his mind. Could he convince Benne never to run for public office? He hoped the dreams of running for office hadn't become a sickness with him. Could Benne possibly understand about IAGO? But who would believe IAGO actually existed? Early in life Val learned how easy it was to manipulate a man's emotions, how much it took to buy his devotion. He understood mankind. Because he knew the key men of IAGO, he knew IAGO well. Knowing men like Benkhanhian, their enormous egos, their love for money and power, he therefore knew the philosophy behind IAGO. God in all His glory couldn't imagine the evil behind this consortium of atheists, or how much evil was done in His name. How easy it was to delude, torment, tease and tempt people, swaying them to a cause.

Magnifying his own involvements a hundred times, he knew the magnitude of IAGO's forces. It was this very fact that kept Val uneasy and apprehensive. He had decisions to make, and one he'd made for certain; not to impart any of his thoughts to Benne until after the Pyramids and other properties belonged to the Erice family, lock, stock and barrel.

Glancing up he saw the mother squirrel and her babies looking quizzically at him. A sweet, tender smile played at Val's lips.

"How easy it is for you to live. You have few worries, other than to provide food and shelter for your family. Man's existence is fraught with too many complications." He tossed aside the stick and headed back along the path, his thoughts shifting, oddly enough, to Neiland Milton's administration.

Before Milton's election Val had seen IAGO plotting to elect their man to office. Now, a wall of silence had been cordoned about the White House preventing the public from observing or learning of the intricate maze of complications brewing within the Oval Office. The men under Milton's immediate command were of one breed; all wore the invisible stamp of IAGO robots on their faces, their mode of dress and comportment corresponded to a familiar blueprint. They would bear watching, thought Val.

Val wished at times he could engender more enthusiasm over the politics of his country, but it was hopeless—he knew too much. He chafed constantly at the fact that the public had no idea what went on behind the scenes or that IAGO existed at all. What would they think if they knew that IAGO, a master puppeteer, coordinated and jockeyed the politicians into positions best serving them?

He could no longer afford to be a frontier hero and champion the rights of the people, not if it jeopardized the lives of his family. Val knew that Benkhanhian and his consortium of bloodless men could rely on his undying love for his family to keep him silent. If he failed in all else, Val promised he'd never fail what remained of his family. They were all he held dear in the world. If his silence insured their lives, then he'd pay the premiums with this same silence.

Benne, with Monk Garret, was at home waiting for Val when he returned to the house. After paying his respects to Val, Monk left with Sadge, Benne's albino German shepherd, for a brisk walk. Sadge was still coolly indifferent to Benne's bodyguard. Christina, after an outpouring of her love for Benne, retired to the kitchen to help cook a lavish banquet of food for him.

In the study, Val sat with his son, listening attentively as Benne brought him up to date on the Pyramid business. Drink in hand, Benne waited for his father to explain the urgency of this trip.

Val laid it out carefully, meticulously explaining what had transpired. "It's taken a long time, but we're there. The land is ours."

"You did it, Pop. You sly fox, never hinting at your victory." Benne grinned, unable to subdue his excitement. "How the hell do you work these miracles? No one can watch wits with you. They shouldn't try," he exclaimed proudly.

Val shrugged. "Long ago I learned that to survive you must be different. Patience, Benne. Patience allowed me to endure. I wish I could teach you some of its far-reaching benefits."

Benne, nodding in his usual placating manner, asked, "When do the Sicilian Dons close negotiations?"

"We go to Mexico to finalize the deal. Send a courier there to meet them. We turn over the money—they hand us the deeds. How about Renzo?"

"No!" Benne shook his head. "I don't know what he's up to, Pop, but I don't like what I'm hearing. For starters, Tina's had him under surveillance for longer than I dared express disapproval. It's nothing tangible, but I know he's not loyal."

"Is such surveillance necessary?"

Benne shrugged, and gazed solemnly out the window. "He's up to no good for the Erice family. Tina's got plenty on him, but I gave her my word I would say nothing until she's collected all the proof she needs. Trust me, Father, let me keep my word to her."

Father? The formality Val once craved caused him to

shudder. He tossed aside a paper clip he'd been toying with and glanced at his son whom he loved with great passion. A look passed between them, one that sent Val into a mood of quiet desperation.

"Feel free to discuss anything with me," he said quietly.

Benne's eyes glistened with strange lights. He wanted to tell Val what Tina had uncovered without betraying her. He couldn't.

"Very well," said Val despairingly. "If not Renzo—who?"

"Me. I'm right for it. I can fly a plane."

"No. No private planes. You take a scheduled commercial flight, no private junkets to spotlight your movements."

Benne argued the merits of flying a private plane and getting to and from his destination without the usual delays. Val argued the safety of traveling in numbers with less chance of foul play.

An hour later they were in agreement. Benne would travel to Mexico transporting a million dollars. Emilio would act as courier, getting the money to him, turning it over to Benne at the Beverly Hills Hotel where he kept a bungalow. It would appear as if he were there on some motion picture business. His destination, highly confidential, would be withheld until Emilio Aprile arrived. Questions, pro and con, tossed on the table and examined carefully, were finally settled.

Benne had been observing his father closely during their discussion. Noting the tight lines etched into his otherwise smooth countenance, he asked, "Are you all right, Pop? I mean, are you feeling O.K.?" At Val's astonishment, Benne added, "Larry Sharp was in Vegas last week expressing his concern over you to Jerry and me. He said you refused to undergo a series of tests he ordered for you recently. Why?"

"For a doctor, Larry Sharp has a big mouth," Val snapped with obvious irritation. "Whatever happened to the privileged doctor-patient relationship? Is confidentiality no longer a word in his vocabulary?" He gestured impatiently at the tolerant smile on Benne's lips. "I'll tell you why. I don't trust him."

"Why not?" He refilled his drink and sat opposite Val.

How could Val reasonably discuss his concern without seeming paranoid? Could he tell Benne that Sam Linden's recent death, labeled a coronary, was really from a lethal injection for knowing too much and foolishly threatening

111

certain political figureheads? Could he tell Benne he expected much of the same?

He chose his words carefully. "Benne, my son, tell me what you'd do if after a doctor examines you and takes numerous tests, advises you you're suffering a cardiovascular problem—"

"Take his advice," insisted Benne before Val made his point.

"—and you went to another physician for the same tests and the diagnosis was entirely different . . ."

Benne, staring at the double-headed griffin in the curio cabinet, jerked his head around. All else was irrelevant. "Are you saying—" Benne moved in closer to Val. "Just so I understand fully what you're saying—you're telling me—"

"Precisely."

"Larry Sharp?" Benne found it incredible, and offered temporary balm. "Go for a third opinion."

"I did."

"And?" Benne set his drink down, his eyes fixed on Val.

"He concurs with the second opinion."

"Larry could have been wrong. Tests get mixed up—"

"For what I pay him, he can't afford to be wrong."

Benne moved to the curio cabinet and removed the griffin from it. He returned, placing it on the desk. "First tell me about Larry Sharp. Then, Pop, you'd better finish telling me about this—uh—figure."

Benne sat heavily in the chair opposite Val, a strange expression in his eyes. Val's eyes fell to the double-headed griffin, then searched his son's face. *First Tina, now it's Benne wanting to know more. If only I could tell you everything, my son. If only I could unburden my soul to you. First, there are too many questions in my own mind which must be dealt with.*

The atavistic Sicilian stirred in Val. "Not now," he said firmly. "When our transaction is completed in Mexico and you return to me, we'll talk. Nothing is urgent."

However provoked Benne was he knew it was futile to press his father. Val asked various questions about TFL involvements. Catching the gist of his inquiries, Benne, no fool, asked,

"Should I be concerned with any possible skullduggery beyond our apparent involvement in Las Vegas?"

"When you return from Mexico *after* the land deal is

secured, we shall deal with Renzo. Meanwhile make no political deals, until after we talk."

Benne shook his head in amused disbelief. "You knew? You already knew. Does nothing escape your attention?"

"My pain is I know too much."

"I hadn't planned to accept the senatorial bid. I admit I've enjoyed the courtship rites," Benne said with solemn imperturbability.

"Courtship rites have seduced stone statues on occasion," Val said ruefully.

Benne laughed good-naturedly. He ground out his cigarette and leaned towards Val. "Have you talked with Whip lately?"

Val questioned him silently.

"Too bad he's not like Ted. Can you get to him, Pop? Shit, sometimes he blasts off like a malfunctioning rocket. He's gotta lay off the investigation he's spearheading in Las Vegas."

A knock at the door brought Jerry Bonfiglio into the room. They all greeted each other warmly. Benne fixed him a drink.

"Which investigation?" pressed Val, picking up the conversation.

"Uncovering the identities of the real owners behind the gambling syndicates in Vegas. He won't let up on it. He won't listen to me. It's a little premature and will ruin all I've worked on!" Benne said, exasperated.

"He's trying to pierce the corporate veils, now?" Val frowned. "Why now?"

"If he does," interrupted Jerry, "you know what it means. If he focuses too much attention on TFL, he'll scare them off. They'll submerge again the way they did after Joey's kidnapping."

"Talk with him, Pop. Tell him to wait."

"I have no weapons of negotiation with that man," Val said ruefully.

"Maybe you do," said Benne shifting gears. "Suggest to Whip if he holds off on the Vegas investigation and cools his interest for a while longer, I'll give him the name of the men who conspired to kill Ted Shiverton."

Silence. More silence.

Val could hear his heart beating. His eyes met Jerry's in open-mouthed astonishment. They both focused on Benne. Moments passed before Val could articulate his feelings. "You realize, my son, the position you've put

113

yourself in?" Val was petrified with fear for his son and his family.

"I know." Benne was solemn.

"I heard nothing. You said nothing. Forget it. Ted's dead. What good can be done resurrecting bad memories, fears, God knows what else?"

Benne's face screwed up in confusion as he studied his father. Turning to Jerry, he made his displeasure known. "This isn't my father seated across from us speaking from the emerald of his conscience!" Turning to Val he expressed his irony. "You've never permitted me to abuse the truth with the carelessness you've just suggested, Father."

Father, again. Why should it disturb me?

Val began to wind up a parental dissertation. "Benne, your father has always appeared invincible to you. In the past you've credited me with omnipotent and omniscient powers. You've made me the bravest warrior to enter an arena. But hear me, the face of time falls upon the world. Things which pain like a dagger in your belly heal, scar over and you become less sensitive to pain. In time you go on living, forgetting the suffering, pain and anguish it takes to live. We bow and smile when we don't wish to bow and smile; we eat when we don't wish to eat; sleep when we've no need of sleep. Often we are defeated. The bravest forge on. Others who aren't warriors fall by the wayside, devastated at the first signs of defeat, never to rise again. You think I'm different from most men? That I'm impervious to the hurts, sorrows, and humiliations that besiege a man in his lifetime?" Val shook his head thoughtfully.

"The deaths of your sister Lucia, Jimmy and of Bob Harmon, should've proven your father to be neither omniscient or omnipotent. He neither knows all there is to know, nor is he all-powerful and indestructible. He is merely human. Above all he's human and therein lies the vulnerability. The death of Ted Shiverton left me feeling less like the all-powerful, all-knowing figure of my past. Not you, nor I, nor anyone can prevent destiny from pointing her sinewy fingers of destruction at the world. There are some things in life which must be accepted, examined, then set aside as an object lesson."

"Pop," Benne interrupted. "Talk to me plainer. You've never resorted to using such evasive rhetoric with me. You taught me to be brief, state your mind and conclude your reasoning. Now, I ask you—what's on your mind?"

114

Val wagged a hand at him in defeat. "All right. All right. I'll speak with Senator Shiverton. I don't promise you miracles. He still blames me for his heartaches. He's never stopped loving Tina. Because of me it took over a decade before he got together with her." He looked at Jerry, and gave him the eye. Jerry nodded and left father and son to talk in private.

When they were alone Benne gushed with questions. "Whip got together with Tina? What do you mean?"

"You don't know about your sister and the man she's loved for years? What kind of a brother are you?"

Benne was flabbergasted. "Tina and Whip? You mean —Tina and Whip Shiverton are—"

"In love. From the time they met it's been the same."

Benne's eyes lit up in devilment. "Whaddya know about that? How do you know?" he asked, puzzled. "I don't get it. She told you about her love for the senator, yet she hasn't told you about her trouble with Renzo?"

Val hastened to explain. "She's said nothing to me. Before she left for Las Vegas, following Ted's funeral she stayed in Manhattan to do some Christmas shopping and got snowed in. Renzo had called me, so I put out feelers for her. She spent a week with him at the townhouse. She even went to Europe to be with him—"

"That's all you can say? You aren't upset by your daughter's scandalous behavior?"

"She's a big girl. She's suffered the sins of her father long enough. She's entitled to any happiness she can get."

Benne shook his head. "More than ever, Pop, our family has got to get together pretty quick. Tina thinks you won't approve of her getting a divorce. She's afraid of what you'll say. Meanwhile she's sitting on a time bomb."

"She's in danger?" Val sat up uneasily.

"Very likely."

"Tell me everything." In all his talks with her she'd said nothing.

"Even if I violate Tina's wishes—destroy my word to her?"

"Better to violate her wishes and destroy your word than lose your sister."

"Then promise that if I tell you, you'll not give me away, unless she brings it up first."

Val nodded. "It isn't necessary to remind me of a sacred trust."

Benne opened the door and called to Jerry, who was sampling some of Christina's fantastic veal birds. He

115

came scurrying along the hall with a small plate containing more of the delicacies.

They talked, father, son and lawyer, who was like another son to Val. When their talk had ended Val was white-faced and shaken. "There's only one punishment for treachery and betrayal from one as close as Renzo," he said in a voice Benne had never heard before. "It shall be done at the proper time and place. Meanwhile you continue as if you know nothing. Advise your courageous sister to do as she's done. Don't let her know we've spoken, but give her all the support she needs. If you tell her of our talk, it might cause her to change her comportment and make herself too vulnerable. Understand?"

Benne understood. He began speaking of the mysterious men behind the TFL combine, of higher-ups who were inextricably embroidered into a picture he couldn't fully understand.

Val cleared his throat. He told explosive information to Benne. He took his time explaining the particular strategy he employed during the liquidation of his many assets. Briefly he discussed his encounter with the IAGO bigwigs. He rekindled Jerry's memory of the day he spent aboard *The Galatea* and stressed the need for continued secrecy and silence and the maintenance of a low-keyed profile. Then he meticulously began to fit together the pieces of the puzzle, beginning with TFL and how it fitted into the bigger puzzle of IAGO.

"It appears highly improbable that the Erice family should become involved with men of such international reputations until you understand that the fate of the Shiverton family is inextricably woven into the fate of the Erice family. One thing jarred me when I met aboard Harmon's yacht with them—the detailed accounting of my financial report. However, conspicuously absent from those reports were any mention of the Shiverton fortune which served as the nucleus for my own financial manipulations and ultimately the bulk of our fortune. Not once was reference made to Shiverton or his previous holdings. This factor if analyzed at its fullest implication would have distorted IAGO's picture of the Erice empire. Since 1929 the names Shiverton and Erice have, in certain select circles, been synonymous. Why wouldn't they mention it?" Val insisted, as he paced the room pausing now and again to glance at the inclement weather and impending storm.

Benne offered a temporary balm. "By the same token,

Pop, it could've meant you had covered your tracks pretty well through the numerous corporations you constructed to obstruct nosey competitors and the world in general from knowing where the power lay."

Jerry agreed. "We've gone to great lengths and expended considerable effort to veil your involvements, Val."

"Yes. That's true. But remember, those financial statements included properties once belonging to Shiverton. Those financial wizards of IAGO would have stumbled onto it—no? Even if they weren't looking, it was spelled out for them in the old records. See, it doesn't wash. Why spotlight Erice with no mention of Shiverton?"

Jerry, about to argue the point, deferred to Val when he noted the urgency in his blue eyes. "In reviewing the old Shiverton files, I stumbled across information which may be pertinent to us now. Thirty years ago it wasn't. Our records show a positive tie-in between the late Commander Shiverton and IAGO. It's possible the old man was a part of IAGO at one time," added Val. "To what extent, I don't know and probably will never know. Follow me so far?"

Benne, sitting in the chair opposite Val, slouched down comfortably, his fingers folded, touching his lips contemplatively as he listened intently. Jerry poured himself a cup of hot coffee from the sideboard and sat near the fire sipping it.

Val, sparked with enthusiasm, continued. "We all know that sometime, somewhere along the way Shiverton and E.L. Lamb didn't hit it off. There was bad blood between them. Recall if you will the countless antitrust suits filed by the government against Shiverton. Lamb had instigated all of them. He was pressing Shiverton unmercifully. Then what does Shiverton do? Eh? Does he fight the suits in court? Does he go after Lamb like the predator he was? The way he combated every other man who obstructed him? No. Shiverton sells his oil stock, trades it in for a real estate bonanza and walks away from millions. Easy millions. Against his usual character and reputation as a fighter, he tosses in the towel, neither contesting E.L. Lamb or the government." Val poured himself a stiff bracer of bourbon. He mopped his forehead with a linen handkerchief, and stared off at some inner scene enacted in his mind, for several moments.

Jerry and Benne wondered where this all would lead.

"Why didn't Shiverton contest E.L. Lamb? Why? Why?" Val moved along. "For thirty years I gave little thought to these questions. I made them occupy no part of my own consciousness. It wasn't my affair. It was a part of someone's past over which I had no control. So, I gave it little importance. Now, after all this time, it becomes vital that the Erice family survives. Survive we must, even though it appears that we're bound up by some curious twist of fate in an insoluble maze of complications with the Shiverton family. I refuse to be sucked up voraciously by this invisible whirlpool of international power, conflict and intrigue. Is that so difficult to understand?" Val continued.

"I had no reason to question Shiverton's earlier dealings. While studying the Commander's strategy I learned the money he received from an outright sale of his oil interests didn't amount to the same capital he invested subsequently in real estate. Where did the enormous sum come from? I checked it out. To be brief, the loans came from IAGO."

Benne rotated the hammered gold lettered ring on his finger, and tilted his head in amazement at his father's words.

"Shortly after my encounter with the men of IAGO aboard Harmon's yacht," explained Val, "I went to Europe, conferring with them at their invitation. They intimated they wanted my full support for their presidential candidate, Neiland Milton. They gave me a year to decide. By then I'd already decided to support Ted Shiverton. Naturally the men of IAGO conveyed their displeasure with a rash of insidious threats.

" 'IAGO always gets what IAGO wants,' they said to me in parting." Val moved about the room.

"Val Erice wouldn't buckle under to their directives. Now, you both know the reasons behind the liquidation of assets we didn't own in clear title. Why the decisions concerning the Community Federated Bank were made . . ."

Jerry poured three cups of coffee from the silver carafe on a serving cart and placed them on the desk, respect and admiration for Val in his eyes.

"My full support in the election went to Ted," Val said. "I proceeded to make myself invulnerable to outside forces, nearly succeeding. Shortly after Ted's inauguration I went to Sicily on business, detouring to Switzerland where I visited for a time with Danny Shiverton at the drug rehabilitation clinic. I was intercepted and asked to be a guest of Benkhanhian at his estate near the Riviera." Val sipped his coffee gingerly.

"They let me know instantly what they wanted—Ted Shiverton."

"They wanted *Ted?"* Benne expressed his amazement at the 180-degree turnabout. Jerry's eyes riveted on Val in stupefaction.

"They intended to own him, body and soul. Whip was next in line. They put the proposition to me, insisting on reimbursing me for Ted's total campaign indebtedness so he'd be beholden to them."

Benne sat perched on the arm of his chair, his face impassive at the implications involved. Was it for this Val asked him to back away from the senatorial bid in Neveda? Val continued.

"They knew everything. *Everything!* They knew that Erice money backed the Shiverton campaign, that it was I who suggested that Ted buy up all available television time during the last leg of the campaign. How could they have known this, I asked myself, when only Ted and I had been privy to the conversation? Electronic devices, naturally. I quickly set about making periodical sweep-ups to make sure my office and home were free of any listening devices. I held my own counsel, and could confide in no one—not even you or Jerry unless it was extremely vital."

Val held them a captive audience for nearly three hours. Finished, he had presented a clear picture of an impregnable society of political gargoyles who with Godlike superiority sought to control the world. Both Jerry and Benne were left with a taste of ashes in their mouths following the incredible tale of power. They were solemn, their faces drained of color, their features implacable. Val sat down in his chair, his expression ponderous. "Shortly after Ted's election he came to me requesting a special service only I could do for him." Val proceeded to tell them what Ted had requested.

"Then Ted had contact with IAGO?"

"I didn't ask." He threw open a window, to clear the smoke-filled room. Dabbing at the fine line of perspiration on his forehead, he left the window ajar and returned to his seat at the desk.

"He knew of their existence," Val said, cleaning his glasses. "Feared them enough to ask me to compile information on them through my European connections. I don't think he knew of his father's tie-in with IAGO. It gets confusing at this point. Bear with me." Val placed a nitro pill under his tongue and fixed his glasses.

"Then Commander Shiverton was part of this cartel?"

119

Jerry asked, a knowing expression in his eyes. "It figures."

Val, exhausted, observed Benne's reactions. "The look in your eyes is asking how the Erice family figures in all this. Some things can only be explained by destiny . . ."

"Pop!" Benne's protesting voice intervened.

"I know, I know. The generation gap can be exasperating. That's what you're thinking. Whenever I defer to destiny or fate you younger, well-educated men disdain it. You scowl and twist your faces with forced tolerance as if you confront something distasteful. I admit you're too young to think in archaic terms, but indulge an old man, listen to his story." He began to speak in narrative form, as if he were speaking of himself through the eyes and lips of another.

"Long ago before his birth the forces of destiny conspired to elevate Valentino Erice up the totem of power, causing his life to be inextricably enmeshed with the lives of the Shiverton family. Ted Shiverton, an obscure dark horse candidate, through Val's efforts was suddenly thrust into worldwide prominence by his presidential victory. Through the efforts of Jim Harmon, IAGO thrust itself upon the Erice family. The Erice family didn't buy what IAGO wanted to sell. The Erice family settled in Las Vegas, suddenly bringing itself to the apparent scrutiny of IAGO by being in competition with the TFL Corporation. We all know that Joey's kidnapping was part of a planned conspiracy to manipulate the Erice family. Bravo, we're in accord. It then follows that the initial encounter between Benkhanhian and Erice at the Villa Garibaldi must have been all part of the same plan, no?" Val paused a moment.

"Listen, whenever it began, it began and for too long has been too much a part of us. If I hadn't resented the grotesque and giant shadow of IAGO looming over us, posing threats to the very essence of freedom for which I've striven in my life, I might have acquiesced, and none of this sordidness would have surfaced."

"What you mean is," began Benne, with a modicum of pride, "if you were a lesser man you'd have let them step all over you, put the screws to you. Right?"

Jerry agreed then added somberly, "Los Cuaycos, Cuba, Nevada, the presidential election, the Fishman deal, Community Federated Bank and I can't tell you how many other involvements—yes, even Joey's business—the kidnapping. For two decades the TFL Corporation—all right, all right, IAGO—has been hovering over Erice affairs. What the fuck do they really want, Val?"

Benne's eyes narrowed thoughtfully as he dragged on his freshly lit cigarette. He studied Jerry enigmatically.

"Good question," said Val, nodding slowly. "Someone attempting to intimidate me, and hoping I'll throw in the towel, is getting impatient. For what? What have I done —and why should they want to destroy me?" Val wet his lips with a sip of water. "It's simple to solve this puzzle if you can view it objectively . . ." Val sat back in his swivel chair and turned it from side to side absently, his fingers touching together contemplatively. "Because I someway, somehow befriended the Shiverton family—" Val held up a restraining hand, waving Benne off until he finished "—I get the crazy impression that the old man, Commander Shiverton, made a pact with the devil in a deal in which he forfeited his sons in return for a sizeable fortune."

"You mean he turned Ted and Whip over to IAGO in some deal he made with them? Benne shook his head refuting the theory, a tolerant smile curving his lips tentatively.

Val's hand flew back into the air, halting his son. "Hear me out. Here's the capper. The man Shiverton hated most in the world was E.L. Lamb—a charter member of IAGO—" Val paused, dramatically waiting until he had their rapt attention "—and the father of the first-born son, Ted."

"Jeezus Christ!" Benne exclaimed, biting the cuticle on his little finger, nervously. He was stunned.

Jerry was stupefied. His face had blanched. He sat forward in his chair, elbows on his knees, hanging on to Val's every word, marvelling as he did at Val's composure. He was fully aware how heavily burdened Val had been by the weight of this knowledge. Still it wouldn't sink in to his mind as truth.

"They tried their best to seduce me. Even offered the presidency to one of my sons!" scoffed Val, unaware of the shock he'd instilled in his listeners. "Bastards! Did they think I was some schmuck of a hayseed?" he cursed in a rare staccato of irritational outburst.

"Ted Shiverton is the son of E.L. Lamb?" Jerry was wiped out at this information. "E.L. Lamb, head of TFL, the power behind Neiland Milton, the man Ted defeated at the polls? The man backed by IAGO? They *wanted* Ted Shiverton? But why? It makes no sense. No sense at all."

Benne concurred. "Why would— Well, why— ?"

Val sighed. "I've already revealed too much. It's best I don't expose either of you to any more until after the

121

Vegas land deal is cemented. As it is I've broken one of my cardinal rules by telling you prematurely of my involvement. I did so with the thought in mind that if I should suddenly meet with an accident, or be found dead at mysterious hands, you'd both be aware of what had transpired and guide your actions accordingly. If anything should happen to me before I'm able to resolve the family business you and Tina take over for the family. It's all contained in these papers—" He held up a thick packet.

"You're serious!" Benne said, aghast. "Pop, you're serious, goddammit! All that other stuff about Larry—you weren't being hysterical, you know something else, don't you?"

Val lifted his heavily burdened eyes to meet his son's. "When you return to Vegas, you be careful. Watch yourself every minute. You and Tina both. Get Richie to double the guard on both of you. That's an order," he insisted.

"I suggest sending Richie back here to be with you."

Val shook his head. "So that you don't mistake my preparedness for fear, let me tell you I fear no man. My days, like those of all mortals on earth, are numbered. I should dislike to die serving any man's purpose but my own. However, if it's to be so ordained, I'll accept it, with meticulous preparation. And, now, Benne, Jerry, forget all we've discussed. Erase it from your minds. What matters is Benne's final step in this last journey of adventure for the Erice family. When all is completed, the family shall meet in Las Vegas to celebrate and have a last family meeting. I promise, by then I shall have discovered that illusive factor to guarantee us peace of mind. This shattering disturbance of IAGO descending upon our family like a plague must cease."

During dinner that night, Val, seated at the head of the dining table, stared quietly and interminably into the lighted candles as the others relished the delicious home cooking. Fully spent from the earlier catharsis, he should be feeling less heavy hearted. He tried concentrating on the humorous stories Benne was telling his mother about Las Vegas. Monk Garret sat at the table opposite Val, eating quietly, speaking only when spoken to and drinking sparingly.

Lulled into a semi-meditative state, Val found himself once again gazing into the flickering lights of the candle. He was happy that Benne monopolized the conversation, keeping Christina smiling and talkative. Several times Val's eyes grew heavy as the soothing flame relaxed him. Iridescent colors of the spectrum in fluttering vibrations formed a haze around the sputtering flame.

At one point Val lifted his eyes to catch the inert expression on Monk Garret's face. Val gave a start, blinking hard. For a split second the ghoulish apparition of a ghostlike figure formed before his eyes, the features of Monk Garret embedded in a black wavering shroud. Once again Val blinked hard, trying to erase the burning image from his eyeballs. Still it persisted. He quickly picked up a candle snuffer, and extinguished the flame.

In the next instant he felt the back of his neck swell. His hair stood on end as if a cold gust of wind had blazed a trail along his spine, chilling it. In an instant of disassociative reaction he felt compelled to gaze upon the face of Monk Garret. In that instant Monk's eyes held Val's. For mystical reasons he didn't comprehend Val received signs of precognition that he couldn't decipher. Later, when he had occasion to recall this moment and reexamine what had taken place, he realized it had been an omen of what was to come. If Val's awareness had been such that he fully understood he'd have taken steps to circumvent the tragedy that would soon befall the Erice family.

They hugged and kissed their beloved son unashamedly in parting. Val and Christina stood at one side of the entry watching Benne, Jerry and Monk Garret climb into the sleek sedan that would transport them to La Guardia.

Earlier, in parting, Val had reluctantly shaken hands with Monk Garret and said in a quasi-deadly tone, "Protect him with your life—or answer to me." Monk nodded without replying before he tossed Benne's bags into the trunk of the car. It was obvious he didn't want to tarry.

With his arms around his wife's shoulders, Val watched the limousine pull away from the house and wheel easily along the gracefully curving driveway, disappearing through the gates as the guards waved at them. Val said nothing to his wife about the inexplicable feelings surging through him.

He felt the webbed fingers of death hovering over the Erice family like a mushroom cloud that would suck them all up into a vortex from which there was no escape.

They turned to enter the house. Christina exclaimed, "Look, Val, it's beginning to snow. Isn't it beautiful? There's nothing like the first virginal snow of winter. It's so clean—so wispy and sheer as angels' wings."

Val glanced up into the dark curtain of night and saw

123

things of which he chose not to speak. As he closed the
door behind them, he stole another glance at the ominous
shadows of nightfall and tried to subdue his thundering
heart.

What is it? he asked himself. *What is it that causes my
heart this suffocation and strangles me so that I cannot
breathe?*

He did not know.

CHAPTER TEN

The scent of her perfume wafting to his nostrils brought Benne's head up from where it was buried in a copy of *Daily Variety*. He saw her enter the Polo Lounge, ambling by him with the free swinging hips and enticing walk that had excited millions of fans on the silver screen. He knew her immediately.

Her makeup was more pronounced than usual; her blonde hair was tousled, a bit bedroomish for the sedate surroundings; her flesh-colored jumpsuit, too provocative for any public place, was eye-catching, designed to turn every head in the room. Mau O'Mara, or Dancey Darling, thought Benne, was still a dishy broad. He was unable to take his eyes off her. How long had it been? Damned if he didn't still feel that rush of excitement.

She sat nearby with a repulsive looking man, her agent, no doubt. Observing her he frowned in recollection. Scuttlebutt had it that Dancey Darling had hit the skids. She was through, careerwise. Her reputation as a weirdo on sets, holding up production, doing everything she could to sabotage a picture, had been bandied about town, reaching the environs of Vegas. Everything was negative; she'd gone from bad to worse. Benne, giving her the onceover, saw no visible signs of the bummer she'd been on. Yes, indeed. She was still some dish.

Finished with his eggs Benedict, he was sipping his coffee when her irate and caustic voice cut into his thoughts.

"You cunt-eating sonofabitch! Get outa my life! You've fucked it up long enough, selling me out! Take your fucking script and get lost. You don't have Dancey Darling to sell under the counter no more!"

Heads turned her way. The Polo Lounge, abnormally packed today, was moved to curiosity by the loud fishwife ruckus.

The man with Dancey, a heavy-set, swarthy-faced man, turned beet red, his cigar falling from his thick pasty lips.

He glanced self-consciously about the room, turning pale at the sight of gawkers and reporters who hung about for juicy morsels of gossip to sell to Tinsel Town columnists. Shaking like a pile of melting jello, Fatso picked up his script that she had flung unceremoniously across his chest and punctuated his wrath with a stubby cigar.

"You'll never work in pictures again, you phony, no-talent whore!" Fatso's voice carried too well.

"Get lost, Jake," she muttered sullenly. "Get your fat ass out of my sight. You can't buy me for that fucking piece of shit you call a script. If I don't get signed to do *Tropics,* I don't work for you again. Now get out of my sight before I puke all over you."

Benne nodded to Monk Garret, seated next to him, watching the scene unfold in fascination. Monk rose to his feet and moved silently towards Dancey's table. He tapped Jake on the shoulder.

"Get lost, Buster. You heard the lady. She's got no eyes for you." His voice was sweeter than honey, yet lethal as cyanide.

Jake's features engorged with blood as he studied the deadpan expression. No one had to paint a picture for Jake Levy or explain the threat couched in those velvet words. Script in hand Jake slipped out from behind the table totally without grace. He blustered out of the room.

Benne moved towards Dancey. "Hi, friend. Looked like you needed help."

She didn't glance up at him, instead fumbled about inside her bag for a cigarette. "Get lost, pretty boy. I got no time for poolside Romeos." Tossing her box of Shermans on the table she searched for her lighter.

"I never knew you to talk with a mouth full of shit," Benne said flatly with reprimand. His words took effect.

Dancey's head jerked up; their eyes met. "If it isn't the Hawaiian stud. What slimy cunt hole did you creep out of?"

Benne cringed for a brief instant. Slowly he removed his dark glasses and slid into the leather booth next to her, observing her with close scrutiny. Her skin was sallow, the hollow caves under each eye covered by makeup. Her hands shook as she removed a brown cigarette from a pack and placed it between her full yet tightly drawn lips. Benne extended his lighter, clicked it on. She accepted the light, inhaling deeply, then, exhaling a long smoke spiral, she batted her thickly fringed lashes at him indifferently.

"You don't really mean what you just said," he told her softly. "It's good to see you. God knows I've tried reaching you." He swiftly bridged the gap since they last saw each other.

She listened attentively, yet edgy and high strung, her eyes widening at times, then disbelieving but reluctant to challenge him. She seemed as vulnerable as she had been when they first met.

"What happened in Honolulu? I was sorry to have rushed off like I did. My brother had been kidnapped—"

"That's why you left?" Her blue eyes widened, misting with tears she fought hard to blink back. "You *didn't* use me, get what you wanted and toss me back on the beach like any pebble?"

"We didn't know each other long enough for you to assume so foolish an idea." He ordered drinks from the waiter. "The same for Miss Darling. Bring mine to me from my table, Eric."

"Yes, sir, Mr. Erice. Right away," replied the obsequious man.

Mau struggled with Benne's words. "You're right. I did assume too much. That's my problem, I suppose. But we did work well together."

"For one night—"

"A day and a night—"

"Yes, less than twenty-four hours."

"A well-packed twenty-four hours," she smiled faintly.

Benne also smiled as a tingle in his loins stirred him. "You still have plenty of what it takes to excite me, Mau." He cleared his throat suggestively. "What was that all about—with, uh, Jake? That his name?"

Mau explained. She told him she'd been ill for a time. "But, I'm fine now, really I am, Benne," she said with too much urgency. "It's just that I need a good property. I read *Tropics* the other day. It's what I need to make a comeback. The flick will make me. I mean, bigger and better than ever. Instead this crum bum Jake Levy keeps bringing me crap! Porno scripts! I wouldn't shit on them, they're so bad!"

"You were hard on him, here, before the world to witness."

"Not hard enough, Benne. You don't know what I've gone through."

"What happened to your agent at William Morris? I spoke with him before you left for England."

"They weren't doing enough for me. I quit them." She grew sullen, puffing on her brown cigarette, averting her eyes, hoping he wouldn't see the truth in them.

Benne knew better. He knew the agency had dropped her for being such a ball buster and hung up on drugs. "Are you still on junk, Mau?" he asked gently, his voice just above a whisper.

"No!" she jolted too quickly, as defensively as most addicts do when pushed to the wall. "They call me hard to work with because I'm a perfectionist. They call me a ball buster. I walked off the last picture because the producer was cunt-happy between his sojourns with little boys. The director was a no-talent slob who couldn't tell the camera lens from an asshole. The assistant to the producer was something else. A lesbian yet, who was after my body around the clock. Jesus, Benne, how much can a person give to her fucking job? They wanted me outside and inside and left nothing for me. Well, dammit, I gotta have something left for me, don't I?" Her voice grew hysterical and anxiety-ridden, loud and resonant.

Benne glanced around, not embarrassed in the least by her emotional fervor but sick at what the other eavesdroppers would make of it. Dancey Darling's stellar performance would become the topic of conversation for many a day in this catty town.

"Benne, you don't know how tough these starch-assed prick lovers can be. A woman's got no chance. Every fucking picture for the past ten years has been all male casting. Oh, once in a while they put a token woman in a flick so the moviegoing audience doesn't get suspicious. You wonder at the growing rash of homosexuals in the nation when theaters are peppered only with *rough, tough* men on the screen? What a laugh! Those rough tough he-men, turn into she-men at night in the boudoir. This whole fucking town is run over with homosexuals and a woman is treated like so much shit!" Mau was really steamed. "They forget it was a woman who gave birth to them—or they wouldn't be here!"

Benne asked her, "If you got the lead in *Tropics,* you think you could handle it? I mean no temper tantrums, no drugs, just concentrated effort and good hard work?" He was growing uncomfortable and wasn't sure why. Monk had left the room. Benne filled with disquiet, didn't wait for Mau's answer. "Look, come to my bungalow, Mau. Tell me all about it, will you? Suddenly I don't like this place."

"Come to *my* bungalow, we'll be more comfortable," she insisted as excitement crept into her eyes.

Benne nodded. He helped Mau up and moved out around the table. Catching sight of Monk near the bar, Benne eased up the inner tension. He nodded to Monk in passing.

Ten minutes later they were in Mau O'Mara's bungalow talking over champagne cocktails. "Did you see my last two pictures?" she asked him.

"I've seen them all. What a question."

"They were box office successes—netting plenty for the producers."

"I don't follow the trades that much —"

"I got an Oscar nomination for the last—"

"I heard. It made me very proud."

All the while she talked, she moved about the room, drawing drapes, casting the room into partial shadow, bringing the bar cart nearer to them, inducing the feeling of romance. She sat next to him on the white sofa and lay her head on his shoulder. Slowly she lifted her face to his, her pink wet lips moist and inviting.

Benne reached down and kissed her, tenderly at first. As he saw Mau unzip the zipper of her jumpsuit, exposing her full milk-white breasts, his hands caressed her gently causing the fine hairs on her body to stand up.

"I almost forgot how good you are, Benne," she whispered. "C'mon, let's go into the bedroom." She stood up, slipped out of the remaining pants and pranced about totally nude. She picked up the champagne bucket. "You bring the glasses," she whispered in Dancey Darling's most provocative voice.

Moments later they lay side by side, naked on the large bed. The draperies were drawn and only the dimmest haze enveloped them. Benne's mind lingered on the way she had undressed him. She had unhooked his belt, unzipped his fly, pulling up on his thin sweater and laying her moist, flushed face against his suntanned, hairy, well-muscled chest, inhaling the fragrance of his cologne. Her arms had encircled his lean body, slowly tugging at his trousers until they fell free to his ankles. He stepped out of them and kicked them aside. Benne broke from her grasp, and whipped off his sweater. Mau had sunk to the floor, to her knees, burying her face in his pulsating crotch, teasing his cock with her tongue, caressing it with the side of her velvety face, letting her long blonde hair whisk by it to create further erotic sensations.

Benne stood watching her for a time, enjoying each delicious moment of her expertise. Yet something kept nagging at him, a feeling that went deeper than sex. The same thing he recalled about her after he'd left Honolulu. Her vulnerability, the need to protect her. *Dammit,* he told himself, *stop with this protection shit. She can take care of herself!*

At one point, his excitement grew uncontrollable. Pulling her to her feet, he held her close and tilted up her chin, kissing her ardently until his passion was aroused intensely. He picked her up and tossed her onto the bed.

"You forget, Mau, I wanna be the man! There's time for cock loving, later." Benne, who loved the furnacelike intensity of a woman's loins around his manhood, didn't put down oral copulation. He enjoyed it as much as most men did. But to him, there was no feeling greater than performing the act as nature had intended.

"Don't you like the way I suck you?" she pouted.

"I like anything you do," he whispered. "We'll get to it." What he didn't tell her was he resented that most women used sucking as a power trip, a way of making her partner feel that she was the dominant one between them, that she could control his ejaculation. Not the other way around.

Benne was a good lover. Once on the bed he made certain all the juices were working for her before he entered her. And by the time he did, she was begging for it. As his hands caressed her breasts, he noticed a loss of elasticity in them, since their previous encounter. They felt different to his touch, somewhat like breasts that have endured a pregnancy or abortion. He said nothing, refusing to allow it to influence his excitement as he moved over her body, spreading her legs apart with his knees.

"Are you going to put that monster inside me?" she asked playfully, exaggerating, a wide-eyed innocence. "You're going to fuck me like I've never been fucked before, aren't you?" she whispered, lifting her body to facilitate his entry. "I love it, Benne. I love it. Oh, don't stop—don't ever stop," she gasped, feeling his warmth inside her, his fullness, the security of his tumescence probing her, enjoying her and stirring her to the heights of emotion.

"Yes," hissed Benne, his eyes burning brightly. "You love it this way, don't you. Tell me you love it."

"I do. I do. I really do, Benne. I love the feel of you inside me. You make me feel like a real woman! God, don't stop. I wish I could feel like this always," she said repeatedly.

They dissipated their desire, then started all over again, fucking, resting, fucking, resting, for nearly five hours. Benne, unable to hold back any longer after watching her continuous orgasms, finally uttered a low, growling sound of animal noises. He exploded inside her. She came with him once again in a violent continuation of spasms and involuntary shudders of delight with wild thrusts until the hot rush of cum flooded her body and she felt the contraction of his manhood inside her relax totally.

Benne, fully spent at the exertion, fell exhausted to one side of her, slowly regaining his strength. His eyes were closed as he let the euphoria spread through his body. He felt Mau slip out of his arms and pad across the floor to the bathroom to do whatever it was she did after such frolicking. If he'd opened his eyes, if he'd been able to recuperate faster from the exquisitely torturous orgasm he'd just enjoyed, he might have given thought to what Mau was doing with the champagne.

How could Benne have known that of all the women in the world Mau O'Mara would be the one woman who would sell his life cheaply? She brought his doctored drink back, placing it next to the bed on a night stand. He trusted her. She wouldn't betray him—not her.

Mau slipped back into bed alongside him, her warm hand using feathery touches to manipulate his placid manhood. When it refused to respond so quickly, she slipped between his legs and, taking it into her hot mouth, worked it gently with a well-practised tongue. Her body was damp with perspiration as she worked with increased fervor.

Benne, beginning to feel the stimulation, cocked open an eye and smiled tenderly at her. "You're insatiable, you gorgeous cunt."

"Flattery will get you everywhere," she muttered, pausing in her artistry. She was drenched with sweat and shaking slightly. She hoped Benne wouldn't guess at her agitation. "Hand me the champagne, please," she whispered.

Benne reached for it. His throat was so parched he sipped half the glass before handing her the remains. Mau lifted her body off him, sprang to her feet and pranced to the champagne bucket. "Go ahead, you drink that. I'll get me another."

He drained the contents of the glass and held it out for more. Mau refilled the glass. Benne sipped from it, and placed it next to the bed as he lay back against the pillows unaware of the strange look she gave him.

"Know what I'm gonna do for you, Darcey Darling, my sweet little cunt?" he asked huskily.

"No. Tell me," she urged playfully.

"I asked you earlier if you could handle the lead in *Tropics*. Well, sugar, I'm gonna see to it you get the part." Benne's eyes swept the ceiling and fastened on her as she lit a cigarette for him. She placed it between his lips.

"Just how do you intend doing that, Mr. Hollywood Big Shot Producer?" her voice came back playfully. Mau reached over for the towel on a nearby chair, wiping her moist face with it, her eyes never leaving Benne's face.

"How?" Benne's eyes snapped open. "Maybe you don't know who owns Snowbird Productions, eh, girl? You're looking at him, Dancey Darling. You're looking at him. I guess I can use a little clout since I'm financing the picture, eh?" Benne tried to lift his head off the pillow and couldn't. He felt a simultaneous hot rush—a glow shoot through him accompanied by the sensation of plummeting through space. He tried to move against the sensation of swimming through a sea of sucking mud pulling him down, down into the viscous fluid. "Mau," he called to her.

Mau rushed to his side and turned on the night light. "God! What have I done?" Her hands flew to her drawn, frightened face. *Benne owned Snowbird?* Was it possible he could have helped her?

"Benne! Benne! Wake up. I'm sorry! God, I'm so sorry!" She tried to tell him what she'd done, but he was beyond hearing her.

"Mau—" Benne, using herculean strength, forced his eyes open. The last thing he saw was Mau standing over him, her left arm across his body trying desperately to help him up. She was ranting, raving about something; he couldn't make it out. He heard nothing. Then he saw it. In a split second of awareness he saw the angry tracks on her inner arm. Before he could acknowledge what had been transmitted to his brain, he felt the presence of two shadowy forms coming at them, one shoving Mau out of the way. He vaguely saw the outline of a man in dark glasses with snow white hair bend over him. As a sharp needle jab pricked Benne's arm, his last touch with consciousness was a scream, then merciful blackness.

132

* * *

Three days later, Emilio Aprile stopped at the desk in the lobby. They rang Benne's room to announce his arrival. Moments later Monk Garret appeared, nodding to the CPA to follow him. He told Aprile that Benne was in the shower and would be out shortly. He fixed a drink for him, and left just as Benne appeared.

"Pretty snazzy here in California, eh, Benne?"

"Emilo!" he exclaimed, shaking his hand vigorously.

"I am here to deliver a package," he said, returning his warmth.

"Good. It's ready at last."

Aprile glanced up as Monk returned to the room. He disliked the man instinctively.

"You can go, Monk," said Benne crisply, understanding Aprile's reluctance to speak before another person.

"In case you want me I'll be in the Polo Lounge."

"Who is he?" Aprile asked with a grimace of distaste.

"My bodyguard for a long time. Why?"

"I don't like him," said Emilio bluntly.

"You didn't like Richie, either—remember?" Benne smiled.

"It's different with Richie. This man is a stranger."

"Emilio," said Benne with patient tolerance. "You didn't fly from New York to express your dislike of Monk Garret. Suppose we get down to business?"

"Are you all right, Benne?" Emilio asked solicitously, studying his face. "You look pale. Ah, maybe you get too much nookey, eh?"

In the past, having always been able to converse freely with the CPA, Benne might have told him how he really felt these past three days, but aware that what he said would get back to his father and cause him needless worry, Benne refrained from discussing his health except to say he felt tired. "They told me I had the twenty-four hour flu, old friend. Whatever it was it hit me and I went out like a light. Outside of a few nightmares, I don't recall a thing. I woke up this morning having lost two days—"

"You're O.K. now? Eat something—chicken soup. Restaurant food can tear your insides up. Too much drinking, the wrong food, no rest can screw up the system." He unlocked the manacles from his wrist and briefcase. "It's all here, including your instructions." He tossed the flight jacket onto the bed.

"The dough's sewn into the lining. Whatever you do you

133

tell no one nothing. I mean, you make it look like you're gonna get the dough from another courier who's already waiting for you in Las Hadas."

"Las Hadas? Where in the hell's Las Hadas?"

Aprile unfolded a map of the Mexican west coast and indicated the spot just above Manzanillo and south of Puerto Vallarta. "I got your tickets to Puerto Vallarta. There you'll make a change to another airline. A private hotel plane will transport you to Las Hadas. The Sicilian Dons will be there waiting to take the money, giving you all the deeds in return. And, Benne—" Aprile glanced cautiously around the room. "You sure it's safe to talk?"

Benne shook his head, a peculiar look creeping into his eyes. "No, I'm not sure." He couldn't shake off the foreboding he sensed of late.

"Now, you tell me!" Aprile snorted with reprimand. "Come with me." They walked into the bright white bathroom. Aprile turned on the shower and water taps. "Listen, one of the Dons has important information to pass on to you about Shiverton's assassination. *Capeeshi?* You take the information and mail it to yourself in Las Vegas. Don't take any chances and carry it on you. You got a P.O. box in Vegas?"

Benne nodded.

Aprile was disturbed. "You should have told me sooner. We could've come in here to talk." He shook his head, disturbed.

When they finished their business, Benne asked Aprile to stay for dinner at least. Aprile refused. He thanked Benne profusely, but he was firm. "I took the liberty of calling some old friends I haven't seen in years. They will pick me up here." Glancing at his watch, he muttered, "In about an hour. Mind if I stay with you a little longer?"

"Make yourself at home," said Benne as he finished dressing.

He took a few aspirins followed by a glass of water and grimaced as Emilio watched him. They made small talk for a while, mostly about the climate and the California way of living.

Emilio left Benne's bungalow accompanied by a couple of well-known thugs of the underworld. He wasn't aware that the reason he left the hotel alive was due to the formidable company escorting him to LAX. Bullmoose Rosario and another hulking brute, known in more select circles as The Angel, both school chums from the old days, flanked him as they left the hotel, boarded a limousine and moved on to the airport, busily talking over the old days.

Hired assassins, about to move in, hesitated due to the imposing reputations of these Damon Runyonesque characters.

The only comment Aprile made about Benne when he reported to Val was that he didn't look his usual self. "I don't trust that Monk Garret, Val. Don't ask me why. But if you've got some time maybe you should put a few of our friends on standby, just in case. He's an ice man, Val! An ice man!" He shuddered visibly.

Val, studying his old friend, needed nothing more than his few words to tell him he fully agreed with the suggestion. "I already spoke to Benne about my feelings, Emilio. He rejected the idea, insisting it would bring too much attention to him. I agreed the operation should be wrapped in secrecy, both for Benne's protection and for the Dons in Las Hadas. Now, despite my son's wishes, I'm inclined to follow your suggestion."

By the time Val's instructions reached Richie's ears and Richie got to Benne at the Beverly Hills Hotel, Benne had checked out.

Three days later, Val paced the floor in his den with marked agitation. He didn't know why he felt so nervous. He attributed it to a change in medication made only a week before.

Emilio Aprile arrived at the Long Island mansion, interrupting his frenetic pacing, to get some papers signed. For a few minutes they chatted informally as they sipped Campari on the rocks.

Val's private phone rang. He picked up the receiver. "Yes," he said, signing the papers before him. Suddenly, the pen fell from his hand. His eyes glanced at Aprile in alarm.

"This is Valentino Erice . . . Benne is my son . . ."

Aprile's eyes riveted on him intently.

At the other end of Val's line, a solemn, monotoned voice was speaking words Val didn't want to hear. "This is the Federal Bureau of Investigation . . . Your son's plane exploded over the Sierra Madre Mountains in Mexico. I'm sorry, Mr. Erice, all passengers were lost . . ."

Val was prostrate with grief. The phone slipped from his hand into his lap.

". . . Hello! Hello—are you there?" came the filtered voice reaching up at him.

Val looked at Aprile. "He's dead. My son is dead. They

135

killed him. There's no one left. They all died, Emilio . . ."

Aprile sprang to Val's side. He picked up the phone.

"This is a friend of Mr. Erice," he said. "Be kind enough to repeat the message. My name is Emilio Aprile, I am an employee and a friend."

Emilio listened solemnly, his sorrow-filled eyes fixed on Val. His heart sickened and sank.

The story broke in every newspaper across the land. Val's phone rang incessantly into the night and for the next several weeks. People from all over the world called to offer him their sympathies. When he could he ordered six of his most trusted men from the old days to join with the FBI's Disaster Squad to help search for the remains of the plane and survivors with the desperate hope that Benne might be alive.

Val and his wife flew to Las Vegas to be closer to the Mexican scene for a time. They were two forlorn and aggrieved parents mourning the loss as they'd mourned for their other dead children.

One night while they were alone, before the final report made by the Disaster Squad in which all hope was abandoned, Val sat on the sofa, holding his wife's hand in his. His hair was snowy white, and this last disaster had aged him ten years. He confessed his feelings to his wife.

"It's over, Christina. There is no fight left in me. They've taken Benne." A sob escaped him. Christina had never seen him like this and she grew frightened.

"Oh, God, how can you allow this to happen to us? What have we done to anger you so?" cried Christina, in supplication to the invisible God who had caused such strife in their lives.

Val put his arm around his wife and for a time they cried together. When it was over, Val dabbed at his eyes and blew his nose, as did his wife. He held her closer in his arms, speaking in comforting tones.

"Christina, my beloved," he began somberly. "For a while the Erice family must bow out of life. We cannot afford to let anything happen to Joey or Tina."

She nodded knowingly, her face relaxing into lines of fatigue. She was aware he was trying to lull her into a false security, but at this point what else could he do? "Somehow, some way, we have made the gods angry," she said. If this simple statement could account for all that had happened in their life . . . Another time Val might have contested such words and taken time to explain their utter absurdity. But at the moment he had neither the will nor the desire.

That night and for many nights to come the Erice family did not sleep, suffering the untimely departure of their beloved son Benne.

Now, some eight months after Benne's death, Val, sitting at the deathbed of his beloved friend, Emilio Aprile, wondered how many more tragedies would befall the Erice family before they awakened to the fact that they were doomed.

His vivid blue eyes reflecting the lamplight on the nightstand to the left of the motionless body were growing dim and empty. Val's lips had grown a deathly pale, his face haggard; he could no longer endure the cold waves of apprehension shuddering through his body. Still . . .

Still, there was David Martin. He had to muster the courage to face David Martin. He sucked in his breath sharply, and leaning forward in his chair cut a sharp eye towards Richie.

God, how he wanted to believe that David Martin was truly his son Benne, resurrected from the ashes of the plane tragedy!

BOOK TWO

He that keepeth his mouth keepeth his life; but he that openeth wide his lips shall have destruction.
—Proverbs 13–3

CHAPTER ELEVEN

Val Erice snapped out of his reverie. He glanced at Richie, then at his watch. They had been in Emilio's room nearly an hour, taking more time than they intended on this night that promised to give the explanations of many mysteries, hopefully including Emilio's murder.

Val's tired, swollen eyes, the repositories of feelings of loss and anger, lingered on the lifeless, mutilated body of his old friend, incapable of shedding any more tears. His entire life had flashed before him during this past hour and he thought, *I cannot tolerate more tragedy!*

The bloodied stump where Emilio's hand had been hacked off to sever the manacled briefcase had stopped bleeding. Richie had wrapped the remains in a thick towel, hiding the amputation from sight, as if this act might restore life to the dead man.

Val rose heavily to his feet. Moving to the large window, he surveyed the glittering of lights and traffic in the street below. The desert fairyland was coming to life, yet, standing in the presence of death far above the activity, he could feel no excitement for the spectacular man-made oasis and the amazing part it had played in bringing life to an area of natural desolation. Val felt only empty despair at the loss of his oldest and most trusted friend.

Who had done this unspeakable atrocity to Emilio? What had been in the briefcase that had sealed his death? It would have been simpler if he had spared Emilio more time he might have had a clearer insight into the reasons why he was murdered.

Behind Val, Richie covered the waxen body with a sheet and stood at attention awaiting his instructions.

Val, turning from the window, shook his head forlornly. He was greatly subdued, the fight almost gone from him.

"What shall I do, my Don?" Richie asked him quietly.

"There is nothing left to do, except find his killers," replied Val. "For that we must wait. Let him rest until I decide what must be done." He sighed heavily, moving to the outer door of the suite. "Come, Richie, for now we return to the penthouse to meet our guests and pretend none of this happened."

He glanced back at the bulky form under the sheet before opening the door. "You are to say nothing to no one. Understand?" He turned the handle of the door and paused again, his clear blue eyes leveled on his bodyguard.

"We go prepared to combat this new man in our lives, this David Martin, eh?"

Richie, a peculiar glint in his eyes, was prepared to contest so provocative a statement, then changed his mind. He was weary of so many catastrophic events in his Don's life. But as usual he allowed his mind to become the silent custodian of his inner feelings and thoughts.

"I come with you right now," insisted the bodyguard, taking a last look about the room before locking it up.

"It's all right. Take your time. What can happen here?" replied Val, wagging a hand at him, then suddenly stopping, his hand frozen in mid-air.

Richie's look of incomprehensible bewilderment stopped Val cold. Before he could point to Aprile's body for answer to his careless remark, Val acquiesced. "Very well, walk back with me." He made a disorganized gesture and left with Richie at his heels after locking the door.

A hundred bits and pieces of business and countless other nagging problems suddenly loomed insurmountable. Val had to clear his mind, set all the problems aside to prepare himself for the most important ordeal of all, confronting the man who claimed he was Benne Erice.

Across town in a sprawling, rented ranch house, the Bureau of Secret Intelligence prepared for the culmination of their plans. Ted McKenna sat playing backgammon with Phil Soldato. Neither of the crusty agents was able to concentrate on the game.

"Think Martin will fare all right?" asked Soldato after his last roll.

"He'd better! He'd goddamned well better come out like a champion or everything we've worked for will go down the tubes."

McKenna slammed the leather dice box on the table, got up and sauntered across the rustic, cozy room, stretching his arm and back muscles. At the well-stocked bar he poured himself a stiff drink, and gulped it down in a fast swill without expression.

Soldato, glancing at him, shook his head in disbelief. *Sonofabitch! When in five years had McKenna taken a drink?* He reached over and flipped on the remote switch of the TV set. The backgammon was shot for the night. They were both edgy—too edgy to work up a lather over a damned game.

In Benne Erice's old penthouse suite, David Martin put the finishing touches to his toilet. The former FBI agent, reluctantly recruited for this highly covert, near-suicidal assignment, had always imposed a moral ethic on his life. He was a driven man. The guilt he had suffered watching his mother's sacrifice had nearly driven him into the far reaches of neurotic behavior. Fortunately he'd come to terms with himself these past six months, during his indoctrination, especially after he'd learned about his true origin. The thought that he was of the same heritage as Val Erice had been mindblowing, after believing himself to be Irish all his life.

He stared at his image in the mirror, seeing only his face, visible as if it were reflected from a crystal ball, a convex distortion of his conscience. A thousand things flashed into his mind, mainly how he'd fare after this confrontation with the Erice family and friends. His feelings of trepidation weren't unfounded.

To hell with this chickenshit feeling of fear. You've a job to finish, one you've prepared for and have been computerized to see through. Get yourself together, man, and get cracking!

Bolstered by this last-moment resolve, he finished dressing.

Tina looked stunning. She'd selected a black Qiana jersey floor-length gown with a halter top and low V-neck that clung to her firm, flawless body, outlining every curve and sensuous movement made as she artfully arranged the flowers David Martin had sent to her and her mother. Her frosted ash blonde hair, in a careless style, gave her a provocative, bedroomish appearance. In her late thirties, the polished sophisticate of 1975 looked more enchanting than she had at age twenty. She glanced up as Val entered, walked to him and kissed him affectionately. She gave him a nod of approval, rolling her eyes. "You are something else, Pop. Mmmmmmmmn! Who else is coming tonight?"

Dressed impeccably in black tie, giving no indication of his deep sorrow over Emilio Aprile's fate, Val widened his eyes as he took in his daughter's appearance. He gasped audibly, scowling in mild reprimand. "I'll never grow accustomed to the freedom and permissiveness your generation indulges in, Tina. Is that thing you're wearing called a gown or a handkerchief?" He watched her counting the places at the formal dining table ladened with magnificent crystal, silver and Royal Doulton china.

Tina laughed. She lit a cigarette from a taper on the candelabra. "What began as a simple family dinner has multiplied to twelve."

"Besides the family and an intimate few, the senator and Amy will be here," he said, pouring himself a few drops of Strega.

Tina gave a noticeable start. Her hands trembled at the anticipation of seeing him again. "Whip Shiverton is coming here?"

"Our family might be too emotional to see through a skillful imposter. An objective opinion is always helpful." Val sat down comfortably on the sofa in the living room.

"You still think I don't know my own brother." Her mild teasing was merely a ploy to conceal the sudden rush of excitement unnerving every fiber in her body.

Val glanced up behind Tina towards the outer hallway.

"Ah, Renzo," said Val amiably, as his son-in-law entered the room, dressed exceedingly well in dinner clothes. Val noticed the friction spark between Tina and him as they avoided each other expertly. *What a champion she is,* Val told himself, sighing regretfully. *If only she were a man.*

Renzo busied himself behind the bar, critically inspecting the brands on the bottles. "Gotta make sure they brought what I ordered," he said pompously. "Ya gotta watch the help constantly. Stay on top of them, else someone always thinks he's smarter than you. Yep, it's all here." He opened a bottle of chilled Dom Perignon and removed three chilled glasses from the refrigerator below the wet bar. He poured the pale amber fluid into hollow-stemmed glassware, handing the first to Val, the second to Tina and holding the third glass in his hand, toasting fashion. "I thought it fitting and proper that the three of us should make the first toast. To the long health and continued success of the family." Renzo flashed his well-practiced smile.

144

"You'll forgive me if I toast to the safe return of my son, Benne." Val held his glass out before him and waited for them to touch glasses. They drank. Over the rim of his glass Val casually observed a flicker of annoyance in Renzo's eyes.

"Now then," said Val, smacking his lips. "When can Christina and I expect to see some grandchildren running about the house?" You aren't getting any younger—" he broke off in mild reprimand.

"Exactly what I've been telling Tina all these years. She's your daughter, Val. Maybe you can convince her it's time. In a few years I'll be finished. I'll have no more seeds left to plant."

Val was so fascinated by the new personality oozing from Renzo that he leaned sideways in his chair to observe him. He also caught the curious glow in Tina's eyes, an undisguised look of pure animal hatred. It flashed briefly, then quickly vanished, shielded by a finishing-school politeness and years of inbred restraint.

"If Tina must be convinced to bear children," said Val indifferently, "then she isn't ready. A man need never convince his wife, unless he himself is unconvincing."

The arrival of several guests saved Renzo from embarrassment and prevented further comment on a distasteful subject. Jerry Bonfiglio and his wife arrived both sporting golden bronze desert tans. After paying the proper respect to their host and hostess they were promptly served champagne by a servant who appeared as if from nowhere. Richie and Captain Ferraro arrived next, followed by Amy and Whip Shiverton. Amy wore a stunning beige chiffon. Whip was in black tie. Perfumes, colognes and other feminine scents permeated the air deliciously and mingled with the fragrant and appetizing scents of food that stirred their appetites.

Tina stood to one side as the guests passed through the group shaking hands warmly, embracing or nodding politely. Unable to move, momentarily she was assaulted with a host of memories of the precious time she had spent with Whip. How long ago? It was inconceivable to her that so much time had passed and still her memories of him were clear, the smell of him still lingered in her mind, and the rapture they had exchanged was . . .

Impulsively she stepped forward to embrace Amy, her stunning gown clinging excitedly to her appealing figure, her free-swinging mass of frosted hair curiously agitated by her mounting fervor as Whip approached her. She

145

turned to him, hoping no one else saw her trembling hand extended towards him in what to others must appear as a polite yet indifferent encounter, as all the while she flushed internally with alternating hot and cold tremors as she attempted to still her racing pulse.

"How good to see you once again, Senator," she said throatily. Their eyes met and held, a wealth of emotion flaring between them.

It was Whip's turn—he'd had so much more experience at covering his emotional nature—to bow politely as the electricity between them sparked causing them both to glow excitedly.

"You are a stunning wench," he whispered *sotto voce*. "I should have come for you before this," he added, while his face was masked expertly by the well-practiced, set smile of a politician.

Their hunger for one another, their desire in that moment became apparent to only one man in the room, who, standing next to his wife greeting his guests, caught sight of the lovers. Renzo tensed, his features hardened.

Tina was first to break the connection between them. Whip's unexpected appearance, the strength of his face so close to hers, the very smell of him had caused her a moment's consternation. Never had the desire for him been as overwhelming as it was now, this very moment. Whip, suffering the same desire, quickly forced a veil of reserve to curtain his longing. Tina gazed about self-consciously and breathed easier when she saw the others were too busy talking to have witnessed the magic between them.

Unable to resist Whip leaned in and whispered softly, "You're more exciting than when I last saw you."

Blushing to her toes, Tina averted her eyes and fastened them on an approaching waiter. "Dom Perignon for the senator, please."

"I can't tell you how happy I am that Benne turned up alive and well after so long," began Whip in a voice meant to be overheard.

Tina took a glass of champagne for herself and clinked glasses with Whip. "It's a miracle—truly a miracle. We are so grateful."

"Where's the guest of honor?" he asked after sipping his drink.

"Probably in his room growing weak at the prospect of passing inspection before the lot of us." Tina laughed lightly.

146

"Does he insist he is Benne Erice?" Whip seemed moved to curiosity.

Tina shook her head. How could she talk about Benne when her heart was pounding furiously, skipping beats in Whip's presence? In order not to communicate her love for him to the others, she was forced to collect herself and speak evenly. "No. He has no memory—not of us, not of anything that happened before the crash. Amnesia of sorts, the doctors tell us." She filled him in on David Martin's story of the incidents leading to this night.

Whip listened as intently as the other guests. Tina was more delighted that Whip showed such interest in her brother's plight. Perhaps with them all together she might one day explain her love for Whip . . . Then, suddenly remembering her resolution concerning their personal life, she tried to remain aloof.

As the conversation peaked elsewhere in the room Whip leaned closer to Tina. "Why haven't you called me lately?" he asked.

She faltered, shaking like a windflower. "You, better than I, should understand. When I thought I'd lost my brother—"

"I thought we understood each other. That I love you."

"That's not fair," she whispered, agonized. Her mood changed abruptly. "It's so good of you to come, Senator," she said with an elevated voice as Val approached them. "Please excuse me." She moved towards Amy, suddenly aware that Renzo's cold appraising glance had been fastened on her.

"Thank you for taking time from your busy schedule to be with us in our happiest hours, Senator," Val said cordially to Whip.

Whip's head tilted politely to Val but his eyes were caressing Tina's body as she moved sensuously through the room. In that brief moment no one existed for Whip but Tina. Feeling Val's probing eyes on him, he finally managed to speak.

"I sincerely hope this man turns out to be Benne."

"As Tina said earlier, it's a miracle. A prayer come true."

"Then there are no doubts in your mind?"

"There are always doubts, one way or another. In this instance, perhaps more than usual." Val's voice was softly speculative. "Tina swears by him. I view the startling resemblance more subjectively than I should. I'm counting on your objectivity, yours and Amy's, to help tide me over this ordeal."

Whip slowly swirled the pale amber champagne in his glass, staring at it, hoping he'd give neither himself nor David Martin away.

"Come, Senator," Val said, steering him towards the terrace. "I'd like nothing better than to take you on a Cook's Tour of the casino, but our appearance together might set the wrong tongues wagging."

Whip laughed amiably as he followed Val onto the terrace. They stood for a time gazing at the panorama of glittering colored lights along the Las Vegas Strip that were pale in contrast to the enormous coppery glow of a magnificent desert sunset to the west of the city.

Val kept trying, with difficulty, to eject the image of Emilio's lifeless body from his mind. In his grief, veiled by a lifetime of skilled practice, he'd managed to find time to place a call to the dead man's mistress in New York. The woman, Maria Rossi, would be arriving in the morning by plane. He sighed deeply, recalling the burst of tears that met his ears when she heard of Emilio's death. Turning from the sunset, and trying his best to keep his thoughts of the tragedy on the back burners of his mind, he studied Whip silently as he sipped his champagne.

For several awkward moments Whip flushed with self-recrimination at the hatred he'd held for Val Erice all these years. He wasn't sure when or if the animosity had left him, but being here among the Erice family he realized he should have taken the means to mend the broken bridges between them long ago.

"Somewhere along the way," began Val without preamble, "things went wrong for us. Too bad we haven't enjoyed the rapport Ted and I did." Val raised his hand to silence the objection forming on Whip's lips. "No, no, let me finish. I should have taken measures to have righted the misunderstandings between us. Why were we so out of step with each other?"

Whip, stunned that Val had seemed to read his mind, shrugged noncommittally. "Believe me, it's all in the past."

"Was it your own guilt that colored your relationship with my daughter to the point that you denied your love for each other?" Val sighed dolefully. "Don't upset yourself. Indulge an old man. It's sad you allowed the hemlock between us to rob you and Tina of so much happiness. You'll never recapture lost years."

Whip smoked his cigarette in a burning silence. Here stood the only man in the world who might shed light on Ted's death and he still hadn't uprooted the foolishness of his past thinking.

"You had nothing to fear from me. Ted and Amy knew it instinctively. You remain unconvinced to this day." The glittering electronic nightmare of Las Vegas was coming to life. Val placed his drink on the nearby table, and sat down, with a gesture to Whip to join him.

"Now, then, Senator, tell me why you denied Benne the request he made of you prior to the fatal trip he made."

"Fatal?" Whip took the chair next to Val. "Then you don't believe this man is your son? Isn't Benne alive after all?"

Val shrugged. "A slip of the tongue. For six months I've lived with his death. His resurrection will take time. Benne asked you, out of respect, not to pursue the investigation of casino owners—pointedly, the TFL combine. You denied him the cooperation Ted would have granted in a second. Why? Give me an answer I can understand."

"I admit it may have been a foolish mistake," said Whip.

Val was relentless. "There've been no charges—no subpoenas—no indictments—nothing," he insisted bitingly. "Tell me why there's no in-depth investigation of Benne's fatal air crash."

"You keep saying *fatal*," Whip insisted. "The FBI hasn't abandoned the project," he lied. "Now that Benne's alive, perhaps he can enlighten them. That is, if it is, uh, Benne."

"Yes," said Val, solemnly. "If it is Benne."

"Then there's reasonable doubt in your mind—"

Val made a disorganized gesture. "Anything new on Ted's death?"

Whip's lips tightened. "President Milton has politely refused me further access to the Justice Department files in areas pertaining to the matter."

"Because you tipped your hand," said Val reprimandingly. "A nod from you, patience on your part, might have helped Benne obtain the information you've needed."

Whip, fully annoyed, was losing patience. "Val, preliminary studies of those men Benne suggested to me as part of a conspiracy uncovered no substantiating evidence connecting them to subversive activities. Evidence leading to the participation of foreign nations in a conspiracy to assassinate Ted, became nothing more than hearsay. Nothing tangible crossed my desk. Floor to ceiling vaults overflow with testimonies of those who came forward to confide in us. Not even a hotshot Philadelphia lawyer could have strung together enough facts to build a case that wouldn't have been tossed out of chambers in a preliminary."

"You wouldn't give Benne an inch," Val remonstrated bitterly.

Whip was slowly coming unglued. "Benne came to me with a farfetched story, *without* supportive data, suggesting that Golden Enterprises aren't what they appear to be on the surface. He indicated that behind Golden there stands a monstrous monolith, TFL, a holding company manipulated by a cartel of super power brokers in what he described as an international conspiracy—"

"Benne told you all that?" Val asked sharply. Their eyes caught and held. "It would have served you well, Senator, if you had believed him."

"The men he described are industrial giants. Such men have no time to play political monopoly."

"You forget where the trail led when Joey was kidnapped?"

"I checked Benne's story straight to the point where facts evolved to fiction. I repeat, I found no substantiating data to support his theories," said Whip evenly.

"Tell me, Senator, when a man intends to commit a crime, you think he bothers to write out a paper that will give you the substantiating data you speak of?" Val snorted contemptuously.

"I needed facts, Val. Not even I can go off half-cocked, lacking the necessary ingredients to make up a case."

Silence. Interminable silence. Soft music reached their ears. Whip watched the smoke curling upwards from his long-ashed cigarette. He butted it in a cylinder of sand.

"I may have made mistakes, Val, but I've had more successes than failures, otherwise I couldn't have remained in the Justice Department, nepotism or not. Shortly after I became Chief Counsel to the President, I discovered the gross incompetence of men in whom the American people placed their confidence to run the government, men who subsequently deceived the government and devised a secret means of self-protection when their careers were on the line. Many misplaced loyalties kept the peccadillos of these incompetent, criminally minded men from reaching the public's eye. Dammit, Val, I'm trying to tell you that I found no supportive evidence to indict countless top-ranking politicians. Some may have been old acquaintances of yours. What I needed from Benne was supportive evidence to make the charges stick!"

Whip, angry at having to be apologetic, walked to the edge of the roof garden, staring into space.

Across from him Val glanced at his watch, wondering where David Martin could be. He checked the impulse to summon Richie to go in search of him. *I'll wait fifteen more minutes.*

At the Golden Oasis, Manny Marciano sat behind his desk glowering at Calous Agajjinian. "Goddammit, your boss is here and right under his nose you come to my place? What the fuck's wrong with you?"

"I didn't mean for Aprile to get killed. He put up a fight. They had to finish him. We needed the records. It's the only way to protect Renzo. You'll take care of Lefty and me—I mean you'll see we get protection until this blows over?"

Marciano hated finks. He hated this fink more than most. This sweating human abacus was second to Aprile's wizardy with numbers. Two bit fink jerk. Under hooded eyes he muttered, "Yeah, yeah, sure, sure. We'll take care of you." His eyes fell on the alligator briefcase with the gold initials, E.A., and the broken handle, dangling with manacles and covered with dried caked bloodstains.

"Ya hadda bring it here with you?" He was incensed.

"I had to place it in a safe receptacle. No one should have access to it until my work's finished. This is the only place I could think of where Mr. Erice's got no juice."

"Whassa matter, a public locker at the bus station's too good for you? Val may have no juice here, but he's got friends all over the joint. If not Val, you can sure as hell bet your uncircumcised prick Benne had friends here."

Aggie took umbrage at the reference to his old-fashioned genitals. The whores were talking again, filthy little bitches! And with what he paid them for their services! It griped him that Marciano should make a jest over it.

151

"Since Benne's a thing of the past," he quipped coolly, "we don't have to worry, do we?"

"Get your ass back to the Pyramids. Ain't Val got some shindig planned for this creep who says he's Benne?"

"It's for the immediate family. Just don't bet your Gucci shoes on this man being Benne. Renzo says he couldn't have survived, Tina swears it's Benne. Who ya gonna believe? He acts like he don't know me."

"You better pray it ain't Benne. While we're at it, I think you and Lefty had better take your vacation."

"How do we explain it to Mr. Erice?" Aggie's brows shot up.

"Shit, I don't care how ya do it. Get Renzo to send you someplace. Go to the Islands. I don't want you around when Val starts fitting the jigsaw together. By the time he thinks of sending for you, it'll be too late for him. Got it?" About to wave him off, Manny changed his mind. "Listen, you and Lefty leave right away. Yeah, yeah, tonight. I'll handle Renzo. I'll tell him to say you're scouting property in Hawaii. Get your asses out of here before Aprile's body is found. Now move. Haul ass!"

Aggie left and moved as swiftly as his legs could take him, anxious to put distance between him and the Erice family.

CHAPTER TWELVE

They were going at it hot and heavy on the terrace. Whip fixed himself a drink. "Americans are so easily fooled. The more mistakes their leaders make, the more popular they become. Americans' need for hero worship exceeds their stupidity and apathy. Give them a roof over their heads; money to keep them solvent from month to month; a television set to keep them hypnotized and de-sensitized to the pain of living and they won't give a fig what happens to their country."

Val noticed a remarkable change in the attitude of the young Harvard punk who had stepped into his office years ago.

"It's a sad commentary," Whip continued, "to think the White House is so dazzlingly attractive it can lure only the most corrupt. An honest president is a rarity. They've tried seducing me. I've been intimidated, threatened, cold-shouldered, nearly ostracized by the present adminis-tration because they know I'll discover the truth behind Ted's death. I still forge on."

Val listened intently.

"Let them all lie and cover up—news media, all of them. They can deceive the people, but they won't suc-ceed in pulling the wool down over my eyes. They figure half the evidence will disappear. It's buried in the na-tional archives so the public doesn't learn the truth. Shall I tell you what's buried in those rubber-stamped files? Gross errors in deeds and judgements made by *infallible* office holders; illegal involvements of some of our na-tion's most revered political figures. Some would make Mafia activities pale by comparison."

"Senator," said Val evenly. "For too long you attacked organized crime from the sanctimonious pulpit of the Senate Rackets Committee. Pity you didn't know you were being led down the garden path like an obedient ox with a ring through its nose."

Whip stiffened imperceptibly. He bit back the need

153

to defend his position. He chose in place of rebuttal to light a cigarette, hoping to camouflage his indignation.

"They distracted you with fringe issues to command your attention and occupy your senses around the clock," Val continued glancing at him through lidded eyes. "You did only what *they* permitted you to do. You must have considered yourself a special, tin-badged maverick doing something worthwhile for your nation, eh? Well, Senator," he temporized, pausing for effect as he nodded his head in recollection. "For a time you actually made the earth stand still—you did. You knocked heads in the Justice Department making it clear they were all to contribute in the effort against organized crime. You succeeded in performing the impossible, all right. The department cooperated, didn't they? They didn't fake it. Did you ever consider your unique position? Your brother was President. You had no worries. You weren't like the politically appointed officials who feared subversive attacks from their enemies. You dealt from a position of strength—a strength that gave you the results you sought."

"What you're saying, Val, is that agency heads in the past feared to surrender their power for a common effort?" Whip grew reflective at Val's nod.

"You brought a spark of life to the Justice Department, and your actions were often helped by the passage of new laws which increased the jurisdiction of the FBI and made certain crimes federal offenses, which in the past had only been state offenses."

"But," began Whip in mild protest, accepting the left-handed compliment with a right-handed slap.

"Ah, there's always a but. You made too many enemies in wrong places. You fought organized crime while the real corruption hid behind a smokescreen of political expediency. The corruption festering within government you conveniently labeled, 'gross errors in judgement by your peers.' Vile, contemptible, totally unqualified politicians—political cripples—sat in their insulated offices behind a protective curtain of 'old alma mater manure' and remained corrupt, bought by outrageous men of power. Yes, Whip, men like me."

"I didn't come here to be raked over the coals! Why do I permit you to—"

"Because I speak the truth and you see it as such. You'd do well to cut into the belly of the cancer where it all begins—inside politics. You know why you stay,

154

why you don't walk out in a huff? Because you need something from Val Erice . . ."

Whip flushed hotly, trying to subdue his outrage.

"Benne was about to stumble onto the identities of the men who conspired in the Los Cuayos revolt, quarterbacked the Far East involvement and unquestionably called the plays on Ted's death. The proof you needed. What did you call it? *Substantiating evidence?*"

Whip leaned forward. Instinctively his eyes darted about the terrace. This was what he'd come for. Amy was right. Val knew plenty. He'd always known. Chief Bowman had sensed it. McKenna and Soldato had echoed this sentiment. Getting David Martin to take Benne's place had been a move in the right direction. But would it all hold up under the scrutiny of this formidable barracuda? Whip began to see things in Val that he could admire. Unquestionably it was reason for his discomfort—admitting to something he'd denied for the better part of his life. By the holy beard of Saint Patrick, why hadn't he been gifted with 20/20 vision before this? All the time wasted . . .

"If you'd listened to my son, given him some assurance of future cooperation, something, he might not have been set up to be killed in that explosion. Now, he's back— if it is my Benne—without a memory." Val grew silent for several moments.

"You know, Senator, I fear so gravely for the lives of my family that I feel inclined to prevent Benne from cooperating with you when and if he should regain his memory."

Color flooded Whip's face. How could he tell Val the man impersonating Benne wasn't his *real* son? The deception ate deeply into his conscience. He thought with concern of Tina and what it would do to her when she learned of the farce.

"What would you have had me do, Val?" he asked quietly.

Val momentarily lost his cool. "What would I have had you do?" he echoed back. "Great God of thunder, man! You're the lawyer—the lawmaker, yet. You say you needed facts. Very well, did you make any attempt to pierce the corporate veil of TFL? Any attempts at all? You probably stopped at the names of those fronting the holdings for the benefit of the Gambling Commission," he snorted contemptuously. "Names that mean less than

155

a fifteen-cent stamp!" Val stopped abruptly, a look of bewilderment on his face as he forced himself to inhale a deep breath of air, trying as he did not to reveal his intense discomfort.

Whip, instantly alert, studied Val's face as it drained of color. "What's wrong? Are you all right?" he asked with genuine concern. He watched as Val opened a small gold case he removed from his jacket pocket and inserted a tiny white pellet under his tongue. A sudden awareness swept over him.

"Is it your heart?"

Val nodded. After a moment he appeared less discomforted. "It's nothing, really. Old age creeping along at too rapid a pace."

Then on a different tack, "I find it incredible that you haven't progressed more than you have in your investigation—" Val paused, and peered about, seemingly concerned with possible eavesdroppers. He glanced at his watch, the slightest trace of a frown evident in his clear blue eyes.

"I'm concerned with the fact that our guest of honor hasn't appeared. He's late." He added, "I'll leave you with a few provocative thoughts, Senator, before getting back to my guests. You are aware of the factions backing the Tabasis regime before Delfino Cratos and his left-wing vultures ousted the dictator, no? Who scripted the Swineherd Bay fiasco?"

Whip glanced into those mocking, contemptuous blue eyes, searching them as if he might see the answers there. He had missed nothing, not a beat or inflection in Val's voice. His own voice was barely above a whisper. "Neiland R. Milton."

Val didn't move a muscle as he looked into Whip's eyes. They wore a strange expression, but a look he felt to the tip of his toes.

"I—I don't see what you're driving at," he said finally.

"The Tabasis regime was backed by the silent, manipulative genius of an international cartel of business men, industrialists, financiers—" Val arose and turned up the volume on the music. He indicated for Whip to follow him to the edge of the terrace. He snapped off a sprig of fresh mint from a cluster growing in a huge pottery crock and inhaled its bouquet appreciatively.

"It's their, uh, custom to finance certain movements in various nations for, shall we say, enormous profits? While you, Senator, were kept busy bulldozing organized crime

156

and syndicate involvements for penny-ante profits, these giants played for huge stakes."

Keep going, Val. Tell me more! Whip fairly shook from the tension of trying to subdue the excitement rising in him. Outwardly he gave Val the impression that nothing connected in his mind.

"Don't you see?" Val was puzzled by Whip's apparent dullness. "The Shiverton political machine was never intended to triumph over Neiland Milton. You were superb, Whip. They all said so. They hated your guts, never counting on your unique talent. My, my, the difference in the popular vote was scant."

Whip caught up with him, playing the game a step ahead of Val. "What of the Baggio brothers? Facts support the evidence that they ordered Ted's death. Garnet, Coswalski's killer, is tied to them." His eyes narrowed intently.

"Bullshit. Mere camouflage," said Val. "The Baggios are talkers, not doers. See how easy it is to divert the pragmatic man skilled in legal mechanics, trained to base his findings on logic and facts? You of all men should know that the most illogical of facts come to life to prove a solution in countless crimes. Not every crime is as scientifically exact as a jigsaw puzzle, designed to fit together securely, piece by piece, to form a final picture of symmetry and perfection."

"That of course is academic."

Val ignored the barb. "You legal giants seldom acknowledge your own potential in becoming master criminals. You do yourselves a disservice in this respect. If assessments could properly be made, I promise, more corruption would be uncovered within your political structures, more double-dealing, than in the whole of organized crime. Criminals in those early days of vast corruption couldn't have existed if there hadn't been a hundred men more evil and corrupt using the weaknesses in the law to guide them into deeper waters."

"You were saying, Val, something about Milton—"

Val held up an apologetic hand. "Forgive me for rambling. There's so much to impart to you." A deep and audible exhalation came from Val as he held eye contact with his guest. "I hadn't intended saying this much. I wanted to wait until tomorrow when we could talk without the pressure of guests and a homecoming party . . . I suppose we can talk until Benne arrives."

Concerned at the obvious tardiness of the honored

157

guest, checking his platinum Piaget, Val glanced over his shoulder through the glass window. Turning back, his voice dropped in volume.

"Information that might never reach your ears is often afforded me through my former associates. Benne had certain information—a mere straw in a haystack of intrigue. Nevertheless, enough for you to have arrived at some conclusive evidence of TFL's involvement in this international cartel. Benne told me your reaction to his information and we both despaired. Is it possible, Senator, that you could be a part of that same system—men going about blinkered and earmuffed, unwilling to believe that corruption exists among your own kind, within your so-called honor system; that you permit a self-protecting veil of invisible threads to shield those men who hold themselves above reproach?"

"If you're saying there's little difference between the titans of organized crime and the men who run the politics of the nation," pressed Whip, "I've already made that assessment."

"In such a comparison, believe me, men like my former associates would come out less blemished. They disdain the system for obvious reasons. If the assassination of the President took place within their system, they'd not permit it to keep a lid clamped down on information that would shed light on the crime, burying it in the national archives for seventy-five years. They'd know the identities of those responsible for the crime and in their own way would have wiped the slate clean. In their system, there are few unsolved crimes." Val paused momentarily.

"What about Bob Harmon, or your own son, Jimmy?" Whip countered.

Val Erice's head whirled around. He withdrew from the assault like a wounded tiger. "The books are not closed yet," he retorted in a deadly voice, much like the one Whip hadn't erased from his memory after their first encounter many years before.

"I didn't mean to stoke up bad memories." Whip apologized. "I have to remind myself to keep the proper perspective."

"You see only what you want to see," Val snapped in mild annoyance. "It boils down to just that. But don't despair, Senator, not many people can perceive a situation from all angles at once."

Their conversation ended abruptly at the sound of

Tina's voice calling to her father. "Benne's here, Pop. You can pick up where you left off, later."

Val's hand reached out to hold back Whip's arm. "We'll talk tomorrow. I'll explain in detail to you the business I did for Ted when I went to Europe for him four years ago."

Whip's brows arched imperceptibly. "Business? For Ted?"

Val extended his arm, leading the way inside, nodding his head. "For Ted."

CHAPTER THIRTEEN

David Martin was half an hour late for dinner. Dressed flamboyantly in the manner of the late Benne Erice, in a white dinner suit with diamond studs, no tie on a ruffled dinner shirt, he swaggered into the room. Every eye in the room zeroed in on him. Tina swept across the room, to save him from panicking. Linking her arm in his, she eased him through the numerous introductions. Her warmth put David at ease as she guided him through the introductions from one guest to the next.

"He says his name is David Martin," Tina was explaining to the others. "I tell you he's my brother Benne. He simply can't remember, since the accident." She pulled him towards a stunning red-haired woman. "This is Amy Shiverton, David."

David bowed slightly, kissing her hand. "Hello, Amy."

"—And this is her brother, Whip Shiverton."

David, totally unprepared for this eyeball confrontation, was jarred momentarily. "Uh, Senator," David bowed slightly, shaking hands with Whip. Martin felt instant tension between them.

"Have we met before?" David stared at him, blankly. "How did you know I was a senator?" Whip asked tightly before anyone jumped on the *faux pas*.

David gave a start and covered expertly, tilting his head, aware every eye was on him. He grimaced, trying to recollect.

"I don't know. It sort of came out that way. Odd, I got the distinct impression we've met before. Have we?"

Good, thought Whip. *He extricated himself superbly.*

"Perhaps. Perhaps we have," said Whip blandly.

It was a ticklish situation for both Whip and Martin. Whip had only met Martin once, after the plastic surgery was performed and his face was still swollen from the surgery. Whip wouldn't have given a wooden nickel for the entire fraud and told them they were insane to attempt to deceive the Erice family. Now, staring inscrut-

160

ably at Martin, he was hard put to tell the difference between the impostor and the real Benne. It was uncanny to witness this remarkable resemblance.

It didn't matter that Whip stared at David, because the entire party's eyes were riveted on him, trying to find a discrepancy in his behavior or manner on which they could base their suspicions.

Whip retired to one end of the room sipping his Dom Perignon. He hated being party to this deception and experienced pangs of guilt watching Tina glowing in a rebirth of hope. It was a shitty thing to do, but what recourse did he have now? The impeccable impersonation had been dreamed up long before he entered into the conspiracy with Bowman. Tina was made of sturdy stuff. She'd weather the storm now brewing on all fronts. What he hoped was that if his participation in the fraud was discovered, he could explain it in a way so as not to incur her hatred.

While the light chatter ensued and David explained as best he could about his accident, Whip turned his attention on Renzo, his loathing for the ex-bookie increasing. Having seen him so often on celluloid, he felt he knew him well. Whip considered him too handsome, too physical and obviously too intent on his own pleasures. How on earth could Tina have allowed herself to . . .

A twinge of guilt shooting through him brought a flush of perspiration to his brow. He blotted the moisture with a handkerchief, wondering if this scheming, plotting and toying with human emotions was vital to the BSI's success. Could they have obtained their goals through other means? Aware that his presence had thrown Martin off kilter briefly, and of the difficulties facing an agent under cover, he also knew there could be no predictable reaction if the threat of discovery loomed nearby. He retired further from the family dramatics and took a seat at the bar, one foot on the stool rung, the other firmly on the floor.

He placed his glass on the bar, only to have it refilled before he could protest. Glancing back again, he caught an undisguised look of loathing emanating from Renzo as he stared at David Martin. Whip's eyes quickly traveled to Martin, studying his controlled and relaxed manner as he bowed, smiled and mixed with the guests. *Christ, what guts it took to foist this deception!* Whip's strange and unpredictable concern for Martin eased off with the announcement of dinner.

David Martin . . . David Martin . . . David Martin
. . . Was he really Benne Erice? This question was running rampant in the minds of the dinner guests. Tina and Richie had accepted the fact. The others toyed with numerous contradictions, not about Martin's appearance, but in the chain of events leading from the accident to this moment. They searched Martin's face microscopically, hoping he didn't pick up on their doubts. They politely contained themselves waiting for the moment Val might ask them for their opinions. Meanwhile they all ate with gusto the array of succulent food prepared by Christina and the galaxy of talented chefs, cooks, and pastry experts loaned from the exotic kitchens of the Pyramids.

Jerry Bonfiglio and his wife, unable to take their eyes from David, had not been prepared for the shock of seeing the reincarnation of Benne. Jerry had read the extensive reports submitted by the FBI's disaster squad; he'd talked with the crew of men Val had personally hired to scout the mountains for bodies. Those reports indicated there could have been no survivors. Yet here stood the living testimony that the FBI wasn't always accurate.

Jerry studied Tina every moment he could. No one was as shrewd as Tina; she had accepted him totally. He hadn't seen Tina as alive and vibrant since before Benne's accident. When he wasn't observing Tina or David, Jerry's eyes lingered on Richie. Something was wrong; he sensed it. Richie was edgy and wore a mask, one defying you to read his mind. Oh, how he wanted to engage David in a conversation and speak only of things Benne would know! What use would it be? Val made it clearly understood that the guest of honor was suffering with retrograde amnesia. Was it for convenience? Jerry contented himself with the delicacies spread before him.

Long ago when he first joined Val's organization, he'd been told, "When the time comes for you to be involved, you'll be told everything." Very well, he'd do what he'd always done, wait until he was fully involved.

Amy had been in Benne's company often enough to have been thoroughly charmed by him. She'd fallen prey to his audacious wit and behavior over the years. He'd been a caution in his formative years but had grown into an astute young man, both in business and politics. Once he'd flown to Florida on a mission for his father. He took the time to take Amy sailing one sparkling sunshine day and she recalled his sensual animal magnetism as he rigged the sails on the 32-foot sloop, how his muscles rippled in perfect coordination when he raised the jib under sail with expertise. He sailed with a seaman's precision and rode the crested waves of the windswept tropical sea like a young sun god.

Later at the club Amy noticed how the women stared at him, straining to catch his attention and how Benne laughingly ignored their blatant, suggestive looks with the attitude of a man who knew his own worth and didn't have to prove it.

Something dynamic about Benne communicated itself to everyone he touched, from a mere street urchin to a—president?

Amy sighed. Ted had been very fond of Benne. But that was long ago. Her green eyes misted, then, looking towards Val, her heart melted. How awful it had been for him. So much tragedy, for both the Shiverton and Erice families.

Sipping her wine, she touched her lips daintily with her napkin and glanced at David. *Please be Benne,* she prayed silently. *For Val's sake, be Benne.*

Aware of his mission, what must be done in the role he'd been primed to play, David Martin, feeling the inscrutable eyes upon him, felt as if he were walking a tightrope stretched across an open pit of hungry crocodiles. He got the distinct feeling that dinner, as fabulous a spread as it was, was planned with a diabolical plot to trip him up in some way. When three choices of entrées were presented in this lavish banquet, his programmed brain did a neat shuffle and he selected only the food that Benne had loved passionately. He chose lasagne over ravioli, eating his salad with his entrée of stuffed baked veal birds and lemon sauce, selected over beef *braciole.* He drank water with dinner, and poured anisette into his espresso. When desserts were artistically presented on stunning silver trays, he picked the *canoli sans citron,* passing up the honey-soaked *pinolatti* and *sfinghi,* lamenting that he had no more room in his stomach. "Save these for later," he told Christina, rolling his eyes in appreciation of the feast prepared for him.

David turned to Val, asking politely, "Mind if I remove my jacket? These monkey suits aren't designed for comfort." He laughed, noting Val's eyes were misting. He also noted that Tina's dark eyes lit up with an *I told you so* look she transmitted to her father. Benne had always detested confining clothing.

The talk over dinner had been subtle, easy, in a light

vein, nothing pertaining to David Martin's recent experiences or Benne's accident. Finally dinner was over.

As the guests left the dining room, servants moved about in the background and drew the folded mirrored doors together, shutting off the room from the living room. David handed his jacket to Tina as he sauntered across the room to the bar. He prepared after-dinner drinks for them as if he'd done it all his life.

"Let's see, Strega over shaved ice for Pop. Green crème de menthe over ice spritzed with seltzer for Amy and—" He nodded in Christina's direction. He turned to Renzo. "You fix Tina's. She never likes what I make." His voice, so much like Benne's, had a chilling effect on the others.

Martin marveled at his own dexterity. So far, so good. Had he been too sure, too slick, too complaisant? Before surrendering the bar to the professional mixologist, he glanced at the keenly observant police chief, Frank Ferraro, calling to him, "Hey, Ciccio, aren't you drinking?"

Aware that an answer was expected, the captain indicated the demitasse in his hand. "The espresso is fine." Ferraro hadn't been clued in on what he would encounter at dinner. Now he wondered why Val hadn't confided in him. Could the fingerprints on the dice cup have belonged to Benne—or to this man, Martin? Martin's voice arrested his thoughts.

"You gotta have something," Martin insisted, reaching for a bottle of Parfait d'Amour. He poured a tiny glassful for Richie. Holding the bottle in midair he caught Captain Ferraro's eyes and gestured to him. Ferraro shook his head. Martin shrugged indifferently and watched Richie down the elixir.

Martin grimaced. "Ughhh, you might as well drink pure sugar."

All this behavior brought tears to Richie's eyes. Every gesture, each word, every moment was proving conclusively to Richie that Martin was indeed Benne Erice.

Captain Ferraro had observed everyone's reaction to Martin. He wasn't in the least convinced that the man was Benne. Subtle differences detectable only by observing Martin with detachment had surfaced clearly in Ferraro's mind. Oh, he looked like Benne, acted like him, but little things Benne did with his eyes that Martin didn't do triggered negative responses in the police chief. Gestures, mannerisms, meaningless to some but telltale for others who'd shared intimacies and little secrets with Benne. What was it Val had said earlier? Martin suffered with retrograde amnesia? Then time will tell if this is Benne Erice.

Meanwhile he found himself fascinated by the goings-on. If this wasn't Benne, who was he? What brand of insanity was it that would risk so daring an impersonation? No one in his right mind would dare perpetrate such a dangerous fraud. Would they? The presence of this man Martin, his convenient lapse of memory, the risky business itself disturbed his cop's sixth sense. Something didn't compute. Shit, if he didn't know better . . .

Val's voice waded through his thoughts. He turned to his host as did the others. "This occasion calls for a toast," Val said, raising his glass in midair. "To our beloved son, Benedetto, and his safe return to the bosom of our family."

Only then did Christina come forward to embrace David. Val gave his sanction. This was their son. The tears she'd held in check since the news reached her rushed out with an emotional outpouring of love and gratitude to God for sparing his life. She stroked his face tenderly and, holding it between her slender hands, kissed him profusely.

Beneath Martin's tan his face reddened; he shuffled awkwardly from one foot to the other. All eyes were on him as he led Christina to the sofa, where he sat alongside her comforting her. It was a touching moment for which no amount of training could have prepared him. He faltered uneasily.

"Forgive me if I cannot reciprocate your feelings. I wish I could feel as you do, but I have no memory of you—" His eyes met Whip's and he felt like shit. *Christ, only a fucking rat would put a woman through such torture!*

For most of the night, as others talked with Martin about his accident, Christina had listened intently. Now she held his hands, searching them, committing them to memory, admiring their strength as any mother does. His long, slender fingers had caused Christina to envision him growing up to be a skilled surgeon. She smiled, recollecting the accident that had ended all such illusions . . .

How old had he been—five or six years old, when she sent him to the store to bring home a quart of milk? On his return trip, trying to maneuver the handlebars of his bike with one hand, the milk in the other, he'd been in a hurry to get home before dark. Benne accidently fell down and the glass from the broken bottle had cut deeply into the tendons of his left thumb. Benne had begged his mother to say nothing to his father or brothers. At this age he was uncoordinated and clumsy and lacked the agility his brothers possessed. He detested the razzing he got, so in a secret pact only he and his mother shared the confidence. For many years after the injury healed a definite X-shaped scar remained. You saw it only if you knew it was there in the first place. The possibility that Benne was alive and had outwitted death had brought many things back to Christina that the family hadn't thought about.

Now, as she stared at his hands, caressing them, she opened his left palm, pressing it to hers, turning it over. Imagine, her Benne was alive. Val confirmed the truth. No one could fool Val. What a brilliant idea, cooking so much food. Only the real Benne would select his lifelong favorites, she told herself.

Earlier Amy had confided that she felt certain this man was Benne. Christina's hopes had soared. Now, as their eyes met across the room, Amy nodded reassuringly once again. Christina felt even more joyous as a wonderful warmth and feeling of love coursed through her.

Senator Shiverton was aware that something was expected of him, something more cerebral and logical than a mere assumption. He hoped David Martin would understand his untenable position and be able to maintain his equilibrium during the next moments. His objective and unbiased opinion about the man Martin was what they expected. Whip couldn't disappoint them.

For a few moments he engaged Martin in conversation, asking subtle but leading questions concerning the accident. Most questions were similar to those Martin had already been asked repeatedly by most of the interested parties since he began playing this dangerous game. Martin responded admirably. He didn't sound well-practiced.

"You have no recollection of me, Benne?" asked Whip.

"Sorry. Afraid not, Senator. Only a vague feeling that we've met before."

"Yet earlier you called me Senator . . ."

"Sorry, sir, I can't explain that."

"I was looking forward to continuing our conversation concerning the Golden Oasis business," said Whip. "I admit I was wrong not to take into consideration the suggestions you outlined at that time. When I think that I might've been able to deter the catastrophic events that happened subsequently—" Whip's voice cracked, as he paused effectively. "I'll never forgive myself. Do you recall anything we discussed?"

Silence spread like a pox in the room. David, stunned, tried to collect his wits. *Fuck! What's the Senator trying to do?*

Val, inwardly incensed at Whip's apparent lack of prudence in discussing private business without discretion was unable to conceal his displeasure. He noticed how quickly Renzo's interest piqued at the mention of Golden business. He watched Tina's husband move away from the bar, easing himself into the circle of conversation with an undisguised look of interest glittering in his green eyes. Val also noticed the decided reticence David displayed towards the senator, as if he dreaded locking horns with the astute politician.

Discreetly Val tried giving little importance to the conversation. For an instant his eyes met Richie's. In that instant they were both thinking of Emilio Aprile's tragic death. Earlier when Tina asked about Emilio and why he wasn't present at dinner, he was forced to endure his daughter's hostility when he explained the CPA had urgent business elsewhere. Whereupon Tina had snapped, "You could have delayed the work until tomorrow. This is Benne's homecoming!"

He'd have to make special arrangements with Captain Ferraro. Pangs of remorse at having to conceal his friend's death ate at him. David's insistent voice interrupted his thoughts.

"I keep telling you I don't recall any of our previous conversations, Senator. Assuredly it's not a pleasant situation for either of us and in this case you have me at a decided disadvantage." The instant change in Martin's speech pattern, the aloof tones and the formal manner in which he pronounced each word carefully with a sparseness of emotion became instantly noticeable to all present. He continued. "It's becoming increasingly clear how much you've all agonized over my accident. For all your sakes, as well as my own, I wish I had instant recall."

"It was merely my intention to spark your memory," persisted Whip gently. "That's why I brought up the Golden business."

"Then," said Martin crisply, "refresh my memory, sir. What exactly is the Golden Oasis? Are you talking about the hotel here in Vegas?"

Val bridled with displeasure. His sapphire eyes under bushy brows sparked with thought. *What the devil is Whip trying to do? He's not that naive. He knows what should be and shouldn't be discussed.*

"Actually," continued the senator, "I should have said TFL. Does that spark your interest, Benne?" Even as he spoke to the BSI agent, Whip's eyes were on Renzo, testing his reactions keenly. He continued to speak to Martin. "TFL, the Texas, Florida, Louisiana Corporation, is a holding company controlling Golden Enterprises, Golden Grove, Golden Oasis, Golden Banyon, Golden Tri-State, on and on *ad nauseum.*"

Why Whip indiscriminately bandied about these names was incomprehensible to Val. He reasoned that Whip was no dummy, no impudent underling ignorant of the consequences of dangerous talk. But what was he up to?

Martin, more rankled than Val, met Whip head on. "Monopolistic practices?" he queried. "My, my, why doesn't the Gambling Commission shoot darts into such manipulations? TFL must pack considerable clout to flirt with antitrust laws."

Whip tilted his head indulgently. "You speak with facility about such things. Are you familiar with corporate laws? Charters?"

Martin, blinking, cocking his head from side to side, hedged artfully. "A moment ago you triggered a light in my mind illuminating certain dormant areas . . ." He paused, grimacing in annoyance. "Sorry, the lights went out again."

"Then suppose we talk for a time. Perhaps I can turn them back on," suggested Whip.

Martin looked annoyed. "If I had a wish I'd ask for total recall." Geared to answer a thousand carefully rehearsed questions, he grew provoked at Whip's constant pressing. The thought struck him that there had to be a purpose to his madness, but what was it? Couldn't he ask straight out? Why the fencing?

Val saved the occasion. He disguised his obvious displeasure with Whip's persistence. "Physicians have warned us not to rush his memory, Senator." He saw no point to this discussion in Renzo's company. With elevated politeness he suggested that the men retire to the next room for a game of *Scopa.*

168

The men moved in a body to the game table across the room and sat down in flamingo velvet chairs. Richie lifted the octagonal table top, revealing a miniature gaming table, containing a roulette wheel, a crap table layout, chips, dominoes, checkers, a backgammon board and cards. He reversed the top, setting it back into place, and tossed a fresh deck of cards onto the green felt top.

"Benne," asked Richie. "You remember how to play the game?"

"We'll find out pretty quick, eh, Rich? You refresh my memory if it fades, eh?" David sat down on one of the chairs, his eyes scanning the others. He had labored thousands of hours preparing for these moments.

"You haven't seen anything, Senator," began Renzo, seating himself grandly at the table, "until you've seen Sicilians playing *Scopa*."

"Good, then, I'll watch," replied Whip, lighting a cigarette.

Whip watched the foursome for a time; then, unable to understand the dramatic concerto of eye and hand gestures, although he found it amusing, he grew disinterested and walked out on the terrace. Tina left the women and followed him. They exchanged polite conversation about Whip's involvements in the Senate hearings and the recent political turmoil and shakeup in President Milton's administration.

Renzo's concentration on the card game was waning. His eyes scanned the couple on the terrace periodically until he began to grow annoyed. He relinquished his hand to Jerry Bonfiglio and excused himself on the pretext that he had to check the action in the casino. He stopped at the bar, poured himself a Beefeater, downed it and left the penthouse.

As he made his way down in the elevator to the casino, Renzo admitted that the presence of Senator Shiverton had ticked him off. Watching Tina's reaction to Whip had thickened his concern. He had good reason to be shaken up. Having heard enough about Whip's estrangement with the Erice family for so long, he reasoned that his presence here at such a time wasn't kosher.

After his last encounter with Jolie Barnes in New York, and the discovery of the secret surveillance equipment, he felt paranoid. When he arrived in Las Vegas he quickly set about debugging his quarters. The complete sweep revealed a saturation of listening devices. The whole thing struck him with a fear he hadn't experienced since he left New York following Danny Shiverton's dope involvement. Renzo's paranoia increased when he began to fit bits and pieces together. He recalled vividly the night he showed up in Washington like a goddamned, idiotic cuckold with injured pride and found Jolie in the hot embrace of her Mr. X. He felt certain that he had fixed the hot cocksman for good. Yet when Jolie returned to Vegas, she never mentioned the incident. True, her behavior had been out of sorts, but she went about doing her show as usual.

One day, things dovetailed for Renzo and he asked himself countless questions. Why had Jolie kept the matter of the gunshot wound to herself? Normally she'd discussed many things with him. Why hadn't the papers made any mention of it? After all, Jolie was a celebrity whose name would have made instant headlines unless the story had been quashed by higher-ups. Her behavior following the assassination of the president, when he watched her inner disintegration, should have tipped him off that something was connected. Now, as the elevator plummeted down to the lobby he asked himself the questions that plagued him, questions he'd refused to acknowledge in his mind. Even now, he might not have resurrected these thoughts if it weren't for the curiously appraising look Senator Shiverton had tossed his way several times during the course of the evening.

Emerging from the elevator he wound his way through the crowded casino, nodding to some and gesturing to others, en route to his office. Suddenly he stopped in his tracks. The issue he'd refused to face and laughed at in the past struck him right between the eyes. Was it possible—was it really possible that Jolie had balled the president? Ted Shiverton? He paled at the thought. Then as quickly he suggested to himself—was it possible he'd taken a pot shot at Ted Shiverton that night in Washington? Hot and cold tremors shot through him.

By the time he inserted the special key into the lock on the office door and entered, locking it tightly behind him, Renzo's brow was a river of running sweat. He wiped his face with his hand and shook the moisture from it in a repugnant way.

Whip Shiverton had guessed at Renzo's involvement! He knew it. The icy reserve when they met earlier, the cool indifference, the obvious assessment in Whip's rapier scrutiny had told Renzo the score.

Damn! Renzo moved away from the door, crossed the

thickly carpeted office and plopped himself down in the comfortable upholstered chair behind the sumptuous desk.

How in the hell could he have figured Jolie and Ted Shiverton? Jolie and the president! He'd known it all along—yet forced the idea from his mind as ridiculous and farfetched.

Mister X was Ted Shiverton? Goddammit! The lights had been dim, her lover's back to Renzo. He hadn't seen Shiverton's face.

Renzo reached into the cabinet of the credenza behind him, retrieving a bottle of Jack Daniels. He gulped the fiery liquid straight from the bottle. He gasped for air as it burned his insides for a few brief seconds.

Dammit to hell, Renzo. This ain't no time to cry over a deck of stacked cards! You gotta make the best of an intolerable situation, ya hear, kid?

He gulped more firewater and set the bottle on the desk. He paced the floor, wringing his hands together, pulling at each knuckle of his fingers until they cracked loudly.

Jolie had given him no indication that she suspected him of the shooting. He knew her. She was an up-front broad who couldn't hide a hangnail from him. Yet hadn't he found the hidden camera and the bugs? What could it mean? Maybe she hadn't been in on it after all. Maybe because she kept company with the president they kept track of all her other lovers, or the men she fooled around with, eh?

Maybe he'd been smart to keep away from her this past year. Since Benne died—or disappeared—Renzo had hardly strayed from home. Jolie hadn't made overtures to him either. Food for thought? Plenty!

From the moment Benne had taken over the complete management of the Pyramids, slowly pushing Renzo out of the picture, Renzo had swallowed his lumps of displeasure, cowed before his brother-in-law, and fought off his jealous hatred on the surface. He had remained as in line as any man in his circumstances could.

Only yesterday he had talked with Marciano. The former big city hood, disgruntled with the obvious return of Benne to the scene, had cautioned Renzo.

"Don't do anything to screw up, kid, or it's goodby Charlie for us."

"Are we that close?" Renzo had asked.

"We're that close," responded Marciano, holding up his thumb and forefinger with little space between them. "So, play it by ear, kid. No more fucking around. It'll soon be over."

What Renzo hadn't known and probably never would was that six months before Benne's dreams had crumbled over the Sierra Madre mountains, Marciano and his gilt-edged associates had begun to wind down plans to cut into the Erice empire. When Manny told Renzo their problems would soon end, Renzo had pressed for more information. Marciano obliged.

"With what's gonna happen to your fresh, smart-assed Harvard punk boss, Benne Erice, we're gonna have the whole pie to ourselves, kid. We're gonna be wheels, you and me. By the time we finish Val Erice will pull out of Vegas and sell his holdings for peanuts. With no one to run the business, he's got no eyes to stay out here. Benne'll be out of the picture pretty soon and Joey in the east wants ta stay there. That leaves you and his daughter. And his daughter ain't no chip off the old block, eh, kid? So, that leaves only you to run the joint, no?"

When Renzo was clued in to rendezvous with Dancey Darling he agreed, but balked when he heard he had to be accompanied by an unknown companion sent by the "old man" in Dallas who, despite Manny's protestations, overruled his objections. Renzo had never quite got over the company of that white-wigged vulture who wore dark glasses to conceal his features.

Renzo knew nothing of the existence of IAGO. As a matter of fact, beyond the clout of TFL, even Marciano knew very little.

Men like Marciano and Renzo Bonaparte were small potatoes and like nonessentials would be expendable after their dirty deeds had been executed. Why it never occurred to either of them that they were mere flunkies to the men of IAGO was perhaps due to the fact that they were given a taste of power. True, it was a mere sampling, compared to the power exuded by the TFL corporation and its mentor, IAGO. However, basking in the limelight, with pencil power and the juice to supply life to the bloodline that ran the small world of each gambling casino, their egos wouldn't admit that they could be expendable. Instead, they believed that in dealing with the top dogs, their position and in-depth knowledge of the countless double dealings and unique machinations in their field would render them invulnerable to any mysterious mishaps. They actually believed that an invisible shroud of untouchability protected them.

Renzo polished off half the Jack Daniels before placing a call to Marciano. *Sonofabitch thinks more about that fuckin' crop of hair springing outa that cue ball-headed garden than he does our own hide.*

In moments he was spilling his guts to Marciano, reporting the disturbing presence of Senator Shiverton and the juicy bits of information spouted about the TFL holding company.

Marciano considered this news about Golden holdings to be far more important than the untimely resurrection of Benne Erice. However, he didn't let on to Renzo how he felt.

"So, the old man, Val, accepts him as Benne?" he asked, chewing on a cigar between his teeth. "Look, kid, everything's under control. Just lay back and act natural. It'll be over with before you know it. Something's cooking. But I can't let you in on it right now."

"O.K. O.K. I got nothing else to do but trust you, Manny." Renzo replaced the phone in its cradle, feeling more depressed than ever. Something was wrong, he felt it in his bones. But what? He sat back in his chair, lost in his thoughts.

Ten minutes later, he realized he couldn't procrastinate any longer. He had to get back to the penthouse. He picked up the phone and dialed an in-house number.

Calous Agajjinian's room didn't answer. Frowning, Renzo placed a call to Lefty Meyer's room. No answer. He called the hotel operator.

"Any messages from either Lefty or Aggie?" he barked into the mouthpiece.

"No, Mr. Bonaparte," replied the girl in a tired voice.

"You're sure?"

"One moment, please." She rang off. She returned in moments.

"No, sir. There's nothing."

Renzo cut her off, slamming the phone hard in her ear.

The private phone rang just as he was about to leave. It was Marciano. "Listen, kid, I forgot to mention that Aggie and Lefty took a vacation to the islands. Ya might say, uh, for their health, got it?" He laughed superficially. "Lemme ask ya, anyone causing a stink about the bookkeeper yet?"

"No. There ain't no sign of him. He disappeared just the way Shorty Levin's body did. I tell you, I don't like it. Manny? Are you there? . . . Hello . . . Hello!"

"I'm here . . . OK, no sweat. We take a step at a time. Go back to the party, I gotta think." He hung up before Renzo could protest.

Renzo replaced the phone. He straightened his tie before the mirror, mopped the sweat from his brow and put himself in order before he left the office. He moved through the crowded casino oblivious to everyone and brooding internally.

Marciano chewed his cigar to shreds, considering everything Renzo had reported. He could understand the missing body. It was a shrewd move on someone's part.

But there was more to rankle Marciano. His involvement with TFL, where he was never accepted as one of the boys. At top level he took orders from Tex Merkel out of Dallas. The relationship, mutually advantageous and in existence since Manny settled in Las Vegas had taken a strange turn in recent months.

When was it? A call had come from Howard Hughes. Manny, thinking it was a joke, hung up. A half hour later verification came from Dallas. Indeed the caller had been Hughes. Would Manny honor the man's call next time? Manny, floored, admitted he'd an inclination to rap with the man from Las Vegas. Unaware of the politics behind the call, he had boasted to Renzo, "When a man like H.H. needs Marciano to talk business with, it means only one thing, kid. We're on our way. You hitched your wagon to the right star."

Renzo had never doubted Manny. With a wariness spawned in the getto, Manny confided much to Renzo, but didn't tell him everything. The only interest Hughes had in Marciano was to gather bits and pieces of old Erice family skeletons that wouldn't stand the scrutiny of the Nevada Gambling Commission.

Hughes's associate, a briefcase lawyer in a Brooks Brothers suit and a haircut reminiscent of the Shiverton New Horizons men, arrived in Marciano's suite a few days after the call in which Hughes had asked Marciano to be candid about Benne Erice. Could Manny explain why Benne was buying up so much land in Las Vegas? Marciano was hesitant to speak out.

"I understand you've been hot around the collar and quite vocal after the Fishman stock deal on the Pyramids," said Hughes on the phone.

"What's one thing got to do with the other?" muttered the former Brooklyn syndicate boss.

"Meet with my man, Marciano. He'll explain."

He had sat opposite the lawyer in the privacy of his office. The lawyer had put several questions to Marciano. They locked horns instantly. The Hughes mouthpiece had framed his questions in such a way that Marciano, no sidewalk dummy, saw through the flimsily constructed plot to defame the Erice family. In the actual showdown Manny became aware that the questions asked of him were slanted towards learning more information about Val Erice than of his son, Benne, as originally proposed by H.H.

"Listen, you motherfuckin' son-of-a-bitch," began Manny in his usual genteel manner. "Marciano admits to being many things in his life, see? A hotshot bookie, gambler, extortionist, pimp— even a hit man in the long ago past. But two things he ain't—a stool pigeon or a fool!"

"But—but," the lawyer tried to speak up.

"Don't give me no buts," he snarled angrily. He saw immediately the role H.H. had planned for him and declined the offer.

"Look, Buster," he lit into the ashen-faced lawyer. "If your boss wants ta talk with Marciano, that's one thing. You don't think I'm gonna stick my neck out for a tinhorned mouthpiece who's probably wired for sound, do you?" With these words Manny stood up behind his desk and ushered the panic-stricken young man out the door unceremoniously by the seat of his pants.

Twenty minutes later Manny's phone rang. It was Howard Hughes. "Why didn't you cooperate with my legal agent?" he asked sternly.

Not to be outfoxed or duped Manny shouted in a fit of temper,

"Listen, Mr. Hot Shot. I don't give a friggin' damn who you are. You ain't using Marciano for no goddamned snitch. You pull that kind of shit on me and Buster, you're gonna feel my clout. Just don't pull no scams on Marciano, you hear? That kinda dough you ain't got. Not enough to buy my soul!"

"Would a hundred grand soothe your feelings and pave the way to your soul?" Hughes asked tightly.

"Not even ten hundred grand, Mr. Hot Shot! I don't do business with ghosts!"

"There are other ways," the mogul had said before hanging up.

"Fat chance!" Manny screamed into a dead receiver.

An hour later, a call came for him from Houston. Tex Merkle's west Texas drawl rasped over the phone with a slight chuckle. "Ah heah H.H. got to ya, mah boy."

"No, no, no, no," Marciano insisted. "Ain't no one got to me 'cepting you, Mr. Merkle."

"Ah want ya ta know it's all right ta cooperate with H.H. He's one of the boys."

"Whaddya mean one of the boys? You mean he's part of TFL?"

"Ah can't take time ta explain. Just cooperate."

Manny protested vehemently. "Oh, no. No, no, no. I ain't gonna be a stooge for anyone. Look, how long you know me? A long time, eh? You never asked me to break no code of my people. I ain't gonna do it now, not for that weirdo."

"Sorry ya feel like that, mah boy. Believe me, ah've made every effort ta keep things on an even keel. We're coming close to a showdown and we need those properties. If we can't obtain them in the usual way, boy, we'll do it our way. The last plan with Fishman fell apart. We aren't about to let this deal go down the tubes, ya heah? Let me suggest that ya cooperate with H.H. Y'all understand, doncha?"

Manny was silent, deathly silent, for a long hard moment.

"You want me to sign my death warrant, is that it? I don't know nothing, Mr. Merkle. If I wanted to cooperate there ain't nothing I could tell, uh, H.H.," he said in a voice dripping with sarcasm. "Besides, he's got so much *chutzpah*, why don't he find out his own way? He owns enough men, don't he?"

Mercifully Merkle took him off the hook. "We'll talk about this later when I get to the desert, mah boy," he had said before ringing off.

Manny stood before the mirror in his apartment examining the slight fuzz growing on his head. Any other time he'd have been ecstatic, but with the problems pressing on him like a dead weight he finished the cursory inspection of the new growth of hair and poured himself a large bourbon and soda. He returned to his seat recollecting the wrath he'd incurred from Howard Hughes for refusing to cooperate. The son-of-a-bitch had even tried cutting the Golden Oasis's garbage pickup for a time until Manny sent his army of pack rats to infiltrate the Hughes domain. He had literally turned loose an army of pack rats on the Hughes properties. The garbage trucks were at the Golden Oasis within an hour. Every exterminator in Las Vegas and vicinity worked overtime to kill the onslaught of rats.

Not once had Manny seen Hughes. At least the prick could have had the decency to appear in person to ask him to perform so important a mission where his life could have been at stake.

Grunting with displeasure, he fell into the chair behind his desk. He kicked off his Gucci loafers and propped his feet up on the desk comfortably. Visions of what Frankie Fortune had done to himself when he learned of Val's true position in the hierarchy of the Brotherhood flashed across his mind. Even later, many years after his deportation, when Fortune had tried sticking it to the New Orleans Dons with foul shipments of badly cut, low grade heroin, the fate Frankie received was clearly imprinted in his memory. The papers all claimed Frankie Fortune had died of natural causes, a heart attack. *Hah! That you could shove up a donkey's ass and turn him into a swan!* There was no way they could spoon-feed that crap to Manny. Frankie had the strongest heart of any man he knew. Someone had gotten to him, silently and swiftly. The Brotherhood's brand of justice had been dispensed in retaliation for Fortune's manipulative double-cross. There was more.

In Manny's mind, Fortune's death had finally balanced out the books for the death of Mario Martinelli and Val's brother years before.

His thoughts flashed back to Howard Hughes and he reached for an antacid pill to combat the ulcers burning holes in his stomach.

Shortly after Benne's accident, scuttlebutt about the mysterious exodus of Howard Hughes from Las Vegas had lit up inner circles of the gambling world like supercharged slot machines paying off perpetual jackpots. Rumors had it that this redoubtable eccentric had been ordered to flee his domain by more powerful figureheads, men whose identities none of the local boys dared speculate.

Ah, who de hell cares, anyway!

Marciano waved his hand in the air around him as if he were trying to make a point to an invisible companion. He pulled a wrapper off an imported stogie, bit off an end savagely, spitting it out from between his thick lips. He took time to wet the other end, rolling it over his tongue. Then, lighting it, he drew on it as one might pump a fire bellows. He didn't enjoy smoking, but he liked using the stogie as a prop when he talked, punctuating his words periodically with it, the way he'd seen the Texans do on occasion, whenever they favored him with their company.

He lay back in his chair, his eyes closed meditatively.

CHAPTER FOURTEEN

Marciano was pissed. He crossed to the wall opposite his desk where a row of slot machines installed for his pleasure became an outlet for his jangled nerves. He began pumping silver dollars into them. He could think more clearly if his hands were kept busy.

Renzo's recent behavior bugged the shit out of him. Shortly after Benne's plane crashed over Mexico Renzo began asking questions about Val and their past association in the old days. He wanted to know why Val Erice had always been held in high esteem. Manny obliged him for a time, reminiscing, drawing a fairly accurate picture of those abrasive days, turning it oblique at will to bolster his involvements when his ego demanded it. He spoke of Val respectfully, hesitantly careful to make no disparaging remarks about a man he still held in high regard.

Pulling the lever of the slots with increased momentum and yanking hard on the handles as he went from one to another, he listened as a few coins tinkled into the tray. He hardly saw them as one hand inserted the coins and the other yanked the handle. His compulsion with the slots became as obsessed as his mind as he pulled out the painful drawers of his past, critically inspecting their contents. He recalled how many times in the past his life had been on the line and how Val Erice had miraculously come to his rescue.

It was true, he owed his life to Val. That was what pissed him off. He dropped three more coins into one of those new machines that took you five bucks at a time, yanked hard on the handle, thinking the time had come to install a button to operate the greedy fuckin' one-armed bandits. Automation would only make them greedier and greedier . . . Greed. Greed was what caused his flesh to quiver. Greed, the cause of his last, near fatal kiss of death, was synonymous with one man, Aldo Napoli . . .

* * *

On a cold, blustery winter day shortly after the end of World War II, Aldo Napoli's boat docked in New York Harbor. Napoli, as greedy as he was insanely courageous, had beat a murder rap, judiciously avoiding it by exiling himself to Europe before the war. His racket dollars made him a big man in Italy. He bought land and lucrative political jobs in the Mussolini era. After Il Duce's disgraceful downfall, Napoli's monetary clout permitted him to infiltrate A.M.G.O.T. (Allied Military Government of Occupied Territories) and make himself indispensible to the Allies and local governing forces by initiating a black market that reaped millions for high-ranking U.S. military officials and lined his own coffers to the point of obscenity.

The war ended. He was back, no longer forced to run his rackets by proxy and prepared to rebuild his organization into an international cartel for the distribution and sale of narcotics.

There were, as Napoli saw it, three drawbacks to his plan: Manny Marciano, Larry Aiello and Alfredo Antonini. All had to be eliminated or his dreams would be ground into dust.

Marciano, a formidable power in the hierarchy since Frankie Fortune's exile, presented the greatest threat to Napoli. Aiello, protector of Napoli's domain during his exodus, efficient on the one hand, had been grossly negligent in permitting the competition to flourish. Last, but far from least, was a newcomer, a cruel, vicious, highly immoral, coldblooded killer without conscience who'd elevated himself to power by killing all the competition standing in his way.

None of Napoli's friends could explain how Antonini had become too powerful to be touched. Rumors circulated wildly through the underworld that this butcher of men was backed by a formidable, anonymous financial combine. Disbelieving this, Napoli put out feelers. He learned that the Five Families had bitterly opposed Antonini because his solution to any problem was a swift, silent knife or a fiery trail of blistering bullets. The Mafia hierarchy was waiting for the right moment and the right provocation to rid themselves of this malignancy. Displeasure at Aiello's lack of disciplinary action in Napoli's absence to restrain the frenetic mass slayings spearheaded by Antonini in recent months had incurred the wrath of the High Council. When nothing was done to curb the madman's insanity, the High Council reacted only by an overwhelming silence. This fact gave Aldo Napoli a secure feeling in what he intended to do.

Since Napoli's return, Antonini kept a low profile; watching, waiting, wondering how a reshuffling of power would affect his operations. Antonini was the star at center stage, the immovable object. The Mafia high command was the impenetrable force.

Napoli, based at his old penthouse in Jersey, met daily with trusted old cronies. He was back and ready for action. "Pass the word," he told them, then lay back waiting for word from the Five Families.

Nothing. Silence. Napoli gave it more time. Two weeks. Three. Four. More silence. Napoli burned. He fumed. Fuck 'em! Fuck 'em all! Napoli, no cherry at interorganizational problems, tackled this matter with meticulous expertise. The extinction of Aiello and Antonini was a foregone conclusion. The annihilation of Manny Marciano would take more than a swift knife to the jugular or a speedy bullet to the brain.

Napoli, a shrewd, conniving, street-wisened bimbo who'd always exercised varying degrees of prudence with an old country wariness, knew he could accomplish none of the three objectives without the full cooperation of the Five Families, or at least a nod from the High Commission, a coterie of the highest placed men in the Mafia hierarchy, formed in his absence and now governing the course of their collected destinies. Napoli had been warned of the elaborate changes made in his absence to which he must adhere if he wanted in on his old operations.

No apprentice in the Mafia, he knew the order of command and what happened to mavericks who cut away from the herd without sanction. But how to get back in their good graces was the point.

The hierarchy saw Napoli as a man addicted to fast, high living; a publicity-crazed, headline-making loudmouth who offended the conservative dignity of their all-powerful consortium. His careless shennanigans and vulgar displays of wealth added to their contempt. To them he was a tough, two-fisted hood who was unable to refine his behavior to the high calibre manner to which they'd elevated themselves in his absence. "He's learned nothing!" they disdained. "Nothing at all!"

"That's what they think? Napoli has learned nothing?" he shouted when he got the word. He paced the confines of his office spewing forth his indignation. "I'll tell you, my friends, Napoli has learned plenty! So I don't live behind high walls and electric fences with armed muscle checking who comes and who goes like some of the *goombahs*. I live the way I want. As long as I attend to business who the fuck cares what they think?"

For days he paced the floor, wearing a path into the deeply piled carpeting, pondering his next move. Shrewd enough to know his action could trigger a bitter power struggle among his contemporaries, he explored all possibilities. It suddenly came to him—he held the trump card he'd carried all the way back from Naples. He knew the identity of the man who carried the Mafia sceptre!

He couldn't fail! The bull-necked, raspy-voiced Mafioso sorted through his crafty mind for the proper tools to reach Valentino Erice. Awareness of Val's closely guarded secret burned his guts like acid. The intelligence of Val's strategy struck him and he was stunned by the genius of the man's planning as he fitted the pieces together from the death of Don Antonio to the present. The puzzle became whole. How much homage should be paid Erice for such brilliant and impeccable planning?

When, wondered Napoli, had a Sicilian, saturated with so much power, remained obscure, never boasting of it or using it to intimidate? Was this a blueprint for power not readily understood by his contemporaries, for the future demonstration of even greater clout? Having discussed this very subject with Luciano and Genovese back in Naples, all agreed and were baffled by the underplaying of such strength. The situation, unprecedented, confused them all.

Napoli was exhilarated by this knowledge, determined to put this brilliant strategy to work on his behalf, to his full advantage. He'd show them all that Aldo Napoli was no *cafone*, no imbecile peasant!

By the end of the week, Phase I went into action, the slaying of Larry Aiello. Napoli was faced with the revolting blundering of an incompetent hit man. Whether by accident or design, Aiello suffered only superficial wounds. The newspapers had a field day at Napoli's expense:

"ALDO NAPOLI PLANS TO BE BOSS OF ALL BOSSES! . . . The bloodiest battle in Mafia history has commenced . . .

The steadying influence of Val Erice intervened swiftly

and silently behind the scenes to halt any retaliation by the Families until the High Commission passed judgement on the headstrong and foolish stepson. Napoli's strategy to flush Val Erice into the open had worked.

They met at the height of one of the winter's worst snow storms, in Jersey City, in the conference room of the BCA Building (Broadcast Corporation of America), a legitimate business owned by Val. The room was plush, paneled in rich walnut and rich cordovan leathers. Val sat at the head of the gleaming walnut conference table. Richie and his two men positioned themselves behind Val. He removed his fur collared black chesterfield, tossing it, together with his homburg, on the nearby chair, and proceeded to peel off his leather gloves.

Aldo Napoli arrived with his men and deposited their pieces with neutral men provided on such occasions. His men took positions behind him as Val motioned him forward. He took a seat two away from Val and sat down. Aldo wore dark tinted glasses to conceal a cast in his eye, a congenital weakness he despised. The slightest eye movement, interpreted countless ways by his infamous associates, necessitated keeping the abomination veiled for he had every intention of maintaining a poker face when playing the dangerous game of Sicilian roulette, in which all the chambers of the gun are loaded.

He contemplated the elegance of Val Erice. Having tasted the sweetest of all nectars, unlimited prestige and power in Italy where he'd been wined and dined with the aplomb afforded royalty, Aldo felt none of the sudden panic or humility Frankie Fortune had experienced on learning that Val held the power of the double-headed griffin in the Mafia hierarchy. Napoli, irked at Val's inscrutable silence, spoke up without preamble or apology.

"Aiello had to go." His reptilian eyes were intent on the ornate ring on Val's left hand, defiant and testy.

Val spoke in well-modulated tones. "Your foolish action against Aiello is looked upon with contempt by our brothers." Removing a gold watch from his vest he flipped open the lid and placed it before him on the conference table, twirling it with a finger.

"If you'd asked him, he'd have gladly removed himself from your organization. He takes little pleasure in being a *Capo*, preferring instead to garden on his estate." Val's icy detachment unnerved Aldo.

Napoli, drawing on his cigar, deliberating Val's words, stared intently at his adversary. "That statement is as irresponsible as it is foolish in my mind," he rasped. "Aiello would have killed me before I got to him."

"A man," said Val icily, "whose entire life has been a succession of killings, disposing of anyone in his way as he rises to the apex of a success mirrored in his mind cannot hope to understand my words. You can't teach an old dog new tricks, if he's deaf, dumb and blind to any words but his own. You're a hard man to convince and too impetuous. Why did you want this meeting? Certainly not to speak of closed accounts?"

"I know where the power lies." He pointedly stared at the griffin ring on Val's finger. "Without your sanction I won't get to first base."

Misunderstanding Val's silence for approval, Napoli laid out his plans in detail. An hour later, with still no comment, no overt approval or disapproval by Val, Napoli lit up a cigar.

"Well, whaddya think, Val?" His grating, rasping voice went on, speaking Sicilian when he wanted to be understood, otherwise resorting to his Brooklynese slang.

"You, Luciano and Genovese make plans that don't necessarily include me. What do you want from me?"

Napoli cleared his throat. "Marciano goes. If I take matters into my hands, he'll be past history. I don't want the wrath of the families on my head."

"At least you don't lack for brains. What makes you think the others will go along with you?"

"Two things. What makes them bend in the wind? Money and power. They'll make so much money, prohibition income will be pocket change to them. It might serve them well to learn where the true power lies and why you've kept it a secret these many years. They—"

"There's that much money in narcotics?" asked Val, shoving aside the couched threat.

Aldo leaned in conspiratorially. "If you only knew you wouldn't sit there trying to charm me into avoiding a war between the families. Dammit, it's worth ten wars!"

Val raised a pontificating hand. "Nothing's worth anything if you aren't around to enjoy it. Killing Marciano will rob you of a good man," he said about the man who'd ordered the death of his brother Martello. "He's loyal. Kill him and you'll be dead before Satan stokes his furnace preparing for you. There's Antonini to be reckoned with," said Val distastefully.

"Yeah, yeah, I heard of him. What sewer did that rat crawl out of?"

"Men like him are a disgrace to us and blacken our name," despaired Val, shaking his head regretfully. "The rate of crime within our jurisdiction in your absence has diminished, paving the way for an expansion of business interests. Maintaining low profiles, we've invested in legitimate business bringing us higher profits without obvious risks. We've got gambling interests in Cuba. The Cubans made us a proposition we could neither refuse or ignore. If we invest a million in each hotel we build, the total cost to us is twenty-five grand. Already the profits are worth the trouble. We're in Los Cuaycos with higher profits."

"Peanuts," growled Napoli. "Peanuts. I don't care how legit you get, it's peanuts to what I propose. Look, we don't need a big stake. We'll use the same network Luciano used for the booze he imported. Val, I'm talking billions! No more penny-ante rum-running days we chased around during prohibition. Dope is the thing. Narcotics—any form."

Val spoke tersely. "I speak. You don't listen. I tell you things are different, you don't hear. War brought changes. Legitimately we've got no more pressures, no payoffs. We've evolved to first class citizens. We like it. Why won't you understand?" Val watched the stubborn setting of Aldo's jaws. There was no dissuading him. "Very well, I'll talk with the Commission. It's all I can do for now."

Aldo, clearing his raspy throat, hawked up phlegm. "You don't understand, Don Erice. Wouldn't the Commission find it interesting to know where the power lies?" he insisted for the second time.

Val glanced at him as if he were an insect. Behind him Richie tensed. In the silence only the muffled droning sounds of a forced air furnace were heard. The guns stiffened.

Val clucked his tongue against his teeth, shaking his head negligently. "You've shattered the illusion. I thought you had brains—"

"Put in a good word and I'll forget what I know."

"You're five years too late. The others already know. What need have you of extortion now?" Val's disgust was evident.

"Can't blame a guy for using his best shots," he said weakly.

"I'll put your words to the Commission. You'll hear shortly."

They parted in silence. Before Val could act on the

talk he had with Napoli, that tough Mafioso took matters into his own hands. Two hired hit men arrived from New Orleans. Within twenty-four hours they committed the act the High Commission had viewed with reluctance; Alfredo Antonini was gunned down in a downtown Manhattan barber shop. Before the hit men departed in their getaway car, the news reached Val.

A national conclave was called immediately. Police harassment when Mafia Dons met recently in Chicago, Cleveland and Appalachia, when their comings and goings were noted by FBI and state police, brought about what Val felt was foolproof planning for the Dons. An unchartered bus picked up the arrivals at the airport; their flights from seven different destinations had been coordinated to arrive within minutes of each other. They were deposited at a seaside manor on Long Island belonging to a business associate of Val's presently in Europe.

Among the notables from Chicago, Detroit, Las Vegas, Miami Beach and New Orleans, plus the local New York Dons, was Manny Marciano. Learning from his spy network that he was fingered for death, he pleaded for the Commission's protection.

Val's services as moderator and mediator, both sorely needed for the amicable settlement of the many issues facing them, proved invaluable. His wisdom, experience, authority, fairness and cool-headed approach instilled an air of calm to their meeting.

Finished with the lavish banquet prepared for them, the Dons lit up cigars and took their demitasse in a splendidly furbished drawing room of the mansion. The Aldo Napoli business wasn't the only reason the High Commission had met with dispatch. The traditional unity and long-established cohesion and discipline within the brotherhood was at stake.

The elders felt they must enforce stricter lines of jurisdictional demarcation in narcotics, gambling and labor fields at once. The Mafia and its role in organized crime was under investigation. The fanatical probing of Senator McClellan's anti-rackets committee was becoming embarrassing to the Mafiosi. Unwanted, dreaded publicity from newspapers and magazines spotlighted Mafia activities garishly. Law enforcement agencies on the take who chose to deny its existence because of political influence or payoffs found the pressure from mavericks in government was forcing them to view the Mafiosi and their pernicious involvements through different eyes. Mafiosi enjoying the total freedom from police interference and total anonymity began to squirm uneasily.

They finally got around to Aldo Napoli. They listened to him, to his grandiose plans for the large-scale smuggling of heroin to the States. He told them what he'd told Val and came prepared with a projected plan of inestimable profits on a graph.

Having listened attentively they put the issue up for discussion.

Marciano spoke up first. "I ain't gonna argue with you, Aldo, but how come I don't get the nod from Frankie or Lucky in person? They tell me lay off the stuff while the heat's on."

"I just arrived from Naples where I lunched with Don Salvatore every day for two weeks," said the well-dressed, evenly tanned Don from Las Vegas. "He gave me the same word. 'Lay off of dope until I give the word.'"

"That's good enough for me," said the New Orleans Don. "Running narcotics will expose my men to too many risks with the Feds. They're dying to bust us the first chance they get."

"I agree," said the craggy-faced Don from Chicago. "We don't need these complications while the heat's on."

Aldo glanced at Val Erice for intervention. Val shrugged, shaking his head. "Try to understand. Drug trafficking is dangerous, too dangerous for us to involve ourselves. The insidious menace of heroin and an increase in crime in recent days have caused the police and legislators to adopt harsher measures than before. For the first time, jail sentences of ten to fifteen years are imposed on drug offenders. Under new federal laws, the death penalty can be imposed. To have worked so diligently all these years and, because of greed, gamble it away is a foolish act."

The Dons nodded in agreement.

"Somebody ain't getting their stories straight. I'm telling you both Lucky and Vito gave the word. You're tossing away billions!"

"Try to understand, Don Napoli," urged Val. "This publicity over drugs has affected us all by drawing attention to every man with an Italian name. We don't intend to bask in the raw spotlight of ignominy to which our people were subjected and falsely accused in 1890. My own political connections promise no assistance. Our juices won't lubricate the machinery of narcotics. Do you understand me?"

The subject of narcotics was closed. The subject of

Antonini's murder was open and they all glared at Napoli with deadpan faces. Something was up. What? He squirmed uncomfortably, aiming his rancor at Val. "I did you all a favor, for Christ's sake!"

"Didn't it occur to you why Antonini was permitted to live despite our loathing of the man and what he represented?" He took time to explain. "We have White House connections on the island of Los Cuaycos. Things have been going smoothly, until Antonini's death. You see, Don Aldo, it came to our attention that Antonini recently sent his, uh, agents to Los Cuaycos to make deals without the High Commission's sanction, in serious breach of brotherhood rules. We took no action against him because we were about to learn the identity of the men backing him in these powerplays. Word reached us that a group known as the TFL combine, spreading plenty of greenbacks, is trying to ease us out of the picture. If Antonini had a foot in the door it stands to follow he represented TFL. We didn't pay our dues to be eased out by oil well jockeys. We don't trespass on their oil wells and resent their inclination to move against our investments. Our contacts in high places have been persuaded to understand, sympathize and strengthen our positions."

Val studied Aldo Napoli and didn't like what he read in the stubborn vice overlord's mind. He ordered Richie to keep a stiff surveillance on Manny Marciano.

"We've got to prevent a killing, Richie. Meet with his lieutenants and form a cordon of protection around him, understand?"

Richie understood. He set the ball in motion. With Manny's own men they foiled three attempts on their boss's life.

The conclave had ended on a sour note for Napoli. His project had been strongly opposed, the Commission voted to lay off narcotics for the time being. The Jersey rackets boss took umbrage and despite concessions made to him to restore his power if he remained in line, Napoli's greed and obstinacy superceded reason. He was intent on bankrolling his own narcotics operation without the protection or cooperation of the Five Families. In due time the world of Aldo Napoli would be doomed.

Two weeks after the conclave, following the third attempt on his life, Manny had been told by his own men and with brutal candor that he owed his life to Val Erice.

Marciano, his decision made in lieu of the circumstances in which his life was threatened, appeared at the Wall Street offices of Global Enterprises to pay his respects and thank Val for his compassionate concern. Val sat opposite the man who'd ordered the death of his brother listening to Manny talk about his plans to leave New York and settle in Vegas.

It wasn't until after Napoli's arrest in 1958 when he and fourteen codefendants were caught for promoting the sale of narcotics and sent to prison for conspiracy to sell that Manny could breathe easy.

Now Manny paced his penthouse at the Golden Oasis possessed with conflicting emotions. No question he owed his life to Val. Goddammit! How long can a man remain beholden to another? He'd kept his nose clean, minded his own business and kept within a rigid framework of decency, but he took orders.

If he didn't execute those orders, he'd be replaced in a second. It was dog eat dog, now. He never expected Val to become a heavyweight in Vegas. And Benne, what a sharpie, a chip off the old block. They all played for high stakes where only victory counted.

Now, Benne was back—or someone doing a damned good imitation of him. This knowledge pressed on him like a two-ton weight. Should he call Val and tell him this bum Martin was counterfeit or let him deal with his own problem? Trouble was it was his problem as well, if this bum Martin turned out to be some creep thinking to ease himself into a good thing in a confidence game.

Shit, what I am thinking? Who can fool Val? The minute he asked himself this question he felt the sweat pour through his pores like tiny faucets. His own crime against Val had gone undetected, hadn't it? No one had accused him of Martello's death. It would have been over long before this, he felt sure, if Val had suspected his guilt in the matter.

Manny poured himself a stiff bracer of Jack Daniels and gulped it down. He whipped off his golf cap and examined the fuzzy growth. "Sonofabitch," he muttered, still marvelling.

Manny stood erect as a sudden thought pierced his mind. The feds! Could it be the fuckin Feds who planted Martin?

G'wan, Manny, you're nuts! Shit, there ain't a chance in a million they could even clone anyone to look like Benne. Recently the word clone had come into his limited

189

vocabulary. He'd been taken by the meaning of such a modern-day wonder.

He flung open the terrace doors and stepped into the pulverizing desert heat, allowing the hot sun to invigorate his body. Glancing down into the thickening city traffic, at the tall obelisk buildings blocking portions of the landscape that once was visible for miles without obstruction, he breathed deeply, trying to relax and unwind. But thought, like a malignant cancer, returned to plague him.

Renzo . . . Renzo . . . Back to Renzo. With Benne out of the way Renzo had eased himself back into the saddle and had taken to his task, grimly determined to impress someone. Who? Was he trying to make up for his stupidities over the years? Was it possible that Renzo, in estimating the Erice fortune, considered he'd fare better if he reversed his loyalties, spilling all he knew to Val, to insure his financial future?

Such thoughts had kept Manny awake nights worrying until he realized he held the trump card. How many deaths had he been responsible for? Jimmy Erice. Bob Harmon. He'd supplied drugs to Danny Shiverton. Then there was this recent business with Benne—and the Dancey Darling conspiracy . . . Nah, the kid would be dead if he tried shifting loyalties.

He gazed out at the increasing traffic Manny had helped to bring to this desert outpost over the years, transforming Vegas into an architectural nightmare. Renzo's face refused to cease intruding in his thoughts. He hated thinking adverse thoughts about the kid this late in the game; however, with the persistence of little old ladies dropping nickels in a slot machine, it ate at him.

It wouldn't hurt to insulate himself with some protection. He wasn't in this with the Texans to take unneeded chances. From here on it had to be a sure thing. He waddled back inside, determination on his face, and made the effort of placing a twenty-four-hour surveillance on Renzo. Better safe than sorry! Then he called a private number and asked to be sent three of the newest and kinkiest broads to service him. What he needed was a fuck to end all fucks. In his condition it would take the artistry of three chicks well schooled in their craft to relax him.

He poured a tall Jack Daniels into his gut and burped loudly. Fucking ulcers were burning holes in him. He'd be damned if he'd give up drinking to pamper them. The doorbell rang. Manny pressed a button on his desk releasing the lock. In they walked, a sultry brunette, an expensive-looking blonde, and a ravishing freshly scrubbed red-head. Their faces were fixed with plastic smiles.

Renzo returned to the penthouse to hear Tina suggest they all catch Jolie Barnes's show at the Golden Oasis. David Martin glanced at Renzo and said, pointedly, "I caught her show the other night, here." He rolled his eyes suggestively. "Are you telling me, Tina, I knew her before my accident?" He winked at Richie, beaming at him from across the room.

Whip Shiverton declined. He wasn't prepared to encounter Jolie this early in the game.

Amy knew it was foolish to try to coax her brother to forgo other business; she merely nodded. Val rose to his feet, stretching. "You all go on ahead to the competition to see Miss Barnes. It's long past Christina's and my bed-time." He turned to Renzo. "Why you permitted Miss Barnes to slip through your hands is a mystery you can explain tomorrow when we meet with Aggie and Emilio Aprile." Van winked at David. "Perhaps Benne can change the young woman's mind and bring her back here where she belongs. He's been known to melt icebergs on contact, eh, Benne?"

"What the hell's everyone so uptight about?" Renzo said tartly, unable to let it pass. "So what if she left the Pyramids? The new act we've got coming in starring Dancey Darling will outdraw Jolie twenty to one. Then you'll see the strategy I put together for the hotel."

"Dancey Darling?" Whip raised an inquisitive brow. "Since when has she done stage work?"

"Since I got the idea to use her box office draw here at the Pyramids. We're building a whole new show around her. I tell you, she'll be a smash."

Val, listening intently, held Renzo in focus. "We'll see how your strategy works when we put Aprile to work counting the box office receipts, eh, Renzo?"

Surprisingly Renzo kept his cool, even though a surge of hot discomfort shot through him. "That's the real test, isn't it? The box office receipts."

Renzo's jaw muscles writhed at the sight of Val embracing David Martin in parting. Jealousy knotted his stomach; his fists balled in spasmodic jerks.

"We'll see each other in the morning at breakfast, son," Val told David softly. His eyes caught Whip's glance briefly.

"Tonight I must ask God's forgiveness for my lack of faith."

Martin, flushing until Val disappeared with his wife into the next room, picked up the tempo, teasingly pressing Tina, "Are you telling me I knew Jolie Barnes *that* well?"

"You more than knew her, Benne," Tina laughed as they went out the door, leaving Renzo alone. She flung her husband one last look before closing the door.

Renzo, his voice choked with anger, cursed aloud, "Fuck 'em! Fuck 'em all! I'll show them who's who!" At the bar he poured himself a stiff bourbon and popped a few uppers as the servants moved quietly behind him, cleaning up after the guests.

Renzo returned to his own suite of rooms. He hadn't been sharing the apartment with Tina since David Martin appeared on the scene—not after the way she blew up at him over Harmon's death. S-h-i-t! In his room he glanced at the clock; it was nearly midnight. In half an hour the uppers would work and he'd return to the casino to keep his eyes open. He had to find Aggie and Lefty. What the fuck happened to Emilio Aprile's body?

He pulled off his tie, slipped out of his dinner pumps, removed his jacket and lay back on the sofa thinking about Jolie, Val, and the meeting in the morning when Aprile didn't show, and a cluttering of crazy mixed-up things that suddenly began complicating his life. *Fucking broad! Couldn't she have been more patient—for a little while longer . . .*

A month after Whip Shiverton enlisted Jolie's aid in his future plans, Las Vegas was stunned by the news that she released to the press—her termination with the Pyramids Hotel combine. She announced that she would finish the term of her contract but would no longer work under the Pyramids banner on grounds too personal to be aired. Instant pandemonium broke out between casino entrepreneurs and the wild bidding for her talent commenced. Gossip columnists and trade journal reporters had a field day speculating over Jolie's reasons to change her residence.

Jolie refused all personal interviews with the exception of one, the toughest of all, with Barbara Walters of ABC.

"Why?" asked Miss Walters, "did you make this broad jump into the enemy camp? You're the hottest property in Las Vegas and it must feel great to have the competition

192

upping the ante over you. But don't you have points in the Pyramids?"

Jolie gave her old friend a scoop. "You're the first to know, Barbara. I sold my points. In all fairness to my old boss, Mr. Bonaparte, I'll remain until the end of my contract."

No one watching this televised interview was as shaken or as irate as Renzo. He left his office and beat a hot path to her door and screamed uncontrollably at her. "You can't do this to me! Now I'm back in the harness, you make me look like a schmuck!"

"How can I make you what you already are—a schmuck?" she asked with revolting sweetness. "You divorce Tina and I'll forget the Golden Oasis."

"You're out of your fucking mind!" he countered hotly.

Jolie held up the freshly inked contract. "Does this look like I'm fucking out of my mind?"

"You can't do this to me."

"I've done it."

"Give me more time. I swear it'll all be mine, soon."

"You've had all the time I can spare. Benne's out of the way. What's holding you back?" She tossed the contract on the desk. "You even took care of him, didn't you? Don't lie, Renzo. I know you too well. Besides, Beauty, you talk in your sleep."

Renzo had a moment ago felt tired, bereft of energy, as if he could no longer summon the strength to combat her. Now he came awake. His spine tingled. Warning lights dotted his mind, chilling him. "It's not that easy, Jolie. Big money deals take time." He chose to ignore her last remarks.

"So? Take your time. Take all the time you need. Meanwhile I'll be at the Golden where big things are happening."

"Yeah, yeah, kid. Big things are happening all right," he muttered. *If you only knew, it's me making them happen.*

At the termination of her contract she moved into her newly furbished suite at the Golden Oasis, where Marciano and his staff feted her royally at a shindig drawing raves from the press and reported in all the trades and syndicated theater columns the world over.

The moment Renzo heard the news via the trades, his thinking went into high gear. He knew there was no dissuading Jolie. What then could he do to turn her departure into a personal success of his own? Nothing could have been more newsworthy when Jolie's intent to leave the Pyramids was shoved onto the back burners in the trade papers, obscured by the startling announcement that the Pyramids Hotel had just signed Dancey Darling to headline Cleopatra's Barge.

Instant speculation spread like wildfire about what was considered the shrewdest move in Las Vegas. Imagine Dancey Darling headlining an act on stage, in person! It would be the hottest act ever to find its way into Vegas, if it could be pulled off. There wasn't a man or woman who hadn't thrilled to her on the big screen who wouldn't pay plenty to see her in person. Screw the bad publicity she'd been getting. She was still Dancey Darling!

Reservations poured in, flooding the Pyramids' phones the day the announcement hit the trades. Manny Marciano, hotter than a pistol when advised of Renzo's *coup de théâtre*, picked up the phone to chew him out. "You fucking prick! What the hell's wrong with you, hiring that junkie, hopheaded cunt to work for you? You realize she could blow your cover to hell and back?" He exploded furiously.

Renzo tried but was unable to cool him off. It was like trying to stop a ten-ton Mack truck with an upraised fist.

When he finally got Manny cooled down to where he'd listen, Renzo tried to explain. "Listen, Jolie's departure left me in a helluva fix. I had to come up with something to explain to the old man—my father-in-law. Dancey's got to be the biggest draw since Elvis Presley. I can control her. You forget she'll do anything for a fix. Her loyalty is to me. I can make it work, Manny. Old Renzo hasn't lost his touch."

The silence at Marciano's end was like the beginning rumbling of an active volcano. His voice was equally as deadly.

"She's a mainliner with a five C-habit a day. Can you control that? Look, I ain't trying ta put ya down, kid, for trying. But, you'd better fucking know what you're doing. She's been speedballing, stardusting, and goofballing it when the fences dummy up to her. Shit, man, she's even gone to croakers for the stuff when her connections cut her off."

"I know, I know, I know . . ." Renzo muttered brokenly. "I tell you, Manny, I've got her under control. There ain't a bagman who'll sell her without my sayso. We've been feeding her blanks from time to time, see? To cut down her habit."

"What are you, a missionary all of a sudden?" rasped Manny.

Renzo's stomach knotted and churned violently. "I need her box office draw, Manny. I tell you I can control her. All she needs to make her work is a big Sicilian cock inside her and enough junk to keep her happy. I'll get her down to where she'll only be chipping, you hear? She won't be coasting while she works here. Whadda I need? Two weeks of solid show biz stuff. After that who gives a fuck? If she's a solid hit, I'll cross that bridge when I come to it. If she's a flop—it ain't no skin off my nose."

"Just so you understand where I'm coming from, kid, ya better listen and listen good. My nose smells trouble, hear? If she fucks up what I've worked for—you'll be the one wearing a concrete kimono. You'll be buried in the desert as buzzard bait."

Renzo was stupified. This was the first time Manny had ever threatened him. They'd had words before, angry words and lousy temperament exploding all around them, but not like this.

Manny himself was surprised at his own words, but no regrets followed. "I mean it, kid. This is the first time you've done anything so flat out stupid. It's fucking crazy! *You're* fucking crazy!" He hung up.

Manny hadn't told Renzo anything he hadn't already told himself a thousand times. He deliberated two full weeks before contacting her agent. She'd never remember him. A mainlining junkie couldn't have remembered him, in that dark, dismal flea trap, the Sinaloa. Hell, he couldn't have made her out if he didn't know her from her pictures. What the hell! He'd handle it. He had the wherewithal to keep her kind of woman happy. All that cunt needed was a good screwing by a real man, who could feed her a line of bullshit on the side. He'd already sunk fitty grand in her career, getting the show together. The reports from Hollywood were encouraging. She was busily at work learning dance routines with a six-man back up. Renzo didn't depend on reports from her agent, he'd sent his own scouts in to check rehearsals at the Peck Dance Studios on Robertson where the choreographer was working his butt off putting the show together. They reported, "The broad's got plenty of magic, boss. Believe it or not, she's behaving."

Renzo's aim was to prove to Val he had more on the ball than ten Bennes. One thing Val understood was numbers. Numbers talked.

By damned, he'd done it! Ten solid weeks of booked

reservations for both dinner and late shows. More came in daily from their Los Angeles, New York, Chicago and Miami booking offices. That meant long lines at the casino, plenty of spenders while waiting for showtime. He'd already planned to bring a planeload of biggies from Hollywood for a rousing opening night, just for moral support. Sinatra planned to attend. Dean Martin, even Carson booked reservations for more than two dozen guests. The list of superluminaries was formidable; the Pyramids would make show biz history.

Screw Jolie Barnes! Screw them all! He intended to make Las Vegas sit up and take notice of him. He should have felt elated. He didn't. He'd never felt worse.

The man they all accepted as Benne was here on the scene. Jolie had left him for good, causing him to lose face among his peers. What really stuck in his craw was the way Tina had boldly led her guests to the Golden to pay homage to the woman who'd left him high and dry. She knew how to stick it where it really hurt.

Renzo, alone, licked his wounds, reflecting on the wisdom of bringing a tiger into a lion's den.

At the Golden Oasis, Marciano lay naked on the bed, serviced by the three whores. Trixie, the blonde, was paid and sent packing. Something about her reminded him of his wife and it turned him off. The brunette, Titanic, with enormous, oversized silicone boobs that bounced, shimmied and shook, remained, with the redhead, who entered Manny's room provocatively flinging him her usual, "Hi, I'm Dallas. Come fly with me."

Manny dug Titanic, proficient as hell with her oral manipulations that drove him into a frenzy; she had the most educated tongue in Vegas. But his eyes were on Dallas. Jaded in his sexual proclivities since he came to Vegas, where hot and cold running broads in all sizes and descriptions were as abundant as gambling chits for your dough, it took a helluva scene to get Manny going; a *ménage à deux, à trois, à quatre*—any kinky scene in numbers moved him.

Dallas, a stunner, mounted him, burying her boobs in his face as he sucked greedily on her nipples; Titanic meanwhile serviced him orally, cock, balls and ass. Watching Dallas, fantasizing a solo sojourn with her, he shot off a load in less time than it took a jackrabbit to sprint through a bed of cactus. It surprised the shit out of him,

196

and made him take another look at Dallas with more discerning eyes. Fuck! She'd whammied him!

While he rested, a lesbian act. Shit, in no time he was worked up again. They knew what they were doing, keeping one eye on his pulsating cock. Pausing, they lit up a joint. Instantly the acrid sweet smell of pot reached his nostrils. Titanic held the joint towards him. Taking a toke from the reefer, he muttered, "There's plenty to drink, cunts." Another toke. "This is great grass." Pot, hash, even pill freaks he could take—but he nixed anyone on horse. He'd seen too many cunts fucked on it.

Titanic felt a buzzing in her head and wetness from her cunt. "Y-e-a-h," she stretched the word. "This is the best. Christ, I'm almost coming."

Manny grabbed her breasts, giving them a squeeze, then worked the nipples, those rosy-brown hard ons, until she felt pain. "Fucking bastard," she muttered through lidded eyes. "You wanna play rough, sweetie?" She came at him, connecting to his face with a loud stinging slap. Manny's cock shot up. Titanic, laughing as Dallas sat before him masturbating, spilled a vial of cocaine onto her long fingernail and snorted, first through one, then the other nostril. A faint numbness, at once icy cold, the powder exploded in her brain. Through glazed eyes, she caressed Dallas, and laid her down on the bed. Instantly they were at each other, sixty-nining, much to Manny's delight.

He watched them, one hand caressing Titanic's ass, the other on Dallas's tits. The women squirmed, writhed and moaned in delight, making noises Manny always found appealing. Something about two broads making it . . .

Manny suddenly wanted in. He shoved his cock into one of them, not sure who. Titanic screamed in orgasm, clutching at him. "Faster, faster, you fucking prick! Don't stop!" she screamed in sheer agony. Manny complied, his hoarse voice barely able to make himself heard as he collapsed on the bed, his breathing heavily labored. He strained to move. Titanic sprinted for the bathroom leaving Dallas to fend for herself.

Manny caught his breath, returning to earth, and raised himself slightly to find Dallas sitting up on one elbow watching him, an amused smile on her freckled face.

"Too much for you, Mr. M.? You aren't a tough customer, you're just a pussycat."

"So, a pussycat? Wanna make another C-note? I'll show you, pussycat."

"Just so you aren't too kinky."

"Nothing like that. You turn me on. First time, I swear."

She stared at the fuzzy new hair on his head. "Your wife here?"

"Nah. In Arizona buying a house. Dumb broad. I build a gold mine in Vegas. She fucking wants to live in a desert. There ain't enough desert here? Shit, that's life, ya take the good with the bad."

Titanic reentered the room. Manny told her, "Take what you think you earned from the top of the chest."

Taking in the cozy pair she shrugged indifferently. Pulling a C-note from the thick pile, shaking it delicately in the air, she asked, "This O.K.?"

"Take another and get lost."

Titanic took the bait and grabbing her jeans and shirt in one hand, her boots and tote in the other, dressed as she left.

An hour later, surprised at the passion he'd worked up over Dallas, he said, "Believe me, kid, this ain't happened to me in a long time. You've gotta be what the doctor ordered. Hey, you wanna be my girl?"

The wheels turned in Dallas's mind. "A girl's gotta make a living."

"Hell, I'll make it worth your while, kid."

"Call me Dallas, not kid. How much worth my while?"

"Whaddya make now?"

She laughed. "Depends on how many Charlie Schlongs I get."

"Charlie Schlongs? What the hell's a Charlie Schlong?"

Dallas began by telling him about David Martin, raving about his big cock and his lusty appetite with broads. Manny listened, vaguely at first, then, as she rambled, he learned that Richie had hired her again for a romp in the hay with his boss Benne Erice. But when she went to his apartment, it turned out to be the same Charlie Schlong who'd given her three C-notes, David Martin.

Still, most of what she told him went in one ear and out the other. He made his deal with her. "You be my girl for a while and when, and if, we find we're good for each other, we'll take it from there. Fair enough?"

Dallas shrugged. Her eyes were on the pile of hundreds on the bureau top. Manny, catching this, waved her on.

"Go ahead, honey, help yourself. No more than five— get it?"

Dallas squealed with delight. "Got it!"

She sprinted across the room and lifted each bill carefully. If she played her cards right . . . She counted mentally. Five a night three or four times would come to— maybe two grand? Phew! She ran back, placed her arms around the huge apelike shoulders.

"Oh, thank you, Manny, baby. I'll be your girl."

"G'wan, get dressed and split. I got work to do." He was suddenly brusque with her. He slipped into his robe and waited until she was dressed to see her out of the apartment.

She kissed him on the lips. Manny patted her round ass, squeezing it as she left, and locked the door behind her.

He was in the shower, feeling invigorated from the blow jobs and the needlelike spray of hot water awakening the nerves in his body, setting it atingle, when it suddenly struck him.

He jerked shut the shower door, grabbed a towel, dotting at the wetness, his face screwed up into a puzzled frown. Then he wrapped his body with the towel and grabbed the phone off the wall.

He growled into the phone at the operator. "Get my wife on the phone. Arizona—someplace, uh, Tucson, I think. You've got the number, Natalie. Call me back the minute you got her. On my private phone," he added, slamming down the receiver.

In the living room, Manny poured himself a stiff glass of bourbon. His heart was beating too fast; he could feel it. The excitement was too much for him. When the phone rang, he couldn't answer it immediately. Finally, on the fourth ring, he managed to remove it from its cradle. Words wouldn't come.

"Manny?"

Finally, he managed a "Yeah, yeah."

"Well, what do you want?"

"Lannie? It's you. Uh, oh yeah. When are you coming back?"

"Manny, is something wrong? You don't sound like yourself."

"No. Nothing's wrong. I just miss you. When you coming back?"

"Oh, for pity's sake. I just got here two days ago. I planned on staying at least a week."

"Talk to me, Baby," he said quietly. "I miss you."

"Oh, I get it," she said, relief evident in her voice. "You just feeling horny again? Is that it? You want me to make with the sexual fantasies again? You can't wait, can you? O.K. Who do you want me to be now? Which of the sexpots turned you on?"

They spoke in low voices. Lannie, a former showgirl, had snared Manny, marrying him a year ago. They fantasized nightly over the other gorgeous women, mentally making love to them, the stunning sexy wenches of screen, stage and girlie magazine centerfolds. Manny finally got to the point he intended to reach in the first place. "Tell me about Jolie Barnes and what's his name?"

"You mean Benne?" queried the obliging Lannie. She'd had an affair with Benne before she met Manny. "Why him? Let me tell you about Renzo and me—"

"First Benne and Jolie . . ."

Manny listened, his eyes narrowing in interest. He feigned ejaculation, breathing hard, and heard his wife laugh. "Did ya use the vibrator, Lannie? Good girl. Stay the week. I missed you and wanted to jerk off with you. Is that so bad? Hey—it's better I jerk off with you than fuck the broads in the joint."

A smile of satisfaction stretched over his lips. So, it was an impostor taking Benne's place! Could he have fooled Val so easily? *Benne's dead! There was no way he could've come out alive. No way. We'll see how this ball game is played.*

At the slot machines he fished five coins from the tray and inserted them in the proper slots. Yanking the handle hard, he turned away thinking about the hoax being perpetrated in the Erice arena. Clanging sounds of coins spewing forth from the machine plus the loud clanging sounds of bells stopped him cold.

"The fucking machine paid off!" He screamed with delight. "A fucking jackpot! Manny, this is your lucky day!" he squealed.

CHAPTER FIFTEEN

Christina Erice sat bolt upright in bed, the image of David Martin's left hand flashing before her eyes. *Sweet Mary, Mother of God!* There'd been no scar on David's hand! On her feet, she paced the floor, smoking incessantly. Scars could disappear over the years, she rationalized. How long ago had it been—thirty-some years, for pity's sake.

She stewed and fretted until a gnawing hard knot formed at the pit of her stomach, twisting her intestines until she could hardly breathe. God, how she wanted David to be Benne! For herself, for Val, and for Tina especially, who'd deteriorated after Benne's reported death.

God, she'd searched his face, his eyes, his nose, noticing the same fine lines and scars on his handsome face. His body, strong and supple, couldn't be counterfeit. It had to be Benne. It had to. *Lord save us if he isn't!*

If it wasn't Benne . . . If it wasn't Benne, then who was David Martin and why would he willingly assume Benne's identity? What sort of man would play so foul and loathsome a trick on an unsuspecting family? Why would he do it? For what gain?

. . . Holy Mary, Mother of God, pray for us . . .

Christina, hardly ever taken into Val's confidence in matters of business, wasn't so sheltered from his affairs that she couldn't recognize a danger to him and their family by this imposter, if he was an impostor.

Christina rose from her bed, and walked out onto the terrace into the torrid heat of the desert night. She had to come to a decision—she had to! She wrung her hands and paced the carpeted roof garden, filled with anxiety.

Perhaps if she talked with David Martin, mother to son, describing the incident in their lives when they shared the secret of his injury? No, that wouldn't do. He had no memory. *Jesus, Mary and Joseph!* She came to an abrupt stop. Had she looked at the right hand, in the right place? No, the left hand—or was it the right? Now she was confused. Besides, she reasoned, she hadn't worn her glasses. God knew she couldn't see close up without them.

She dashed inside, turning on the night light next to her bed. She studied the lines on her hand. Then, putting on her glasses, she glanced at her hand again. There was a difference. Without her glasses she couldn't see most of the fine lines between the usual deep lines on a human palm. She fell on the bed heavily, a sigh of relief expelled from her lips. She sank back against the pillows, her eyes closed, breathing deeply. *I worried over nothing,* she thought, as sleep engulfed her.

The next morning, she awakened early. She showered, dressed in her robe and went into the kitchen to fix coffee for herself and Val.

She carried in a tray of coffee brewed as he liked it, with a plate of confections Val loved, but had abstained from for a long time. One or two wouldn't hurt, she thought. Placing the tray on the nearby table, Christina sat on the bed alongside Val as he stirred awake. He yawned, sat up, sniffing the air gingerly with appreciation, his eyes lighting up at the confections.

Val had sipped his first cup of coffee and devoured three cookies before she expressed her earlier fears. In an emotional outpouring she mentioned the absence of scars on David's hand. She hadn't worn glasses, perhaps that explained it. "Val, before confiding in him, will you search for the scars?"

He listened intently, and reached over to pat her hands tenderly, nodding reassuringly. "Don't worry. It will turn out fine. You'll see, my dear."

"Then you're sure it's Benne? You believe it with your heart?"

"Do you?" His voice was quiet, solemn and probing.

"I believed it, until I recalled seeing no scars." Her eyes lit up brightly, the need to believe urgent. "He could have had them removed surgically." Anything to dispel her fears.

"Anything's possible," Val said, shoving aside the tray. He rose from the bed and walking into the bathroom, turned on the shower. He poked his head out at his wife. "Ring Richie's room for me. Tell him it's time to pick up Maria Rossi."

"You sent for her?"

"She's Emilio's woman. It's only right that she be summoned."

"Yes," she said picking up the phone. "You did right."

Christina passed on Val's instructions when Richie came on the line. "I'm on my way," he muttered sleepily.

Val had confided to Christina that Emilio had died. He told her nothing of the cruel way in which he'd met his Maker. "Say nothing to no one yet," he cautioned.

"It's not necessary to caution me, Val. I've known my place from the beginning."

Val, wincing at her candor, said nothing in rebuttal. He showered, reconsidering her words, wondering how she'd take to the presence of Maria Rossi and what must later follow. He dreaded the encounter; but what choice had he? Val had made no spur of the moment decision in summoning Emilio's woman to Las Vegas. He needed straight answers only she could provide. Erroneous information had been disgorged; he was ready for truth.

Finished with his personal grooming, he dressed himself in casual grey flannel trousers and a grey silk shirt, thinking of the conversation he'd had with old Doctor Barone yesterday.

The man had grown senile, forgetful, incoherent of speech. Val had a difficult time making himself understood. Once the amenities were over he got to the point, asking him the name of the woman who'd worked for him so many years. Val, ashamed to admit it, couldn't remember Emilio's woman's name.

"Maria Rossi!" came the aging man's voice.

"Maria Rossi?" he echoed back, wondering, as something nagged at his mind. "Maria Rossi?"

"Maria Rossi," the doctor shouted again. "Whassa matter, Val, you don't know the mistress of Emilio? It's the same woman who helped me deliver Bennie when he was born." He gave Val her phone number and hung up before Val could properly thank him.

The bells rang. Doors opened in his mind. Maria Rossi —tall, thin, angular, in her fifties, a striking woman with white streaked hair.

He'd seen her with Emilio once or twice recently, but his recollections of the woman who accompanied Dr. Barone to his house in Long Island, after Genny Martinelli delivered Benne, was vague, hazy, and impaired by the passage of time.

Five years ago Emilio confessed his affair with Maria, insisting he was too old to marry her, but expressing his desire that she be well provided for after his death, since there was no one else in his life. He didn't want her devotion to go unrewarded, since she'd filled an empty vacuum in his life and given him happiness and companionship. For this reason Val felt a responsibility to notify her of Emilio's death after he got her number from Dr. Barone. Maria, no hysteric, expressed profound grief and genuine sorrow. Many years in the nursing profession with the visibility of death around her every hour of the day had provided her with excellent control. She insisted on coming to Vegas and transporting his body back for burial. Val made all the arrangements, cautioning her to say nothing to anyone about the matter.

A silence fell upon them when Val entered the living room. Maria Rossi, seated next to Christina on the pale blue damask sofa, dabbed at her red-rimmed, swollen eyes. Christina consoled her.

Val, at her side, commiserating gently, took her hand in his. "I can't express the deep sorrow I feel at the loss of so dear and valuable a friend," he said. "I share your loss greatly. Emilio has been like a brother to me, Signora Rossi."

"Have you found his killer?" she asked with remarkable control.

Christina, alarmed, glanced from Maria to Val, questioning.

Before Val could reply, Maria continued, "Why would anyone kill him? He never harmed a soul. He was a good man . . ."

Val nodded. "No one knew better than I. These things happen. When they do, they leave confusion, questions that cannot be answered, and too many sorrow-filled people behind to mourn the departed." He released her hand and poured three glasses of red wine. He handed one glass to Maria.

"Shall I leave, Val?" asked Christina, sensing his need to speak intimately with the woman. She too, had to do some thinking.

"Please, my dear, remain. I need you concerning some old business." He handed her a glass and held the third in his hand. "First, we drink to the dear departed soul of a beloved man. May his soul rest in peace for all eternity."

They clinked glasses and sipped in silence.

Maria watched Val bring a wing-backed chair into their circle and sit down with a confidential air. Christina remained on the sofa next to Maria.

"Something is wrong," said Maria. "Apart from Emilio's death."

Val placed his wine glass on the low table before him. "Nothing to frighten you, my dear. It's against my nature to trouble you in such moments when you are aggrieved. Is it true, Signora Rossi, you were present at the birth of my son, Benne?"

"It was me. Don't be formal. Call me Maria."

Christina froze.

"Do you recall much about that night?"

"It was a long time ago . . ."

"A very long time ago. You won't be faulted if your memory has dulled."

"My memory is sharp," she said defensively. "I recall everything about that night. I admired your courage, how well you bore up in light of the tragedy."

Christina and Val exchanged perplexed glances. Val frowned. Dr. Barone had really grown senile. Christina sat forward.

"Tragedy, Maria? What tragedy do you speak of?"

Maria tensed. Wary, apprehensive, ill at ease, she wasn't sure what was expected of her. She glanced from one to the other.

"Suppose you start at the beginning," suggested Val quietly.

"Why would you wish to dwell on unhappy moments? I dislike stirring ashes of painful memories."

"Explain, if you will, step by step, what happened after you arrived with Dr. Barone." He stimulated her memory. "It was a hot night, you arrived shortly before Mario and his wife left my house . . ."

Maria sat stiffly upright, sipping her wine delicately, wiping her lips primly with her fingertips. "The baby had already been delivered, as you know. We took Christina upstairs to her bedroom, where the doctor examined both mother and child, to make certain there were no abnormalities, then I let you nurse the infant for a time," she added glancing at Christina.

"Dr. Barone insisting on examining the placenta—the afterbirth. I went downstairs into the room the child was born and found nothing. In the laundry room. I found the bloodstained sheets. The placentas were rolled in newspaper in the garbage pail."

"*Placentas?* There was more than one?" Christina's shrill voice jarred Maria.

Maria, nodding, continued. "I brought them to Dr. Barone and when he saw two placentas, he was as astonished as I."

Christina's hands flew to her lips in shock. She was aghast. Her eyes took on curious opaque lights; she trembled visibly as a flood of old thoughts punctured her consciousness. *Oh, dear God,* she mumbled internally. *What next?*

"Dr. Barone instructed me to say nothing to Christina or you until after he spoke with Mrs. Martinelli. Later I learned that he did speak with the woman and she informed him one child had been stillborn. She withheld the information so as not to inflict sorrow upon you, since you'd already suffered the loss of two children."

Christina's face had drained of color. She sucked in her breath as faint recollections came at her in the form of images that had haunted her over the years, like spectral dreams which had no beginnings, no ends. Vaguely she recollected the euphoria, the giddiness brought on by the amount of bourbon she had consumed that night. She tried to go back over the events of that night and failed. After so many years how could she recollect every detail, every second of what had transpired? All she'd ever been able to do was piece together a lingering feeling of emptiness that had persisted over the years.

Twins! Imagine, twins! Aggrieved, she turned to Val. "Why would Genny keep such a thing from us?" she despaired. "The excuse she gave the doctor isn't enough." Suddenly she gave a start.

"Val! You don't think . . ." She stopped short.

"It's all right," he said, trying to console her, telegraphing silent signals to say nothing else. "Perhaps Genny thought she was doing the right thing. It's regrettable the doctor didn't inform us. But let's not burden Maria with our affairs." He turned to the former nurse. "I'll take you to Emilio now."

"Yes, I would like that," she said, rising.

"Uh, one more thing, Maria. Did the doctor keep the death certificate of the deceased infant on file?"

"I recall he made the birth certificate out and sent it to you. I also recall thinking it odd that he kept the death certificate on file for so long without sending it to you. In time we forgot about it."

Richie arrived with the albino German shepherd, Sadge, Benne's dog. Val instructed Richie to take Maria to Emilio. "I'll join you momentarily."

His immediate attention was showered on the frisky and elated dog, ruffling his neck, petting him enthusiastically.

The animal barked excitedly, scooting about, wagging his tail happily.

"What does it all mean, Val?" She referred to Maria's words as well as the sudden appearance of Benne's old dog. Sometime during the night someone had flown to Long Island and brought the animal here to Las Vegas.

"I'm not certain. But I intend to find out," he said solemnly.

"You think that—"

"Not yet, Christina," he said, trying to calm the animal. "If Martin should turn out to be Benne's twin, the implications are too grotesque to contemplate. He'd have to be a desperate man to attempt so dangerous a deception as to pass himself off as Benne. It's this desperation that I question and find frightening." He leaned over to kiss her, compassionately. "Keep Sadge out of sight until I ask for him, will you? There's my girl."

Christina walked into his arms, melting against him, her arms encircling his waist, her head on his chest as she listened to his heartbeats, a sprinkling of tears down her cheeks.

"Oh my dearest, what you must be experiencing." She was disconsolate, bordering on heartbreak. "From the first day I saw you, when you came to live with us, I fell in love with you. Over the years I've come to respect you, thanking God every day for bringing me so wonderful a husband and father to our children. You've kept me sheltered, immune from most hurts, Val. Perhaps too much so. I've always trusted your judgment—still do. But, for once, will you listen to the woman who adores you? What precious time is left for us, let us spend it together without more separation. I don't think I could live without you."

Val held her close, inhaling the fragrance of her cologne, her daintiness, and the very essence of her. At their age, the tenderness between them was genuine. She'd given him freedom to do all he'd done in his lifetime. Now it was one last plea for her tolerance and understanding that was needed.

"It's nearly over, *cara mia*. I have to enter the arena once more. We'll be together as you wish." He lifted her chin so their eyes met and kissed her forehead, the tip of her nose, then, lightly, her lips. "Now, go, before I forget I've work to do. I promise I shall not permit myself to become vulnerable to anyone."

"Not even if he is our son?"

She took the dog and left Val standing, watching her, profound thought etched into his features. He was tired, but this news disintegrated the fatigue and gave him a new rush of energy.

For the next few hours Val performed the necessary duties required of him as Emilio's friend and employer. He arranged for Maria, under the strictest of security, to accompany the body back to New York. She agreed to keep the entire affair quiet after Val confided, "It's the only way I can hope to uncover his killer."

He arrived back at the penthouse office around noon. Urgent calls from Captain Ferraro had stockpiled. He returned the call and listened for a time to the officer's frustration pour from his lips.

"Something crazy's going on, Val. The prints from the dice cup have been identified, here and in Washington. Get this—Washington reports they are Benne's prints. Locally they don't compute. How the hell do you figure it?"

"Did you check them with Benne's prints on file with the Gambling Commission?"

"Got the report in front of me. Godammit! Something stinks to high heaven. They don't check with those sent to Washington, but two telex inquiries sent to the FBI confirms them as Benedetto Erice's."

Val pondered a moment. "Keep this to yourself, Frankie. I'll get back to you in a while." He rang off. No matter how skillfully he masked his frustration, Val was beginning to crumble bit by bit.

A hot, brilliant silence fell in the study permeated with the fresh smells of new leather, wax and tobacco. Val sat with hands folded on the desk, in a stark solitude in which there were no sounds as he pieced together the parts of a puzzle he'd labeled David Martin. His heart pounded in his ears.

He reached into his shirt pocket for a nitro tablet, slipped it under his tongue, waiting for the discomfort to pass and the angina to subdue. Then, pursuing the only avenue open to him, he placed a telephone call to David Martin.

Fifteen minutes later David joined Val on the sunlit terrace, freshly showered, shaven and wearing casual Levis, an open shirt and sandals. A bright smile spread across his face.

For an instant when Val caught sight of him, his heart

quickened. He thought, *Benne, my beloved son, it's really you! All this other business is merely a nightmare* . . .

"Hi!" said David, ogling the serving cart ladened with chafing dishes with food for lunch. "Can't think of anything I need more than a hot cup of coffee." Martin stopped abruptly, paling under his tan at the sight of the albino shepherd, who jumped up and sprinted forward with a few loud barks only to stop suddenly in his tracks, eyeing David with deference as he sniffed the air, faltering again, then sauntering over to him, turning abruptly, curling up, and lying down at Val's feet, gazing at Martin in what appeared to be contemplation.

"Hi, there, boy," said Martin. "Where did you come from?" he mumbled, careful not to call the animal by the name he'd memorized. In that moment he died a thousand deaths, thanking the Lord the animal wasn't belligerent.

Val, feigning indifference to the animal's reaction, poured coffee into their cups. Behind them, a brilliant backdrop of desert stretched to infinity in the haze of the sun's glare. The white buildings clustered to their left, bleached whiter by the sun, were impossible to look at without benefit of dark-lensed glasses. Val had removed his. David wore none, but shade from an umbrella on a glass table shielded him from the hot glare temporarily.

Val, seated opposite David, sipped his coffee while David consumed scrambled eggs and sausage. Richie was seated nearby engrossed in the morning papers, shaded by a planter box containing a *ficus benjamina* with full green foliage.

"Who are you, David Martin?" asked Val quietly, his voice barely audible to him. "You aren't my son Benne. So, tell me, why the diabolical plot to stamp out a carbon copy of him?"

Val's voice, cold and deadly, brought a reaction from Sadge. He tensed, growling low in his throat until Val's hand signal stayed him. Richie's head jerked up, his eyes darting to Martin, tensing uncomfortably, wondering what Val was up to. It was a tight, crucial and shattering moment in which Martin's face drained of color. Val remained resolute, his blue eyes sparking as the moments ticked off.

Well, thought Martin, *here it is*. What he had feared would happen had happened sooner than expected. *It was the animal's reaction*, he rationalized. *You can't fool a dog*. Benne's cologne, his clothing, nothing had fooled the albino. The bomb had exploded. There was no way for Martin to go. He knew Val was on to something. If he lied or continued the farce he'd lose everything he'd worked for. If he spoke the truth he just might survive. He gambled against the greatest odds in history, one in a million.

"I am the son of Mario Martinelli. You remember him, don't you?"

Val's lips parted, expressing his utter amazement for one brief moment. The moment passed and Val turned stony.

"Is this another lie, another deception? Will you not be honest with me, now that your life depends on it?"

"I'm speaking the truth," David said tightly. The food had turned into a heavy ball in his stomach.

Val wagged his hand in a gesture of resignation. "Mario Martinelli and his wife never had a child. Genevieve was barren." It was a simple statement that signalled the truth to Martin.

Astonishment moved across his face like a tidal wave. He stammered, "But I've a birth certificate. I was born November 20, 1934 in Brooklyn, New York to Genevieve and Mario Martinelli. Later my mother changed our name to Martin. I never knew the name Martinelli until recently. We moved to Buffalo when I was very young."

Val grasped the implications long before Martin did. Something instinctive, something innate in his nature telegraphed the truth to him. His somber blue eyes met those of his bodyguard's for an instant. He noticed Richie's sudden paleness, the alert stance of an animal ready for the kill. In the maze of confused emotions, Val thought that nothing in his long and varied career had prepared him for such an excruciating moment. As he turned his eyes back on David Martin, Val couldn't help thinking it was all a part of a mad scheme concocted by a wizard of the lower depths. Things like this didn't happen. It couldn't be real—but it was. Perhaps in time he could accept it.

Benne, my loving son, is dead. Now, here is Benne's twin brother taking his place. His son, whom he hadn't seen—not even at birth—had suddenly materialized before his eyes. Imagine! It seemed a millenium passed before he could rise to his feet. Totally overwhelmed by the truth laid out before him, Val excused himself. Sadge sprang to his feet to follow him as if Martin didn't exist.

"Please remain here, Mr. Martin, until I return. Richie will remain with you." It was a polite indication that he wasn't free to leave.

Martin, himself staggered by the implication of Val's earlier words, struggled internally for some explanation for what Val had alluded to. He searched his memory for recollections of the woman who had raised him as her own. As the small germ of truth threatened to rise in him, he felt a sinking sensation. He poured more coffee for himself and lit up a cigarette with trembling hands, and stared off into space, in silence.

Val found Christina almost as he left her earlier, curled up on a corner of the sofa wearing a pale blue kaftan, reading her Bible. She glanced at him, alerted by the expression on his face.

"Now can you tell me what this is all about?"

Val glanced at his watch. It was not quite 11:00 A.M. "What time does Tina awaken?"

"They came in late. She left a 1:00 P.M. call." She studied her husband critically, a sinking feeling at the pit of her stomach. "Val?" she called imperatively. "What does it all mean?"

In the past half hour Val had aged a decade. He sat down next to his wife on the sofa searching for an easy way to explain the confounding enigma that had just unraveled in his mind. Sadge curled up at his feet, unwilling to let Val out of his sight.

IAGO was suddenly forgotten. The Shivertons became incidental. Renzo's deception, Emilio's death, Tina's frustrations, the corporate troubles—all became meaningless. No one and nothing else mattered at this moment except Christina and his personal life with her. He feared the emotional insulation she'd built up over the years might disintegrate, but he only knew of one way to talk — straight out.

"What does it mean, my dear? What does it all mean?" He sighed despairingly. "It means that David Martin is our son. Benne's twin brother. The infant we never saw and knew nothing about didn't die as Maria Rossi thought, but was plucked from us by Genny Martinelli to raise as her own son. God rest her soul."

He held Christina's hands tightly. "Do you understand what I'm saying? David Martin is the flesh of our flesh, blood of our blood, the seed of my seed who sprang from your loins."

For several moments a look of insane confusion caused

211

her eyeballs to glitter unnaturally. She stared straight ahead, her lips moving, her voice agonized.

"And Abram said, Lord God, what wilt thou give me seeing I go childless, and the steward of my house is this Eliezer of Damascus? And Abram said Behold, to me thou has given no seed: and lo, one born in my house is mine heir. And behold the word of the Lord came unto him, saying this shall not be thine heir; but he that shall come forth out of thine own bowels shall be thine heir . . ."

"Christina!" Val shook her gently. "Christina!" He reached over and picked up the Bible from her lap. He closed it and lay it on the table nearby, then held her in his arms, rocking her gently to and fro.

"What kind of world is this, Val? I thought Genny was our friend," she muttered at last.

"We have more important things to consider than the kind of friend Genny may or may not have been. Until I learn what devilish plot has made our own flesh and blood assume the identity of his twin brother, it's best you do not permit yourself to become attached to him."

It was more than she could endure. "As usual I'll do as you wish. But, Val," she added significantly, "Whatever you do, remember he is our son."

Val made a disorganized gesture. He kissed her forehead and left her. In moments he was back on the terrace. Richie was a mess. Very little was making sense to him. Martin, in a meditative silence, sat forward as Val approached. He watched as Val removed a small white pill from a gold container and slipped the pellet under his tongue.

"What will you do now, Mr. Erice?" he asked politely.

"Whoever planned this chicanery nearly succeeded, Mr. Martin. Nearly everything, with the exception of a mother and son's secret, was taken into account. I admit you nearly succeeded in the flimflamming. Incidently, may I see your left hand?" Val asked.

Moved by the peculiar request David glanced down at his hand curiously. He offered it to Val reluctantly, wondering. They had been so meticulous in their planning, so exact . . .

Val tried desperately to locate what in his heart he knew didn't exist. He told Martin the secret Christina had shared with him that morning. "No one could have known the existence of such a scar except for Benne and

212

his mother. Those artists who attempted to create you in Benne's image, beyond the work of God, didn't include it in their blueprints."

"What will you do with me now?" Martin pressed, almost glad the farce had ended.

"What would you have me do with my own son?" Val countered softly.

Martin flushed in annoyance. "We both know I'm not Benne. Why continue the farce?"

"Who speaks of Benne?" Val was unable to subdue the internal agony he felt in this instant. "Would it shock you to learn you are really Benne's twin brother? You were taken from us the night you were born by a neurotic and profoundly obsessed woman whose desire to bear a child manifested into a compulsion to steal one. Yes, it's true. Mrs. Martinelli plucked you from my wife's womb the night she bore twins. How she got you out of our house without detection and raised you staggers my imagination. What courage! What insanity! But then, no power is as mystifying as the need for woman to procreate."

It was a pivotal moment. The action of this drama assumed a quick and catastrophic new turn, a reversal of postures, one which presented severe complications and acute emotional trauma to all the players. None was as affected as David Martin.

He was unable to catch his breath. Gasping, he managed to speak above a whisper. "If you're trying to make me feel shabby, you've succeeded. This is—too incredible."

"You prefer it to be a coincidence? The same birthday, coloring, eyes, build. We were very close, Mario's family and mine." Val explained how it was with Genny, a registered nurse, barren, mentally distorted by her obsession. He explained what happened atfer Mario was killed and how Genny left Brooklyn like a thief in the night.

"It's even more difficult for me to understand," Val said sadly.

"It's true what my Don tells you," spoke up Richie. "I myself saw you at the door the night Mario died. Thinking you were Benne, I insisted on taking you back to Long Island. Mrs. Martinelli told me I was mistaken, that you were her son, David."

David chainsmoked. Dark shadows out of his past shifted and moved before his eyes. So much came together in his mind, unusual emotions he'd experienced in

213

the past of which twins often complain: elation when in the throes of depression, depression when in the throes of elation.

Val continued to explain what he'd learned from the doctor and nurse in attendance, about the two placentas, a death certificate and all Maria Rossi had told him. "Coincidence, Mr. Martin?"

Undeniable evidence in the chain of recollections shook Martin to the core. The atmosphere for him became like molten lava issuing forth from the mouth of an angry volcano—dangerous, tricky and frightening.

"You're my father?" he asked Val incredulously.

"If it distresses you imagine how I must feel to learn that my own flesh and blood is part of a diabolical plot against me and his own family. It's a plot I fail to comprehend and because I don't I'm more distressed. Why would you want to impersonate Benne? What purpose would it serve? I'm not a stupid man, so, tell me why I fail to perceive the wisdom and the direction in which this fiendish conspiracy is headed?" Although Val's voice was soft and underspoken, his words were sharper than a two-edged sword.

David rose to his feet mulling the phrase over in his mind. *Val Erice is my father!* His face creased in frowns as he moved over the bricked patio. Never in his life had he conceived of this reality. To suddenly be told he was the son of a man he'd been conditioned to despise, that his life had been falsely directed, that he wasn't who he thought he was all his life was mind-boggling. Rigid training, extensive and gruelling hours of discipline, conditioning and pain added to the erection of barriers standing guard over his emotions had brought him to this end. Caught now, in an unexpected confrontation between his past and present, the tension of the past months exploded. Martin could only release the constriction through long, hard laughter. How McKenna and Soldato would take this new development tickled his fancy in a perverse way. And what about Senator Shiverton? He laughed ironically.

Watching him, Val grew stonier. "I don't appreciate your brand of humor," he snapped.

"No," said Martin. "You wouldn't. If you only knew how much it took to bring us all to this point, you'd laugh all right, sir. You'd find it very amusing. So I'm to call you Pop?"

Val's lips tightened grimly.

"Is it safe to speak freely here, sir?"

"Richie, turn up the volume on the music," requested Val. "Now you may speak with ease," he told Martin.

"You've got me—as the saying goes—by the short hairs, caught redhanded in a plot I haven't the right to divulge, even if you threaten to kill me." He held up a restraining hand against Val's objection. "Perhaps if you'll send for Senator Shiverton—"

Val tensed. *"The senator is aware of this absurd deception?"* Val's fingers drummed the glass table.

"Well, the senator only recently entered the picture. It's best you get it straight from him. I'm a special agent with the Bureau of Secret Intelligence, formerly with the FBI. He'll vouch for my credentials."

"A son of mine with the FBI? Now the BSI? The plot thickens. The implications are too grotesque to consider."

A half hour later, at Val's request, Senator Shiverton arrived. David hastily revealed his true relationship to him. Whip, having spent the majority of his life involved in intrigue and counter intrigue, had developed a sophisticated veneer insulating him from unsuspected developments, but this information devastated him. He stared from Val to David incredulously. Martin shrugged helplessly.

"It's as much of a shock to me, Senator, as it is to you."

Whip was at once instantly apologetic once the reality of Val's words penetrated.

"If any hint of your relationship was known, I'm certain the BSI would have employed other means to get to you," he muttered.

"Why was it necessary to 'get to me' through any scheme?" Val's eyes were still on the son he'd known nothing about.

"If we can discuss this new development, someplace where we won't be overheard—" Whip began.

Val drew himself up coldly. "We have nothing to say to one another." Val walked to the edge of the terrace and gazed out at the panorama. He felt a suffocation around his heart. The stress and anxiety of the past few days were taking their toll. He'd taken more nitros than he did ordinarily. Having taken Benne's suggestion to get a third opinion on his health, when it concurred with Dr. Sharp's diagnosis, his confusion had increased. Reluctantly he'd taken Larry Sharp's prescribed medication in addition to the Percodan for pain. Never forgetting Sam Linden's fate, Val seemed overly wary in this respect, bordering on paranoia.

Mistaking Val's silence for hostility and fearing he'd lost his confidence, Whip hastened to explain. "Believe me, Val, Martin's impersonation of Benne was never intended to hurt or destroy or implicate you in any conspiracy. It wasn't the BSI's intention to jeopardize you or your family."

As Val contemplated the attempted farce, lies, hypocrisy and downright deception, he felt his own personal integrity constrict. He felt as vulnerable as a battle-scarred warrior sinking into the murky waters of final defeat.

"Give me one reason why I should ever speak with you again, Senator?" Val asked, drained of politeness and civility.

"Ted Shiverton's brutal death," said Whip quietly. "Is it reason enough?"

Their eyes locked.

"Look, Val," began Whip, gesturing animatedly. "All this has been perpetuated due to my inability to communicate with you. I take full blame for my own inadequacies, my stupidity in not dealing with you on a more direct basis as Ted might have done." He paused to light a cigarette. "Shortly after Ted took office it seems he stumbled upon something rather astonishing. It begins, I suppose, with a group of men known as IAGO . . ."

Eight hours later they were still talking. They'd been joined by Ted McKenna and Phil Soldato. News had already been imparted to Chief Bowman who was on his way westward. Lunch and dinner had been served. The guests had removed their jackets and occupied the sprawling den, their jackets off, shirts open at the collar. Richie and his men stood guard at all the exits. No food or beverage entered the penthouse without Richie's inspection.

Cigarette butts were piled high in ashtrays. Empty coffee cups and soda bottles accumulated. The men, more relaxed, were still raptly involved in their discussions. Following dinner, the meeting continued.

CHAPTER SIXTEEN

Renzo Bonaparte knew something was up the instant he saw the activity surrounding Val's penthouse suite. A burning itch of curiosity incubated in his brain. He picked up the phone, called Tina's suite to see what he could learn. She hung up.

Tina angrily instructed the operator to tell all callers she was out of town on business and wouldn't return for several days. An odd thing to do in view of her family's presence in Las Vegas. But Tina had no choice.

Pacing her bedroom, wearing a turquoise silk kaftan, she smoked incessantly, pausing intermittently to study her battered and bruised face and body in the mirror. Angry splotches, swollen and red, had raised blueish weals on one side of her face and along the left side of her breasts and neck. Perplexed at her appearance, wincing at the painfully stiff areas of her body, she aggravated her memory, trying desperately to recall what had happened to her.

In Val's penthouse, the summit meeting was going hot and heavy. McKenna and Soldato, thunderstruck at David's true identity, berated themselves for not having guessed the truth; it was there all the time, staring right at them. Could they have been too close and unable to employ the proper amount of objectivity? The birth certificates, with near identical statistics, too close for coincidence, had thrown them. Perhaps they should have checked Mrs. Martinelli's background more carefully, admitted McKenna ruefully. Numb at the turn of events they found themselves staring at Val with awe and apprehension. After stalking him for so many years it was natural they should harbor animosity towards the man, after nurturing preconceived notions that put him on a level with those giants of IAGO. Observing, listening as their notions were shot down, one after another, both men became filled with considerable discomfort.

Disturbed particularly by Senator Shiverton's candor in discussing IAGO freely with Val, Whip hastened to explain to them, out of Val's hearing, that here was the one man who could tell them plenty.

"He can fill in the missing links, tie up the loose ends that for a quarter of a century have baffled the BSI."

Chief Bowman arrived in the middle of the night by jet and, taking all precautions to conceal his movements, checked into a modest motel on the Strip under a cover name. Then, dressed in casual clothing like a gawking tourist, he took a cab to the Pyramids. He rented a car under another cover and drove to a rendezvous where the others had gone to meet him, a rambling ranch house away from town.

It was a warm, pleasant night with a full moon overhead that grew paler as the dawn approached. A slight wind ruffled the tumbleweed across the desert and brought a gust of warm air into the house. The smell of bacon and eggs cooking brought a smile to Chief Bowman's ruddy face.

After a hearty breakfast, the chief was apprised of the recent developments concerning David Martin. Bowman studied Martin intently, listening as McKenna filled him in on the true facts surrounding his birth. The shock and disappointment was apparent in Bowman's eyes, as he listened to McKenna.

"So you see, Chief, it's best we disqualify Martin at this point."

David protested vehemently. "Listen, I know how you all view me and my importance to this cause. Our main objective was to get close enough to Val Erice to learn all we could about IAGO. I don't see why you think I should be disqualified. We're close enough to Mr. Erice. He's indicated to Senator Shiverton that he'll cooperate as best he can. In short he's an ally—not an enemy. Wouldn't it be perfectly justifiable for me to remain as Benne Erice and learn who was behind the conspiracy to kill him and why? There's got to be a reason beyond the obvious one—that someone wants Val Erice out of the Las Vegas action."

Val never took his eyes off David. "I thank you for that," he said. He glanced about the warm, rustic house belonging to Captain Ferraro. It was the only place they could hope to remain hidden from the prying eyes at the Pyramids.

Val listened as the agents and Senator Shiverton discussed their strategy. He experienced a feeling of suffocation; his breathing grew more labored. Once or twice he'd gotten to his feet and walked to the front door, inhaled a few breaths of clear early morning mountain air above the desert and then returned to his chair where he observed the others, saying little or nothing as if he were viewing a motion picture and feeling little or no involvement.

It seemed impossible to Val that he could alter the course of destiny. His personal involvement in this unfolding melodrama seemed inevitable. He was amazed at the information the agents had compiled about him. Whip's voice arrested his attention.

"Due to David's uncanny resemblance to Benne, they got the courage to infiltrate your world, to learn more about IAGO."

Val's concentration hadn't left David. To think he was really the seed of his loins both excited and dismayed him. How different would things have been if he'd grown up under Val's guidance? How much different . . .

"Will you, Val?" Whip repeated as Val glanced at him. "Will you cooperate—confide all you know of IAGO?" Whip moved closer to him, his eyes intent on Val's face. Whip peered intently at him, a curious expression forming on his face. "Val?" His voice alerted the others. "Val! What is it? What's wrong?" He spanned the few steps between them quickly. "McKenna! Chief! What's wrong with Val?"

David knelt at Val's side, chills shooting through him. He stared at Val's face, noticing the apparent clouding of his eyes, the trembling of his soundless lips.

"Jesus Christ! I think he's having a stroke," cried David in alarm. "Senator, quickly, in his pocket. He's been taking some pills recently."

Whip searched frantically through Val's sweater pocket and retrieved the gold pill box. He opened it and slipped a pellet under Val's tongue.

"We'd better get him back to town—to the hospital— a doctor—some place where there's help for him," urged David.

"Hospital," McKenna sorted through his mind. "Southern Nevada Memorial. It's on our way back."

Whip was sick. "We were that close," he said, holding his thumb and forefinger together, with barely a slit of light between them. "That close to answers and this has to happen."

The BSI agents slumped in discouragement. David was irked that they were so insensitive to Val's condition. But he refrained from saying anything lest it be misunderstood. After all he'd spent more of his life in law enforcement—hardly any at being Val's son. The role was new and uncomfortable. He picked Val up in his strong arms and carried him to the car outside.

"We'd better get a move on," he said gruffly. "If we save his life, it might not be a total bustout!"

Driving back towards the city, with Val propped up in the back seat of one car, a dark gloom settled on them.

"What a rotten break!" cursed McKenna.

"You're jumping the gun," Martin snapped. "Don't call in the mourning ghouls yet!" He stole a glance at Val. This was his father. He felt nothing a son should feel. Like the others he viewed Val as the possible answer to their problems. Now fate had jimmied up the works with the proverbial monkey wrench.

"Martin," said Chief Bowman, "when we arrive at the hospital you admit him. As Benne Erice you can remain with him and draw little attention. We can't risk some son-of-a-bitchin' nosey reporter roaming the halls, sniffing out a story."

"What do I say if the same nosey reporter suggests to me that Benne Erice is dead? You forget I've only recently been resurrected . . ."

"It's a chance we'll have to take. If the worms come out of the woodwork at least we'll have you in our sights."

McKenna and Soldato gave him a weak smile.

"Fine. Just fine." Martin dourly caught the full implication of the chief's words.

"We've come this far. We must see it through."

"Even though I'm not David Martinelli? Val Erice is my father."

"Goddammit, Martin! You're an employee of the United States government. A trusted federal agent. Genealogy has nothing to do with your sworn duty. You'll stay on the case until I can think of a remedy for this confounding mess. Meanwhile no one is to know you aren't Benne Erice. You don't have to publicize the fact— just don't deny it."

Martin shrugged. "You're a little late. A few already know."

Whip turned around in his seat. "Who knows? Who did you tell?"

"Me? No one. Richie was present when Val lowered the boom on me. His wife probably knows—even Tina."

"I'll handle Tina. Possibly his wife," Whip told Bowman. He turned back to David. "Think you can handle Richie?"

David shrugged dubiously. "He's loyal to his boss. I'll do my best."

Val was conscious, but unable to speak or move. Subjected to a partial paralysis induced by the medication he took, his inability to speak or move frustrated him and for a time terrified him. Fully aware of the goings on, yet helpless to communicate, he lay back viewing it all with cool objectivity.

The new medications. He should have guessed it. Earlier Whip inserted the white pellet into his mouth. He couldn't reject it. As it melted in his mouth, he could feel a hazy cloud of confusion and dizziness. Earlier when talking to Captain Ferraro he felt the same clumsiness; forgetting something in the middle of a sentence; the inability to articulate. Since his arrival in Vegas he'd taken more medication to calm his heart—more than he was used to, increasing his disorientation. Perhaps at the hospital the medics would catch it. Hospital! How could he tell them not to admit him under his real name? *Call Richie . . . Richie will know what to do.*

"Can you hear me?" asked David gently, looking at Val. "Can you move at all? Your eyes—what about your eyes?"

"Knock it off, Martin," McKenna's gruff voice interrupted him. "Can't chance aggravating his condition. Let the doctors examine him first." He leaned forward in his seat. "Take a right at the junction, Phil."

The sedan crawled into the circular drive of the emergency entrance. Martin jumped out of the back seat and rang the emergency bell urgently. A sleepy-eyed medic emerged.

"Step on it. Heart attack victim here!" he shouted.

Once Val was on the gurney, being wheeled into the hospital, David waved the others off. "See you at the hotel." He went in with Val and registered him under an alias, John Goodrich.

A resident intern verified Val's condition. He'd suffered a stroke. The extent of the damage wasn't known. He needed tests, further study. Could David tell them the name of the patient's physician?

David couldn't, but he'd get the information as soon

as possible. He ran the length of the corridor to the phone booth and made a hurried call to the Pyramids. Unable to reach Tina, he wondered at the message . . . out of town? He called Richie and told him what had happened to Val. "Don't use his real name," Richie insisted loudly. "I'll come right away."

"Richie, tell Tina. No one else."

David spotted Richie through the door of Val's room as the bodyguard reached the second floor from the stairwell. He sprang to his feet, drawing Richie inside and explaining to him that it was vital to Val's welfare that his own identity wasn't revealed. "At least not until Val recovers."

"Val's agreed to cooperate," said David. "It's the only way we can find Benne's murderers."

Richie was not sold yet. "First I talk with my Don," he said. "I see my boss first, then we talk."

Richie saw for himself the condition Val was in. Unable to hide his dismay, he asked, "What happened?" He leaned in closer to Val, asking in Sicilian, "Can you hear me, my Don? They want me to cooperate with them. How do I know this is your wish?"

From Val came nothing; no gesture, no response, not even an eye flicker—nothing! All his life Richie had taken orders. It was unacceptable to him that he should move on his own volition. An idea struck him. "My Don, first I go see Jerry. I tell him about this. I will obey his instructions. Are we in accord?"

Still nothing from Val. No matter how earnestly Richie searched Val's immobile face, no sign came to indicate what he should do. "I go make a telephone call to Jerry," he said. "At least I tell Tina."

"I don't think you should. The more people who know, the less his chances of pulling out of this."

McKenna and Soldato entered the room conspicuously, their stiff-necked stealthy moves telltale. They went to the far wall and glanced out the window.

Richie stiffened. "Feds. I can smell them a mile away." David glanced at his associates and smiled. It was true, they gave themselves away.

"Friends," said David, softly. "They're friends. Let's go get Tina and her mother. They should be here." He signalled to the men. They nodded. "Tina doesn't answer the phone. Some message about her being out of town is what I got from the operator," he told McKenna. "I'll

222

be back as soon as I can," but meanwhile, you know where I can be reached."

David and Richie arrived back at the Pyramids. In the casino, they skirted the crowds and went towards the rear exits.

"Benne!" A voice in the crowded casino called to him.

Martin and Richie both searched the faces in the crowded room, trying to locate the source of the voice.

"Benne?" said the voice, hesitant and unsure. "Is it really you?"

Martin and Richie stared hard at the stranger, their eyes searching the man's face, which was concealed by large aviator glasses with intensely dark lenses. Martin's eyes went blank, but his voice and demeanor were Benne's.

"You got me at a disadvantage, buddy. I don't know you. My name's David Martin. You got me confused with someone else."

The stranger slouched in a careless pose, leaning against a slot machine, wore his thick mass of white hair frizzed out, like a black man's natural. The rest of his face was covered with a thick brush moustache. He backed away. "Yeah, yeah, I guess I'm mistaken," he muttered, staring closely at Martin and eyeing Sadge warily.

David got the distinct impression that the man was disguising his voice. Sadge growled, baring his fangs.

They lost track of the white-haired stranger and forgot all about him as they made their way to the Erice penthouse. Unknown to either of them, this white-haired man who incurred Sadge's wrath and hailed Martin as Benne had been photographed by a BSI agent. McKenna's man, while in the posture of a tourist, had lucked out, taking several photos of the man.

An hour later, McKenna and Soldato scrutinized the enlargements of the white-haired stranger but failed to identify him. The chore was difficult due to the dark glasses, the bush moustache, and the white wig, which both agents felt certain were a disguise employed by the stranger. Annoyed and disturbed by the incident, they stewed for a time, then passed the photos out among the skeleton crew of men with instructions to find the white-wigged stranger and do their damndest to get a set of prints off him. Something about the man's nonchalance, the attitude of a man too sure of himself, irked them.

Returning to the business at hand, they patiently awaited the results of the test made at the hospital, hoping to pinpoint Val's ailment.

CHAPTER SEVENTEEN

Tina, reviewing every moment from the time she returned to the Pyramids following the Jolie Barnes show, was unable to recall what had happened to produce the unsightly bruises and welts on her body and face. Such things don't happen without reason or explanation, she told herself as she seated herself at the white directoire desk. She picked up a white quill pen and began listing on a pad all her movements: arrived home; couldn't sleep; showered; washed hair; took two seconals; still couldn't sleep; tried to read; couldn't concentrate; dozed off and awakened groggy, disoriented; too much booze.

She paused, trying to jog her memory with what she'd written. She recalled trying to wade through a hazy euphoria of reality and dreams. She wrote: storm—sudden electrical storm; thunder; lightning; scream.

She stopped writing, her memory amply stoked. She recalled sitting bolt upright in bed, awakened by the loud roar of thunder. Lightning flashes had illuminated her room. Her throat was parched; she drank water from a glass on her night table.

Rolling over she tried to doze off again. She awakened with a start this time, soaking wet with perspiration. She took off her nightie, kicked off the coverlet and plopped tummy down on the bed, covering her head with a pillow to drown out sight and sound. Boom . . . boom . . . boom . . . the sound of her racing heartbeats made her anxious. Wide awake, as if her instinct was trying to warn her of an inherent danger, she tensed. Was it possible someone was in her bedroom?

Listening for movement like a cat sensing danger, Tina felt herself submerge into euphoric density. Her eyelids threatened to close. She tried to stay awake, but was unable to under the powerful persuasion of the sedation doing its work. Her body fell limp against the pillows. Despite the slowing down of her senses, there came a few brief moments of clarity in which she felt a sharp jab in her upper arm. Through the narrow apertures of her partially opened eyes she discerned a fuzzy, hazy shadow hovering over her. Behind the ambiguous shadow, outlined sharply by a flash of lightning, she saw nothing and heard only the howling of a desert simoon.

She'd tried struggling, but her body, like rubber, was unable to cope. A husky voice was muttering words she couldn't understand. She wanted to struggle. A sharp slap across her face felt as if she'd been struck with a cotton club—she felt no pain.

"Bitch! No one can hear you, even if you scream!" the same muffled voice whispered.

Tina's head ached throbbingly; her eyes were aflame. Vaguely she felt the body of a naked man next to hers. Something told her to fight him off, but her body refused to obey her commands.

A narcotic injected into her upper arm began taking effect. However it was that she remained coherent in the next few moments before oblivion engulfed her was little short of miraculous. She inhaled a familiar fragrance, one that so repelled her, she felt an involuntary retching coil up in her stomach. Giving vent to this powerful process, her body jackknifed and her arms flailed wildly about. Somehow she accidentally activated a recording device kept secreted in a drawer of her nightstand. She recalled nothing after that.

The next morning shortly before noon the incessant ringing of her phone startled her into wakefulness. The sound of rushing waves at high tide turned out to be the heavy pounding of her heart. She stared fixedly at the phone for several seconds before reaching for it. As she did, her body became a testimonial of aches and pains she hadn't experienced before.

The room spun around for her as it did when in the throes of alcoholic stupor. She shaded her eyes from the blinding light streaming through the sheer window casements, wincing at the stiff yet burning sensations on her face and around her eyes. By the time she'd picked up the receiver, the caller had hung up.

She fell against the pillows, eyes closed, sniffing the air, puzzled at the strong scent of a man's cologne—the odor was so strong. Tina turned her head and sniffed the pillow next to her and turned away in distaste. She lay back again trying to think. One eye cracked open, then the other. She stared fixedly at a point across the room, seeing nothing in particular, wondering why she felt so terrible. Meanwhile her hand groped for a cigarette from the nightstand.

Yes, a cigarette would help. Maybe coffee. Plenty of coffee.

She lay there smoking, watching smoke spirals drift to the ceiling, until she came fully awake. She lifted her body to a sitting position, her eyes reacting painfully to the light. It was then she noticed the wild disarray of her bed. Before she could think about the disorder her attention was caught by a swooshing sound. She cocked her head to listen, her eyes skirting about the room. It came to her that the sound was coming from her nightstand. She opened the drawer and saw the spent wheel of her tape recorder swooshing—swooshing—swooshing. Annoyed by it she merely snapped it off, giving it no further thought. On her feet, a dizziness came upon her and she fell against the bed until the lightheadedness passed.

The room and its contents did a wild fandango in her head.

"Fucking Valium," she muttered, waiting for the indescribable dizziness to leave her. On her feet again, she managed to navigate her rubbery legs towards the bathroom, hanging on to furniture, the wall, anything to get her there.

"Christ! What a hangover," she muttered aloud. She hadn't taken that much Valium, she recalled, flipping on the light switch. Tina suddenly froze at the image reflected back at her from the bathroom mirror. Her face screwed up into a puzzled, pained expression as she traced lightly with her fingertips the weal marks, the swelling, puffy discolorations and dried bits of caked blood on her face and eyes where most of the damage had been inflicted. There was evidence of more caked blood around her swollen lips where she'd been struck by something sharp—perhaps a ring.

Tina knew imagination had nothing to do with what had happened to her. It was for real—pains and all.

When she became aware of the stickiness between her legs she panicked. Only one thing could have caused the dried semen. She blinked, hoping to activate her memory. Somehow a man had raped her. Was that the motive behind all this? She rushed to her walk-in closet, and worked the dial on her wall safe. She quickly scanned the contents; her jewelry was intact.

In moments she was in the shower using both hot and cold water beating on her body to invigorate and revive all her senses. Wrapped in a thick terry robe, she made a fresh pot of coffee on the tile-topped island off the dressing room area.

Aspirin, she thought, would help her heavy head. She took two, and brought her coffee back into the bedroom; she stared at the telltale bed covers. It was true; someone, a man, had been there—who? At that moment, as her head began clearing Tina gave thought to the tape recorder.

She sprang to the night table, rewound the tape and pressed the play button. By the time the taped scenario played itself out, Tina, trying with all her strength to control a violent rush of anger, reached for the phone. She had to talk with someone—her father. No, perhaps Richie? No, it would have to be Benne. He'd have to remember what happened before his accident. As luck would have it, no one answered his phone. Not her father, not Benne or Richie, not even Whip had left a message.

Now that she'd figured it all out, she was itching to confide in someone. Where the hell were they? Something was wrong. She called her office and told her secretary to try to locate someone, her father, Richie, Benne—no, not Renzo! She hung up and continued her sporadic pacing. *Benne, wherever you are, call me, please!*

Richie and David Martin had just arrived in Martin's suite at the hotel where he showered and slipped into fresh bluejeans and a shirt. Richie sat across the room from him, the albino dog at his feet, watching David Martin, still unsure of his position in this strangely unfolding melodrama.

The phone rang. They exchanged glances. Martin picked up the phone. Tina's voice overwhelmed him.

"Benne! Thank God I reached you. Come to my place right away!" She hung up before David could reply.

Holding the phone in his hand he glanced at Richie. "It was Tina. She wants to see me right away. She says it's urgent."

Richie gave him an apologetic look as he crossed the room. Taking the phone from him, he dialed Tina's private number. When she answered he said, "It's Richie. You wanna see Benne?"

"Right away and don't tell anyone," she instructed him before hanging up.

By the time they reached the penthouse, Tina was

dressed in bluejeans and matching shirt. She opened the door, grabbed David's arms and pulled him inside before Richie could protest. She slammed the door in his face and talking through the door, told him he could enter after she was through talking with her brother.

Whatever protests Richie might have made froze on his lips. He pulled up a chair from the end of the hall and positioned himself dutifully outside the door. He removed his piece, checked it and shoved it back into his shoulder holster. It had been a long time since he actually wore a gun.

Inside, David stopped in his tracks when he saw her face.

"What in hell happened to you?" he asked, following her into the bedroom, where she poured coffee for him. He felt more at ease, thinking she'd been told nothing about the deception foisted on the Erice family by the BSI.

"Never mind, Benne. Do you remember anything we discussed before you left for Mexico? Try, for God's sake, try to remember about Renzo and me."

"I know only that things between you aren't right," he said guardedly. *Tina, you're my sister—actually my real sister* . . .

"You can't remember what I told you?"

"I'm sorry, honey. Really I am."

"It'll come back to you. I want you to listen to this. You might not understand at first, but I'll explain it later."

David listened to the tape twice through. He heard mumbled words, heavy breathing, a whisper of garblings and a few words out of context. He placed little significance on it and wished Tina would explain. The thought of Val at the hospital without next of kin worried him considerably.

Tina obliged him by telling the entire story. "It's proof of Renzo's guilt, don't you see?"

David shook his head apologetically. The puzzle she'd provided proved too complex. "Just tell me what you've concluded, Tina," he said finally.

She nodded. "Renzo was responsible for Jimmy's death. Bob Harmon, too." And she filled him in on all the rest, his plottings and schemings to control the Erice fortune, what she surmised of the incident leading up to Jimmy's death. This time when she played the tape, the broken sentences and hazy words made sense. David jotted down

228

words between the grunts and groans and when he strung them together they came out in a sentence:

"*O.K. little miss big shot—you're gonna get pregnant if it's the last thing I do. If I have to keep you drugged until we have one in the oven—*"

Laughter, muffled movements, and heavy breathing associated with sexual excitement, mingled with words like "*bitch, cunt, cock teaser,*" didn't affect Tina one bit. David marveled as he watched her throughout the trying ordeal.

"Look, Benne, look at my arm—the needle marks," she said rubbing the discoloration of blood vessels in her upper arm. "I knew it couldn't have been the Valium alone that made me feel so badly."

"Why do you stay married to him?" David stiffened with anger.

She shrugged. "I've waited all these years—" she began, her throat thickening. "Now I'm sure how it happened. Renzo doctored the drinks at the Seaside Tavern. I know it was him. He tried to get me pregnant so I'd be forced to marry him. He intended to get me any way he could. Why didn't I see it then? Don't you see it? The m.o. is the same. He couldn't take the countless rejections then, so taking matters into his own hands he eliminated the competition. He needed the security of a grandson for Pop to keep me married to him until his plans are finalized. Oh," she fumed internally, "how diabolically clever can you get? Following our wedding night, when Renzo made no mention of the fact that I wasn't a virgin, my Sicilian mind worked overtime. Knowing how Sicilian men revere virginity in their brides, you can be sure if he weren't aware that he'd copped my virginity he'd have thrown it in my face and suffocated me with the guilt. Yet never once did he mention it! Not once!"

As Tina pieced it together David found himself emotionally distraught at the ignominy of the deed. He wished he could come closer to it, the way Benne might have, since they both shared brother and sister intimacies. His loathing for Renzo and men of his calibre was raw and pure. He glanced at his watch. It was time to tell her about Val. But Tina, taking him by the hand, led him into the breakfast room off the terrace, where she poured hot coffee for them both.

"The one thing that baffles me is why Renzo was so foolish in harming our brother Jimmy." She pursed her lips thoughtfully, and gazed out on the terrace.

"It's possible he didn't know Jimmy was there. His

anger might have been directed at someone else. It's pure conjecture on my part," he added when Tina's eyes brightened.

"I think you've got it! The owner of the tavern is the only one who could have told Bob what happened to me. Renzo must have returned to get even with the owner—that's his style. Jimmy happened to be at the wrong place at the wrong time. As long as Bob Harmon couldn't remember what had happened, he was safe." Tina sipped her coffee and set it on the glass-topped table, her memory in reverse gear as she thought back to that tragic New Year's Eve.

"Bob was excited about something that night, he kept saying he had to talk with Jerry . . ."

Amy Shiverton stood frozen outside the door on the terrace. She'd been probing around the cactus plants making cuttings to take back to Florida with her. She had tried not to listen to the unraveling of Tina's story but Tina's last few words had stirred her memory. Dressed casually in jeans and a silk shirt, and her red hair tied with a Calvin Klein scarf, she pushed back the drapes and entered the room, about to speak out, when she noticed Tina's deplorable bruises.

"What happened, Tina?"

Tina, slightly annoyed at the interruption, shook her head indifferently. At any other time she'd have been far more courteous, but her business with David was important. She poured a cup of coffee for Amy, but turned her attention back to David. Amy, however, interrupted them, stopping Tina cold.

"Bob Harmon called me that same night," she told them. "Danny took the message. The message was: *Tell Jerry I remember everything.*'"

Tina paled. "Bob said that? He remembered everything?" To David, "That reinforces what I believe." She frowned thoughtfully.

"Oh, my God!" exclaimed Amy as the sudden realization struck her. She stared at them. "Danny!" Her hands flew to her face, her head shook with disbelief, but in her eyes was the truth. "Val—where's Val? I've got to talk with Val," she said, growing enormously excited.

"Who's Danny?" asked David.

"The senator's youngest brother—Amy's kid brother," said Tina, stopping at the implication. She turned back to Amy. "Danny! That's it, he's the only one who can really tie Renzo into this sordid mess. Drugs—" She stopped at the sight of pain on Amy's face.

Amy muttered, "Val, I must see Val . . . Oh God, I'm so sorry—"

"We'll all go see him," said Tina. "It's time this is finished."

"Uh, Tina, that's what I came about—"

A knock at the door. Richie entered, stern disapproval on his face. "My Don is waiting—did you forget?" Catching sight of Tina's face, he felt for the security of his Browning with one hand, and held Sadge back with the other.

"We came to take you to your father," David said quietly.

"What's wrong. *Your* father?" She frowned. Two nights ago it had been settled. Val officially called him Benne. Her head angled from one to the other. "Something's wrong, isn't it?"

David took her hand in his. "We think he's had a stroke."

"And you're just telling me?"

"You haven't been answering your phone, remember?"

A half hour later the three women, Christina, Amy and Tina, arrived at the hospital with nothing else on their minds except Val's welfare. Christina was admitted first. Dressed casually in beige pants and matching shirt, she entered removing her dark glasses, creeping softly across the sterile room, her worried eyes searching her husband's pale face. In the shadowy room, Val appeared asleep. She leaned over him, kissing him, smoothing his snowy hair off his tanned forehead. Val was motionless.

She pulled a chair up to the bed, sat and prayed silently, her well-manicured fingers intertwined with his. All at once her eyes widened at the pressure she felt on her fingers. Val's blue eyes, opened wide, stared straight ahead.

"Val, can you hear me? Can you talk? Do you need anything?"

He remained motionless; no flicker of life in him, nothing to indicate he sensed her presence. She repeated her words, stressing her love for him. Tears sprang to her eyes, seeing him so helpless at the mercy of others; he'd never been as vulnerable as he was at this moment. For the first time she was forced to consider a life without him and she became afraid.

231

A nurse came in quietly and touched her shoulder. It was time for her to leave. Tina came in behind her, kissed her mother before she left. Father and daughter were alone.

She studied Val's placid face. Somewhere a radio was playing. Sounds from the corridor echoed dimly in the background. Tina sighed despairingly. "Oh, Pop, what happened? Can you tell me? Shall I send for Dr. Sharp? He can be on the next plane here."

Val saw his daughter peripherally, noting the swelling and bruises on her battered face. He felt a rush of parental alarm.

"I want to help," persisted Tina. "Tell me what to do," she implored, sitting on the bed facing him squarely. She shoved her dark glasses up on her head, searching his face, stroking it gently, lovingly as she searched his eyes. Tina suddenly gave a start. Val winked at her, then cautioned her to silence with his eyes.

"You sly fox!" she hissed at him, her hands on her waist ready to lay into him. She was cut off by his whisper.

"Lock the door," he said without lip movement.

She shook her head. "Can't, there's no lock on it." Sliding off the bed she admonished him. "What game is this, dammit! You've scared us half to death."

"Be silent and listen," said Val sternly. "Lay your head on my shoulder so I can talk without being overheard." Only that morning feeling had returned to Val and with it, tingling sensations of movement. Considering what had happened to him, what was bound to follow, he wisely said nothing to anyone of the improvement—especially to none of the hospital staff.

Tina nuzzled his neck. "First, I've got some good news. Renzo killed Bob Harmon and Jimmy. He planted a bomb at Seaside—"

"I know," Val told her. "For a long time, now."

She drew back in horror. "And you didn't tell me? You let me go on living with that vile bastard?" She stared at him in anger.

"Tina! Take care. To keep me alive, bear with me. This is no time to air our differences."

Shaking angrily, she obeyed him. Too many years of obedience and acquiescence was ingrained into her mentality, forcing her to comply.

"Forgive me," he said repentantly. "Danny Shiverton confessed his part in the sordid affair when we met in

Europe last year. We'll talk about it later, after I leave here, if I'm alive. Before the nurse returns . . . quick . . . your arms around my neck, your ear close to my lips so you can hear me talk. The hospital scans each room on a monitor. Check on it . . ." He gave her a list of instructions. Tina listened intently and left at the appointed time, when Amy was ushered into the room.

At the sight of Val, so helpless, Amy, in an emotional tizzy, grasped his hand in her trembling fingers. Then, quickly to avoid the eruption of tears, she turned and fled the room. Val hated putting anyone through such torment, but there was no other way. They'd understand when it was finished. Meanwhile, he had all he could do to concentrate on an inner state of meditation and control; he couldn't risk betraying his position.

An hour later, Tina, carrying a briefcase, returned to the hospital alone. Nodding to some of Richie's men stationed in the outer corridor she slipped unnoticed by the nursing staff at the far end of the corridor. Seated at Val's side, her eyes located the closed circuit TV scanner. Earlier she'd stopped by the central scanning room, noting one male attendant manned the monitors. She learned the ICU were under constant surveillance; PCUs (progressive care units) were scanned every ten minutes; some areas, six times an hour; the rest were monitored twelve at a time at fifteen-minute intervals, allowing for emergencies. She had ten minutes with her father without surveillance.

"When the lens is dotted with an ultraviolet eye, you're on camera," she whispered to him. "Now, we can talk."

"To make certain I don't shock them," he told her when she leaned over to kiss him, "turn my bed to the window. If I suddenly come on camera they won't see us. It will give us more time."

Tina wheeled the bed to face the window, grateful it was on casters. She opened the blinds onto a stunning desert landscape. She fluffed up Val's pillow and helped raise him to a sitting position. "Why the Browning magnum? You've never used a gun before."

"Is it secured to the false bottom of my briefcase?"

She nodded.

"Good. Remove the handcuffs, clasp one to my wrist, the other around the handle of the case. If I need the gun, I can press the spring lock."

"What's going on. Pop? Can't you tell me?"

"No questions. Trust your father. You understand all

233

I told you earlier? David is really Benne's twin—not Benne. You are to treat him as if he is Benne—you understand?"

"None of this makes sense."

"It will. Now, lean in closer to me, light of my life, and hear me well. When this is finished, take your senator and find your happiness while you can."

"You know about him—about us?" She was as fascinated as she was appalled. He had something up his sleeve.

"I know. I've known a long time. In the end love is all that counts. Anything else is illusion. Remember what I say."

Father and daughter spent a few precious moments together, trying to beat the clock. He tried desperately to school her on certain matters should something happen to him. "Papers, Tina, in the private file at home in Long Island, will enlighten you." Tina tried to protest, to desperately sway him from this role he'd chosen to play against people of whom she had no knowledge, but before she could cite a dozen reasons to dissuade him, the door burst open. A freshly starched and irate head nurse stood indignantly before them.

"What is going on?" asked the dry-faced woman. "John!" she shouted at the attendant at her heels. "Turn this bed around instantly! Put all the plugs back into their proper sockets!" She waded through the dangling cords hanging impotently from a panel, that disconnected lifesaving devices from Val's arm, bleating hotly at Tina. "You couldn't have cared much for your father's welfare! Twisting hospital regulations to suit your fancy!"

"I thought my father would enjoy watching the sunset." She kissed Val and picked up her empty tote, sweeping past the indignant nurse. "Sorry for the inconvenience. You have many patients. I only have one father."

Tina breezed out of the room.

"You just make certain all the emergency outlets are properly connected. Have central scanning control zero in on this room without hesitation. Get on with you, and hurry back," ordered the nurse. Adjusting the sheets around Val she spotted the manacled briefcase attached to his wrist. She exploded.

"I've had about as much of this cloak and dagger burlesque as I can handle. Where did that come from? Take it off!"

Val stared stonily into space as he had since his arrival.

The nurse leaned over him and peered into his eyes. She waved her hands before them; not a blink, not a reaction came from Val.

Staring at him intently, searching his eyes, she trained a pencil flashlight into them. Was that a flicker of dilation she asked herself, or the golden fleck in his natural blue eyes?

She performed the act again, snapped off the light and left the room. Walking along the corridor, the nurse bit the insides of her lips. She entered a pay phone booth, dropped a coin and spoke confidentially to her party. She turned and glanced at the scattering of Richie's men in the corridor as if she were counting heads and spoke again.

"I can't tell you any more," she said softly. "The federal agents take alternate turns guarding him, with local police and a rash of others. You'll have to figure it out from your end."

CHAPTER EIGHTEEN

On the morning of the third day, eight redfaced, sweating, blustery men, four belonging to Richie, the others local undercover officers, were nailed to the carpet by the explosive police chief, Frank Ferraro.

"You snakebitten sons of bitches! You stand there, all of you, and dare tell me you don't know where he is? You expect me to believe that *Mr. John Goodrich* vanished into thin air under your very noses and none of you saw it happen? By Christ! I'll have all of you stewing your asses in jail for the next six months!"

The men, dazed, embarrassed and totally baffled by the incidents leading up to this blistering excoriation by Captain Ferraro, could find no words that would ameliorate the circumstances. Nothing unusual had happened. There had been no disturbances, nothing to initiate the slightest suspicion in their minds. They had taken turns checking the hospital room consistently before and after any hospital attendant or nurse entered to dispense medication to the patient. They didn't know how or why patient Goodrich had disappeared, they protested to the angry police chief.

By twelve noon, the entire staff at Southern Nevada Memorial had learned that patient Goodrich was missing, that an abduction had taken place.

"No one vanishes into thin air!" protested Captain Ferraro. He glanced accusingly at Richie's men, chastizing them with a glaring silence, then added, "I can see a cop mucking up, but where the fuck were you experts?"

Richie had left earlier for the Pyramids and returned with Sadge. He huddled with his men for a time, their mortification self-evident by their hangdog expressions. Richie, leading the dog on a choke chain, entered the room formerly occupied by Val and received an immediate reaction from the animal.

Sniffing the air gingerly, Sadge pranced to the bed, sniffing at the crumpled sheets. He jerked forward so hard that he nearly gave Richie a whiplash, heading towards the sliding glass doors leading to a sundeck. Richie slid back the door and Sadge leaped up, putting his paws on the top of the redwood railing. He barked loudly several times, fell to the floor, circled about, still sniffing, then elevated his forepaws to the railing again.

David Martin moved in behind Richie and watched the dog's behavior intently. Captain Ferraro peered carefully about the area and glanced thoughtfully at the two-story drop, making mental notes of everything. Richie studied the scuff marks on the deck flooring as instant awareness set in. His voice was dispassionate and fatigued.

"Here's the way they got him out." He shook his head regretfully.

"No one watching this exit?" David asked, studying the bushes and lawn below them hypercritically.

"Who knows what those fucking assholes were watching?" griped Ferraro, watching the BSI agents file into the hospital room, aware of what they were thinking. The news of Val's abduction chafed them. They bridled angrily at the obvious blundering of both the police and the private bodyguards. Their concern and indignation over the turn of events was immeasureable.

McKenna especially lit into Captain Ferraro like a two-ton jackhammer. "You assured me this was your jurisdiction—that your men could handle it. You'd better produce Mr. Goodrich in the next twenty-four hours or you'll hit the skids in Vegas so fast I might charge you with conspiracy and don't ask for what! I'll think of something to nail you with!"

Richie scowled darkly. He leaned towards Martin.

"He's got no right to talk to Frankie like that. My Don and Frankie are tight." He immediately walked to where Captain Ferraro stood, whitefaced and tightlipped with indignation at the dressing-down he received from McKenna. It was as if Richie, by this gesture, let everyone know whose side he took. But as much as Captain Ferraro appreciated his trust and faith, it didn't alleviate the shame he felt knowing his own men had brought dishonor to him through their carelessness.

Whip, fearing for Val's life, remained in seclusion in his suite at the Pyramids. He couldn't risk letting the newspaper editor, Hank Greenspawn, have a field day speculating on his presence in Vegas. He had to stay put until Chief Bowman rendezvoused with him.

Captain Ferraro had instructed the hospital management to keep the information under wraps, threatening them with punitive measures if someone leaked the information to the press. He hadn't counted on the swift communication between nurses, interns and other employees who were on a retainer with several local reporters and had already phoned in the scoop. But then, what did they know? Who the hell was John Goodrich and why was he so heavily guarded? That was what they aimed to learn more about.

It fell incumbent on David to tell Tina and Christina about Val's disappearance. Amy comforted Christina, trying to assuage her fears. Tina, under David's scrutiny, took the news with subdued interest. He was puzzled; this wasn't the reaction of a loving and devoted daughter over the mysterious and possibly disastrous disappearance of her father. Renzo, who was present, made a futile attempt to comfort Tina, only to be shunned by her, as if his very touch had contaminated her. Flushing with embarrassment at the obvious rebuff he made a hasty exit.

David and Richie met with Whip Shiverton and the other BSI agents. Shown photos of the man in a white wig who'd hailed him a few nights before, David could not identify him. Richie labored over the photo thoughtfully.

"Any of you get a handle on him?" asked Phil Soldato. McKenna shook his head. "He's disappeared."

"Disappeared?" snorted Richie. "All he gotta do to disappear is take off the wig, mustache and glasses, no?"

"You recognize him, Richie? I mean without the disguise?" asked David, a flash of hope in his eyes.

Richie wiped his face with a huge hand, stretching his jaw reflectively, and shook his head. "I go feed the dog," he said.

Renzo went to his office, locked it electronically and placed an urgent call to Marciano. "Did you hear, Manny? The old man's been snatched!" He was unable to disguise the delight in his voice. Taken off guard by the statement, Manny asked him, "The old man—who?"

"Val Erice is missing from the hospital. A real snatch job, eh, Manny?" An edge of newly formed respect glittered in his voice.

"Listen, kid. Don't lay that on us. It ain't our doing."

"If not you—who?"

"Shit, I dunno. Bet your ass I'll find out."

"Do that, Manny, and be quick, hear?"

"Take it easy, kid. Take it easy," purred Manny, thinking. "Listen to me, this could be a blessing in disguise."

Renzo wasn't about to be pacified. "I've got everything riding on this last toss of the dice. Just make sure we don't crap out!" He hung up abruptly. The sudden reversal of their usual roles was a new experience for Renzo. He was sweating bullets. He wasn't certain why Val's disappearance should shake him in this manner. He only knew that it did. He had to learn what happened.

He pondered Marciano's words, wondering how Val's kidnapping could be a blessing in disguise. The longer he considered it the less merit he found in the words. *Dammit!* He'd never wanted Val rubbed out. Only to step down and let him, Renzo, run things. Or if, as Manny often insisted he would, he'd sell his holdings for peanuts, Renzo could take over like gangbusters with the sizeable loot he had managed to skim off the tops of the casino receipts for a long time.

To hell with that right now. He poured himself a stiff drink and took a downer, washing it down with the Beefeaters gin. The red flag alert was up in Renzo's mind as he paced the floor, creating a paranoia that wouldn't dissolve. He figured that anyone who could snatch Val out from under Richie's protection and Ferraro's cops could do likewise to him—or kill him. He was more expendable than Val. If they got him, getting Renzo was a cinch. His eyes fell on a postcard from Hawaii. Goddammit! For two cents he'd fly there to get answers from Lefty Meyers and Agajjinian. Where the fuck was Emilio Aprile's body? All he heard was silence—silence—silence! There had to be a fucking body around someplace!

Who had snatched Val Erice? First Aprile's body, then Val? Nothing computed. Renzo placed a call to an old crony of his in New York. He needed six gunsels, undercover, for protection. Despite the fact that the underworld network would flash the news to the right spots before the gunsels could arrive, he made his request.

"Renzo," said the raspy-voiced old man out of his past, "You're a dead man."

Renzo hung up the phone as if it had become a fiery piece of molten steel in his hand.

"*Renzo—you're a dead man!*" The old man wasn't clowning.

Wiping the disbelief and the sweat from his face, Renzo sat and thought for nearly an hour.

The paranoia passed. Fuck! Why should he be scared shitless? Marciano was on his side and together they had juice. Inhaling deeply several times to relax himself, he did a few jumping jacks to work out his circulation and left his office. Sauntering through the casino, his eyes everywhere, he could feel the electricity in the air. *Act natural. Make it appear to be business as usual. Don't say nothing to no one, until it's official,* he told himself, thinking about Val's disappearance. It was a desperate attempt on his part to relax, but nothing could stop his guts from writhing and twisting.

Nodding to two security guards, he instructed them to remain at his side as escorts at double their salary until further notice.

He sauntered through the casino, the guards behind him, as employees glanced up questioningly at him in passing. All at once he noticed a thickening crowd across the lobby of the hotel, where bedlam ensued. "What the hell?" he muttered aloud, nodding to the guards. They flanked him as he moved forward towards the hullabaloo taking place.

Cameras clicked incessantly. Light bulbs popped. The crowd, gathered six deep, oooohed and ahhhhhhed. A cordon of bellmen and security guards moved in, flanking two stunning women, protecting them from autograph seekers and devoted fans, who were screaming and calling out,

"It's Dancey Darling! Dancey in the flesh! Get her autograph! Wow, it's Dancey! Over here, Mary, look over here! She's terrific! What a sexpot!"

Renzo heard the shouts and craned his neck to see above the crowd, thinking, *Shit, I forgot all about her arrival.* A feeling of momentary exhilaration swept through him. Forgetting his troubles, he patted himself on the back mentally for having had the foresight to hire Dancey Darling.

He moved out of the way of an onslaught of fans trampling one another just to catch a glimpse of the blonde superstar and her beautiful companion.

Stopping at a florist shop, he entered and greeted the pleasant-faced clerk cheerfully. "Send six dozen American Beauty roses to Dancey Darling's suite. And, Penny, call room service for me, will you? Send a magnum of Dom Perignon also." He wrote a message on a plain white card. "Put this with the flowers and booze, will ya?"

Penny, a trim, petite blonde in her early forties, nodded, picking up the card and entering her instructions on a notepad. Picking up a house phone she ordered the champagne sent to the flower shop as she watched Renzo leave the shop. When he was out of sight, she placed another phone call on a private phone, speaking softly.

"She's just arrived. He just sent her six dozen red roses and a magnum of Dom Perignon. Yes, Renzo—the boss."

CHAPTER NINETEEN

A few months before David Martin arrived in Las Vegas Princess Jamila Rhadima Izmur, alias Jaqualine Devon, returned to Los Angeles from a trip along the California coast with Abdul Harrim. She was filled with nostalgia and with a deep desire to communicate with her brother, Ali.

She'd lived with Abdul all this time, sharing a life of excitement, drugs, and generally good times. They spent time lounging on the beaches or exploring the cities along the coast; often Abdul had to meet with someone in San Francisco, Santa Barbara or San Diego. She was amazed how many exchange students there were in California.

Jaqualine was enchanted with San Francisco, enthralled with Carmel and amused by the droves of free thinkers who congregated at Nepenthe to share community baths and the latest psychological jargon. She wondered at the countless Americans who seemed in dire need of psychiatric help, feeling contempt for these apathetic people in a land of plenty, where daily miracles were taken for granted, who'd never known the depths of degradation to which a human soul can be subjected by starvation or war.

This weekend, having visited Hearst Castle at San Simeon, Jamila had grown nostalgic and withdrawn at the splendor that reminded her of what she'd left behind in the Middle East.

Driving along the Coast Highway in a subdued silence, Abdul sensed her mood and realized it was more than the usual depression she experienced from drugs. The traffic on the highway was intense. Abdul turned off, and drove along Sunset, following the winding road through numerous canyons until they arrived in Westwood Village.

They stopped to buy some falafels, and took them to the apartment, wanting to spend a quiet evening alone. But the apartment was filled with Bahar's friends. Observing them with impatience, Abdul worked his irritation into genuine anger. The presence of certain men disturbed him. Before anyone saw her, he whisked Jaqualine into her bedroom.

"What the fuck's going on with Bahar?" he sputtered, pacing before her, collecting his thoughts. "Stay here. Don't come out until I get rid of them."

"What's wrong? Who are these people?"

"It's best you don't know. They are no one you should encounter. What's that son-of-a-bitch thinking?" He lit a cigarette, inhaling deeply, and composing himself. "Remember, now, don't come out until I send for you," he said in an abrasive manner that was unlike his usual way of speaking to her.

Jaqualine hated these moods of his, but she nodded submissively. He'd been wrestling with these curiously argumentative people for months and was always short of patience with them. Abdul lacked the subtlety at times to suppress his indignation. Now, curious, she went to the door to listen. A wave of voices came at her. She heard murmurs of protest, doors opening and slamming shut. Moving to the window she saw the men filing out below her, huddled together and still talking. She'd seen their faces before, but knew none of them well enough to speak with. They were companions of Bahar. The shadows of night obliterated their features as they took off in different directions.

Returning to the door she listened again. Bahar and Abdul were arguing in a dialect she could understand only slightly.

"It's arranged," Bahar was saying. "The President's mistake in siding with Israel once too often will prove his downfall. Shortly he'll be forced to resign. Our mark is to be groomed for the office of president. There's little time. We must set the ball in motion. If the Prince supports him, so will the other Arab nations and all will be lost to us. Those who stole our Palestinian homes must be annihilated . . ."

The rest was garbled. Jaqualine frowned thoughtfully. She'd listened to Bahar's radical talk since she began sleeping with Abdul. Something about their relationship bothered her, but it was nothing she could pinpoint.

For a long time, she had felt an excitement about her own work, and immersed herself in it so completely that she had paid little heed to Bahar's comings and goings. She was involved with a motion picture company with affiliations in the Middle East. Her expertise in five languages was a tremendous asset to the company and had brought her swift advancement from secretary to head of foreign film rights and distribution. But there was more to interest her.

She saw a way, using the medium of film, to bridge the enormous gaps between the East and the West, and a way in which she could be useful to her brother by producing films.

Today at Hearst Castle, as they ambled about the magnificent structure, she had missed Ali achingly. If she could only convince him . . . Her thoughts spiraled off. It had been hard to concentrate lately. What could be causing the holes in her memory? She reached for a joint and lit up, allowing the euphoria to envelop her. Her hands began to shake uncontrollably, but she paid them no mind. A soft knock at her door brought her head up.

Abdul entered, holding the door ajar, his face a mass of storm clouds. "Come into the other room, Bahar wishes to speak with you." His voice, resigned, acquiescent, alien, threw her momentarily. The earlier attitude in which he'd cursed Bahar had evaporated. It seemed Bahar was issuing orders to him.

Bahar, smiling tightly, handed her a newspaper from Amman, Jordan. Jamila's photo was sprawled across the front page. She was dressed in the fatigues of a terrorist, holding an M-16 automatic rifle in a menacing pose. She glanced questioningly at him, then quickly translated the copy: "Princess Jamila Izmur, sister to Prince Ali Mohammed, has defected to the Feyadeen. With terrorists from the Popular Front Organization she led the ambush which killed Sheikh Ali Shammar Jebel and his two sons. . . ."

"Who is this woman? What is happening?" she asked Bahar in a piercing voice, as a sinking sensation gripped her.

Bahar, watching her reaction, said, "Princess Jamila, heartsick over the serious problems with her people, has joined the Palestinian rebels. She has become a heroine of the resistance forces by fighting for the freedom and rights of her people."

"B-but th-this is untrue!" She slammed the paper on the coffee table. "This isn't me. I never posed for such a picture." She laughed as if they were playing a monstrous joke on her. A look at Abdul's stony face and she sobered. "What does this mean in plain language? Who is responsible for this?" She tossed the newspaper down in disgust. Only then did she notice more papers, more photos of someone impersonating her. She did a slow burn as the picture started to form in her mind.

"Why was it necessary to concoct such lies? I am not a traitor to my brother. I was merely unable to handle my personal life the way he handles his. I've never been a member of the resistance. I demand that you see that my brother is made aware of my whereabouts and of my neutrality in this intrigue of yours." It came together in her mind suddenly. "So that was it, Bahar? That's why you've been so generous, paying all my expenses. You found that I could be an excellent tool to incite the civil war you've been anxious to bring about. You with all your crazy talk about overthrowing governments! Civil wars can be crushed before the first shots are fired!" she exclaimed scathingly. "Or doesn't recent history make a dent in your thinking?" She pivoted and accosted Abdul.

"You, too, Abdul? All this time you've been using me, keeping me under your thumb while you and Bahar conspire subversively to bring my brother's empire crumbling down around his head. Well, it won't work. My brother knows I would never betray him."

They both remained quiet as she vented her wrath at them. A hard glint formed in Abdul's eyes as he leveled them at Bahar.

"Tell her!" he commanded sharply, his former servility absent from his features. "Tell her, goddammit!" he repeated.

Bahar made no move. Abdul furiously strode to the desk. He turned over the news clippings.

"Take a good look, *Princess*," he snapped sarcastically. "You're dead! You might as well be dead! The Prince has disowned you publicly. Over two years ago!" He slapped one paper against her breasts, forcing her to take it.

Jamila stared at the photos on the desk. There were so many. There she was, in militant poses. The captions described a variety of terrorist activities that she supposedly led: "Jamila Victorious in Border Dispute Against the Enemies." "Jamila—Heroine of the Hour—Blows Up Enemy Tanks." "Jamila and a Handful of Palestinian Rebels Forces the Oppressors to Reconsider New Restrictive Laws."

Jamila was stunned. Slowly she glanced at the paper in her hands. Photos of Ali glowering blackly stared up at her. The copy read: "Prince Ali Mohammed Izmur publicly disowns his sister. He says, "She was always a rebel, unable to accept the Moslem ways.'"

Jamila felt sick. She tossed the paper down on the desk in disgust. Bahar sat back in a languid pose, a supercilious grin creasing his face.

"You know you cannot return to your homeland," he said. "Not now. You'd risk being punished as an insurrectionist against the state."

She was shaken. The thought that Ali would believe such treachery was inconceivable, yet when she recalled her own vicious behavior to Valerie Shiverton and all the other women Ali had chosen to be in his harem . . . He would believe her capable of anything, including spiteful hatred and vindictiveness. She recalled the brutal whipping she'd been subjected to, just to show her she had no right to interfere in his life. Ali never really understood the love she held for him.

Well, to hell with it. To hell with all of them, especially Ali. If he really believed all that phony propaganda, she'd give him something to really loathe. She casually re-examined the photos. "Jamila the heroine of the hour." She liked the sound of it. She liked the feeling of importance. How many years had she been here in America? Too many. Too many, during which time she felt like a nobody. The thought that she could actually be that girl in the photos made her pull back her shoulders and stand erect.

She didn't see the triumphant look in Bahar's eyes as he exchanged knowing glances with Abdul. She moved to Abdul's side, held his hand tightly and looked into his eyes lovingly, dependently.

"What is it you want from me, Abdul? I'll do anything you say." She laid her head on his shoulders, waiting for his full approval. Again she failed to see the knowing, satisfied looks passing between the men.

Abdul lit up a joint mixed with angel dust. He passed it to her. She took a hit and returned it to him.

"This is what we have in mind," began Abdul, his arm around her as they sat on the sofa opposite Bahar.

CHAPTER TWENTY

The house was ramshackle, dilapidated, built of loose, rotting, weatherbeaten clapboards that looked ready to blow away if challenged by a good gust of wind. Brooding at the center of a lonely stretch of desert land, the structure was reminiscent of the povertystricken homes of itinerant workers during the Depression.

The center of the building sagged; the front porch, two feet lower than it had been originally, sagged. An aura of condemnation hung over the house.

Its interior was far more dismal and shabby; torn wallpaper was peeling off one wall, while others were filthy with grime and dust, with a maze of spider webs in every corner. A metal cot was shoved against one wall, containing a badly soiled, bare mattress and a stained pillow of mattress ticking; a rumpled sleeping bag in sad need of laundering was shoved to one end.

Rats scurrying across the room paused periodically to stare at the intruder to their private domain, then moved on to scavenge what they could from numerous discarded fast-food containers tossed carelessly against a blackened fireplace. On a soiled and dilapidated sofa with yellowed stuffing visible through badly frayed, gaping holes, was the object of their curiosity: a man, fast asleep, wearing only shocking pink nylon briefs. His body glistened with profuse sweat from the intensity of the heat.

On the floor were a scattering of open girlie magazines. Most were yellowed and worn with frayed edges.

Nearby on a rickety wooden crate lay a white Afro wig, a matching mustache, a pair of sunglasses, eyebrow pencil, and a vial of spirit gum lying on its side next to a hairbrush thick with strands of white synthetic hair. A dark business suit, white shirt and black string tie on a wire hanger were suspended from a nail on the wall. Two hand-tooled western boots stood upright against the baseboard under the suit. One boot was orthopedically designed to correct a slight deformity and stood two inches taller than the other. Nearby an open cosmetic case held a variety of makeup. The lower drawer of the case was filled with barbiturates and dangerous narcotics with the usual artillery for their use. Next to the case lay a silver-handled collapsible cane and a closed piece of luggage.

The place was filthy; the stench, unbearable. Rat droppings scattered about the room added to the disorder but apparently had no adverse effect on the indolent man. Filter cigarettes, a few joints, a half-eaten candy bar were scattered on a broken orange crate next to a battery-operated, phallus-shaped hand vibrator.

Totally incongruous in the room was the three-by-five poster of a stunning film star posed provocatively in the nude; her expression and posture certain to evoke titillating response. Nearly four dozen eight-by-ten glossy photos of the same woman in similar poses were tacked around the border of the large poster. The famous, sensual, pouting lips and well-formed breasts that she touched with caressing fingers teased all onlookers.

Beneath the poster, a ramshackle table had been pushed against the wall and covered with a spotless white sheet. It resembled a consecrated altar. The only sunlight in the room forced its way through a grimy window and became a spotlight focused brightly on the tabletop where an accumulation of gleaming, immaculately oiled and cleaned handguns, rifles and automatic weapons lay in lethal array. Under the mock altar, a cache of bullets, shotgun shells and a Polaroid camera with a stockpile of unexposed film were illuminated.

Occasionally a squeak or screech could be heard as the rats nibbled on food, scratched at wood shavings or shredded clumps of paper with their sharp claws. These sounds were intermingled with the steady breathing, intermittent snores and wheezing from the sleeping man.

A slight buzzing sound, amplified by the silence, sent the rats scurrying. The man's eyes snapped open. He didn't move immediately. His eyes fell on the wristwatch fastened to his outflung left arm. Noting the time, he sat up. He turned off the wrist alarm with his free hand. He reached up to wipe the dripping sweat off his face and rubbed his hand against the sofa to dry it.

His left hand caressed the tumescence prominently outlined under the nylon shorts. Pulling them down below his hips, taking out his hard cock, he began caressing it with a pleasurable motion that brought a sappy expression to his hard features. He relaxed, well pleased with the swelling size of his tool. The man's one desire in life had been to get it up to this size when he fucked a woman. For some unknown reason buried in his subconscious he hadn't been able to achieve this desire. To compensate, he'd fantasize on awakening from a nap, hold himself caressingly, telling himself what an incredible size it was, at the same time enormously excited by it.

His cold eyes, filled with lust and desire, gazed across the room at the large poster and the photos on the wall —at the one woman who to him personified sex. Dancey Darling.

His hand increased its momentum, working feverishly in a rapid up, down and around movement. His eyes narrowed. He licked his parched lips as his free hand moved across his body and reached for the battery-operated vibrator. He chanted, "Fuck me, baby. Fuck me, Dancey Darling. That's it, you sweet fucking cunt. Do it to me."

His hand turned on the switch. The familiar humming sound seemed to increase his frenzy.

His eyes closed tight. His body writhed, twisted and jerked from side to side, then leaped into the air several inches as he ejaculated. Loud, groaning sounds scratched his throat as his sperm shot out in yellow, jelly-like blobs, spurting onto the sofa and floor. The rats went scurrying into hiding at the loud sounds.

Finished with this ritual, the man lay quite still. His eyes snapped open, and fixed once again on the sensuous pose of Dancey Darling. He exhaled heavily.

"Y'all are gonna get yours, Dancey," he said when his breath returned and his labored gasps had disappeared. He glowered at the poster dispassionately. "Fucking junkie cunt!"

CHAPTER TWENTY-ONE

Dancey Darling was in seventh heaven following the warm reception she received in the lobby of the Pyramids. "They haven't forgotten me at all," she told her secretary, kicking off her sandals the minute she entered her lavish suite of rooms. She tossed aside her tote bag and thrust a bouquet of American Beauty roses someone had handed her at the airport towards her secretary and quickly shimmied out of her Oscar de la Renta pink silk shirtwaist, doing a few pirouettes about the room.

Jaqualine Devon set the roses aside and quickly pulled back the lapis lazuli-blue coverlet. "Rest a while, Dancey, you're too wound up."

"I'm too excited to sleep," the star bounced back, peeking through the sheer curtains covering large windows that overlooked the penthouse terrace. She smiled submissively at the scowl on Jaqualine's face. "All right, I'll try and nap for a while."

She plopped herself face down on the king-sized bed between fresh azure sheets; piped-in music soothed her jagged nerves. She closed her eyes, hearing only the movements Jaqualine made as she padded about the room, unpacking her wardrobe and hanging it in the large walk-in closet.

Periodically Jaqualine gazed at Dancey to assess the star's increased nervousness. Her old insecurities ate away at her constantly; the thought of the Vegas stage show was frightening. She needed constant approval and reminders that everything would be fine. Jaqualine had been with Dancey several months. Dancey's impression of Jaqualine was that there was more to her than met the eye. Her good breeding was visible; her apparent knowledge of a variety of subjects both intrigued and fascinated Dancey. Jaqualine gave no indication of volcanic inner impulses. Then why did Dancey sense something of a rebel in her?

When she hired Jaqualine and the girl moved into her

Brentwood home, Dancey had appraised her critically. Jaqualine was a stunning woman and Dancey, on impulse, asked why she hadn't chosen a show business career. "You have the looks to make it."

Laughing at the absurdity, Jaqualine retorted, "Not I. It's not my cup of tea. False and predatory friends, more anxious to eat you alive than say a kind word, frighten me."

Her answer satisfied Dancey. There'd be no competition to clash with. Jaqualine entered Dancey's life at a time when she needed a great deal of moral support. Dancey was fighting for her life. She had no time to concern herself with anything else.

Jaqualine unpacked her own bags in the adjoining suite, her thoughts centered on a complexity of concerns. She was well aware of Dancey's insecurities. She had found the star to be a fiercely driven woman, enduring long, arduous hours of dance rehearsals, backbreaking routines and fatiguing sessions under the tyranny of a vocal coach. Dancey was a woman who, in a sense, contradicted everything Jaqualine had thought about American women— that they were weak, ineffectual, inadequate and parasitical.

She knew that Dancey's future hinged on her success in Las Vegas. She'd heard the rumors of Dancey's insecurities. She'd witnessed pivotal moments in rehearsal, when her shaky career could have ended. But at the eleventh hour something would occur to snap Dancey out of her tantrum and put her back on the track.

Observing Dancey's frayed and jagged nerves, her hairtrigger anxiety, ready to blow at the slightest provocation, it became apparent to Jaqualine that something fiendish ate away at the cinema star. Whatever it was, she had confided nothing to her secretary.

Jaqualine had put the last of her things away and glanced about the room. They were here at last. The first steps of a long journey had begun. She paused a moment and looked in on Dancey in the next room, sound asleep, her fingers tightly clasped around a gold locket worn around her neck night and day. She was never without it. She'd never volunteered to explain it to Jaqualine or allow her to get a better look at it. Each night upon falling asleep and later on awakening, her hand would clasp it tightly, as if it were a security blanket.

Dancey wasn't asleep. She tried to nap and couldn't. The excitement of Las Vegas, the culmination of long, exhaustive work, had ended on one plateau. She was prepared to climb to another to realize the fruits of that labor. Dancey fingered the gold locket, aware of Jaqualine's unspoken curiosity over it. Dancey had no intention of revealing the significance of the locket to anyone, nor the inscription inside it.

What Jaqualine didn't know was that the locket, containing an intimate photo of Dancey and Benne Erice, taken at the Beverly Hills Hotel before she betrayed him and sent him to his death, had been a gift from him. The thought of Benne and his undeserved fate lay heavily on Dancey's conscience. She tried dismissing him from mind when she felt the familiar accelerated heartbeats of anxiety racing helter-skelter inside her body. Turning over on her back, inhaling deeply, she gazed at the ceiling, following the trickles of light seeping up over the drapery heading at the window, playing a complexity of iridescent patterns above her head.

She thrashed about restlessly, closing her eyes against the vague vignettes forming in her mind. Memories she'd been forced to deal with and thought she'd neutralized in her mind began rearing their ugly heads.

I'm under the same roof where Benne lived, worked and loved. Oh, God, forgive me. Haven't I had enough punishment?

Sitting upright in bed against the headboard, her fingers clasping the locket, her body oozed with perspiration. She blotted herself with one end of the sheet, her fingers feeling the grooved numbers etched inside the locket. Dancey had the numbers 711-222 etched into the locket so she'd never forget the license number of the late-model Mercedes she'd seen pulling away from the Sinaloa Club the night she'd met with Benne's betrayers and become part of that unholy trio of death. Memories of that night had been vague. She'd been in bad straits, hurting and in desperate need of a fix. That night she could hardly recall the cab ride to the Bel Air Hotel where she'd parked her car. Once she'd paid the cabbie off, she got into her sportscar and driven the short distance to her home in Brentwood.

She'd scoured the mailbox; found the drugs left her; recalled little afterwards, strung out on barbiturates and heroin. A few days later, during moments of lucidity, she'd turned on a Channel 2 newscast and caught a brief blurb about a plane exploding over the Sierra Madre Occidental range in Mexico. Listening to the grisly report of Benne's death as his photo flashed on the screen, she had fallen into a state of shock and despair, collapsing in her home in near hysteria. For weeks and months she felt certain that retribution would come from someone, somewhere, for her participation in the deed; the growing paranoia plagued her every living moment.

She had kept afloat on heroin, refusing to allow reality to enter her consciousness, unable to endure the persecuting pain of guilt. The knowledge of her betrayal nearly annihilated what remained of her ego. In her eyes she became the vilest of all creatures with no right to live. She had overdosed three times. Saved on each occasion, recovery brought her more intolerable guilt.

Oddly enough the same guilt that caused her to seek death became the instrument psychiatrists used to pull her out of her depression, trying to stimulate her determination to kick the bloodsucking, insidious drug addiction.

Several psychiatrists tried but were unable to wean her off drugs. Drug-oriented sanitariums, highly recommended, had detoxified her and placed her on a regimen of tranquillizers, their doses lowered daily. What followed was numerous psycho-therapeutic rap sessions, the inclusion of nutritional foods and supplemental vitamins to help reduce the shock done to her mind and body.

Nothing helped. The craving for heroin was still there in the wings of her mind, waiting like a seductive and enticing whore to be beckoned back into her body.

One day while in a session with her therapist, the clear realization that she'd stupidly and willingly, under the influence of this insidious drug, sacrificed a human being in exchange for the grossly debilitating, monstrous drug, hit her square between the eyes. It produced in her the needed effect to combat her feelings of worthlessness. Backed into a corner, she had to choose between life and death.

In that pivotal moment, Dancey found the courage to make decisions and concluded she couldn't exist with the duality of her nature thwarting her at every turn.

The survivor instinct deep within her fought for her life, desperately reaching out and trying to grab hold of reality. In moments of lucidity she begged God's forgiveness for her gross misdeed against Benne, promising that in some way she'd right the wrong she'd done. How? She didn't know. She knew only that she must try, or she couldn't have endured the struggle back to life.

There was more—much more. Her psychiatrist, Dr.

Kadir Bushar, introduced her to a clinical psychologist, Abdul Harrim. If it hadn't been for Abdul . . .

Dancey sighed. She owed everything to his kind, loving care. Abdul had moved in with her several months ago and was partly responsible for Dancey's rehabilitation. They became lovers. The intense infatuation was equal. Through Abdul's efforts she hired a secretary, Jaqualine Devon, whom she considered a priceless jewel. Now they both occupied very special places in Dancey's life. But Abdul Harrim . . .

She thought she knew everything about making love. Compared to Abdul, Dancey was a neophyte. She missed him dreadfully. She and Jaqualine had flown in from LAX and because she wanted her own car at hand, Abdul was driving it in from Los Angeles, in time for the grand opening this weekend.

Abdul's urging had caused her to accept the contract offered by the Pyramids Hotel when her agent presented her with Renzo's proposal. At first she refused outright. A Las Vegas show! She'd never hack it. Her agent insisted; she resisted; Abdul persisted and discussed the potentials in a logical manner.

"This mystery man who is willing to back you in this new career is no fool. He knows you've got the stuff it takes or he wouldn't invest a dime in you."

Dancey had argued, "Me in Las Vegas dancing and singing before a live audience? If I can't face the terror of a camera how do you imagine I can face an audience of thousands? Oh, no, not me. I won't commit professional suicide."

"But, my pale moon flower," Abdul said softly, "the old you is dead. You are the new Dancey Darling, brave, spirited, a woman who knows what she wants in life and is going to get it."

"No," she said wistfully. "You're speaking of Maureen O'Mara. She is the gutsy one. She's the one with courage, not Dancey!"

"I've never met Maureen O'Mara. It is you who has what is needed."

By the time Abdul finished using his persuasive talents, the idea sat well with her. She had nothing to lose and everything to gain. It could be a new career. The added security of knowing someone cared and believed in her talent helped to mend her fractured ego.

She and Abdul played games trying to discover the identity of the mysterious philanthropist who had staked her to this new career. Abdul suggested she should accept it as a gift from Allah, who always guided his people in strange and mysterious ways.

She was floating on a new high, the high of living, of working towards a reasonable and realistic goal with acceptance of herself by not demanding the impossible.

"There's no way Dancey Darling is gonna fuck up," she told Abdul one night after a deliriously exciting love tryst with him. And she meant every word.

When her agent told her she'd open at the Pyramids Hotel, her first instinct was to refuse. The hotel belonged to the Erice family. She grew paranoid. Had they somehow learned of her participation in Benne's death? Did they seek retribution?

In permitting her mind to freeze around the idea that this stint in Las Vegas would be a death trap, she had allowed fear to twist and torment her beyond reason.

Abdul took her in hand. "You're letting your imagination play games with you." He spoke calmly, reassuringly. "In the past your thinking was guided by your drug habit. You were a junkie! You thought, connived, scammed, manipulated others, yes, even sold your soul for the price of a fix. But you're no longer a junkie. When will you accept it and think rationally??

Oh, Abdul, what will I ever do without you? she thought, unaware she'd become an unwilling pawn in a dangerous game.

Dancey's eyes moved about the restful, comfortable hotel room. It was hers until the end of the contract. Two days of rehearsal to familiarize herself with the enormous stage in that overpowering room called Cleopatra's Barge, and then opening night.

Opening night! What if they don't like me? What if I bomb? What if the crowd boos me? It can happen . . . Stop it, Dancey! Stop doing this to yourself!

Jumping off the bed, she pulled back the draperies, letting the bright sunlight into the room. Catching sight of the six dozen American Beauties, she pranced across the room, opened the card and smiled. The card read, "Bushels of success for my star! Renzo Bonaparte." The magnum of Dom Perignon caught her eyes. Her smile broadened at the card. Renzo again. She'd like to meet this Renzo—whoever he was.

Glancing at her image in the mirror, she concluded she hadn't looked better in her life. She no longer resembled living death, with black bags under her eyes. a sallow, sickly complexion and the haunted eyes of a drug addict. Even her body had fleshed out in the right places, firmed by the vigorous dance rehearsals. She'd regained her old seductive curves over which many a palpitating male had fantasized.

She began to dislodge the long hairpins from her topknot, letting her silvery blonde mane cascade onto her shoulders.

"Jaqualine!" she called aloud. "Where's my string bikini?"

Wearing slim Levis and a sheer see-through blouse, Jaqualine carried a tote bag into Dancey's room and placed it on the bed, removing the contents. "Going for a swim?" She handed her the bikini bottom.

"No—out on the terrace for sun. Be a luv and open the Dom Perignon for us." Dancey placed the abbreviated wisp of fabric on her body, tying the strings properly, and tossed the bra top back at her secretary, winking mischievously. Jaqualine tossed it aside, and poured the champagne for them.

"To the best and brightest star to capture the heart of Las Vegas," she toasted. They clinked glasses and sipped.

Dancey tilted her head teasingly. "Better than the reigning star, Jolie Barnes?"

"Better," replied Jaqualine mildly, surprised that Dancey had bothered to learn about the competition.

"I'll have to go some to beat her time. But thanks, anyway. Jaquey," she paused a moment. "You've been a real friend, more than I could have hoped for. I get the feeling you shouldn't be dedicating your life to me. You've too much to offer someone . . ."

Jaqualine waved her off with a scarf. "Put it on your head. The sun's disastrous for blondes."

Dancey sipped the champagne, drained her glass and, pouring more, moved out through the glass doors. "Don't let me stay in the sun more than an hour. Got it?"

Jaqualine nodded. "I'll be in my room if you need me."

The intense desert heat rushed at her. The sun felt invigorating as Dancey strolled to the edge of the roof, glancing at the city scene stretched out in both directions for miles. Below her, men were putting the finishing touches to a sign announcing DANCEY, just plain Dancey. She had arrived! To be called by her first name meant she had it made.

She was so excited by what she saw, she had to calm

down. She returned to the chaise longue and sat on the hot seat until her body adjusted to the heat. For two cents she'd remove her bikini bottom . . . Glancing cautiously about to spot a peeping Tom, Dancey tensed briefly, then blinked hard, her eyes fastened on the naked torso of a man standing in the adjoining patio, stretching, soaking up the sun as he worked a piece of rope over his head. It wasn't his nudity that startled her; she'd seen enough naked men in her life. Something about him . . .

In that instant, David Martin, sensing her presence, turned to face her. Their eyes held briefly. About to smile apologetically, his own expression froze at the horror in Dancey's eyes; a rush of incredible fear caused her to gasp aloud, clutching at the gold locket at her neck.

"No! No, it can't be you!" She fell into a faint.

David called to her, pulling on his shorts, shouting, "Hey, are you all right?"

She did not move; she just lay there in a heap on the terrace.

He sprinted over the obstructing iron railing between the two patios and falling on one knee at her side, rubbed her wrists. Then, when she failed to respond, he picked her up bodily and carried her inside.

Jaqualine, startled by his presence, caught sight of Dancey in his arms and ran towards him. "W-who are you? What happened?" She motioned to the bed. "Over there. Put her on the bed. What happened?" she asked again.

"Don't really know. She caught sight of me and fainted. The Vegas heat can be prostrating if you aren't used to it."

"Thank you. I'll take care of her now, uh—" she faltered.

"Benne. My name's Benne Erice," he said, recalling Bowman's admonition to keep up the Benne Erice identity. "I live next door. If I can do anything—anything at all—my family owns this hotel. We'll do our best to accommodate you. Does she faint often? I think you should call the house physician," he suggested, glancing at Dancey's labored breathing.

"Thank you, she'll be fine." Jaqualine's voice was curt and aloof although she found him exciting. With the exception of that ghastly scar along his cheek . . .

"Who is she?" He jerked his head towards Dancey. "She's a dishy-looking broad."

"I'm sure Miss Darling will appreciate your chivalry." Her voice was deliberately colorless.

David, one foot out the door, when he caught the name cast a hurried glance over his shoulder. "Uh, Dancey Darling?" He watched Jaqualine rub her wrists vigorously. "Uh, take good care of our star, will you?"

David sprinted back over the hot roof, lifting his feet as quickly as possible to prevent burning them. He was frowning, his brows knit into a scowl. *Dancey Darling! Fuck! Another monkey wrench to gum up the works! As if we didn't have enough problems to sort out . . .*

On the roster of Benne's paramours, quite close to the top of the list had been the name Maureen O'Mara AKA Dancey Darling. He'd never seen an assignment so fraught with complications. What else could go wrong? Val's disappearance had all the earmarks of a kidnapping. *A kidnapping! Fuck it! What ill timing!*

David had been working around the clock with a covy of agents glued to the phones with recording devices, hoping for a call from Val or his abductors. Neither David nor Whip believed this to be the usual kidnapping for ransom.

Craving sunshine and air, David had gone out on the terrace, never thinking he'd encounter the likes of Dancey Darling. No question, she'd mistaken him for Benne. Believing him to be dead, her reaction to Martin had been a natural one. Scowling blackly, he reentered the apartment ready to blast away at the imbecile responsible for placing Dancey in the suite next-door.

"Who was the bright-eyed genius who allowed her to move in next door? I thought we vacated the top floor? Dammit, she's here." He wiped the sweat from his face with a towel and poured a glass of ice water from a carafe.

"Who's here?" asked Whip brightly, entering the living room. He was wearing tennis shorts, no shirt. He carried a brief in his hand.

"The new star attraction—Dancey Darling."

Whip frowned. "Here? Next door?" He glanced at McKenna. "Move her. We don't need added pressures on Dave—not the kind she can furnish."

"Any news about Val? No word? Nothing?"

Chief Bowman shoved his Ben Franklins further up on his nose. "Helicopters scouting the area report seeing nothing unusual."

"By now, he could be halfway around the world," said David.

"Halfway around—" Whip expressed his concern. "You don't suppose he was spirited out of the country? Is it possible IAGO would—? They wouldn't, would they?"

The BSI didn't relish this theory. It meant more headaches on top of the ones they already had.

"You suppose Val knows more than he indicated?" David sat on the edge of the sofa nursing his third glass of ice water. "For Christ's sake, the TFL wouldn't flirt with a kidnapping!"

"They did once—with Joey Erice," said Whip. The others didn't buy this. They analyzed and conjectured and theorized.

David excused himself. He needed a shower. The others brooded over coffee, and sorted through the IAGO files.

Whip retired to his room and paced the floor thoughtfully. He had hardly given Dancey a second thought when Renzo mentioned she was headlining the next show. He had too many things on his mind. He wanted nothing to start between them again. Maureen O'Mara had been fun, exciting and spiritually uplifting for him. However, Dancey Darling was a totally different personality incarnated in Maureen's body. A demon at times, she was possessive, demanding, far too schizoid for his tastes. Madly obsessive and filled with insurmountable paranoia, her insecurity had spilled over into all her relationships. She'd become deeply involved in the drug scene, too much so. He hadn't minded smoking a joint or two, but that was his limit.

A year ago he'd run into Dancey at Marty James's Malibu pad. Among Dancey's entourage had been some of the strangest weirdos he'd ever seen. Whip found them all too freaked out on pills. He should have smiled and gone on. But there were the good old days in Malibu to reminisce over. He ended up at Dancey's pad in Brentwood, in bed with her. What really disturbed Whip, during their sexual intimacy, were the photographs Dancey had shown him—pictures of himself and Dancey in some of the lewdest poses he'd seen.

Astounded at first, he peered at them, trying to suppress his indignation, until he realized they weren't of him at all. His face had been superimposed on the body of another man.

"Don't worry, Whip darling," she'd explained. "I just miss you so much that seeing you in these poses with me, helps me to fantasize, so I can get over the lonely nights of missing you without too much pain."

That night Whip had just restrained himself from clouting the stupid bitch. From the moment he left her home, he refused even to speak her name. Her calls were not accepted. She was just too dangerous in her present state of mind.

She was here, now, next door. It was a bad omen. What was it David said before taking a shower? *Dancey had fainted at the sight of him.* Why? He paced the floor, chain smoking and thinking. He was on to something, but what? Something remote nagged at his memory. Had Benne and Dancey ever been an item?

Suddenly, enormously excited, he returned to the next room.

"McKenna—"

"Senator?"

"Let's back up a bit. In Martin's briefing, what was fed to him concerning the relationship between Benne and Maureen O'Mara, or Dancey Darling?"

He thought a moment. "You'd better ask David." He tapped his forehead. "He's got it all stored up here. I have it stored in a file back in Washington. Why?"

The BSI agents looked up, their eyes on Whip questioningly.

"Just a hunch . . ."

The woman on their minds was just being awakened by her secretary. Jaqualine broke open a vial of smelling salts and held it under Dancey's nostrils. The pungent fumes caused her to avert her head sharply with a sudden jolting return to consciousness.

Her words were jumbled at first. "No! No, it can't be you! You're dead! You're dead!" she screamed aloud and sat bolt upright in bed. She was drenched in perspiration. The scarf had fallen from her head, her hair was disheveled. She was frightened and distraught.

"Who was it? Who was that man I saw?" she shrieked at her secretary.

Jaqualine tried to calm her. "Just a neighbor who brought you inside when you fainted. I hope the sun doesn't always have this effect on you, Dancey. You'll have to keep out of it."

Dancey shoved her hands away as if they were contaminating her. Her hysteria shot up and her tongue became caustic. "I asked you who he was! Didn't you ask? Are you in the habit of letting strangers in our apartment without asking names?"

Jaqualine was seeing another Dancey, someone totally alien to her. Her face had contorted into a mask of ugliness.

"He said his name was, uh, Benne Erice. Yes, that's it. His family own the Pyramids—"

Dancey's face twisted into fright, her lips into an ugly leer.

"You lie! You're lying to me! Why are you doing this? Who are you?" she cried savagely, filled with suspicion. "Who put you up to this?" Her lips curled back over a violent flash of teeth.

Jaqualine's astonishment was total. "I'm not lying. Please rest, Dancey. You've been working too hard." She tried to hold Dancey gently, pressing against her shoulders, trying to get her to lie back on the bed.

Dancey turned into a madwoman, all arms and legs, as she shoved Jaqualine away from her with herculean strength.

"It's not Benne. Benne's dead! Don't touch me!" She wrenched away from Jaqualine's grasp and scrambled off the bed. She screamed, uttering imprecations, with rising hysteria and became totally unmanageable. She began throwing things at her secretary, anything within reach. A vase of red roses went hurtling across the room, smashing against the wall, the flowers flying everywhere.

Jaqualine fled into the adjoining room, slamming the door behind her. Reaching for the phone she called the house physician. In the time she'd worked for Dancey she hadn't encountered such violence. Advised that a day might come when her employer might need considerable help, Jaqualine had prepared for the eventuality. She usually kept a small medicine bag at hand containing the necessary drugs to sedate her. Because she hadn't needed them in the past she had left everything in Brentwood.

Dammit! Damn Ali! Damn Abdul! Damn Bahar! Goddamn them all! Why had she permitted herself to enter into this crazy business? She even had to share her lover with this crazy wanton woman. *And what for? What for, in the name of Allah?* Hatred and madness contorted her features as she walked the floor awaiting the house physician. She felt she was at the edge of insanity.

Her mind raced back to the first time she'd found

Dancey and Abdul together in bed. Her jealousy had been unendurable. She had wanted to sink a knife into both their lousy hearts. For a minute the amorous couple on the bed had stared at her in stupefaction. Then Dancey in her drunken stupor suggested that Jaqualine climb into bed with them. Jaqualine had all she could do to keep from flying at Abdul to wipe the silly smirk off his lips.

Later, after Dancey had fallen into a sedated sleep, Abdul had come to her, in her own bed. She felt an inner revulsion for her spineless, prideless crawling to him. What had she done to herself that she lacked the strength to walk away from him? Despite the turning-in of her own anger, she was still furious that Abdul could come to her after having prolonged sex with Dancey.

"You—you male whore!" she yelled at him. "That's what you are, a male whore!" She hurled vile obscenities at him in all the languages she knew. They had fought that night. Jaqualine had pounded her fists against him, scratched him, drawing blood. She kicked him and bit him. Abdul did nothing except hold her, pinning her arms back tightly until her fury had subsided. When she quieted down he spoke to her softly.

"You think I enjoy myself with that broken-down gutter tramp?" He smoothed her hair off her face, stroking her gently, his words hypnotic. "I cannot stand touching her. She is an obscenity to me. But for that day in the future when we can live in peace and security in our own land, I will do anything. No sacrifice is too great. It's you I love, Jamila. When will you believe what I tell you?"

She had fallen into his arms at once, submissive, melting against him. His words erased all the bad memories. Then she got fired up again. "Would you love me if I were not a princess? If my brother were not the great wealthy Prince Ali Mohammed?"

Abdul gave her a look of long suffering and buried his head in her firm breasts, playing with those twin beauty marks with his tongue.

"When will you understand it's not a matter of wealth?"

She'd kept her silence during her arousal, unable to resist the magic he performed on her body. Only Abdul could provide the fuel that kept her drug habit under control. She had closed her eyes, obliterating everything from sight and mind except the excitement of that moment.

Jaqualine was brought out of her reverie by a loud knock at the door. She ushered the doctor into Dancey's

262

room, by now a shambles, and stood to one side as the doctor examined her. Dancey was spent, exhausted and pale, fraught with terror. She looked quite mad. The gold locket, torn from her neck, had been flung across the room. "He's dead! He's dead!" she sobbed repeatedly. "Stop playing tricks on me!" she hissed as the physician jabbed her with a hypodermic syringe filled with a sedative.

Dr. Jake Saperstein, in his fifties, dressed casually in bright orange slacks and an open yellow shirt, peered at Jaqualine through horn-rimmed glasses in a searching, professional manner, as he snapped the disposable syringe in two, discarding it in a wastebasket. "What happened?" he asked, jerking his head towards Dancey.

"What did you inject?"

Doc Saperstein's brows shot up. "Why? Are you a doctor or a nurse?"

Jaqualine bridled angrily. "She's a former addict. Some things don't agree with her. It might start the craving up again."

The doctor snorted. "There isn't such a thing as a *former* addict," he said gruffly. "Pillhead or mainliner?"

Jaquey faltered. "Uh—heroin among other things."

He nodded knowingly and tossed aside the towel. "You don't look so hot yourself. What are you on?"

"I beg your pardon?" She drew herself up icily, at once hostile.

Dr. Saperstein shrugged. "Yeah, yeah, none of you are on anything. You don't take a thing. That's why there aren't enough hours in the day for me to handle all you people who don't take anything!" He snapped his bag shut. "It's nothing she'll get a bad reaction from." He handed her a card. "Call me any time. We can't let anything happen to our new star."

Jaqualine frowned. "I hope you'll be discreet. She's been clean a long time. She's worked hard to get her act together."

"Honey, the only reason I'm here for so many years is I'm deaf, dumb and blind. Get it?"

She scribbled the voucher he presented without contest. She cringed at the hundred-dollar charge, aware she was buying his silence, not his services. He gave her another long, hard look, one which made her squirm uncomfortably, then left. She locked the door behind him.

Leaning heavily against the door, Jaqualine sighed in relief. Her eyes picked up a glittering object on the floor nearby; the locket. She picked it up and walking to the bed pulled a coverlet over Dancey. Pulling the drapes, she returned to her own room, leaving the door ajar.

Captivated by the mysterious locket, Jaqualine examined it under a lamp and pulled it open. Astonishment was in her eyes. She couldn't be mistaken—it was Dancey and—and this man Benne Erice.

Her brows drew together in a puzzled frown. What was it Dancey had been screaming? "It can't be Benne! Benne's dead!"

She turned it over and studied the numbers, 711-222.

The shrill ring of her telephone startled her. She picked up the receiver. "Miss Devon here."

"Miss Darling, please. Renzo Bonaparte calling."

"I'm sorry, sir. She's sleeping."

"Well, wake her up. This is the boss."

"Can't do that. She's very tired. I'll have her call you the moment she awakens—"

Renzo hung up abruptly. Jaquey shrugged and replaced her phone. She had more on her mind than to be concerned with his hangups.

Obviously, thought Jaqualine, pacing the floor, one hand clasping the locket, Dancey knew Benne Erice quite well, judging from the intimacy of the photo in the locket. Yet, the man who called himself Benne Erice acted as if he barely knew her.

Earlier she had sensed that something peculiar was happening, and felt more certain of it now. She picked up the large scrapbook Dancey kept at her bedside, containing newspaper clippings of Ted and Whip Shiverton's political careers. Dancey, secretive about her relationship to each man, had confided more to Abdul than to her. Later when she and Abdul were together, Abdul would replay taped recordings of their conversations.

She recalled Whip Shiverton briefly. Their encounter at Ali's Rome villa might have blossomed into a worthwhile one if Ali hadn't burst in on them unannounced with—uh, what was her name? It was so long ago, how could she remember? She had questioned Dancey about the senator without being obvious. What kind of a man was he? What were his political intentions? How badly had he fared after his brother's death?

It had taken a while, and in time Dancey seemed more inclined to discuss the Shiverton brothers more freely, speaking frankly about their romantic sojourns.

Recently she had stopped discussing them. Jaqualine

got the distinct impression Dancey was growing suspicious of her unending inquiries.

Jaqualine confessed her concern to Abdul. "She's getting suspicious of me, I can feel it. I just can't ask any more."

"You must. Everything she tells you is being recorded."

"Why?" she asked in innocence.

"It's best, Jamila, that you do as I ask without asking questions. The less you know, the better for you."

"Are you involved in something desperate? Tell me, Abdul."

He looked away, unable to meet her probing eyes. "If I said yes, what then?"

His candor threw her. "I—don't know," she replied truthfully. "You'd best stop calling me Jamila," she cautioned.

"You see? What earthly good would it do to tell you? It would mean one additional worry for me." He paused. "I did? I called you Jamila?"

"Then it *is* desperate," she said in dismay.

That night, Abdul, as he had on every other occasion, replied by letting his body grow hard against hers, touching, caressing, petting, stroking her until her skin rippled with passion. "Yes, yes, it's as desperate as I am at this moment. I want to fuck you every minute of the day and night—"

"When you're not fucking that whore."

Abdul grabbed her face, fiercely forcing her to look into his eyes. "I am speaking with you. When we're together nothing else counts. Do you believe me?"

"Oh, yes, Abdul," she moaned, "Do it to me morning, noon and night," she wailed aloud, rising to the heights of delirium.

Her thoughts, interrupted by the shrill ringing phone, ended abruptly. She picked up the receiver. "Yes," she said dully.

"Is it you?" came the voice on the phone.

"Yes."

"Can you talk freely?"

"Wait a minute." Laying the phone down Jaqualine padded barefoot across the room. Dancey was fast asleep. She closed the door partially and picked up the receiver. "Yes, within limits."

"The medication is on its way. Uh—he's there."

"Where?"

"In the suite next door. Why the need for the drugs? Is everything all right?"

"I'm not sure. Something happened. The pieces don't fit. How can you be sure he's here? Why would he be?"

"Bahar wants you to learn all you can . . ."

In the penthouse Tina occupied, several FBI agents with wiretaps on her phone, waiting to hear from Val's kidnappers, sat before their electronic counters watching their screens. One agent tapped his partner gently. "What do you make of this, Jim?" he asked inquiringly as he listened to an open channel.

"How can I hope to learn anything? I can't barge in on him. What if he recognizes me?" said Jaqualine's voice.

"Then give him a cover story. Quick! Hang up!" her caller advised when he heard a familiar click on their line.

In her suite, Jaqualine did so with dispatch.

The agent named Jim cursed aloud. "Too late, goddammit! It could mean anything. We better report it to the chief."

Jaqualine, staring at the phone, wondering why Abdul had hung up at the clicking sounds, considered the matter. Who would think of tapping Dancey's phone? It didn't make sense. She walked to the bathroom, opened her overnight case and popped two aspirins, chased down with water. She brushed her long hair for a few moments, wondering what business Senator Shiverton would have in Las Vegas. Her mind churned. Why would he choose to be here now—why?

She went back to the living room and curled up on the sofa, poring over the scrapbook.

Renzo sat glumly in his suite pouting like a school kid. The idea of having to talk with a go-between annoyed him. When he called his star he wanted her to answer, not some Miss Goody Two-shoes who clanked sabres with him, refusing to comply with his orders.

He had planned everything to the last detail. Dinner with Dancey, here in Benne's swinging pad that had all the trappings. A rush of water trickled from a three-tiered fountain into the sparkling turquoise waters of an abstract-shaped swimming pool between the living room and bedroom. In the bedroom guests could observe an assortment of porno films designed to turn on a frigid spinster. In addition, there was a display of electronically controlled lights, that were spellbinding. All of it was perfect for a dish like Dancey, thought Renzo, ambling about, his critical eyes making a last-minute inspection. Then Renzo changed his mind. Considering Dancey's background, he decided it was more appropriate if their first dinner and a romp in the hay took place in Dancey's suite. She'd be more comfortable there. The phone rang. He picked up an extension nearby. It was Tina.

"So, my wife decides she has a husband?" he said sarcastically.

"Move your star attraction out of the penthouse. You have no business putting her there without checking with me," she ordered crisply without preamble.

"Why?"

"Benne says so, that's why. They don't want any nude distractions pussyfooting around. They're doing business."

"Yeah, well, it's gonna hafta wait until tomorrow. I can't bother her. She's tired."

"I'll send the maids to pack their belongings and transfer them into one of the bungalows. Since when does the hired help rate a two-hundred-dollar-a-day suite? Are you so desperate to impress her?"

"No need for smart talk. She stays the night. Tomorrow when she's in rehearsal I'll personally see the move's made. Tell Benne it's not the proper time. He'll understand even if his family doesn't. Hey—don't hang up! What's going on up there? I can't find out a thing. What have you heard from the old man?"

Oh, how she wanted to tell him what she really thought. But as her father's daughter, she had a role to play—and play it she did. "You're right. We'd be fools to display such bad manners to our new star. She might mistake it for a lack of faith in her ability to perform. Tomorrow is fine."

"Tina?" She threw him with this acquiescence.

"I hear you."

"That's the closest you've come to making sense in a long time. You're O.K., kid."

Tina slammed the phone down on him.

Renzo turned on the stereo. Jolie Barnes's voice came at him from all directions from the powerful speakers rigged to bounce off every wall in the room. Her sultry voice stirred powerful memories in him. He angrily switched the stereo to a medley of Tony Bennett songs. His hands shook noticeably as he turned on the water and stepped inside the brown Italian tiled stall shower.

Renzo finished his toilet with meticulous care. He was filled with great expectations for the evening. He took time to check with several department heads in the casino. Things were under control. He wanted to call Marciano, to describe the tremendous change in Dancey. His spies had told him she was clean. Renzo knew what that meant. She had to be watched every minute. One mistake, one moment's weakness, could trigger off the whole cycle again, like that one drink did to an alcoholic.

He didn't call Manny because he had no answers to the other questions he was sure to ask. He hadn't seen Richie, Benne, the senator or the others holed up in Val's penthouse. He knew by the room service tabs and by questioning his key personnel that there were nearly a dozen men up there. He could understand the Feds on the job in a snatch case. He wondered why they hadn't questioned him. Meanwhile his job was to run the hotel and casino as usual.

An hour earlier Joey Erice had called him. He was flying west. To pry him away from his business something heavy had to be afoot. Joey would level with him tomorrow. At least he had one ally in the Erice family. Renzo had helped him in the matter of two abortions when two of Joey's broads got caught. Yeah, Joey wouldn't want the family to know about his indiscretions. He was one mistake Val had made. Joey was so unlike the rest of the family it was pitiful. No balls! No balls at all.

Renzo sauntered to the bar, poured himself a half glass of Beefeaters gin and downed it straight. His mind focused on Dancey.

Forget this other crap, Renzo, baby. Tonight you're gonna have yourself a fuckin' ball. You need it, kid. Imagine, Dancey Darling is straight!

CHAPTER TWENTY-TWO

The brilliant coppery sun was setting and over the floor of the desert cooling winds ruffled the sand and chased tumbleweeds across the topaz-colored desert onto the walkway of the ramshackle cabin.

The sweating, indolent man inside stood facing the large blown-up poster of Dancey Darling, his hand steadily holding the .345 magnum. He took careful aim at portions of Dancey's anatomy. Slowly, very slowly, he squeezed the trigger.

Click . . . Click . . . Click . . .

The sounds were loud. The gun wasn't loaded. The man grinned. He came a few steps closer, then took careful aim once again, fixing her temple in his sight. His finger squeezed slowly again. Click . . . Click . . . Click!

A sickening grin spread like a malignancy across his leathery, weatherbeaten face. He walked back towards the mock altar and picked up a silencer, attaching it firmly to the barrel. He glanced up at the poster again, this time holding the gun to her temple. He made a clucking sound with his tongue. Then, still grinning, he made exaggerated movements as he removed the gun and placed it back on the table.

The approaching sounds of copters flying overhead brought his head up, angling to one side as he listened. He skirted to the open door, staying back in the shadows, and peered up into the brightly colored sky. He tensed and listened. For nearly fifteen minutes the Army helicopter circled the isolated old house. Apparently satisfied there was nothing amiss, the chopper flew off in another direction.

The man pulled out a velvet-lined box from under the table and began packing the firearms meticulously in their proper niches, securing each weapon except the .345 magnum. He put the ammunition in its proper place and shut the case, locking it. He brought it to the door and placed it on the floor.

He glanced at his watch. It was 8:30 P.M. The desert outside was a pool of darkness. A haze of city lights illuminated the sky on this moonless, starless night. He lit a small battery-powered flashlight and finished dressing. Then he stood in his black suit, white shirt and black string tie, rubbing the toe of each boot against the back of his trouser legs. He slipped the magnum into a specially built boot holster and, limping slightly, went out the open door.

Housed in a flimsy lean-to attached to the ramshackle building stood a white '75 Pinto hatchback, in sad need of a washing. He opened the hatchback. He went back into the house, reappearing with the small arsenal, putting it into the rear of the car. Inside the house, he removed the poster and other photos of Dancey Darling, ripping them to shreds inside a bucket. He opened a bottle marked *acid* and tossed the contents onto the picture shreds. In moments the prints disappeared. He never used fire, when acid was foolproof.

The acid, packed in a corrugated container, was placed into his valise. He set the white Afro wig into place on his head and applied the mustache with spirit gum. Finished, he opened the cosmetic case, flipping back the upper half. He scanned the narcotics and syringes, then, satisfied, transferred the tray to the false bottom in his valise. He packed everything in the rear trunk of the Pinto, locking it. Back inside the house his discerning eyes searched every niche under the powerful beam of the flashlight. It was clean, nothing telltale. He left it as he'd found it.

In moments he was driving towards the bright city lights illuminating the black horizon. He stopped a mile from town at a public pay phone, dropping a coin, dialing a number, listening intently. He was off again, stopping this time to buy a couple of Big Macs and a coke. He polished off the fast food in the car.

At 10:30 P.M. he pulled into the parking lot next to a post office, parking near a Mercedes with the Arizona license plates 711-222. He waited, searching the deserted area. Convinced no one was observing him, he quickly transferred all his gear into the Mercedes, placing the arsenal in a built-in compartment out of sight; only the valise remained in the Pinto.

He locked the Mercedes, and got back into the Pinto, driving along the strip towards the Golden Oasis. It was 11:00 P.M. when he pulled into the Golden's employee parking lot and chose the spot furthest from the hotel's entrance. He sat for a while, his piercing eyes everywhere;

270

it was quiet. He got out of the car, closing the windows, leaving the key in the ignition, careful to wipe away all prints. He took a cane from his valise and leaned on it, looking thirty years older.

"Sorry, you can't park there, old man. You'll get a ticket without an employee's sticker on the wheels."

Nodding, he got back into the Pinto, glowering fiercely. Starting up the car, he backed out of the space and cruised to another place at the edge of the lot. He emerged five minutes later, having drawn thin surgical gloves on his hands. He left the key in the ignition again.

Leaning on the cane for support, carrying the valise in his other hand, he limped between cars, staying well in the shadows. He was sweating copiously. Two more jobs and it was finished; this one and the last hopefully the next day. Then the world was his. He'd netted enough dough to retire for life without financial worries. He slipped by the parking attendant unseen before entering the side door, where he peered about and exited through another, emerging at a point some fifty yards from where he'd entered the Golden. His eyes peered about, soon spotting what he was searching for, a dung-colored Volkswagen. In moments he'd hotwired it, gunned the motor, and made off with it.

Once on the Strip, he breathed easier. Tonight, the job would be a snap—the last one might prove complicated. *You pay your money and take your chances,* he told himself.

It was 12:00 midnight. He abandoned the Volkswagen at the rear of the Sands Hotel and checked his appearance in the rear view mirror; wig, mustache, glasses, all in place. Out of the car, his transformation into a withered old man began; cane in one hand, body bent over it, valise in the other, laboriously making his way to the hotel, favoring the orthopedic boot. Inside the hotel he limped to the front entrance and stood outside until a brightly uniformed doorman flagged the first cabbie in a long line waiting for fares. He helped the old man board.

"Where to?" asked the driver, peering at his fare in the rear view mirror.

As if afflicted with the palsy, his trembling voice muttered, "T-the P-Pyramids, p-please, y-young f-f-fella."

Dancey couldn't stop laughing at Renzo's humorous stories.

"You should be in show business," she chided him.

He'd arrived with an entourage of waiters wheeling serving carts heaped with gourmet foods and wines to please a queen, and tactfully introduced himself. His mood was overly pompous and overly serious. It struck her funny bone.

"Please come in. I'm overwhelmed, since I'd planned to go to sleep early tonight."

"Nonsense, I insist we celebrate your new contract and your new career together. I'm Renzo Bonaparte."

"Ahhhhh," she murmured knowingly. "The roses and Dom Perignon." Dancy swept past him as the expert waiters set up the intimate table for two. Renzo opened a fresh bottle of champagne and poured two glasses. He took both with him, leading the way to the terrace. "Shall we, until my men are ready for us?"

She smiled enchantingly, always a sucker for romance and gallantry. "Why not?" Her azure blue silk kaftan revealed every delicious curve in her body; her hair, piled high atop her head with wispy strands corkscrewing on her face, gave her a bedroom appearance, begging for seduction. Her makeup was sparse; a few freckles were visible; there was a little pink lip gloss on her petulant lips and her Estée cologne was fresh and alluring.

They moved along the terrace, warm desert breezes stirring the air gently, and went to the edge, overlooking the glittering neon and gaudy lights. Dancey stared at her own name up in enormous lights, larger than she had seen earlier.

"You'll own it all one day," said Renzo. "Like the feeling?"

Dancey turned abruptly to him, nodding at first, then something inside her triggered another response. "Have we met before, Renzo? You seem familiar to me."

You seem familiar to me—not, *you look familiar*.

"If we'd met you wouldn't have forgotten me, I promise." He kissed her fingertips with Old World charm, evoking throaty laughter from her.

"You don't lack class, for sure." She accepted the champagne.

"Then, honey, let me lay it all out for you up front. I'm the man who bankrolled your career." His innuendo was unmistakable.

Her head angled sharply; her smile faded. "I should have said you've got balls. But that's O.K. 'cause I'm an up-front broad. I gave my secretary the night off. One

272

look in your eyes told me what a stud like you had in mind."

"I'm *that* obvious?" He laughed uproariously.

Renzo's polite cordiality threw her. He displayed a charm that dazzled her. Later she would wonder if this impression of him was colored by her own insecurities. During dinner he remained pleasant. Over coffee and liqueurs, she fairly glowed as he described his expectations of her performance. "You'll be the toast of Vegas, New York and Hollywood. I tell ya, I've got faith in ya, kid."

Once again, Dancey glanced critically at him, the inescapable feeling that she knew him refusing to abate. They had both been drinking a lot, each for different reasons: Renzo to relieve his tension over Val's kidnapping and the havoc created by the federal agents running rampant in the hotel; Dancey to bolster her courage for the show's opening, knowing how much rested on her success here in Las Vegas.

Renzo's thoughts trailed to his irrational behavior a few nights ago when he'd snuck into Tina's boudoir, a desperate man. Ready to make a pact with the devil to get into Tina's good graces, he'd drugged her. A kid was the answer. He shouldn't have waited so long . . . *What's the use, it's gone too far. Fuck it! You're with Dancey Darling, Renzo. Live it up—the broad's ripe for the picking!*

Behind her facade of smiles, Dancey was also thinking, about her encounter with Benne Erice. No one could fool her. It *was* Benne! Awakening from the sedation, she had missed her locket instantly. Jaqualine claimed she'd taken it to the jewelry shop to have it repaired. Dancey felt naked without it. *For tonight, forget it. Tomorrow you'll lose yourself in rehearsal. You have no time to believe in ghosts,* she told herself.

Dancey snuggled up to Renzo, her hand on his upper thigh.

"Renzo," she whispered, feeling a glow from the drinks. "Who owns this hotel? I mean who is really the boss?"

"The Erice family. My wife's family." He wanted to say, *I'm the boss. One day soon I'll own the whole place.*

"Erice," she repeated vaguely. "I read the son was killed in a plane crash—the same family?"

Renzo tensed. *Fucking cunt knows damn well what she read. What the fuck's coming off? Had she recognized*

273

him? Was she playing games? He had to make sure. "Yeah, something like that. Only I guess he didn't die. He survived the crash but don't remember nothing. Amnesia is what he's got."

"You think he didn't die?" She sat up, reining her fear. "Don't you know for certain?" Her stomach coiled into a knot. *Benne's alive?*

"Sure I know for sure. Do we hafta talk about him? I came here to get acquainted with my star. So, let's get acquainted."

"O.K." she muttered colorlessly. "Let's get acquainted."

He started with hot kisses on her too-willing lips. It was no good—not this way. He wanted to do it the right way.

She was tense and needed relaxing. They both fumbled awkwardly. He wasn't dubbed the greatest cocksman east of L.A. for nothing. "Relax, kid, relax. This ain't gonna get far if you stay so uptight."

Dancey needed no further coaxing. On her feet, she pulled at a few snaps, undid a zipper and stood before him naked. She was breathtaking. He gasped with pleasure. Her overt sexuality shook him. He laughed uneasily. "Dammit, what the hell's wrong with me? I can't get it up. I'm acting like a fucking, snotnosed cherry!"

"Give it time," she soothed. "It happens with most men. I guess they're awestruck about being with Dancey Darling!"

"Fuck that!" he muttered, drawing her close to him, kissing her smooth white belly and those full rounded breasts with strawberry puckered nipples. Everything he planned to say dried up in his throat. He caught a glimpse of her face; she was reacting to him, melting under his skilled hands and lips. So what was wrong with him? Picking her up in his arms he carried her to the bed; he removed his clothing quickly. His urgency to perform increased his anxiety and communicated itself to her. Dancey rolled towards him, tracing the outline of his body with a fragile, fluttering finger.

"That's some body you have, superman," she purred.

"You ain't so bad yourself, kiddo," he muttered, taking in her beauty, thinking as he did, *Here's the body millions of men lust over, right next to me. And where the fuck am I?*

He tried to squirm away from her touch when her warm hand slowly stroked his upper thigh, getting closer—closer—closer.

Renzo rolled over out of her grasp. He was apologetic. "I don't know what's gotten into me. Tired, I guess. Look, it ain't got nothing to do with you, sweetie. Believe me."

The hell it doesn't! I can't get outa my head that she's a junkie cunt! What the hell's wrong with me? Renzo had never wrestled with his conscience before. Morality had never entered into his relations with women. He'd fucked whores, from a two-bit hooker when he was a street kid in New York, to high-class five-hundred-a-night call girls, with a helluva lot of freebies in between. But here was the Queen of Sheba, Cleopatra, and Salome lying next to him and he couldn't perform.

Dancey eyed him coolly for different reasons. His use of the vernacular set off an alarm in her head. *Where have I heard that voice before? Something—something about him . . .* There was more. The deeply rooted feeling of rejection was threatening to rise in her again. She just didn't have what it took to get him hot and bothered. She was nothing—a real nothing. If the world only knew she had no sex appeal at all.

Renzo moved off the bed, furious with himself, and puzzled. He poured two drinks, and doctored them from a vial he removed from his pants pocket. He sipped his, handed her the other as he stroked his deflated cock. "Wouldja believe this ain't happened before?" he said, suddenly reverting to his old Brooklynese slang. "It's the strain I'm under. Give it time, I'll perform like magic. What the hell, we ain't in no hurry, are we?"

He watched her sip her drink. The glittering gold amulet around his neck caught her eyes. She blinked hard in the dim lighting; her memory did a dizzying foxtrot trying to fit pieces together in her mind. "What's your sign, Renzo?" she asked, sipping her drink economically.

"You mean this?" He glanced at the disc. "December. Don't tell me you're one of them sign-happy broads? Shi-i-t! I've had my fill of them. Sagittarius, baby—sexy, eh?"

Benne was Sagittarius, too! That's not what disturbed her. The drinks were getting to her. Renzo removed the glass from her hand and leaned her back against the pillows, as the buzzing in his groin came to life. His impotence of the moment had passed. Sensing her momentary confusion he held her closer.

"Don't worry, babe," he whispered. "Renzo will take care of you. Relax, pretty baby, I believe in you. No one has the faith I have. Just do what I tell you and I'll be there always—"

He continued to sweet-talk her, caressing her quivering body, tracing the outlines of her breasts and nipples with a fluttery tongue. She sighed ecstatically, her earlier doubts and fears fading, replaced by mounting excitement. Her body writhed and responded to his expertise.

"Mmmmm, you're good," she whispered. "You're real good."

"You ain't seen nothing yet, baby."

"No, but I'm feeling something like I've never felt," she whispered, avidly holding on to his tumescence. She angled away from him and looked down. "I don't believe it. It can't be real," she giggled.

"Believe it, sweet cunt, it's real." He sucked greedily on her nipples, as Dancey felt his pulsating cock swell.

"I could easily become addicted to you," she sighed. Tensing, her body coiling, her eyes wide and stunned at the pleasure, she climbed to higher and higher plateaus. She screamed aloud as she spiraled into ecstasy, her body bouncing frenziedly until the orgasm passed. Drowsy, curiously languid, she wafted in euphoria. Was it possible, what she felt? *I swear I feel a drug high. A painless fog where nothing matters* . . . Pictures flashed on her consciousness, subliminal images: two men seated opposite her in the Sinaloa Club, one in a white Afro wig. A golden Sagittarius amulet spun about her head. Renzo's words: "Benne didn't die. He survived but he's got no memory." No memory! *Was it possible he'd have no memory of me at the Beverly Hills Hotel?*

"What's the matter, sweetie? You aren't with it, are ya?"

"Yes, yes, I hear you." She rolled over on her side facing him. "Put it inside me, Renzo. That always does it to me. I gotta feel your big prick inside me to really turn on," she whispered sensually.

His sexual urgency was under control. "It's my turn to show you," he murmured, knowing she was ripe, aroused by his ministrations and the irritant he spilled into her wine. They both were aroused and aware. Dancey thought the scent of roses had never been as intoxicating as it was during these moments as Renzo brought her to climax after climax until she was spent and begged for mercy. Renzo finally ejaculated, forcing her for the last time to climax with him.

The phone rang shrilly. Dancey didn't budge. Renzo

nudged her. "Answer your phone. It could be for me." He glanced at the time on his watch; 10:45 P.M., still early.

Dancey muttered a sleepy "Hullooo . . ." and handed him the phone. "For you, boss."

Renzo frowned thoughtfully. *Sonofabitch! I can't take a minute off. They track me wherever I go.* He barked into the phone. "Yeah, it's me . . . You sent him up here? Goddammit! Maybe I didn't want no one to know where I am! All right! All right!" He handed the phone back to Dancey.

"Sorry, babe, I've gotta leave you for a while. Give me a little sample of what I can expect when I return, will ya?"

She puckered her lips and gave him a lazy kiss. Her head was still hazy. Had she heard him clearly? She turned her back on him.

When a knock came at the door, Renzo walked over and opened it slightly. It was one of Manny Marciano's men. "Sorry, Renzo, the boss wants you over there on the double. Some kind of trouble." He spoke in confidential tones.

"Now? Right in the middle of—" His voice broke off as he listened. "O.K. Did anybody see you coming up here?"

"Naw—I was careful. Look, I'll wait for you at the usual place. I'll drive ya there and back. You got too much fuzz in the joint to suit me." Renzo closed the door and turned back to Dancey.

Dancey was wide awake. She was cold. She couldn't remember ever being as cold as she was at this moment. She rubbed her arms and pulled the sheet up around her. "Where are you going?" she asked him possessively. "Sure you'll come back or shall I lock my door?"

"Both. I'll be back, and lock your door. You just be here."

In the bathroom Renzo showered and dressed hastily wondering what was so urgent to make Manny send this schmuck to fetch him. He snapped off the bath light, and stole a glance at Dancey. "I'll let myself in with a passkey. Keep the bed warm. Shit, if you're so friggin' cold, turn off the air conditioner."

Dancey, still shivering, her teeth chattering, sprinted off the bed and snapped off the air conditioner. The highs had left her; the lows, hitting below the belt, twisted her stomach. She ran into the shower and let the hot water rain on her for several minutes. She still felt spaced out—from what? In a robe, she opened the terrace door and felt the warm rush of air. Her agitation increased; her knuckles kneaded the palms of her hands nervously; the old insecurities plagued her.

She wasn't good enough or he wouldn't have left her. She couldn't wait until Abdul arrived. He never left her like this. Where was he? Jaqualine said he planned to leave Brentwood in the morning. She wouldn't see him until tomorrow! She smoked as she paced the terrace, staring at her name in lights. What a power trip it was to see it.

She felt dizzy. Flashes of Renzo's amulet sprinted across her mind, followed by a staccato of Benne's image; repetitions of the old images she thought were buried and done with; the dim interior of the Sinaloa; the white-wigged weirdo; the sleek jaguar, Midas, who badmouthed her, his golden jewelry and Sagittarius. What was it he told her again and again? "I don't trust junkie cunts! What I'm saying is I think you'll fuck up, babe."

Those words had burned in her memory for too long. That same speech pattern, the use of those same idioms. Was it possible? Could he have been Renzo? Midas and Renzo, one and the same? A feeling of weakness came to her and in a split second, Dancey came to a decision. She glanced towards the next penthouse, and walked to the adjoining patio. Lights shone through the window casements; she could hardly see inside.

She shuddered, chills sweeping through her. It was shortly after eleven. Did she dare chance it? If she didn't she'd go crazy. A few moments later, Dancey, shaking like a leaf, frightened, with her old insecurities mounting, walked through the open door.

"Hi," she said, her voice just above a whisper.

David was startled. After a moment's awkwardness he set aside the book he was reading and stood up graciously. He was wearing Levis, no shirt, and was barefooted.

"Hi, neighbor. It is Miss Darling?"

She stared at him, hard, critically, with piercing eyes, despite the terrible pounding ache in her head. She had to know once and for all. "I thought I was Mau to you, Benne. Have you forgotten me so soon?" She moved in closer to him, her eyes assessing the scars. "That from the accident?"

He nodded. "Forgive me. I don't remember much. I'm a fool not to remember you—but I promise it's not on purpose."

"Nothing? You remember nothing about us? Nothing? You don't remember the Beverly Hills Hotel before you left for Mexico?" Dancey felt a severe pain in her stomach. "We were there together."

"Were we now? Damn, I'd give anything to remember. The best of all memories seem lost in a maze," he lamented, feeling the coiling knot of tension squeeze his insides.

"We spent nearly a week together—"

"Please, enlighten me. May I fix you a drink?"

She sat on the sofa arranging the folds in her robe. "It would be much simpler if you remembered."

"My dear, you fainted dead away when you saw me today. No repeat performances, please. Your secretary loathes me."

He handed her the drink, and toasted. "To your new career!"

Dancey drained her glass and placed it on the coffee table.

"Benne," she began, looking him straight in the eyes. "It was me. I can talk about it because I've come to terms with myself. It doesn't ease the pain to know how you've suffered at my hands. I've lived with the truth until it nearly killed me, that and heroin." She erased the frown between her brows.

He shook his head. "What do you mean it was you? What was you?" he asked lightly, uncertain of what was coming off.

"I set you up. The trip to Mexico," she explained when he drew a blank. "I betrayed you, understand? You'd better remember 'cause I'll never be able to level with you again."

"Just a moment, Miss Darling," he said, his breath coming in gasps, "so that I get this straight. Are you telling me—"

"Yes. Yes! Yes! Exactly. It's all my fault. I was mainlining at the time. Lower than the lowest gutter rat without principles or morals. You know what a junkie is? Yes, that. Exactly. I sold your soul for the price of a few fixes." She was shaking uncontrollably, tears streaming down her face. She was wretched, agonized, and wouldn't last much longer in this state.

"They kept sticking you needles, sodium pentothal, I think, just so you'd tell them the details. They wouldn't let me stay. I pleaded with them not to hurt you. But they got you to tell them everything. Oh, they were good,

Benne. They kept me floating in heroin until it was over. Later, after I learned you'd been killed—I mean it was in all the papers and on television. You'd been killed is what everyone thought."

Dancey told him her story. She was wringing wet with perspiration, alternating between hot and cold chills.

"The shock of seeing you—"

David came closer to her and took her hands in his. "It takes a helluva lot of courage to tell me this. I'm not sure if I should despise you or thank you for your honesty."

"I'd rather you forgive me, Benne. Please. So I can go on living? I know I don't deserve it. By rights you'd be justified if you killed me for being so weak as to cause the death of another human being. It's been ghastly . . ."

"Please, tell me about it. Tell me all you know," he urged. "Perhaps you can help stoke my memory." How else could he encourage her to keep talking?

Dancey's eyes peered about the room. "Are—are we alone? I mean he isn't here, is he?"

"Who?"

"You know. That awful person you kept at your side all the time." Dancey shuddered in revulsion. "That bodyguard of yours."

"Oh, him," David said absently. "He died in the crash."

Dancey shuddered again. She collected herself and began to explain her involvement, describing the meeting she had at the Sinaloa Club with two comparative strangers. She began to describe the weirdo and in doing so brought curious excitement to David's eyes. He reached for a stack of photos on the coffee table, pulled out one of the wigged stranger who'd hailed him as Benne in the casino and thrust it before Dancey. Startled, she grasped the photo and stared at it.

"That's him. That's Whitey!" She backed off, suddenly suspicious. "But, how—where—who is he?"

"We don't know, but do go on, Dancey."

With a degree of reluctance she described the man she'd labeled Midas in her mind. Behind them the bedroom door opened. Whip Shiverton, about to enter the room, took a look at Dancey, and catching a warning glance from David retreated quickly, leaving the door slightly ajar. He could hear them clearly as she finished telling David about that night's ordeal.

David comforted her as best he could. He stood up and taking her hand in his led her back to the terrace.

"It's late and you'll need your rest, Dancey. Tomorrow we'll have breakfast and you'll tell me more. Look at me, I'm alive, see? Don't punish yourself any more." He hoped she couldn't really see how he felt in these last moments.

"Others were killed, Benne. A day hasn't gone by since your accident that the weight and guilt of my actions hasn't pressed on me, eating at me like a dreadful malignancy. It's consuming me . . ."

He soothed her, consoled her, but his voice was a dark cloud hiding his true feelings. He leapt over the patio railing, then picking her up in his arms swung her over. For an instant she clung to him, then, as thoughts and panic prevailed, she backed off.

"You understand I'm not certain. I can't be sure it was Renzo . . . I mean it was dark—very dark at the Sinaloa. And that gold amulet—Sagittarius, and his speech pattern . . . Oh, Benne, I can't be sure. Maybe you'd better wait until I can be more positive it was him."

"I understand. Now, go to sleep and we'll see each other for breakfast, O.K.?" He kissed her forehead lightly.

She glanced up at him through tear-filled eyes. "That's not the way you used to kiss me."

"Perhaps I'll remember who I am soon enough so I can remember how I did everything," he said suggestively. "I need time."

Dancey nodded and watched him leap back over the iron railing and disappear inside. Instantly she had misgivings. What had she done? *You stupid, stupid cunt! What the fuck have you gone and done? You have no proof it was Renzo. So what if he wore a zodiac amulet? There must be millions of men born under the sign of Sagittarius! Remember what the shrink told you? The low opinion you hold of yourself, the sado-masochistic tendencies—the need to punish yourself. You just betrayed the one man who had courage to stake you to a new life. Some loyal cunt you are!*

Dancey couldn't calm down. She tried to fall asleep. Renzo's cologne kept wafting to her nostrils from the bed linens where only a short time before they had coupled passionately.

Fear, doubt and guilt twisted her brain into a pretzel of anxiety. Cold sweat poured off her. The constant churning of her stomach squeezed her insides until she could hardly breathe. What ludicrous burlesque had she performed by spilling her guts to Benne? *You're disgusting, Dancey. Loathesome. And downright certifiably sick!* She grabbed for the remainder of the champagne.

She gulped it down. It wasn't enough. She needed more. Frantically searching through her cosmetic case for a pill, something, anything, to rid herself of this bitchy, crawly, burning sensation as compulsion locked its grips on her, she suddenly remembered. She raced to the connecting door, unlocking it frantically.

"Jaquey! Jaquey! Where are you?" she screamed hoarsely. Her burning eyes felt swollen and distended and her vision was becoming impaired. She remembered Jaqualine had left for the movies or something.

In the bathroom she tore Jaqualine's cosmetic case apart searching for a quaalude—nembutal—something—anything. There was nothing—not even a joint. She ran back into her own room, her fists clenched hard in an effort to steel herself against the throbbing pains shooting through her legs. Suddenly she stopped cold by the image of herself in the wall mirror. Collecting herself, she inhaled deeply. *No! I won't give in to you. I won't start again! I won't. Oh God, help me, don't let that monster back into my life!*

With this affirmation fixed in her mind, she was still helpless. Her willpower had melted completely, giving in to her powerful imagination where pictured vividly in her mind was the feeling of contentment derived from drugs. She picked up the phone defiantly, giving in to the horrendous and fierce compulsion propelling her actions.

In less than ten minutes a bellman knocked at her door. One look at her and he knew her story. She merely handed him a C-note. He took it, hesitant, somewhat dubious. "Dunno if I can score this time of night—"

She tossed him another hundred. "I'm desperate," she said softly.

He wanted to ask her if she was mainlining or how much of a habit she had. The junk coming into Vegas recently had been laced with strychnine. It was a bad scene. But he thought of the two hundred bucks she'd given him, and thought, *Who the fuck cares? By the time Miss Blonde Bombshell leaves Las Vegas I'll be rich.*

Ten minutes later he returned with a small bag. In parting he told her, "Listen, you don't know me. I don't know you. If you need me, tell the head bellman to send Walter—got it?"

She slammed the door in his face and ran to the bed, dumping the bag's contents on the sheet. A dozen reds, quaaludes, two bags of heroin and four joints. She stared at the stuff, entering into mental combat, arguing pro and con the thousand reasons she knew for not starting up again. Then, without the artillery to fix heroin she snorted it, as if her conscience had cleared any impediments that might deter her. She felt the icy cold impact instantly. She'd been clean for so long, the slightest bit made a difference. She was on fire; the cold sweat running down her body felt like burning ashes. The compulsion to imbibe further raged unassuageable.

Oh God, take this pain away. I can't stand it. I can't live through it! She was in the bathroom. Her skin was crawling. She peeled off her robe, unable to bear anything touching her. In the bright fluorescent lights, she looked ghastly. She let the tap water flow and sprinkled the cold water on herself. Nothing helped. Slowly she filled the glass with water. The six red capsules were lined up in a row. She stared at them. *Just one,* she told herself. She took two and chased them down with water. She picked up the others and with the other stash, she shoved them under her mattress. She didn't want Jaquey to find her stash even if it didn't amount to much. Anyway what harm would two reds do her?

The narcotic rushed her senses. She paid little heed to the thought that her tolerance to the drug was minimal. Lying naked on the bed she felt a warmth engulfing her and calm came over her, untying the knots in her stomach one by one. As the usual euphoria descended she inhaled deeply and exhaled in peaceful contentment as a thousand images began their march across the recesses of her mind; a kaleidoscope of pictures from her past, broken and disjointed, making little sense. She dozed off.

One floor beneath the penthouse apartments, in a room directly under Dancey's suite, the bent figure of an older man leaning on his cane was admitted by a bellman carrying his luggage. He tipped the porter modestly so as not to bring undue attention to himself and wagged him impatiently out of the room. In a quick transition from old man to a strapping, vigorous one, the new guest straightened out his body and locked the door, gingerly rubbing the small of his back. Slipping the chain lock into place, he tossed his coat onto the nearby chair. He pulled off his wig and ran his fingers through his salt and pepper hair, scratching here and there. Glancing at his watch he noted it was midnight. He set the alarm for 2:00 A.M. In a flash he'd shed his Western boots and wriggled his toes contentedly. He dug into his valise for a joint, lit it up and lay back on the bed taking hits from it.

Visions of Dancey Darling floated across his mind until she came alive for him in his imagination. She was nude next to him, offering him her charms. In his mind's eye he reached out and held her breasts in both his hands. Grabbing her head in a sudden lunging move he forced her to take his cock in her mouth. His hands were busy working her over, exploring, penetrating, as he writhed on the bed, muttering, *Oh, yes, suck it, baby. You know you love it. Tell me, I wanna hear you say that I'm the only one who really knows what it's all about—that no one can love ya like I do. S-s-saaay it b-baaaby! Put that sweet juicy cunt on my mouth. That's it, baby. I'll suck you as you suck me. Ahhhhh.*

His fantasy was livid and real. He pulled out his engorged cock and masturbated with frenzy.

"It wasn't nothing you couldn't have told me tomorrow, Manny. Goddammit! You sure have a knack at wrong timing!" He thought about the many times in the past Marciano's urgent calls had interrupted what otherwise might have turned into pure magic. They sat opposite each other in Manny's office.

"Listen, kid, when I hear the big wheels are here and they haven't contacted me, I worry. What's happening over at your joint? I hear you got the Feds breathing down your neck."

"You heard right. Are you sure your side had nothing to do with Val's disappearance?" Renzo smoked nervously, his lips tight as he inhaled and exhaled.

"I told you before no. But I can't be a hundred percent sure . . ." He avoided Renzo's probing eyes.

"Oh, fine. That's real fine and dandy. Now at the tail end of our hard work you tell me you ain't sure of your people. Who else can it be?" Renzo's annoyance was visible.

Manny didn't answer. His fingers were absently probing the new growth of hair on his recent transplant. His mind was elsewhere. *Fuck, it ain't right that the old man don't call me. He ain't never done that before. What the hell was it all about?* What really bugged him was the report he got not long ago about the white-haired weirdo being in town. One of his men had seen him less than an hour ago pulling into the Golden Oasis parking lot. He could've been mistaken, but his man was too reliable.

"Aw, maybe it's nothin' to be worried about, eh? You sure nothing else but the snatch is on their minds—the Feds I mean?"

Renzo, shrugging imperceptibly, broke open a chocolate-covered cherry he took from a silver plate on the desk. He slurped the insides and wiped the corners of his lips with a swipe of his hands. He reached for a tissue nearby and smiled with a childish grin. "Always loved cherries," he admitted, then sobered again.

"The senator still there?" Manny's brows wrinkled in a frown.

Renzo nodded. "He don't show himself, but the tabs come back with his signature on them. Something's cooking. I can't even get to my wife. She won't talk to me."

Now Manny was really worried. "In other words you don't really know what's happening." He smirked. "Can't get a tap on their phones? No surveillance?"

"Can't do the impossible. Every bug's been swept out. The taps on the phones ain't working. As for the cameras —there aren't any in the penthouses. Tina has seen to that. So, buddy, we're up shit creek."

"What about your men—the waiters?"

"My men can't get on the penthouse detail. The FBI and BSI are working their own men for security reasons."

"Then," said Manny firmly, "we sit tight." He got to the real reason he summoned Renzo. "You ain't making it with the star attraction, are ya, kid?"

"What the hell is this? Do I give you the third degree? Sh-i-it, you gotta leave me some privacy."

"Does she recognize you? You're walking a tightrope, kid."

Renzo's agitation increased. His eyes followed Manny's gestures carefully, marking time for the right opening. "Listen, Manny," he said, finally. "Wanna hear something that'll blow your socks off? The kid's straight. That's right. For nearly six months."

Marciano wagged his hand. "G'wan, you got rocks in your head. Once a junkie always a junkie," he muttered sardonically. Manny suddenly froze as he studied his friend of many years. His eyes narrowed suspiciously. "Hey, you ain't falling for junkie cunt, are ya, kid?" He made a few animal grunts in his throat and shook his head at the frightening possibility. "Look, kid, trust me, eh?

In all the time we know each other—have I steered you wrong? I'm telling you, stay away from her. She's trouble."

Renzo frowned thoughtfully. He leaned up against the slot machines, unable to siphon off his resentments and inner tension.

Manny continued with scorching contempt, "You think I pay a stable of informants for nothing?" He leaned forward intent on getting through to Renzo, his voice dropping in volume significantly.

"Word is out there's a contract on her," he said with the proper menace.

Renzo stiffened. He paled instantly and searched Manny's eyes for the truth. It was there and in spades. For several moments he was unable to speak. He sank into the chair opposite his host. "They won't touch her, not here in Vegas—will they? I mean it would be bad for business—for all of us." His arms jerked into the air in a gesture of helplessness. "You realize how much I got invested in the broad? Nah, no one in their right mind would do the job her." He tried convincing himself of this.

"Who the hell said anything about them being in their right mind—the ones who put out the contract?" Manny countered. "Somebody thinks she's a threat. Do I have to spell it out, kid?" His jowls drooped in disgust. "Sonofabitch. You know the score. Didn't I tell you you were crazy to consider the junkie cunt in the first place?"

"They wouldn't do it in Las Vegas," Renzo kept repeating as if he were in a sodium pentothal trance. He thought of a dozen reasons the city's image had to be maintained and couldn't be besmirched with any trace of scandal or murder.

"What the hell's wrong with you? They'd do it at the pearly gates with St. Peter and a band of angels watching if they took a mind to."

Renzo looked white and shaken. The hard-nosed entrepreneur swiveled around to face his host, as he crumbled internally bit by bit. "What shall I do, Manny? What the fuck do I do now? She opens in two nights!"

"Pay her off. Use any excuse, but get her out of Vegas. What happens to her after ain't none of your business. This way no shadow of suspicion can fall on ya, see?"

"This is why you called me, isn't it? You knew I was with her. You're keeping tabs on me, ain't ya?"

Manny shrugged. "I got a lot of dough and dreams tied up in ya, kid. I don't want nothing ta happen to ya."

"You have anything to do with the contract?" the

street-wise kid from the lower East Side asked straight out.

"No. But that ain't saying I didn't think of it," Manny said with as much honesty as he could muster. "The idea of you gettin' close to someone who can finger you just don't set well with me. I'm telling ya I don't know who put the contract out. I got a good idea—but I ain't sure, see? Just use what I told you. You know what to do, kid. You ain't so dumb you can't figure it." Manny rose to his feet and scratched his crotch. "Look, I was in the middle of a blow job when I got the word, eh? See what I do for you? G'wan, get back to your joint." He wagged Renzo off and headed for the door at the end of the room.

"Thanks, Manny. I'll never forget it."

"Do the right thing, kid. Ya hear?"

All the way back to the Pyramids, Renzo's head whirled with mad and insane thoughts. He took the service elevator to the penthouse. First, he was ordered by Tina to get Dancey out of the area. Now, Manny really laid a big one on him.

He opened the door to Dancey's suite with his passkey, uncertain how to break it to her. Christ, he'd have to pay her a fortune to cancel her contract. Hell would break loose when the trades got wind of it. What would he say to them? Worse, what could he say to Dancey? He couldn't lay it on straight and say, "Look, kid, someone's gunning for you. A hitman is stalking you. Go someplace and disappear." No. He couldn't do that. He'd tell her the boss—the owners decided to book another act. No—that was no good. She knew it couldn't be so flimsy an excuse.

He looked down at her asleep in the buff, so innocent, so beautiful. It would be a shame to knock off a dish like her. *Who the hell would wish her dead? Not Manny. The wheels from Texas? Manny had never really confided everything to me. When this blows over, I'll insist he tells me who the big guns are.*

Renzo sat on the edge of the bed. What could he do? Awaken her, tell her to pack her things and get out? Watching her, her breasts so appealing, he felt himself grow hard.

Goddammit! This fucking shit can wait until tomorrow—can't it? What the hell could happen tonight? Besides, there ain't no one can tell me the hit will happen in Vegas. They're too smart to let it happen here.

Dancey stirred in that instant, feeling his presence. She gave a start and sat up, suddenly apprehensive. Had he come back to harm her? His face in the soft glow of lights shining inside from the patio wasn't that of an angry man. He seemed perturbed but not vindictive. *Oh God, what have I done? Maybe it wasn't Renzo at all I'd met at the Sinaloa. Maybe a thousand other men wore Sagittarius amulets on chains around their necks.* In her condition could she have been so accurate? Here was the only man who gave her a chance for a comeback and she'd fingered him as Benne's betrayer. *Dear God help me!*

In that instant Renzo's heart went out to her. He reached for her and held her in his arms. He had no idea what was whirling round in her brain and she couldn't read him.

"It's O.K., babe. Things are gonna work out just fine. You leave it to Renzo," he murmured, fondling her, caressing her. And Dancey felt vulnerable to his ministrations.

Earlier they had experimented with each other and found what best suited them. Both were sensuous and able to divorce love from sex and place the act in its proper perspective. They both made love as if their very lives depended on it.

To Renzo, the excitement of Manny's words coupled with the dangers involved merely heightened his urgency with her. She wasn't Jolie Barnes—but sure in hell ran her a close second. His physical excitement in this instant, with all the outside factors working to stimulate him, was like nothing he'd ever experienced. He abandoned himself to the beguiling illusion, and why not? He'd paid plenty for it.

Feeling the insurmountable guilt from her earlier remarks to Benne Erice, Dancey was torn and agonized. She'd been crazy to spill her guts without actual proof! Her shrink was right. Accusing the man who in her hour of need had set the ball rolling in the right direction was the shabbiest thing she'd done to herself. The act could rebound and destroy her. Her repentance was such that she clung to Renzo fiercely in an outpouring of emotion that communicated so savage a sexual desire to him, he was left gasping.

There was nothing she wouldn't do for him to make up the damage she'd done him—nothing! It was either that or go out and fix.

Renzo reached for a small box and opened the lid. Dancey recognized the amyl nitrate, and made no objections. In the past she'd tried everything—anything. She was worthless now, so why not?

Renzo thrust his pulsating tumescence into her mouth. She coughed and choked at first, then took it despite the uncomfortable position. Renzo's eyes became glazed with lust as he rocked his pelvis to and fro. Then he turned her over quickly, withdrawing, and with his free hand broke the ampule under her nose. Dancey felt the sudden rush of pressure as her brain exploded. Her heart felt ready to burst through her breasts. He pulled her into a knee to chest position, slapped her buttocks smartly and shoved his hard shaft inside her abruptly. She screamed and moaned and writhed under him, but he held her firm.

"Like a dog, woman. Feel my hard cock inside you."

Orgasm after orgasm burst in her head as he slammed hard into her time and again. She was trembling with pain and a wild desire as she mentally flagellated herself. He made her feel as she felt about herself, suddenly—totally worthless. There was no love between them, no tenderness, merely his assertion of power over one he had no respect for. She felt his alienation, so different than he'd been earlier. Almost as if something had happened during his absence to make him change. But it was all right for Dancey. Let him treat her like this. Then in due time she'd feel no guilt. The hurt was tucked away beneath her armor.

Dancey was drunk. The champagne and reds were doing a number on her all right. The depression reduced her anxiety and the heaviness in her stomach and pain in her anal area was negligible now with the numbness of drugs and alcohol interacting. She wasn't sure what Renzo was doing but he kept busy.

"You got a vibrator?" he whispered huskily.

"Doesn't everyone?" she remarked acerbically. "It's in the bathroom."

If he took umbrage at her tone of voice he didn't show it. He returned in moments with the trusty little hand job and plugged the cord into an outlet. "Here, use it," he ordered gruffly. Dancey held it and directed it onto her clitoris. She squirmed. The vibrator felt like a hundred pricks at once and set her off exploding with orgasm again. Renzo sucked on her nipples until she moaned with ecstasy. Then, hardened by the picture of her coming alive under the vibrator, he shoved himself into her again. He hardly moved. The vibration from the machine stimulated him to such heights that he wasn't able to hold back. The bed thundered under them for several minutes as they climaxed together with excruciating pleasure. Then all was silent.

Fifteen minutes passed. Renzo could hardly move. He glanced at his watch. It was 1:30 A.M. He squinted his eyes together and peered at the luminous dial and set the alarm for 2:00 A.M. He needed a half-hour to recuperate. His body went limp and he fell sound asleep. Dancey was totally out of it, engulfed in euphoria.

CHAPTER TWENTY-THREE

One floor below the penthouses the man in suite 1400 awakened at the buzzing of his wristwatch alarm. His eyes blinked wide. Turning off the alarm, he limped to the bathroom to splash water on his face and then returned to the bedroom and got to work.

He tossed the valise onto the bed; opened it, removing a pair of faded blue Levis, a Western shirt, a reddish-brown wig and mustache—the brown was more sedate than the white Afro—and laid everything on the bed. From a small black bag inside the valise, he removed a syringe and a vial containing grams of heroin. Breaking the seal, he shoved in the needle, drawing the heroin into the syringe, and capped it with a rubber tip. Wrapping it in a tissue he slipped it into his pocket.

The moment his boots were on he was ready to adjust the white Afro wig on his head; the mustache was next. Observing his handiwork in a mirror, he checked the .345 magnum in his boot holster. Satisfied, he replaced it.

The man was methodical, painstaking and exact. His heavy face became a stone mask over which he placed his wraparound dark glasses. He checked the locks and safety chain on the entrance doors, turned down the lights and slipped out the patio doors. Moving with the facility of a man familiar with his surroundings, he swung himself bodily over the ledge overlooking the busy city streets below him, grasping the rungs of a fire ladder affixed to the building, making his ascent one step at a time until he reached the water tower on the fifteenth floor. Moving stealthily over the top of the tower he lowered himself easily and soundlessly down the other side onto the terrace and, creeping along the wall past the potted fern, he paused a few inches from the open door, peering about before stepping into the room between the sheer curtains.

He moved with lightfooted agility on the balls of his feet towards Dancey's side of the bed, stopping abruptly at the sight of the man lying next to her. A flickering of annoyance crept into his icy eyes as his hand reached for the syringe. The soft suction sound of the rubber tip being removed stirred the silence. Testing the needle, he made a quick expert jab in Dancey's upper arm. She stirred only slightly, jerked at the shock to her body, and became rigid. He stared down at her voluptuous breasts, the blonde curly hair at her crotch; his free hand stroked the bulge in his trousers. His narrowing eyes on Renzo, he snapped the syringe in two and shoved it into his pocket. He had had other plans; finding Renzo in bed with her thwarted him. For two cents he'd have finished him off. The bastard deserved to be annihilated, but the freebie wasn't going to come from him.

Still . . .

Standing over Renzo, magnum in hand, the silencer inches from Renzo's temple, the man removed his glasses. Slowly, very slowly his finger began to squeeze the trigger. Unexpectedly, he suddenly stopped and withdrew the gun, shoved it back into his boot holster. Backing out of the room as soundlessly as he had entered it, he thought, *Missed you this trip, Renzo old boy, but believe me, your day is coming soon.*

In less than five minutes he was back in his room on the fourteenth floor, shoving the gun and silencer into his luggage. He tossed the broken syringe into the toilet, flushing it down the drain. With the movements of a quick-change artist, he removed his clothing, wig and mustache, and donned the Levis and Western shirt, setting the brown wig and mustache into place. He drew himself up, throwing out his chest and appeared to have added both girth and height to an impressive stature. Swaggering about the room, critically inspecting his reflection in the mirror, he was satisfied with his handiwork. Everything except for the white wig and mustache was crammed into the valise. He wrapped the black suit, white shirt and string tie into a newspaper. He took a last look about the room, opened the door with a tissue in hand, and left, closing the door behind him. Passing a laundry bin, he casually tossed in the paper bundle and swaggered off, whistling a tune.

Renzo's wristwatch alarm sounded, awakening him with a start. It took a moment to orient himself. Glancing at Dancey's nude body, remembering, he smiled vaguely and pulled himself off the bed. She was something else. Too bad he hadn't started with her a long time ago. Things might have been different for them both. Thinking about their earlier encounter made him horny. His cock was greedy. Renzo thought, *What the hell! Maybe one more time?*

He moved closer to her, snuggling against her, his pelvis moving rhythmically. "Dancey—wake up. See what I have for you."

She was unmoving. Renzo reached for her, turning her towards him; she flopped like a rubber doll without control.

"Jesus Christ!" he gasped aloud, quickly reaching for the light switch, choking when his spittle went down his windpipe. His eyes bulged from their sockets; she was white as flour, foam escaping her nostrils and lips; her eyes were like glassy blue and white balls, swollen and distended. No one had to tell him Dancey was dead. He grabbed her arm, searching for the telltale artillery; there was none, not in her or on the floor nearby. One pinprick on her upper arm was visible; a few drops of coagulated blood trailed into dried spider webs. Renzo leapt from the bed like a man possessed and dressed in a frenzy, his brain whirling maddeningly.

Manny was right! They did it to her—right under my nose. Fucking bastards! They could've killed me! Get outta here, Renzo! On the double!

How he got to his suite, Renzo didn't know. He showered, shaved, and wrapped himself in a thick white terry robe that matched his pasty complexion. Pacing the floor erratically, the shaken man had guzzled nearly a fifth of Beefeaters before he found the wherewithall to make up an alibi for his whereabouts when Dancey was killed. Manny and his gofer would swear he'd been at the Pyramids earlier. So he didn't return to Dancey's suite. He came straight here. His prints would be all over the place. So, he had dinner with his star, earlier, then left. He picked up the phone to place a call to the pit boss in the casino.

"Just checking, Harry. Is everything all right?" He yawned loudly. "Fell asleep a few hours ago . . . just woke up. Can ya handle it without me? I'm really knocked out."

Harry Cohen, a burly oldtimer with casino know-how, muttered, "Go back to bed. I'll handle it. Any news about Val?"

"Not yet," he replied, managing to sound concerned. He hung up, cursing himself for returning to Dancey's room. He should have known Manny wouldn't have steered him wrong. *Fucking asshole. With all the cunt you've had in your life, you couldn't have passed this up? Whoever killed Dancey ain't interested in you, Renzo.*

Jaqualine Devon found Dancey the next morning. Dr. Saperstein pronounced her dead and suggested calling the police after informing Tina. Captain Ferraro and his men arrived shortly after 10:00 A.M. to conduct their investigation. Following a rushed autopsy the coroner declared death was due to a heroin overdose. The inability of the homicide investigators to locate the artillery used to induce the drug made it murder.

In the privacy of his office Renzo admitted being with Dancey the night before, swearing an oath that Dancey was alive when he left her. "Be reasonable, Frank, why would I kill her? I had a lot of dough tied up in her—dough I'll never get back."

Captain Ferraro checked his alibis; they were tight. Renzo, scratched off the list of possible suspects, left an unsolved case in Captain Ferraro's jurisdiction.

By evening of that same day Las Vegas felt the shock waves of the happenings at the Pyramids. Val's kidnapping, although not official, became a concern for all casino owners. And their star had been murdered. Renzo brooded visibly over two facts; the first that Jolie Barnes would remain as uncontested star of Las Vegas; the second that he hadn't been killed with Dancey. His call to New York, when an old crony advised him, "You're a dead man, Renzo," ate at him. He relayed the information to Marciano.

"Stay on your own turf, kid. Stay cool. I'll try to find out what's coming down."

Renzo's name was on David Martin's mind as he recounted to Whip Shiverton his fears concerning Dancey. Last night, after Dancey left David's suite of rooms, Whip, who'd heard most of her confession, discussed the state of affairs with David, coming to no real conclusion, except that she'd shed light on the probable conspiracy behind Benne Erice's death. Now, David insisted he should confide his knowledge to Captain Ferraro.

Whip disagreed. "First we tell Bowman. Can't take the chance of blowing the case. We still have Val to be concerned over. Dave—I don't like it. We should have heard by now."

"Then we must proceed with the idea that Val is either dead, or it wasn't the usual kidnapping. Perhaps Val went

294

voluntarily—" He was interrupted by the sound of soft knocking on the door. They exchanged concerned glances. Among the BSI agents, Tina and family members they had arranged a code. Whoever knocked on the door didn't know the code. David sprang on the balls of his feet to the vicinity of the door, gun in hand.

"Who's there?" he asked.

"Jaqualine Devon. Miss Darling's secretary. I want to speak with Mr. Erice."

David tossed the automatic to Whip; he shoved it under a sofa cushion as David opened the door. "Please come in, Miss Devon. May I present Senator Shiverton."

Jaqualine faltered; she hadn't expected to confront him so soon. Quickly lowering her lashes, she tried covering her discomfort. She nodded and directed her words to David. "Uh, I have something of a personal nature to discuss with you."

"Feel free to speak before the senator," he urged.

In the moments that Jaqualine tried to comply with Abdul's instructions she felt Whip's eyes studying her intently, as if he were trying to place her. She banked on the considerable changes in her appearance since her initial encounter with Whip serving as a barrier to his recognition of her.

"I won't take too much of your time, Mr. Erice. I have something I'm sure Miss Darling would want you to have." She dangled the locket before him.

Whip glanced from David to the young woman, thinking that something about the girl seemed familiar. David began to speak words of sympathy.

"We are still in a state of shock over her unfortunate death . . ." He didn't take the locket, instead added, "If you can explain anything the police would like to know—"

Jaqualine took David's hand and pressed the locket into it.

David displayed puzzlement. "Why would she want me to have this?" he asked.

"Open it, please."

David complied. "Yes, I see why you'd assume what you did. Thank you, Miss Devon. You're very kind."

Jaqualine's attitude took an instant turn. "The police might be interested in knowing what happened to her when she caught sight of you, Mr. Erice. She's been off drugs a long time. She was trying her best to rehabilitate herself. Yet one look at you, and she became a basket case for several hours." She continued to explain how Dancey, in such dire straits, had to be sedated. She grew hostile and accusatory.

David, exchanging concerned glances with Whip, kept up his cover. "What you're saying is you think I killed Dancey?"

"Can you account for your whereabouts last night?"

David laughed ironically as McKenna and Soldato entered the suite of rooms with their passkeys.

"I see nothing funny," snapped Jaqualine, growing uneasy at the new arrivals. They stood by, silently listening and observing her with interest.

David, sobering instantly, admitted tersely, "Death is never humorous." David turned to McKenna with exasperation.

"You explain to Miss Devon, will you, Mac? She thinks I killed Dancey Darling." He pivoted quickly and left the room.

Whip Shiverton continued to search her features critically, admiring her splendid bone structure. His eyes became fixed on the twin moles over each breast, visible in her cleavage. Jaqualine's attention shifted from one man to another as feelings of disquiet shook her. She watched as McKenna removed his credentials from his wallet and showed them to her, before steering her across the room to the oversized sofa.

"Please sit down, Miss Devon. Tell me all you know."

A half hour later, Jaqualine muttered weak apologies to David. She balked when Ted McKenna suggested she should remain in protective custody until they had more concrete information concerning Dancey's death. "I must handle the burial arrangements for Miss Devon. Why must I remain under protective custody? I did nothing wrong."

"I'd like to think I was a friend to Miss Darling. What can I do to help you?" Whip's eyes refused to leave those twin moles.

"I can handle everything," she said curtly.

"They're only trying to help, Miss Devon. It may not be safe for you since her death was really murder—not suicide. Let me see what I can do." Whip huddled with McKenna out of hearing distance. "Let her handle the funeral and other business. We'll keep her under twenty-four-hour surveillance." He confided his feelings to McKenna. "Mac, did you ever get the feeling you know someone and can't place them? That's how I feel about this woman—Devon. Listen, this is what I want you to do. Get a handle on her that passes the stiffest security clearance. I'll get Tina to offer her a job with the publicity department here at the Pyramids. I predict she'll jump at the chance. If she does, I'll know I'm on to something. I have to fly back to Washington to pick up a file."

"Before we learn anything about Val Erice?"

"It can't be helped. If this Devon woman is a part of what's forming in my mind, she already knows too much. It's possible she remained here to to learn more about our activities." Whip shook his head, trying not to infect McKenna with his own thoughts. "Objectivity is what's needed in this case."

"Who the hell do you think she is?" whispered McKenna, subduing his voice. "It would help us in checking her out."

"Yeah, I suppose it would. Say, Mac, when David was with the FBI, wasn't he involved with uncovering some radical, subversive groups?"

"You don't miss a trick, Senator. Martin was deeply involved in such work."

"He'd know the cream of the lot, wouldn't he? Look, here's what you tell her . . ."

Jaqualine, back in her suite, was packing Dancey's belongings when a knock sounded at her door. She moved to the door swiftly, half hoping it would be Abdul. It was Tina.

"Miss Devon?" Tina studied the girl, intrigued by her rare beauty. "Miss Jaqualine Devon?"

"Yes." Jaqualine's eyes narrowed in a hasty appraisal of Tina.

"May I come in please? I'm Tina Bonaparte. Senator Shiverton sent me in to speak to you. I'd like to hire you to work here in the publicity department at the Pyramids." She breezed into the room. "I'm dreadfully sorry about Miss Darling. You can't imagine how awful we feel. Have you been with her long?"

Jaqualine nodded, closing the door behind her. "Please sit down. I was packing—"

"I'll get on with it. What experience have you had?"

Jaqualine gave her background in film distribution and promotion, describing her skills. Tina listened avidly as she studied the young woman in whom Whip had suddenly shown interest. A woman in love paid attention to specific details in another woman in whom her lover expressed interest. She noted the dark new growth of hair at the scalp; dark hairs growing in under bleached brows; the shape of her hands and fingernails; the way she moved about and spoke with a slight trace of accent; her choice of words and how she arranged them in a sentence. Even the shape of Jaqualine's lips, full and pouting, seemed familiar to Tina. Or it could have been the overpowering scent of the woman's perfume that stirred her sense memory. That was the one indulgence Jamila had permitted herself, to remind herself of her homeland; it was an unusual fragrance, thick with a musk base seldom worn by American women.

As intently as Tina studied Jaqualine, the princess in turn studied Tina, certain they had met someplace.

Tina left Jaqualine's room with a polite air, assuring the girl she could find some place for her at the Pyramids. She stopped next door, and knocked in the code: three short knocks followed by a steady staccato. The door opened. Tina sighed deeply, instantly reminded of the reality of her own problems. Her father was still missing. She toyed with the idea of telling them all she knew. She was weakening, and despite her promise to her father to keep what she knew to herself, she gave it twenty-four hours. If Val didn't return, she'd unburden herself to both Whip and David.

It was arranged. Jaqualine Devon would be escorted to Hollywood to prepare for Dancey's funeral. Two undercover agents would accompany her for protection until she could be returned to the Pyramids. Whip had guessed correctly; she had jumped at the chance to work at the Pyramids under Tina's supervision. In her absence, the BSI went to work. A full-scale investigation of Jaqualine Devon commenced. They uncovered all they could about her.

David requested special files be dispatched to him from FBI headquarters in Washington. A courier arrived six hours later. David pored over thousands of photographs as gallons of coffee were pumped into him.

The room was a shambles; files were strewn about at random on the large conference table. Empty coffee cups, cigarette butts piled high, and candy wrappers crumpled carelessly filled wastebaskets. Stacks of glossy photos were piled in several groups.

"It would help, Senator," said David, wearied by the strain, "if you could remember where you met and why she seems familiar."

As fatigued as the others, Whip stretched his weary bones.

"Yeah, well, I can't. Nothing registers. Maybe I was wrong. It was a wild guess." On his feet, he stretched again, and yawned. "I'll be on the terrace for air."

He left them sorting, sifting through papers, restacking the photos.

A rush of exhaustion struck Whip as he sauntered about the terrace. His eyes catching sight of a chaise, he sighed, thinking he could sleep an eternity if he just touched the pillow. A hundred thoughts tried to jar his thinking, but he tried to hold to just one guiding thread to carry him through this labyrinth of mystery. He lit a cigarette and stood for a time smoking, looking out at the jeweled carpet of manmade lights and glitter.

A wisp of perfume wafted to his nostrils. Turning he caught sight of her in the patio to his right.

"Tina?" he called softly, hoping not to startle her.

She turned as Whip climbed over the partition separating them. She quickly dabbed at the tears she'd been shedding quietly.

Whip drew her into his arms and held her tightly. She lay her head on his shoulder, trying not to give in to the flooding torment of tears hiding behind her eyes.

"Why have you kept away from me?" he asked softly. She shook her head, unable to reply.

"We must talk. We must fix this thing between us. We've gone our separate ways long enough. I want to marry you."

Tina shook her head again. "Don't say that. You and I can never marry, Whip. I'm not the woman for you. I would only complicate your life."

Whip pulled her close to him, tenderly, stroking her head. "We've all been through hell," he muttered.

"I can only think about my father—"

"I understand."

"Where is he, Whip? Where can he be? Do you have any idea?"

"If I did, he'd be here. If it takes the Marines to get him back we will, I promise. All we can do is wait—"

"Whip—" Tina pulled back her head and stared into his eyes. For a second time that day she wanted to tell him Val wasn't paralyzed—that he hadn't suffered a stroke. If only she hadn't promised her father . . .

Passion sprang up in him. "Yes, luv, what is it?"

"Just hold me—hold me tight." She was unable to stop trembling.

They kissed, tenderly at first, then with increased passion, Whip's earlier exhaustion was replaced by an excitement surging in his loins. "If we could be together just for a while . . ."

Tina moved back out of his arms and searched his face in the dim shaft of light coming through the windows of her apartment. "You look tired," she whispered, stroking the fine lines of fatigue etched into his face. She noticed the slight touch of gray at each temple and suddenly a deep sigh escaped her.

"You're right. We've been apart too long." She smiled wanly. "Our love has survived many catastrophies, hasn't it, Whip?" She wiped her tearstained face with a tissue and sniffled. "When I saw you in her arms, I swear—" Her laughter fell in a long ripple. "I should be ashamed. That happened so long ago. I really don't blame you. I mean, Ali explained about his sister at lunch . . ."

Whip stared at her, unable to understand what it was she was talking about. "What are you raving about, woman?"

"—But, seeing her here again, I'm not so certain I can still condone the relationship. But then, I'm not the epitome of virtue either. I'm still married . . ."

Whip was thoroughly lost. "Tina, please. I know we're all under a strain, but, honey, you aren't making sense. Who in the hell are you talking about? Who did you see in my arms?"

"The princess, uh, you know who," insisted Tina, searching his eyes.

"Princess?" His eyes were fixed on her. "Jamila? Are you still thinking about that? You just said Ali explained my innocence—" He stopped. His face lit up.

Tina was dismayed. "You see? She still causes such a reaction? And now she's here with your sanction? Why, Whip?"

Whip wasn't listening. "Tina, you gorgeous, wonderful woman you!" he exclaimed exuberantly. He gathered her in his arms and whirled her about in wide sweeping moves. He kissed her with a loud smacking sound. "You've saved my day!" he said.

"Look, leave your door open. I want to come back later to tell you how much I really love you." Her protests were smothered by his kisses. New life teemed in Whip as he hurdled the planter box obstruction, making his way back to where the others labored under the workload he'd given them.

They glanced up idly when he passed and entered his bedroom. Picking up the phone he placed several calls, one to Rome, Italy.

"I wish to speak with Mrs. Ali Mohammed Izmur, Operator," he spoke clearly into the phone. "Uh, Operator, make that Mrs. Valerie Shiverton Izmur," he said when he considered that Ali might have several wives.

He thought about Valerie's recent wedding to the prince. He hadn't been able to attend the ceremony. He felt badly that he hadn't given her the moral support she had wanted. Amy had gone, much against her wishes, but to comply with Whip's request.

"Yes, Operator. This is Senator Shiverton. Is she there? Yes, I'll wait . . . Hello . . . Hello, Valerie? Yes. This is Whip. Fine. Everything's fine. You? Good. Valerie, is the Prince there? Is he? Where? I see. Tell me, whatever happened to Princess Jamila?"

Whip drew the phone away from his ear. Her shrill voice nearly split his eardrum. "Calm down, Valerie. Now, that's better. She's with the who? Ali's disinherited her, you say?"

Whip jotted things down in a notebook, his face a symphony of concentrated thought. He hung up the phone after a while and sat there quietly. Within him his brain roiled with thought as he attempted to piece together the enormous puzzle.

Valerie had told him Prince Ali was in America—Las Vegas to be exact. What she said about Jamila certainly didn't compute. She insisted that Jamila was in Beirut, affiliated with the Palestinian resistance. Only yesterday she and several of her terrorist friends had walked into the International Bank and at gunpoint had robbed its coffers of an enormous sum of money. Valerie had added that Jamila was a terrible embarrassment to Ali.

Whip stood up and slapped the sides of his thighs contemplatively.

Well, he thought, *how about them apples?*

Valerie promised to send him in the fastest way possible a stack of news clippings about Jamila, "the bravest heroine in the Middle East."

He returned to the other room. When they saw his expression the agents despaired. "Something terrible has happened to Val?" David Martin Erice tensed.

Whip made a abstract gesture. "Hmmm? No, no, noth-

301

ing like that. It's about this, uh, Jaqualine Devon. I want her every move checked out. Who she speaks with, where. Where she lives. How long she's worked for Dancey. Her credentials. Check her visa, passport, everything!"

Chief Bowman studied him. "You're on to something —what?"

Whip sat down and propped his feet on the table. "I wish to Christ I knew. Look, let me lay it out for you. Maybe you all can fit the pieces together."

BOOK THREE

And when he reached to touch
The stars . . .
They crumbled into dust.

CHAPTER TWENTY-FOUR

A sprawling ranch house renovated into a desert strong-hold stood intact and foreboding ten minutes from Las Vegas. Well armed, wary eyed guards manning the estate with magnum shotguns and sweltering in the broiling sun began to breathe in relief; the brash, westerly sun had begun its descent. A scattering of Dobermans, sniffing a section of their enclosure cocked their heads, listening. Frisky Mustangs, corralled for breeding, pranced about playfully, nuzzling their mates. Giant jack-rabbits, darting in and about cactus beds scavenging for food avoided the periodic fusillade of bullets spewing from the guns of bored guards who had nothing better to do than take out their frustrations on the game. Other than the usual natural noises of a barking dog, a horse whinny and crunch of boot heels on the high bricked wall, the exasperation of desert silence affected all residents.

Most affected perhaps was Val Erice, inside an enor-mous, air-conditioned, well furbished suite of rooms, where he lay quietly on a large four-poster bed; his ears and eyes were committing every sound and visible artifact on the stone and wood walls to memory.

He had had little else to do these past few days but eat, sleep and experience the ennui of a helpless man. He did have plenty of time to recollect what happened the night of his abduction from the hospital, shortly after he re-ceived his nightly medication.

He had dozed off. An hour later, he awakened, sensing the presence of others. One of the shadowy figures bent over him seemed familiar; his features, in partial shadow from the dim lighting, jogged Val's memory. He'd had little time to dwell on the man's identity; wrapped like a mummy in a sheet, bound tightly with a rope, he'd been lifted from the bed, transported to the balcony and low-ered to the ground below. Lifted once again he was transported a short distance and placed on a cot in a waiting vehicle. It happened swiftly, methodically and without incident.

He heard a motor start up; the vehicle took off with normal speed. Ten minutes later they arrived at their destination. The scenario earned Val's respect; it was timed perfectly; none of the numerous guards in the hospital corridor had heard a sound.

The briefcase, still manacled to Val's wrist, hadn't been touched. One alteration to his appearance, however, was the signet ring; the double-headed griffin. His hesitation in displaying the symbol was quickly dispelled by solid thinking. An obvious factor was that he was alive. He asked himself, why? Other, prominent and important men had been wasted; why not him? His enemies must be concerned with possible retaliation. Val clung to this thought. The ring was vital. It must remind them of their own vulnerability.

In all this time Val continued to act as if he were still afflicted with the same mysterious symptoms for which he'd been hospitalized.

Footsteps padding along the outer corridor approached. Val tensed. The footfalls ceased; the door opened. A man entered, shutting the door behind him. Val's eyes, opened wide, concentrated on a distant point, enabled him to see peripherally without eye movement. He sniffed the familiar scent of a man's cologne. Something about the interloper was familiar. A voice from out of the past addressed him. "We meet again, Mr. Erice." Val did not react. "Too bad we gotta meet under these circumstances. You ain't coming out of this alive. You gotta know that, doncha?"

The man turned on a small bedside lamp. A man in a white Afro wig stood over him; the same man who accompanied Renzo to the Sinaloa; who greeted David at the Pyramids; the same man the BSI was combing Las Vegas to find; the killer of Dancey Darling. Of course Val knew nothing of his recent involvements; his familiarity with the man went beyond the wig and mustache. Even without the disguise Val knew him. He remained motionless.

From under his sweater lapel, the man removed a long, sharp pin. "The doctors say you suffered a stroke and some paralysis. You don't mind if an old pro makes doubly sure?"

306

Val, bracing himself, focused his concentration on an internal center as he'd done in the past, practising self-hypnosis and the denial of pain. When the pin was jabbed into his hands, Val did not react; his features remained immobile. There wasn't even an involuntary reflex.

Satisfied, the man replaced the pin and observed Val, deliberately watching for the slightest hint of awareness. "You can hear me, I know you can. It's only decent to tell you what happened to Benne. For whatever it's worth, the dude passing himself off as Benne is an impostor. I oughta know."

Monk Garret pulled off the Afro wig and the mustache, smoothing his salt-and-pepper hair into place, his eyes on Val. Not a muscle moved on Val's face as Monk thrust himself closer. Never in his life had Val been more moved to do murder than at that precise instant. Standing over him in an arrogant pose was the man everyone had presumed dead with Benne. It took superhuman effort for Val to contain himself during Monk's compulsive post mortem of his successful contract—the elimination of Benne Erice.

"Sodium pentothal worked magic in prying loose his tongue. We used a broad to lure him. He went out like a light; our specialists moved in and did the brainwashing once we knew his destination. We implanted the post-hypnotic suggestion of using a private jet for the final leg of our journey. Benne left the details to me; another suggestion. I planted a stiff in the plane, dressed him up, my clothes and ID; just so's there'd be the proper number of corpses on the plane . . .

"Look, Mr. Erice, there ain't no hard feelings, see? It was just a job to me. I planted a bomb to go off at the right time so there'd be little left to identify. It had to look like an accident—a malfunction or something. But someone had already beat me to it—you see? They rigged the plane before I did.

"Benne caught on to me a long time ago. He said nothing. The minute we were airborne he says ta me, 'Monk, you're one of the guys that wasted Ted Shiverton —aren't ya?' He was one smart cookie, Benne was. There was no way I could let him live after that. I had to blow out his brains, along with Jake. I parachuted out. Half-way to the earth I heard the plane explode—not once, but twice. Like I told you, there were two bombs. That's for the record. If it's any consolation, Benne didn't suffer.

Hear what I'm telling ya? Ain't no way Benne can be alive. Monk Garret does a foolproof job. Whoever the impostor is, it's gotta be for something big." Monk moved to the other side of Val.

"Before your lights dim forever, my boss wants to talk with ya. Ya wanna sit up? What can I do for ya?" he asked solicitously, pulling Val's body to a sitting position.

"Like Richie is devoted to you, I'm devoted to my boss. So no hard feelings, eh?"

No hard feelings? God give me strength. Val fought the rash of violence churning through him and the vivid pictures of his son Benne, helpless against this fiend, his skull shot off, before the bombs blew him to kingdom come.

Garret leaned closed to Val, his beady eyes piercing, probing, attempting to puncture the invisible veil between them.

"To think anyone got so close to me with a near hit boils my blood. I couldn't have gone down with Benne!" he hissed in outrage. "Since you ain't going no place but six feet under when my boss finishes with you, you might just as well know who planted that second bomb: that dumb prick Marciano—him and that no-good son-in-law of yours, Renzo." Monk stiffened instantly.

The door behind him opened. Monk moved to one side as two men entered; one walking, one in a wheelchair. Dr. Larry Sharp pulled open the drapes, admitting the bright rays of sunset into the room. Val stiffened imperceptibly, recognizing him at once.

"How's my patient today?" asked Sharp, approaching the bed, allowing the wheelchair to pass before him. "You should have returned to normalcy by now." He lifted Val's wrist and with his free hand rolled back Val's eyelid.

Still no reaction from Val. Sharp examined him; pulse, blood pressure, temperature. He nodded to the older man in the wheelchair and left the room with Monk Garret, leaving the two men to talk.

The Golden Eagle himself; the old bird, the clout behind Carlini in New Orleans, the high and mighty power and glory of TFL, a vital arm of IAGO, sat facing him. Val had done it. He'd flushed the old bird into the open.

E. L. Lamb's features had settled into a mask of obstinate sullenness. Here was a driven man, impelled by a burning hatred, whose life reflected this hatred. In his

308

eighties, it was difficult to imagine him ever being a brave, fiery youth of great passion, capable of loving. His dry skin was stretched like parchment over his skull; he was bald, but concealed it with hairpieces or caps. Today he wore a perforated white golf cap. Cosmetic surgery periodically performed kept his excess wrinkles from turning to flab.

He sat rigidly, his hands flat on his knees, committing Val's features to memory in studied watchfulness. Gradually, Val adjusted his faraway focus until his eyes returned to normal vision. He met the red-veined eyes of his captor. Lamb sucked in his breath, his stiff lips parted by a spurt of cracked laughter.

"You're a clever man, Mr. Erice," cackled the oil impresario who had no equal in the western hemisphere for wheeling and dealing. "You won't live long enough to brag about your cleverness. It all ends here. Ah'm speaking of your life, boy."

The smells of the desert were heavy and musty. Val gazed past Lamb to the cactus-filled solarium where succulents and vivid bromeliads bloomed in breathtaking beauty. Val studied the exotic blooms, wondering how to approach this embittered eccentric.

As a woman feels the fetus in her womb growing to maturity Val felt his strength returning to him. He gazed back at his host inexorably. Slowly he brought himself to a sitting position, dropping his legs over the side of the bed to face Lamb. His wrist, manacled to the briefcase, brought the leather bag to his side on the bed. Lamb's beady eyes focused briefly on the case, then fixed on the glittering diamonds on the ring of the double-headed griffin.

"Since you've already decided to interfere with my destiny and claim my life, why do you honor me with your presence, Ace?"

Lamb winced at the familiarity. Ace, a nickname given him early in life, short for American Common Enterprises, was a name used only by a select few. Lamb cackled gleefully, tickled by Val's casual bravado. The potentate slapped his knee, forgetting the ring.

"Ah'm curious, mah boy, what it is makes a fella like you tick. Ya see, there ain't a dangblasted thing ah don't already know about ya."

"We're even, Ace. I, too, know all about you. You have no secrets I don't already know."

309

"Secrets? My life's an open book. Speak up, I can't hear ya, boy."

"An open book?" Val hooted mirthfully.

Lamb was rankled by Val's lack of fear and his audacity. Hatred oozed from his small eyes.

"Let's not waste time. Why did you bring me here, Ace? I've waited long enough for you to show yourself."

"Ah respect a man who knowingly walks into a trap," he told Val, a smile of crafty ridicule lighting up his face.

"Good. Suppose we begin with why you've declared a personal vendetta on the Erice family. I mean in addition to the one IAGO dealt me during the Shiverton presidency."

Lamb's cackling laughter filled the room.

"Ya got guts, Erice. Ah mean ta tell ya, ya ain't gonna see the morning sun rise tomorrow, an' here ya are giving me orders. Ah almost wish we'd met years ago before ya decided ta champion those yellowbellied, slimy sons of a blackhearted rattler. Those Shiverton boys is who I mean."

"Why? You think you and I might have something in common?" he asked, choosing to ignore the last half of Lamb's statement for the time being.

"We're both born predators, Erice, after the same thing —wealth and power, like two peas in a pod."

"God forbid," muttered Val.

"What's that ya said? Speak up, boy. Comes a time, when a man's mah age, some of his hearing goes." Lamb moved around to a chest along the wall, and opened the chest revealing a well-stocked liquor cabinet. He poured a stiff bracer of bourbon in a glass, held it towards Val.

Val shook his head. Lamb gulped the drink swiftly, wiping his lips with the back of his shirt sleeve.

"Like ah was saying. Ah'm a little deaf, but ah ain't lost mah senses. Don't make out ta me ya don't favor the anonymity of shadowed places just as ah and mah contemporaries do. We all live in the same manner— we're the power behind the thrones in the world, ya might say. But as ah see it, ya made one big mistake, else ya wouldn't be here preparing ta meet your Maker on mah orders."

"Ah. I chose to back Ted Shiverton. That's it, isn't it?"

"That's telling it straight. It became your Waterloo."

"What perplexes me," said Val, choosing his words carefully, "is why a man should be so intent upon breaking his son's back. Did you hate him so much you couldn't have forgiven him with a father's love for any wrong unknowingly done to you?"

Lamb sweated copiously. His face grimaced as he watched Val slip off the bed and pour himself two fingers of bourbon, the briefcase still manacled to one wrist. The room fell silent.

"Bring them words by me once more." His eyes glistened like a diamondback's.

Val obliged him, repeating his words loudly.

"You lie!" he hissed. "You lie!" Lamb jumped to his wobbly feet, raging, shaking a bony finger at him. "Ah could kill ya for telling them lies. What's wrong with ya? Ya make it hard for me to be decent to ya in your last hours."

"It's the truth," Val said quietly. "Ted Shiverton was the son of your loins. Think, man, think! The last night you lay with your beloved, you begged her to leave her husband, but she turned you down, pleading for your understanding, but only after you both had conceived the child who grew up to be Ted Shiverton."

Behind Lamb's stony face, his bright fiery eyes were turning back in time, focusing on the scene Val was describing.

"Then," continued Val, "in anger you married a woman known in certain circles as Carlotta. Yes, Ace. I know Carlotta. You know exactly how I know her so I won't humiliate you by bringing up her sordid past."

"Ya lying, sidewinding sonofabitch!" he cackled in that high falsetto voice. "Ah ain't about ta show ya mercy—"

"I don't ask for mercy. Not when I have proof."

If Lamb heard Val's last words he gave no indication. "Monk will return to finish ya off. I guarantee I'll show ya no quarter for speaking of mah wife so dishonorably."

"I'd never speak dishonorably about a woman who brought me as much pleasure as Carlotta did, Ace." He changed his tack. "You never forgave Shiverton for taking Miss Austin from you. You promised to break him. But one giant obstacle thwarted you. IAGO. You both belonged to IAGO and they refused to condone such immature behavior, since it threatened their existence. They could afford no world spotlights shed upon them."

Val moved towards the patio door, pulling it open. The intense desert heat rushed into the room. Val inhaled it deeply, then turned back to his host. "It was IAGO who backed Shiverton's play in business after your braying asses in Washington filed anti-trust suits against them. That's right, Ace. Why look surprised? Isn't that IAGO's specialty—backing both sides in any confrontation?"

Falling against his chair Lamb looked as if he'd been embalmed.

"You ordered your own flesh and blood assassinated—murdered at your own hand as if you yourself had pulled the trigger of those abominable weapons." Val was exquisitely relentless, yet surprisingly gentle with the older mogul.

The crusty, hardbitten old man, a survivor, cocked a wary eye at his adversary. "Who else knows about this?"

Val explained about his systematic investigation of Lamb. "You were a tough one to ferret out, but not impossible. I have letters you wrote to Mrs. Shiverton, photos of you both as children and later sweethearts. Included are letters she wrote to you and didn't mail. If these letters were to find their way into Senator Shiverton's hands, I fear he couldn't ignore you in the matter."

"Ya better give me them letters! All that memorabilia is mine. I'm warning ya, turn it over ta me."

"How can I do that? I've been abducted—at your hands." Val sat at the edge of the bed, his bare feet crossed at the ankles. "I'd stake my life that the entire state of Nevada is looking for me. I left a letter with my bodyguard to be opened at midnight tonight. They'll know who to look for. You'd better deal with me now, while you can, Ace."

Lamb's face jerked, his jaw muscles twisted and writhed as a shudder passed through him. Despite the hot desert air permeating the room he felt chilled to the marrow. His fists clenched together involuntarily, the knuckles of his fingers showing bony white. His head tilted back against his chair, his puffy eyes closed. The color of his skin turned a ghastly saffron yellow in the dim lighting.

Val watched him, wondering over which of the many complicated routes of thinking he would embark upon. He waited patiently, stretching his ankles, rotating them for circulation.

Lamb, his eyes closed, had been thinking back to the night he had begged his beloved to leave Shiverton; his voice, barely above a whisper, said,

"That night we made love for one last, memorable time. She begged me to understand why she couldn't leave our love child, Amelia, in the hands of her husband. Later—

312

I didn't count the months—when she gave birth to a son, I felt defeated, the very hope yanked out from under me. Can ya understand?"

The shock of his stunning words struck Val. Amy, too?

"That's when mah hatred for Whitman Shiverton multiplied in mah mind. I swore ta eliminate every last son that bastard ever sired—if it took mah life. He represented everything evil in mah life. He stole mah sweetheart, laid claim to mah daughter, but when he tried ta break me in business, Ah made mah move. Ah should have killed that lousy lying son of a cobra years ago, with mah bare fists. He took mah sweetheart and my daughter from me," he lamented. "For me mah life was over."

"And you subjected the innocent to your wrath," insisted Val sternly. "You married Carlotta on the rebound, and she ended up in a sanitarium. You did to her what Shiverton did to your sweetheart—persecute her for your own shortcomings. And look what you did to your own son!"

The oil titan's twitching, jerking face resembled a skull and crossbones. For a quarter of an hour he ranted, objecting to Val's cutting remarks; at times incoherent, at times with clarity. He couldn't endure the truth from Val's lips, not from the enemy he'd sworn to kill. His arrogance and pride began to disintegrate before the eyes of this comparative stranger who brought him unendurable emotional trauma by retailing his personal sorrows and carefully guarded secrets.

Nothing in Lamb's questionable and shady business life could fragment his composure as Val had done on this day. Pulling himself out of his wheelchair he moved heavily, clumsily towards the open solarium, his boots scraping heavily along the Italian tiled flooring. He stood in the open doorway, his fragile, ancient body illuminated by the sun, his back a black shadow to Val's eyes. His bony head was lifted skyward, the lights of another, more terrifying world reflected in his aged, yellowing eyes.

"Do ya know the feeling of madness, Mr. Erice? You must. All power-crazed men like us experience such feelings from time to time. Every day of mah life since I can recollect, ah've been possessed by a raging demon, driving me. More so since Shiverton took from me the only things that counted, my beloved and our daughter, Amelia, named after mah own dear mother."

Val closed his eyes to shut the sight of Lamb's pain. He

wondered how he would feel if he learned suddenly that Tina and perhaps Benne wasn't the blood of his blood. Lamb's piercing voice cut into Val's thoughts.

"Ah don't contest your words because it's true. Ah did the things you accuse me of doing. But ah swear ah never knew Ted was mah son!" His balled fists struck against the door jamb. "Goddamn, it was cruel of her not ta tell me!"

A sob shuddered through Lamb's scrawny frame. Observing him, Val felt certain that he heard Death rattling nearby. But, he wondered, whose? His or Lamb's?

"Ah'm too old ta be facing such truths," continued Lamb. "Ah married up with that woman Carlotta an' she bore me the three sons ah sired. They ain't one of them worth the price of a saddle. Too much money, ya see? Not enough spine. Money don't make men—it makes nothin, unless they got the stuffings . . ." He broke off and peered at Val darkly, filled with suspicion. "Ya ain't just feeding me a line of bull about them letters, are ya?" His reptilian eyes boring in Val's read the truth. Turning away he lifted his face to the heavens, crying aloud. "Mah God! Y'all forgive me, hear?"

The poignant moment passed. Lamb, quickly recuperating from his brief vulnerability, changed tack in his approach to Val. Watching the oil mogul, Val marveled in fascination at the changes flooding the older man's hard-bitten face.

"What's your deal, Erice? Ah know yer hankering for one, so talk!"

Val angled his head in amused silence. He yawned and scratched his head thoughtfully, as if he might be considering something spectacular.

"Yer life for them papers," bargained the old horse-trader. His bony fingers shook noticeably.

Val laughed. He shook his head tolerantly. "You forget, Ace, wherever you travel, I've already been there. My destiny is not as clouded as yours. I'm aware of the treasures to be found at the end of our journey," he said enigmatically. "You aren't." Val stretched his arms and rubbed the small of his back.

"What will your friends at IAGO say when they learn you've taken the destinies of several lives into your hands? Ted Shiverton, Sam Linden, possibly Hughes when you learned he intended to keep the Houston men out of Vegas. Don't deny it. Neiland Milton's next, you said. Then me."

314

"Y'all wait a dangblasted minute, boy. Lying ain't one of mah vices. Ah already told ya that ah arranged for Ted Shiverton's demise, God help me. But ah'm telling ya Sam Linden's and Neiland Milton's fate came directly from IAGO. As for you—" He stopped short, his leathery neck bristling with anger at having walked into Val's trap. Then he cackled harshly, aware that he held the royal straight flush in this card game of wits. His eyes were intent on Val's ring as he collected his thoughts.

"Since ya won't be leaving my ranch alive, Mr. Erice, there's no reason ya shouldn't know the truth." Lamb shuffled painfully across the room and sat down in the wheelchair again.

"Sam Linden moved against orders just as Milton's done since his reelection. Sam Linden chose ta fight the Hughes land acquisitions, getting us all upset. For a time, Milton complied with his orders through the first administration. But of late there's been too much hanky panky with money. Hughes made himself too visible in Las Vegas. His thirst for power outside of IAGO became too obvious. What Hughes attempted ta do is convert himself into a one-man IAGO. His repeated efforts ta bend the American government ta his will through bribery brought about the wrath of IAGO. Power madness can make a man dangerous. Do ah have ta paint you a clearer picture?"

"But," said Val, tentatively. "There have been too many, uh, assassinations of late, right? You're letting Milton commit political suicide instead." Val shook his head in amazement as Lamb lifted a thin forefinger with an expression of delight.

"Exactly!" exclaimed Lamb with joy.

"One thing about IAGO. They know how to bust a man's balls. How did they get a fighter like Milton to agree to retire from office? How, without putting up a fight?"

"We believe in force, strength, power and conquest. We are a strangely cohesive group. Make no mistake about that. It's our real strength. The ultimate stupidity in men like Sam Linden, Hughes and Milton and their *personal* lust for power is appalling ta us. They were too greedy, Mr. Erice. Too greedy. They thought themselves immune to the power of IAGO. Strong, fearless men with bright intelligence is what IAGO needs, not pussyfooting, yellow-bellied lizards who turn tail in a whirlwind." Lamb sighed

315

heavily, shaking his head regretfully. "They jus' don't make men of our calibre no more."

Val raised his hand to his mouth and behind it smiled grimly.

"Strong, fearless men with bright intelligence?" Val paused. "You mean like Ted Shiverton? The very potential needed desperately in a world leader was embodied in the heart and soul of the man. And you, for selfish reasons, saw fit to diabolically snuff out his life." His voice dripped with contempt.

"Mah God! Can't ya see its bustin' mah guts, man? Ah told ya I didn't know ah had sired that maverick. Ah don't give a cactus pear for Milton. Bigger men far more dangerous than Milton have been busted—"

Val laughed off the other's discomfort. "C'mon now, Ace, your newspapers blew the affair out of proportion. They crucified Milton. Why don't you deal with him as you did Sam Linden and what you had in mind for me?" Val pressed. "A syringe filled with instant mortality would have kept the lid on all the sewage."

About to reply to Val's charges, Lamb became recalcitrant. "*Had* in mind for you?" Lamb's cackling voice echoed through the room. His black eyes in their yellowish whites were obscene with gloating. "It's a good act you put on of being fearless," he snorted.

Val walked back into the room from the edge of the patio, sighing heavily. He shook his head regretfully as he made his point.

"I told you, Ace, death is an old friend of mine. Years ago we made a pact. Before escorting me through St. Peter's gate she promised to let me do my bit on earth." He stretched again. "Too bad we can't go for a walk. This room is too confining."

"The hand ah intend ta deal ya is your life for those personal papers." Lamb's voice was unusually quiet.

Val turned to face his host, and laughed heartily. "You not only underestimate me, Ace, but apparently you aren't listening. You take me for some fool, like Linden or Milton? I told you you can't threaten me with death— and you don't hear me. I'll repeat, my affairs are in order. I've left no open tracks. However, we may have another bargaining point. Do you mind if I remove the manacle from my wrist? It's getting cumbersome."

Lamb watched Val slip a key into the bracelet and unlock it, placing the case on the bed. He rubbed his irritated wrist gingerly and turned to face the oil man.

"My private papers for your promise and IAGO's to never again interfere with Erice business," he began. "Next, you are not to interfere politically with Senator Shiverton. If he should learn that you spearheaded his brother's assassination you'll let the chips fall where they will and not obstruct him by inventing a confusion of cover stories to disguise the main issue. In addition you are never to breathe to a living soul your true relationship either to Amy or to Ted."

"You ask too much."

As if he hadn't heard Lamb's lament he outlined further provisos. "You'll withdraw from any and all political machinations—including your affiliation with IAGO. You're old enough to retire gracefully. Then you, Larchmont and Merkle will dissolve TFL and all its holdings."

They argued, negotiated, talked again and renegotiated. They drank coffee, had a snack, and negotiated some more. During all this time, Lamb kept squinting at Val's ring, but never asked about it. As the talk continued Lamb's indignation was colored by his selfish determination to best Val in the manipulation. When he thought Val was too hardnosed he growled, "You'll never get away with it."

"Get away with what?" Val countered with a steadying calm that rankled Lamb. "I've no guilt for crimes the magnitude of yours or TFL's. You must admit, Ace, I do have bargaining power. But don't take my word. Talk to your advisors. Put it to them that I have in my possession volatile information that could dethrone you, upsetting American Common Enterprises worldwide. A nation of people can be incited when they learn your interests under the clout of IAGO have accelerated the oil crisis. Your man, the despotic prince, has kept his country producing oil, using slave labor, at slave wages, while simultaneously increasing the costs far beyond—"

"Mistuh Erice! You've gone too far."

"If you're going to repeat yourself, I rest my case." Val tapped a sheaf of papers Lamb had been eyeing ever since he removed them from his briefcase. "Suppose you take a look at these. You must know what I have here . . ."

Lamb fastened bifocals into place over his large, pockmarked, bulbous nose and picked up a few papers with trembling hands. As he perused them, the colors on his parchment face alternated from cherry pink to a leadlike paleness.

Val, possessed of infinite patience, stood at the entrance

of the solarium determined not to budge an inch. He'd stick to his guns. Periodically he'd glance at Lamb, awaiting the mogul's decision. Like a warrior doing battle with a mortal enemy Val felt he'd exhausted every ploy and all the efforts of friendly persuasion he knew.

The aged, hardbitten atheist who had parted company from religion when his one and only true love married another man had shown no tolerance or belief in a power other than his own. Yet presently, as he read the compilation of papers, his bony fingers clutched at a black onyx cross in his hands, manipulating it nervously as a superstitious gambler might finger a lucky coin. "It's mah good luck piece," he told Val.

This self-made, vinegar-faced man with a voice to match, a highly combustive personality frayed with self-doubt, had lived his life with money as his God. A loner, a devious schemer, he'd lived by his wits until the age of twenty-two when he discovered the supreme power of money and the monied man who could be anyone and anything for a price.

Ezekial Lazarus Lamb, the scammy wheeler dealer, became an independent entrepreneur; a respectable name for a fast-talking, hustling con man without scruples, ethics or morality. The rest of his billions had been earned by the same means of treachery, deceit and betrayal.

Val had gambled his life to smoke this man into the open. Now, he wondered, would it pay off?

Twice Monk Garret knocked on the door to check with his boss. He was brusquely told "get your ass back to where ya belong. If ah want ya, ah'll call for ya."

Val spoke up. "One other stipulation to my offer, Ace. I want Monk Garret."

Before Lamb protested another voice called out, "Not a chance, Mr. Erice. You see, he's my man." A stiffly accented British voice preceded the shadows of the men approaching in the semi-darkness.

CHAPTER TWENTY-FIVE

"I repeat," said Val, his steadfast eyes on Lamb, with no need to glance up; he recognized the voice from his past.

"I repeat I want Monk Garret. He killed my son."

The sweat glistening on his skeletal features, Lamb set aside the papers, viewing instead the shadowy forms advancing into the room. Removing his cap, he mopped his sweaty pate with a napkin, nodding a silent greeting to the newcomers.

"So, we meet again, Mr. Erice," said Mourous Benkhanhian, moving into the light. Val cursed inwardly, aware that the presence of the IAGO chieftain complicated his involvement with Lamb. He nodded to Benkhanhian, his eyes sweeping past him to rest on the handsome features of an Arab dressed in desert garb.

"Be satisfied," Lamb piped up, reinforced by the appearance of his companions. "You're getting enough of mah hide."

"Monk Garret—or no deal." Val held his place firmly.

"You ask too much," quipped Lamb defiantly, stopping short at an upthrust hand by the Arab.

The Arab bowed with deference to Val. "It's our understanding your son was returned to you, Mr. Erice. There is no need to push and shove. We need Monk Garret. It's a question of mere mathematics to us."

Under the wide arc of light Val saw the Arab more clearly defined. He shrugged imperceptibly. "Your man Garret insists the man posing as my son is an impostor." Val saw the exchange of annoyance flickering in their eyes. "Monk assures me he killed Benne by a direct gun shot to his brain, then parachuted to safety before the plane exploded." His words came hard.

"My son will never return," commiserated Lamb.

The IAGO hammerhead, Benkhanhian, staring tentatively at Val's signet ring, mumbled, "Then who is the impostor?"

"Suppose you solve that riddle. You're supposed to be the shrewd braintrust—not snake-oil pushers," countered Val, with an air of indifference. The appearance of Benkhanhian and the Arab threw a monkey wrench into his plans, weakening his position against Lamb. His strategy to push Lamb into a corner using the fear of IAGO's wrath to insure his position floundered. Now, forced to reconnoiter, he stalled for time. Focusing on the Arab, he extended his right hand to him cordially.

"I remind myself that IAGO is never one for polite manners," he said. "I've heard a great deal about you, Your Highness, from my daughter Tina. You impressed her when you met her in Rome."

Ali Mohammed, thunderstruck and momentarily thrown off balance, shook Val's hand, but was not prepared for his next remarks.

"You succeeded in gagging Valerie Shiverton, do you now intend to romance the senator?"

Benkhanhian laughed with coarse guffaws, shaking his head incredulously. "I told you he was an exceptional man, Your Highness. Something special, wouldn't you agree? It's uncanny how he perceives our strategy. Too bad, Val Erice. In refusing to join us, you've deprived us of a formidable ally."

Val shuffled into the adjoining bathroom to relieve himself, mulling over his conversation with Lamb. The old horse trader never mentioned Benkhanhian; in retrospect Val realized their conversation had been taped, filmed and viewed by these IAGO potentates. He sprinkled cold water on his face and dried himself, thinking of the Arab pirnce. Ali Mohammed's presence here could mean only one thing; he was a rising power in the hierarchy of IAGO. With these additional considerations, Val concentrated his efforts into converting this setback into success for himself and defeat for IAGO.

For an instant, before he turned off the light and joined the others, he wondered how his family had taken his disappearance.

When he reentered the bedroom, Benkhanhian was scanning the sheaf of papers through his bifocals, perched on the end of his nose. Prince Izmur was peering at the fading desert scene. Lamb seemed ill at ease, evidently irked by Benkhanhian's pontificating aura of superiority. On spying Val's entrance, he asserted himself.

"Ya can't have Monk Garret," he repeated.

320

"Then we have no deal," said Val tersely. "In addition I want Marciano and Renzo Bonaparte."

"You know about them, too?" Lamb asked with a sneer on his face.

"Why won't you believe me, Ezekial? I've known for a long time. I was very close to Ted Shiverton. He confided in me as a son might to his father. He was gravely concerned over your pact with the Arab nations." Val turned the overhead lights on, bringing all their faces into sharper focus. "It's pointless to rehash old issues."

Benkhanhian mumbled, "If you'd only complied with our directives. I explained our mission long ago. We are the illuminated of mankind with a responsibility to propel the lesser endowed man to his destiny. Ted Shiverton might have been alive today—"

Val gave Lamb a sharp penetrating glance. E.L. Lamb quickly averted his eyes. "Who can combat the forces of destiny?" he said.

"IAGO doesn't combat destiny," said Ali Mohammed. "We propel her, control her, insuring our results."

Val moved to his bed and sat down, his alert eyes taking in the scene. First, Lamb, a skeletal old man dressed outlandishly in western garb, pathetic in his attempt to defy death. Next, Benkhanhian, an older, Humpty Dumpty of a man, less emaciated than Lamb. Last, Prince Ali Mohammed, champion of the new breed, vigorous and vital, whose mentality was steeped in new and revolutionary technologies spawned in the age of the atom. Men like Izmur, Ted and Whip Shiverton, and his son Benne were sharp, and more knowledgeable about the future than the men of Val's generation. One day soon, this Arabian prince would become a power to reckon with, prophesied Val, despairingly.

As if reading Val's thoughts, Benkhanhian spoke out. "I have recently named my successor, Ericc." He motioned to Ali. "Prince Izmur will soon replace me."

Val nodded to Ali. "Congratulations. It would be interesting to hear from your lips what you'll do when the Israelis push back your borders and confiscate your oil. If they should rule the oil empire, what will your people do?"

Ali bowed coolly. "I never speculate over uncertainties. Hypothetical questions are a waste of time."

"But," pressed Val, "if it became a reality?"

Ali frowned. "Believe me, what you suggest could never

321

become reality. Knowing in advance the outcome of a situation is dependent on knowing the whims and caprices of those involved. A wise man eliminates all eventualities not in keeping with his plans." Ali had little patience with men long past their prime. Yet this man Val Erice hardly seemed to fit in the same category as Lamb and Benkhanhian. He addressed himself to Benkhanhian, "Perhaps you should convince Mr. Erice of his limited bargaining power. If you'll excuse me, much has to be set in motion." He salaamed to the others, but before leaving tossed back the flap of his *cuffiah*. "I am as enchanted with your daughter Tina as she is with me. Did you know that, Mr. Erice?" He left them, but his presence was still felt among the others.

Val felt a sudden dread descend upon him; the hidden meaning behind Ali's words burned lividly in his mind. He didn't think he'd lost much ground at this point, yet as he searched his mind for ways to combat these supporters of political assassinations and international terrorism, he forced himself to reconsider Prince Izmur. Val had made it a point to learn as much as he could about Ali Mohammed; his wealth, social status, connections in Zurich, IAGO connections, and promiscuous romantic flings. None of these things affected Val more than Ali's last words: "I am as enchanted with Tina as she is with me!" Val knew exactly the nature of the threat couched in that seemingly innocent remark. He shuddered inwardly, never more as discontent with himself as he was at this minute for not having confided more in Tina after she left Rome. Now as he glanced at the two moguls he had to take a different tack. If his earlier weapons of negotiation were ineffectual, he had to find some that would cut deeply and wound his adversaries.

"How absurd we are," admitted Val with candor. "Here we are indulging in daydreams—fantasies, if you will—acting as if we were eternal." He scoffed ironically. "The world will hardly mark the deaths of three men who for a short while rented space on earth and paid their dues. Neither shall we be mourned in the manner Ted Shiverton is, who will be mourned by the world for years to come." He inclined his head.

Lamb squirmed uncomfortably; Benkhanhian scowled. Neither had any use for such terminal words.

Recently, Lamb had updated his will to make certain the IRS wouldn't get the largest chunk; he had made dual grants to the cities of Dallas and Houston, to provide for a memorial to him; a multimillion-dollar museum of art, a gesture from one of the first oil pioneers.

Benkhanhian, in meditative silence, wondered why he'd bothered to travel this vast distance at his age. The threat of failing health kept him in morbid fear of death. Now, listening to Erice, the old fears swept through him. Once again he fastened his eyes on Val's ring, aware that it was a psychological spur appropriately manipulated to subtly intimidate the men of IAGO. *Blimey, what ruddy courage. This bastard can never be a loser. Though we dispose of him, somewhere, somehow, the hand of the double-headed griffin will reach out and do the same to any of us.* He chuckled to himself, tapping his thigh impatiently. A game plan had been put in motion; it must be played as they had cleverly implemented it. Besides, it would be gratifying to see how this bloody scheme turned out.

They paused for a light supper: rare, thinly sliced beef, a tossed chef's salad and frozen sherbet. Coffee was served to them back in Val's room. A tray of fruit juices was placed next to the oval table where they continued their talks.

The moon had risen above the horizon, the desert air had turned chilly. They were stalemated. Val, involved in negotiations long enough to know things must fall into place mutually, was fatigued. Lamb perused the documents with noticeable melancholia. Benkhanhian reread the papers. It all took time.

Why, wondered Val, was Lamb so adamantly loyal to Monk Garret? Why did Benkhanhian come to Monk's defense? Hit men were as expendable as a private in the army. They were the guns, that's all. It wasn't reasonable for men of Lamb's and Benkhanhian's stature to be sentimentalists. Then why such loyalty to the gun? Lamb, whose money belt had bought and sold men with the ease of buying and selling commodities over a counter, had some reason to show unmitigated loyalty to Monk, and Val intended to discover that reason.

In the next few moments, Val became a skillful tailor who began to fit together the pieces of a conspiracy. Slowly, it was coming together in his mind.

Lamb slammed the last of the papers on the table, sucking at his dentures to remove food particles. "Might as well get to it," he said, swilling down a glass of pineapple juice. "How soon can ya get the originals to me?"

323

"Are we in agreement, Ezekial? You know my terms."

"Ya don't get Monk Garret." He added quickly, "Don't call me by that ridiculous name."

"Then we've no deal," said Val, undressing and putting on his pyjamas. He slipped into bed, between the sheets. "Go ahead, call Garret—or Larry Sharp. Prepare the syringe. Induce the cardiac arrest." Val held up an apologetic hand. "There are so many players in this farce, I keep reminding myself you control them all."

Benkhanhian, fascinated by Val's dramatic panache, smiled tightly. Val gave them no quarter. "Monk murdered my son. It's only fitting that you give him to me. I can understand your reluctance to sacrifice him since he also assassinated Ted Shiverton—"

"You're an endless fountain of information and getting to be a constant source of pain to me," Lamb spat acidly. "Too screwing smart for your own good—"

"Any time you're ready," called Val with a calm designed to rankle his hosts. "Oh, yes, Ezekial, make sure it's a swift finish, will you? Death, no fickle mistress, doesn't approve of indecision."

"Ya dangblasted, gutsy, stud bull bastard!" cursed Lamb. "Ah won't be pushed!"

"Just trying to be helpful," said Val, smoothing the sheets.

"Ya think ya got it figured out, do ya. Unlucky for you."

"You're a maddening man, Ezekial," insisted Val in a light vein. Despite the bluff he perpetuated, Val knew something provoked the oil man. It wasn't characteristic of either Lamb's or Benkhanhian's natures to put up with the nonsense Val was dishing out.

"I assume the contents of these papers are true," said Benkhanhian in his Churchillian accent.

"I don't deal in falsehoods."

"You can't have Senator Shiverton," said Benkhanhian. "You—"

"No deal," insisted Val.

"—see he already belongs to us."

Val's brows jackknifed.

"Once," continued Benkhanhian, "you suggested that I buy my own congressmen and senators. Do you recall?"

Val recalled it vividly.

"I did as you suggested. Senator Shiverton will be the

next American president." Benkhanhian lit up a cigar, puffing expansively on it. "The reason you can't have Monk Garret is, as Prince Ali said earlier, a simple question of mathematics. We need him. You may not know this but Monk Garret is a specialist in his field with another job to do for us before retiring. After this mission—" Benkhanhian spread his hands in a speculative gesture, "if you're so inclined, you can do as you will."

"That's the straight of it?" Val asked, aware he'd have to make concessions.

"How sure are we that you'll deliver all the original documents—that you won't cooperate with the Bureau of Secret Intelligence?" The IAGO chieftain rolled his cigar over his thick lips.

Val's brows raised slightly and fell softly back into place.

"What purpose would it serve for either of us to deceive the other? What would we gain? Everything loaned to us on earth is about to be passed to the next inheritor—the next manipulator. We had our time and it's nearly over. Why not bow out in majesty?" Val suddenly knew it was futile. He had failed to convince these titans, and they were besting him. They would get what they wanted with or without him. In these moments, under these circumstances, the power of the double-headed griffin was impotent. It was nearly over. For the first time Val felt the bitter elixir of defeat. It had all been for naught.

"Ah'm not a man of hasty decisions," said Lamb. "Ah'm a man who retires early every night. It's past my bedtime. Ah'm free to take these copies with me, since y'all have the originals?"

Val merely looked at him. They were still playing, he thought sadly, watching them leave the room. The IAGO chief paused at the door, to say, "I admire your ring," before closing the door behind them.

Val, more depressed than he could ever remember being, sprang from the bed and locked the door. He brushed his teeth in the bathroom, then, returning to the bedroom, closed and locked the sliding glass doors. He shoved a straight-backed chair under the door knob, hoping to deter an unwanted visitor. He snapped open his briefcase, pressing a hidden lock and releasing a hidden compartment. He removed the Belgium-made Browning magnum, checking the full clip with approval. *Good girl, Tina. You filled the clip.* He entered the bathroom, and placed the gun on

325

the marble commode as he disrobed and showered, relaxing for a time. Finished, he dried himself and took time to shave, ridding himself of a three days' stubble. In the bedroom again he donned a fresh pair of pyjamas his host had provided and hopped into bed between the sheets, the Browning under the sheet at his side. He pressed a button on the panel next to the bed, turning on an overhead TV set.

Johnny Carson was beginning his nightly monologue. Val got up, and removed the chair from under the door, padding back to bed, where he concentrated on the Carson jokes. Within moments, he saw the handle of the door turning. Dr. Larry Sharp entered the room, syringe held upright in one hand. He was followed by Monk Garret who moved with his usual swaggering gait towards the bed.

"Sorry, Val," said Larry Sharp. "I never thought it would come to this. By now you must know, they own me body and soul. Make it easy on yourself, cooperate. Roll up your sleeve."

"You'll do it yourself. I won't aid and abet you in my death," said Val evenly, his eyes trained on Monk, who had every intent to accomodate the doctor, by force if necessary. Under the covers, Val's grip on the Browning tightened. It was now or never.

He squeezed hard. It was a direct hit to Monk's shoulder. Garret, shocked, moved for his gun. Val, by now above the covers, shifted his weight to his left side and fired again and again. The explosions were deafening. Dr. Sharp, panicked, lay flat against the wall, petrified as he watched blood spurt from the bullet punctures in Monk's chest and stomach. He shouted, "Don't shoot me! Don't shoot me!" like a squealing pig.

Val faced Sharp, their eyes meeting in silence. Taking careful and deliberate aim, Val fired four times at his target.

"You'll live, Sharp," said Val in a scorching voice. "You'll never perform surgery again—without hands; but you'll live. I'll see to it." Sharp's howling, painfilled voice echoed loudly.

Val waited, watching the physician sink to his knees as he stared at the sickening bloody masses at his wrists. The sound of running footsteps drew nearer.

Val quickly leaped to the wall at one side of the door as two hired hands, guns drawn, burst into the room, stopping short at the bloody scene. "Try anything and you'll join Garret," said Val. "I don't want to kill either of you, but if I must, I will." He relieved them of their weapons, ordered one to sit down and the other to summon his boss.

E.L. Lamb padded his brittle-boned frame hurriedly into the room, aided by his hired hand. He stood frozen at the door, his features blanching, a half-crazed expression forming on his face. Larry Sharp writhed in agony, trying to subdue the pain, in near shock as he stared dumbly at his bullet-shattered hands; whimpering sounds escaped his lips. Lamb's disbelieving eyes moved to Monk Garret's bloodied body sprawled grotesquely on the floor, then traveled to the gun held in Val's hand.

"What have ya done?" he bleated, bending over to retrieve the syringe Larry Sharp had dropped.

"I've helped you make up your mind," said Val sternly. "You may have time to waste, I don't. I'm a man of decision."

Lamb, shaking uncontrollably as if afflicted with the ague, mumbled, "We'll have to get Sharp to the hospital."

"Sharp can wait. First take me to the phone," Val insisted.

As he followed Lamb along the corridor leading to a large room with overhead beams and an enormous fireplace along one wall, Val commanded sternly, "Tell your men to back off." Two armed guards entering the large room paused. The oil man waved them off, muttering, "It's all over. It's finished."

He motioned Val to the desk at the other side of the room where two telephones rested in their cradles. "Make your call, Mr. Erice."

"Ezekial, need I caution you to do nothing foolish while I make my call?"

Lamb simply waved Val off as he sank into a nearby chair, crestfallen, defeated, his empty eyes staring stonily ahead at nothing. One hand, holding the hypodermic, dropped over the arm of the chair. Watching him closely Val dialed the operator. When she came on the line Val instructed her to get the Pyramids Hotel, extension P-1000.

"You can dial the number direct, sir," came the sterile voice.

"If I could dial, I would," retorted Val. "Please oblige me."

A frantic Richie answered. As Val laid out his instructions to him he removed his eyes from Ezekial Lamb for a split second. But that was all it took for Lamb to jam the needle into his arm and push the plunger. Val shouted into the phone.

"Hurry, Richie. Bring an ambulance!" He slammed the phone and rushed to Lamb's side.

"Ah ain't about to go to prison after mah long and remarkable career," muttered Lamb, a look of satanic glee etched into his lean, haggard face.

A pained expression crossed Val's face; he was touched so deeply his eyes filled suddenly with tears. "We could have worked something out," he said quietly. He removed the syringe from Lamb's arm and ran back into the bedroom where Larry Sharp had curled into a ball against the wall, weeping, moaning with pain. The sight of Val rushing at him with a crazed look in his eyes caused Sharp to cringe and retreat further from him.

"The syringe—what was in it, Sharp? What was it? Is there an antidote? Tell me, you sonofabitch, scum of the earth! Tell me!"

Sharp fell heavily away from Val's arms. He was dying or close to it. Val stared with disdain at the cowardly dog. Rushing back along the corridor to the living room, feeling the fatigue of the past days, he ran to Lamb's side and shook the older man. "Tell me, what was in the syringe?" he persisted. "Tell me so we can save you!"

"It don't matter none. There's little time for me. Ah'm the sorriest sonofabitch that ever lived. God forgive me for killing mah son. Ah didn't know. Ah just didn't know—they ordered his death. They didn't know."

"Where's Benkhanhian?"

"Gone. He left it up ta me." Lamb coughed, unable to catch his breath; his face was engorged with blood, the vessels at each temple writhing like angry red worms.

Val placed his gun on the sturdy oaken table, to help the dying man. He shook his head sadly, a terrible passivity sweeping over him. He hadn't wanted Lamb dead, but alive. Alive to explain a number of things to Bowman, Whip Shiverton and the others. Here was the one man who could plug up all the holes, link together the chain of events.

"You can't die now, Ace! Not now! Dammit, not now!"

Val wasn't certain how long he stood there, helplessly trying to revive Lamb; thinking of questions he wanted to but couldn't ask.

A deafening explosion burst all around Val; then another and another as his body jerked violently, twisting as he made a valiant effort to locate his assailant. Sharp bolts of pain seared his chest; his spine burst into fire. An armed guard, creeping cautiously forward, had discharged his gun. Another explosion burst the guard's body open, propelled into the air by the bullets fired from Richie's gun as he and Captain Ferraro's men moved in, a few seconds too late.

CHAPTER TWENTY-SIX

Jaqualine Devon had left Las Vegas with the two BSI agents, constructing an elaborate design for her escape. Neither the time nor the place was set in her mind, but at the first opportunity she would do it.

The mortician at Westwood Memorial Chapel greeted them and announced that Dancey Darling was not quite ready to be viewed. "I'll need a half hour longer," insisted the pasty-faced, fish-eyed man. Jaqualine excused herself to go to the powder room, unaware she'd find the perfect opportunity to extricate herself from the agents. One of the burly, six-foot men stood guard outside the door, while inside, Jaqualine saw her opportunity and took it, beating a hasty retreat through an open rear window.

Within moments she had crossed Glendon Avenue and, cutting through a busy parking lot, entered the United Artists Theater, pausing first to purchase a ticket. She quickly detoured to the powder room, dropped a coin into a pay phone and dialed a number. Waiting for Abdul to answer, she tapped her foot impatiently and bit off a hangnail. His lazy voice came on the line and she rattled off in frantic Arabic, "It's me. I've run away. What shall I do?"

An hour later, Abdul, sulking noticeably, drove her through the thickening Saturday afternoon traffic to an apartment across town on Fountain Avenue in Hollywood. He parked the steel gray Volkswagen in the street and led her cautiously inside the dated Normandy-styled building that once had been as posh as the fabled Garden of Allah.

Slipping a dead bolt into place, Abdul watched Jamila smoke incessantly, pacing before him, speaking in short bursts of explosive speech, half English, half Arabic, giving him a play by play description of her involvements since they last spoke.

Flinging off her jacket and tossing it onto the sofa, she sat on one arm of a chair, facing Abdul imploringly. "For the love of Allah, don't ask me to go back. The senator is suspicious. I know he recognized me. He never took his eyes off me, studying me, hoping some clue would connect in his mind. After all," she added, rising to her feet, pacing again, wringing her hands compulsively, "you are not dealing with a fool. He was the attorney general—an astute man in government." She spun around wild-eyed. "And the woman who interviewed me—"

"—Woman? Which woman?" Abdul searched her eyes piercingly.

Jamila's hand whirled about her forehead in a gesture of confusion. "I've met her someplace, I'm sure. I cannot place her. I've tried. Somewhere, we've had a previous encounter." Just then, memory sparked. Her mouth hung agape.

"Abdul—I do know her," she began tentatively, realizing she must explain and bracing herself for the worst. She laid it out for him, explaining in detail her encounter with Whip when Tina and her brother stumbled upon them in a passionate embrace. "*She* is the senator's lover. Not Dancey Darling! Oh, Abdul, what fools we've been, pursuing the wrong woman." She laughed. Abdul was unable to join her. His features became stony as he listened, the highly intricate ramifications far too frightening to speculate over.

Freaked out by now, Jamila jumped from subject to subject, making it impossible for Abdul to follow her. He tried unsuccessfully to calm her rising hysteria. For an instant the princess caught sight of her reflection in an unflattering mirror and grimaced distastefully. She felt like a hypocrite dressed in black pretending to mourn someone she loathed and told Abdul so. His attempt to soothe her frayed nerves resulted in making her more hysterical. "Find someone else for this stinking job. Count me out. It's getting too risky."

"It's a helluva time to be telling me this, Princess," he said calmly, while fuming internally over the upsetting information given him at this late date. Giving no outward reaction of his displeasure he went into the kitchen and returned with a few articles he'd taken from the refrigerator.

Jamila watched him intently as he sat before the coffee table, spreading out cigarette papers, dried parsley and bags of angel dust. He commenced slicing and chopping through a small mound of white crystals with a sharp double-edged razor blade, converting it to a powdery substance.

331

Annoyed by his calm manner she ground out her cigarette savagely against the fireplace and, turning to him, demanded answers to a few bothersome questions.

"Why would anyone kill Dancey? You're sure it was none of your doing, Abdul? Or Bahar's?" Her eyes were piercing and accusatory.

"Use your head, Princess," he countered, sifting the dried parsley with the white dust, mixing it meticulously before pouring the mixture onto the thin papers. "We needed Dancey. She was vital to our plans. Why else do you think I encouraged the filthy tramp?" he insisted, rolling the joints, twisting each one carefully.

"Then who?" she hissed. Watching him critically she tried to contain her fright and dull her over-active imagination. "Who killed her? Dammit, Abdul, it's becoming too complicated. It's a nightmare! And this Benne Erice thing. Abdul, he wasn't even *Benne Erice!*"

Abdul stopped the business with the joints. His eyes narrowed.

"Explain, please." He lit up a joint, took a hit and handed it to her, watching as she did likewise. He lit a second joint for himself. "Relax, Jamila, relax. We haven't come this far only to have it blow up in our faces."

Jamila stood at the window, growing more subdued from the drugged smoke. Turning back to Abdul with less hysteria in her voice, she explained what had happened when she took the gold locket to the man she presumed to be Benne Erice and accused him of some underhanded involvement in Dancey's death.

"They are all federal agents, Abdul. I threatened to go to the police, just as you suggested, to tell them what I knew. Well, this man Benne—or David—or whoever he was, requested one of the agents to set me straight. They were BSI agents. The Bureau of Secret Intelligence, Abdul! They were thick as thieves!"

Abdul led her calmly up a short flight of steps to the bedroom. Once inside the modest room she continued to magnify the situation, hoping to convince Abdul of the high risks involved if she should be forced to return.

"I'm frightened, Abdul. When I agreed to their plan, the job and protection offered me, I got the feeling I was playing right into their hands. I can't go back. I won't! Something disastrous will happen. Why can't I make you understand?"

Abdul, still silent, removed his sweater and handed her

two quaaludes. "Go ahead, Princess. You need to relax." His voice, itself calming to her jangled nerves, was soft, solicitous and husky. "You may be right. I promise to give it serious consideration. You naughty girl," he cooed. "You should have told me long ago that you were acquainted with the senator. For now, forget it. We have more important things to do, my sweet princess."

A spray of light from the streetlight beyond the dusty windowpane lit up the rumpled bed coverlet. It picked up the discarded black dress and undergarments at the foot of the bed. Feminine panties and bra of wispy nylon were draped over the chair. A partially opened closet door revealed a row of jeans and shirts hung on wire hangers. On the bed two naked bodies moved in feverish tempo.

Abdul, expert in matters of the flesh, with the endurance of an iron god, knew how to use his expertise to bend any woman into submission. Jamila, having long since lost any outer crust of toughness she had in the past, had gradually become overly dependent on Abdul. Beyond the perimeter of his arms she could think of nothing; she was his slave without will or volition to act on her own. He kept himself under complete control until his companion climaxed into physical and mental exhaustion. She would beg him to bring her to the last ultimate high, and this begging, this animal-like pleading became to Abdul symbolic of his unique hold over women and infused him with a sense of power unequal to anything he'd experienced, except hand-to-hand combat on a battlefield, when the rush of exhilarating power he felt was too overwhelming to describe.

This supremacy over women afforded him a strong sense of identification enabling him to reinforce his own personal importance and high standing in one of the splinter groups of the Feyadeen. His reputation as a composed, clear-headed, perceptive and sagacious man of inestimable bravery and temperance, always in full control of himself and his women, spread among his peers, elevating him to a lofty position where he became admired and sought after by his leaders for special assignments demanding such attributes. Abdul had devoted precious time to Jamila, using her resentments against her brother until she was ready to commit herself fully to the Feyadeen even if it meant opposing the prince. The success of this mission clearly guaranteed that Abdul would become first in command next to their venerable leader, Al Fatmah

Ahmed. This was what Abdul lived for, what he dreamed about. No one, nothing could deter him from fulfilling this dream.

A low wailing, a gasping deep inside Jamila started in her groin and traveled upwards until her body jerked and trembled with increasing spasms as Abdul's throbbing manhood exploded inside her. Holding her pinned under him so she wouldn't thrash about and injure herself, Abdul watched her in this highly sensuous moment of his supremacy over her. Pouring streams of molten fire in her he joined in uttering low grunts and groans as they both twisted and gyrated in undulating rhythm. Their pulsating bodies finally grew motionless as their sexual urgency abated.

It seemed to Abdul that an eternity passed before he heard her slow, steady, labored breathing. Pulling away from her slightly he studied her relaxed face in the shaft of light from the street lamp. "Jamila, can you hear me?" he cooed softly.

"Umhuh," she muttered.

Satisfied, Abdul began to chant to her in Arabic, words he'd spoken over and over for the past five years during these moments of heightened awareness. Subliminally these words and impressions were reprogramming her subconscious mind.

He is a sympathizer, a lover of Jews. You know he is our enemy. The suffering of people means nothing to him. He is a tool of the oppressors. The capitalists who believe only in profit squeezed from the blood of our people . . . You will always be aware of these truths and act only upon the word of the black-maned lion of the desert . . . The Lion of Judah!

Jamila was sound asleep. At 8:00 P.M. Abdul arose and crept soundlessly out of the room. In the sunken living room he picked up the phone and made a hurried call. "Get here quickly," he whispered into the mouthpiece. "We must talk."

Abdul had showered, dressed and brought two cold beers into the living room by the time Bahar let himself into the apartment. Taking another look into the bedroom to make sure Jamila was still asleep, he returned to Bahar's side, greeting him quietly. Instantly they were immersed in conversation. Bahar listened with the intent eyes of a cobra ready to strike. He was furious when Abdul revealed Jamila's presence and the reasons for her exodus from Las Vegas.

The dim candle glow flickering from the coffee table threw their features into grim shadows. Abdul sipped his beer and wiped his lips on the back of his hand. "I'm inclined to agree with her. Why take unnecessary chances? Our time will come. With federal agents sniffing around, I can understand her dilemma. She was unable to learn what the intrigue was about."

"I *know* what happened. One of the hotel's VIPs was kidnapped."

Abdul's eyes lifted to meet the black eyes of Bahar. "What lousy timing." He lit a joint, took a toke and passed it to Bahar. "Then she's right. This is no time to be parading our wares in the heat of someone else's battle. Have you any idea who killed Dancey Darling? Her death turned the spotlight on Jaqualine Devon. That unexpected bit of business and the fact that Senator Shiverton could recognize her . . ."

Bahar's eyes turned to dangerous ebony points.

"Why," he asked with trepidation, "would the senator recognize her? For what reason?"

When Abdul explained Jamila's foolish attempt at seducing Whip in Rome and how she subsequently met Tina Erice, Bahar's indignation was uncontainable. He took his frustration out on Abdul. "You should have reported this to me long ago!" He took another toke of the pot, shaking noticeably.

"I could report nothing sooner. I learned it only tonight." Abdul's calm showed signs of dissipating. "I tell you it's unlikely she'll be recognized. She's a different person altogether. Her hair, cosmetics, manners and speech have altered considerably since you first met. Is it not so?" He wiped his sweaty palms against his pant legs.

"Pray to Allah you are right." Bahar continued to discuss their plans, exploring possible alternatives.

In the bedroom, Jamila, trembling uncontrollably, awakened with a premonition. Her swollen eyes, unable to focus in the darkness, turned everything hazy and distorted. Nausea churned her stomach; hot and cold chills coursed through her. Wafting between wakefulness and slumber, she was plagued by a drug hangover sapping her strength, further distorting her perception.

Jamila grabbed her head between her hands and rocked to and fro, hoping the movement would alleviate her anxiety and disorientation. How many times had she promised herself to stop popping pills, smoking angel dust, hash, even pot? *How many times?* In her increasing paranoia she felt the entire world to be her enemy. She'd undergone a personality change, unable to recognize the old Jamila; she couldn't cope with the guilt she felt.

Her love for Abdul had cost dearly. She no longer possessed the courage to contact her brother Ali Mohammed to explain that she'd taken no part in terrorist activities against him or their country. How could he believe her? As a criminal desperately wanted by Ali's government, she was lost to everything she revered as home and family. Tears of remorse sprang to her eyes. Balling a hard fist with one hand, she shoved it against her mouth to stifle a loud sob, while simultaneously fighting the compulsion she felt to bang her head against the wall. How wretched could she feel? She wanted to scream and tear her hair out by its roots.

Voices from the next room drifted in clearly through the open door. Ploughing through the drug haze she tried to understand them. She was assaulted by the words she heard.

"If it's true he recognizes her she is of no further use to us."

Abdul's words became a nightmare in her ears. She blinked hard. *Abdul! It was Abdul!* If Bahar had spoken those words, she might have been more forgiving. But, Abdul? The man who had professed to love her more than life itself all these years? The man whose slave she had become?

Bahar's voice was equally clear. "Do what must be done. We cannot risk jeopardizing our plans at this stage." Then Abdul spoke with authority.

"Let us not rush into this. We've invested time and money in her. Might it not be feasible to extract further ransoms from the enemies of her brother for conspiring against the state?"

Bahar's negation came in the form of an indictment. "The prince has already disowned her. She is of no use to his enemies in government. Only in the role planned for her was she of importance to us."

Abdul concurred. "You realize shortly we must take a stand. Peace talks with Israel are an insult to the Arab nations. We can no longer tolerate their occupation of East Jerusalem, the West Bank, Gaza and the Golan Heights. We Arabs must become a cohesive strength with determination to restore our rights. Bahar, do you realize the time will come when those we consider to be our oppressors in our land may join us to fight against those nations who are determined to be influenced by the Zionist Jews in the United States?"

"From where did you learn this?" Bahar's voice grew deadly.

"Where else? From our leader, Al Fatmah."

There commenced an argument between them, spoken in a dialect with which Jamila was unfamiliar. She heard a loud sound as if someone had pounded a table with his fist. Bahar's enraged voice of loaded venom cut through the room.

"Very well. If these orders are true and you have become my immediate superior I defer to your judgment. But make no mistake, Abdul, I will check it out!"

"It would be foolish if you did not do so," muttered Abdul.

In the living room the two men faced each other with obvious acrimony. Bahar was the first to bend. "Very well, since you are now in command, it is futile for me to tell you what must be done." He took his leave, slamming the door.

Abdul locked the door behind him. At the desk he removed a small black duffle bag and opened it. He drew forth a few items and proceeded to fill a syringe with fluid. He placed the filled hypodermic on a tissue, dusted his hands off on the seat of his pants and closed the bag, tossing it under the desk. He opened his black leather portfolio, removing an array of paraphernalia used in his psychological studies at UCLA. Shuffling through a stack of 4x6 cards, he stopped at a photo of an enormous black-maned lion, which he shoved into his sweater pocket. Carefully picking up the syringe on the tissue, he approached the bedroom door, walking softly on the balls of his feet.

Suddenly, from someplace in the building, came the deafening sounds of a stereo blasting his eardrums, bouncing off the walls, reverberating like crazy until someone had the good sense to lower the volume. Startled, irked, then relieved, Abdul continued on his mission. He knocked softly on the door and pushed it open.

"Jamila—" Abdul stopped short.

Jamila was gone. The wind blowing through an open window caused the lace curtain to flutter and billow. Sprinting across the room to the window, his fiercely stern eyes peered outside at the narrow walkway leading across the rear of the property to both side streets on the block. There was no one in sight.

Abdul pulled in his head and snapped on the overhead lights. The black dress and lingerie were still scattered about. The closet door was ajar and on the floor lay two empty wire hangers.

Abdul spent the next half hour in the Volkswagen searching for Jamila. Then he returned to the apartment, an enigmatic smile forming at the corners of his lips. He sat at the desk, the photo of the black-maned lion propped up before him, scribbling notes into a notebook.

CHAPTER TWENTY-SEVEN

The midday calm of the Sicilian coastal village of Castellammare del Golfo is drenched in the pale saffron sunlight that falls on its countless red cupolas and scattering of brick-red tiled roofs. The narrow, winding streets and alleyways are deserted. It is siesta, a time when the inexorable sun prostrates any living creature who ventures out in it. There at the water's edge, not far from the ancient castle on the cliff, stands the tower, its tip shaped like a pyramid and on its four sides the double-headed griffin: two griffin heads, joined on a pedestal with the sun circle at its center.

Val Erice is approaching the tall edifice. Around him are men wearing the ancient order of the Cornuti, the insignia of the western army of Sicily in Roman times. The men bow to him reverently in passing, paying homage to him, as they might to their most exalted leader.

A dark cloud passes over Val, a mist-like apparition, shifting and thinning as faces begin to form one after another, the faces of Benkhanhian, Von Rhome, Lord Harrofian, the Texas oil moguls, E.L. Lamb, Tex Merkle and Larchmont. The faces appear and then disappear. Superimposed over them all is the face of Ted Shiverton; it is a sad, sorrowful, almost forlorn countenance thinning as various scenes of his tragic death form and dissolve.

The face of Prince Ali Mohammed Izmur forms, and around him are the images of Tina, Whip Shiverton and Benne Erice.

"Val? Can you hear me?" Christina's anguished voice attempted to penetrate the hazy veil hovering over her husband's consciousness. Her turbid eyes, swollen from the countless tears she had shed, studied his features minutely; she was unaware of the struggle taking place in Val's mind as he lay on the hospital bed in the intensive care unit.

* * *

Tina stands as a bride, waiting to be joined by her husband. Two men, dressed in formal attire, approach her. One is Whip Shiverton, the other, Ali Mohammed. Tina extends her arms towards Whip, but something causes Whip to recede from her grasp. Ali Mohammed approaches her, his arms extended as if they contain a strangely magnetic force drawing her into his arms. The picture shifts and Benne's smiling face appears over this scene, then David's face alternates with Benne; first one, then the other, then the two in rapid succession.

Val's face tightened and contorted. There was a reaction on the monitors on the wall behind his bed. The EKG showed a marked disturbance. Christina, noticing these changes, moved closer to Val, to comfort him with her voice.

"I'm here, beloved," she said softly, smoothing the lines in his forehead, critically observing each movement he made. She clutched his hand tightly in hers. "It's me, Val. Can you hear me?"

A few days ago the Chief Surgeon had removed the bullets lodged dangerously close to Val's spine and that had shattered vital nerve centers. "Time will tell if he'll be ambulatory or confined to a wheelchair for life," came his pronouncement. "That is, if his heart holds out," he added bleakly.

Christina and her daughter had accepted the news grimly, determined not to fall apart. Christina had remained at Val's side, refusing to leave him. Now, after four days, he was responding. His eyes briefly opened and rolled upwards, returning to focus vaguely on her face. Beyond the hazy milky substance veiling his sight, he saw her, acknowledging her by raising his brows and letting them fall.

Val's ebbing strength couldn't gather its forces to utter a syllable in the weightless, euphoric fog acting as a barrier between himself and reality. A giant tear escaped the corner of one eye and trailed along the side of his face.

Christina dabbed at it with a tissue, cooing to him, "I love you, Val, come back to me . . ."

His lips, soft and rubbery, were unable to shape words. She placed her cool face next to his as she repeated her love to him imploringly, hoping he heard her.

Words came to Val from a different level of consciousness; his voice was strained, hoarse and weak. "How dark is the sea, beloved. How still; how very dark . . ." Behind

340

the curtained darkness of his eyes he struggled valiantly to make contact.

"I gathered sea shells and showed them to Jimmy. Jimmy called to you, saying 'there's mamma.' I looked and saw my beloved, the cherished love of my life."

"Val, speak to me. Tell me you know it's me at your side," she beseeched him.

"The children are sleeping. Nothing is awake, my beloved. We are alone—the night belongs to us. Come, let us make love."

Sitting next to him, listening, aware of his delirium, Christina relived every fantasy. She smoothed back his cold forehead, kissed his pale lips, one wary eye cocked on all the lifegiving appliances piercing his body.

"Christina, beloved, look at the stars with me. Hold my hand and we'll spiral towards heaven. We fit together like eternal lovers; let us carve our future into eternity and never part. Look! Look! A star streaking upwards towards God; it bursts into a thousand lights. Our hearts beat in tune—tell me; have I remembered to tell you how much I love you?"

Her face streaked with tears, Christina leaned over Val, holding him tightly, her body convulsed with sobs. Val's eyes snapped open; he couldn't move, constricted by a heavy weight on his chest. He blinked, sniffed the air; the familiar scent of his wife's perfume ushered him to reality. "Christina?" he whispered.

Pulling away, she stared at him, joyous tears streaking her face. "Val! You're awake. Do you know me? Where you are?"

"What foolish questions," he said weakly. "Why do you cry?"

"Because I'm happy, that's why." She fussed over him, kissing him, smoothing the bed covers. Elated at both his recovery and the rambling soliloquy of his love, she couldn't disguise her rapture. Then, recalling the doctor's words, she became subdued. "Don't talk. You'll be fine. You need time—"

Val searched her eyes until a thick curtain of darkness descended again; he relaxed into a peaceful languor caused by the drug.

"He'll be like this for a while," said the nurse, removing the respirator; he could breathe on his own.

Having marveled at the vigilant, precision-like teamwork by efficient nurses and lifesaving devices at work to

341

save her father's life, Tina, awed by their professionalism, now observed them removing the glucose pipeline that had fed Val intravenously for so long. They disconnected all the other apparatus. The crisis was over, thank God.

"Where's Joey, Mom?" Tina asked when her father wafted back to sleep. "He should have been here by now." Her face, pale with taut lines, showed her concern for her father and her anger at her brother's neglect. There was more on Tina's mind, too, disturbing her.

Christina merely shrugged and kept her eyes on her husband.

Richie sat in a straight-backed chair across the room, unaware of his own discomfort. He awaited orders from his beloved Don, orders to combat the grave injustices afflicting the Erice family. Periodically his eyes met Tina's. They both shared the same disturbing thoughts; concern that the family business left in Renzo's hands, even for a brief time, would prove disastrous. Without word from Val their hands were tied. *Or were they?*

An hour later Joey Erice arrived. He embraced his mother and sister and moved to his father's side. He asked the usual questions; how, what and why? Tina answered as best she could. For a time Joey sat by Val's bed staring at the thin, gaunt face, his thoughts kept well in check.

Tina had no time to explain about David. Joey glanced about the room. "Is it true Benne's back? He wasn't killed in the accident?"

"We'll talk later, Joey," she said quietly. "Back at the hotel." She leaned in closer to her mother. "Call us when he's fully conscious, Mom. Now the danger's passed—"

"For Christ sake, Tina," Joey scolded sharply. "Your husband can handle the place. Have some faith in him."

Tina's shock was such that her eyes met Richie's and she blinked hard. In a tolerant voice she tried to explain. "There's a few things you don't know, Joey—"

"Stop trying to castrate Renzo. How can he feel like a man if you wear the pants?" Joey snapped snidely.

"Joey—" Her voice contained a muted anger. Tired, anxious, worried and under great strain, Tina still couldn't permit his remark to pass. "You don't know what you're saying. Butt out, will you." She paced the room, agitated, and worried sick over her father's fate. Greatly displeased at having left Renzo at the helm during this critical period, her instinct screamed at her to go back. She finally blurted, "Look, I'll be at the hotel when you want to talk."

"Your duty is to stay here with *our* father!" Joey spat at her.

Dumbstruck and offended by his abrasive manner, her voice loaded with biting rancor, she countered, "Look who's talking duty all of a sudden!"

Their mother gave them a sorely wounded look at their lack of consideration. This was not the time nor the place to air their differences.

"I'm sorry, Mom," apologized Tina. "You stay here with Mom," she told Joey, tersely. "Pop might be pleased to find you at his side for once in your life." She prepared to leave.

"What the hell is that supposed to mean?" Joey was irate.

Tina turned to him, sharply searching Joey's eyes.

"We'll talk later," she said sternly. "Then you'll explain why suddenly you look upon me as a woman who takes joy in emasculating her husband. What do you know of anything?"

She and Richie left the ICU ward of the hospital and walked quickly along the highly waxed corridor floor past several worried visitors awaiting word about their loved ones. Tina snapped orders to Richie faster than an exploding firecracker.

"Tell Jerry I'm calling an emergency meeting in my office. Find Senator Shiverton. I must talk with him. Make sure David is there, hear?" She got into the waiting limousine, with Richie at her heels.

"Is your Papa going to be all right?"

Seated next to him in the rear seat, Tina placed her hand on his arm compassionately. "We'll all pray loud and clear so God will hear us, O.K.?"

An hour later she sat with David, Jerry and Richie in the office in her penthouse taking the proper action to insure that nothing catastrophic would occur during this critical period. Tina's burning concern over a possible Marciano-Renzo covert alliance and their possible skullduggery was made apparent to her companions. To her relief, they concurred with her. David listened, marveling in fascination at Tina's astute business know-how.

"The extent of their treachery isn't known. Renzo, if given free rein in the next few days, could ruin the Erice family," she told them somberly. "It's not exaggeration.

343

What's our remedy, Jerry? An injunction restraining him from setting foot on our property until you implement the proper measures to dissipate his clout with the Erice organization? Then, do it! At the same time commence divorce proceedings against him. Use what you need. I have plenty of grounds—and Jerry, no community property. If I could find a way to strip him of everything he's acquired since our marriage—"

"Don't be bitter, Tina," David suggested lightly.

About to say something, Tina changed her mind. She nodded to Richie. "Put only those you can trust in key positions. Take all of Renzo's men out of the counting rooms. Give them a month's pay and wave bye-bye to them."

"Immediately," said Richie, pulling his large frame out of his chair. "I go right away. I can use the emergency crew until we rearrange our men."

As Tina, David and Jerry debated the need and wisdom for the swift employment of drastic measures, they were unaware that elsewhere in the hotel other wheels had been set in motion.

Having long prepared for an emergency, Renzo Bonaparte, that street-wisened sharpy who conspired, schemed and plotted his way to the top of the Erice empire, began stockpiling nearly a million dollars in large bills in a secret compartment in his office. When the FBI and BSI spun a cocoon of silence around their activities at the Pyramids, Renzo, no dummy, concluded it would only be a matter of time before his and Marciano's involvements would be spotlighted.

Now he had grown wary and in his wariness declared a state of emergency. In his office he began to fill a leather satchel with his loot, when an impatient knocking on the door brought a flicker of annoyance to his eyes. Glancing furtively about the room, he shoved the satchel in the walk-in safe, out of sight, leaving the door slightly ajar. Shuffling languidly across the room, he pulled back his shoulders with nonchalance and opened the door.

Two federal marshals, credentials in hand, entered the room, and began an instant litany. Stopped cold by the warrant shoved into his hand, Renzo challenged them with his quick-tempered wrath. "What the fuck's going on?"

"You're charged with the assassination attempt on the late President Shiverton," retorted a ruddy-faced marshal with a grin. "Want I should read you your rights?"

Before Renzo could wave him off, the officer read them. Handcuffed, Renzo was instantly whisked away to a federal facility where by law he was entitled to make one telephone call. Only one person could bail him out of this mess.

Manny Marciano was nowhere to be found when Renzo's frantic call reached the penthouse at the Golden Oasis. Although no newspaper account of the shootout at E.L. Lamb's ranch had reached the public, news had a way of infiltrating the gambling network of Las Vegas even before it happened. Marciano had already flown the coop. His sudden leave of absence took him to Tucson where he secluded himself with his wife in their new home. Renzo, meanwhile, left word for one of Marciano's lawyers to contact him and arrange for bail.

For two days and two nights, Renzo paced the floor of his cell, his cool slowly dissipating. Two BSI agents appeared on the scene and began pressing him to turn government's witness.

"Tell us what you know about Marciano's affiliation with the TFL Corporation and we can deal with you on the other charges."

Renzo grinned inwardly, gloating like a content fat cat. Their case against him was flimsy. Else why would they try for a deal so soon? His feelings of elation evaporated when other charges were leveled against him. Income tax evasion was always the kicker. And he knew they could stick it to him.

Phil Soldato flew to the federal facility to slap Renzo with that last charge. Seated languidly in the sterile counsel's room Renzo's lips exploded with loud guffaws and laughter at the agent's charges.

"What the shit are you guys trying to pull off? Digging into a grab bag of surprises until you come up with one you think you can stick me with?" He made clucking sounds with his tongue and shook his head in admonishment.

"Suit yourself, punk," said Soldato stonily. "You can softshoe through the act or do a foxtrot with balls and chains around your ankles." Soldato slammed his briefcase on the wooden table before him. "Suppose we *dig* into the *grab bag* for another surprise, Renzo, buddy." He flourished another warrant. "How does this one grab you? You're charged with the murder of James Erice." He dug into the case again. "And how about this little ditty. You're also charged with the murder of one Robert Harmon."

Renzo's smile evaporated instantly. His indolence dissolved. He sat forward in the stiff-backed wooden chair, the cigarette between his fingers falling to the floor unnoticed. "Who the hell are you? Where the fuck did you get them pack of lies? Oh, I get it. You're trying to con me into ratting on Marciano. Is that it? Well, you're blowing up the wrong asshole, pig. Renzo don't fink on anyone, especially Marciano."

"Yeah? No kidding? That's the way you figure it?" Soldato placed the two warrants on the table and shut his briefcase. "That's some loyalty you got for someone who's got none for you. See ya in court, Renzo, buddy."

Soldato made a hasty retreat, leaving Renzo with a raging inferno of suspicion in his mind. Unaware that he was a most sought-after trophy between several factions, Renzo returned to his cell, thinking black thoughts about Tina. Later, in his awareness that Marciano was the only real link to the deaths of Jimmy Erice and Bob Harmon, he began to reconsider his position. With him out of the way on murder raps, Marciano could rake in all the glory. *Sonofabitch!* Why had he ever confessed his *pecato* to Manny? Well, if it came to push and shove, he had enough on Manny to send him to hell.

What Renzo didn't know was that he owed his life, momentarily, to the quick thinking, shrewd acumen of Senator Whip Shiverton. Aware of the competition for Renzo's hide, once his treachery became known to the Erice factions, Whip had to exert his influence to keep him alive. Twist an arm and Renzo might be induced to part with information to help solve several mysteries concerning TFL. All Whip and the BSI agents could do at present was to exercise patience.

The lid, clamped tight on Marciano's and Renzo's involvements in betraying the Erice family, had prematurely been opened and examined when Monk Garret refined their dealings and passed them on to Val. Locked inside his memory, behind a postoperative coma at the edge of his consciousness, it would remain there indefinitely.

Renzo's incarceration had brought Tina's problem with him to an abrupt halt. The treacheries and deterioration of their relationship were over and Tina didn't want to think of him again. Knowing she could retire to her quarters without having to see him and be reminded of his perfidy granted her a modicum of relief.

Unfortunately Joey Erice insisted upon hanging up the dirty wash, refusing to believe the worst about Renzo. They discussed the matter in Tina's office in the company of both Jerry and Richie. The tension was fierce, emotions at a high pitch.

"I can understand your reluctance in believing me, Joey," Tina said tightly. "I know how Renzo scrambled your brains, calling me a boozed-up broad who indiscriminately popped pills. The fact that you believed him, drawing your own conclusions before asking me, personally, if he spoke the truth is something I won't forgive. I am family, Joey—not Renzo. His blind ambition and greed caused our brother Jimmy's death and Bob Harmon's, too. Everything Renzo has ever done from day one was premeditated and calculated, including marrying me, just to get control of the Erice fortune."

Joey was unmovable. The accumulated efforts of both Jerry and Richie in convincing him of Renzo's treachery and shady dealings perpetrated against the Erice family hardly moved him. Jocy had been told the truth about David the moment he arrived from New York, before he saw Val at the hospital. That David was Benne's twin was as farfetched a tale as this cynical New Yorker had ever heard or could swallow. Even later, when his mother explained what Genny Martinelli had done the night the twins were born, Joey didn't relax his skepticism. By the time he came into actual contact with David, his attitude had become hostility and he went out of his way to avoid him.

"I don't understand your attitude, Joey. I'm trying real hard," said Tina, biting back her rancor. "You should be glad there's another one of us alive."

Joey gave her a look of fermenting anger, refusing to discuss the situation. "It's your problem, Tina. I have enough of my own to contend with." Without further ado he left the penthouse and returned to New York.

Fortunately Tina was compelled to bury her nose in the urgent business at hand and fill vacancies in the organization left by Renzo's absence. Unable to locate either Lefty Meyers or Calous Agajjinian she was forced to hire a private auditing firm to check out the books. She jockeyed a few key men into more responsible positions. She only hoped to God that the firm she hired to audit the books didn't come up with something scandalous and bring the

IRS down around her neck. That would be all she needed.

Forced to sit at the helm of the Erice business, Tina wasn't sure she liked the enormous responsibilities heaped upon her slender shoulders. Like it or not, she was doing it. That was what was so amazing to her. The time was ripe and she was ready, without consciously preparing herself for the ordeal.

No time for daydreaming. She had urgent work to do.

CHAPTER TWENTY-EIGHT

Chief Bowman and his BSI agents were unhappy at finding themselves at the center of an overwhelming and unsoluble puzzle. Bowman was brooding inwardly. His squareset, pugnacious face and his bearish appearance were never more indicative of defeat than in these moments as he paced about the Erice penthouse.

Seated opposite him, slouched into a deeply cushioned brown velvet chair, Senator Shiverton's grim face indicated his exhaustion. His dull, smoky blue eyes stared at some inner vision of complexity as he reflected on the fast-moving events of the past week. How had it all gotten out of hand? He'd flown back to Washington on urgent business for a day and returned to find the agents stymied over the curious events related to E.L. Lamb's death. Worse, the agents in charge of Jaqualine Devon returned to report how she'd given them the slip. He was incensed and frustrated.

In this atmosphere of gloom and depression McKenna and Soldato, stretched out on a sofa, reflected the inner turbulence of Chief Bowman. How could they have anticipated the complication greeting them at E.L. Lamb's ranch house? Their attempts to interrogate Dr. Larry Sharp were foiled on two counts: the heavy sedation administered by his personal physicians and strict orders by his lawyer forbidding him to talk.

David entered the room kicking off his shoes, stretching his toes as he walked, trying to relax and allow himself relief from the tension coiled in him. He came from a conference with Richie and was left with disturbing thoughts he couldn't discuss.

Soldato, on his feet, his face lined in thought, paused briefly, an empty look in his eyes, then quickly left the room. David padded about the room barefooted listening to McKenna's laments with a bright-eyed alertness, although he needed sleep.

"Be grateful," he said, "for Richie's discerning eyes or

we wouldn't have made the progress we did." David pulled back on a poptop of Tab, guzzling half the contents before adding, "At least we know who killed Benne. Ballistics in Washington proved conclusively the bullets embedded in Benne's skull match those fired by Monk Garret's magnum. The message just came through on the telex."

Chief Bowman stopped his incessant pacing when David flopped down heavily on the sofa. "How's Val?" he asked concernedly.

The men retired to their previous gloom when David shook his head. "The prognosis is dim. He may not pull through."

Bowman cursed aloud. "There goes IAGO. All the roads leading to them are muddied again. Goddamit, we've been sealed off once more. Might as well admit it. We failed." He moved sluggishly towards the window, the weight of his disappointment like a suffocating anchor pulling him down into a deeper melancholy. For a thin dime, he'd chuck the whole fucking IAGO conspiracy! His red-veined eyes scanned the far-off desert scene beyond the edge of the terrace.

"All this makes us laughable—totally ineffective. To have come so far and so close, only to fizzle out so outrageously, is unacceptable to me."

McKenna offered him balm. "At least we put the screws to TFL. Lamb is out of the way. We've got Larchmont and Merkle. They'll come under Grand Jury indictment for tax evasion, for openers, possible anti-trust laws, and God knows what else. Once we start checking into their financial frauds, stock irregularities and manipulations of international currencies—"

Soldato had entered the room a moment earlier in time to hear his partner's spiel. His face was twisted into an ironic leer. "You mean you *had* Larchmont and Merkle," he said ruefully. Biting his underlip tentatively, he handed Bowman the message.

Chief Bowman's disgust became apparent as he read. He crumpled the message, hurling it savagely on the desk. "That tears it! Two accidents; one to look like an accident, the other to resemble suicide. Concussion, cerebral hemorrhage, suicide, murder, take your choice. No matter what you pick, Larchmont and Merkle are dead!"

Whip scrambled to his feet, retrieving the crumpled message. He spread it out, unwrinkling it on the desk. "How reliable is the source?"

"Our men have been on their case since the wind down

began. Someone got to them, somehow. Lamb's death triggered something off." Soldato opened a diet cola and poured it into a glass over ice and sipped it slowly. "Our men claim the jobs were professional." On a lighter vein he added, "With those three big wheels shot down we've at least stopped TFL—haven't we? That's not so bad, is it, Chief?"

Whip lit his last cigarette and tossed the cardboard box aside. He picked at a tobacco fleck stuck to his lower lip, muttering something about giving up smoking. He opened the desk drawers, searching for and finally locating a half-filled carton of Shermans. He tossed them on the desk, closing the drawers with his knees. He sat on the edge of the desk dangling one leg before him, taking his time, puffing on the cigarette. After a few drags, when his thoughts were ready, he began to air them.

"Corporations of that magnitude are never out of commission, Phil. They just live on and on," he quipped balefully. "Faces change, as do the names behind the entities, but the principles behind their formation continue to permeate the world, corrupting everyone who finds an affinity to their precepts. IAGO's lifeline will keep TFL alive." Whip's voice, soft at first, grew more audible.

"All isn't lost, Bowman," he said, pausing to collect his thoughts. "Our file is thick—thick enough to bring about a Senate probe." He smiled tightly, "That is, with a little help from my friends. Grand juries in over a dozen states are waiting to jump on to the shady dealings various public officials and key politicians have become party to for an exorbitant sum of money. Recently large parcels of land were quietly taken off the state's acquisition lists and sold to various Golden-owned subsidiaries for a mere fraction of their worth." Whip glanced at McKenna knowingly. "Does the M.O. ring a bell, Mac?" He continued when McKenna's eyes sparked in recollection of the modus operandi employed by Deacon Hawes after World War II when brand new trucks were gobbled up for peanuts and resold for five times what he paid.

"If we pursued each deal we'd uncover those public officials on the take as well as the sums of money paid in bribes. Our files are formidable. We'll use my probe network. If we aren't welcome at the front door, there's always the rear."

Chief Bowman was suddenly infused with life. "You think we can prove that IAGO is the parent behind TFL?"

Whip shrugged with a feeling of optimism. "We can

give it a helluva go. When the shit hits the fan, you'd be surprised what that fertilizer can do. The most unlikely things rear their ugly heads."

Ambivalent and unsure, Chief Bowman continued pacing. "You think a Senate probe is the right way to go after them?"

"I'm not sure of anything," Whip said with infectious candor. "Look at it this way. Your approach in the past has been highly clandestine. Where did it get you? What can we lose by letting our enemies know we're on to them? And if we just happen to flush a few of those IAGO-philes into the open under a spotlight—"

Half dubious, half hopeful glances and exasperated silence greeted him. The BSI knew they were stalemated. With the big guns of TFL dead and Val in a touch-and-go situation their case had been shot down. Where could they go from here?

Perched on the arm of the sofa David made a sensible suggestion.

"Suppose we search through Val's papers in Long Island. He mentioned the records he documented over the years."

Bowman nodded. "We can ask your family's cooperation in turning them over to us—or subpoena them."

"My family!" The words, alien to him, brought about an instinctive change in David. After a moment's reflection he suggested that Bowman give them time to recover from the shock of recent events. "If such information exists, in time, when Val's health is more stable, I'm sure I can obtain the family's cooperation."

The BSI agents grew wary. David felt awkward and ill at ease. Whip Shiverton came to his rescue.

"David's right. Let's cool it for a while. I guarantee you, Chief, the file on IAGO is far from closed."

After Whip outlined his plans, the men of the Bureau of Secret Intelligence left Las Vegas with uplifted spirits and returned to Washington where they began to put together the bits and pieces that hadn't computed for a while. They left behind a crew of agents who would remain in the shadows, yet guard Val Erice with their life until he fully recovered.

While Val lay in the hospital floundering between life and death, David Erice was seized by a profound depression. Since he learned his true identity, he had experienced a gradual metamorphosis in his thinking and feeling. A ganglia of complicated thoughts flashed on his mind creating unnatural confusion which was upsetting to him.

After weighing the facts surrounding his recent turmoil, his former associates wondered how they might have fared if they had been thrown into a life so diametrically opposed to the lives they had lived in the past. It was not an easy judgement to make.

Awkwardness, defensiveness and uncertainty had never been part of David's personality. On the contrary he'd been sure of himself in the years spent with the FBI—as sure as any agent can be.

On the plus side, the many months he'd spent during his indoctrination to Benne's life had helped him adjust to the mindboggling shock that he was indeed Benne's twin brother. Having acted the role it helped lessen the stunning impact and for a time he managed to feel comfortable.

However when Val revealed the relationship, he felt, oddly enough, as if a heavy burden had been lifted from his shoulders and despite the many ramifications it presented he felt free. Later, upon reflection of the enormous burdens connected in this new relationship and faced with unanticipated and complex problems, it became obvious to him he could no longer remain with either Bureau. With Val close to death, his position as son and heir became a vital consideration.

Chief Bowman took David off the hook, in a manner of speaking.

Empathy flowing between them required few words. Perceived instantly by Bowman was the duality, the war raging in David. Having been programmed to recognize his new family as former enemies was creating irreconcilable problems for him. Shortly after Val's abduction the BSI chief had cornered David for a heart-to-heart talk.

"In good conscience, Martin, I can't ask you to remain with the Bureau, nor can I ask you to bend your loyalties either way now that your real identity has been established. It simply cannot be done. You'd end up a suicide or in the looney bin, of no use to anyone including yourself. Take time to examine your priorities, will you?"

David left his apartment to keep an appointment with Tina. He found her pacing about in frustration, moving art objects about her suite from one place to the next, then replacing them in their original niches. She glanced up at him, her manner changing instantaneously to a more relaxed one.

"I'm happy you came, David. We must talk to decide

353

what must be done." Taking his hand in hers she led him to the sofa.

Before Tina could bombard him with what he felt was coming, he took the initiative. "You've been swell, Tina, really. For all concerned it's best I go away for a while to sort things out in my mind." He made a disorganized gesture. "There are so many considerations. I mean—well, you know—things are happening too swiftly. I can't catch up."

Tina watched him closely, unsure what he was driving at.

"We didn't expect such calamities, David. We must overcome them. We're all Pop's children so it's best we put our heads together—"

"Tina!" His stern voice cut her off. "You don't seem to realize what I attempted to do to the Erice family!"

"I know what you tried to do—but that was before you knew who you are. You're my brother, the flesh and blood of our parents. You can't deny your heritage. The genes of our forefathers are buried as deeply in you as in me. We are what we are and can be nothing else. No matter what you think you've done no matter who you worked for, you are still David Erice. You are Benne's twin brother and a part of me." She sat next to him, her dark eyes boring into his. "Pop would want you to take Benne's place," she added softly.

Emotion pouring through David inhibited his articulation.

"Did he actually tell you this? I mean what about Joey? He's downright antagonistic towards me. Truly, I had no part in my abduction—"

"You think we don't know that? Listen, because you weren't raised to know all about your heritage—" She paused. "Don't be impatient. It will take time to learn. We don't ask for miracles, David." She stood up and poured coffee for them. "It's Vienna with cinnamon, the way you like it." She handed him a cup.

"About Joey. He hasn't the stuff needed for this business. Pop never imposed his will or his thinking on Joey when he saw his own individuality being expressed in a different way. You're more like Benne and me. Sharper, I think, because you didn't have things handed to you on a platter." She smiled wanly. "I'm not putting Benne down, I loved him deeply. You must know that by the way I took to you at first."

David listened and sipped his coffee. For a time Tina

talked randomly about Val's philosophies, of the precepts he'd taught his children in life as well as business.

"I can't tell you what to do with your life," she added, noting his somber, reflective mood. "But consider why destiny brought us together—I mean how things fell into place after Benne died."

Several moments of thoughtful silence passed. "If you choose to remain apart now that we've found each other, you'll be haunted the rest of your days by the things you should have said when opportunity knocked. The family counts in life. When the eleventh hour approaches we turn to each other for support."

Reflecting upon the sterility of his loveless childhood, David sensed the truth of her words. He had accepted his fate aware that his actions and thought processes had been geared to meet the requirements of a loner in life; a loner, a self-contained man who had erected rigid defense mechanisms to keep love and other emotional attachments from intruding upon him. He never understood how to reach out to anyone, to become a part of anyone else's life. At Quantico he'd made an excellent recruit because he lacked emotional attachments that could mean instant death to an agent in the field.

Tina's total acceptance of him from the moment they met, her warmth and infinite trust, caused a wealth of deeply hidden emotions to surface and color his thoughts and action in varying degrees. The onslaught of events in recent weeks brought about affinities and compassionate responses where before there were none.

"It won't take long to learn the business," urged Tina. "I'll teach you all I know." She tried to dispell his hesitation. She gave no thought to the impassioned fervor with which she desperately wanted him to fill Benne's shoes. It would be a while before she realized that she subconsciously tried to palm off on him responsibilities she didn't want for herself.

"I promise I'll give what you say deep consideration," David told her before leaving her to her own thoughts.

The superstructure of power created by Val Erice in his lifetime was never more formidable and unshakeable as it was becoming in the days during his recuperation, despite the numerous attempts by outside forces to uproot it.

Christina took her husband home to Long Island where she personally could tend him and zealously watch over him with the aid of carefully selected physicians. Objecting strenuously to this at the outset, Tina finally deferred to her mother and concentrated on the monumental task of convincing David to learn the family business.

Upon conferring with Val the first opportunity he could after the coma lifted, Jerry Bonfiglio was urgently requested to push David ahead as swiftly as possible to learn the family business. Richie, fully determined to return to Long Island to remain at Val's side, was instructed by Tina to remain at David's side and school him as best he could in all the matters David should know. Hedging artfully, Richie became submissive only after Tina promised to let him return to Long Island the moment Val was strong enough to enjoy his company.

Both Richie and Jerry found it difficult to lay themselves bare before David; Richie because he hadn't received orders from Val himself, and Jerry because he couldn't accept the story of David's being Benne's twin. The lawyer's skepticism impeded their progress for a time.

Sensing their duality, David shrugged it off for a time. When he made his own decision to do the best he could and accepted the role of being Val's son, embracing it on all counts, he was unable to handle their reluctance. One day while they were in David's office, he could take no more.

"I am David Erice now. What must I do to prove my loyalty?" he demanded of them. "I want to find every last son-of-a-bitching bastard that brought this trouble upon my family. If you won't cooperate, I'll find someone who will!"

His words, spoken with vitriol, cowed Jerry and Richie and changed their attitudes somewhat. David knew it would take time to win their confidence, that he'd have to behave in a way to convince them of his loyalty. Oddly enough he never felt more sincere than in the moments these words were spoken.

Within months the Pyramids operation returned to normal. David, at the helm of operations, wisely hired and fired key personnel until their loyalties could belong to no one but him. He rehired Jolie Barnes and proceeded to back her in a new Broadway production earmarked for instant success. He gathered together the fragments of Snowbirds Productions, the motion picture company that splintered after Benne's death, and whipped it into shape by purchasing film properties of high calibre.

Jerry and Richie watched David's acumen spiral into a

Midas touch as he created new monetary resources for Erice Enterprises.

Three months after Val returned to Long Island, Richie was hastily summoned to Val's side. The early spring sun slanted brightly through the windows of Val's bedroom. He was sitting in his wheelchair, having just finished with the therapist who arrived daily to help him exercise his lower limbs to keep his muscles from atrophying. He squinted against the sun's rays as he awaited Richie.

Richie's first glimpse of Val shocked him when he noted how thin and gaunt Val looked. His face was ashen, the lines of pain etched deeply into the sunken hollows of his cheeks. Quickly composing himself, Richie kissed his Don's hand. He sat down alongside of Val and remained there in secret conclave for better than five hours.

When Val unveiled his plans to Richie, his old friend and obedient servant hesitated, fully concerned over Val's state of health to be undertaking such responsibility. However, one look at his bright azure eyes sparkling with life dispelled Richie's fears.

The next morning, shortly before noon, Christina stood at the door of the Erice mansion, an expression of fear and concern drawn clearly on her face. She watched as Richie helped Val into the rear seat of the limousine. The driver folded the collapsible wheelchair into the trunk of the Mercedes. Nothing she could say or do would alter Val's decision. Having learned long ago that she was helpless in such matters, she resorted to her former posture of watchful waiting and praying. She waited until the limousine was out of sight before closing the door. They had promised to be home by 7:00 P.M. How many hours before she could stop praying?

"It's like old times, my Don," said Richie, flushed with pleasure at sitting alongside Val as they drove through Brooklyn.

Val nodded, his alert eyes peering out both windows. "Brooklyn had changed since the old days. A bright cosmetic applied to it disguises the old ghettos of our youth. I fail to recognize the place."

Richie nodded. "Many of our old friends live in palatial manors along Lakeshore Drive. They've come a long way since the old days."

"So have we, my friend," replied Val. "So have we."

A cautious, hawk-faced guard peered inquisitively when the limousine approached the iron gates of the elegant

357

mansion he protected. The driver anounced, "Don Erice to pay his respects to Don Patruccio."

At once obsequious, upon recognizing Richie, the guard tipped his hat respectfully to Val. He pushed a lever housed in a wooden box on a concrete pillar. Instantly the iron gates swung open admitting them. The limousine drove on through along the gracefully curved drive towards the stately mansion set several hundred yards back on the well-wooded property flanked by tall poplars.

Lifted into his wheelchair, Val was propelled inside the house where a warm and effusive greeting ensued between host and guests. Within moments the men sat down before a warm and inviting fire in the spacious oval library. They sipped wine for a few moments, then Don Patruccio excused himself to make several telephone calls. Within the hour Don Patruccio became host to eight former formidable heavyweights from the five Mafia families of the early days. Don Miguel, the former New Orleans Don who'd made Brooklyn his home for a few months of the year, sat with his old cronies, drinking wine, chatting and exchanging fond memories of an era long since past.

The sojourn of pleasant talk passed. Getting down to business, they began to painstakingly balance out the old books of account. A nod here, a look there, a hand upraised in agreement and the conclave of snowy-haired men began preparing new balance sheets on their profit and loss ledgers. Five hours later, the conclave ended. The old friends embraced, teary-eyed. There was no need to promise cooperation; the word had been spoken, the deeds were as good as done.

Before Val reached Long Island, the grand old emeritus Dons had taken their case to the streets, cashing promissory notes among the snitches. For so many years they had nurtured stables of informants. Word spread like a carefully guided missile among a select few that Val Erice needed information. Then they waited.

Christina watched Richie bidding Val a fond adieu unable to deny that whatever had taken place that day had given Val new life.

In Las Vegas, Richie went about his business in relative silence. Two weeks following the Brooklyn conclave, Richie was lunching with Tina and David on the terrace of the penthouse.

David, grinning, was boasting, wanting compliments from Tina. "Well, tell me, have I or have I not done a good job for a neophyte in the business?"

"Do any better and I'll be taking a trip around the world." Tina grinned, winking at Richie. She shoved aside her salad.

Although she smiled radiantly, David saw through her thin disguise. Something was nagging at her, something she hadn't confided to him. David looked up past her as Jerry entered the sunlit terrace. One look at Jerry's somber face subdued David's greeting.

"Hi, Jerry," said Tina. "Come join us for lunch—" She stopped when Jerry thrust out his hand, holding a wire.

"It's for you, Tina." Jerry's eyes held Richie's.

Tina wiped the corner of her lips with a napkin, accepting the wire from him, scanning it quickly. Without expression she remarked, "Renzo's just hung himself." She caught the secret looks between Richie and Jerry and lowered her eyelids.

Reaching for the wire, David read aloud: "Renzo Bonaparte found dead this A.M. He hung himself with his belt." Glancing at the others he wisely kept his thoughts to himself. Inwardly he brooded, wondering how this would affect Senator Shiverton and the BSI.

In Washington, Senator Shiverton blew a gasket over the report of Renzo's death. What he'd tried to prevent had occurred despite his precautions. "Goddamit!" He cursed aloud, wondering who the hell had leaked Renzo's whereabouts.

"It was an inside job," lamely admitted the prison authorities to Chief Bowman. The information didn't abate his temper.

"One brand of Mafia justice," Bowman related angrily to McKenna and Soldato. They needed Renzo's help to carve through the TFL conspiracies. Before they recuperated from this setback and before they deliberately set about plotting the wrathful trajectory of Mafia justice, they were dealt another blow to impede their progress.

Manny Marciano and his wife were both found brutally murdered one morning by the servants at the new residence in Tucson. The killings were among the most vicious of all gangland deaths. Both had suffered multiple stab wounds. The authorities concluded that the brutal, sadistic knife thrusts seemed to have been performed by a specialist —a surgeon, perhaps?

Val received Richie in Long Island. Richie gave him a full and detailed report as told to him by their old friends. When he finished, Richie spoke in sincere, almost plaintive tones.

"I'm getting old, my Don. These old bones are weary. They can no longer endure the fast pace of living." He made a gesture of hopelessness and continued, "Once the mind becomes conditioned to old age—" Richie stopped. He noticed that Val was staring out in space at some inner picture taking place in his mind.

Val appeared weaker as if his strength were slowly being siphoned off. He signalled to Richie to lean in and listen closely. Barely speaking above a whisper he outlined his plans. Richie nodded and straightened up, his dark eyes fixed on Val's.

"Then, my Don, after that may I retire?"

Val nodded. His eyes blinked affirmatively. Richie kissed Val's hand and returned to Las Vegas.

The next day Jerry Bonfiglio arrived in Long Island to sit in counsel with Val. They remained in a huddle the entire day. The following morning after a hearty breakfast he left for the airport. He returned to Las Vegas weighed down with an enormous load of responsibilities. Conferring in secret with Richie, he relayed Val's instructions.

The next morning Richie flew to the Hawaiian Islands with friends. They remained there a week and returned to Las Vegas where the friends departed to places unknown. A week later a news clipping arrived in Richie's morning mail.

The news item indicated that two vacationing American tourists, who apparently were not accomplished boatmen, had encountered a squall en route to Maui. With no ship-to-shore radio aboard the sailing vessel, to summon the Coast Guard, in an effort to save themselves they had attempted to swim to shore. Since the authorities claimed that the boat, leased to Irving—Lefty—Meyers and Calous Agajjinian of Las Vegas, Nevada, found intact near Maui, had not capsized, it was assumed that the men had been caught in the undertow prevalent in the area and had drowned.

Richie placed the clipping into an envelope and mailed it to Val in Long Island. With the rest of his mail, Richie picked up a copy of the Las Vegas *Sun,* whose headlines glared out at him. "Senator Shiverton Demands Senate Probe of Conspiracy."

BOOK FOUR

You'll never own the earth, the moon,
The dazzling stars above,
Until you learn they'll all be yours
The day you learn to love.

CHAPTER TWENTY-NINE

It's a well known-fact in Washington, D.C. that the real work of the Senate is accomplished in committees, in party caucuses, chance encounters in the cloakroom, in various hideaway rooms scattered in the nooks and crannies of the Capitol and at certain hours in the private dining room; but certainly never within the confines of a senator's office.

In one of those special hideaway rooms in the new Senate Office Building, Senator Shiverton was bringing to a close one very special session with a select group of his peers.

"And that, gentlemen, is as far as we go for the time being. Suppose we knock off for the weekend; give you time to digest the contents of the briefs I'm leaving with you . . ."

On his feet, Whip collected his papers and with his aides left the room; and in his wake several stunned senators were absorbed by the blistering information imparted to them. A hush prevailed among the room's occupants as they anxiously perused the numerous documents to which Whip had periodically referred. After attempting to digest the volatile data, one senator tossed the papers aside glumly, suggesting to his companions,

"We'd best continue this meeting and speculate on the sanity of Senator Shiverton."

Provocative information of such inflammable content, coming at a time when scandalous upheavals in the nation's capital were becoming commonplace, didn't sit well with these skittish public officials, who wanted to maintain low profiles during these, the last days of the Milton administration.

It seemed that President Milton—by resolving a recent Middle Eastern crisis by clanking American armor with an iron fist, thereby forestalling Russian aggressors, militarily too weak to challenge the U.S.—had managed with bold audacity to keep the balance of power in a status quo position in those crisis nations, much against IAGO's wishes. Gravely displeased by Milton's initiative in working against IAGO's interest with the Arab nations, IAGO history repeated itself. Their misbehaving prodigy in the Oval Office would be shown how IAGO handled rebellious behavior.

Milton, fighting desperately to the last with ineffective weapons at his disposal, couldn't combat the forces of IAGO; they owned the press and heavily influenced other media. To whom, then, could Milton look for support—the Congress? Hardly. Over half the Washington politicians belonged to IAGO. To whom could he turn for justice—the Senate? Too many senators were in hock to IAGO.

IAGO, under a shroud of anonymity, began jockeying into position a new group of chessmen primed to play according to their game plan. The Age of Aquarius in Washington had turned into the age of catharsis; an avalanche of confessions from outgoing officials were forced on the shocked people of the land as public officials disclosed their scandalous conduct. Congressional and Senatorial committees formed to combat this plague infecting The Hill did not know which issue they should address themselves to: the scandal tearing away at the core of Washington's politics, threatening to destroy the nation's political chain of command, sabotaging their credibility, or Senator Shiverton's outlandish report concerning the covert activities of an ignominious, insidious, mysterious entity threatening America—the world, in fact—by some ridiculous worldwide conspiracy?

What was it Shiverton had called this conspiracy? IAGO?

As the remaining senators pondered these questions, Whip and his aides breezed through the halls in the new senatorial building and rode what are affectionately labeled the "Swift Chariots of Democracy," the open subway trams that linked Congress with the subterranean garage where their limousines waited.

Dog tired, the strain of his concentrated involvement on his features, Whip settled back into the rear seat of his limousine, two aides seated opposite him in jump seats, as the sleek sedan wheeled outside into the bright Washington sunshine, heading for Georgetown. Kevin O'Brien and Tom Murphy, his bodyguards, sat in the front seat next to the driver. Whip's law clerk sat next to him in the rear.

All the aides, thoroughly engrossed in the earlier happenings of the meeting, were studying their briefs intently. Whip pulled his horn-rimmed glasses into place, scanning the contents of the reports he'd delivered earlier.

"You shook them up good, Senator," said Jack Payne, a young Texas lawyer who'd come to Washington to serve as a clerk in Whip's office. His contribution was a keen mind that offered research acumen second to none. "When you stipulated that twenty-two senators were already the property of IAGO, I swear I thought they'd crap in their BVDs." His west Texas twang was infectious. "Well, suh—"

Whip glanced at him questioningly. "Well, suh, what?"

"Well, suh, I've assiduously compiled a list of senators who in recent months have dissented, those who've fought you at every turn, those who through innuendo or by other means have cast aspersions on you for suggesting IAGO has already infiltrated American politics and retained a lethal stranglehold on key officials—all those who've used any platform available to them to deny IAGO's existence."

Whip closed his file. "Get on with it, Jack."

"Don't you see, Senator?" Jack Payne handed him a yellow legal notepad with names scribbled on it. "Take a look at the count. I just finished the list. There's twenty-two names on my pad."

Whip scanned the list, a wide grin stretching across his face as he looked back at his aide. "You guys from think tanks ain't bad at all, my friend." With that Whip yahooed so loudly he startled the other passengers.

Whip tore the sheet from the pad. "You got a duplicate list of these names?" he asked the aide, who'd just become the man of the hour in his eyes.

Payne nodded. Whip leaned forward. "Give it to O'Brien."

O'Brien turned in his seat and glanced questioningly at Whip.

"Get that to Chief Bowman as fast as possible. We'll drop you off at his office. Tell him to put a tail on each of these men. Twenty-four hour surveillance followed by complete security dossiers. He can get them from the files. He knows which. And Kevin, drive back to Georgetown, got it?"

The limousine dropped Kevin O'Brien off at the Justice Department. It took off again, heading for Washington Circle and M Street. Whip settled back in his seat and smiled at the slim, mild-mannered, nondescript man seated next to him. Jack Payne pushed gold-rimmed glasses into place and returned the smile.

"Jack, you son of a gun! You did it to them!"

"No, Senator, they did it to themselves. Their vigorous protests and attacks on you is what did it. It flushed them into the open. Perhaps we should be conservative. A few of those names on the list might belong to innocent men. We'll know soon enough."

"Why the bloody devil didn't I think of that?" Grinning like a Cheshire cat, Whip shook his head gleefully in anticipation of Chief Bowman's report.

The staggering summer heat of Washington always caught the city off guard. Air conditioning was always in need of repairs at the wrong time. Whip's townhouse, no different than the others, was sweltering inside. The men quickly stripped to their shirtsleeves and tossed their briefcases on the large conference table Whip had set up in the room adjoining the study. By the time Whip hit the study his jacket, shirt and tie formed a trail behind him. He'd removed his shoes, peeled off his trousers and had one leg inside a pair of tennis shorts when the phone rang.

McKenna on the line asked, "Can you talk, Senator?"

Whip flipped a switch to hook the scrambler in on the line. "Shoot," he said. Anyone listening in on a tap could hear nothing intelligible now.

"The woman you asked me to check out doesn't compute," McKenna muttered. "A courier will reach you in about twenty minutes with all we've got on her."

"Be more specific, Mac."

"The woman you have in mind is a Palestinian terrorist. Hot stuff in the Middle East. She's not the Devon woman. Where the devil did you get the idea—"

Whip cut him off. "It's not possible. Did you check Devon at the other end? I mean where did she emigrate from?"

"We checked the Department of Immigration. As far as we know she came from Beirut, under the name Jaqualine Devon. The woman you identified, Princess Jamila Izmur, is playing havoc with her terrorist playmates over there."

Whip's face knit into a thoughtful scowl. "Mac, you better try learning where Devon's passport was issued and backtrack. Find out who she is—the whole make, get it?" He hung up, dismayed.

A half hour later Kevin O'Brien arrived carrying an opened package in one hand. Entwined around the fingers of his other hand was a golden chain from which dangled a diamond-studded scorpion.

"What the hell is that?" asked Whip.

"Dunno. It came in the mail for you. I checked it as usual the moment I got in, opened it to see if you'd been sent another kind of goody. *Voila!* Them's real diamonds, Senator—and pure gold."

"You know about them things, do ya?" Whip cracked easily, taking the amulet from the other's outstretched hands.

"I've paid for enough in my time," cracked O'Brien ruefully.

Whip turned on the desk lamp and peered closely at the jeweled charm. It was exquisitely done. He laughed lightly. "Scorpio's my sign, but it's not my birthday for a long while. So it can't be that." He glanced at O'Brien. "That's all? Nothing else with it?"

O'Brien handed him a folded sheet of paper. Whip gave him a scathing glance, as he unfolded it. He read the contents:

"Will the bearer of the diamond-studded scorpion call (714) 473-3311? Be prepared to identify yourself by your date of birth, year and dog tags when you were a major in the army.

"You want I should look into it?" asked O'Brien.

"Such a provocative gift deserves first-hand consideration." He'd already begun to dial the number. He waited for someone to answer at the other end.

"Please identify yourself," said a soft voice, obviously disguised.

"I've misplaced my dog tags. How else may I identify myself except to thank you for the diamond scorpion?"

There was noticeable hesitation at the other end. In fear of losing the other's confidence, Whip suggested, "I'll give you the number to call at the same address to which the scorpion was mailed—"

"Does fig wine mean anything to you?"

Whip gave a start. He blinked hard as if this might stimulate his memory. "The fig wine forbidden by Moslem law?" he asked as a stimulating jolt shot through him. "The most delicious of forbidden fruits?" He heard a loud gasp followed by a sigh of relief.

"Praise Allah, it's really you. You must make it possible for us to meet. You are my only hope."

"Where are you? I'll dispatch someone immediately for you."

"No! Only you. They'll kill me if they find me. I have been hiding. Please come to help me."

"Where can I find you?" Whip asked, double checking to make certain the scrambler was working. *A helluva time to think of it, Whip old boy.*

"Call me back at this number in five minutes. I shall give you proper instructions." Jamila told Whip.

Whip jumped to his feet, highly agitated, pounding his fist into the palm of his hand repeatedly. "It's got to be her, Kevin. McKenna's got to be wrong. Jaqualine Devon and Jamila Izmur are one and the same. They have to be. What in hell is rupturing McKenna's spleen?"

"Sorry, Senator, I can't help you."

Whip stared at O'Brien without really seeing him.

A half hour later when a parcel arrived by courier from McKenna, Whip saw for himself why McKenna had come unglued. A portfolio was filled with newspaper clippings and glossy photos captioned by headlines: "Princess Jamila, Heroine To All True Palestinians!" "Princess Jamila Leads Terrorist Bombings Against the Oppressors of Her Nation!" "Princess Jamila, Publicly Disowned by Prince Ali Mohammed."

Whip shuffled through the same photos and clippings Bahar had shown to Jamila. He was flabbergasted. He propped up the glossy photos on his desk and spread the other clippings out before him. Training the desk lamp on them he studied the photos critically, careful to detect any superimpositions. Jogging his memory he admitted that the Jamila he'd met in Rome looked more like the girl in the photos than did the Jaqualine Devon he met in Las Vegas. Whip bit his underlip contemplatively trying to recall everything Valerie had told him when he called her in Rome. She attested to Jamila's terrorist activities.

What in hell's coming off here? How is it possible that Jamila and Jaqualine are one and the same? It makes no sense—none at all!

Whip shook his head as if to clear out the cobwebs of uncertainty and ran his fingers through his thick shock of hair in frustration. Picking up the phone he fairly barked into it.

"Operator, this is Senator Shiverton. I'm requesting an emergency priority. My code is XPI 1-222 . . . Yes, I'll wait."

"How may I help you, Senator?" asked another voice on the line.

"How long before you can get me a location and identification of area code 714, 473-3311?"

"Twenty minutes, sir."

"Make it ten. It's a life or death situation."

"It always is, senator."

Whip leaned over his desk as he peered intently at the photos propped up before him. Deluged with countless questions, he picked up the diamond scorpion and dangled it before him. This was no nickel and dime store merchandise. The stones nearly totaled five carats. The phone rang. He picked up the receiver.

An apologetic operator, sorry that she'd taken so much time in getting back to him, finally got to the point. "It's in the vicinity of Idyllwild. It's the Dysmus Fellowship Society."

"What the hell is that?" Whip asked crisply.

"A drug rehabilitation center—a half hour from Palm Springs."

He muttered his thank yous and a polite, "You've been most helpful," and rang off. He studied the name he'd jotted down on his pad, and once again studied the photos on his desk.

The following afternoon, after touching down in Las Vegas to pick up David Erice, Whip's jet soared through southwestern skies and landed in the sweltering heat of the Palm Springs Airport. A helicopter stood on stand-by. They boarded the chopper. The rotors whirled noisily as the plane lifted off, heading towards the mountains.

Fifteen minutes later they were circling the Dysmus properties. Through binoculars, Whip and David studied the sprawling complex of buildings nestled in the mountains. A flurry of young people, both male and female, were engaged in various sports activities.

Whip lowered the Zeiss glasses, and nudging the pilot, gestured below. He cupped his hand around his mouth, shouting,

"The recreation yard under our belly!"

Nodding, the pilot observed the area meticulously. He circled about and began the squat down.

Whip, David and O'Brien jumped out of the chopper, peering at the handful of people staring at them. A half hour later the stalwart trio and Jaqualine Devon piled back into the helicopter. The rotors turned sluggishly overhead as the copter lifted off and putt-putt-putted into the sky, heading back to Palm Springs.

Jaqualine had lost twenty pounds. A mere shadow of her former self, she was nervous, awkward and fidgety. It was apparent that she was uptight, inordinately distressed and self-conscious. They had moved so swiftly she had come away only with the Levis and shirt she wore and a large leather shoulder bag.

The chopper's loud rotors precluded conversation. Once back in Whip's jet, enroute to Killadreenan Downs in Virginia, Whip patted her hands reassuringly. She seemed unable to talk.

"Just rest. We'll have plenty of time to talk at the farm," Whip said.

David Erice sat across from her on the plane, his eyes skimming from the report in his hands to Jamila's face. It was difficult to read his face, Whip thought, but it seemed apparent that an unspoken mutual attraction had sprung up between David and Jamila.

Once at the farm house they listened to her story, the entire incredible tale, beginning with her departure from the palace in her homeland to her meeting with Bahar Bahar and later Abdul. It was miraculous she'd survived so harrowing an experience and gotten away before she'd been killed. Despite her dissipated and somewhat bizarre appearance and the fact that both men felt compassion for her, they each experienced mixed emotions based on various loopholes in her story. After reading the report on her condition, David felt she needed more time to recollect the episodes of her plight. Whip concurred, yet was unable to give her the full benefit of a doubt.

Jamila's bizarre appearance was attributable to the four-inch growth of black hair that sprouted from her head, ending in faded, bleached out, straw-like fibres frizzed out unbecomingly around her shoulders. Enormous black eyes, haunted with a startled expression, stared out at them. Without benefit of cosmetics she resembled a frightened, displaced war orphan.

"A few calories, a trip to the hairdressers and a shopping trip to purchase a few feminine frivolities and you'll be good as new."

"I'll need more than that," she sighed forlornly as panic flashed in her eyes. "You won't let them find me—please?"

Both Whip and David sensed a paralytic fear gripping her; her alarm seemed genuine. Following dinner she appeared fatigued.

370

Whip suggested she rest and tell them the rest of her story in the morning. Jamila shook her head stubbornly; she poured wine for them with the grace of a gazelle.

"You've both been too kind. I'd prefer getting this off my chest, if you don't mind," she replied.

They both watched her critically; David perhaps with more hypercritical eyes than Whip. He was unable to come to terms with the doubts plaguing him; she was to him a mass of contradictions. She didn't tell them why she had rebelled against her brother's tyranny—if it was tyranny she'd escaped—and didn't speak as a sister would of the brother she was supposed to revere. David's gut reaction, something he trusted infinitely, made him eye her with suspicion and distrust. He got the distinct impression she wasn't being honest; something disturbed her deeply.

Jamila felt his distrust. It made her self-conscious and aware that she'd have to convince David more than Whip. Nevertheless, in directing her next words to Whip, she spoke with downcast eyes. "It is my sincerest desire, in my supplication to Allah, that my brother, the Prince, when you explain my folly to him, will forgive me." She became hesitant. "However, it will not ameliorate my guilt, unless I, with great humility, prostrate myself before you and confess I was part of an assassination plot." She swallowed hard. "I beg you, forgive the foolishness of a stubborn child."

Whip and David exchanged glances, telegraphing unspoken volumes. Whip's heart skipped a beat and he sat forward in his chair, his eyes intent on her. David's mind stopped, his hazel eyes skimmed past her and held on the early twilight scene beyond the window, hoping to suppress his agitation.

"The plot, as yet not dismantled, is geared to, uh—" Jamila hesitated; she reached for a cigarette. Both men reached towards her with outstretched lighters. She took the one offered by David. After exhaling a long smoke spiral, she completed the sentence dangling over them. "Uh—geared to assassinate you, Senator."

Disturbed by Whip's apparent calm, she prevailed upon him not to take her words lightly. "If they hadn't discussed killing me in cold blood—if I hadn't overheard their intent, I might still be with them plotting your death. May Allah have mercy!"

Tears swam in her eyes, illuminating them like sparkling stars in the candlelight reflection. "That I was so easily manipulated, so vulnerable to their evil, is frightening."

371

"You speak of it easily enough." David's voice was accusing.

"Yes. Yes, I do, now. Praise Allah!" She glanced from one to the other. "Recently thoughts of my involvement have pushed me to the brink of madness." Shivers passed through her body on this hot summer night. She rose to her feet, rubbing her arms to stimulate the circulation. Moving about with frenzied actions, pausing to examine a few artifacts, she struggled with words, faltering with marked hesitance.

"I am so ashamed. Can I hope to explain the inner loathing I feel for myself? The doctors insist I have a long way to go. They begged me to remain for therapy until I could cope." She paused with involuntary hesitation as if something frustrated her and she was examining her options before speaking.

Whip attributed Jamila's faltering speech to a possible translation from Arabic to English. David, however, far more knowledgeable in certain matters, understood the impediment in her speech was the result of her addiction. He wanted to assure Jamila that the slurring of words and hesitation in her speaking pattern didn't disturb him. Jamila beat him to it.

"Forgive me. After so many years on drugs, angel dust, cocaine, pot and Allah knows what else—" She paused with a glassy-eyed stare. "Abdul—h-he—t-they knew just how to control me." She kept flicking her nails against the nails of her other hand.

"I'm sorry, Jamila," Whip said compassionately. "It must have been hell for you."

"Why do you have to be so nice?" she wailed, wringing her hands.

Whip grew silent. David's intent eyes never left her.

"Please believe what I tell you, Senator. I may not get the courage to do it again. I must tell you all I know."

"And rid yourself of the guilt?" David's wrath was inexorable.

"Yes! Yes, and rid myself of guilt and any participation I had in the dastardly deed. Once I leave your protection I know I'm a dead woman," she fired back at David with rancor.

"We'll report it to your embassy—" began Whip. He was cut off instantly.

"No! Not them! Only to my brother! Oh, please, I don't trust the ambassador—none of them."

"Who are the people involved in the plot to assassinate

Senator Shiverton? Who is behind it? On whose orders are they acting?" David pressed.

Jamila returned to the table and sat down. She poured a demitasse of black coffee and sipped it. "A branch of the Feyadeen, the terrorists. I don't know who is proclaiming the orders, but there is one man with whom you should be familiar, Senator. Do you recall the name Bahar Bahar?"

It took but a moment for Whip to conjure up the young man's image. "He came a long way from West Berlin. And Rome, too." He frowned. "Wasn't he the same man who lost a leg in the attempt to kill me in Rome?"

"My brother's Doberman mangled it badly, but it wasn't a total loss. The physician repaired it and stitched it together . . ." Jamila paused momentarily arrested by the look in Whip's eyes.

David opened his briefcase and laid it out on the table near the desk. Out of force of habit, he carried his automatic in a specially constructed holster compartment built into the case. He removed a sheaf of papers from the leather folder and perused them as Jamila continued to speak.

"You aren't taking me serious enough, Senator. I can tell by the way you're acting that you think this to be a figment of my imagination."

"On the contrary, Princess—"

"The man in full charge, but who gives the impression of being low man in the chain of command, is—" She stopped, noticeably disturbed.

David glanced over at them, his ears cocked attentively.

"He is— uh." For an instant Jamila seemed unable to form her words. It was as if some internal struggle was impeding her progress.

David thought, *It's either the drugs or genuine fright. Which?*

Jamila steeled herself as if to gather courage to utter the words. "A-Abdul—A-Abdul H-Harrim. There are others. Perhaps I might identify them in some way?" On it went. Things formed an alarming pattern in David's mind. He pulled Whip aside when Jamila went to the powder room and vocalized his concern.

"I don't like it, Whip. It's best you get the Chief and Mac here. Perhaps Mac can bring the file of subversives the FBI has accumulated."

Whip shrugged off the suggestion, then he laughed lightly.

"Once an agent always an agent, eh, Dave?"

He hardly let the words penetrate. No one and nothing was going to stop his call to Chief Bowman. He went into the next room to place the call, flipping the switch on to the scrambler.

An hour later the BSI chief and his dynamic duo, McKenna and Soldato, arrived. Refreshed with drinks and seated comfortably they sat listening to Jamila repeat her earlier words. McKenna studied her in fascination, thinking what a stupendous hoax had been perpetrated upon Prince Izmur and his government. This fact alone led him to think more about the Arab leader. A few things didn't compute. Perhaps the same blatant loopholes that had disturbed David earlier? It was shortly after midnight when Jamila finished talking.

"When they intend to strike, Senator, is not known to me. Their plans were foiled by the untimely death of Dancey Darling, you see."

"Is it fair to assume we could eliminate any and all of your former companions as suspects in her death?"

"How is it possible to suspect any of them?" Her eyes widened at the inference. "Dead she would have been of no use to them. Is it not so? Through her they had hoped to learn more of the senator's plans."

Whip grew more disenchanted by the minute. Having heard the story several times by now, the truth lay brutally upon his mind.

The men of the BSI eyed Whip, sharply aware of his feelings; was he targeted once again for assassination? Unable to sit still, Whip became mobile, fussing with the coffee for his guests. Their overly compassionate looks disturbed him.

"Permit me, senator." Jamila bowed and took over pouring the coffee. She went into the kitchen, returning with cream and sugar and a fresh pot of coffee. She busied herself like a hostess.

Chief Bowman, brooding visibly, sat hunched over in his chair, his stark white hair resembling spun snow in the dim lighting. *When I can no longer hide my feelings behind a bland mask of indifference, I'm showing my age.* Listening to this ugly plot unfold before him like sickening pus-filled sores spreading on a rotting body distressed him. *How much more can the senator take? What a sobering thing to listen to the actual mechanics of his own death plot!* What disturbed Bowman was the time element in this plot. How long had it been planned? Since Whip's trip to West Berlin? *Why in the name of all that's holy did anyone want to kill him?* he wondered. *What had Whip done to be considered a prime target for assassination? What could he do? What would he do?*

Questions mounted in the chief's mind. He wanted to put it straight to Whip and ask him why he was such a threat to these people? Certain that Whip would shrug and play dumb, he thought, *What the hell's the use bringing the subject into the open?* Perhaps another time . . .

Seated at the table where McKenna had spread out a number of glossy eight-by-ten photos of every subversive terrorist known to the FBI and BSI, Jamila set aside a half dozen. At the doubt registered in McKenna's eyes she hastened to add, "If they weren't exchange students they used student visas to get into this country as I did."

Jamila continued to shuffle through the photos. McKenna moved towards the serving cart to pour himself another cup of coffee. Chief Bowman was absorbed in the medical records David had managed to retrieve from Dysmus. Whip and David were busy talking about a related matter. Soldato was reviewing the news clippings.

Several photos of Israeli guerrilla fighters had been added to the terrorists' photos. She stopped at the sight of one guerrilla in particular who wore a sleeveless vest emblazoned with a black-maned Lion of Judah. Her eyes fixed on it piercingly, then they flattened and became glazed. Copious perspiration dripped from her brow. Her eyes left the photo and came to rest on David's automatic tucked into the briefcase not far from her. Slowly she reached for it. Her manner was tentative, but eventually, when no one focused on her, her hand tightened around the blue steel weapon. She raised it, pointing the barrel at Whip. Words played over in her mind, like a recording: *He is a sympathizer, a lover of Jews, a tool of the oppressor. Your trigger mechanism is the black-maned lion of the desert.*

David saw her first. "For the love of God—no!" he yelled, making a flying tackle for Whip, tumbling him unceremoniously from his chair as two shots rang out.

McKenna dove towards Jamila and knocked the weapon from her outthrust hand. The room was in an uproar. David, closest to the girl, studied her trance-like state; passing a hand before her glazed, unseeing eyes. The men closed in on her. David shook her, gently, without getting a reaction; then more forcefully.

"Can you hear me, Jamila?" No reaction.

375

David slapped Jamila's face. She responded, Blinking. "What happened? What is it?" The look she got from them caused her to recoil, her eyes widening in fear.

Bowman was at the desk, sorting through the photos. "You were looking at something here. What interested you?"

McKenna emptied the clip of the automatic and tossed the empty gun on the table, the clip in his jacket pocket.

"I'm not s-sure," she said, reluctant to look at the photos. She felt faint.

"Please take a look." Bowman spread the photos before her.

"She's been programmed," said Whip flatly. The others nodded knowingly.

"Shit!" muttered Soldato. "That's fuckin' all we need."

Jamila was scanning the photos, her eyes falling once again on the Lion of Judah emblem. The triggering mechanism popped in her brain; words paraded across her cranium. *He is a sympathizer, a lover of Jews who must be destroyed!* Jamila furtively reached for the empty gun and held it firmly in her hand.

David, moving to stop her, was immobilized by Soldato. They all watched as she turned slowly, raising the gun, pointing the barrel at Whip. There were two loud clicks, followed by twelve more. Whip, frozen as a statue, had turned a sickly ashen color, his eyes dulled to a smoky gray as he watched Chief Bowman remove the empty gun from Jamila's hand. In a monotone, he talked to the girl.

"It's over, Jamila. You've killed Senator Shiverton. You no longer have to obey the orders in your mind. Will you show us what triggered your impulse?"

Jamila was still in outer limbo. Bowman nodded to David.

"Keep an eye on her."

Bowman studied the photo of the Israeli fighter. The young man in the picture was leaning indolently against a jeep, carrying an M-I rifle. Around his waist were hooked several grenades. Four companions stood in a huddle in the background. Mountains and desert formed the far distance. They were sipping Coca-colas, and all were dressed comparably.

"I'm not a goddammed specialist," he said sullenly.

"Get Dr. Leonard Paul," he snapped to McKenna. "He'll know what must be done." He turned to Whip. "Meanwhile, Senator, she's too dangerous to you to keep her here."

Jamila was coming out of the programmed trance. Soaked with perspiration, she shook noticeably. "Please," she said tremulously. "I am very tired. May I go to sleep now?"

Bowman nodded. "Get one of my men to stay with her all night," he told David as he moved out of the room with her, leading Jamila by the elbow.

They went up the stairs to the bedroom she'd occupy. At the threshold she held on to David's arm. "What will they do to me?" she asked, suddenly curious.

"Don't you have any recollection of what you just did?" He studied her features intently.

"Did I do something terrible? What did I do?" she asked.

"You passed out," he lied. "If you've told the truth, you've nothing to worry about."

"It's true," she said forlornly. "David—I'm afraid of what my brother will do. The prince is a hard taskmaster."

"If you told the truth, you've nothing to fear," he repeated noncommittally.

A smile played at her lips, one laced with bitter irony. "From you? From my brother? Or from the Feyadeen? In making peace with one faction, I've fired up the wrath of the others—and Allah knows how many more."

David took her hands in his, comfortingly. "Don't worry. Things will work out." He stopped abruptly. "Why would you fear your brother?" The thought nagged at him.

Jamila exhaled heavily in resignation. "The Prince is ambitious for our nation. He has introduced much of your technology to our people. He wishes to modernize and bring us into the twentieth century with as few labor pains as possible."

"It's a commendable gesture . . ."

"There are those among our people, strict adherents to Moslem laws, who object. There could be civil war . . ."

David frowned, wondering where this would lead. "This would be the problem of your people and the prince—"

She searched his eyes. "Perhaps you wouldn't understand. The senator might. Tomorrow I'll discuss it with him. You see there are many others involved. People the senator met in Europe . . ." She yawned, suddenly fatigued. "Good night, uh, David.",

He nodded quietly. She closed the door behind her. David walked along the upper hall and descended the steps, thinking on her words. *There are many others involved. People the senator met in Europe . . .*

He found them involved in a heated discussion. They all questioned the integrity and honesty of Princess Jamila Rhadima Izmur. Poised languidly in the doorway David listened to them for a time.

"It's a trap, I tell you, Senator. From the first it was geared to lure you into her confidence. Now we know," said McKenna, glumly staring at the gun. "When I think it could've happened before our eyes—"

"It didn't," Whip retorted. "So let's take it from here."

David walked into the room and removed a manila envelope from his open briefcase and handed it to Chief Bowman. Bowman studied it with pursed lips before opening it. He looked up at David, commenting, "I thought you were through with the BSI."

David shrugged sheepishly. "It's not that easy breaking with old habits. Besides, I've got a personal interest in this."

They all glanced at him questioningly.

"I've got a sister who's head over heels in love with the senator. I just don't want anything to happen to him."

Whip flushed. The others nodded knowingly. Bowman's attention fell on the medical records of Jaqualine Devon while at Dysmus. David explained the reports.

"Jaqualine Devon was found wandering the streets of West Los Angeles, Westwood Village to be exact. On a Saturday night the Village is usually mobbed. Musical acts working for handouts entertain on nearly every corner. An arcade is open where vendors deal in jewelry, artifacts, arts and crafts—you name it. It's easy to get lost in such a setting." David lit up a cigarette, and inhaled deeply. Letting the smoke out through his lips he continued. "Various cults and religious groups frequent the place, seeking handouts and donations. The Dysmus group found Jaqualine wandering the streets, heavily dosed by drugs, irrational, screaming that someone was trying to kill her. At first they thought she was suffering the usual delusions and paranoia of the effects of prolonged drug abuse. The report attested to by two Dysmus youths further declared they took her to their bus waiting to take the entire group back to Idyllwild. They arrived at the foundation's headquarters some four hours later where Jamila was kept under restraints until resident physicians sedated her. The following week she was kept on a daily reduced dosage of tranquillizers until she was slowly weaned off the most debilitating of drugs, PCP. Remission has been exceedingly slow. Recurring attacks and symptoms have prevailed despite the lack of drug intake. Such is the idiosyncrasy of the drug. PCP, an exceedingly dangerous drug, can with prolonged use cause severe brain damage."

David sipped the rest of his wine. He held the bottle up and waved it before the others. There were no takers.

"Senator, do you believe the girl's story?" asked Bowman.

Whip was staring intently at Bahar Bahar's photograph. He shrugged and held his hands up before him with a woebegone expression.

"The story checks with what my sister-in-law told me. It's very possible the Feyadeen found her double and collected a ransom until they decided they could work both ends against the middle. By championing the princess, making it appear she joined them, making a national heroine out of her, they attempted to lower the prince's prestige. If the prince cannot control his sister how can he control his nation? You see? It was a disgraceful act."

David picked it up from there. "By keeping the real princess under wraps in America, changing her appearance, they gave her a cover as they marked time for some future retribution."

"By her own admission she had never revealed having met me previously," added Whip. "She was a natural to get to me. As sister of a reigning monarch in a foreign land it wouldn't seem out of line if she made supplication to me over her dilemma. How much easier the job for them. They kept her plied with drugs, fed her that bullshit about the corruptness of capitalism and hyped up the degradation of their own people by oppressors, who interestingly enough turn out to be their own leaders supposedly corrupted by capitalism. And they led her to believe her brother had disowned her—that the real Jamila Izmur could not return to her country without being severely punished for crimes perpetrated by her proxy, the hijacker, the terrorist who blew up border patrols and machine-gunned to death those who defied her.

"They did jobs on her head, accelerating the increased paranoia, until her depression warped what little remained of her ego. Add to this the continuous raid on her emotions by a man who controlled her sexually as a pimp controls his whores on the street. It's conceivable that Jamila's psyche became frayed and splintered and she lost all control. The final straw came when she overheard a plot to kill her by the same man who had made love to her for five years. Isn't it therefore believable that when she revealed to them that I could identify her as the real Princess Jamila, her usefulness to them was over?" Whip wiped the sweat from his forehead and pulled back the sliding glass doors to the patio hoping to find a vagrant breeze to cool him off.

"It's believable when you sew it together like that with calm reason. But we don't know their full motivation. We're second-guessing it," said McKenna reflectively.

The men grew quiet. Soldato spoke up. "It could still be part of a conspiracy. She could be setting you up like a sitting duck, Senator, preying on your sympathies. If they programmed her to kill you, they could have programmed her for everything else leading to it." He shook his head dubiously, unsold on Jamila's veracity.

David, one of the doubting Thomases, leaned forward in his chair, his elbow on his knee, his chin cupped in his right hand. The next moment he was verbalizing Chief Bowman's unspoken thoughts.

"Why do they want to kill you, Senator? What purpose would your death serve? What have you done to them— or intend doing? Is there something you haven't told us? I mean—" he raised his chin, dropped his elbow and sat back in his chair, his eyes boring holes into the man who was about to turn Washington politics inside out by his revelations of IAGO. David paused, frowning. "You didn't decide to begin this subcommittee business until recently, so it couldn't be that. The first assassination attempt was in West Berlin, wasn't it?"

Bowman nodded dourly. "And the second happened right here at Killadreenan—*after* the Berlin incident."

"I'll ask once again, Senator, is there something you haven't told us? Something you might consider trivial and unrelated? Something you're purposely holding back?"

Whip avoided David's eyes. In his subsequent nonchalance as he shrugged and shook his head it became doubtful that the others believed him. Even when he emphatically emphasized,

"No, nothing I can think of." The agents, too sophisticated in their jobs to be fooled, saw a different Whip in those brief moments.

"Suppose I contact Prince Izmur and suggest he may have been the victim of a hoax and probe his thinking if it were established that his sister is innocent of the charges against her?"

380

"Why not tell him the truth straight out?" David prodded.

Silence ensued. Whip was absorbed in other thoughts.

"Senator?"

"Hmmnn?" Whip glanced at the others. "You don't deal straight out with men of the calibre of Prince Ali Mohammed. You rely on protocol and decorum and do things through the correct channels—unfortunately."

Whip's imperviousness to the anxiety of the others concerning motivation on the part of the Middle Eastern terrorists to assassinate him shook the agents. Discreetly they kept their thoughts to themselves.

Bowman spoke up. "Until all the facts are checked, we accept nothing as gospel. Meanwhile it's imperative the princess be kept under wraps—tight security in the hands of specialists. Got that, Senator?"

Whip smiled at the overtones of an order.

"Dr. Paul is a genius in programming and deprogramming subjects. The man gets damned good results. He'll find the trigger mechanism. Any objections, Senator?" The chief grew insistent.

Whip shook his head. "Just remember she's the blood relative of an important leader."

"I don't give a damn if she is the sister of Jesus Christ, Senator. In her state of mind she'll be treated the way she should be treated, got it?"

"You're right, Chief. But Jesus Christ doesn't happen to control a goodly portion of our much needed oil. Got that?"

Chief Bowman bit back a sharp rejoinder as he compiled his papers and stacked the photographs in a neat pile to keep his fingers busy and subdue his temper. Nodding to his men, they prepared to depart. Bowman brushed by David and remarked, "I'd have thought you'd be so caught up in becoming a highfalutin' gambling impresario you'd have no time to be playing cops and robbers, Dave."

Hanging his head to one side, a sheepish expression creeping into his features, David grinned. "Tell me how one changes the habits of a lifetime overnight and I'll have it made."

David locked the doors behind the agents and returned to the study in time to hear an aggravated diatribe burst from Whip's lips.

"What a goddamned stew to be brewing! Between this business with Jamila on the one hand and the Senate

381

subcommittee breathing down my neck on the other hand, waiting for more revelations, there aren't enough hours in the day to do either any justice. Dave—you think you could stash Jamila away someplace while this joker works with her to deprogram her?"

David, uncertain of what Whip was getting at, muttered, "Anything's possible."

"I don't want her to slip out of our hands. Not until after I meet with Ali Mohammed. We have some things to settle."

David's interest was piqued. "She must be kept away from you, you understand? For your own safety. Look, I can spare a few days away from Las Vegas, just for added insurance until the expert arrives to do his job on her."

"Good. Perhaps the deprogramming can take place out of Washington. I just don't want anyone to get wind of what's happening."

"I understand. I think I can handle it."

Whip glanced at his calendar watch. "Where in hell is Tina? It's not like her not to call me. It's been a week since we last spoke."

"She's on the island with Val."

Whip's head angled around sharply. "Nothing serious, is it? I mean, Val's all right—"

"It's still touch and go. We can't be certain of anything. Look, Whip, I'll handle Jamila. I've bought a ranch in Las Vegas—a perfect place, sequestered and inaccessible except by helicopter. I'll arrange for this Dr. Paul to work with her there at least until after she's deprogrammed." David frowned noticeably. "Why the fuck do you really care what happens to her, dammit!" His anger flared and he wasn't sure why.

Whip stretched his arms and yawned. He opened the patio door and inhaled the warm night air. "Political expediency and international good will, my dear Dave. Even if Prince Ali has disowned Jamila and despite what you've read about her impersonator hijacking planes and causing terrorist pandemonium, the stories must be corroborated before we draw our own conclusions. We cannot turn her over to her brother, nor can we serve her up on a gold platter to the CIA—or the Feyadeen. Dammit, not even to the prince's ambassador—not until we've satisfied ourselves of the truth in this matter."

David slumped into a chair, his eyes fixed like dagger points on the photo of the Israeli guerrilla that had triggered Jamila off. "Who do you suppose he is? Or any of the others for that matter. The sight of him triggered off this urge to kill you."

"Don't know. I'll leave it to you experts," piped up Whip, preparing to leave the room. At the door he paused and said matter-of-factly, "For kicks, Dave, why don't you check the Dysmus Foundation?"

David Erice grinned as he glanced up from the photo. "I've already put feelers out on them, Senator. I'll have the answers in a few days."

"You're good, Dave. Maybe you shouldn't have left the BSI."

Laughing goodnaturedly David retorted, "The pay was lousy, the fringe benefits worse.

Whip laughed, waved him off and left the room. David sat in the smoke-stale room refreshing his memory of Jamila's behavior and words from the moment they picked her up in Idyllwild until the photo of the Israeli guerrilla fighter triggered her off lethally. So steeped was David in his old way of life he'd managed to tape-record most of her conversation. *Thank God for old habits!*

Dog tired, David finished listening to the tapes at sunrise. He had expected no miracles and got none. He decided, however, to take the cassettes to the bureau in Washington and let the lab technicians analyze them. Modern technology made it possible to determine truth and deceit differentials by recording speech patterns graphically to clearly indicate any emotional stress accompanying the words. It would help.

Having never met Dr. Paul, David wondered how the specialist would take to performing his work in Nevada instead of Washington. Moreover how would Chief Bowman take to his interference?

The phone rang. About to pick it up he stopped. Lights on the panel indicated the call had been answered somewhere else in the house. He lay back to catch a few winks.

Tina was speaking to Whip. "Sorry for disturbing you so early. Can you come to the island this weekend, Whip? My father wants to see you—to talk with you."

Clearing the thickness in his throat and rubbing the sleep from his eyes as new excitement shot through him, he managed, "Yup, I'll be there. Hey—I love you."

"I love you too," muttered Tina at the other end.

CHAPTER THIRTY

Whip spent the entire weekend with Val at the Long Island mansion, hardly aware that Tina was alive. Val and he had breakfasted, lunched and dined together in seclusion, talking for long hours into the night. Before he left for Washington the following Monday morning, Whip held Tina tightly in his arms. His features were strained and he appeared weary and exhausted.

"Sorry we didn't find time together, honey. I'll call you the moment I can. Maybe next weekend, huh? We have to talk, Tina—you and I."

They kissed lingeringly. Breaking the embrace with noticeable reluctance, Whip sprinted to the waiting car. Kevin O'Brien revved up the motor in the sleek Jaguar XK-E. The sportscar took off along the drive and out the gates.

Tina sighed heavily and closed the door after them wondering what Whip and her father had discussed so secretively. Moving through the great house, casually attired in blue jeans and shirt, her thoughts skipped to other pressing matters, for she too had been burdened recently with realities she had never before contemplated.

A half hour later Tina moved along the wooded path behind the Erice house pushing her father's wheelchair along the narrow dirt walkway through the woods permeated with the smells and colors of autumn. The sounds of her leather boots crunching pebbles underfoot to the accompaniment of snapping twigs as the wheels of Val's chair cracked and crunched everything in its path amplified as they moved forward into the early afternoon of splintered sunshine.

The beauty of nature fell upon them. The woods were a wonderland of brilliant, burnished fire, deep verdant greens, golds and pumpkin orange on this late day in a September Indian summer. The day was quiet. Not one bird chirped. It was as if the whole world had suddenly stopped for these few moments. This world was in vivid contrast to the perpetual excitement and activity Tina had encountered daily in Las Vegas. The contrast startled her.

"I had forgotten it could be so beautiful here. Shall we stop for a few moments, Pop? Look! Over there by the bridge. Is that a fox?" she squealed with childish glee.

Val nodded. They both watched the red fur fluff disappear under the bridge. Val's eyes shone unusually bright in the slanting rays of the sun parting the overhead trees. Color had seeped into his complexion. He was dressed leisurely in Levis, shirt and sweater, with a lap robe over his legs to keep them warm; his constant complaint was the feeling of inexorable cold in his lower extremities.

He gazed contentedly at the tranquil scene. Here the woods were drenched with dank coolness, beneath the wispy weeping willows with low hanging limbs extending to the earth. He watched as two riders on horseback raced through the adjoining property laughing ecstatically.

Instant nostalgia engulfed both Val and Tina as the sounds and smells of galloping horses from across the field assailed their senses. Striated sun streaks penetrating the thicket glowed with life and suddenly everything, the day, the sounds, the smells, transported Tina back in time to her youth when she and her brothers frolicked playfully in the nearby fields. Jimmy had pushed her high up on the swing that once hung from the oak tree, now empty. She saw herself and her brothers running barefoot along the babbling brook, tossing rocks on the surface of the water.

The scenes dissolved and Tina, dismayed, said, "Remember how it was when we were growing up, heaping monumental problems on you night and day? How did you put up with us? Did you ever think we would grow up and stand on our own two feet?"

Val nodded and gazed into the distance, seemingly tuned in on the same scenes Tina had seen in her imagination. He smiled. Daily, more speech returned to his lips, filling him with reassurance. These past several weeks with Tina had been a tonic to him. The two days spent with Whip, however, had drained him and left him more debilitated than he realized. Both Tina and his wife had scolded him, insisting he should rest. In good conscience, Val refused to consider their words. He could not be deterred from doing what he beileved to be his duty.

Tina had arrived two weeks ago carrying with her a

small package the hospital had forgotten to return to Val when he left Las Vegas. On her arrival, Tina confronted him with the article contained in the small box; the jeweled ring of the double-headed griffin. That day Val had studied the ring gravely, his eyes slowly lifting to meet Tina's.

"They insisted it was yours. I recognized it. When I returned from Europe you promised to tell me all about the statue of the double-headed griffin you keep in the curio cabinet. Has the time come yet?" she'd asked him pointedly.

Val, with no rebuttal prepared, and no retreatable avenues open to him, proceeded to explain in detail. It was a line of conversation ultimately leading to the reason Val had asked Tina to come. He laid it all out for her, IAGO, the E.L. Lamb affair—everything. Now, as he gazed upon his daughter, thinking how like a small child she was with her hair parted down the middle and caught at either side in sections banded by elastics, he sighed heavily wishing he hadn't had to overburden her. As his daughter she deserved to know everything, if only to come to terms with herself before making the one vital decision. He should have told her sooner, he knew it.

Now his eyes rested on Tina and he smiled with pride. She was exceptionally bright, well educated, knowledgeable on numerous subjects, poised, damned attractive and for the most part had demonstrated a clear-thinking objective mind in business. How, he wondered, would Tina fare in matters requiring broad perspicacity? His keen blue eyes observed her incisively, weighing the pros and cons of her personality, character and intestinal fortitude against the issues with which she would have to cope in the near future.

She sat opposite him on a portion of the split rail fencing listening to the rustling leaves falling from overhead maples and oaks as a soft flurry of current tunneled them to their destination. Tina lit a cigarette, inhaling deeply. She tucked the pack into a side pocket of her jeans and crossed one booted leg over the other stretched out before her.

"You smoke too much," Val said with parental tolerance.

"It's hard to break the habit." Her eyes followed the trail of two bright varigated orange oak leaves that fell onto Val's shoulder. Leaning closer to him she removed them, twirling them around by their stems. Inhaling the woodsy scents of earth and autumn appreciatively, Tina glanced into the sleepy giant pepper trees a-hum with bees.

"Have you considered all I've told you, Tina?" Val asked softly, watching the leaves spinning in her fingers.

Tina grew thoughtful. "As a child, when I first saw the griffin in your study, I was curious. Now, you've told me what I've known and denied in the past. It took time to come to terms with myself and no longer deny my heritage. It made life easier for me—not perfect—just easier. The question is—can I handle it?" She shrugged dubiously. "To answer your question—yes, I've considered everything."

"It's not the ring or the bronze figure I speak about, Tina. We've already discussed the responsibility of perpetuating the power you agreed to assume. That business is no longer on the agenda. You know perfectly well what I refer to."

Both their attention was momentarily captured by a yellow canary flying down from a tree limb and alighting on the ground a few feet from them.

"I'm referring to Whip Shiverton, Tina."

She gave him a sharp look and sighed heavily, averting her eyes. "I know. I guess I've been trying to sweep the pieces under a carpet to avoid confronting the issue." Why tell him of the countless sleepless nights she had spent crying over the futility of their relationship? She'd grown thinner and paler these past two weeks; her *joie de vivre* had dimmed considerably. "If it's not meant to be, it's not to be."

"You love him enough *not* to marry him."

Tears swam around in her head and she snapped it back hoping to dissolve them, but a few escaped, spilling onto the soft contour of her cheeks. She brushed them quickly off her face.

Val, watching her, sighed wistfully and with obvious sadness.

"The secrets contained in my heart impose a terrible burden on me and you. Since my accident, I've recorded them on tapes in my study. I was unable to write—" He glanced at his useless right hand. "They are in the file room in chronological order. Only you and I remain alive with the true knowledge of Ted and Amy's birthright. I entreat you, keep this information inviolable."

"You ask a great deal from a mere woman."

Val was unable to suppress a smile. "This from my Tina who insisted that she be spoken to as if she were my son?"

Tina blew her nose with a hankie taken from her jean pocket.

"I can't help if your first assessment was right. Maybe I shouldn't try to shoulder this responsibility. What about David? He's your son, too!" She flared with a trace of militant rancor as if this statement might eradicate her responsibilities.

Thoughtfully silent for a moment, Val's soothing voice reached her. "The way a tree is bent during its formative years is the way it grows for the rest of its days. As it matures it gathers luxuriant creepers and parasitic leaves in great abundance, so the tree itself becomes so smothered it is no longer recognizable. Wading through the welter of foliage in some instances in order to discover the tree's true identity takes time." His hesitation was brief.

Cocking his tiny head, the yellow canary watched Tina, then turned to eye Val warily. Both Tina and Val watched the bird, making no move to frighten it.

"David is doing fine," she said softly. "He's taken to the business as if he were born to it, just as Benne did. Sometimes I think he even has more on the ball than Benne." Because she suddenly felt intense disloyalty to Benne, she stopped talking. Leaning over she picked up a dry twig. The sudden movement and noise frightened the canary. It sailed upwards into a shaft of air with spread wings, landing on an overhead tree branch.

They watched it. Tina dragged on her cigarette, exhaling resignedly. "O.K., Pop. I'll do it. Two years from now, God willing, you'll explain it to David yourself." She wagged a hand at him. "All right. All right. But if you *shouldn't* be here," she broke off, a catch in her voice, "I'll tell him myself."

Val had told her everything, including what transpired those last tense hours before tragedy befell him. He confided the betrayal of Dr. Larry Sharp, indicating the importance of thinking at the level of your adversaries and being steps ahead of them in anything they might conspire against you. She felt a surging anger at men like Sharp who deliberately deceive their fellow men. Realizing that soon she too would be guilty of the very deception she detested she became quiet. She filed all that Val told her, including her deep-rooted feelings in the matter, into

388

neat little niches in her mind for future reference when needed.

In short Tina held the answers to all the questions plaguing the BSI. During his sojourn with Whip, Val had questioned him and imparted many vital answers to vital questions—but not everything, and for a purpose. Tina asked her father if she should allow the BSI or Whip to inspect his personal papers. Val had replied by asking her to table that question until after she'd been briefed on other matters.

It was almost over, thought Val, leaning forward in his wheelchair to stretch his back muscles. Tina moved over and began to rub his back gingerly. He sighed appreciatively, then thought clouded his senses. Recent headlines about upheavals in the Middle East had been alarming. Peace talks had been scuttled, renegotiated and rescuttled. No doubt the heavy hand of IAGO was planning a coup —but what and how would it affect his beloved country?

He had to and drop the bomb, thought Val, he had to apprise her of future options. Tina had stopped rubbing his back and sat down again, stretching her legs before her. She picked up a twig and tossed it into the lazy stream of water.

"What do you think of Prince Ali Mohammed?" he asked as if it mattered not in the least to him.

She turned abruptly. "For goodness sakes! What kind of a question is that?" She was taken unawares. "Now why did you suddenly conjure up his name?"

"One day he will be head of IAGO, if he isn't already."

She was still thinking as a woman. "Why should this news be of earth-shattering importance to Tina Erice?" she laughed amiably.

Watching her carefully, Val prepared his next words meticulously.

"It is possible that the lives of Prince Ali Mohammed and Tina Erice are inextricably bound together."

Disconcertment flared in her. *Had Whip mentioned Jamila to Val?* She hoped he hadn't bothered her father with insignificant nonsense. She'd even tried to keep Dancey Darling's involvement in Benne's death from Val. Nothing would be gained by the revelation. It would only make Benne a weak man in Val's eyes. It was agreed that neither Jerry or Richie would mention this to Val. "Now, why this sudden interest in Prince Izmur? What a thing to say."

"Did you ever wonder why he swept Valerie off her feet so soon after Ted's death?"

"For the usual reasons, I suppose. They were attracted to each other." She smiled reproachfully. "Standards aren't the same today as when you and Mom were young. Valerie has always lived with money. Oh, Pop who the hell knows—or cares. What are you driving at?"

"Think, Tina. Think. Keep IAGO prevalent in your mind. Remember how they tied Joey up into ribbons once? Think of Bob Harmon's father—his personal and business involvement with IAGO. Think of the Fishman affair in Vegas, Benne's triumph and the faked kidnapping of Joey." He enumerated other instances, refreshing her memory. "IAGO nearly always gets what it wants."

Watching and listening to her father Tina's mind was still dulled by the intense learning process to which she'd been subjected recently. Val's silence honed her mind into activity. The thought that formed in her mind became unacceptable; still she asked the question aloud to test her internal conclusions.

"Why does Ali Mohammed's marriage to Valerie stir you to disquiet, Father?" Even as she asked it she refused to give the answer life in her mind. She wasn't prepared for the barrage of images and thoughts parading across her cranium.

"A-are y-you t-trying to say that he has some ulterior motive—is keeping her under his—uh, wing?" She was on her feet pacing in the dust before Val's wheelchair, a mass of quivering thoughts and feelings, her hands thrust deeply into the pockets of her jeans. Her activity caused more leaves to rustle and swirl through the air falling on Val's lap and on her shoulders.

"Long-range plans are IAGO's forte. Think long-range plans, Tina," Val suggested, trying to stimulate her capacity for logic. "What if Whip should run for the presidency?"

"He said he won't, Pop."

"What if he does?"

"No chance of that." She spoke with utter confidence.

"Tina!" He swung his wheelchair around sharply to face her.

"He won't." Tina's voice was cutting. Her hands trembled.

"Tina—and if he does?"

"Why do you keep insisting? He won't. He *won't!* Pop, if he does, we can never be married!" She stopped short.

A warm flush surging through her. "Is this what you've been trying to tell me? Is this why Whip left here this morning as if we'd never known each other? Is it?" She stopped pacing and stood directly before him, looking him square in the eyes.

Val didn't reply. He merely stared at her hoping the answers to all he'd taught her would jell and she'd come to the proper conclusion. *There's so little time, Tina. So little time.*

A wave of irrepressible anguish welled up in her. "You know something you aren't telling me, don't you? Why don't you just tell me straight out and stop this guessing game?" She stopped as it began to dovetail in her mind. At first her eyes grew disbelieving. She shook her head tentatively. The words refused to form on her lips.

Val nodded his head knowingly. "Whip *will* become president. IAGO has courted him for some time. It's only a matter of time before he accepts. It's his destiny. No one, nothing can prevent this."

Tina shook her head and averted her eyes as if this very gesture would prevent Val's words from becoming fact.

"Everything is falling into place," Val continued. "It's taken a few years; now the bait is too alluring. Having found the key to Whip's thinking they've seen fit to lock things into place along the way." He gazed into her stricken, terrified eyes.

"No. I won't believe this. Whip has a mind of his own. If he really loves me he won't run," she said in a half-hearted voice that wrung Val's heart.

"In a contest between love and destiny who will emerge victorious?" Val coughed slightly. He bent his elbow, rotating his shoulder, and sucked in sharply, frowning at the severity of pain he felt.

Tina, instantly solicitous, pressed, "What's wrong, Pop?"

He shook his head. "Just some discomfort. Nothing I can't handle." It grieved him to watch the torment in her eyes. Better now than to be caught unaware later. "We were discussing—"

"I know you love me and would do anything to see me happy," she began. Her love and respect for her father precluded her acceptance of this as frivolous talk. "What you're telling me is killing me. I've loved Whip for so long there is no one else. You tell me I can't have him—that I'm about to lose him to some vague undefined force you call destiny. I can't accept this. I won't!" She sat down on the split rail fencing and with a twig savagely drew geometric patters in the dirt.

Val sighed despairingly. "Was my first assessment correct?" He made a gesture of hopelessness. "You can't handle a man's responsibility. You're too emotional. You can never see the truth of anything in such a state." He stopped when he saw her defiant expression.

Tina, speaking in a strained voice, began to talk, hesitantly at first, then with more impetus.

"If Whip becomes president and Valerie is still married to Prince Ali Mohammed, and he controls the children—" she began. "What I mean is— Whip's inclination might be to hesitate, relax his aggression in a confrontation with Prince Ali." Tina's eyes smoldered in thought. "Would he be inclined to favor Ali's government—right or wrong —in any controversy? America's inclination has been pro-Israel . . . Would Whip take a stand against Israel?" Tina, on her feet before her father could see her expression, refused to give birth to the possible consequences of such an act brewing in her brain. "Pop! Whip wouldn't bend like a reed in the wind. He's a man of principle!"

"Principle has little to do with politics, my dear daughter. I've explained in depth the ramifications involved, so don't become naive with me. A peace settlement could be secured this moment if the monetary remunerations were sufficient for all parties. The key word is money. Money is power."

"It's confusing, is what it is," snapped Tina. "Daily, politics change and shift. First, it's the Arabs against the Israelis, then splits in the Arab world bring enemies together to fight for a unified cause. The Palestinian rebels, against their oppressors who were infected by capitalism, are now preparing to bed down together. Who can keep track of this mishmash?"

Val smiled at the use of the vernacular. "Tina," he explained patiently, "the entire situation is so complex . . . If Machiavelli himself were alive and viewing it, his confusion would be total. Russia, eying the picture with careful and protracted deliberation, could swoop down and control the Middle East in a moment. Her troops positioned to aid her allies, already occupy the fringe areas surrounding the oil emirates. In addition she supplies arms to the resistance, the terrorists who spout radical ideals akin to Marxist precepts. If the Middle East falls into Communist hands, America will be crippled. Without oil to supply industry and transportation . . ." His face

392

darkened. "Whip is needed in the White House to help assuage this international crisis. When the time comes, you will tell him the truth about Ted and with Amy's clout as a blood descendant of E.L. Lamb and papers to prove it, they can perform with plenty of power on the oil industry's behalf. You see, your personal feelings must be set aside."

Tina crossed her hands over her breasts, and gave him a soulful, woebegone look. "What a two-bit melodrama, Pop. To think Tina Erice must put her country before her own love and desires. Very well, so we don't run blissfully off into the sunset, Whip and I!" she snapped dryly, breaking through the affectation. She placed a fresh cigarette to her lips and lit it with obvious agitation. Clicking her lighter shut, she puffed on the Sherman for a time. She thought it unfair to be singled out for so great a sacrifice. Didn't her love for Whip and his for her mean anything at all? Couldn't it transcend all earthly matters?

"View your relationship with Whip with the objectivity you viewed Renzo—"

"That was different. I felt only disgust and loathing for him—not love! Detachment was easy!"

"—and in this detachment came the answers." Their eyes locked.

"You're telling me the stage is set, that the players have moved into position and things are falling into place. That no one, especially not Tina Erice, can circumvent the outcome . . ." She smiled mischievously. "What happens if I can convince Whip not to become president? Then where will Prince Ali Mohammed be? The whole fucking world for that matter?" Tina bit back her lip, regretting the profanity, aware that Val detested it.

Val was dismayed, but not at the profanity. "You are incapable of recognizing the truth," he said despondently. "I have failed with you, Tina. Whip must become president. Only then can he defy IAGO and bring about the defeat of any conspiracy on the part of those nameless, faceless giants in the shadows who are making the world bend to their edicts. Should IAGO gain control of the Middle Eastern oil, they would indeed have reached the pinnacle of world control. They must be stopped. Whip is the only one who can accomplish this—why can't I make you see?

"I talked long with Whip pointing out that the only solution to this incredible situation is for a united control of the earth's natural resources. They should be owned jointly by all nations and doled out according to their needs. If the world doesn't destroy itself through nuclear missiles, it will destroy itself with greed and avarice. My last act upon earth is to try to make this a better place for my children and their children. For what other purpose was I born? I can only pass on to you what I've gleaned in my lifetime. The only truth I will take to my grave is, I was on earth once and did my best to improve it during my stay."

Tina would later regret with great remorse that she wasn't listening as sharply as she might have been. For the moment she was thoroughly rattled. Confusion swirled around her head like the swift images of a merry-go-round. "Pop, you tell me Whip must become president, that it can be no other way for him. Oh, Pop! You're driving me crazy! Why can't I grasp what you're saying? Am I so obtuse? The way I see it, Whip is damned if he runs and damned if he doesn't! And I, Tina, am caught in the middle!" She turned the wheelchair around so he'd be facing her as she plopped down on the felled tree trunk.

"You're forgetting all I've taught you about being a huntress like Diana the warrior," he said quietly. His breathing grew labored. Tina became concerned.

"You've exerted yourself too much. It's best I take you back to the house." Worried, she became solicitous of him.

Val shook his head stubbornly. "I've been trying to make you understand your relationship to the world—not to any one or more persons—but to the world. I've tried to convince you of the importance of assuming responsibility for being here. You must make every act on earth count since you'll be here only for a limited time. Have you forgotten the precious teachings I imparted to you, teachings that came from your grandfather and myself?"

For several moments he refreshed her memory. "The power of which I speak is that personal power you've stored inside you all your life. You are a strong woman, Tina. God knows you've been through hell these many months since my accident—even before. Suddenly you act liked a wilted flower because the womanly instinct to be comforted and protected stirs in you. You've rid yourself of enormous problems, Renzo for instance, now you flounder because the burden is gone and your inner strength is at peace. You handled that threat with amazing coolness. You didn't once come running to me crying, 'Solve my problem!' You didn't give way to self-pity; instead you became a champion of survival. That, my daughter, is power. In your present exhaustion and concern over me—" he wagged a hand at her to ward off interruption, "you permitted old insecurities to cloud the issue. Be tired at times, lie back to reconnoiter your strength and strategy, but don't give in to self-pity, to the need of a strong shoulder to cry on. Find inner assurance from an internal source that builds your confidence, whispering you can handle matters yourself. Listen to that inner power and you'll need no one in whom to confide and so dissipate your powers."

With no weapons of rebuttal handy, Tina grew thoughtful. He was right. How many times, when things seemed darkest for her and she'd given in to feelings of longing and despair, had something deep inside her nudged her, shaking her into sensibility?

Val was telling her to recognize that power, nurture it. "It's a strange commodity, an intangible. In order to have power to command you must have it to begin with. Joey had no such power. Not even Jimmy. Benne had it for a time, but for a while he was dictated to by his loins—" They exchanged quick, sharp looks.

"As for David—" Val tilted his head speculatively, "only time will tell. Remember this, Tina. In any battle between the will and the imagination, the imagination emerges victorious."

Tina faced Val, eyes askance.

"You've been forced into power battles before and emerged victorious. I've watched you. There is no doubt, not a shred of doubt in my mind. The power of the Erice family belongs to you."

Tina experienced a moment of unparalleled confusion. "What if I don't have enough power?" How could she explain what she felt?

Val sighed heavily. He did not smile. His eyes were piercing.

"Death is always waiting in the wings observing the goings on. When power wanes Death just taps your shoulder."

"I don't want this power you speak of! I have no reason to possess it," she cried in anguish. She lay at his feet on the ground, her head on his lap. Val stroked her head gently, with affection. He lay his head back against the leather headrest, his eyes watching the sky through the treetops. The September sun was beginning to turn a blood red. "Life is only as hard as you make it, child. Teach your spirit to become impassive, do nothing or say nothing to betray your feelings; you'll always be the victor in a battle for power."

"I know what you're doing, Pop and I love you for it. You're just preparing me so I won't be disappointed if Whip and I don't marry." She dried her eyes. "If all this talk about power is to bolster me against the shattering of my emotions—O.K. then, I understand. Judging from my past sprinting record, you're right. I can overcome anything if I set my mind to it. You took a long way around to get to the point, Pop."

She pulled her hair up off her face and neck. Pulling the elastic bands off each ponytail, she wrapped each tighter. Tina felt an attack of anxiety brooding behind her outward calm, ready to erupt.

Watching her, Val shook his head in amusement. She was still a child in so many ways. "I have no fear you can't handle yourself where Whip is concerned. Once you know you cannot marry him and why you must not, you have the power to abstain. My concern is—" Val clasped Tina's slender hand in his and patted it with his other. His sudden remoteness caused a pang of overwhelming concern to surge through her.

"Pop, what is it? What are you trying to tell me?"

A sudden gust of wind traveling across the wooded path swirled in its wake cornucopias of dust. She turned slightly to watch the course of the wind following its movement.

"Promise me one thing, Tina." He couldn't bear to look at his beloved daughter knowing what torment she must be suffering. Her full lips, usually smiling broadly and somewhat mischievously, wore the brooding, troubled look of a suffering woman pleading for reassurance from him. Instead he had to plunge the lance of ultimatums into her guts. "You must never, never marry Prince Ali Mohammed."

In an instant, Tina's head riveted about, eyes fixed on her father as her brooding expanded into an expression of mirth and laughter. On her feet, she swung her arms about freely.

"Ali Mohammed? Me? Pop, you've got to be kidding! Why would I marry him? He's already married to Valerie." She scooped up another birch branch and pulled off a few remaining dead leaves, striking it against her

396

boots. A sudden mental image of Ali Mohammed came upon her mind, as he was the day they lunched by the sea in Ostia Antica. What had he said to her?

"My dear Tina, you are extraordinary. You have the gift for life. Everything around you comes to life in your presence. You smile and the sun rises in heaven. We'll be together, you and I. Mark my words. When we do it will be because you will it so."

Her smile evaporated at the memory of these words. Simultaneously Val's recent words became superimposed over those of Prince Izmur. *In a battle between the will and the imagination, the imagination will emerge victorious.*

Tina smiled ingratiatingly. "It'll never happen, Pop." She whirled about to face him, her smile disintegrating. "Pop? Are you all right?" She moved in closer to him, studying the inert expression in his blue eyes. "Pop!" Her scream was stuck somewhere between her vocal cord and her mouth. She called to him frantically, but he didn't respond. Unsure if he'd lapsed into unconsciousness again, she fell to her knees, taking his hands in hers, rubbing them, to stimulate life in him.

"Pop! Please answer me. Dear God in heaven, please. Please!"

Val had died while she laughed at his last words. Tears sprang into her eyes and rolled down her cheeks. She wasn't certain how long she sat there at his feet staring up into his face.

After a while she closed his eyelids and brushed her own tears aside. She thought back to the earlier part of the day when he insisted on being wheeled out onto the grounds surrounding the house. He'd been infused with supernatural energy. It was as if he'd willed himself to remain alive until he'd finished telling Tina all there was to tell her. She dug into her pocket and retrieved the jeweled ring of the double-headed griffin.

She stared at it, slipped it onto her index finger where it fell loosely to one side. She squeezed her eyes shut against the anguish she felt. Her luminous wet eyes glowed and she held Val's still warm hand in hers.

I don't know how I'll do it, Pop. I heard all you've told me. You'll be proud of me, you'll see. You'll never regret entrusting me with the power. Somehow, someway I'll do the Erice family justice. If I could only perpetuate what you've taught me . . .

Tina removed the ring and replaced it in her pocket.

She tucked Val into the chair securely, arranging the lap robe tightly so he wouldn't fall and, turning the wheelchair around, retraced her steps over the path Val had walked thousands of times in his life. Recollections came at her like a montage of pictures; her impressions of her father, his life, the burdens and hardships he endured, his strict adherence to principles and philosophies of awareness and humanity. She burst with pride and felt an overwhelming urge to shout to the world: *Here is a giant among giants!*

Easing the chair away from the wooden bridge, she was unable to subdue the thousand recollections of her childhood when Val was always there to help her over the painful hurdles of living and growing up, as he did with all his children. The love he held for his family was indescribable.

She neared the house, sensing his presence in all living things. The weeping willows, gesticulating in the slight breeze, seemed to sense he wouldn't be walking the lane again. Chipmunks, scurrying busily, chittering, chattering, nibbling food morsels, stopped their activity to watch them pass.

Sadge came loping towards them, pausing some twenty feet away, sniffing the air, muttering a low whine, then leaping, spanning the distance between them, stopping once again, whimpering, keeping his head low, sniffing cautiously, his eyes intent. Tina had never seen such a hangdog expression on the animal's face. He fell into step behind her, whining softly.

Chills shuddered through her as she passed the gazebo where both her parents had sat in the past watching their children at play. How would she explain this to her mother? She felt a suffocation of spirit, a stranglehold upon her when flashes of her enormous responsibilities came to her, dwarfing her by their breadth and scope. Disturbing Tina equally as much as the death of her father were the reasons why she above all Val's children should be the keeper of the power.

Pausing at the rear entrance of the house to collect her strength and inner fortitude she couldn't abate the rush of emotions that assailed her.

Oh, David, why didn't you come into our lives two years ago? Maybe none of this would have happened. Two years! Two whole years must pass before I can confide in you. You know what can happen in two years?

* * *

Richie, an aging, fleshy hulk with slightly stooped shoulders, moved along the guests with ursine tread and quiet rectitude, shaking hands solemnly, tears spilling freely along his gray, expressionless face as he made introductions with poise and dignity. When he wasn't at Tina's side, he stood shoulder to shoulder with David Erice introducing him to the old trusted family friends.

People from all walks of life poured through the heavily guarded gates, admitted only by special invitation to keep out the nosy media. Judges, city, state and federal politicians came to pay their last respects. Show business personalities and superluminaries gathered to laud the memory of Val Erice.

That her father in his lifetime had commanded the genuine respect of so many people was mindboggling to Tina. Dressed in a simple black silk shirtwaist Tina moved through the circles of men and women listening as Richie imparted information relating to the old days, regretting that she'd been so sheltered from that former life of her father's.

The impressive funeral cortege, a mile long, ended, following the service at the Sacred Heart Church in Brooklyn, at the family crypt in a marble mausoleum, where the bodies of Lucia, Jimmy and Benne had been interred. Never more aware of death than at this moment, Tina shudderingly observed the accommodations for all remaining members of the Erice family within these cool marble walls.

The litany; holy water sprinkled onto the bronze casket; overbearing odors of incense; bland parrafin; a mixed profusion of flowers; strong and inspirational eulogies; the wet-eyed mourners. It was all there, but it didn't faze Tina. She thought, *There has to be more to life than such an ending.* None of it, as memorable as it was, was good enough for a man like Valentino Erice.

It was over. She consoled her mother in quiet, soothing tones, feeling none of it was real. Standing next to Christina, she guided her mother over the marble floor into the bright sunlight to the waiting limousine.

Christina had coped formidably throughout the trying ordeal. Once in the seclusion of her house, she walked among Val's possessions in his study, her hands caressing his chair, desk, books, and she broke down into a torrent of tears.

David consoled her, comforted her in her grief. His

words pacified the raw aching sorrow in her heart, for the truth of death hadn't fully settled in her. How, she wondered, would she face life without Val?

A doctor arrived to administer a sedative to calm Christina and allow her to catch up on the sleep she desperately needed.

Tina began the monumental job of locating all the Erice holdings and scrutinized each carefully with an eye to their importance in her scheme of things.

CHAPTER THIRTY-ONE

Two months after the date of Val's death, Tina and her brothers buried Christina in the vault next to her husband in the marble mausoleum. She had lost the will to live. Not even Maria Rossi's companionship helped to ameliorate Christina's sadness. As one half of the whole, unable to exist without the other half, Christina wanted to die; her wish was so great she'd made it happen.

Five months spent watching her father's predictions become realities helped Tina to understand his character and destiny in ways that reinforced the beliefs she had entertained in the past. She thought Val was a superior human being who carved a name for himself in ways of which the average man had no conception. Changes occurred daily in her, subtle changes obliterating the Tina of the past. Unwittingly she was paying heed to certain atavistic stirrings within her crying for expression. The gradual metamorphosis would extend itself over a prolonged period of time to help insulate her against the abruptness of change, allowing her to come to better grips with the future.

Tina had holed herself up in Val's study, listening to the steady tranquillity of his voice as on tape he spoke to her of matters so electrifying they infused her with a bold excitement. Constant changes all around her thrusting her suddenly into unfamiliar territories, combined with the unpredictability of exploring unknown areas of her father's numerous interests, were intimidating to Tina, to say the least. Slowly, an insouciance spread through her, an imperturbable attitude of inpregnable mental strength, growing stronger each day, supporting her through the most anxious of days until she no longer felt emotional. Detachment was setting in, and she saw things more clearly than before, all the things Val had strained to teach her.

She found it chaotic to follow the chronology of events Val had documented years before. Listening to his voice making adjustments to the earlier documents confused her. For a time she abandoned the written documents for the tapes until she came to know intimately the curious cast of players who dominated her father's life, including those giants in the shadows always hovering close.

Benkhanhian she found to be incredibly intriguing; a curiously fascinating man, certainly no counterfeit, a one-of-a-kind man. Broadly brushed across her mind, in bright colors, those international power brokers were beginning to form real pictures of a world quite remote from hers. The budding realization that her father belonged on the same plateau of accomplishment as the IAGO cartel overwhelmed her. Her father's accomplishments grew in her mind; adjustments in her thinking process shifted accordingly, enabling her to view the overall picture in a clearer perspective; her earlier fears became nonexistent.

She wouldn't be human if she hadn't felt a pressing urge to share this new-found knowledge with someone else. How many times had she picked up the phone and dialed Las Vegas to talk with David and tell him all about it? And how many times had she hung up before the call went through, when she recalled her promise to Val? She'd renew the vows and her compulsion would abate. *Two years pass swiftly, Tina, then, come hell or high water you can tell David everything.* She would repeat this over and again.

Reams of information crammed into Tina's brain reduced the intimidating stature of IAGO. She no longer questioned why she'd been the recipient of Don Antonio's legacy, instead she spent her spare time studying the origins of her ancestry, aware that once she embarked upon this journey into the unknown it would be irrevocable.

Today, Tina's thoughts turned to Valerie Shiverton Izmur, recalling the day she'd found a letter from Valerie that had found its way into the file room without having been opened.

Alone in the house that day shortly after Val's funeral, Tina had gone into the study to turn on Val's tapes in the daily ritual she had formed. His voice, bouncing off the walls from speakers, had produced an eerie feeling:

When the world is in your hands, tap it lightly, take only what you need for your time on earth. When you've made your pact with death, be prepared to turn the world over to another master for safekeeping.

These words, his intonation, something caused Tina to

choke up. She snapped off the recorder, fighting back the tears that welled in her eyes, and before she permitted herself to engage in maudlin histrionics she went into the adjoining file room to search for the confidential files of the Community Federated Bank.

The instant Tina heard their voices she knew she should have made her presence known. What little devils kept her inside the file room? It was too late now. Through the crack in the door she saw Jerry and David remove their jackets, David pausing briefly before the desk, his eyes intent on the bronze griffin. He sat down in the leather swivel chair. Jerry stood before him, one hand stroking the cold bronze figure pointedly.

"I cannot put it off any longer. Val died before title could be passed to you. Normally it would have gone to Benne. Under the circumstances it has to be you." Jerry began to fuss about the desk, picking up candles from the curio cabinet and placing them near the bronze figure.

Tina froze. The air in the file room was stifling her. She was tempted to rush into the room and tell them how it really was. Her fingers fondled the griffin ring on the chain around her neck. Why couldn't she budge? All she had to do was place one foot before the other and move. She couldn't do it. Jerry's word's trailed into the room, filling her ears.

"By conferring title to you—"

"Title to what, Jerry?" David was puzzled by both Jerry's cryptic words and his discomfort.

In the file room, Tina picked up a letter and fanned herself. She listened to Jerry's words.

Jerry explained. Listening, David believed a hoax was being played on him. Tina, also listening, felt an inner suffocation. Whatever it was, the closeness in the room, lack of oxygen, something caused her heart to pound deafeningly in her ears. In these brief moments Tina was possessed with a mad thought. *Could I possibly shirk my duty, avoid my obligation to my father's last wishes? Let David assume all the burdens? Could I get away with it? Do I dare? Dear God, I'm only a woman!*

Giddy and sick to her stomach she clutched the wall. Only then did she notice she held an unopened letter from Valerie Shiverton Izmur in her hand. In the blur of her eyes she noted the postmark had been two months before. How had it found its way into the file room unopened? Before she could ferret out the answer Jerry's words caught her attention.

"It's only a titular title, David. Hardly any of the old school are left here . . ."

Tina thought, could she somehow, some way marry Whip after all? Her mind raced ahead. Stuffing the letter into her sweater pocket, she connived mentally.

"The valid assets are the valuable connections in Europe," Jerry's voice continued. "Many of the older men, still alive, and to whom tradition means everything, have instilled their next of kin with their pragmatic teachings. These men rank high in government. Should it become necessary in your lifetime to need a special favor—no matter how large or small—to be the possessor of the double-headed griffin is tantamount to getting what you want. Countless doors, normally closed, would be open to you."

"Why the fuck would I want, uh, *special favors?* Nah, forget it, Jerry. Put all that junk away. We'll bring it out one day and have a good laugh." David waved him off.

Jerry's stunned expression and total disconcertment at David's lack of respect for the ritual shook him. He had opened the wall safe behind David's chair. Unable to find the griffin ring he needed to complete the rites he frowned thoughtfully.

Tina fingered the ring around her neck, polishing it with her fingertips. Her eyes clouded with thought. *Why hadn't Jerry consulted her? Was it possible Val had failed to tell him he had passed the power on to her?*

"Don't make light of this," Jerry was telling David. "Look, I can't find the ring so I'll perform the ceremony symbolically."

"You're intent on this foolishness?" David regarded the lawyer gravely.

"I have no choice." Jerry removed a folded sheet of frayed and yellowed parchment from an envelope. "It's my duty as *consigliere* to your late father to speak this invocation. I must abide by it. What you do in the future concerning this is your business."

The whole thing was unpalatable to David. He watched the lawyer place four scented candles on the desk at each corner of the bronze figure and light them. The sandlewood essence wafted to his nostrils. He barely observed the marked sobriety with which Jerry undertook the task, hardly hearing him speak the required ritual formalized eight centuries before. His hazel eyes took on a supernatural topaz glow in the reflected candlelight, his mind clinging to the last of Jerry's words:

404

"When the world is in your hands, tap it lightly, take only what you need for your time on earth. When you've made your pact with death be prepared to turn it over to another master for safekeeping. Don Valentino Erice is dead, long live the Don!" said Jerry, wrapping it up.

Much to David's embarrassment, Jerry leaned over to kiss his hand. "Your wishes are my command, my Don."

David withdrew his hand hastily. "C'mon, Jerry, cut it out! Cut the comedy," he blurted in annoyance.

"It's no comedy, David."

"Just like that, I'm a Mafia Don!" David's scorn, cynicism and total condemnation exploded. "You don't expect me to buy all this!"

"With the Erice name comes certain responsibilities . . ."

"Well, goddammit, I wasn't prepared for this! I didn't mean to imply—" David hesitated when he saw Jerry's obvious discomfort. "Dammit, man, it's inconceivable to me that I should suddenly—well, all at once—with no forewarning—" He stopped. On his feet he searched for the proper words to express his anger and confusion. He stared at the bronze griffin and shook his head, wagging his hand at it. He began to enumerate a long list of reasons why he couldn't accept the new role inflicted upon him and stopped. They sounded inane. Assessing the situation with trepidation he shook his head negatively. "It's just that, well—"

Listening, Tina understood the things to which her father had alluded prior to his death, concerning David. Tina had expected too much; she expected him to be exactly like Benne, not merely his twin. She understood, now that they were separated by two different worlds. Each was constructed of a unique set of ideals and beliefs. Although Erice blood flowed through David's body, what was contained in his mind, the thoughts with which he'd been programmed, was what determined the man.

Tina had just come face to face with her destiny. What would be, began long before her birth; no power on earth could prevent her destiny from being fulfilled. A sadness fell upon her, and in this sadness came the realization that no personal will could dissuade her from the role destiny had selected for her.

Without hesitation, reluctance or misgivings, she opened a file drawer, and removed an envelope. She opened the door to the study, her face somber, her manner precise; she walked into the room. Catching sight of her, Jerry suppressed his astonishment, the greeting frozen on his lips. His silence drew David's attention to her; he stopped midway between an effusive smile and a spoken greeting. Jerry must have glanced from the ring around Tina's neck to her eyes a half dozen times before he got the picture.

David rose to his feet as Tina thrust the envelope in Jerry's hand. "Sit down, David, Jerry has something to tell you. You'll be happy to know you've been relieved of a cumbersome burden."

Jerry, scanning the contents, mopped his sweaty brow. He should have guessed all along . . .

The relief instantly apparent in David's features following Jerry's recitation was duly noted by both the lawyer and his sister. David's subsequent puzzlement and consternation was vocalized instantly. "Tina," he began, leaning forward on the desk, where he'd casually propped himself, "you can't mean—what I mean is, you don't intend to carry on with this antiquated foolishness, do you?" Frustrated, he shoved his sweater sleeves to his elbows. "I mean, why? Why subject yourself to—to—"

"Because Pop passed the power to me," she said artlessly. "Don't try to dissuade me. I made no effort to influence you to accept the role, so don't use any cleverness to make me break my vow to our father."

"Fair enough," he muttered in annoyance. About to leave the room, he paused briefly. "Tina?"

She leveled her dark eyes on him questioningly.

"I thought you should know. Jolie Barnes was found dead in her hotel room. Did you hear about it?"

Her composure shattered, she stared in shock. "Why? How?"

"Don't know. I thought you might." He nodded to Jerry. The lawyer left the room. David closed the door behind him. "I happened to stumble on S.S. 1144. I viewed the films—"

"And?" She arched her spine instinctively; the fine hairs on her neck stood on end.

"It was a—I mean, you had nothing to do with it—did you?"

Tina's eyes turned dull; she muzzled the opprobrious rebuke surfacing. "If you knew your sister better, you'd have no need to ask such a question. I had nothing to do with it."

"I believe you," he muttered half-heartedly. "Tell me," he asked scorchingly, "what else comes with my inheritance?"

Equally as scathing, she asked, "Monetarily speaking?"

"You know I mean no such thing. I mean that—" He gestured to the double-headed griffin.

"Nothing you need concern yourself over."

"Really." He sank into a chair. "I'm not burdening you with what should be my responsibility?"

Tina couldn't believe the aloofness and sudden caution with which they were speaking to each other. She tried to circumvent this detachment, but couldn't. "Your loyalty to the Erice family is all that's expected of you. In two years the picture might change. Until then—"

"Two years?" The announcement tied to a timetable sounded discordant. "Why then?"

Tina explained Val's wishes, watching his pained expression.

"I dislike such discipline exacted of me. I'm a free soul."

"I see; you've had no discipline in the FBI or BSI?" Her dissident voice filled with reproach incited him.

"And I'm not in the habit of telling my troubles to a woman," he snapped acerbically.

"I'm your sister. Should that fact alienate us?"

"I don't intend for this to turn into a regular donnybrook between us." At once apologetic, he gestured wildly. "Sorry, so much is happening. On top of it I think I'm in love."

Tina, melting instantly, grinned with understanding. "That's great. Who's the lucky woman?"

David, walking to her side, pulled her to her feet, embracing her affectionately. "I knew you'd wish me well. Whip thinks I'm crazy. We've known each other a short time, but I'm sure it's love."

"Tell me, is it serious? I mean, wedding bells serious? Who's the lucky girl?"

"The princess, that's who. Jamila." David grinned, sappy-eyed.

Her smile evaporated; her instant reaction was too acute for David to pass it by. His elation siphoned off into a trickle; he backed away, searching her eyes. Tina averted her head as she moved in closer to the fire. *Steady, Tina, don't alienate him. Never come between lovers—it will prove disastrous.*

"Are you madly in love with her?"

"What kind of a question is that?"

"Is it the 'I can't live without her and wanna marry her'—or 'do you wanna play house for a while'?"

David fell heavily into a chair, exhaling air from be-

407

tween his lips. "Boy, Tina, you're tough. You're tough, do you know that? I'm not sure. Does that answer your question? You know, Tina, if it weren't for the fact that being a brother is totally new to me, I'd tell you it's none of your damned business."

She nodded. "You're right. It isn't, up to a point. The only responsibility I have is to what's left of our family. You and me. I won't let you jeopardize that relationship. Is that plain?"

"How does my love for Jamila jeopardize you or us?"

"I can't tell you. Please trust me."

"That's not good enough. That answer won't buy you an ounce of loyalty. You've gotta tell me more."

"I will in two years. Help me keep my promise to our father."

"In two years Jamila and I could be dead."

Tina paled. Her eyes closed. The truth of his words diminished her resolve; still she was unable to accept his words.

"This isn't the brave, mighty, persevering David Martin who risked his life in a daring conspiracy to defraud the Erice family. Is your lack of control such that you'd risk so much for a mere slip of a woman?" She marveled at her own audacity. "For Christ's sake, David, live with her, love her, do everything you dream of doing but don't marry her—not for two years. Is that too much to ask?"

David's sullenness stopped cold. "I promise nothing. I'll think on it."

Tina shrugged. "Fair enough."

"I presume you've heard of Whip's plans?" he said tentatively.

Tina fingered the buttons of her shirt. She nodded glumly.

"Does he have your blessing?"

"He has my love—not my blessing. I would have had it differently."

"Why? I thought you two hit it off."

"We've been in love for years."

"So?"

"C'mon, David. The future American president cannot afford to be associated with the daughter of Val Erice— let alone marry her." She tried to keep the stinging tone from her words.

David's compassion was instant. "Oh, Tina, I'm sorry. I'm really sorry. Christ, this has got to be tough on you."

He came around to her side, pulled her to her feet and held her close.

"Go ahead, cry if you want. You deserve better than this."

Tina pulled away. "I don't want to cry, David. Really. I've shed all the tears I intend shedding on a matter over which I have no control."

David searched her eyes. "You're some woman," he said quietly. "Some woman." Then he laughed lightly. "Speaking of women, I know this is the era of women's liberation, but tell me, Tina, how are you gonna explain a woman wearing the double-headed griffin to some of those Mustache Petes around here?" He grinned.

She glanced at him, rolling her eyes in a gesture of mock superiority. "Don't laugh. I asked Pop this very question when I wanted to dissuade him from passing the power to me. And he tossed a few passes back at me. It's true, he said to me, no woman in over a century had involved herself in the activities of the brotherhood—not since the death of one Principessa Eleonora Scarlatti. It seemed this woman of royalty had joined forces with Mafia-armed bandits when the French Bourbons controlled the island of Sicily. She had committed herself to the Honored Society, as the Mafia was called, and became the most vicious, bloodthirsty and despotic leader of the underground resistance forces, dedicating her powers to rid the island of its barbaric oppressors. In her day she was a most unusual woman.

"Well, David, after Pop died, I did some research of my own." She waved her hands in the air about her. "Right here in this most formidable of libraries." She indicated her healthy respect of the room's contents. "Naturally I was curious to learn more about the woman who reminded Pop of me. At first I resented Pop's analogy, until I read how the princess survived the tormenting conditions inflicted upon her. She suffered gross humiliations at the hands of her oppressors. She was tortured, nearly starved to death, and forced to suffer physical hardships, but the young noblewoman lived to give her enemies a taste of their diabolical cruelty that became a legend among her people. Her courage and total dedication to the cause are still spoken of with reverence in the interior villages on the island."

"Tina—" David studied her with mixed emotions. "You don't seriously intend to pick up the gauntlet."

409

In the ensuing silence, Tina chose her words cautiously.

"To be connected with me would mean Whip's annihilation in politics. The Erice family will support him much in the same manner we supported Ted. Perhaps you too should remain on the sidelines."

"Another penalty for wearing the Erice name?"

Tina let the remark pass. "Whip led me to believe he would never seek office at a high level. For a time I allowed myself to dream. Well, the bubble burst. He changed his mind. For a time I felt lost. But I'm all right now. You see, politics is in his blood. He was born to power. He can no more help abate his obsession for the presidency than I can help being my father's daughter or you his son. I would be the eternal impediment to his career. You see, it's best that I walk away."

David brooded. "Not long ago we talked. The presidency was remote in his mind. It's my fault, I encouraged him," he admitted, warming his hands before the fire. The shrill ring of the telephone startled him. He watched Tina reach for it.

"Did it ever occur to you, Whip is using himself as bait?"

Tina waved him off. "Yes, he's here." Placing her hand over the mouthpiece she called to him. "It's for you, David."

He picked up the phone and motioned her to remain when Tina prepared to leave him. "Yes, Jamila. I'm fine, honey . . . What's that?" He paused to listen, frowning. "Did he call you personally? He's sending his jet for you —again?" His voice strained. "Hostess a dinner for him at Killadreenan, again? I suppose I can fly there from here. But I'd feel better if my men go with you. Is it his intention to publicize this, uh, this gala?"

Tina stood looking out at the deserted tennis courts, thinking that no one used them any more. She'd have to make some changes about the house. Her heart was possessed with such fear she tried to keep her thoughts active. It was the kind of fear that terrorizes you in the night and dissolves your power of speech.

It's happening, Pop, just the way you predicted. So soon. Why did you wish this burden on me? Why?

David's mood descended into morbid depression. He'd hung up the phone and stood at the bar pouring a tumbler full of Chivas Regal. He couldn't believe Jamila was flying to Virginia without first consulting with him. They'd had an understanding, she had confessed her love to him and he to her. Now as he considered the developments, more than personal jealousy was involved. He reassessed the implications of this move. Why hadn't he been able to dissuade Jamila from going to Virgina?

"I asked if you'll miss me for a few weeks, David? I'm flying to Rome in a few days." Tina tried to change his mood.

He whirled about to face her. "Rome? What in hell's going on in Rome?"

"Valerie Shiverton Izmur has asked me to be their houseguest. Seems she's terribly lonely for America and wants to see a familiar face. I need the rest and diversion."

David set his drink down. "Tina, there's more to it than that. Hey—you forget I was part of the BSI for a long time. I know more than you can imagine about IAGO. I also know that Pop left a great deal of important data he compiled on IAGO and Ted Shiverton's involvement. Need I tell you that Prince Ali Mohammed is highly suspect in a conspiracy aimed against Israel and the United States?"

"Why are you telling me all this?" she asked with polite disdain. "What does it have to do with me?"

David searched her eyes intently, but was unable to pierce the screen behind her eyes. "Richie has told me a great deal. Jerry has filled me in on more. What I already knew with the bureaus has made me far more shrewd than you give me credit for. Promise me you won't do anything foolish."

"Like what, David?"

"Nothing. Forget it." He turned from her, then whirled around, incensed. "Dammit, I just found you. I don't want to lose you because you've got some godamned notion you have to fulfill a godamned promise made to a dead man!"

Silence descended. "That *dead man* was my father—our father."

"He was unfair to ask this of you. You lived with a lousy rat because you were led by tradition. You should have cut the bastard loose the moment you learned he had gutter rat morals. But did you? No! You stuck it out— and for what? So many miserable years—"

"—taught me plenty," she retorted. "It prepared me for the next two years. What I learned was invaluable."

"That again! Two fucking years of keeping everything on the front burners can ruin what it is you're cooking."

A long, sustained look stretched between them until Tina changed the subject. "Will Jamila be hostess for Whip at Killadrecnan?"

"Yes, dammit! And it's fucking well foolish on his part,"

411

he snarled in a way that indicated the touchiness of the subject. "I don't like it! He knows how dangerous it is to Jamila and himself to flaunt her in the public's eye. There are bound to be reporters and cameramen—Dammit! She's not well enough to be—"

"What did you mean earlier when you said Whip was using himself for bait?"

"It should be self-evident to someone like you, Tina."

"I suppose so." She had expected more from David.

"You can't be persuaded against the trip to Rome?" he asked solicitously. He felt a sense of relief that Tina hadn't picked up on his real terror. Jamila was not ready to be thrust into Whip's company yet.

The shadow of a smile forming on her face told him nothing. He asked her outright if anyone could influence her to remain.

"No. No one. Don't recruit a militia to dissuade me."

"Why this sudden interest in the former first lady? Rumors from Rome are hardly complimentary."

"Like any other human, I suppose she's had her problems."

"Tina, you will be careful? She's heavily into drugs. Word's out she'd taken the cure so often she'll never recuperate."

"It's amazing," began Tina, chilling a bit, "what having a former BSI agent for a brother can do for a girl. She gets to hear all the dirt."

Frowning, as a deep flush spread over his face, David spun on his heel and left her. Tina wanted to bite her tongue. Why had she snapped at him? She missed Benne so much. She really didn't know David at all. It was unfair of her to confuse them. She moved to the window, peering out at the gray drizzle, in time to see Jerry and David enter the limousine. They hadn't even said goodbye to her. A well of loneliness engulfed her.

Blinking back the tears brimming her eyes she returned to the desk to reread Valerie's letter, wondering if David's assessment was correct. Dispassionate in her own evaluation, she tried reading between the lines, only to feel more strongly that Valerie was in trouble and needed help. Coupled with the compelling urges that drove her in recent days Tina thought she might very well be the one to aid Valerie. First she had some personal business of her own to handle.

She tried not to think of Whip, David and Jamila enjoying themselves at Killadreenan, and concentrated on the mission before her.

Elated or depressed? Which should she be? One part of Tina called her a fool, suggesting she should take immediate steps to stop this foolishness; the other smiled secretively, content in knowing she was doing the right thing, Yet how could she be certain? She wondered if her father had vacillated as she was doing. Had he been plagued by apprehension and self-doubt when he embarked on journeys into unknown territories?

Elation, exhilaration and secret plotting came and left her giving in to a profound soul-searching and later self-approval. By the time night fell on the big lonely house Tina's mind had accepted the blueprints of her future endeavors. Decisions were made and, by God, no one could dissuade her from this one act she believed vital to her sanity.

The following three days brimmed with activity in preparation for her trip to Italy. Richie was called to the island and listened to the outlining of her plans. Asking for his cooperation she wasn't surprised at his hesitation in complying with her requests. His austere and loyal obedience, despite his stupefaction at her intentions, were what she'd expected, and what she received. Following an afternoon of telephone bouts with overseas operators in both Rome and Palermo, Richie, with utter exhaustion, reported all was in readiness.

"You are certain you don't wish my presence? With your permission—I cannot dissuade you from going through with this?"

Tina considered his words carefully and asserted herself firmly. "If what I have attempted to do becomes an impossible task, I promise you, my dear friend, I shall not hesitate in calling for you to join me."

The following day Richie drove Tina to Kennedy Airport and waved until she disappeared into the accordion-pleated tunnel permitting passengers to board the 747 aircraft. So many newfangled contraptions, thought Richie, so many changes had occurred in his lifetime that he no longer recognized the world. *Perhaps it is the Lord's way of telling us that our time on earth is at an end,* he told himself, *by confusing the world and all around us until we are out of step with our surroundings.*

He watched the 747 taxi out to the landing strip and rev its engines for takeoff, thinking that the end to a very special era had come to an abrupt halt when Val died.

Imagine! A woman walking in the shadow of the double-headed griffin! Incredible. What had his don been thinking to make so shocking a decision? The honored brotherhood would roll over in their mausoleums to hear such earth-shattering news. A woman . . .

CHAPTER THIRTY-TWO

The monotonous droning sounds of the 747 were lulling Tina to sleep. Her eyes read the time on her solid gold, diamond-studded Corum watch. Four more hours to Rome, she thought, slipping a leather marker between the pages of the book she was reading and closing her eyes.

Numbed by the death of her parents and the abrupt finish to her romance with Whip—which she found intolerable—she felt as if she were sleepwalking through a labyrinthian nightmare from which she was unable to awaken. So much had happened to create a void in her that for a time she experienced a savage rebellion against that illusive, unwritten law called duty. Then, slowly, came apathy and a dullness that for a time quenched the very will to live. Gradually the inspirational teachings of her father took root and she experienced a rebirth. The changes in her thinking were becoming more definable and to her the growing awareness of these manifestations more palatable.

Tina accepted the hot coffee from the bright-eyed, soft-spoken stewardess and nibbled on the cookies on the tray. When she finished, she noticed that most of the plane's passengers were asleep. She switched off the overhead light, settled back in the reclining seat and determined to nap awhile. Thought gave her no peace. For a time she reflected on the less complicated days spent growing into womanhood, her education both at Miss Porter's and Vassar, her love for Bob Harmon, learning high fashion at Bonwit Teller, the invaluable friendship with that clever hustler David Meyers, Las Vegas, her bitter marriage to Renzo, her closeness to Benne, even her love affair with Whip Shiverton. All of it had been curiously integrated and stored in her mind along with Val's teachings, and now it was all sifting together, forming the perspective from which she would be making judgments in the coming days.

It was clear that Tina's cool, analytical absorption in her

recent plans had brought about numerous and surprising contrasts in her present and past thinking. She felt like a new woman. But despite the infusion of new energy and power, Tina wouldn't have considered herself much of a woman if, despite Val's stern admonitions, she hadn't attempted to combat the forces of destiny for the man she loved. She'd made countless attempts to lure Whip away from politics.

Six weeks after Val's death, following a period of prolonged study of Val's tapes and private papers, Tina felt she could cram no more into her head. She had agreed to meet Whip at the Manhattan townhouse where he'd retreated to siphon off some of his senatorial pressures.

The first winds of winter brought an abrupt end to the long Indian summer. Howling winds swooping down on New York attempted to convert the falling rain into snow. Shivering in her fur-trimmed leather coat despite the hot gush of warmth coming from the heater in the Ferrari, Tina emerged briskly from the car, quickly relinquishing her car keys to the gargantuan, spiffily uniformed doorman who touched his cap in recognition of her as she breezed past him into the building.

Tina had sensed something amiss the moment O'Brien, munching a celery stick, grinned when he let her in. With a quick jerk of his head followed by an eye signal, he indicated Whip was in the study and lazily mentioned something about the short fuse on which Whip was operating that day.

Whip's brooding when he saw Tina dissolved into a grin of delight. He made a beeline for her, sweeping her into his arms and whirling her about, bestowing a rash of passionate kisses on her. Hot brandy and eggnog before a fire followed. Try as he did to keep his spirit elevated, Tina saw through the deceptive attempt and was filled with disquiet. He was either unwilling or unable to relax.

"What do you say we fly to Aspen and get in some skiing?" he suggested about to scramble to his feet. Tina pulled him back to the alpaca carpeting alongside of her and kissed him lingeringly. Coming up for air she whispered lovingly,

"What's wrong, Whip?"

He held her tightly, holding her warm supple body against his, trying desperately to feel and to stop the thinking process enslaving him. He sighed deeply. "I'm sorry, baby, I'm poor company. Senate committee meetings,

416

investigations—it's all taking its toll. Say something, honey, tell me what to do."

"You expect a mere woman to tell her impressive lover what to do?"

"No. Just tell me you'll stand behind me in all I do. Val indicated to me he left tapes," Whip continued, "and personal papers concerning his involvement with IAGO. Are they available to me, Tina?" He searched her eyes. "I may need them to back up my previous statements to the committee."

"If I disagreed with you, will it make us enemies?"

Whip, staring at her in a peculiar isolated manner, intimidated her, deterring her momentarily. Undaunted she continued.

"Are you interested in my thinking? Will it change the course of our destinies?"

"You sound more like Val each day."

"Or will you do as you've already decided to do?" She ignored his last remark.

Whip took the eggnog from her hand and placed it on the table nearby. He drew her to him, kissing her ardently. "I've missed you. Three months is too long without you."

"Me too," she murmured.

"You're really going after IAGO?"

His reaction was instantaneous. Concealing his annoyance, he transformed it to a mood of conciliation. "Now, what does a pretty girl like you know about IAGO?" he asked facetiously. Scanning her voluptuous figure in her tailored jeans and open necked silk shirt he traced the outline of her body with his fingertips.

That's when Tina, try as she did to keep her silence, couldn't and began the windup. "What do I know about IAGO? I'll tell you what I know. You're so distracted by IAGO you are alienating your peers. Can you really do anything about IAGO's proliferation of power? Can you indict them, bring them to heel? Take punitive measures against so pervasive a force? Can you charge them openly with the illegal manipulations of people and nations? Let me see, can they be charged with conspiracy to defraud? Or of influencing government officials through financial contributions to make them exempt from the law?" She paused. "Let's see, what about the influencing of foreign policies in nations to further their own interests? And destroying the credibility of any material witness against their interests by any means at their disposal? Oh, Whip," she exclaimed plaintively, "They are inhuman, these men

417

of IAGO. Twenty-four carat gold and oil runs through their arteries. They wield a brand of clout that is utterly inconceivable to the average man."

In the silence, Whip's voice struck her as lethal. "What gives you the idea I am an average man, Tina?" His resentment tightened his lips grimly.

She should have stopped long before. Now the silence, too thick to dissolve with a loving sigh, a murmur, or acquiescence, wouldn't melt his resolute anger. Before Whip could offer a rejoinder, Tina continued making pirouettes on the rapidly thinning ice.

"My father buried information about IAGO within him, not because he feared them. Following his encounter with the men of IAGO *after* recognizing their strength, when he realized you don't enter into combat with such a force, you outfox them, he began to diligently and strategically put his affairs in order. Unassumingly, without fanfare, he took measures to make himself immune to their ploys. The word is *immune*."

Whip sat observing Tina through new eyes. Obviously he didn't share her point of view, and appreciated less her candor. Despite what he construed to be a personal attack on him he didn't refute her. Taken by her keen insight and intelligence as she revealed more concise knowledge of IAGO, Whip became aware that Val had confided a great deal to her. This awareness lessened his indignation yet left him with lingering concern over the reasons Val had imparted such information to her. What really stuck in Whip's craw was the way Tina was playing her cards too close to her chest, to please him.

Later, after a long sexual interlude, they lay quietly next to each other on the oversized bed that held fond memories for both. Whip lay on his back, his head resting on his hands. He was thinking that neither he or Tina had performed with their usual sexual prowess. He had to forcibly block from his mind any vagrant thoughts that might interfere with a memorable night of lovemaking. When had sex ever taken a back seat to thought in the past? Was he disturbed? Damned right. Yet as he explored the possible reasons for this they eluded him. Gathering his skill at covering his thoughts he turned towards Tina and resolutely took his fill of swollen kisses from her lips, hugging her tightly, muttering half spoken, sometimes indiscernible words.

"We've both been through hell, Tina. We should have motored down to Killadreenan for the holidays instead of staying cooped up inside by the lousy weather." He rolled over onto his back. "You didn't like my suggestion of Aspen. How about Snowbird? I hear the powder's just perfect."

Tina rolled over on top of him, her warm body trembling over his. Cupping his face between her slender cool hands she searched his smoky blue eyes intently. She could feel his body harden under her as he had in the past when thought wasn't a part of their lovemaking. But she had to make him understand somehow.

"Whip, my beloved, resign as senator. Give them notice or whatever you do. Get out of politics. Write. Teach. Or if you love skiing so much let's go skiing around the world—anyplace. Do what you've dreamed of doing, but get out of politics before it's too late. You said yourself, the odds were against you in this IAGO business. Twenty-two senators wear IAGO dogtags. Doesn't that tell you something?"

Tina, feeling a sudden chill, wondered what forces he was marshalling while he digested her words. What complicated balances of love, desires, duty, willpower or expediency did he weigh in his mind? Indignation, irritation, exasperation, acrimony and a half dozen more emotions surfaced as Whip, bridling egotistically, shoved her to one side of the bed, unsure of how to best describe his feelings. He got up, lighting a cigarette with unsteady hands, irked by her unyielding manner. Dammit! He hadn't known how stubborn she could be at the wrong moment.

He shook his head in total frustration. "I can't believe you said that. *Resign? Give notice?* You must be mad to suggest such a thing. Is that what it is?" He turned on the bedlamp and searched her face. "Are you not in possession of your senses?"

"No. Just in love with you."

Her words stopped him cold. He fell across the bed, uttering a sigh of anguish and pulled her into his arms, holding her, rocking her until he felt the pounding of her heart against his. One hand deposited the cigarette in an ash tray, then, holding her tighter, he stroked her lustrous hair lovingly off her face, lifting a tendril and placing it with the thick shock spilling against him. When his voice returned he had to speak his thoughts.

"You of all people, Tina, beloved, would lose all respect for me if you found yourself saddled to a quitter."

"I wouldn't. I wouldn't, darling, really I wouldn't. Once

419

my father told me to take my man and be happy with him. 'Love is all that really counts,' he said." She averted her eyes and lay her face against his heaving chest hoping to conceal the truth from him.

"Val wouldn't have spoken those words in his forties," he said ruefully. "Those are the words of an impotent man whose use to the world has passed."

Tina stiffened. "No one can tell you what to do, can they?" she fired at him defensively. Crestfallen and defeated in this hopeless cause they both grew combative.

"That's right." He picked up his cigarette, puffing on it until it nearly burned his fingers. He ground it out in the ashtray exhaling tightly. "No more than anyone can tell you what to do. We're both alike, Tina, and a bit headstrong. Maybe we're too alike . . ."

Easing herself away from him she reached for a robe and wrapped herself in it, trying to ward off the chills pervading her spirit. She fought off the impulse to tell him everything—everything Val had made her promise must wait for two years. *Why? Why had she made the promise?* Watching the inner agony registering on her face, Whip attempted to pacify her, misconstruing her anguish.

"Some things cannot be understood, Tina, so don't try. I've been a loner for too long to put up with interference at any level. I won't permit anyone, not even you, Tina, to dictate my actions."

"I see. What are you really after? Power? Is that why you're bent on courting death?" She sighed deeply. "I can't talk you out of it."

"Really, Tina, don't be so dramatic." His features turned stony, his jaw muscles twitched as he ground out his cigarette. Checking a backlash rebuttal he stalked out of the room, down the stairs and into the study.

Tina grabbed his terry robe and charged after him relentlessly.

"That's what you're doing, you know, flirting with death!" She angrily flung his robe at him. "Do you think those senators and congressmen will let you air their dirty laundry without fighting back? Twenty-two senators and how many congressmen? What gives you the unmitigated gall to think they won't attack with every weapon at their disposal?" She watched him put on the robe.

"I won't live in fear. It's against my nature—"

"Then, don't." Her voice was deliberately colorless. "Die!"

Shocked at her brutal candor he retorted blackly, "Damn it, Tina, stop it! Shut up, will you?" He yanked hard on the belt.

Her voice fell to a whisper. "That's what'll happen if you persist in this folly. That's not all. You've no idea the problems that can arise for your loved ones—accidents that aren't accidents—"

"Tina! Stop! I get the picture, dammit!" Grabbing the brass stoker near the fireplace he jammed it hard into the dying coals, trying to revive the fire. He tossed more dried twigs on it with wooden shavings. When they caught fire he tossed in a few smaller bits of wood, then added a log. Staring into the fire he dusted the shavings from his hands.

"The great Whip Shiverton is his own man. No one influences him," she snapped, equally as caustic. "Just count on this, Whip. The moment you lay the full evidence before that body of your peers you'd best count on employing more bodyguards than O'Brien and Murphy. Twenty-four hours around the clock. Here, in Georgetown, Killadreenan, and any- place you decide to hang your sheepskin. You'll be a moving target for a hundred paid assassins lying in wait—"

"Did David tell you—" Having exploded furiously, Whip stopped abruptly, aware David would have not told Tina any of the plot Jamila had revealed. He felt foolish.

"Did David tell me what?" Picking up on his *faux pas*, she gave his words sharp and speculative consideration. What could David tell her that would set Whip off like this? How it happened, she couldn't explain. The thought of Jamila sprang to mind. Taking little time to ponder this, and recollecting what her father had confided before his death, gave rise to several womanly conspiracies that refused to cease whirling around in her head.

"I haven't abandoned all thoughts of, uh, Jamila what's-her-name. Oh, yeah, Jaqualine Devon, too. Just because I haven't brought up the subject—" She fixed her eyes on the bright fires igniting on the hearth. "I know David is keeping her hidden at the ranch in Vegas. Very little escapes me."

"So I understand from what went on in—what was that room called? S.S. 1144?" Whip was unusually fang-toothed at the moment.

Tina's face, drawn tightly, flushed with crimson. They regarded each other in a splintered silence. Whip thought,

She'll never forgive me. It will never be the same between us.

Tina was also buried in thought. Now, added to her weariness and anxiety was an enormous pain and withdrawal from Whip, and a deep regret that something precious had just been shattered, possibly beyond hope of repair.

"S.S. 1144 was something that had to be done. I merely did what was necessary to cure the evil," she said simply. What stirred in her imagination were her father's words concerning Prince Ali Mohammed, for truly in these brief moments she clearly saw the beginning of a plan to lure Whip by using Jamila as bait. It wasn't the correct plan, but Tina, engaged in subjective thinking, was allowing her imagination to soar, the very thing her father had attempted to discourage.

"Perhaps it's best I leave. I suddenly feel unwelcome here." She moved towards the door.

Whip reached out for her hand and drew her towards him.

"I didn't mean it, Tina. It's the spoiled brat in me talking. Once in a while he comes back and I have to shake him into taking a back seat. Come, let's sit down by the fire and start all over again."

She fell heavily onto the sofa beside him, curling her legs under her, unsure of what she should say. "You will be careful, won't you? I mean in everything you do. Suddenly I'm afraid for you—for us." She felt terribly alienated. Nothing functioned right; not her heart or her mind. It was as if everything that meant anything had suddenly stopped.

"Whip?" She prodded again. "You will be careful—"

"She's right, you know. You should be more careful."

Tina and Whip, abruptly startled, turned sharply to stare at the intruder, sighing with relief at the sight of David Erice.

"Didn't mean to eavesdrop, Senator. You oughta keep your doors locked. I could've been anybody." He removed his topcoat.

Tina jumped off the sofa, flew into his arms and lavished kisses on him. "Look at you! Whip—come take a look. He's had all the scars removed from his face. When did this happen?" she asked David excitedly, viewing him from different angles. "You look so much like Benne now, it's even scary."

"Tell you all about it later," he said shaking hands with

Whip. "Tina, will you go home? It's your mother—I mean our mother. She's taken a turn for the worse. Maria Rossi called me and I flew here to get you."

Tina stared at him quietly.

"It seems she's lost the will to live."

"I'll pack my things. Will you call the airport and book a flight? You can drive my car back." She took the stairs two at a time.

Whip made the call, hung up and called his pilot to get the jet ready. "It's too late for a commercial flight, I'll have my man fly Tina home," he told David, pouring two Chivas on the rocks for them. Whip plunked himself down on the sofa and handed a drink to David. He stretched out comfortably.

"I hope it isn't serious," he said. "About Christina, I mean."

David shrugged, a concerned expression fixed on his face.

Whip tossed down the scotch. "How is, uh, the princess doing?"

"Slow—slower than the doc had hoped. I suppose it just takes time. They graphed out the photographer of the Israeli fighter to the quarter inch and taking each section and blowing it up they've tested her reaction. They've even tried sodium amatyl—pentothal—nothing of enormous consequence to report yet. In her rare off moments, she's actually quite charming. We've learned a great deal about her background—"

"How much longer before she's actually deprogrammed?"

"Why? What's the rush? She can't hurt anybody where she is. She's under constant guard."

"I've a few things in the fire that need tending to. The possibility of keeping Jamila on tap for future negotiations with the prince are beginning to look better each day in view of the botched-up attempts at peace in the Middle East. Prince Ali Mohammed's power as lead spokesman for the coalition of Arab nations in opposition to Sadat's stand in the entente is becoming formidable. There's so much, Dave, so very much happening—"

David turned from the fire where he had warmed himself and approached Whip, taking a seat facing him, and sipped his scotch. "Tell me, Senator, are the rumors true?"

Tina hadn't meant to eavesdrop. She had quickly donned jeans, sweater, scarfed her hair and hastily thrown things into a bag and was coming down the steps when David's next words, reverberating through the hall and bouncing off the walls to pierce her consciousness, turned her to ice. She grabbed the bannister to steady herself.

"Those in the know say you're laying the foundation for the presidency with this senate committee probe. Is that it?"

In the study, Whip's intent eyes were fixed on David.

"Tina and Amy would become basket cases overnight, if the rumors are true."

Running his fingers through his tousled hair, Whip bit his lips contemplatively. His silence to David was an indictment. David, leaning forward in his chair on one elbow, drew his own conclusions.

In a tone of voice bordering slick political apology Whip muttered, "I've made no such plans."

"Let me put it another way. Will you run for the presidency, Whip, in the coming elections?" insisted David gently.

Whip, staring at David and hardly seeing him, seemed to be miles away; his ears felt congested and his vision hazy. He'd heard David speak but hadn't assimilated much due to the unnatural panic spreading at the pit of his stomach.

Neither of the two men saw Tina standing at the threshold, a bit in the shadows, almost as if she didn't want to be seen.

"You're accustomed to ponderous responsibilities as well as an overwhelming sense of power, Senator. Exactly the kind a man in the White House must deal with. Your enemies know you to be chilling, despicable, yet a highly principled man who can't be bought. Unpredictable events exploding all around you have succeeded in strengthening your resolve." David continued despite the glowering looks he received from Whip. "You've been criticized, God knows how much. Your highhanded tactics in the aftermath of tremendous pressures have left much to be desired."

Tina retreated further into the shadows and sat down at the bottom steps of the staircase, shaking because she dreaded the outcome yet desperately needing to hear Whip's thinking.

David's voice rambled amiably. "—But, you've never been accused of panicking under the gun or reacting in fear or blind desperation. Pragmatism is your forte, Whip. I know, because I've been watching you carefully for a long time."

In the study Whip stared at Tina's brother as if he couldn't be done wondering at him, curiously interested in knowing where he was coming from.

"I've seen your assessment of frenzied and tempestuous acts emerge under a tight and logical framework of cause and effect . . ."

"Jezus Christ! What the hell is all this supposed to mean? Talk straight, man. If I didn't know better I'd swear you were priming me for the very thing I said I wouldn't do."

"You *want* to be president, don't you?"

"No!" Whip sprang to his feet, gesturing with disorganized abandon. His face screwed up in a frown. He waved David off, then paused to stare at him intently.

It seemed a natural break for Whip to sidle to the glass sliding doors and peer out into the darkness. The wall separating the terrace from his neighbor's was windswept and rainy. He turned on the patio lights and saw the first snow fall, turning the water puddles into pockets of white snow that slowly thickened into a film of iridescent crystals. Whip was very tired.

"If you're considering it, Senator, I want you to know you have my full support. The Erice support, that is."

David's words tunneling at him from across the room stunned Whip. He pivoted on one foot; their eyes met. Whip seemed baffled.

"You tell me that despite everything else you've said?" David nodded. "Despite what happened to Ted? Or the dangers that would automatically be heaped upon us?" Whip was flabbergasted.

"You've often said fate is unreliable. She can be quite dependable if you read her early in life," insisted David.

"You say that when your life has been fraught with inconsistencies?"

"Hey, I've only recently learned to read the signs. All my life I've known something wasn't the way it should be—"

Whip's rebuttal splintered in midair when he sensed the need in David to talk.

"As a child it seemed I was living a life that was propelled in strange directions, invariably drawn to an unknown destiny with no permanence. Here I am—how many years later?—as testimony to those earlier feelings. You, Senator, were lucky. Raised to know who you were and where you were headed you set your sights on a destination long ago. Now, because you've suffered temporary

425

defeat by the forces of destiny, you're in limbo and you've stopped spiraling towards that goal. You're confused because you've misread your fate. If you are destined for the White House, you'll wind up there no matter what detours you take or how many in your path attempt to divert you."

"You and Tina are getting to sound more like Val with each passing day," confided Whip.

David shrugged and watched Whip pour two steaming cups of coffee from a percolator on a sideboard. "He was my father. I wish I had truly known him. He was a very special man—a very, very special man. I'd have given one of my balls to have known Benne," he said wistfully. "He was the lucky one, to have been endowed with Val's teachings."

"Not so lucky. He's dead," Whip stated flatly, handing David a cup of coffee and sipping his gingerly. "Might as well hear it from the horse's mouth, kid. I've too many enemies to be considered prime material for the presidency. And that, my Las Vegas entrepreneur, is the end of that."

Tina stood in the partial shadows of the hall, her hands clenched tightly until her nails dug into her palms.

"Not if you seal the IAGO file," David said tentatively.

Whip turned livid. "I don't believe you said that."

"Take a lesson from Val," continued David, undaunted. "When he became aware the stakes were higher than he could handle, he withdrew from the arena, reconnoitered and planned his strategy accordingly. It didn't make Val gutless or afraid. He simply maintained a low profile while deciding the next play. He withdrew from the spotlight, put his affairs in order and in so doing insured his family against future attacks. A brilliant tactician, Val had the sense not to tempt fate."

"What the hell's going on?" Whip exploded. "First a tonguelashing from Tina, now you? Is the family ganging up on me?"

"Hell, man! We don't want anything to happen to you!"

"You're saying I should close my eyes to all that's happened?"

"No. Not that. But, *after* you've become president . . . Think of the powers at your disposal. You can cut the cancer of IAGO out. I don't have to tell you how, senator."

Whip exclaimed ruefully. "You know how many men

426

have tried to doublecross IAGO and what happened to them?"

Tina's heart sank. How could she win when the fates had joined against her? David was learning from Jerry the very things Val had asked her to keep in abeyance. Perhaps not everything, she thought, but it stood to reason Jerry knew the intimate details of Val's operations and how he had handled matters in the past. As Val's *consigliere* and legal brains, Jerry had on occasion been Val's right arm. Voices coming at her brought her back to the moment.

"I prescribe a trip for you, Whip," said David with warmth. "A trip. A rest. A journey to foreign soil. Gain a new perspective. Meanwhile table the senate probe or drop it, dismiss the committee. Use any excuse you consider necessary. Just forget IAGO for the time being. Meanwhile Jerry and I will start winding things up. On your return we'll rap and outline a campaign for you. After all you are the best, Senator. Remember what you did for Ted's campaign . . ." David grinned. Whip's face was without expression. "Look, I know you're out to get every last mother's son who's been on the fat take from IAGO. Whaddya say we do it up right? From the president's podium, miracles can happen."

Whip smiled grimly. "Say what you will about destiny, but I find it dammed unreliable. For instance," insisted Whip, "I never in a million years would have believed we'd have this talk tonight—or at any other time."

Tina had heard enough. Wearing the inner tattoes of fear and insecurity within her mental framework well concealed, she entered the room.

"Ah, here she is." David moved towards her. She kissed her brother and offered her cheek to Whip, numb and devoid of feeling. Whip tried to read her expressionless face, wondering how much she'd heard. He explained that his pilot was taking her to Long Island as they moved towards the front door.

"Signora, avete fame? Desiderate un aperitivo?" The soft-spoken Italian stewardess intruded upon Tina's thoughts. "Are you hungry? Would you like a drink?"

"Si, per piacere, portatemi una lista."

The stewardess left to bring Tina a menu.

The jet soared through the darkness high above the clouds as its passengers dined in splendor; some watched the movie, some chatted over drinks, others read. Tina reopened *Zanzara* to her place in the book and tried to concentrate on the story. She kept turning pages, retaining nothing. She went back a few pages and reread them. Whip's face kept forming on each page, his voice echoed in her ears. Before tears welled up in her eyes she closed the book, turned off the overhead light, and closed her eyes tightly.

Following her mother's death, Tina remained alone in the mansion facing many decisions. Deep within her she knew it was graduation time—time to go forward and not look back. The transition shouldn't be difficult, she told herself, and soon learned the sad truth; it posed the most difficult problems she'd ever encountered. So, when Whip called her a week before Christmas she had agreed to fly with him to Aspen. Part of her prayed desperately that she could convince Whip to change his mind.

Harassed by the press in Aspen, they were forced to flee. Tina, in desperation, suggested they fly to their mountain retreat in Lake Tahoe. She called David, asking him to make the necessary preparations for them.

They arrived four hours behind schedule, cold, hungry, tired, exasperated by the storms and delays, yet as excited as school kids hiding from a truant officer as they skilfully evaded newshounds in Reno who'd been tipped off in advance by the disgruntled ones left behind in Aspen.

Eggnog, hot brandy, the scent of juicy steaks barbecuing on the indoor grill as they explored the great house with its vaulted ceilings made them forgo the momentary excitement of taking a bath in the hot tub at one end of the master bedroom. Immediately following supper . . .

Who could ask for anything more? thought Tina, as they ate before an intimate fire. She was desperately aware that the eleventh hour was approaching. This was her last chance; could she convince Whip to turn from politics? Was she fighting a losing battle?

Gold help me. Only You can make this the merriest of Christmases.

That night their love was sweet, tender, fulfilling and promising. Neither marred the memory by dealing with matters of consequence.

Three blissful, memorable days passed. *Heaven couldn't be as perfect*, thought Tina. But, on the fourth day . . .

It was in the hour before dawn that the prevailing winter storm, having reached its zenith, was on the wane. The bellowing winds, bending snowladened branches of Ponderosa pines mercilessly, shaking storm windows, rattling the rafters, were abating. Tina awakened, tears streaming down her cheeks. Her thoughts had been taken up with the deaths of her parents, the uncertainties of her future with Whip or without him and a resolution to the nerveracking predicament.

Important to Tina's sanity was to confront Whip and ask him his intentions outright. It was too late to sweep it all under the rug in hope that it wouldn't happen. Whip's reluctance to bring the situation to a head and her own ambivalence in the matter was detrimental to them both. No more pacing, no more marking time. She promised herself to get the problem resolved once and for all.

Shortly after breakfast, the storm subsided. The sun, like a breath of spring, pierced the clouds, spreading a translucence of pale crystalline pastels on the winter mantle of snow. Whip wanted to go for a drive in the jeep, insisting they'd been cooped up too long. After careening over the snow, jostled about for half an hour in the vehicle, Whip pulled up abruptly at the edge of a steep, snow-covered ravine. Tina shoved her snow goggles up on her forehead under her blue fox parka and peered about at the tranquil panorama, so still she could hear her heart beating.

A shaft of bright light lanced sharply through purple shadows of a yawning canyon, baring a blanket of snow so vast and blinding it swiftly and painfully contracted the irises of her eyes. Hastily pulling the fur parka close to her face to ward off the icy blast of the chilling wind, she let the goggles slip back into place shielding her eyes. Both had dressed warmly but neither Whip nor Tina were prepared for the below-zero temperature when the sun hid behind the gathering of new storm clouds on the horizon.

Glancing apprehensively at the sky Whip started up the motor and backtracked, at times careening sideways over the rapidly forming surface of crystal hardness where chipmunks, foxes and rabbits skirted about without leaving tracks. They both felt an intense desire to return to the warmth of an invigorating fire.

"Look!" shouted Whip. "Over there!"

Tina's eyes came to rest on a spectacular sight. A grand old stag stood majestically on a slight rise overlooking the snow-covered crags, an omnipotent patriarch overseeing his domain. In that instant, she was so reminded of her father that involuntary tears escaped her eyes.

Whip squeezed her gloved hand hard. "You promised, no more tears." They were approaching the edge of the property. "On the brighter side, Val and your mother were lucky to have a marriage where everything worked."

"I know. But she couldn't live without him. That tells me something. Marriage should keep the fire of two lives burning at all times, not one alone. Who was it that said, you can give each other your bread, but don't eat from one loaf alone?"

Whip, preoccupied with thought, didn't answer. The sun, hiding behind clumps of dismal gray clouds and mist, cast dark shadows on the dun-colored snow creating a somber, reflective mood between them. By the time they reached the house Tina felt a wedge of indefinable desperation forcing them further apart. Once as close as two human beings could be, they no longer seemed able to confide in one another as in the past.

How difficult it must be for him, she thought, watching Whip refill her coffee cup. She'd seen evidence of his melting resolve in the wake of popular demand and pressures brought to bear from the close confidants urging him to run for the presidency in the next election. Whip, complacently and with good humor, had refused the challenge repeatedly, no matter how tightly the bit was maneuvered. She began to realize what her father meant when he insisted Whip's future was inevitable. She watched the formation of an embryo, just as the development of a picture from a negative takes place in hypo solution, as the inner scaffold of growing optimism and belief infused him with the needed confidence to make his bid for the highest office in the land. This recognition and awareness both frightened and oddly enough strengthened her fortitude and courage.

Tina set down the coffee and walked over to him where he stood looking into the flames of the fire. She tugged on his arm. He turned to her questioningly. Reaching up she pulled his head down to meet hers and kissed his coffee-flavored lips lingeringly. He backed away slightly.

"What's that for?"

"Do I need a reason to kiss you?"

"Hell no." He scooped her into his arms ardently. "Mmm. Give me some more."

Tina laughed. "Careful, Senator, I might seduce you here and now."

"If you think I'm considering a marshmallow roast—"

They both laughed. She pulled him towards the large

430

overstuffed chairs before the fire and sat down very close to him.

"Do you miss Las Vegas? Once you wouldn't leave the place."

Tina sighed. "When I'm with you I miss nothing."

"Why not?"

"Why not? Because I'm content in your company."

"Despite what's happened?"

Tina shrugged and slipped off her fur lined boots. "I'm taking one day at a time. Right now the moment is about to make my day perfect."

"And if something happened to mar that perfection?"

Here it comes. God give me strength. Quietly she said, "Nothing you can do will mar that perfection."

"Hmmm," he muttered. "If something happened to end our relationship—what will you do?"

Tina didn't reply. Instead she put a stack of carefully selected records on the turntable. She retrieved a bottle of Mumms from the refrigerator and sauntered back into the living room.

"I'm going to soak in a hot tub until I warm up. Join me, Whip."

A half hour later the mood had altered considerably. They were relaxing in the laminated wooden tub, sipping the champagne. Between hot kisses and loving embraces the blood in their veins warmed up enough for them to feel alive.

Dressed warmly in thick woolly robes they roamed about the house again, looking at ways to improve upon what both agreed was an exceptional job of decorating. Massive earth-colored macramé hangings, covering an entire wall in some instances, were woven and coiled in abstract designs incorporating a wide variety of fetishes; bird feathers, brass rings, wooden images, figurines and shells. An amazing collection of fine animal skins and Indian artifacts graced the walls. Colombian art works were artfully displayed on built-in wall shelves. A towering fourteen-foot totem pole in the foyer surrounded by Boston fern varieties, croton for color and sturdy corn plants under growlights, made a dramatic entry. They ended up back at the fireplace listening dreamily and lazily to the random mood music.

An hour later they were in bed together. Whip's arms were wrapped tightly about her. She felt shivers run through her as his lips took little playful nips of her ears, lips, cheeks and, working his way down, fairly devouring

431

her breasts. It was always like this, thought Tina. He'd be miles away from her for weeks and she never really knew the extent of his aching for her until they were together. He wasn't vocal about his love except on occasion when the need for her intensified. Once she was in his arms, she felt the deep need and desire for her in him. She aroused him more than any other woman could, he'd told her until it was etched in her consciousness.

"Love me, Tina. Love me forever as you love me now," he whispered fervently between honeyed kisses, voluntary and involuntary thrusts, strokes of pleasure and a deeply felt anguish.

Her strong yet gentle hands caressed his neck and shoulders, rubbing, kneading, feeling, trying to erase the tension she felt knotted under his hot skin. The intensity of their lovemaking became eager, desperate and frenetic as each tried to fill the other's needs. Tina couldn't bear to let him go; she'd relived a life of longing for him in these hours spent with him. She desperately attempted to swim through tangled memories, past the heat of desire nudging aside the insidious thoughts primed in her by her father before he died.

They were terribly in love, yet behind their love was lurking an unknown, unnamed terror which both refused to seek out, face or discuss. Sated sexually they lay close together, plagued by thoughts.

Whip propped up a pillow under his arm, raising himself on one elbow, and looked down on her. His fingers traced the contour of her cheekbone, chin, forehead and nose. "You aren't really complicated, you know. Nor temperamental. Nothing about you is shrewd, cold, calculating or tyrannical."

Tina cracked open one eye, then the other. A burst of laughter exploded from her lips. "You just described Tina Erice as a young, naive woman *before* she married Renzo." Sobering instantly she pulled a pillow under her breasts, turning on her tummy to face him. "You'd better take another look," she said. "You really don't know me. I *am* complicated. I *am* temperamental and I *can* be cold, shrewd, tyrannical."

He wrapped his arms about her soft, quivering flesh and bones, feeling her arms embrace him and cling to him as if her life depended on it. He stroked her hair off her forehead, muttering, "Shhhhhhhh, don't talk. Let's just feel —feel each other as we did the first time we found each other, when time had little meaning for us. In some odd and indefinable way you became the essence of all women, everything I want in the woman I planned to spend my life with."

Tina stiffened. About to pull away from him, she was unable to avoid the onslaught of his passionate kisses. After a moment she gave up trying and yielded to him wholly. Earlier she had felt tired, but she would not allow herself to sleep. *Put on blinders, if you must. But feel, feel, feel, Tina. Do as Whip does—live only in the moment and to hell with tomorrow . . .*

Catapulted to full arousal, in the midst of this passion came their audible gasps and low gurglings from deep in their throats, sounds of unrestrained lovers.

If once they had seen shooting stars whirling around inside their heads, tonight they saw electrifying comets of whirlwind force. If once they had waded amid the expanding horizons within their mental peripheries, tonight they swam willingly to the very edge of the swollen, pulsating universe and gazed tremblingly upon the face of God. . . . Slowly, indefinably, in exquisite perfection they spiralled back to earth locked into a stillness in which they were mentally and physically spent.

Whip could feel life returning to him, the tingling sensation coursing through him as his blood began its charted journey through his veins and arteries. Reality came back and in this reality he felt replete. Tina lay heavy on the crook of his arm, motionless. He managed to disengage himself without disturbing her. On his feet, with a comforter wrapped about his nudity, he felt chilled despite the warmth permeating the room from the fire on the hearth. His brooding thoughts were rapidly germinating.

He strolled in bare feet to the large glass door and stood for a time gazing at the snow-covered deck in the hazy glow of illumination from the exterior spotlights; what appeared to be shadowy apparitions in the night, swaying, eerie silhouettes caused by the falling snow and tree branches shuddering in the wind, yawned into grotesque designs and became reminders that he could procrastinate no longer. He must tell Tina. He had to be fair. There was no other way.

It was true. Since his trip to Europe when he had set his sights on a particular goal, he had permitted himself to be influenced by the past; the death threats and assassination attempts on his own life had been deterrents. A pattern had formed, and it was clear in his mind that the death threats intensified when, by basking in the spotlights of attention, he became too visible. This awareness both angered and inhibited him, followed by an introspection into his cowardice, if it was cowardice, that made him overly cautious, unwilling to become a pawn to an unworthy cause. He'd never considered himself a coward; the thought of fear was incompatible with his nature. Yet he could not live under the threat of constant death and not take it seriously. Not any more. The time had come to remove the thought from his consciousness, uproot the very word death and go forth to conquer or be conquered himself. It was that simple. Delete the word assassination from his vocabulary, erase the thought of death.

Whip inhaled a deep breath, and in that moment of decision knew there was no other way but to do what he must. He padded back along the thick llama-skin carpeting, sinking into its furry softness until he stood at the bed staring down at her sleeping form.

"Tina . . ."

"Hummm?" she muttered sleepily.

"What would you say if I tell you I intend to—"

Quick as a bolt of lightning, as if she'd been programmed in this response electronically, she sat up and blinked hard, allowing her eyes to adjust in the darkness. A cold sweat beginning at her toes worked itself upward until she began to shiver. She moved on her knees closer to him, and placing her slender hand over his lips silenced him. Inching slightly away from him, she searched his eyes.

"The rumors aren't true. Tell me you won't run. You can't. Oh, Whip, I won't let you." She didn't cry. Tears didn't flow as they might have in the past. Her good breeding precluded maudlin histrionics. However, she was unable to disguise the changes already taking place in her as a slow steadying force, quieting her, created an indomitable newborn force. Everything she'd dreaded, prayed against, even worked against since the death of her father was slowly coming into place. The intangibles were indescribable. An inner power, the foundation of which was laid at a time when she was unaware, took hold of her to steady her.

Studying her in the illumination from the fire, watching these intangible changes occurring in her, he was unable to assess what it was he felt. A complication of thoughts vied for first place in his mind. *You're stalling, Whip. Tell her. Make her come to terms with the reality. You can do it—if you want.*

A wild roaring wind fairly shook the rafters, agitating

the storm windows. Its echoing, cavernous howling continued to belch and sway for several long moments, bringing concern to their eyes. They ran to peer through the large bay window, watching the snowfall thicken in the storm. Whip removed the comforter from around his body and rewrapped it around the two of them bringing her closer to him. All this reminded him of their first love affair when a winter storm kept them snowbound for a week. He tightened his hold on her, and tried to swallow the thickness in his throat.

"I'm tossing my hat into the presidential ring, Tina," he finally said, straight out.

Tina pulled slightly away from him, and managed to slip out of his embrace. She sprinted for the closet and wrapped herself in a thick robe. He hadn't asked her. He told her in a simple statement. He wanted no opinion, no argument, no rebuttal, just her approval. Trembling she tightened the belt around her waist and ambled into the dressing room area where she plugged in an electric percolator filled with coffee. Returning to the bedroom she found Whip seated before the window, the drapes pulled back, staring at the falling snow that was rapidly working itself into a fullblown blizzard. She sat down heavily on the bed, defeated.

He was thinking in all his life he'd never met or loved anyone like Tina. Now it was about to end. Here with her, life was simple, uncomplicated, not in the least demanding. Something had happened to Whip in those three days he spent with Val Erice on Long Island.

He'd learned a great deal. First and foremost, he was a man of destiny. Val knew it all along. Even Ted had known it. Why, then, had he been the last to know? Yes, the very last to become aware of it. Goddammit! *Even Tina knows it,* he thought as he sat staring out into the flurry of snow into infinity. He had sensed it; now, he knew it for certain. David knew and made him face what had been germinating in his soul for so long. A man of destiny . . . *A man of destiny!*

Standing in the shadows behind him, off to one side, Tina watched him as a tingling numbness pervaded her body. In these moments Tina considered the tragedies that had befallen both the Erice and Shiverton families. Unable to equate the senseless and tragic deaths she wrung her hands in frustration and returned to the dressing room for the coffee, torturing herself with self-condemnation. How could she continue to keep the secrets locked up in her

435

breast? Why had she promised her father? She was inwardly shattered, bewildered and wild-eyed as she sank against the door. She couldn't let Whip see the agony she felt.

Whip's thoughts increased his wretchedness. He arose from the chair at last and approached the fireplace to toss two more logs into the fire. He stood leaning one arm onto the mantel watching the new logs catch fire until the snapping, popping, crackling sounds abated. He hardly heard Tina reenter the room carrying a tray with coffee. They both remained silent.

The darkness was lessened by the soft radiance of light coming from the fire. Outside the howling wind fiercely competed with the inner monologue of thoughts sprinting across their minds.

"I'd make one helluva president, Tina," he said quietly.

"I know. I've always known."

"Then you know what it means." He turned to her, half hoping.

She nodded, her eyes intent on the fire. "An American president must have a wife. You must have planned for this. Have you decided who?"

"I thought you understood. I want to marry you." His heart stood still as he searched her fire-lit features. "Tina, look at me. Listen to my heart."

"The daughter of Val Erice could never marry an American president." Her eyes on the fire remained steadfast, intent on the misty apparitions. For an instant she swore she saw the double-headed griffin loom before her in the spitting fire. She closed her eyes abruptly.

"You can't mean that! Look, those things can be taken care of easily. A PR firm can gloss over—"

"—the gory details? Why? Deny my heritage—my father—my family?" She shook her head. "Not Tina, not me. I am what and who I am and no one—*nothing,* can alter that fact." She laughed ironically and turning to him, searched his eyes. "The opposition would have a field day with the headlines. 'Whip Shiverton's wife revealed to have former Mafia connections!' No, my love. That's not the dowry Tina Erice wants to give her husband. No. Not me."

Her words erected a barrier of concern in his mind as he stared broodingly into the fire. Something could be worked out, he thought.

His profile formed harsh planes in the fire's reflection.

Watching him she knew she must relinquish him and her love for him. He was forever lost to her, the battle was over.

"If a bachelor can be the governor in California it's time we give it a try in Washington," Whip said half-heartedly.

"What the world needs now is love, sweet love . . ."

The music of Burt Bacharach filled the room hitting them both simultaneously. How many times had they made love to those sweet refrains? Tina placed her coffee cup down on the nearby table. *What the world needs now is courage for the future,* she thought. *There's been too much love.*

Whip's jet picked them up the next day, transporting them to Washington in a strained silence. At the Georgetown townhouse, she repacked and prepared to drive the Ferrari to Long Island. Whip's aides had cornered him, waiting for his approval on the new press releases the moment he broke the news of his intentions to them. It was to Tina a Christmas present she'd never forget.

Observing their infectious excitement pervade Whip's spirit, she knew her father had been right. Whip was to be a man of destiny. Unable to catch his attention, she slipped quietly out the door, boarded the Ferrari and sped off desperately trying to quell the empty feeling rattling about inside her.

Goodbye, my dearest Whip. May God protect you and watch over you for all eternity . . .

Tina snapped on the car's stereo, angry at the tears welling inside her.

My heart cries for you, sighs for you, dies for you . . .

"Dammit! Dammit! Dammit!" she muttered, brushing aside the tears and cursing the sentimental oldies on the radio. Well, she'd fix that soon enough. She whirled the radio dial listening to the blurrrps and bleeeps until she tuned in on something less painful.

"It is time to awaken, *signora*. We shall be arriving at Da Vinci Airport."

Tina, awakened by the gentle touch on her shoulder, smiled sleepily at the stewardess. She collected herself, thinking how she, too, had changed of late. In the past, while in the throes of love, where she once desired to be engulfed and enfolded in Whip's arms by his love, to share his hopes and fears, his wildest ambitions and listen to his most private dreams and fantasies, in their parting hours Tina hadn't experienced the totality she normally felt with him.

Their final separation had not been accompanied with a pathetic and overwhelming desire for self-annihilation as she had envisioned. The end of her life was not in sight. What, she asked herself, did that awareness make her? How was she able to turn her feelings off and on like a hot water tap? Why had this change manifested in her? Was it a subtle way of letting her know the metamorphosis had occurred? Had she become the woman her father expected she would? Detached, clear-sighted, self-assured, strong with an unquestionable self-identification like the huntress, Diana?

Before making this trip she had managed to cram a great deal of valuable information into her head. She'd spent a full day at the New York library searching the files of newspaper clippings in the microfilm library after a computer located all the items ever written about Prince Ali Mohammed Izmur. She had the most salient and revealing information photocopied and took it home to peruse.

In addition to this information Tina compressed more obtained in a brief period of time spent with Don Patruccio and two other ageing and retired dons who no longer participated in business. Discussions with these Mafiosi were not what she'd hoped to achieve, but she hadn't expected much, not even their blessings which she did receive and thanked them for before departing.

The 747 lurched as its power began to diminish in its approach to the Eternal City's airport. Red blinking lights over the bulkhead warned passengers to buckle their seatbelts and extinguish their cigarettes.

Tina glanced out the plane's window at the sprawling mixture of antiquity dotted here and there with modern monoliths, just as dawn peered over the horizon. A curious apprehension, elation and melancholy settled in her, coupled with a mixture of fear and bravado. Undaunted, she forged ahead, ready to step on the threshold of the new life awaiting her. The mental separation had come about; now to insure the emotional dissolution with Whip Shiverton.

CHAPTER THIRTY-THREE

Killadreenan Downs

Whip stood at the rear terrace of the Virginia farm house staring at the verdant carpet of lush farmland; his eyes sweeping over knoll and glade that seemed to stretch to infinity. Satin-coated young thoroughbred horses prancing about playfully in the bright sunlight with arched tails, nuzzling contentedly under overhanging boughs of the giant pepper trees, brought on a sudden nostalgia; he missed Tina desperately.

He couldn't bear the thought of Tina's hurt expression when he finally revealed his political aspirations; he knew she wanted him to shout, *To hell with the presidency! To hell with politics, I want you!* A part of Whip wanted and needed her desperately; a larger part craved the presidency. In recent days he felt this strongly. After all he'd been programmed to become President of the United States; all his life seemed concentrated towards this goal. Built-in mechanisms allowed him to adjust to circumstances with minimum emotional damage. He was a survivor; he did what survivors do best—survive.

Presently he brooded. News that Tina was en route to Rome to visit Valerie had shaken him. He conceded it was no spur of the moment decision and deliberated why Tina chose to renew her acquaintance with Valerie, since a relationship between them in the past had been nonexistent. Tina had paid little heed to Valerie, hardly mentioning her. Now this sudden concern over her welfare was puzzling. Women! Would he ever understand them?

He shut his eyes against the outer panorama of tranquality and the inner turmoil twisting his guts and returned to the house where mayhem was about to erupt. Inside they were all waiting for him: campaign advisers, speech writers, election committee finance people, well-wishers and hangers-on who'd recently jumped on the Shiverton bandwagon; and here he was acting like a love sick pup. Putting himself in order, and drawing a veil over his memory, he moved through the house in the direction of the den where a hum of lively conversation greeted him.

Dressed casually in old Levis, a sweatshirt and tennis shoes, he'd considered lazing about before the onslaught of tight schedules caught up with him.

With committees gearing to work their butts off to get him elected, they had all converged on him for the weekend. The least he could do was participate in their activities. The break with Tina had precipitated a response he'd kept bottled up since Ted's death. What he needed and desperately yearned for was a wild, invigorating horseback ride galloping through the countryside with wind and sun at his back. He no longer could enjoy the simple act of communing with nature without a rash of bodyguards hovering over his shadow. Several near fatal accidents had marked him well; how could he embrace the simple life for which he yearned?

Screw it, Whip. Come off this self-indulgent jackass pity you're wallowing in. This is what you've wanted. You got it, so shape up!

The smoke-filled room was alive with laughter, concern, conjecture, even dissension. Spotting some of Ted's New Horizon men, Whip fixed a smile on his face and plowed into them, shaking hands, slapping shoulders, exchanging wisecracks.

Kevin O'Malley, once advisor to Ted, greeted Whip loudly, a sheaf of scrawled papers clutched in his hand. "We've got it figured, Whip, if you'll cooperate. No need for the opposition to pick up and crucify us on the one weak link that sticks out like a sore thumb—a bachelor president! What's happening on every front page of every newspaper in every city, town, village and one-horse stop? What's the most vital issue before our nation today? I'll tell you." He modulated his voice up one octave when he noticed every head turned his way. "It's oil! We need oil! The scarcity of it is plaguing us and you can bet the Arabs are gonna attempt to boycott the U.S. if every Arab faction isn't satisfied in the ill-fated peace talks." O'Malley had everyone's attention, but he hadn't lowered the boom yet.

"You don't see the answer, do you? Any of you? We'll handle the opposition. Meet the bastards head on. We can't let them force us into a defensive position. So what do we do, 'Mister President' and my fellow Shivertonites?

440

The answer is upstairs in one of your guest rooms. Whip will marry the Princess Jamila Izmur and thus form an alliance with the most powerful Arab emirate."

O'Malley's words exploded in the heads of his listeners like a bomb. Every head in the room turned to him, their glazed eyes computing rapidly, trying to ascertain whether O'Malley had lost his senses or hatched one of the shrewdest schemes in the history of American politics. Cigars and cigarettes hung from loose contemplative lips, long fragile ashes dangling precariously at their ends. Astonishment from the presidential candidate himself: a staccato burst of laughter from him accusing O'Malley of smoking Colombian gold.

O'Malley, too fired up to be shushed, waved his hands wildly before him, demanding in a loud, persuasive voice, "Hear me out. Think of the far-reaching effects of such an alliance. Think! Peace talks are down the toilet. Why? Because the fucking Arabs and Jews, like petulant school kids, can't get it into their fucking heads they're both sitting on fucking time bombs, ready to destroy the fucking world—that in a goddamn nuclear war no one comes up winners. So who sets the example of brotherly love? Our candidate for the presidency. The future prince of peace is gonna show them how it's done. He marries an Arab princess—who, incidentally, filed for American citizenship a year ago—and proceeds to bring Arab and Jew together by setting an example himself. . . . Well, whaddaya think?" O'Malley's teeth clamped tightly over an expensive Garcia Vega, puffing expansively as he scanned their reactions.

The room fell silent. It was a staggering concept. Then affirmations, negations, questions, conjectures and a variety of rebuttals from the men brought about a heated discussion; the pros and cons of this stunning, unprecedented move in American politics were candidly assessed and discussed as if neither Whip nor Jamila had a choice in the matter.

"Dammit, at least it will insure our receiving some goddamn oil!" argued O'Malley, listening to those who opposed the alliance. "You got any better ideas? Then come up with them!"

"Catholic and Arab marrying?" piped up one of the men. "I can just see old JHC sparring with Allah to see which religion will prevail in the Capitol."

"The Jews will interpret the Capitol dome to be a

441

Moslem mosque complete with minaret," said another.

Jack Payne, elevated from aide to head of the finance committee, drawled facetiously in his west Texas accent, "After your second term ends, if things don't work out, y'all can get a divorce, suh."

Whip's glowering eyes sent him reeling back into his protective cocoon. Shrugging imperceptibly as a weak grin transformed his face into that of a foolish schoolboy caught cheating, Payne nursed his Perrier water.

The mayhem abated into a reflective silence. Whip asked quietly, "When will her citizenship papers be finalized?" Some of his supporters couldn't believe Whip would entertain the idea, much less ask such a question. The cigar-smoking, finger-snapping, thigh-slapping O'Malley winked his merry eyes at Whip. They were on the same wave length—a good sign.

"Any time you want it to be finalized, with a little help from our friends," he retorted. Rubbing his hands together, he barked aloud, "Suppose we get down to brass tacks? We're gonna resurrect the New Horizons party and incorporate into the platform everything Ted didn't get a chance to finish."

The men clapped their hands.

"You take care of the courting and romancing, Mister President, we'll handle the technicalities. I can see the headlines: 'Whip Shiverton's Marriage to Middle Eastern Princess Forms Tight Alliance between U.S.A. and the Arab World.' " O'Malley guffawed loudly, pleased with his visionary tactics.

Watching the reactions of the men, their expressions changing to reflect the far-reaching effects of such an alliance, Kevin O'Brien and Tom Murphy sat in the back of the room troubled by what they heard. Murphy, wondering about David Erice's fast-paced love affair with Jamila, was unable to envision the smoothly paved road O'Malley described. O'Brien, plagued with similar thoughts, recalled the days following Ted's death had been no picnic for Whip; the days ahead promised no joy rides. What a damned shame Tina Erice had left so wide a berth for that cunning jaguar, preening and purring about the upstairs guest room. She should have fought a little harder for her man.

"When American voters go to the polls, they'll think Shiverton sacrificed his private life so they can have more gasoline."

442

"I've seen the princess," piped up one of the men lecherously. "I wouldn't call it a sacrifice. She's some dish."

Listening, Tom Murphy thought, *Wherever you are, Tina, girl, you better get on home and claim your man or you ain't gonna have him anymore.*

CHAPTER THIRTY-FOUR

A red carpet welcome far more impressive than the one she'd received five years before greeted her at the Villa Garibaldi. Then, she'd been a guest; now, she was the proprietress of this fine establishment, and a great deal more. The utterly charming Signore Monte Allegro had been with the Villa Garibaldi since Val purchased the property and, unlike some businessmen who occupied positions of trust with obvious efficiency geared at turning over a dollar, carried an air of genuine nobility and gentility that served him well with the more distinguished guests who made the Villa Garibaldi their home away from home.

"What an honor to welcome you back, signora," he said with old world elegance that at times seemed pretentious to Americans, but delighted Tina. Bowing low he kissed her hand and stood at attention awaiting her wishes.

Tina entered the sumptuous suite decorated in superb taste. On the wall behind an ornately carved desk hung an oil painting of her father she'd never seen. Pleased, she allowed her eyes to quickly scan the fireplace, low mahogany coffee tables with mother-of-pearl inlay, dark mahogany chairs, cushioned with brocaded fabrics and several fine paintings on the walls. Several ornate telephones stood on a communications console, with a telex, a tickertape machine and other impressive equipment.

"The pleasure, I assure you, is mine, Signore Allegro. This trip is long overdue. Tell me, were you able to handle my instructions with little trouble?"

His manner was one of total competence and efficiency. He nodded, an enchanting smile gracing his features. "They are gathered in the conference room and await your arrival. The moment you are ready we shall commence."

"Then," replied Tina, smiling back with equal charm, "let us commence at once."

444

From the moment she stepped across the threshold of the richly appointed conference room, every discerning, inquisitive and cautious dignitary present craned his neck to stare at Tina. She was grateful she had selected a fawn-colored Chanel suit with a cocoa silk blouse and fine Spanish leather boots to wear before this formidable consortium of redoubtable members of Italy's Mafia, including high ranking men in government. She was the picture of femininity without frills so as not to offend these masculine men in whom she detected a built-in antagonism for women, delicately layered with the respect accorded the late Valentino Erice.

If she shook in her boots or felt awkward in their presence she gave no outward indication; instead, as they passed before her introduced by Signore Allegro, she acted as if she'd been born to the responsibilities of this role. She smiled through the introductions.

Allegro's cool reserve in their presence helped sustain the mood for which Tina had hoped. Her assessment of Allegro, high as it was, soared even higher when he slipped her a card containing a seating chart of those guests who would remain after cocktails to attend the conference. She acknowledged the accommodating gesture with silent appreciation. Allegro leaned closer to her in an effort to assuage her apprehension.

"Do not be intimidated by them, Signora Erice. In recent years our thinking has been modified by the realities of our times. Our colleagues shall be persuaded to accept the reality of a woman seated at the helm of business enterprises, much as it goes against their grain."

He walked her to the edge of the room overlooking a brick patio overwhelmed by a profusion of cascading blood-red roses, filling the air with their rich sweet aroma. Allegro's deep resonant voice had a calming effect on her. "These are transitional times. Italy, with her share of economic tragedies, from the moment the oil crisis inflated our economy beyond endurance has not been the same. Changes occur daily, hourly, even by the minute. And those terrorists threatening the upper classes are not to be believed. No one is safe on the streets—but absolutely no one!" He gestured animatedly. "Italy is learning —shall I say, the terrorist approach? Having studied the results of the PLO who brought even the great United States of America to its knees when they demanded and got the release of their comrades from Israeli prisons, they now threaten us with the same tactics. Extortion! Kidnapping! What is the world coming to when a man cannot walk the streets of Rome in safety?" He gallantly plucked a choice red rose and handed it to her. Tina thanked him, pressing it to her nose, inhaling its fragrance and letting the velvety petals trail along her cheek.

"Your man in America, Signore Rizzuto, requests you be protected at all times during your stay here in Italy."

Checking a flare of annoyance Tina insisted it wouldn't be necessary since very few people knew of her presence here. Glancing at the others, gathered in clusters sipping wines and tasting the canapes, Tina caught them staring at her again, sizing her up. When she caught their eyes, they simply nodded without embarrassment as if it were a common thing to stare.

"Pray forgive what you might construe to be impertinence," said Allegro, holding up a hand to ward off further contest. "It is a matter of honor that I comply with Signore Rizzuto's request. Two young men have flown here from Palermo for this purpose. I promise they are discreet, very capable and nearly invisible. I shall with your permission summon them. They are the Volpe brothers, Giacomo and Tomasso."

She saw it to be an exercise in futility to explain that she desired no escorts. She had made no impression upon Allegro, none at all. Sensing her discomfort Allegro hastened to explain.

"Your position must be protected if only to add stature to your presence among these personages. It is to your credit that they be present at this meeting."

"I would have presumed the opposite to be true. Alone one displays indomitable courage—"

"No! You would display foolishness." He wagged a finger at her. "In our country, to be protected is a sign of power. Else you would be considered most unimportant."

Tina conceded. "Well, then, when in Rome—" She smiled tersely. "Summon these brothers—Volpe? They shall sit by the door."

"With your permission, Signora. They shall sit behind you, one at either side." He gestured to the two empty chairs behind the head chair at the conference table.

"Since you know the protocol, Signore Allegro, I leave it in your hands." She thanked him graciously.

The names on the seating chart read like an Italian Who's Who. She had no need to memorize their names, only to remember their faces and make certain they never

446

forgot her. Ministers of every branch of the government, well known and highly respected, were engaged in conversation. She recognized several industrialists, financiers and redoubtable politicians currently making headlines in Rome. These names were familiar because she'd seen them mentioned in Val's papers often enough.

As this consortium of power sipped their champagne delicately and nibbled with polite reservation at the lavish banquet of food, Tina noticed that on a nod from a distinguished, darkly tanned man in his forties, the room began to thin down. Twelve men remained before the enormous doors closed behind them.

At precisely this moment, Allegro escorted Tina to the head of the conference table where she removed from her pocket the double-headed griffin ring and slipped it onto her right index finger. She placed both hands on the table in clear sight of the others. The blood-red rose lay across her leather case.

A low hush prevailed. Audible gasps escaped their lips as they quickly gazed from the ring on Tina's finger to her face for some recognizable sign that no chicanery or trickery was being played on them. They found a disconcerting solemnity in her expression. To reinforce their befuddlement the Volpe brothers entered the room; both well-muscled, clean-cut, strapping men in their twenties with unreadable stony faces, taking their positions at either side behind Tina. Familiar bulges protruded under their ill-fitting jackets.

Managghia! This was no joke. In their wildest imaginations, the twelve men would not have believed what their eyes beheld on this day. Hiding their feelings behind expressionless masks with typical Sicilian arrogance, dark eyes burning into hers asking a thousand unspoken questions, they stood tentatively behind their designated chairs, unwilling to be seated.

One hard-eyed man was stoking an internal furnace of wrath. Tina glanced at her seating chart. The man was Don Liborio Ferraro. She raised her cool eyes to meet his.

"But how is this possible?" he asked.

Tina stood her ground. *"Per piachere, signori*—Please, gentlemen, will you be seated?"

Reluctantly they deigned to sit with her in what was to be a battle of wits, undaunting courage and powerful persuasion on Tina's part. To educate a mentality so steeped in tradition to the changing ways of a rapidly moving world was the issue being tested; the imperious male versus the stereotypical subservient female. The arena, clearly marked by invisible barriers, became electric.

On the one side sat the hostile, power-saturated Dons, firm in their refusal to bend a centuries-old custom. On the other side Tina sat regally, head held high in a self-assured posture of strength, unflinchingly gazing upon the room's occupants as a queen might upon her subjects from whom she demanded total obedience. Moments of silence ensued. Tina tingled with new sensations of an unknown power surging through her. In these moments, the tasting of such heady elixir was like nothing else she had ever experienced, short of orgasm. She was hooked, but didn't know it yet.

Don Vincenzo Gatto from Castellammare, a young man in his thirties, was first to trespass the invisible barrier. Flushed with quick recuperative powers from his earlier shock of seeing a woman at the helm, his lusty laughter tore through his throat as if he were infinitely pleased at this new development. The ruggedly handsome, craggy-faced, dapperly dressed construction czar stepped forward and with dramatic panache bowed graciously, kissing the ring on Tina's finger with traditional flourish.

Stepping alertly to one side, he glowered fiercely at the others until they, too, followed his action. Flushed with momentary victory and considerable relief, she mentally committed Don Vincenzo as an ally and reseated herself. The Dons moved back to their places, the most respected in the hierarchy sitting closest to Tina.

A few extended their sympathies to her on the death of her father, adding their highest respect for the man of great personage. She thanked them politely, opened her portfolio and commenced with the business at hand.

"In the true tradition of the Principessa Scarlatta," she began in a clear, well-modulated voice, "I intend to dispel your doubts that a woman has no business occupying this seat." The name, plus the fact that she spoke to them in Sicilian, stoked an instant affinity between them, for they all recalled the legendary folk heroine Mafiosa. For a time they bantered over the woman's exploits.

"There is nothing of earth-shattering importance to which I address myself today. The purpose of this meeting was to meet you and advise you who my father selected to carry on the power of the Brotherhood in America. If I achieve nothing more than impress you with the desperate need for unity among our people, I've accomplished much. Daily the world grows smaller. Communication is instantaneous. All human needs are becoming identical. Environmental problems plague us in matters of survival. In our expanding world of investments there is much to be considered.

"We cojointly have many investments in America as we do here in Italy and other nations. Many Sicilian Americans have made numerous investments in Italy and Sicily which we don't wish to jeopardize. For centuries the Brotherhood has been known for its cohesive strength, my friends. It was my father's desire, as well as mine, that this strength endure."

"Bravo! Bravo!" The men nodded approvingly. So far the daughter of Valentino Erice made sense.

The Dons sat back, lighting cigars and sipping their wine with more ease than they demonstrated earlier. Tina continued.

"For centuries the Brotherhood has fought off foreign oppression. During World War II you even assisted the allies against the tyranny of fascism in ways the world has yet to discover. You contributed to the peace of the world in your own inimitable way, I'm proud to say."

The Dons recollected those trying days that seemed only yesterday. That this woman was echoing their sentiments was not to be believed. They had always been a misunderstood people. This was their world—their own reality. No other nation understood Sicily's unique problem.

"There may come a day in the near future when this cohesion will again serve a purpose. Meanwhile, it is wise to be alert to any real changes occurring in business and among your business acquaintances. Certain crucial events taking place in Mediterranean waters have the capabilities of upsetting the world's economic balance. With the Middle Eastern conflict about to erupt on our doorsteps and conceivably cause the downfall of all mankind we must not remain indifferent or blind to the circumstances surrounding it."

Dr. Lorenzo Fabiano, a well-known lawyer in the Ministry of Finance, observed Tina critically. "What exactly do you ask of us, Signora?"

"First, I convey to you the last request of my father. He asked me to point out to you that the trend in sound investments are the Swiss franc and South African krugerrand. So that I am not repetitious, he said you will know exactly what is indicated and act accordingly."

They were a step ahead of Tina, jotting down her words. "Better than oil?" Don Vincenzo asked subtly.

"No." Tina smiled vaguely and made a gesture of futility. "Apart from oil. Let me state that our financial holdings in South America and Mexico will be greatly affected if the Arab-Israeli conflict is not resolved."

They spoke of investments, the scorching spiral of inflation gripping all nations, of failing economies and far-reaching corporate powers. Tina was quick to observe how soon they ignored the fact she was a woman when once immersed in subjects dear to their hearts and pursestrings: wealth and power.

"Which among you is well versed on the Arab-Israeli conflict?" Tina asked, searching their faces.

Behind her Giacomo and Tomasso sat like statues, motionless. Only their active eyes were telltale of their thoughts. *Imagine, a woman telling these preening peacocks the time of day! A woman! Will wonders never cease?*

The Dons barely flinched at the question she asked with an almost careless ease. Tina saw the slightest, most imperceptible looks pass between them. Her eyes darted towards one man: dark-skinned, slight of build, with finely chiseled features, a man whose skin had been exposed to a brash, scorching sun all his life. He leaned forward in his chair. His piercing black onyx eyes, more Moorish than Sicilian, lifted heavily to look into Tina's eyes. Earlier when Tina scanned the list prepared by Allegro she had noted one name that did not appear to belong: Don Ibrahim Spinoza.

"Is it within the realm of your knowledge to explain what is actually causing turmoil in the Middle Eastern nations, Don Ibrahim?" Tina asked him. "Peace settlements have been frustrated, conciliation seems hopeless. You understand, any investments made in those lands on the tail of peace would mean considerable profits, say to a colleague like Don Vincenzo in his construction business."

Don Ibrahim, pleased at the attention, shook his head and wagged a finger at her negatively. "With your permission, Signora, only long-eared fools would invest in the Middle East in these uncertain times. In those sunscorched lands, there rage cries of centuries-old revolution. Who would have willed such a catastrophe to happen, eh? Prior to 1948 the worlds of Arabs and Jews were exploding, but nothing so violent until Israel aggressively formed its state and expanded its borders at an alarming pace."

Don Ibrahim shook his head ruefully. "It's true, the Arabs, far less militant, less prepared than the Israelis, never expected such acts of aggression in their lands. They were a sorely confused people, irate, overwhelmed at their suffering at the hands of the iron-willed, dogmatic, tenacious Israelis who, in their efforts to protect what they took by force, remain intractable. We all ask, of what use is the United Nations, eh? Resolutions are passed. Resolutions are vetoed. Some, implemented, are not abided by. So, you ask, what will happen? What is taking place?"

Don Ibrahim Spinoza, an Italian Jew living and doing business in Italy and Switzerland, had little reason to side with one faction or another. Since World War II when Italy joined the Nazis as allies, he had renounced his religious beliefs and fled the terrors of the invading Nazis. He was a slave to no religious beliefs for in them he saw his own annihilation. This he could not accept and refused to believe he was put on earth to become a martyr to an inherited cause with which he, himself, felt no kinship. Where was it written that he should suffer the ills of a people he never knew? Lifting his wine glass to his thin lips with long sinewy fingers he stared reflectively into the burgundy liquid as if staring into a crystal ball that would reveal the future. His words came slowly and with perception.

"The Arabs complain, and with good reason. The Israelis are an audacious, outrageous people with over two thousand years of persecution built into their mentalities and are determined to avenge their ancestors if they must destroy the entire world in the process."

Tina studied Don Ibrahim through assessing and evaluating eyes. "What do you say of Egypt's attempts towards peace. Of its efforts to promote peace and stable relations with Israel?"

Don Ibrahim's eyes rolled speculatively, as he rubbed his fingers together significantly. "Egypt's economy is in a frightful state, hurting her painfully with each passing day. For enough American dollars she will agree to most anything. It is this stand that most of us fear. Any stand against the other Arab nations will brand Egypt's

451

leader as a traitor. Then, my dear, the world of the Middle East will surely explode in so many directions, the leftover pieces will not be recognizable—to anyone. America, who needs oil desperately, will certainly be the loser in any event. If they impose an oil boycott . . ."

Don Vincenzo, puffing his long black cigar, added a comment. "The Jews are an unreasonable, argumentative people unable to agree upon any one issue, even among themselves. They are well armed, well trained, gun-crazed guerrillas determined to bring to full fruition the Zionist conspiracy implemented in the minds of American politicians long ago."

Zionist conspiracy! Not again, she thought.

"First, the oil taken from the land becomes the property of the rich and powerful and is transferred from their hands to every nation for staggering sums of money. Now, even the gold beneath the lands and in the waters of rivers and coastal areas glitters enticingly—"

"Gold?" Tina's ears perked up. "You mean black gold —oil?"

Don Spinoza raised an objecting hand. "Yellow gold, Signora. I speak of real gold. Gold like this." He placed his gold watch on the table. "This gold, you see?"

"But, you said in the water—" Tina shook her head. "The costs of recovering deposits of gold from water would be far greater than gold itself."

She studied the expressions of polite interest on the faces of the men, realizing none had any inkling of what she was driving at with the exception of Don Spinoza, who was contemplating her words.

"There is a rumor that a special Arab company has been experimenting in this, uh, underwater recovery of gold. Once the desalinization of sea water was a fantasy, no? Today it is a reality. My understanding is that many brilliant scientists have been industriously at work on this secret project for a long time."

Tina, when married to Renzo, had become adept at acting as if she knew nothing and cared less. Now this attitude was about to pay off.

"Which of the Arab nations promotes this research?" she asked subtly, feigning little interest.

The dark expression in his eyes was enough to cause Tina to back off. However, he surprised her by replying,

"Ahhh. It's a mystery." His expressive and articulate hands performed a symphony of hand movements as if they might help stimulate his memory. *"Si,* a mystery. If

452

one has the desire and proper inspiration to pursue the mystery, *Signora*," he began with unmistakable overtones as to his meaning, "it is not an impossibility to uncover the mystery."

Tina closed her portfolio. She raised her wine glass in a toast. "My friends, we have shortened the distance between us. We know each other now. If I or my family can do any of you a special service, you have but to ask. I assure you that our mutual business interests will be conducted as scrupulously as they were in the past." She stood up, portfolio in hand.

Instantly the Dons were on their feet. She passed among them, smiling in a controlled, unemotional manner. "Please remain and refresh yourselves. Enjoy the comfort of the Villa Garibaldi, my friends."

She stopped a foot or two away from Don Ibrahim's thin frame.

"It would please me if you would join me in my suite, Don Spinoza." She did not wait for an answer. The wiry man stepped behind her, an expression of profound pleasure on his face. The attentive and impressionable Volpe brothers trailed after them exchanging amused looks.

Despite their protests and long faces Tina instructed the Volpe brothers to remain outside her suite and closed the door abruptly before they got in a word edgewise. She faced Don Spinoza, who bore traces of embarrassment to be in a hotel room with a woman. Tina got right down to business.

"What will it cost me to properly inspire you to pursue the matter of which we spoke moments ago?"

Don Ibrahim's face turned a brick color. "But, Signora, it is not for me!" Aghast at her abrupt manner and what she intimated, he held up open palms to indicate his innocence of such base behavior, insisting, "It is for those who must be bribed to part with such information. Our friends in Geneva and Zurich can be most cooperative when their palms are crossed with sufficient gold. You understand?"

"Perfectly. How much?"

Three days later Tina got the information for which she paid handsomely. Don Ibrahim cautioned her, "You are to keep the source of this information in the strictest of confidence. The Ministry of Finance must not be implicated."

Tina drew herself up regally. "You need to say such a thing to the daughter of Valentino Frice?" she asked in a voice that caused the fine hairs on his neck to rise.

"With your permission, I spoke merely words of caution. These men are powerful. To them a life is meaningless."

Tina turned her cool appraising eyes on him. "Have we not shared these beliefs also, Don Ibrahim?"

At once flustered, hesitant, taken aback by her boldness, he was unreconciled to the cold detachment with which she spoke to him. His intestines coiled tightly. "If you desire, signora, I shall be most happy to escort you about the city and show you the Roma of greatness."

Thanking him politely and effusively Tina indicated her time was limited and must be spent economically. "I shall reserve time for you tomorrow—shall we say tea time? Perhaps you can tell me more about the Arabs and Jews and how it is you came to join the Sicilian brotherhood. Ah, yes, and another thing. We shall discuss the retribution to be paid to the forces that killed my predecessor." She looked him directly in the eyes.

Don Ibrahim bowed slightly, trying not to reveal the flickering in his eyes. "I can reply to your second query by telling you I joined for expediency and a desire to live without harassment from unknown forces of evil. It is my pleasure to take tea with you. My tales are plentiful and interesting. As to the retribution you speak of, I shall confer with special men who already know of such things and can bring such a request to an instant conclusion. Might I suggest you discuss this with Signore Allegro?" He kissed her hand with aplomb before leaving.

She closed the door behind him, relieved the ordeal was over. Seated at the Florentine desk, collecting herself, she turned on the desk lamp, scanning the report Don Spinoza had submitted. It wasn't much, but it was tangible; a little ammunition fired strategically was better than none. The words as the top of the page read CONFIDENTIAL REPORT: MURALIZ, INC.

She easily unscrambled the word MURALIZ; it stood for Ali Izmur. The Muraliz Corporation ownership was veiled by several other companies all leading to Prince Izmur. Through this company Muraliz funds were siphoned off to pay the astronomical salaries and expenditures involved in the attempt to recover gold from waterways indicated on the map of Middle Eastern nations.

From the way Tina interpreted the report, the project, underway for the past five years, had suffered setbacks due to the untimely deaths of key personnel in unforseeable accidents that were considered sabotage by terrorists. Included with the report were technical studies, graphs, mathematical equations, secret formulas used in the process and lists of costly expenditures in the recovery of the precious metals. She considered the report with deliberate thought, wondering was it possible that Muraliz was working in cooperation with an Israeli company in this as a joint venture. The name Yakov Shulman & Sons, Inc. crept into the report several times. She shuffled through the papers and returned to her place.

Whoever prepared the summary report alluded to the possible profits should the project prove successful. Because oil was direly needed in nearly every nation, it affected the world's economy. However, thought Tina, when she scanned the locations of the heaviest concentration of underwater gold, whoever amassed sizeable amounts of this precious metal would really control the economy.

The coastal areas from Beirut to Port Said along the eastern shores of the Mediterranean and on both shores of the Persian Gulf from the Arabian Sea to the Red Sea were heavily outlined, clearly indicated the largest deposits.

Tina placed the report into a secret compartment of her luggage as a series of explosive thoughts raced through her mind. The race for supremacy in the Middle East could never be resolved. Surely other nations were involved in similar experiments.

She recalled the information Val had amassed on Benkhanhian, when in his early years he had singlehandedly invaded the Arab world and made a deal for the oil under their lands in the Four Nations Conference. What a visionary he was! Now Ali Mohammed, under Benkhanhian's tutelage, was doing precisely the same thing with gold. This time the entire world would be at their mercy.

Tina thought that in the past years the OPEC nations in a sense had been teasing the Western world, providing them with fraudulent hope so that at the right time, when the need was greatest and prices soared beyond the limit of any nation's endurance, their helplessness would defeat them. This *coup de main* is what Benkhanhian devised.

Tina spent the next morning and part of the afternoon meandering about the boutiques of Rome. Rapturous over Ferragamo shoes on the Via Condotti, shocked at their price, she nevertheless purchased two pairs. She browsed at Roberta's on the Piazza di Spagli and La Mondola at Trinita dei Monti and the leather shop of Renard on the Via due Macelli, but Tina's mind was elsewhere. By one o'clock she hastily returned to the Villa Garibaldi, anxious to reread the Muraliz report and more anxious to speak with Don Spinoza.

At precisely two the Don arrived. Tina had ordered lunch in her suite, on the patio, and in no time she was held spellbound by fascinating tales Spinoza spun for her. She learned about the multifaceted Arab character, that their passion ran high over anything from riotous trading in the marketplace to the abominable manner in which they held their women, treating them worse than slaves. Their mentalities defied classification, insisted Spinoza.

"They are an astute people, cunning as foxes, meticulous in planning every aspect of their lives as if they lived by a blueprint. Their ethics are totally unscrupulous; their word is meaningless; their morals grossly lacking if they have any at all. Yet their hospitality is unsurpassed."

Through Spinoza, Tina learned that the Arabs, a religious people, were considered the heart and soul of Islam, bound together by a common language and a common religion of submission to God's will.

"Their history is as long and violent as it once was dazzling and spectacular. Once a spectacular culture, it evolved through many wars to the ravages of cruel and bloody battles. When finally the Arabs were divided and brother fought brother in senseless feuds, and the waters of the Nile ran red with their blood, their land became a dustbowl, their culture was all but destroyed. But," said Don Spinoza, sipping his delicate wine, "When the final disaster struck, during the siege of the Ottoman Turks in what was the final atrocity, they were rendered totally helpless. Divided against themselves they were unable to unite against the Ottomans. Five centuries of feudalism and corruption followed.

"Without water what can a people do? A drop of water in a land of none is more precious than gold. Without it their world disintegrated into one of unspeakable filth and disease, illiteracy and poverty. The meagerest existence was marked with torturous struggles, squalor, and deprivations from birth to death.

"Is it any wonder that in this deplorable state, in an atmosphere fraught with horrendous hardships, were spawned men without principle, blackguards capable of all sorts of skullduggery and unconscionable behavior, where wickedness, thievery, infidelity, whoredom, betrayal and sedition, even murder ran rampant? For a long while the sheikhs, emirs, pashas and other lions of the

456

desert longed for emergence into the 20th century. Their sons, dispatched to schools in America, France and England, have returned to their lands with revolutionary ideas, new technologies, and hope for their people. After centuries of abuse, indignities, torture and murder they hope to carve oases in the deserts, but their only hope is through the profits earned from oil pumped from the bellies of their lands."

Long after Don Spinoza had left her suite, Tina considered all he'd said. She had hoped to learn more about Ali's people. Perhaps it was already enough, she thought. Don Ibrahim's words concerning the retribution she sought lingered in her memory. "If the guilty are known to you, you have but to whisper their names and it is done. If they are not known to you give us the data, and we shall locate the guilty before the cocks crow seven times. The deed will be done in short order."

She considered his words solemnly. All of a sudden, loud brash voices in a torrent of Sicilian and Arabic assaulted Tina's ears. Following the commotion Tina came upon the Volpe brothers, guns in hand, warding off the advances of two desert-garbed Arabs and a hysterical Signore Allegro, in a desperate attempt to pacify all concerned.

"What is the meaning of this commotion?" Tina asked sharply.

Instantly the sullen-faced foursome quieted down. Allegro ran his fingers through his graying hair nervously. "There appears to be a misunderstanding, Signora. Pray give me a moment or two to unravel the complication." He spoke first to the Volpe brothers who simultaneously, in a barrage of expletives, told him their side.

In Arabic, Allegro asked the intruders to state their case. Listening attentively he nodded and held his hands up to both factions warding them off. He addressed himself to Tina.

"These two men, it appears, are emissaries of Prince Ali Mohammed Izmur. It is their contention they have been sent to escort you to the prince's yacht. Your bodyguards insisted you go no place without them and refused them admittance. What will you have me do, Signora Erice?"

"The prince's emissaries are correct. I am expected to be his house guest at either the yacht or his residence. It's best you explain to the brothers that under the circumstances I shall not need their protection. Thank them. Pay them well for their services. I shall be protected well enough in the prince's care."

Allegro, in rapid Sicilian, conveyed Tina's instructions. The Volpe brothers indignantly shook their heads and with bold gestures blisteringly negated his orders. Unable to take this coarse shouting and acrimonious cursing he wagged them off and, mopping his sweating brow, approached Tina.

"It is most difficult to explain the chain of circumstances, Signora. They are committed to you by a debt of honor owed to your late father who accepted their oath. They will protect his successor with their lives. It is not a matter to be taken lightly."

"This is preposterous! I need no protection. Make them understand, Signore Allegro! You must. I have no need of such protection in America either!" Tina's mouth dropped in astonishment. "They don't plan to return to America with me?"

"But of course," replied Allegro as if it were a normal consideration. "A debt of honor is enforceable to their death. In addition, should they fail to protect you properly, they've informed me that their uncle and benefactor would skin them alive before he personally puts an end to their shameful souls."

Tina was aghast at the absurdity of their contention. Pacing the floor, nonplused at the situation, she voiced her annoyance.

"This is incredible, utterly unacceptable—" She stopped. "Their uncle? Benefactor? Who—"

"Signore Rizzuto, the man inseparable from your father."

At the sound of Richie's name the Volpe brothers smiled, flushing pleasurably, nodding their head affirmatively.

Tina, fit to be tied, realized she'd been outsmarted despite herself. Tossing her hands into the air in exasperation, she relented.

"Very well, they shall remain with me. You had best instruct them on how to get along with the Arabs. They will be in their constant company for the next few weeks. Oh, and Signore Allegro, please see that they are suitably attired in proper fitting clothing. They are disgraceful the way they are!" Spinning on her heels she went back inside the suite to prepare herself for the company of the Izmurs while Allegro attempted an explanation geared to pacify both the Arabs and the Sicilians.

CHAPTER THIRTY-FIVE

The *Scheherazade,* one of the most palatial yachts to traverse Mediterranean waters, stood proud in the harbor of Ostia Antica in the Tyrrhenian Sea. On each side of her in deep folds of somber cobalt blue water, white foaming swirls bursting in low hissing sounds created ripples and undulations on the agitated surface of the sea. An inexorable sun shining on the immaculate white yacht created a glare so intense it was almost impossible for the occupants of a motor launch approaching her to gaze at her sleek lines for long, despite their dark glasses.

The moment Tina stepped aboard the luxury yacht, she was convinced she had entered an enchanting land of makebelieve. Ostentatious living at its apex is what she saw when she cast her eyes upon the lavish display.

Valerie, delighted and gushing over Tina excitedly, plagued her with a rash of questions about America and their mutual acquaintances. Ali's escorts took the Volpe brothers to their quarters and Tina explained about them.

Valerie's eyes lingered on them as they followed Ali's men. "We have so many guests, I hardly know them." She took Tina's hand and gave her a superficial tour of the yacht, chattering like a blue jay as she did.

"Were the American people really disappointed about my marriage to Ali?" She asked the question again and again. "How did they really take it?" Valerie led her through several staterooms, so opulent they left Tina gasping.

"Solid gold fixtures, Tina. Imagine. I wonder what the people back home would say to this?"

"What could they say? It's a bit wasteful," Tina replied, dismayed at the obvious change in Valerie since she last saw her. "No one wants to see others happy if they can't have their share. It reminds them of their own shortcomings and misery. The more miserable those in the spotlight, the happier are the others. What it is is pure insanity."

They went next to the main salon. "Ali is due here soon. He's anxious to see you again. I swear, Tina, since he heard you were coming, he's actually been downright nice to me." Her voice was laden with rancor and bitterness.

As they continued the grand tour, inspecting every nook and cranny, a sudden humorous thought struck Tina; how would the Volpe brothers take to such opulence?

The crew, uniformed in spanking white, were efficient and exceedingly polite. Fresh flowers were strewn about in priceless porcelain vases and Oriental cloisonné containers worth a fortune.

"We get them fresh every day," Valerie boasted, picking a red rose from a vase and handing it to Tina. "There's nothing Ali won't do for me."

Tina heard her, but she wasn't convinced. She wanted to get closer to Valerie to ask her what was really troubling her, but the barriers erected between them were momentarily insurmountable. She didn't sound like the desperate, driven woman who had written Tina a near hysterical plea for help.

Valerie, summoned by one of the stewards, was informed there was a mixup in the menu and the chef needed her presence.

"Meet me on the aft deck in fifteen minutes for lunch," she told Tina, then snapped tartly at the steward in French as she followed him to the galley.

Tina sauntered along the deck heading aft, thinking of the noticeable changes in Valerie. Piercing through the exterior veneer of gaiety, Tina had found a highly nervous, insecure woman in her thirties, looking fifty beneath the mask. Dissipation, etched deeply into her features, was accompanied by alternate periods of depression, disappointment, unhappiness and a noticeable frustration.

Dressed in white jeans and a halter-neck jersey, showing a bare expanse of tanned, firm skin, her long hair piled high atop her head, Tina gazed out at the busy, colorful harbor scene where slick yachts and trim yawls and ketches dotted the sea in profusion. She reflected momentarily on Valerie's life.

If the world had been shocked when Valerie's intention to marry Prince Izmur was made public, the news that she'd borne him a set of twins met with the same unrestrained speculation. Now, Tina had heard, she was preparing to make sordid headlines, the kind that brought no one satisfaction except for those salacious gossip mongers whose deep-rooted envy and jealousy for the extravagant way Valerie lived her life oozed from every pore.

Tina had read about the backyard gossip spewed forth by acerbic-tongued shrews in their syndicated columns and felt somewhat incensed. Valerie, she felt, was too young, too alive to remain chained to a memory. Like any human being she was entitled to live and love the way she chose.

Tina wasn't certain how it was that Whip knew of her plans to see Valerie. A day before she left New York, he had called, upset. "I don't want you going to see Valerie," he had insisted. "I forbid it." He should have known those were the wrong words to persuade Tina to change her plans. "You shouldn't be there, not now," Whip had continued the tirade.

Any other time Tina might have used a different choice of words. "I can't see that it's any of your business what I do," she had told him in a voice that stopped him cold.

"You're right," he agreed. "I was a fool to try pounding sense into that stubborn head of yours." He slammed the phone down more out of frustration than anger.

Tina sighed and turned at the sound of her name being called. It was Valerie breezing towards her. Valerie, a veritable chatterbox, couldn't stop talking. She'd ask Tina a question and before Tina replied, she'd move on to another.

"Tina, I'm so happy you came. We'll have such fun together. Why didn't we get to know each other better in the States? Amy always raved about you." She took Tina's hands in hers and led her to the deck chairs nearby.

"Where are the children?" asked Tina, annoyed by the superficial chatter. A steward was approaching, wheeling a gleaming gold and glass serving cart ladened with iced champagne, caviar and a variety of delectable-looking hors d'oeuvres.

Slipping off her white crocheted beach coat Valerie revealed a sunbronzed body in a postage-stamp bikini, the briefest Tina had ever seen. Her body was still in great shape, thought Tina, as she accepted a glass of Dom Perignon from the steward.

"I could positively live on this forever," Valerie exclaimed, popping the Beluga into her mouth. "The children are all in school in Switzerland. We live there part of the time. Ali insists. They are all fine, really fine. Ali

461

wants desperately to adopt Ted's children. I've been putting it off, at least for the time being." She rattled on in a superficial tone.

"That was a wise move on your part. In a way, they really belong to America, Valerie. Being Ted's children, and Whip's nephew, you know. Besides, Ali has two of his own now." Tina sipped her champagne, totally unsuspecting the deluge that erupted from Valerie as she crumbled beneath her marble exterior.

"Oh, Tina, I don't know what to do." Tears spilled to her cheeks. "Ali loathes me. He wants to divorce me and I just won't have it." She confided this the moment the steward left the area.

"A divorce?" Tina was flabbergasted. It was the last thing she expected to hear and didn't compute with Val's theory concerning Ali's hold on Valerie "Whatever for? I thought you both were the essence of love and devotion. What brought this about?"

"It's too terrible to talk about," Valerie gushed emotionally. She dabbed at her eyes with a tissue. Her eyes darting about the area were telltale of her fright. Tina moved from the deck chair to the chaise closer to Valerie.

"That's why I came. Your letter to me got lost in a shuffle and I didn't get to read it until last week. You sounded so very upset—"

"I am, I really am, darling. Don't you see? Well, how can I tell you?" She groped for words. "It's terribly sticky—" She gazed about again, her eyes darting suspiciously. "You never know who's skulking about, dear Tina. It's about the twins, Rafi and Rahmet. Oh, it's so awkward to discuss, don't you see?" She opened the gilded top of a nearby table revealing a mirror and other toilet articles of fine porcelain and gold, and examined her features narcissistically.

Watching her, Tina experienced a sudden revulsion at this superficiality. She was beginning to get the picture all right and didn't like the scenes forming in her mind. "Valerie, you don't mean what I think you mean—do you?" Tina hoped she was wrong.

Their eyes caught and held briefly. Tina, sickened, turned away. Valerie's past excursions into sexual debaucheries had been spoken of in certain circles, but Tina had shrugged them off as jealous rumors. Amy had broadly alluded to several of the former First Lady's exploits, but never spoke of them in depth.

"Oh, Valerie, it can't be. You couldn't have permitted

462

such a thing to happen. I can't believe you'd be so fool-ish—" Whatever words of chastisement began to form on Tina's lips ended abruptly. *Let he who is without sin cast the first stone!* But for the grace of God, she might be carrying Whip's child in her womb. How could she denigrate another woman for the same thing?

"Oh, Tina, don't become maudlin. Ali knows. That's all that counts. He knows and hates me for it. I swear there have been times he'd like to kill me."

"What a terrible thing to say!"

"It's true. I can see it in his eyes. It scares me to death at times." She reverted to her Southern accent in this emotional outburst.

"You aren't exaggerating? How did he find out? Is it really true? Why didn't you lie? There are times when a lie is more merciful than the truth, for heaven's sake."

"Do you know the law in Ali's land for lying, cheating, stealing and all the other things that go on daily in our country?" She made a facial grimace that defied clas-sification. "I don't blame the princess for joining the reb-els. He disowned her totally. She no longer exists in Ali's mind."

"Then, he doesn't know—" Tina's words ended abruptly.

"Doesn't know what?" Valerie's ears perked up.

Tina lit a cigarette, taking time to decide if she should or shouldn't reveal Jamila's peculiar circumstances. She took a chance.

"Jamila is in America and has been for five years."

"You must be joking!" Valerie's eyes widened enor-mously.

"The Jamila you've read about and believe to be a terrorist is an impostor."

Valerie looked past Tina, her expression frozen.

"Who is an impostor?" asked a deep voice behind Tina.

Turning around Tina looked up into Prince Izmur's green eyes.

"Your Highness," she said bowing slightly, holding her hand out.

Ali bent over her and kissed it. "My wife told me she was expecting you. How good to see you again, Tina." He nodded perfunctorily to his wife.

He was an inch or two taller than she recalled, slightly under six feet, powerfully built and he came at her with just the slightest stoop of his shoulders, head forward, and a fixed stare under thick brows that made Tina think of a charging bull, but much more handsome with those

463

incandescent eyes that were sometimes green, other times hazel. His voice was deep and resonant and his manner, although princely and graceful, was a combination of modern world aggressiveness steeped in elegant Middle Eastern tradition. He was impeccably dressed. His eyes exuded boldness and his lean body radiated a bronze glow that came from hours spent lazing in the sun.

The prince seemingly ignored Valerie, fixing his eyes on Tina as two stewards approached and fussed over him, serving him caviar and champagne with the reverence given a pasha of rare distinction. Ali removed his *cuffiah* and shed his desert garb handing it to one of the stewards. Dressed in spanking white trousers and silk shirt he sat on a deck chair giving orders to his man in Arabic. He turned back to Tina.

"I cannot convey to you, madam, the happiness in my heart to see you once again, I welcome you to the *Scheherazade*. My house is your house. It is my humblest wish that you enjoy your stay with us." He turned to Valerie and in an obvious change of mood suggested that she go below deck and prepare herself for guests arriving within the hour.

Tina watched Valerie submit to his order like a well practiced galley slave, a totally new posture for the former First Lady. She walked away and disappeared below deck.

Ali Mohammed was more than Tina bargained for. Five years had passed since she saw him last. He'd hardly changed except to look more handsome than she recalled. His remarkable resemblance to the film star Omar Sharif was startling except for the emerald green color of his eyes. His sun-burnished skin, flashing white teeth, and a shock of black curly hair gave him tremendous appeal.

Sipping his champagne, he placed the goblet alongside him on the gold and crystal cart wheeled out for his personal use. He clapped his hands twice, dismissing the stewards.

"You were speaking of an impostor, my dear—"

"Yes, I was. I was speaking of the woman who fools even you into believing she is actually the Princess Jamila."

He gave Tina a look that sent shudders to her toes. "You must be mistaken. I have no sister."

Collecting her courage Tina spoke with detachment. "The truth has no importance to his royal highness?" She

464

pursed her lips into a momentary pout. "My, my, you've ended the illusion."

Ali was unable to ignore the remark. His eyes narrowed as he lit a long brown cigar. He stiffened imperceptibly, angling his body slightly towards her, his deceptive green eyes beginning to smolder. "Perhaps it is best you do not interfere with matters you know nothing about," he said at last, staring at the cigar in his hand.

Tina had little time for subtleties. It wasn't her style. "Ah, but I do know all about her. She's been in my country for the past five years. The woman harassing your government is an impostor. It's that simple."

"You are obviously misinformed or mistaken." Ali's eyes blazed dangerously. He rose to his feet, looking down at her serious expression. "It is beyond you to be teasing me. This isn't some joke?"

"It's no joke, your highness. I regret upsetting you. I just thought you should know, if you don't already."

Tina stood up, facing him in an open, frank, and calm manner. Ali reminded himself that here was the daughter of Valentino Erice and she should be reckoned with on that basis. There was neither folly or smugness in her eyes.

"Come walk with me about the deck. Please call me Ali. Then tell me how it is you happen to be so certain that the real Jamila is in America." They began to walk. Ali glanced at his diamond-studded Piaget. "I'm due at an important meeting shortly, but we have time."

"What will you do with her, Ali? Banish her once again? Take punitive measures against her?"

"That remains to be seen," he said in an evasive manner. "If what you tell me can be authenticated I shall make that decision after I listen to your arguments."

They strolled about the deck languidly. Anyone watching could not determine the range of emotions bouncing between them. Ali, listening intently, made little or no comment as Tina told him all she knew about Jamila— all David and Whip had confided. Only in this instant did Tina see certain loopholes in the story and wondered if Ali would be cognizant of them. If he questioned her story he indicated nothing, instead assured her he would take measures to check out the facts. He slickly changed the subject by the time they returned to the aft deck, where Ali poured more champagne for them. He clinked glasses with her. "How long will you stay with us on the *Scheherazade?*"

She shook her head. "I'm not sure."

"You will stay for at least two weeks. I insist. We plan to cruise the Mediterranean with stopovers in the Greek Isles, Beirut, then to my land. You must allow me to show you my country, Tina."

"It's difficult to refuse one as gallant as you," she replied suggestively, causing a rise of excitement in Ali. Before he could act on this hope their attention was taken by the arrival of a sleek motor launch sidling up to the yacht. Six men were climbing aboard the yacht; three dressed in desert robes, and three in Western business suits. They carried briefcases and wore dark glasses.

"It's painful to leave you, my dear." He clapped his hands. Two stewards sprang from seemingly nowhere. Ali addressed one. "See that our guest is shown to her quarters, Akim."

Akim salaamed. Ali bowed over Tina, kissing her hand. "We'll see each other at dinner later." Turning on his heel he approached the new arrivals and together they disappeared into the large stateroom chattering in a mixture of French, Arabic and German.

Tina followed Akim through the labyrinthian passageways below deck until she came to her quarters. Outside her door, looking glum and morose, the Volpe brothers sat in silence, brightening when they saw her approaching. They sprang to their feet, caps in hand, smiling dazzlingly. Tina showed her frustration.

"Truly," she said in Sicilian, "it isn't necessary that you guard me at every moment. There is no danger for me aboard ship while under the protection of Prince Izmur. Enjoy yourselves. Go below with the crew or above deck and enjoy yourselves. Just do not get in the way. *Va bene?*"

They were reluctant and a bit frustrated. Giacomo, the heftier of the two, spoke in broken English. "Far from you, Signora, we shall not be. We shall be watching you at all times." They placed their caps on their heads and moved along the passageway.

Shaking her head in a bemused attitude, Tina thought she should have been firmer. It was a mistake to bring them along. What could happen here?

Tina found Valerie waiting for her inside the stateroom, smoking. She fairly pounced on Tina. "What did he say? Did he tell you, Tina? What will he do with me?"

Tina removed Valerie's hands from her arm gently, and led her to a chair. "He didn't mention you at all. I was telling him about his sister, Jamila."

466

"You actually spoke to him about her? I mean he didn't stop you or demand you not speak her name?" Valerie exclaimed.

"He did, but I told him anyway, Valerie." Observing the tremors in the other woman, the actual shaking of her hands, Tina sat down at the foot of the bed and held Valerie's hand.

"What's wrong? Are you imagining things that don't exist? Exaggerating them beyond reason?"

Valerie withdrew her hands and turned on her in a state of heightened paranoia. She wrung her hands incessantly, sprang to her feet and listened at the door before she flung it open. Finding no one listening behind it, she slammed it shut and began pacing the floor. Tina tried changing the subject.

"What time is dinner, dear? What shall I wear?"

Valerie wasn't listening. "No one believes me. What must I do to convince you that my life is in danger?" Then on sudden impulse she pleaded, "Tina, loan me one of your bodyguards. I shall pay him well. You have no need for two. Please, Tina?"

Tina grasped both her wrists and pulled her closer to her. "Valerie, stop this. You keep it up and you'll make yourself very ill. Your husband gave no indication that he was displeased with you. On the contrary," lied Tina, "he praised you highly, commenting on the marvelous hostess you are to his friends and business acquaintances." If a small white lie could ease the torment in the woman, what harm was there in telling one, reasoned Tina.

Valerie stared at her guest with haunted eyes. Her expression went blank. "He said that?" she asked flatly. "He really did?" She shook her head disbelieving, yet trying to accept it. Her eyes left Tina's face. Vaguely she muttered, "Dinner? Oh, yes, dinner." Her eyes studied the digital clock across the room. "One hour. Wear what you want. Not too casual . . ." She rose slowly, still wearing her string bikini and, with lithe strides, headed towards the door. She paused, looking back at Tina. "I still want one of your guards. Uh—Giacomo—that's the one."

She closed the door behind her leaving Tina perplexed and disturbed.

Tina entered the splendid dining salon dressed in tightly draped white Qiana jersey with a flowing knee length overblouse to match, designed by Cardinale. She wore white sandals. Her only accessories were a chain of platinum around her neck from which was suspended a ten-carat pear-shaped diamond, five-carat diamonds in her ears and a ring on her left index finger of thirty diamonds twisted into a spray with four pearl-shaped emeralds. She was breathtaking, her frosted hair worn off her face, fluffed out to shoulder length.

Several dinner guests stared at her in open admiration. Spotting Tina, Valerie, dressed in a gold lame hostess gown and in a complete change of mood, floated towards her, a bright easy smile on her face.

"My dear friends," she spoke in accented French, catching her guests' attention. Ali glanced away from the cluster of men to whom he was talking. "May I present my future sister-in-law, Tina Erice. She is going to marry Whip Shiverton, the future American president." She waved a glass of champagne in midair in a toast.

Tina's face turned crimson. She tried to interrupt, to deny the announcement, but it was like trying to cap an active volcano as it erupted. Ali's expression froze. Tina caught his look while being propelled by Valerie among the guests, who were introduced faster than Tina could assimilate them. Congratulations came from all sides. She tried to set Valerie straight but there was no reckoning with the former First Lady. Tina, irked by this sham, observed that Valerie came aglow whenever the name Shiverton was mentioned. It dawned on her that Valerie's only claim to the fame she so desperately needed was her connection to the Shiverton family. She'd become a celebrity in the Middle East, Rome, Zurich, Paris, wherever they maintained a home, by virtue of the fact that she'd been the wife of a martyred American president and sister-in-law to a possible future president. She wore this honor like a badge of valor. Being married to one of the world's wealthiest men didn't give her the charge she needed. She had clung like a barnacle to her former life and in so doing was jeopardizing her present and annihilating her future with Ali.

Dinner, boring and stilted, dragged on endlessly for Tina. The language barrier frustrated her. Valerie had monopolized the conversation until Tina felt embarrassment for her. Later after the guests departed, Valerie retired to her stateroom under the influence of drugs and drinks and the exhaustion of talking at a hundred RPMs. Tina was unable to sleep. Changing into jeans and a sweater she went above deck and strolled about aimlessly.

Lights from Italy's coastal cities glittered for miles as

far as the eye could see. A warm night breeze enveloped her in comfort and for a time she stared at the bobbing reflections of light in the frothy waters swirling about the yacht. The ceiling of stars was incredibly close, she thought.

"It's more beautiful on the desert," said Ali, moving in behind her. "There the stars are truly jewels, so inconceivable in size, they can actually light up your path for miles."

"Is it true stars on the desert are magnified many times?" Her eyes scanned the heavens. "Here on the water they appear far larger. Is it a phenomenon?"

"Is it true?" Ali asked quietly.

"Is what true?" She turned abruptly, facing him, fully aware of what he meant, but letting him take the lead.

"Are you marrying Whip Shiverton?"

She turned from him, staring at the reflections of the ship's running lights. "No," she said finally.

Ali's heart felt as if it would burst. He was confused.

"Then what was Valerie jabbering about?"

"She's your wife. You tell me."

"It's not true, then?"

"It's not true."

He moved closer to her, the scent of his cologne wafting to her nostrils, the heat of his body, so close yet not touching, setting hers aflame. He pressed both her hands to his lips.

"I'm happy to hear this. I told you once we would be together one day. Has the time come? Do you want me?"

Flushed by his forward manner she felt awkward. In addition she was unable to abate the rush of excitement shuddering through her. *This isn't the way it's supposed to be. This is insanity, Tina. Stop it at once. You've been in control up to now. Stay that way.* She forced a rush of laughter to spill from her lips.

"You certainly have a charm we hardly see in America. No wonder Valerie fell so madly in love with you."

"Valerie," said Ali tightly, "is incapable of loving anyone." He changed the subject instantly. "I must convey my sincerest sympathies to you, Tina, over the death of your father. The world lost a great man."

Tina looked up into two eyes resembling black star sapphires. "How can you make such an assessment? You didn't know him."

"Oh, but I did. We met once. True, I did not know him

469

intimately. My misfortune. I can see much of him lives in you."

"Yes, it does." Tina wondered why Val hadn't told her of this.

"You were in love with Whip Shiverton?"

Tina lit up a cigarette. "Yes. For a long time."

"Why not now?"

"The conquest of love is overshadowed by the conquest of power. The two are not compatible. You should know this better than anyone, your highness." She removed her hands from his grasp.

"Because I am a man, I know this, accept it and deal with it. It's rare that a woman can accept and deal with this truth."

Tina laughed. "Oh, no you don't. You won't get me into a battle of the sexes. I've been a liberated woman too long. I believe only in facts, not ambiguities, and I never speak in generalities. It's too risky with someone as astute and sagacious as you, Prince Izmur."

"Ali."

"Very well, Ali." She offered him a cigarette from her case. He lit it for her gallantly, then lit his own. They smoked thoughtfully for several moments in silence.

"Why didn't I have the good sense to whisk you off your feet and make you fall in love with me when we first met?" Ali's hand moved closer to hers on the ship's rail and covered it.

Tina's eyes fell upon it. She stared at his hand as it tightened its grip. "I wouldn't have been ready for you then."

Ali picked up her hand and drew it to his heart. "And you are now?" She could feel his pulse quicken, almost hear his heart pounding in his chest.

Tina's eyes met his. Slowly she withdrew her hand. "You are a married man, your highness. What can you be thinking of?"

Ali stiffened imperceptibly. "Yes, you're right. What must I be thinking?"

"We're both creatures of circumstance, it seems."

"No, I prefer to believe we're the leftover victims sacrificed in the battle for power." They began to perambulate about the deck. "I find it impossible to believe that the greed for power can hold men to such a steadfastness of purpose, to such blind persistence in endeavor and sacrifice," she began. "They sacrifice love as if it's the most

470

available commodity in the world, when indeed it's as rare as the underwater discovery of gold."

She felt him stiffen. She felt his eyes on her assessing her remark. His silence was oppressive.

"Since the greed for power burns in the hearts of certain men like the flame of love, what wouldn't they do for power?" he said at last. "They'd slit each other's throats without hesitation and foreswear their souls. The bizarre obstinacy of that greed makes them defy death. Yet, Tina, this same thirst and greed for power has made some men great. It has made some heroic in their attempt to manipulate that power into worthwhile causes."

"No matter how many others are sacrificed if they stand in their way?"

"No matter." Ali puffed indolently on his cigarette. "You have but to look back upon the history of mankind to realize that only a very few are chosen for greatness. As instruments of a recorded destiny they have pushed outward into the unknown in obedience to an inward voice, to an impulse beating swiftly in the blood, to a dream of the future. They are entitled to the fruits of their labor if it benefits mankind in general. The price man pays for his greed for power is the constant reminder of what lies ahead, not the barnacles that affix themselves to his shield weighing him down, preventing him from progress. The mistake you make is in attaching sentimentality to a life."

"What a presumptuous statement to make."

He stopped, grasped her arms and pulled her towards him, to face him. "What would you have me be?" His face was inches from her. "A sniveling dog? A man without spine?"

Tina couldn't speak. Her lips trembled. The effect he had upon her was disconcerting, because she didn't expect it. She tried desperately to camouflage these alien feelings. In a sudden unexpected move, Ali's sensuous lips found hers, covering them in a surprising turbulence of passion felt to the tips of Tina's toes. Her body flushed with new excitement. An overpowering emotion transporting new feelings to her senses aroused her to such heights that she became feverish, suddenly aglow with life. She actually shook by the time Ali released her. Angry at herself for being so susceptible to him, she turned from him and dug her fists into her sweater pockets, unable to isolate her true feelings.

She heard his soft gentle laughter. "It isn't possible that you're afraid of me, is it?"

471

Tina didn't reply. She was shivering and didn't know why.

"Tina, look at me."

She shook her head stubbornly. Ali pulled her towards him again and lifted her chin up to his face forcing her luminous eyes to gaze into his. Her eyes were misting against her will.

"What have you heard about me that puts such fear into your heart? It is fear I see in your eyes. Why? Am I such an ogre?"

Tina was saved from replying by the arrival of Ali's secretary, a young man in his late twenties, dressed casually.

"Forgive me, your highness. An important message has come over the telex," said Damien Le Doux.

Ali released Tina. "Will you have coffee with me later?"

"I'd like to go to sleep," she said softly. "Suddenly I feel quite ill." Her hand flew to her moist forehead as nausea churned inside her. "I really do," she said, breaking away and running below deck to her quarters.

Inside her cabin, Tina threw herself on the bed, hoping to quell the strange feelings spiraling through her body. She felt dizzy. *Mal de mer?* Could it be seasickness? She stood up and moved for her luggage, fishing through zippered compartments before locating the Demerol. She took one, chased down by a glass of water. Too weak to undress she flopped across the bed waiting for the nausea to subside. She dispassionately reconsidered Ali's words, resenting his honeyed manner. Yet something about him . . .

Unable to regain her equilibrium, Tina felt it more sensible to go back on deck in an open breeze rather than remain in the closed confinement of her cabin. Grabbing a sweater she went out.

No one saw the dinghy rowing towards the *Scheherazade*. Under the cover of night, when most of the coastal city lights dimmed and other ships lit up with running lights only, four men dressed in black trousers, turtlenecks and seamen's caps approached the luxury craft.

Tina wandered about on deck passing Ali's office. He was huddled with his secretary, Damien le Doux. She didn't want to give the impression of eavesdropping. She turned the corner and was suddenly caught in a viselike hold, her arms pinned behind her, one hand over her mouth, and a gun at her temple. She could not see her

472

captors in the darkness and was instantly propelled bodily through the stateroom door, where Prince Izmur and his secretary, startled at the intrusion, took in the scene in a glance.

She was frantic, squirming in her captor's arms, glancing from one ominous face to the next.

"You, Prince Izmur, will come with us, or the woman is killed and you along with her," ordered one of the intruders.

Tina managed to bite her captor's hand. He tightened his grip on her, wrenching her arms painfully.

"It's best to do as they say, Tina," Ali retorted solemnly. "They mean business." Ali recognized two of the men of the Feyadeen. "You are signing your own deaths. If a hair of the woman's head is harmed—"

A loud burst exploded in Tina's ears. She felt herself bodily heaved against a wall. Then, as a blurring of images raced in a spiral before her eyes and gun shots burst her eardrums, she cowered away from the bloody scene. Bodies were hurled into the air, falling back onto the floor in pools of blood. Fists went flying, more shots, faces, bodies, all in total confusion. She covered her eyes to shut out the sight.

She felt her hands being lowered, her eyes blinking against brighter lights until she recognized Ali Mohammed, and behind him stood two wide-eyed, grinning Sicilians, guns in their hands, triumph on their faces, pleased and waiting for her praise.

Tina stepped forward, looking at the four dead men. Blood oozed from a wound in Ali's shoulder. Damien received a superficial scratch on his forehead, but those two Sicilians, the brothers Volpe, had saved the day and their lives.

Before Tina could thank them or voice her feelings, Ali's men rushed the stateroom, looking in all directions, instant fear in their eyes. Shouts were hurled in Arabic, questions followed by verbal chastisement. Two of Ali's men leaned over the ship's rail, spotting the dinghy tied to the ship's ladder. More Arabic expletives were followed by apologies and interrogation. Ali hustled them out of his office, his words and eyes infusing them with a burning humiliation. They moved frantically with profuse regret and shame for their lack of diligence in letting such a deed occur. Ali turned his back upon them.

"It appears that I am beholden to your men for saving my life," he said to Tina as one of his men handed him a

473

newspaper removed from the pocket of one of the would-be assassins. In the shaft of light coming from inside the office, Ali read the headlines. His eyes quickly darted to Tina, but he kept silent. Folding the paper he slipped it inside the pocket of his smoking jacket. In Arabic he gave orders to his men to properly dispose of the interlopers.

Ali again thanked the Volpe brothers, shaking their hands and praising them for their quick-witted reaction. He said goodnight again to Tina, and with his secretary returned to his quarters.

For the next week she saw little of Ali. Her every moment aboard the yacht was occupied talking to a myriad of people. Each day there were gatherings of socialites and celebrities. The ship toured the Mediterranean. Often Ali and his retinue of hangers-on remained behind in various ports and would later join the ship by helicopter when new guests came aboard.

The guest list was something out of an international Who's Who. Transported from land or their own yachts to the *Scheherazade* in splendid motor launches, they would stay for cocktails or dinner and go on to the next party. If Tina needed anything, clothing or cosmetics, they would stop and shop in any of a number of exclusive salons in port. Valerie's personal hairdresser lived aboard the yacht and dressed Tina's hair whenever she permitted him.

Then their plans were changed. On the eighth day of the voyage the *Scheherazade* headed back for Rome.

"I don't know why I should feel so relieved, but I do," said Valerie, stretching out on a chaise lounge on the aft deck. "Four galas await me at the villa, but I'll get through it," she sighed heavily.

Tina, taking photographs with her Nikon, moved about the deck, taking as many photos as she could of the Volpe brothers, the crew, Valerie and the breathtaking panorama.

"You'll be able to see the children in two weeks, Tina," Valerie called to her.

Valerie was gone before Tina could tell her she didn't intend staying two more weeks. She continued with her photography, then went below to begin packing.

In Rome Tina was shuttled from yacht to land on a sleek motor launch with Valerie and her personal servants and of course the Volpe brothers, who, since saving the

Prince's life, had become guests of honor and were taking to this luxurious life as if they'd been born to it.

Transported by a sleek white Corniche to the villa, Tina unpacked in her suite with the assistance of a personally assigned servant, wondering why Ali had kept his distance in recent days. Periodically she'd caught him staring at her from across the room, over dinner, past the heads of his guests. He had limited his conversation with her to common pleasantries.

Valerie had also undergone a change in recent days. Not once since her arrival had she discussed her estrangement with Ali. It seemed as if Valerie had become another person entirely. Tina mulled over this and thought that whatever had caused the change had been for the good.

If Tina considered the parties aboard the *Scheherazade* the epitome of opulence, what greeted her at the first of the planned galas was a scene out of the imagination of a surrealist, so stunning it staggered the imagination. The villa was spruced up to resemble a futuristic palace. As she descended the gilded circular staircase she saw what she likened to an artist's conception of the Arabian Nights. Above her was a chandelier of Austrian crystal and solid gold, at least twenty feet in diameter, with no less than a thousand lights glittering from its gigantic frame, and multifaceted oval crystals sounding like bells in their movement. Filmy white silken cloths embroidered with golden filigree hung from high vaulted ceilings and were draped to each wall, each panel billowing in and out, set in motion by hidden fans until the glitter of gold and the tinkling crystal balls became too dazzling to behold.

Stewards wearing gold uniforms stood behind enormous buffets in the dining salon, to assist the guests. A centerpiece in the shape of a thickly maned lion's head had been sculpted out of ice and adorned with fruits and flowers. Golden platters containing spicy meats simmering in rich sauces were placed between platters of jumbo prawns, crabmeat and countless other sea delicacies.

The entire villa was lit by flaming torches outside; inside the lighting was low-keyed and intimate and permeated by floral scents and incense. Tina noticed the common use of drugs, the overabundance of golden bowls of cocaine placed conveniently about the villa.

Tina lost count of the assembled guests and recalled few of their names. She felt more like an observer than a participant in this folly.

475

Valerie's high-strung manner should have tipped Tina off that something was amiss. Her eyes were glittering unnaturally. Others were smoking hash or whatever took their fancy. She thought of what David had told her and grew angry with herself for having put him down as she had. Her preoccupation with their behavior and her own feelings of being out of step with these maddening, superficial people who contributed very little to the world and lived indolent, decadent lives, occupying precious space, surrounded by obscene grandeur, drove Tina outside to the balcony for a breath of fresh air.

She was more annoyed that she was the subject of curious gossip. She had felt them pointing her out, whispering, "That's the future wife of Whip Shiverton." She pretended to be deaf to their remarks. She inhaled the delicious bouquet of the enchanting garden of roses in full bloom cascading down the walls of the villa and balustrades.

"Don't let them annoy you. They mean well. They have nothing more to do than fill their empty, dreary lives with gossip."

"How do you put up with these leeches? I've seen their faces aboard the yacht so many times in the past week," she said tartly. "Don't they ever host a party at their places?"

"What an undemocratic thing to say." Ali laughed heartily.

A servant wheeling a golden cart laden with flowers stopped nearby. Ali bowed graciously. "Please select any flower you desire with my compliments."

Tina shook her head and instead accepted a glass of champagne from a servant. Ali, too, took champagne. He delicately selected a flower for her.

"It's called 'Daughter of a moon virgin' in my country and considered a very rare specimen."

"It's a bromeliad, perfect for gazing at in appreciation but not for wearing," she said sipping her champagne. The pear-shaped diamond at her neck glowed against her golden skin and in the moonlight her appeal to Ali was heightened tenfold. Sensing his emotional reaction to her, Tina opened the conversation.

"I never realized how unworldly I am until this past week as your and Valerie's guest. I can see why Valerie has no defense against you. She's very much in love with you."

"Valerie, my dear, is incapable of loving. Didn't I tell you?"

476

Tina's eyes darted to the four attendants who stood at attention, nearby.

"Do they annoy you?"

"Not annoy—I just feel uneasy speaking in their presence."

Ali clapped his hands. They disappeared. "Better?"

"How do you stand having them around? I like my privacy too much."

"They neither speak nor hear. They know the consequences of such foolishness."

Her eyes leaped up at his implication. She felt uneasy for more reasons than she wished to explore. "This is your anniversary, your highness. Perhaps a toast is in order," she said holding her glass before her as Ali poured more from the bottle resting in a silver bucket. "May you and Valerie be happy forever."

"Don't talk like a child. No one is happy forever," he remonstrated acerbically. "We live as we do because we may die at any moment. I should think that night on board ship when your men came to my rescue would have proven to you the inescapable fragility of life." He sipped the champagne and turned his attention to the sparkling lights of the grand, ancient city.

"Such philosophical gems of wisdom are not for nights of laughter and revelry."

"How right you are. Suppose I show you the rest of the party? Have you been in the fun-and-game rooms?"

Tina hesitated. Their eyes held and Tina, wanting to sever the connection, seemed unable to. She did finally and laughed self-consciously. "I can't imagine what you're talking about."

Ali stared at her, pursing his lips. "You can't be that naive." Ali took another sip of champagne. "Or can you?" he asked deliberately. He set his glass on the balustrade and did the same with the glass he took from Tina's hand.

"You, my dear enchantress, are in for a treat," he said, taking her hand in his and elbowing his way along the terrace, turning a corner, past several party guests.

"*Voila!*" Prince Ali bowed with panache, extending his hand before him.

A large, freeform swimming pool had been built around a grotto with cascading waterfalls surrounded by large decorative rocks and exquisite tropical plants. There was an aviary containing exotic birds in vibrant colors of the spectrum. Naked men and women, making amorous advances to each other without inhibition, were swimming,

477

dancing, and drinking champagne. Earlier, upstairs, it had struck her as peculiar that more guests seemed to be arriving than she saw in the salons. So this is where they'd gone? Ali seemed to be waiting for some reaction from her. She merely gave him a taciturn smile and followed him to another room.

Ali flung open the doors, and revealed a salon made to resemble a theater, where amorous couples on damask chaise longues were watching an unusual tableau taking place at center stage. Other spectators lay about on billowy pillows, mesmerized by the activity in a shaft of light on stage. A scrim billowed out from behind marble pillars in graduated muted shades of blue-black to pale blue mist and, worked by trick lighting, produced an ethereal effect as if supernatural forces were at work. The air was permeated with the erotic scent of musk.

At the center of the dazzling spotlight a golden-skinned woman with hip-length hair the color of anthracite swayed sensuously to the accompaniment of four men playing Oriental music on exotic-looking instruments. The girl was naked, her sensuous body oiled to accentuate every soft curve, each rippling muscle, and each rhythmic undulation. From openings in the sheer scrim came six more dancing girls, each one more enchanting than the first, moving to the beat of the music, clinking finger cymbals, the bells at their ankles giving impetus to the exotic atmosphere of an Oriental bazaar. Slowly the girls began to take their positions, parading their charms before the wildly cavorting body of the goddess at center stage.

It became clear to Tina that their intent was to make love to the golden lesbian. Some sucked her toes and moved along her legs only to be obstructed by another who did her best to bring the goddess to orgasm with her clever tongue. Two dancing maidens were nibbling at her breasts and the last was kissing her lips from overhead in a most sensuous and erotic manner. They assaulted the goddess erotically in ways that left the audience gasping and manipulating one another in heated passion. But, unwilling to miss the stimulating action on the stage, the spectators kept their eyes on the performance, while their hands were busy satisfying their own arousals.

Aware of Ali's intent, and his eyes on her, Tina grew flip.

"Perhaps I should book the act for Vegas," she quipped, refusing to let Ali see she was affected by what she saw on stage. Tina found it difficult not to flush under the

478

intensity of his probing eyes. She felt as if he were putting her to a test.

They proceeded through a corridor to another section of the villa. "You weren't affected by what you saw?" he asked.

Before she could reply Ali reached for her, drawing her close to him. "You can't tell me you weren't moved by the sensuous activity." Once again before she could reply Ali leaned over her, his powerful shoulders pushing against her, his hot lips on hers, tasting, feeling her warmth. Behind her, Ali groped for the gilded door handle, opened it and maneuvered her into the dark room, closing the door behind her.

He kissed her again with renewed passion, his fierce eyes overflowing with desire. Tina, unable to move or breathe, was taken off guard. What disturbed her was that she wasn't fighting him off. Finally she began to writhe, pushing and twisting with all her strength against his firm, hard body. One hand came free and with all her strength it swung to his face and connected with a loud stinging slap. Ali reacted as if she'd swatted a fly. He laughed, easing up a bit.

"I love a tigress," he whispered.

He groped for the light switch in the dark and flipped it on. The moment their eyes adjusted to the brightness Tina gasped. Ali gave a start as a cold rage settled on his features. Across the room on a low divan, in a drug-dazed sexual embrace, was Valerie. Moving over her in a fast rhythmic tempo was the powerful muscular nakedness of Tomasso Volpe, either boozed up or drugged, yet dedicated to the principle of fornicating as if nothing else existed.

As flabbergasted as she was furious, Tina wanted to scream at Valerie, knock sense into her, thrash her until her brains unscrambled. She was embarrassed for Tomasso too, but she realized she had no control over his sexual escapades.

Ali had the good sense to flip off the lights and navigate her out of the door, leaving behind him a well-satisfied Sicilian and a bedraggled, stoned and unconcerned Valerie, who was unaware that her infidelity had been recorded first hand.

Tina was propelled through the labyrinthian corridor, up the back stairs to the main villa. The crashing sounds of the study door that Ali kicked open and banged against the wall caused Tina to recoil. She watched the changes in his face as he forced back the cold rage surfacing in him. In the interplay of his facial muscles flexing and jerking, Tina became aware of the actual beauty of the man. Anger turned his eyes into smoldering black firepots, enhancing his coppery skin and white teeth.

Tina was at a loss, unsure of what to say or do. She was, after all, part of Valerie's Western world. She didn't condone Valerie's stupidity; on the contrary she detested a person who lacked control of her passions to the point that they controlled her.

"Don't be too harsh on Valerie," she said softly. "I don't suppose she can help herself."

Ali's eyes, narrowing, pierced hers like daggers. Lifting a golden cup to his lips he drank the two fingers of brandy he poured and muttered incoherently. His seething anger infected Tina.

"Perhaps I'd better leave," Tina said. "My presence in some way is disconcerting to you."

"You Americans!" he snorted. "How touching. How pleasant and civilized you are. You think I care what that whore does? There's nothing between us. She is free to come and go as she pleases. She can fuck whomever she wants anytime she chooses, but not under my roof when we are entertaining guests."

Tina moved to the door. "I'll leave. I regret you have such low opinions of Americans."

"Wait," he implored her. "Don't go. You do want your, uh, fiance to become president—"

"My fiance?" she queried archly.

"Whip Shiverton."

"No. *He* wants to be president. It's none of my doing."

Ali led her back to his desk. "That's all I wanted to hear. Perhaps this won't disturb you." He opened a desk drawer and, removing a newspaper, handed it to her, studying her reactions intently.

She reluctantly disengaged her eyes from his and let them fall on the newspaper. Photos of Whip and Princess Jamila, laughingly ducking photographers as rice was pelted at them, glared up at her. For an instant her heart sagged and wept. She read: "Future American Presidential Candidate and Middle Eastern Princess Are Wed. The former New York senator officially tossed his hat in the ring in the coming election. How his marriage to the princess will affect Middle Eastern relations was answered by Shiverton himself: 'In my humble opinion

480

this alliance can do nothing but good. It's time America embraces our Middle Eastern friends as brothers.' "

Tina composed herself, and tossing the paper on the desk said, "You see I tried to tell you Jamila was alive." She helped herself to a gold-tipped cigarette from a porcelain box and held still while Ali lit it for her with his gold lighter.

"I've known Jamila was alive for a long while, Tina," he said softly, watching her exhale and tense slightly. "My agents have watched her activity from the moment she was sighted in Beirut with the terrorist Bahar Bahar, nearly five years ago."

The smoke almost careened through her windpipe. "You've known? Even the farce perpetuated with her impostor?"

"Everything. Before she worked for the film star, she was employed by one of my film companies in Hollywood. What was her name—Dancey—"

"Darling. Dancey Darling." She supplied the correct name.

"Yes, the one with so preposterous a name."

"You permitted your sister to be a target for those killers?"

"She constructed the plan of her own volition. Later, my duty was to observe, watch over her and insure her from harm. When her impostor first brought publicity to her moves, of course we were curious of the intent behind the terrorist plottings. It was to our advantage when we learned her activity was merely a cover for the terrorists' underground activities in America. It was the will of Allah that we kept a watch on Jamila," he said, pouring brandy into delicate snifters on a tray. He handed her one and watched her down the drink and refuse a refill. Ali excused himself. "I'll return briefly," he said.

In his absence, Tina hurriedly reread the newspaper and felt a sinking sensation at the pit of her stomach. Before she could intelligently reflect on this—what else could she call it but strategy—Ali returned to the study. She dropped the paper and glanced at him, her eyes moving past him at the appearance of a pale, slender young woman with haunted eyes whom she recognized instantly.

"You remember my sister, the Princess Jamila, don't you?"

Tina, rooted to the spot, was flabbergasted. "I—uh— don't understand." Her eyes darted from Ali to Jamila and back to the newspaper on the desk. "If this is Jamila —then who is the woman with Whip?" Before either of them replied, Tina understood. "Ali," she said quietly, "are you sure? Very sure of this?"

"I would know my sister anywhere," he replied gravely.

"But—how? When? How could Whip be so easily fooled?"

"The switch was made after I escaped Abdul Harrim and Bahar's clutches. Allah was watching over me for certain," began Jamila, moving gracefully towards the serving table to pour wine for them. She brought Tina up to date on what happened after they met in Las Vegas. "In my drugged condition I ran from a man I felt intended to kill me. My brother's agents, covertly watching the apartment house, caught sight of me in my frantic effort to escape and wisely sensing something greatly amiss rescued me, swept me away to a medical facility where treatment was administered to me, and finally I was transported safely to my brother's house, here in Rome."

Tina, shaken, listened and studied Jamila inscrutably to determine the veracity of her story.

"I should have known something far more treacherous was underfoot when Abdul began to work over me in the hypnotic sessions he managed to impress me were vital to our work. I overheard him tell Bahar Bahar that my usefulness to them was over. At first I didn't put it together. It was only after I returned to my brother's house, where I confided all of my involvements, shamefacedly, I confess, that I learned from certain learned men, specialists in mind control and brainwashing and programming, why it was that I suddenly became expendable." She looked at her brother imploringly, her hands shaking as she sipped her wine.

Ali picked up from there. "If the mind rejects something from a moral or ethical point of view, it will fight any suggestions implanted there consciously or subconsciously. In Jamila's case, it was a trigger mechanism she rejected, the Lion of Judah emblem, which is of course a Hebraic symbol and against our Moslem teachings. Had they used any symbol acceptable to Jamila's mentality, they might have succeeded."

"Excuse me," began Tina, as confusion swirled through her mind. "What are you saying? What trigger mechanism?"

Jamila blurted out, "I was being programmed to slay Senator Shiverton—"

Tina whirled about in astonishment, her eyes leveled at Jamila. "P-programmed t-to s-slay—" Tina sank into a chair heavily.

"They brought my impostor to America when I disappeared and—" Jamila stopped at the expression of panic on Tina's face. She glanced apprehensively at her brother.

"—And programmed her to do the job," Ali hastened to explain. As he did, he too was studying the changes Tina was undergoing with dismay. *It isn't over between them,* he thought. He felt a dull thud over his heart. *Her only care is for Whip's safety.*

Tina was wondering how Whip could have been deceived. David too. And the BSI. Wouldn't they have probed into her background enough to know they were sheltering an impostor?

"If it helps to put your mind at ease, Tina," said Ali, sitting across from her, "someone close to the senator must have discovered the woman's intent. It is my understanding that a renowned authority on brainwashing has been working with her in an attempt to deprogram the girl."

Marveling at the way in which he read her thoughts, Tina nodded gratefully. "How do you know all this?"

"The same way I knew of my sister's whereabouts and involvements."

Ali lit a cigarette and handed it to Tina. Behind them, Jamila moved away from them, bowing her head and asking to be excused. Ali nodded and turned his attention to Tina.

Jamila addressed herself to Tina. "Pray find it in your heart to forgive me for any heartache you may have suffered." She left them alone.

Tina had barely acknowledged her. She was thinking that someone had better alert Whip. David! She'd call David.

"I am most curious to learn why Senator Shiverton would marry the woman posing as my sister. Forgetting the fact that she is not my sister—and it's difficult for me to believe he isn't aware of the fraud—the fact that he would marry Jamila, defying his religious beliefs, with the possibility of causing dissension in his own political party, simply doesn't compute."

Tina was staring obliquely at the crystal lighter on the

coffee table. "You're asking the wrong person to dissect this enigma," she said evasively. "All this comes as a surprise to me. Whip's marriage and of course the fact that Jamila has been here with you for so long." She shook her head in reflection.

"Less than a month ago, my brother professed his love for Jamila—rather, the impostor."

Ali nodded. "We've been aware of all her love trysts. Our agents reported the growing romance between them."

Tina picked up the smooth glass figurine, fondling it between her fingers. Ali pulled his chair up closer to her.

"Perhaps," said Tina, with averted eyes, "Whip married the woman for the same reasons you married Valerie. Political expediency."

Ali's eyes dulled. He tensed indignantly and with flagrant audacity proceeded to set her straight.

"My dear young woman, the one thing I did not marry Valerie for was political expediency. Although I admit marrying her for the wrong reasons, pity being one, I divorced her for the right reasons. I am not in love with her, never have been and never shall be. A man does many things in his life that he hopes will ennoble him and earn respect from his peers, or rewards perhaps in a future kingdom."

Tina wasn't listening. Her mind had stopped earlier at the word divorced. "You're divorced?" Another stunning revelation. "And you are still living together?"

He nodded, and picked up one of her hands, holding it between his strong, firm hands. Tina replaced the tiger on the table.

"We must talk, Tina."

"Can't you do it without holding my hand?"

"Does it so repel you?"

"Uh—it's—uh. It's just that—" She slipped her hand out from between his without replying. A knock at the door saved her from responding.

Ali said, "Enter."

Damien Le Doux, Ali's secretary, handed him a telex. They huddled and spoke in a rash of Arabic, incomprehensible to Tina. Periodically they glanced at Tina, speaking rapidly, then the conversation came to an end. Damien left the room. Ali shoved the telex into his pocket. He turned up the stereo and walked to Tina's side, brandy decanter in hand, and poured some into a snifter. He handed it to Tina. "Drink," he said sternly. "We must talk."

484

"Thank you, I've had enough."

"I said, drink it." Without hesitation Tina obliged; then, angry with herself for bending to his authority, she set the glass down on the table. Her eyes lifted to meet his. She wasn't certain what she saw in those split seconds, but one thing was certain, she felt no fear in his presence.

"I know of no other way to tell you. Allah knows I dislike being the emissary of any more unhappiness than you've had in recent months—" Ali took her hands and led her to the sofa and sat down next to her. "There's been an accident—a terrible accident."

As if she didn't already know. The moment she heard Jamila's story she knew what would happen.

"In four days I was scheduled to meet with Senator Shiverton, here in Rome," Ali was saying. "With members of the Arab coalition—"

"You said something about an accident—"

"He was shot."

Tina gave a start and found herself saying, "If this is your idea of a joke—"

"It's no joke. I don't really know the status of his health—"

Tina heard his words as if they were amplified through a tunnel of resounding echoes, unable to unscramble the message in her head. *For pity's sake, he said something about an accident! Fatal?* Confusion upon her, she blinked hard, shaking her head refusing to believe. Ali pressed the telex into her hands. She stared at it, unseeing, but she finally made it out.

Senator Shiverton shot by foreign assassins . . . details to follow.

"There will be reporters here, if they haven't already smelled the news. The paparazzi and their infernal cameras will descend upon us like vultures. You must be prepared to make some comment."

"W-why me?" Tina asked when she regained composure. "What have I to do with any of this?"

"Valerie. Dear Valerie introduced you as the future Mrs. Whip Shiverton. Word's out that you are Whip's former mistress, that you came here to bury your grief at being jilted."

The irony of Ali's words burned deeply and she almost felt like laughing. If laughing weren't so close to tears.

Her glance dropped to the telex in her lap. Her eyes

485

blurred, cleared, then blurred again. She choked back the tears, taking a firmer grip on herself.

"H-how? W-when? W-where did it happen? Who killed them?" She didn't ask why. She already knew that answer. The family was doomed. She'd known it when Ted was killed and feared it during Whip's stint in the Senate. Hadn't she fought against his candidacy for president? She hardly heard Ali's words.

"Their timing was off," Ali was saying. "Our intelligence reports stated the attempt on his life would take place here in Rome. I can see where it would benefit the assassins to pull off the deed in America; the sentencing of a criminal is far more liberal in your country than in ours." Ali was on his feet, thinking as he paced the floor.

Damien Le Doux reentered the study, this time with two more telexes for the prince. Ali studied them intently, shoving one into his jacket pocket.

"Both Whip and the woman he married are dead. Their assailants are in custody, as I presumed earlier."

Tina leaned over and poured herself another brandy from the crystal decanter. She tossed it down swiftly, feeling the burning sensation searing through her throat and upper chest.

"We had been negotiating, the senator and myself. The time has come when all Arab nations must of necessity unite to defend what is ours and not permit other nations to take from us what belongs to us by birthright. Too many lesser powers are in possession of nuclear weapons. Allah protect us from those militant dictators who get their hands on such weapons of destruction. It would mean the instant annihilation of the entire world."

"You Arabs and Jews don't seem to realize this, do you?" said Tina caustically.

"There is no reckoning with the Jews. They demand too much!"

"And so the world must die because Arabs and Jews are too stubborn and too greedy to negotiate over a conference table!"

"I fear it's gone far beyond that, my dear."

What am I doing? What am I saying? Whip is dead and I stand here concerned with the rest of the world that means nothing to me! Val's words suddenly flooded Tina's consciousness.

I've been trying to make you understand your relationship to the world—not to any one person, but to the

486

world. You must make every act on earth count since you'll only be here a limited time . . .

Ali was standing before her shoving another telex into her hands. "This should explain what I mean."

Tina read the telex: *Arab-Israeli Peace Signed.*

"Your American president has persuaded the Israeli and Egyptian leaders to sign the treaty. It is my understanding that the monetary remunerations are phenomenally high."

Tina let the telex fall from her hand and flutter to the floor, the very life knocked out of her. Her father had been right after all about many things. But, she thought, he was dead wrong about Whip. *Whip did not get to become president!*

The brandy had worked its way into her bloodstream, bracing her, elevating her from that plateau of depression she'd fallen into at the news of Whip's death. Now, she listened to Prince Ali Mohammed expound on the things that were eating away at him.

"The question on everyone's lips is, who will prevail in the Middle East? The Arabs believe they cannot give Jerusalem to the Israelis for they will take the world and bend it to their will and all will be destroyed. The Zionists are determined to see their conspiracy to the end. The Arabs on the other hand can be controlled. Because they are steeped in centuries-old traditions and are only now arising from a long sleep, they will cooperate with the progressive Western states. It will take another century for us to catch up with the Western world and time, my dear Tina, will be the angel of the world's destiny.

"It will be a matter of time before my Arab brothers realize they have been betrayed by the Egyptians. Members of the Middle Eastern terrorists splintered from the PLO due to their nihilist credos are being united with West Bank Arabs and leaders from the other Arab nations. The extremists have joined the liberals in a common bond of survival against the Jews. The peace talks and now this treaty have succeeded in doing nothing except to spotlight the treacheries underfoot and split the Arab nations. The slogan, I fear, will be death to all our enemies!" said Prince Izmur dully. "It will follow that all Arab leaders including myself who feel betrayed by the Egyptians will be ready to implement an oil embargo against all nations who help Israel."

"You must not allow this to happen," cried Tina.

Ali rose to his feet and lit up some hash. He offered the glass pipe to Tina; she refused and watched him keenly.

"It is becoming so tiresome. What you ask is slowly becoming an impossibility," he said regarding Tina with gravity.

"The United States policy in the Middle East is tepid and is bound to cause conflicts because they help Israel to consolidate its hold on territories occupied in 1967, thereby obliterating the right of the Palestinians. I earlier attended a meeting with my Arab brothers. They are a most unhappy lot. They give little credence to what the American policy is attempting to do. They believe with conviction that Israel's objective is to isolate Egypt and consolidate its hold on the West Bank. So far," added Ali ruefully, "the U.S. has made a significant contribution to this effort. This attempt at peace will only disrupt friendly relations. Naturally my Arab brothers will attempt to insure survival of the Arab nation and safeguard its identity. This announcement, a phonied-up attempt at peace which America bought with enormous sums of money, will serve only to unify all factions behind the Arab lines." Ali was bitter. "The influence of the Zionist Jew has once again tightened its chains around Wall Street."

Tina only half listened to Ali's rhetoric. If she had listened with every fibre in her mind and body she might have heard the despair couched in his words. She was thinking she had best return home. First she would call her brother David.

"I must return to the Villa Garibaldi. With your permission, I beg to be excused."

"You may use any of my facilities," he suggested. "I shouldn't wish to meet those reporters, Tina."

She regarded him for a moment, then thanked him. "It's best I return to the villa and book a flight home."

"Then I shall accompany you to the Garibaldi with my men."

"It isn't necessary, really."

"Believe me, it is necessary."

Five minutes later Tina had cause to be grateful that she had accepted Prince Izmur's protection. Outside the villa was bedlam. The crowds were horrendous. Trying her best to avoid the swarming hordes of the curious, grasping reporters with their microphones outstretched and shoved nearly into her mouth, and their clicking

488

cameras, with popping light bulb explosions nearly blinding her, Tina allowed herself to be flanked on all sides and guided into a waiting limousine. The Volpe brothers were a stout force, elbowing their way, muscling against the avaricious press. They sat in the jump seats facing her and Ali as the limo snaked its way through the pressing crowds.

Some reporters pressed newspapers against the smoky glass windows for Tina to see. She averted her head, closed her eyes, yet was unable to shut out the afterimage of those Italian headlines that told her Whip had been assassinated.

She felt like screaming. She was shaking, hot and cold chills alternating as her stomach knotted into hard balls with excruciating pain. Twenty minutes later she was safe in her suite. Ali insisted on remaining with her. Too tired to care, too spent emotionally to protest, she hurriedly made her call to Las Vegas and was told there would be an hour's delay. A phone call for the prince came and Ali begged to be excused and retired to the suite he maintained at the Villa Garibaldi for business purposes, promising to return the moment he could.

The Volpe brothers, instructed by Signore Allegro to remain with Tina, proceeded to maintain a solemn vigil in the studio off the foyer. Within moments they admitted a waiter pushing a serving cart ladened with Beluga caviar, pâté and truffles and a large bouquet of six dozen blood-red roses. Bowing before her the waiter handed her a message on a small silver tray. Tina, wondering at the pomp and ceremony, frowned as she accepted the envelope. Studying the curious emblazoned crest on the paper she began to read the contents:

My dear Tina Erice: It's difficult at such a time to express the proper sympathies. Words are inappropriate in times of sorrow and pain. It would please me if you would honor me by taking tea with me before you return to America. Presently I am a guest at the Villa Garibaldi. You have merely to advise Signore Allegro and our tête-à-tête shall be arranged. A devout admirer, Mourous Benkhanhian.

Appalled, seething with indignation and an overwhelming rage at the three-ringed circus going on around her, she wondered why she had received such a letter as well as the flowers and food, from a comparative stranger. What could he want from her?

A call from David was the only remedy to the torturous emotions careening wildly through her.

David talked rapidly. "I'm flying to Rome in the morning, Tina. Don't do anything rash. I'll explain when I see you. Do you hear me?"

"David," she practically screamed. "I can't hear you. Please speak louder. Our connection is horrible. What did you say?"

"Honey, I'm sorry we're so far apart. You won't do anything crazy, will you? I'll get there as fast as possible."

David's voice waxed and waned. It sounded scratchy and cracked through the transatlantic cables as if the very ocean swells were audible, doing its best to drown out his voice.

"Can't you tell me what happened?" she begged.

"Will you have a car at the airport to pick me up? I arrive at ten A.M. your time, Pan Am flight 350."

Tina found herself sleepwalking through the hodgepodged maze of conversation, jotting his instructions on a pad. After hanging up the bad connection, Tina wondered why she did not cry. Didn't she feel anything for him? She had loved Whip desperately, yet not a teardrop spilled. Why?

Whip is dead! DEAD! What am I doing here? Why don't I feel something—anything?

Tina searched her cosmetic case and took two Valium. She wanted to sleep and forget. Perhaps then she'd find some peace. She called the front desk and reserved a limousine to pick up David at Da Vinci Airport the following day. She gave the clerk the flight number and time of arrival and hung up.

Ali returned and closed the door behind him. "It's time, Tina," he began soberly, "for us to talk." He stopped short at the sight of the champagne and the lavish banquet of food.

Tina showed him Benkhanhian's note. "From a friend of yours," she said in a voice oozing with contempt.

He indicated his surprise, but not his pleasure, as he inhaled the sweet aroma of the roses. "He does have impeccable taste, as usual."

"You don't seem surprised that your mentor would wish to talk with me?"

"My mentor?" Ali laughed easily. "He would be pleased to hear you call him that. But it displeases me to hear your innuendo behind the word. Tina, I am my own man. No one is my mentor."

490

Suddenly Tina grew weary, dropping with fatigue. The Valium couldn't have worked this soon, she thought. "I'm tired. If you don't mind I'd like to get some sleep."

"Tina, marry me."

Taken aback, her heavy eyes widened slightly. "I wouldn't relish being part of a harem," she quipped.

"I won't dignify your remark, nor is it worthy of you. For five years, from the moment we met, I've been in love with you. I told you then one day we'd be together. I want you as my wife. We belong together, you and I."

"We hardly know each other."

"When I learned you were in love with my old schoolmate, my heart felt suffocated, crushed. But Allah was merciful. My world changed so drastically it left little time to nurse a bleeding heart and less to come courting you across the ocean. My world—the Arab world—came into prominence. My first obligation, as leader in my nation, is to my people. My personal desires of necessity came second."

Tina yawned. The drug was taking effect. "Please, let's talk in the morning—"

"Tomorrow is too late. I must know tonight. I must hear from your lips where I stand with you."

"It's difficult to think straight," she yawned again.

"Do you still love Whip Shiverton?"

"That's an unfair question. It's unworthy of you, your highness," she retaliated with scorn. Yawning again, she grew dismayed. "Why are you so insistent? Dear me, I took too many valiums. Besides, you're already married." Her words were disjointed.

"I told you we are divorced."

"Why live together if you're divorced?"

Ali took heart. If she weren't interested in him why ask so leading a question? He started to tell her a strange and poignant story.

"Valerie, from the beginning of our relationship, has been ill. The very thing contributing to her illness she is unable to part with. Twice, she's attempted to take her life. She lives in close proximity to me in the best interests of the children, and until I am satisfied she's well enough to return to America where she belongs. She has no financial worries; what I've settled on her, plus the inheritance she received at her father's death, is more than enough to care for her and the children. Doctors who care for her give no hopeful prognosis. She is a self-destructive woman. New drugs, on occasion, have

491

worked marvels to bring her out of her depression, others aggravate her condition."

"How long has this been going on?" asked Tina, shaking herself awake.

"She began to deteriorate six months after our wedding. Constant recurring nightmares of the assassination, you see. She thinks she saw the assassin, and is afraid to speak up because of the inevitable danger to her children. To appease her I've called in highly skilled artists with the secret police of my country and they sketch a face according to the description she gives them. Every time, Tina, it comes out the same face: a film star who was known for his gangster films; someone she associates with evil in the unconscious portion of her brain. She began taking drugs to alleviate the fears and enable her to sleep. She began hallucinating, and took drugs to prevent this. It's been a merry-go-round. She had the best medical attention possible.

"For six months she disappeared from my household. She was found wandering about the fleshpots of Costa del Sol and Cannes, along the French Riviera, taking up with anyone who found her desirable. Lucky for her, no one believed her rantings, nor did they recognize her as Valerie Shiverton. There was little resemblance between the former First Lady and the person she had become."

"Why are you telling me this, Ali?" she said, trying with difficulty to stifle another yawn.

"You fool, don't you know real love when it stands before you? Melt, Tina, become as a clear, running brook that yearns to flow into a strong river and follow its destiny—"

"What happened then?" pressed Tina.

"We found her, brought her home. She learned she was pregnant and because she could not recall who the father might be she went into a deep depression. Obviously she survived. The twins are splendid young men of whom I am terribly fond. Aware that I might have been a contributing factor to her personal tragedy, I felt it best we live apart. She agreed."

"Contributing factor?"

"While she was still married to Ted, we had engaged in sexual relations. This of itself is not earth shattering. She had countless extramarital affairs—"

"Yes, I know. What of IAGO, Ali?"

"*What of IAGO?*"

"Do you not already sit at the helm of this—this consortium of power? Command their vast resources? Do you not venerate these antiquated titans? Involve yourself in their one-sided games of international monopoly?"

Ali laughed tolerantly. "My dear Tina, you read too many fairy tales."

She stiffened. Then smiling indulgently she murmured easily, "I see. That's what you think? I read too many fairy tales?" She nodded smugly, still fighting the languor melting through her body. Instantly she drove a wedge between them.

"Pray tell me, your highness, what exactly is your intent in the Middle East?" If only her mind wasn't dulling . . .

Ali drew himself up regally. In every move, every gesture he was a prince.

"Why should it be of interest to you what my intent is in the Middle East?" he asked, watching her closely. "Why is it of interest to you what anyone's intent is—any place in the world?"

His questions threw her. Why indeed should it be of personal concern? She was unable to reply. The usual reason that any citizen would be concerned over the future of her country was not sufficient.

"You are no aspiring politician, are you? Are you an international financier who has enormous investments to risk, worldwide? Why do you risk getting involved in the boiling cauldron of abrasive politics?"

He walked in closer to her and took her hands in his.

"Marry me, share my life. My strife also if you're bent on a career in politics. Why you'd wish to be burdened by the ponderous complexities of public life are beyond my comprehension. I want you to bring an heir to my throne. Do you realize how blessed our children would be? To think they'd possess the genes of a very special man, Val Erice—and mine of course," he smiled charismatically. Just as easily the smile dissolved and he despaired openly. "Why am I going on like this? If the world doesn't come to its senses there will be no world for any of us. There will be no throne for me or my heirs."

Tina's confusion, aggravated by the sedative, thickened. This wasn't the manner of man she'd come to know through her father's files on IAGO. "Why?" she asked with hesitance, "won't there be a throne?"

"Three more nations are armed with nuclear weapons. If the USA and Russia do not stop supplying the smaller

493

nations with arms, missiles and nuclear warheads—It's time to speak of one world government. One, controlling all nations. We cannot exist in a world filled with adversaries. We must unite in a brotherhood of man. What was vital to the world yesterday has little value today. If there were some way for all nations to share equally in the natural resources of the world . . ."

The last thing she remembered before falling asleep was Ali kissing her, tucking her into bed.

"Go to sleep, my beloved. Sleep with a prayer to your God for our love to endure."

CHAPTER THIRTY-SIX

David Erice stood over Tina's bed looking at her, his face creased with worry. "Tina! Wake up, Tina."

Wafting between slumber and wakefulness, the memories of her fretful dreams combined with the dreadful reality of Whip's death was etched into the pallor of her face and dull eyes as she forced them to open. The invigorating aroma of fresh coffee drifted to her senses and vaguely, as the opaque film of sleep over each eyeball was rubbed away, Tina began to distinguish David's face. In her drugged and euphoric hangover she cried out, "Benne . . . Benne."

"It's David," he said. "David."

She jolted upright in bed, falling into his arms. Tears spilled down her cheeks freely. "David, oh, David, isn't it terrible?"

"It was a foolish thing you did, taking so much Valium. You've been sleeping for fifteen hours."

Tina laid her head on his shoulders, shedding the tears she couldn't cry the night before. David was stroking her hair off her face tenderly, speaking in soothing tones. "I've come here to talk with you, Tina. To prepare you for something. I want you to brace yourself . . ." He nodded to the third person in the room, encouraging him to come in closer.

The tone of his voice alerted her. She reached for a tissue at the side of the bed and blew her nose, dabbing at her tears. It was then she saw him, dimly at first because the drapes were closed, but there was no mistaking him. She sucked in her breath and gasped aloud. "Whip! Oh, my God, what sort of a trick is this?"

He came in closer, and David lifted his tall frame off the bed, giving a wider berth to his sister and the man she loved.

Whip moved closer and gathered her into his arms.

Tina kissed him back, but something stirred in Tina

and it had no resemblance to the love she once felt for him.

"Why?" she asked. "Why the deception?"

Then they explained. Since the assassins, Bahar Bahar and Abdul Harrim and the impostor, were on a suicide mission to slay Whip, the BSI let them think they had accomplished their goal. They released a false story to the press. Whip's intent to be president was unchanged and he wanted to attend the conference with Ali Mohammed and the other Arab leaders to insure a collaborative peace. Unquestionably, Whip Shiverton in the White House would be far more of an influence than even Tina could estimate. Times had changed since Val's world dominated the future of mankind and if he were alive today, Whip insisted, he would be flexible enough to know that the clout of IAGO had dissipated.

They talked with Tina for hours, over breakfast, until Whip prepared for his meeting with Ali Mohammed and his compatriots.

When it boiled down to where Tina stood in all this, she was unsure of her own emotions.

"Tina, it makes sense. Don't you understand? Now you don't have to be the tower of strength, the watchdog over the Erice empire. We have lawyers, and corporate structures governed by laws. There are no giants in the shadows lurking behind us trying to topple our well-constructed towers. Whatever Val told you, whatever it was he instilled you with has no real influence anymore. Even that silly ring—that double-headed griffin—is of no account. It's meaningless."

Tina's eyes sharply cut towards David. She smiled enigmatically and said nothing. David caught the smile as did Whip. Simultaneously Whip glanced at the clock over the fireplace in the study and finished the rest of his coffee.

"It's time for me to meet with the prince," he said, sipping the remains of his coffee. He leaned over to kiss Tina. Angling back from her he eyed her intently.

"It's over between us, isn't it?" he said softly.

"It's all been a dream Whip. It never existed. We come from two different worlds. You could have been a part of mine, but I could never trespass on yours. It's as simple as that."

"You've changed," he said, feeling pangs of remorse.

"I've changed." She nodded, her eyes intent on the thoughts parading across her mind. "Good luck. I hope that you and the prince come together for the benefit of all mankind."

"There can be no other way for the world except through peace. If only I can impress this upon them . . ."

He opened the doors to the outer salon, and was instantly flanked by four men, including Kevin O'Brien and Tom Murphy, who waved to Tina. They all left in a body, snapping to in clockwork precision. Tina caught a glimpse of the Volpe brothers who stared wide-eyed at Whip Shiverton, recognizing him immediately. Tina thought, *This is a story they'll tell their grandchildren about with fierce pride.*

"You're a tough cookie, Tina," said David, pouring the last of the coffee for them. "You're real tough."

"Am I?" she asked absently, lost in thought. On her feet, she paced about in a rustling pink silk kaftan.

"Yesterday when I was told Whip was dead, my sorrow was disguised by the total disorder and chaos of my mind. Earlier, I thought, Pop had been wrong. He told me Whip had no choice but to run for president. News of his death upset me and for a time, I was filled with countless regrets. Seeing him alive has restored my faith to a degree. Pop wasn't wrong at all. The world was changing too fast for him. This I can accept.

"I can even understand when Ali told me IAGO can't exist in so revolutionary and transitional an era in which we live."

"Come home, Tina. Let's get back to a normal life. You'll find a man, a good one, settle down and live with the happiness you deserve. Don't take the unhappiness of an unrequited love to heart."

Tina laughed. "I've already found the right man. Should I say, he found me? I've been blind, I suppose. I should have seen the writing on the wall. Pop told me once, you can seldom direct the course of love, for love itself, if it finds you worthy, will direct the course for you."

"You're talking in riddles," David interrupted abruptly. "Who is this right man you speak of?"

Tina, smiling enigmatically, gazed at her brother, her eyes twinkling mischievously. "Haven't you guessed? It's Ali."

At the blanching of his features as shock waves spread through him, Tina moved closer to him, and put her hand through his elbow, leading him out onto the rose filled terrace.

"Come, David, walk with me in the garden, and I shall

tell you the story of a real man, a prince of a man with compassion, heart, intelligence and love.

"You see, dear David, when the world is in your hands, tap it lightly. Take only what you can use for your time on earth. That's exactly what I intend to do."

10-19